Assassin

Celebrating
30 Years of Publishing
in India

Praise for *Assassin*

K.R. Meera is easily one of the finest storytellers today, a truth proved once again by her novel *Assassin*, translated with characteristic ease and panache by J. Devika. Suspense, fear, excitement, revenge, the intelligent pursuit of a murderer that leads to the discovery of a web of deaths, conspiracies and love-tangles: the novel has everything to make it a highly readable narrative. It unravels against the dark political context of demonetization and its many implications, including the calculated impoverishment of those that need money the most. Here is a layered tale that culminates in an unexpected event with deep personal consequences for the first-person narrator while it works as an allegory of our blood-soaked times.

– K. SATCHIDANANDAN

Assassin

K.R. MEERA

TRANSLATED FROM THE MALAYALAM BY
J. DEVIKA

HARPERPERENNIAL

An Imprint of HarperCollins *Publishers*

First published in English in India by Harper Perennial 2023
An imprint of HarperCollins *Publishers*
4th Floor, Tower A, Building No. 10, DLF Cyber City,
DLF Phase II, Gurugram, Haryana – 122002
www.harpercollins.co.in

2 4 6 8 10 9 7 5 3 1

P-ISBN: 978-93-5629-626-8
E-ISBN: 978-93-5629-627-5

Typeset in 11.5/16 Adobe Caslon Pro at
Manipal Technologies Limited, Manipal

Printed and bound at
Thomson Press (India) Ltd

AUTHOR'S NOTE

Assassin is an attempt to document the times and lives of the women of my generation as personally witnessed by me. It is my own humble experiment with the Indian political truth. Naturally, *Assassin* is very much autobiographical, and although the characters and situations are fictional, the emotional core of the story remains true. Satyapriya has a lot of me in her, and her mother's quirkiness is borrowed from my own.

Assassin wouldn't have been possible without J. Devika, who was gracious enough to take up this translation project despite her busy schedule as a professor and researcher. She has remained my most trusted reader and valued critic ever since we first met, and this is our fifth book together. I thank her from the bottom of my heart for being there for me all these years.

This is my first book with HarperCollins. I express my gratitude to the Associate Publisher (Literary), Rahul Soni, an acclaimed translator himself, for commissioning this book, and Rinita Banerjee for her immaculate and insightful editing.

I am immensely grateful to A Suitable Agency – particularly Hemali Sodhi and Ambar Sahil Chatterjee – for being a part of my journey. There are not enough words to thank my friends and first readers V. Jayakumar, Adv. G. Mohan Raj, author and journalist

P.K. Parakkadavu, Dr Resmi Bhaskaran, Dr Dhanya Lakshmi N., Sadhya K.P., R.K. Bijuraj and Dileep Raj. Also, Thrissur Current Books and DC Books.

Special thanks are due to P.K. Sajan for his valuable help during the initial stage of this translation, and Dr C.J. John, V.V. Krishnan Kutty and K. Sankara Pillai for their valuable inputs in clearing my doubts.

Have you ever faced an attempt on your life? Gauri Lankesh had. I dedicate this book to her.

– K.R. Meera

Assassin

ONE

Have you ever faced an attempt on your life?

A pity, if your answer is no! If only because the soul experiences a tremendous release in that moment. Instantly, body and soul part ways within your living self. They take wing on their separate paths. One thing, however, is certain. It is better to die at an assassin's hands than escape. If you do escape, then say 'swaha' to the rest of your life, which is gone forever, like an offering to a sacrificial fire. Every face you see after will be suspect. Even your own shadow won't seem to belong to you – but to the assassin. You will feel something piercing right through your chest; you will squirm in sudden bursts of pain.

I have been in such a state since 16 November, the night on which I was attacked. The whole of that day was spent standing in a queue in front of the bank. Just eight days earlier, one-thousand- and five-hundred-rupee notes were banned in the country. The government was still making mutually contradictory statements; the new notes were not yet ready. People camped in front of banks day and night. News of them collapsing and dying in queues kept piling. I had reached my workplace looking limp and wilted. I was on the fourth shift. The attack happened when, after work, I was dropped off at the rusted gate of my rented house, just as I had started to push it open. It was past midnight. The company vehicle that had dropped me had not even disappeared from sight when a motorbike came up noiselessly from the dark. Someone who's lost his way inside the housing colony, I thought, and turned. I saw his hand slink between his legs. Ah, an exhibitionist, thought I – a member of that eternal race, sure to outlast us all. Then he pointed something at me. I did not peer again to make sure that it was a gun. I ducked; the sound of a windowpane shattering rang terrifyingly. My consciousness was dripping away but I saw him take aim again. I fell flat on my face. A bullet hit the ground, and the sand and dust got into my eyes. I did not see him aim a third time, but I could foresee it. Clutching on to my life, I rolled towards the road. My good luck or bad – a wild-looking young man, a neighbour whom I had not yet met, arrived there on his hulk of a motorbike after a late-night movie. He braked suddenly and honked repeatedly. The gunman's vehicle sped away, and I escaped.

The young man helped me up. But body and soul had already parted. I am dead, I continued to believe. My limbs stiffened. Still holding me up, honking, and shouting for help, he roused the neighbours. I heard his voice as if from across a river. Death was the bluish-red-tinged bank of a river – such things were revealed to me. I was crossing it, seated atop my bullet-ridden body as a canoe. The river was the colour of flames. The ripples rose as cool tongues of flame towards the sky, the spray of sparks scattered all over.

Some people ran up to us and carried me to the house of our neighbour, Dr Fernandes. The doctor shook me awake gently, splattered water on my face. I was reborn into the disquiets of life with great reluctance.

Completely exhausted, I lay still for about an hour, still craving for the violet shores of death. Akhil Gupta, a Superintendent of Police and a resident of our colony, came up to me in between and asked some questions. I could only babble. He told me that men from the local police would be protecting me. I spent the rest of the night in the house of that 'freaken' young man. I couldn't but help a laugh even in my terrible state when I heard that his name was Mrityunjoy Sen. His mother, Dr Sandeepa Sen, was a teacher at the university. She received me very kindly. Dr Fernandes had given me a sleeping pill; I slept like I was rehearsing death. In the morning, Sandeepa told me that I had screamed twice in my sleep. By the time I bid her goodbye and staggered towards my house, my body had become a damp sheath of leather with soggy flesh hanging inside. A sheath like the one Gurkhas use to keep their knives in. One used to conceal the sharpness of the dagger and to protect the world outside from that sharpness.

The SP and the president and secretary of our Residents' Association were waiting outside, in front of the gate of my house. They were chatting about the wedding of an ex-minister's daughter. I overheard the inspector say that the bride's sari was worth seventeen crore. The optimism around black money vanishing was dimming, it seemed. I led them inside. The broken shards of glass had fallen on the sit-out too. The inspector was observing the premises keenly. He loosened the bullet that had broken the windowpane and pierced a wall. He frowned like a great crime investigator, pressed his fingers on his lips, bent, craned his neck and stretched to examine closely all of the 750 square feet, including a drawing-cum-dining area, a bedroom, a study, a small living room, a kitchen, and a small work area outside, enclosed with an iron grille. He asked me to describe what had passed. The president of our Residents' Association H.H. Reddy and the secretary Atul Shetty encouraged me to speak. Shetty recorded all of it on his iPhone. Maybe it was a case of mistaken identity? Reddy expressed his doubt. A senior scholar had been murdered this way. I, too, remembered the image of the blood-splattered pieces of his round spectacles. Not surprising he died that way, said Shetty. He wrote false stories against the government. Sandeepa Sen also writes such things, Shetty added, lowering his voice. He shot the wrong person, the SP said to himself. For a split second, Samir's face flashed in my mind. But my voice did not rise. The three continued to ask questions which they themselves answered. Gandhis are gone, said Shetty, now the contract killings are going to go up. But only the ordinary folk are bereft of Gandhis, Reddy countered. They were talking about the five-hundred-rupee notes, of course. The SP assured me that soon a detailed statement would be taken from me. He promised Reddy that security in the colony would be increased. Soon, all of them were gone. The house was now empty. My heart was still pounding. I was swamped with guilt and the fear of humiliation. Intense darkness rolled and thrashed about inside my head.

After some time, in came a sub-inspector with swarthy cheeks and eyes that looked as though sorrow had congealed in them forever, accompanied by a pot-bellied head constable and a young woman constable who was at least five feet ten inches tall. They were to record my statement. They asked me the following questions, and these were the responses I gave them:

'What is your name?'

'Satyapriya.'

'How long have you been living here?'

'Sixteen months.'

'Aren't you afraid to live here alone?'

'The woman who used to live here earlier was also alone.'

'But you could have found a flat or a hostel room?'

'Simply can't put up with hostel wardens on top of everything at the age of forty-four.'

'Where were you before you moved here?'

'In Odisha.'

'Why did you move here?'

'Because I found a better job.'

'What is your job?'

'It is in the HR department of a software company.'

'Do HR employees work at night?'

'This is an American company.'

'At what time did you go to work yesterday?'

'At five, in the evening.'

'Where were you until then?'

'I had gone to the bank at ten in the morning.'

'To deposit or withdraw?'

'To withdraw.'

'How much?'

'The ink to mark those who change notes ran out. So I couldn't change any money.'

'Do you think that the motive was robbery?'

'No.'

'Aren't there security arrangements in your company's vehicle? Shouldn't they make sure that you are safely inside your house before leaving?'

'That's the rule.'

'Why have you not complained against this breach of rules?'

'Have not really felt insecure here. The SP's house is just past the bend down the road.'

'All right. What is your educational qualification?'

'Double MA, MBA.'

'Double MA?'

'In Communicative English and Malayalam.'

'You have no relatives?'

'My parents live in my native place.'

'Are you married?'

'No.'

'What does your father do?'

'Nothing nowadays. He is fully paralysed.'

'Siblings?'

'A sister. She died in a car crash.'

'A car crash?'

'On the road. Her scooter collided with a lorry.'

'Was it an accident?'

'That's what the police said.'

'Do you have any enemies?'

'Not to my knowledge.'

'Anybody in the office?'

'There have been disagreements.'

'About what?'

'Work-related matters.'

'Why are you not married?'

'Because I haven't found anyone suitable.'

'Didn't you try putting out a matrimonial ad?'

'No luck.'

'It is difficult to imagine that no man ever fell in love with a good-looking woman like you.'

I thought for a moment and then said, 'Luck in love is directly proportional to submissiveness, not beauty.'

The SI frowned. The woman constable gaped, her eyes filled with disbelief. To change the topic, the SI asked for my identity card. I gave it to him. The head constable copied down the address carefully. The questions continued.

'Have you seen the man on the bike anywhere?'

'I didn't see his face. He was wearing a helmet. All I saw was the pistol in his hand.'

'Can you describe him?'

'The truth is that I saw only the pistol.'

'Did you note down the bike's registration number?'

'No, but I think it ended with 25.'

'So you have no suspects in mind?'

'No. At least for now.'

'That means?'

'My mind feels numb. Can't focus.'

'All right, we will come again. Do let us know if you recollect anything else.'

The police left.

I felt helpless. My memories don't return like that; they aren't kittens tied up in a sack and let out somewhere faraway. They are like banyan trees that send down roots from every branch to cling on to the earth. As the tree grows, these roots grow bigger than the trunk itself. Just the way stories survive even if the one who wrote them is killed, the roots remain even if the trunk is felled.

The sun that noon was like the hole from a bullet that had pierced clean through the crystal sky. The sunlight glinted like broken bits of glass. I swept the house clean. I was still running on the cup of tea that Sandeepa had offered me. Going into the kitchen, I looked for something to eat. I hadn't bought any provisions last week. I was loath to spend the money that I had before the new currency notes reached me. Money, and money alone, protects the woman who lives alone. Yesterday, I was hindered by the government ordering that the indelible ink, used generally on voters, be used on citizens changing their money. The ink ran out just before my turn came.

I found a packet of bread in the fridge. A cup of tea and two pieces of toast made me feel stronger. I then phoned the HR general manager Rakhi Gupta and told her everything. She was horrified. The police think it is a case of mistaken identity, I calmed her down. My colleagues called, one by one. By noon, the manager Shantanu Sir and another colleague of mine, Ali Akbar, came to see me. They told me that the security guard on escort duty in the company's vehicle, who had broken the rule, had been dismissed. Ali Akbar chided me for not having reported him before. Take a week's leave and go home, Shantanu Sir insisted. They left some new notes, so needed in this time of note ban. Ten Gandhis each worth a hundred rupees inside a paper cover. Gandhi's face reminded me of the bullet. Its angry buzz resounded in my ears and inside my head. I was overcome by the fear of death. But I was not so afraid as to go on leave. I was more wary of the police. The unspoken answers to unasked questions scared me. I needed more time to regain balance. I decided to make use of the unexpected leave. After sending Shantanu Sir a leave application, I booked a ticket to my home town on an AC bus that was to leave at 7.30 p.m. And then, I slept like the dead until five o'clock in the evening.

The bus was not crowded. The passengers were talking about currency notes. Most of them were happy that black money would disappear now. The video-player in the bus began to play a movie five minutes later; most people were engrossed in it. I could not concentrate. So I leaned on the glass of the window letting my eyes wander outside. Night, like a knife-thrower, threw daggers of light. My brain was still numb. Though it was an air-conditioned vehicle, the bright slivers hit the windows and pierced my eyes. The fellow was such a fool to have fired at the wrong person, I thought with mild frustration. But what if the bullets had found their target, what if Mrityunjoy had not appeared then? I shivered at the thought. Lost in such reflections, I felt very sleepy. Like a leaf about to fall off in the wind, I dangled between sleep and wakefulness. And then, you know that moment when the leaf falls off its stalk into deep slumber, one that arrives silently, unknowingly, just then, the mobile phone rang, shaking me like a naughty child shaking a tree trunk. I took it mechanically. I could hear a male voice:

'*Khushi rawho…!*'

Before I could say 'wrong number', I heard him speak again. '*Khushi rawho, Satyapriya, khushi rawho, motte bhuley na* … as there is always going to be a third chance!'

I was fully awake. It was a call from a burner phone. The part of the threat that was said in Odiya meant: 'Be happy, Satyapriya, be happy … Do not forget me.'

A bolt of lightning shot through my body. Who was this? The gunman? A third chance? Didn't that mean that two chances were over by now? My earlier brushes with death flashed through my mind. I had come close to it at least three times before. Did it mean that those three times were not accidental? Probably just one was an accident – the other two were murder attempts. He's picked up a gun because they failed. My eyes flew open, and my sleep vanished. Like a half-broken leaf, I hung perilously from the stalk and shook helplessly. I grew clammy with sweat in the chilly air of the air-conditioned bus. I tried to calm down, analyse the facts, and soon managed to retrieve the memory of the three preceding experiences.

The first was three years back, and close to home. It was night, and I was on my way back after visiting an old retainer of our family, Venukkuttan Chettan. The bus stop was close to our house, so I decided to walk home. I had walked some distance when a bike passed by me. The path was deserted. I quickened my pace. The bike reappeared, this time, very slow. When it came up close, the rider thrust out a hand towards me. I thought it was a chain-snatcher. I have always had Amma's quickness in the face of danger. I spun around and grabbed his shirt. He swung a knife; my arm was hurt but he lost his balance and slipped off the seat. The bike moved forward, and he fell down. But just then, another vehicle came that way, and he leapt up, got back on his bike, and sped off.

The second escape, too, was by a hair's breadth. That was a year and a half back, the day after Golla Jayaramulu was killed, the second day after I broke up with Samir Sayyid. To get over the pain, I had gone to Bhubaneswar's Esplanade Mall with Aseema, my co-worker at the company, Advaita. I was standing behind the car and giving directions to Aseema who was getting it out of the parking lot. A taxi that was parked opposite suddenly reversed at great speed. The female security guard noticed and screamed. I leapt aside. The driver, who wore dark glasses and had a handkerchief tied around his head, muttered 'sorry', driving off without bothering to respond to Aseema's angry remonstrances.

The third time was when I was returning from home after my first visit there since I joined this software firm. This was in a train. I'd just finished consuming Amma's packed dinner and was washing my hands in the washbasin near the door when someone pushed me hard. The man was wearing a balaclava and was wrapped in a woollen shawl. He had dark glasses on, and his teeth protruded. I actually fell out through the open door. But luckily, my kurta caught on the broken railing on the door, and with one hand, I was able to grab the door handle and pull myself up. With the other hand, I clutched his shirt. By then, other passengers came up, someone pulled the chain. I escaped again, but that man slipped away.

I tried to recall the gunman. Memory is like a rock formation. When you remove each layer, you see a still body of water below. One in which all is mirrored. I saw that the ones that came on the bike, in the car and in the train, all had the same physique as the gunman. All four times the man's eyes were shrouded in dark glasses. His head was covered, all four times. My heart beat painfully hard. If two of the four were murder attempts, and directed at me, if they were planned, then which ones were they? Who was he? And most importantly, why did he want me dead?

I tried to review the chances of me becoming an assassin's target. Who would bother to kill a woman with no power or wealth? Maybe the ones she hurt. It was when I tried to recollect who I may have hurt that I was actually convinced of something: yes, there were many. If you count, four. The caller could have been one of them. He spoke in Odiya. So maybe it was Prabhudev Maheswari. Did that mean that the first murder attempt was the one that happened in Bhubaneswar? There was something peculiar about that day. On that day, I received a message from Samir which said, 'When love disappears, you have to fear.' That was soon after I escaped the accident at the mall. So maybe Samir, not Prabhudev? I had no clue. All I could do was sit and swelter. As time slipped by, I became a burning candle placed on seat number 12 of a bus in which the lights were switched off. Instead of sleeping, I was melting.

I had decided not to tell Amma any of this. But after I reached home, I was having breakfast when the news appeared on TV. Following 'Note ban: Despondent housewife commits suicide' came the lines 'Mistaken murder attempt: Malayali woman escapes'. In Atul Shetty's video, my face and voice were discernible. Amma, who had just given my father a bath, had seated him in his armchair and was now rubbing some rasnadi powder on his head, was startled for a moment. 'It was nothing, Amme,' I intervened quickly. Amma collected herself. 'But why didn't you say a word?' she complained. Oh, it was nothing, I persisted. But the whole thing – the three gunshots, me rolling on the ground – was described with much excitement on the screen. After that, my father did not take a bite. He would not have even a sip of water. He sat still, eyes fixed on the TV screen.

My mother's brothers and paternal aunt called. I twisted the incident into a joke for them. Venukkuttan Chettan and some neighbours came over. I joked with them too. Venukkuttan Chettan alone did not smile. 'Did the police come? Have they filed an FIR? In which police station?' He went on, looking uneasy. 'Now please don't blow this up and make me lose my job!' I laughed. The best balm for fear is humour. Very soon, I was myself convinced that all that had transpired was just a funny story. So I did not respond to calls from journalists.

After it was all over, at night, when Amma was taking my father to the bedroom in his wheelchair, he gestured to me. I followed them. Then he gestured to Amma to leave us alone in the room. When we were alone, his voice rose, taking me by complete surprise.

'Satyamole, there is something I have to tell you.'

I started violently. This was the first time in many years I was hearing him utter a full sentence. And the first time he was addressing me as 'mole' – my daughter – since I turned nine. I quivered sharply, like a leaf in a tornado. My mind came undone, turned over. In the tears that welled in my eyes, the whitewashed room and my father's bulging eyes and menacing moustache in the framed black-and-white photo on the wall, disappeared from view.

'Satyamole,' he called again. His voice sounded like it was coming from the depths of a lake. I swallowed hard. I was beset with unease, just like I used to be whenever I ran into him during my childhood. 'It's not a mistake … his target…' The reddish hue of a heart in turmoil was visible in his large eyes. 'You, too, may be killed any moment.'

'For what?' I was astonished. What flashed through my mind first was the new revelation that the killer was neither Samir nor Prabhudev. And then, a brief respite, which soon disappeared. If I had grasped what he said correctly, there was another person, whom I did not know, who wished to see me dead. My nerves throbbed. Suddenly, I felt rather important. Who would have thought someone would identify me as an enemy to be annihilated? Someone is afraid – the thought gave me a thrill, a certain pride. I realized that the fear one inspired in others builds up one's sense of security. I could understand my father better now.

Acchan tried to say something but choked and coughed; Amma ran in and began to massage his back, but he still struggled for breath. Like a huge shark beached and helpless, he slipped off the wheelchair, fell on the floor and writhed hard.

I called the neighbours. But by then, his gills had closed up forever. And thus, abandoning me mercilessly in the middle of the endless sea of fear, oblivion and darkness, he swam away towards the shores of death. In my imagination, I saw him waiting on the bluish-red shore of the river of cool flames. I, too, would reach there soon. The heart pulsed, banged incessantly against the ribcage. Who – who was that cruel assassin? And more importantly, why did he want to kill me?

I needed to find out – by myself. What a fascinating task, for a woman who lived in the India of those times!

TWO

I was plagued by a series of misfortunes soon after I joined the degree course in college. The house caught fire in the first year. In the second year, someone mixed poison in our well water. Acchan was stabbed by someone in the third. The next year, he was in hospital, trying cure after cure. The debts mounted, our house had to be sold for a pittance. For some time, we were in and out of the houses of our relatives.

At first, we stayed in Acchan's family homestead, his tharavad. In just about a month, his younger sister, our kochappachi, and her husband had turned it into a veritable minefield. We somehow hung in there for about a year. Then we moved to my paternal uncle's, my kochacchan's. If the earlier place was a red-hot wok, this was a full-fledged firepit. Just when we were considering moving to Valyamaaman's – our senior maternal uncle's – home, both our maternal uncles paid a visit to find out if we were all right. Five minutes into the visit, and they began to bicker, just to provoke Amma. 'Didn't you make a face at me when you were in Class 2?' 'But you pinched me in Class 5!' And then it went on to become a roaring quarrel. All tragedies carry within them some blessings. It was good that they parted, quarrelling, then. We were spared the horrors their wives and children would have inflicted on us.

But in the middle of all that thrashing about for sheer survival, we failed to notice something crucial: the incidents that had unfolded one after another during these three years were connected. By 'we' I mean my sister and myself. Acchan refused to complain to the police about the first two. At the time of the third, the police filed a case. But Acchan insisted that he had not seen the culprit. He had been stabbed fourteen times. He could not walk after that. Never snapped at us after that. Leave alone snap, he hardly uttered a full sentence. He was always lost in thought, until he died. My sister and I invented a game which was about guessing his thoughts.

'The price of a bottle of Scotch whisky!'

'No, no, the colour of the film star Rajani's panties!'

Of course, these were not jokes daughters should have ideally made about their father. But we had to air our desire for revenge against the man in some way! The annual day in my sister's workplace, where she was an apprentice, fell on the day after the stabbing. She went off to attend it. Brought home prizes for elocution and essay writing, poetry writing and painting. I did not go to college that day. I took a peep at him at the hospital that evening. Then for the first time in my life, I watched *Chitrahaar* and other stuff on TV in peace, and left for the hostel early next morning.

But when Acchan vanished forever, I felt a void. The pyre burned me too. When everyone left after the sanjayanam ceremony, I went to the shade of the south-side jackfruit tree. The funerary urn with the ashes, its mouth tied up with bright red silk, that hung from an east-facing branch, rocked gently. I saw it and imagined: he is calling me to him. Maybe he had an afterthought; maybe it was now that he wanted to be loving to me. My heart began to melt slowly as I pictured him waiting alone on the bluish-red banks for the daughter to cross the river of fire. Tears came to me. I pressed my face against the jackfruit tree and burst out weeping. My tears fell like rain on the rough, lichen-ridden trunk. They must have scalded the tree. Don't cry, don't cry, the leaves begged.

That moment, Acchan's last words rose again. 'You, too, may be killed any moment.' I heard the bullet's whizz. The gunman's form began to take shape in my mind. Acchan had not said 'You will be killed'; he had said 'You, *too*, may be killed...' What did that mean? That even my chechi's death was a murder? My hair stood on end. Until that moment I had thought it was an accident. She was riding her scooter. A bike came in suddenly from a side road, she swerved, and a lorry that had sped up from behind knocked her down. I did not try to probe further into it. That was seventeen years back. And anyway, my life had left me half-dead.

The more I thought about it, the more my heart seethed. I did not fear death – but I did not wish to die while my mother was still alive. Now I had to find out if Chechi, too, had been the victim of the assassin. If that was indeed the case, I swore, I would kill him very, very slowly. I had inherited my mother's persistence and father's cruelty. That day, beneath the jackfruit tree, the earthen pot swathed in red rocking from its branch, the enigma of my future seemed resolved. I knew what it was meant for. I must find him. Every life is meant to seek out someone or the other. Is it not true that every life involves another who dismembers the soul? Someone who is present and absent in it at the same time, like an absent solitaire in a ring, absent because the jeweller forgot to set it, or because it fell off?

My pain multiplied. I was beset by fear on the one hand and by the terrible thirst for revenge on the other. Fear and revenge together make a potent brew. Not even for a second can it stop boiling. The walls of the heart are stretched by that immense pressure. Then, it yearns to explode. My assassin seemed to be the keeper of a huge secret, an immense rage. For sure, my father knew him. He could not complete what he had begun to say. The cough choked him. The words died with him. Words and desires accompany humans when they cross the river of flames to reach the bluish-red banks. That is the real tragedy that those who live face. The loss of a human is not too much. Memories do heal the void. But how to retrieve the words and ideas they were going to reveal but could not?

I went to my room and lay down. I had once shared it with my sister. After her death, I did not like staying here. She was everywhere. Even after seventeen whole years. She was tall, with a full head of beautiful hair, a lovely girl with a pretty mole above her upper lip. Her greenish eyes and ever-merry laughing mouth made her very popular. From the day she completed her MSc degree and the PGDCA course and joined a software company as an apprentice, she shored us up. Found us a rented place. Sent me to college. She soon bought us a house, and we regained our dignity in the eyes of our relatives. Even after death, she remained our support, with the huge insurance payment we received.

I tried to control my memories. But they broke the dam and brimmed over the edges of my eyes. Just then, Amma walked into the room. Pulling her hair, loose and wet after a bath, to one side in front of her shoulder, she sat on the cot near me. Her hair was long, it reached well below the cot. I wiped my eyes and sat up. She caressed my close-cropped head. 'What's the use, racking your brains?' she scolded me. I lay my head on her shoulder, feeling helpless. 'If someone's hell-bent on murder, no one can stop them. Are you afraid to die?' she asked.

When we were kids, when Acchan would sometimes beat us or insult us badly, my sister would declare her intention to commit suicide. Amma would always shoot back, 'If you do, you'll be dragged into a hole and buried! You think you'll be kept here dead and stiff?'

'Do you care even a bit, Amma?' Chechi would flare up.

'I will, if you die in some normal way. I'll weep for some days. Then I'll forget. That's all. If you kick the bucket yourself, don't expect a single tear from me.'

That usually quelled Chechi. Later, although she didn't kill herself and died from an accident, Amma did not weep. She had made Chechi Mysore pak that day. When she lay swathed in white on the front veranda, Acchan burst into loud sobs in the bedroom. But not Amma.

She was unfazed. She sat beside Chechi's body, pressing her face on her forehead, for a long time. The injury was to the back of her head. When it was time to cremate her, people had a hard time separating Amma from her. I wailed, banged my head on the wall in total despair. But Amma did not shed a tear. When they took Chechi away, Amma followed them. When they placed her on the pyre, she sank to the ground, and lay there, pressing her face down. The summer rains had fallen the day before. When they helped her up, Amma's face and the front portion of her body were covered with mud. The nurse Sarada Chechi had to sedate her with an injection to calm her. But after she woke up next morning, she behaved as though nothing had happened. She removed from eyeshot all of Chechi's things, her pictures, everything that belonged to her, as though she never had such a daughter. She spoke only of me. If anyone mentioned Chechi, she would immediately stage a walkout.

Soon after my sister's passing, the impassivity that was already a part of her nature, hardened, and impenetrably so. I could never break it, ever. And yet, I tried to provoke her now, and asked, 'Amma, are you not scared for me?'

'If your life is at its end, you'll die. No reason to stop living because you're scared of dying. That's all.'

'Why does he want to kill me?'

'For revenge, what else?'

'Revenge, against me?'

'Against your father...'

'What's the proof of that?'

'The man kept a knife at his waist all the time when he could walk! What for? If not to stay alive?'

'Acchan? Carried a knife?'

'Which knife do you think was used to stab him? His own knife! He never spoke a word about what happened that night. Why do you think? Something he could not reveal happened that night!'

'What could it have been?'

'I'd thought that he must have attacked some woman, and someone must have taken revenge on him for that. Maybe it was the woman herself?'

'Which woman?'

'Some woman he attacked.'

'Could this not be just your suspicion, Amma?'

'Yes, that's precisely what society expects a daughter to ask her mother,' she said. 'Satye,' she continued, 'do some justice to that name of yours. Isn't pretending to not know the truth the biggest violation of truth?'

Amma was angry. I reeled in pain within as though someone had smashed the insides of my chest with a huge iron pounder. My tongue froze. Amma picked up the newspaper, opened it and began to read from page 1. 'How long it has been since I read the papers in peace,' she muttered.

Amma had not a moment of respite since Acchan became bedridden. But was reading the newspaper more important than her daughter's life? I felt a rage rising inside me. As though she had sensed it, Amma thought aloud as she flipped through the newspaper: 'What are the possibilities when a man is attacked but struggles hard to hide those responsible for it? Either he wishes to protect the attacker, or there is some secret behind it that he wishes to keep from the world.'

'Is it easy for a woman to stab someone fourteen times? That, too, Acchan, burly and six feet tall?'

'Seven of the stab wounds were around the waist and ribs, one each just above and below the left elbow, two on the thigh, just one on the back, below the spine…' Amma paused and immersed herself in some story in the newspaper. I was left alone with my confused thoughts. I tried to guess what she meant. When she finished reading, she looked up at me.

'They've started distributing the new five-hundred-rupee notes. Then why did they withdraw?'

'Is that the burning issue here right now?'

'Edi, the attacker was short, shorter than your father. Barely five feet tall...'

I stared at her, stunned. Amma was in the habit of giving us occasional shocks since I was a child, but this was something else. Enjoying my pathetic stupefaction, she continued:

'That's why I am saying, the attacker was a woman. Another piece of evidence is that all the stab injuries were weak. Acchan had tried to fend off the attack and grab the knife. That's why there were wounds on his palm and near the left elbow, above and below. But the spinal wound was serious. Which means that it was the first one. The rest of the wounds were shallow.'

I continued to stare at her, blood draining off my face.

'Who told you all this, Amma?'

'The doctors who treated him.'

'But then, why did the police not investigate this?'

'Shouldn't the victim want that?'

'Why did you not tell the police that it could have been a woman?'

Amma threw a look of pity at me as she shuffled the pages of the newspaper.

'If a woman stabbed him so many times, there was surely something going on between them. She decided to finish off the business herself. Why should I get in the middle of it?'

I sat, my mouth agape, taken aback.

'Why did you not tell me all this for so long?'

'You didn't ask.'

'But I had a reason to ask only recently.'

'I didn't have a reason to tell you until now, either.'

Amma went back to her newspaper. Suddenly, she looked up eagerly. 'Ah, this guy is now the chairman of the corporation?'

I did not ask who. Some guy. Some guy who used to loiter around here when Acchan ran his film production company, a newsmagazine, and a hotel. A smile appeared on her face. 'Didn't you recognize him?

The guy whose house you went to…' It was a derisive smile. My face reddened. I flung her an enraged look. Not willing to concede defeat, I asked, 'Who?'

'Sriram,' she said.

'Oh, him.' I yawned. 'There's a man out there trying to kill me. That does not bother you, Amma. You prefer to remind me of some chap who tried a cheap romance with me a long time back…'

I was angry. Amma folded the newspaper, set her glasses right and looked at me.

'What am I to do if someone's out to kill you? It must be because of something your old man did. You're the one who should try to find out about that.'

'How am I to do so?'

'You're scared of death, aren't you?'

'No, I'm not. But I need to know why I deserve to die.'

'You'll die if you know, and also if you don't. It's better to bite the dust without knowing some truths.'

'But it is better to know some truths before dying.'

Amma threw the folded newspaper casually on the bed, and muttering, 'Just like her old man, won't let me have a moment of peace,' sat up straight. The little knot at the tip of her long hair had come undone; she retied it, and throwing it back, faced me.

'I used to lap up all the detective stories I could find when I was pregnant with you. I had dreamt of a detective son or daughter!'

'Oho! I am most gratified to have found an opportunity to make your dream a reality…'

After a moment, I murmured, 'Detective Satyapriya!'

Both of us burst out laughing. I hugged her from behind. She tilted her head towards mine, her cheek brushed against mine. At that moment, I saw the extremely rare expression of motherly affection on her face.

'But from where am I to begin the investigation?' I asked.

'A detective must start from the lives of the dead...'

Amma sighed. She untied and retied the little knot at her hair-tip, threw it back, got up and left. The tresses tied into that small knot swung like a pendulum below her waist. My mother was a beauty. She could make me laugh easily, she could also disarm me as quickly.

When she left, I picked up the newspaper. The story was on the regional page. It was indeed him. Inaugurating some seminar on women's empowerment. Seeing his face made me want to puke. I folded the paper, put it on the teapoy and leaned back on the bedstand. Outside the window, the money plant that Chechi had planted had spread everywhere. Its leaves were riddled with holes, like someone with unerring aim had shot them repeatedly, I noticed. I was gripped by the fear that someone crouching behind the creeper there could shoot me directly in the heart. I went up to the window with a pounding heart and convinced myself that there was no one. Then, I became engrossed in pulling out the knives Amma had thrust into my heart and examining them.

One thing she said drew me fully to it – the detective novels she had read when she was pregnant with me. Maybe it was the fear and suspense and scare that she experienced then that made me this way. But what could she have read while pregnant with Chechi? She had been the lovey-dovey type. Maybe Amma read nothing but romances then. The memory of Chechi rattled my nerves. Her passing had left inside me a crumbling well so deep, so suffocating, that no one could see its bottom. Whenever I slipped and fell into that darkness within, I experienced the throes of death. I felt a thousand needles pierce my chest all at once. When my memories of her awoke, I paced the room. Sometimes I chewed on green chillies. When they seared my tongue, I felt relieved.

A good detective starts from the lives of the dead. I had two close relatives who were dead. First, Chechi, second, Acchan. Which of the two must I start with – that was the first question. In death, Chechi could claim seniority. But I decided that I would begin with Acchan's as he was senior in age. I waited, sleepless, like an experienced detective, until it was two in the morning. Then, without waking up Amma, I went to Acchan's room.

Have you ever entered a dead person's room alone? That, too, in the dead of night? A pity, if you haven't. Because it is a strange experience. Especially when a soul awaits you there with a secret that is now controlling your very life. I opened the door, stepped into the darkness. The smell of Dettol with which Amma had doused the place to mask the odour of Acchan's shit and piss still lingered in there. I paused for a moment. There's something similar between light and money. You get used to the absence and presence of both, equally. My eyes adjusted to the darkness. I began to see. At the end of the darkness was the cot on which Acchan used to sleep, his chair, his steel almirahs. On the other side of the cot, a wooden box as high as my knee. I began to feel pain for him. The unfortunate man, how the secrets must have choked him! Human beings have secrets because they are insecure; they fall in love because they feel inferior. My case was different. My secrets and my loves were the same. Both arose from my insecurities.

As I stood there, someone whispered close to my ear, 'You can't sleep?'

I whipped around. Seeing a female form with flowing long hair right behind me, I screamed! Amma turned the lights on, and pulling her hair back and tying it up, looked at me with a vexed expression.

'Are you trying to scare the daylights out of people or what? What are you up to, Satye? Why are you screaming in the dark?'

My heart kept pounding even after I went to bed. I tried to sleep hugging Amma. But as I lay there pressing my cheek against her right shoulder, all sorts of doubts assailed me. Was this Amma? Or the woman who stabbed Acchan perhaps? Or was it really Amma who stabbed Acchan? Will Amma turn around and shoot at me, catching me unawares?

I began to shiver. I heard the hiss of the approaching bullet and the click of the gun. This is what I said: never run from an assassin. But I did run, and nothing could be done about it. On the strength of my years. But that killed all the joys of life. To get them back, there was but one way: find my intended assassin.

I lay on the bed and reached out for the newspaper. Then, shining the light from the torch on it, I read the whole report. His speech ran like this:

'Nowadays, more men are subjected to violence than women. There are many women who snare innocent men and destroy their good name. These women are an insult to womanhood. It is such women who fall prey to the gun and the knife...'

A streak of lightning passed through me again. Was it Sriram who had sent the killer? I switched off the torch, lay close to Amma. I reviewed the list of likely killers once more:

Sriram.
Samir Sayyid.
Prabhudev Maheswari.
Swami Mahipal Shah Baba.
Besides these, Acchan's unknown enemy.

So, one of these five. Or all five!

I knew then that I had to read together the stabbing of my father and the shooting I escaped. All of it was connected. Like the way in which roots growing down from the branches seek the roots underground, each sought the other. Like the butterfly that could not cover the vast distance of its journey in a single lifetime and therefore attempted to do so across many generations, the consequences of my father's karma now rested upon me. An exciting moment in the life of a woman who lived in these times!

But, Amma...! My heart ached. My unease began to simmer. Who will tear away my mother from my corpse? Who will lift her up when she sinks to the ground in the rain pressing her face into the mud? Who will wipe off the rest of the memories about me that linger in the house when she wakes up? Who will she go to in the middle of the night, beside whom will she sigh and whisper that line from Kumaran Asan's poem *Chintavishtayaaya Seeta*, 'Narajeevithamaaya Vedanaikkorumattarbhakaraushadangal thaan...' For this agony that is human life, our children are a kind of balm...

THREE

It was during an Onam season that the house caught fire. It was a Sunday. Ayyankali Jayanti fell on a Tuesday. The Onam vacation began on a Friday. I reached home that very day. There had been a power failure there since two days – we lived in a rural area, and it was normal for power failures to last for two or three days or more.

Chechi was at home, waiting for the results of her MSc exam. She was also holding literacy classes on the sly, without Acchan's knowledge. She had found a new boyfriend there. On Sunday, we had gone to bed whispering about him and giggling together. Around two o'clock, the house was filled with fumes and soot and flames. Later, the locals were to describe how the smell of kerosene had carried right up to the bazaar on the farther bank by the wind from the lake. The general conclusion was that a kerosene stove had exploded, a lapse on the part of the cook, Laalamma. The flames spread rapidly over the dried coconut and copra heaped above in the kitchen loft, and then the kerosene in the storeroom and the dry kindling stored under the slab also caught fire, making matters worse. Amma, who woke first, choked by the kerosene fumes, opened the door and found the flames spreading to the dining room. There were buckets of water placed near the open courtyard in the middle of the house, where we washed our hands. Amma tried to douse the fire with the water from those buckets.

Acchan was dead asleep. Amma roused us and Laalamma. Chechi and I ran half-asleep through the thickets of rubber trees to our uncle Gopi Maaman's house half a kilometre away. He quickly sent his workers to help put out the fire. When a crowd gathered, Amma managed to pull Acchan up and drag him to the cowshed. The kitchen and pantry were aflame. The air was filled with soot and fumes. As the locals tried to put out the fire, Chechi and I sat on the outer step of the cowshed, completely overwhelmed. The shifting lights from the Petromax lanterns and kerosene lamps, the sounds of the pulley and of the many buckets being lowered into the well and pulled up again, the hissing of the water fighting the flames – we experienced these as though in a dream. Acchan, however, was still curled up, sleeping. An awful stink from his open mouth hit us right in the face. That stench, combined with the reek of cow dung and cow urine sickened me. I lay down on Chechi's lap and wept.

The same stink emanated from inside Acchan's wooden box. That's why the memory of the fire came back to me. A detective needs, first of all, liberation from emotions. Individual likes and dislikes are not relevant in an investigation. Any search for truth is a temporary renunciation of one's desires. The old wooden box was blackened and mouldy; no amount of cleaning could get rid of the mould. The lock was rusty. The icy chill that it seemed to bear entered my very bones. No, I cautioned the detective in me: do not become a slave to your senses.

On the night our house caught fire, Gopi Maaman's wife Valsala Maami had sent over black coffee in a huge portable jar – the type in which you take milk to be sold to the cooperative society. Amma and Laalamma poured it out for those who came to help us put out the fire. It was not sweet enough. I tried to swallow two cheekfuls, and grimacing, gave it back to Amma. Amma pinched me hard on the arm, almost tearing off the flesh, for not giving in even at a time like that.

The pain nearly blinded me. 'Amma, you are acting out! You are angry with Acchan and taking it out on her!' Chechi tried to intervene. Amma twisted the flesh off her arm too. We comforted each other, rubbing the sore areas.

The day dawned after the fire was put out. It was still hot, the smoke still billowed. The roosters in the hen coop seemed to be in a crowing competition. The magpies and drongos in the trees around the house roused each other. Acchan woke up slowly. But seeing the crowd and the bustle, he struggled up awkwardly, and retied the kaili-cloth tightly around his waist. He ran his hand on his moustache and let out a low growl. Amma had tied her hair up into a bun and draped a sari. She pressed her hands on her hips and threw him a complaining look. Acchan merely rolled his eyes and twirled his moustache.

'Ah, you have woken up, Muthalaali. You didn't feel or hear anything, boss?' the locals greeted him. He went into the sooty, smoky bathroom and had a bath. Then, entering the bedroom which the flames had spared, he took out a freshly laundered silk shirt and gold-brocade-bordered mundu from the wooden almirah and soon presented himself as the rich man, the muthalaali. By ten o'clock, the police arrived.

'This is what happens when the women in the house are careless! No need for a police case,' Acchan declared. A curl of smoke rose from his Rothmans cigarette. The sub-inspector then was Dinakaran Pillai, well known for pulping convicts and making them spit blood. 'Saare,' he began very humbly, 'if we just make a complaint...' 'No need. Didn't I make it clear, Dinakaran Pille?' Acchan's voice grew stern. But he reached out and slipped some hundred-rupee notes into Pillai's pocket. The police team, including Dinakaran Pillai and the case writer Sadasivan Nair, left immediately. Our driver Ulahannan, whom we called Ulahannan Maaman, reached the house on his Hero cycle. When he finished wiping clean our black Contessa car, Acchan left without a word to Amma. The car disappeared, crossing the white-gravel-covered yard, sounding as though glass panes were being crushed under it.

The kitchen was completely gutted. There was nothing that had not turned into soot or had not melted. That day, we ate all three meals brought from the little shop behind the bus stand, Sekharan Pillai's Hotel Mahalakshmi. We had dosa and chutney for breakfast, and regular rice and curries for lunch. Supper was warm parottas, wrapped in a banana leaf, and beef in spicy gravy sprinkled with pieces of fried coconut – a delicacy of those times. Then, after many years, beef was banned. When I heard of it, the old flavours surfaced inside me. I quickly went over to a Malayali restaurant and ordered beef fry. But the zing was missing. How would it not, when fear reigns as you eat? When there is no freedom, there can be no relish either.

That day, before we got up from lunch, our maternal grandfather's white Benz car rode up to our front yard. Appooppan got out, supporting himself on his silver-tipped walking stick. He walked around the house and saw it all for himself. Amma was standing in the yard, with a deadpan expression on her face. He went up and patted her on the shoulder:

'Good thing it burned down. Now we can build a kitchen there in the new style,' he said jovially.

Amma laughed. We laughed with her. Then, in a flash, the masons and carpenters arrived. A temporary shed was built facing west to serve as a kitchen. New kitchen implements, pots and pans were bought. An engineer, contractor, and an army of workers arrived. Only Acchan was missing. That was normal and so we did not worry. Onam was six days away. On the fourth day, they laid concrete on the roof. The painting began the next day. 'The smell of the paint will make the little ones sick,' said Appooppan, and he took my mother and us to the town. We bought a fridge, a mixie, a grinder, and a gas stove. He got us new clothes for Onam. We went to the Prince Theatre and watched *Iyer the Great*. 'We have come this far, let's go visit Ayyaal,' said Appooppan. 'Ayyaal' – 'that person' – was how Appooppan referred to our father. And when he addressed him, he always used the word 'eeyaal' – or 'this person'.

So we drove to Acchan's office. It was a ten-acre compound by the sea, full of casuarina and tall pendula ashoka trees. There was a story behind how Appooppan came to possess it. At the beginning of his career in business, he had gone seeking a room. He found a locked room in the market that looked suitable. He asked about for its owner and went to meet him. The owner was a prosperous man, and his house was a whitewashed mansion full of servants and retainers. The yard was filled with heaps of harvested coconuts. The owner was busy supervising the workers counting the coconuts when Appooppan met him. Appooppan was thin, and did not look prosperous at all; his clothes were worn. The first thing the owner asked him was his caste. When he told him, the owner said, 'Even if I don't use the place and let the termites take it, I won't let you have it.' Stricken, Appooppan came away. But soon, he managed to find a better place. He made a lot of money. Then one day, he heard that the first room he had seen was up for sale. That was the time he had made an enormous profit from the sugar trade. He went again to the big house. But the man there was barely a shadow of the proud owner who had denied Appooppan the room. His copra trade had collapsed, and he was deep in debt. The house was empty and shabby; the yard was overrun with weeds. He owed others one lakh rupees – a lakh, back then, was an enormous sum. Appooppan drew upon his savings, managed to put the amount together, and met him again. He said, 'I don't need your charity – I'll transfer all that I have to you.'

That is how the ten-acre property and all the assets that stood on it came into Appooppan's hands. It stood in the middle of the two roads that led from the market to the seashore. It was only after he got it registered in his name that Appooppan learned that there was a printing press in the compound, near the road on the left. He did not close it down. When he earned a substantial profit from prawn exports, he expanded it and began a weekly magazine. One day, a struggling young man who had dropped out of medical studies and did not have the courage to face his family and the local folk, came there looking for a job. 'Ayyaal' – that person – was my father.

That day, when we passed the Beach Road, it was dusk. 'When I bought this place, there wasn't even a puppy on this beach,' Appooppan quipped, seeing the crowd there.

I never liked the sea. The ever-surging, ever-rolling sea made my heart pound. My sister, however, thought exactly the opposite. Her heart was like the sea. She truly enjoyed the light waves of romance that rose in the high seas and pranced and tumbled merrily towards the shore to share sweet nothings with it, only to roll right back.

Our car entered a large gate over which a large, curved signboard read 'Hotel Vasanthamaalika' and reached the porch. On either side of the building stood the offices of Nityavasantham Productions and the magazine *Vasanthakairali*. I gazed at them, feeling proud. The sea breeze was blowing hard when we stepped out of the car; we nearly swayed. Chechi and I had on the latest fashion of the time, a suit set called the 'Punjabi dress' – a kurta-pyjama suit, with the pyjama trimmed with the fabric of the kurta. We pressed down our kurtas against the breeze as we climbed the steps. Amma, who wore a cobalt blue Binny silk sari, held the edge of the sari close. The doorkeepers wore jackets and red headgear with fan-shaped trimmings of yellow silk sewn on them. They didn't seem to recognize us. They greeted us as though we were guests seeking a room. Appooppan held the edge of his gold-bordered mundu in one hand and the silver-tipped walking stick in the other, and probably just to amuse us, he asked, 'May we have a room, please?'

'Yes,' said the receptionist, moving the register forward, 'what type of room would you prefer?'

'Who is the owner of the hotel?' Appooppan asked.

'Sivaprasad Muthalaali. He was a doctor. Now he is a businessman ... a film producer...'

'All right. Where is he now? Can we meet him, please?'

We looked at Amma smilingly. But she did not smile.

'Not possible today...' said the receptionist.

'But why?'

'Just not possible, Ammava.'

Appooppan began to tap the floor with his walking stick.

'Don't refuse me, chezhara ... we've come from far, just to see him. Don't say that he isn't in.'

Chechi and I swallowed our laughter. Amma's face went pale.

'If you come tomorrow, you can see him ... He has left orders not to let anyone in today.' The receptionist's expression became severe.

'So the man is here! Okay, this is an emergency...'

'No, no, come another time, old man.' The young man was now openly hostile.

'No, Accha, let us leave.' Amma's voice sounded pitiful. Appooppan looked at her searchingly. Just then our driver Ulahannan Maaman ran up. He told the receptionist who Appooppan was; then he turned to Appooppan and begged him not to go up to Acchan's room. Amma looked even more devastated. Appooppan, who had been gay and hearty until then, flew into a furious rage. He swung his cane, walked swiftly towards the lift; the receptionist chased him, imploring him not to go up. But he had got into the lift, and we, with him. 'No, no, no Accha...' Amma entreated. He silenced her with a searing look. Chechi and I were terrified to see our grandfather transformed thus. Chechi gripped my hand tightly.

The lift opened on to the dimly lit fifth-floor lobby with mirrors on its walls that reflected darkly. Appooppan strode towards the room numbered 555. He knocked hard on the door repeatedly with his stick. Amma tried to hold us back, but Chechi pulled free, and holding my right hand, she dashed after Appooppan. Amma had grabbed my left hand. Chechi dragged me forward, and I dragged Amma.

The door opened after three or four hard, long knocks. Acchan's face, livid at the interruption, stuck out, and the moment it saw Appooppan, it turned yellow and withdrew. He tried to close the door from inside, but Appooppan kicked it open and went in. The three of us, holding each other, also stumbled in. Acchan ran to the bed, jumped in, and lay with his face down. The room was filled with the scent of Rothmans and Scotch whisky. On the floor lay a Punjabi dress, a yellow kurta with large white leaf-prints and a matching pyjama, a bra and panty. A teenaged girl leapt up and tried to cover herself with the edge of the bed sheet. But because Acchan was lying on the other edge, she could not pull the sheet from under him. I saw her face only after I saw her pale breasts with blackish nipples and her hairless crotch. It was the film star Rajani. Her first movie was *Aralippookkal*, produced by Nityavasantham Productions.

Chechi and I stood there motionless, staggered. Then, after a few moments, Amma bent down and picked up the scattered clothes. A pretty bra of black lace. A fine pink panty with a red rose sewn on to it. Amma held them out to Rajani. She slipped them on and ran into the bathroom.

It was Amma who stepped out of the room first. I followed her. Appooppan held on to my shoulder as he came out. Chechi took more time. 'Sive, Sive, aren't you coming?' Amma scolded her. Chechi came away too. Appooppan's legs trembled when we got into the lift. But Amma held her head high. She smiled at the receptionist and asked him his name and about his family. Opened her bag and handed him a hundred-rupee note. He took it mechanically. Amma did not weep when we came down the stairs. Nor did I. But the tears flowed from Chechi's eyes. When we were inside the car, she burst out sobbing and fell into my lap. She was always tender-hearted.

All of this – I had wanted to forget. Acchan's wooden box brought it back. I did not linger in my memories. Instead, I began to try the keys that Amma had found, one by one. Though she had dipped them in oil, the rust in the lock proved an obstacle. Amma then called Harish, who drove an autorickshaw at the local stand. He found an iron worker who took apart the lock easily. I handed him two 'Gandhi' notes. The note my mother had given the receptionist at the hotel did not have Gandhi's picture on it. It was of a different colour and size. I tried to recall all the different currency notes I had seen in my life and whiled away a lot of time.

The truth was I was trying everything I could to delay opening the box. The only other time my heart thumped so badly was in that trip to join Samir for a night. It was a massive risk, and it could have literally wiped out everything I had achieved in my life until then. It was to turn my life upside down later. That is why I held back from mentioning his name to the police. If he was not the assassin, it would be dangerous for both of us. And besides, if that was indeed the case, the police would nab him soon enough. I had prepared myself to speak of it in such an eventuality. But for the moment, it was more important to find the assassin Acchan hinted at.

In the end, I decided to open the box. I called Amma, for courage. She was in the veranda reading the newspaper; she pretended not to hear me. I went to the door and called her again. She looked up irritably.

'You open it yourself.'

'What if it is full of gold bars?' I tried to joke. My mother's face looked dour. She recited a couplet:

> *'Vinayaarnna sukham kothikkayi-*
> *-llinimel njaan asukham varikkuvaan...'*

In no way was she going to seek troublesome pleasure to end up in pain ... Amma's head stooped towards the newspaper again.

I went back to Acchan's room. Though Amma was present just two walls away, I felt like I was now all alone on this planet. No detective ever finds out the killer at the very beginning. But she always gets a clue – one that proves crucial later – right in the beginning. I opened the box, trembling.

Right on top, there were loose sheets of paper and some notebooks. The moth-eaten pages were in shreds, like dead termites. When I pushed them apart, there rose an unbearable stench. There was a cardboard box below. It was fairly heavy, sealed with red wax on all sides. When I opened it, the horrible odour spread all over. The same awful smell that had come out of Acchan's mouth on the night our house caught fire. My eyes and nose burned.

There was a half-metre-tall glass jar in the box. Inside it slept a full-grown foetus – all shrivelled up, upside down – like the seahorse in an aquarium. My hair stood on end. My hands shook and so did the liquid inside. The foetus moved. It was formalin; that was why it stank so badly. Acchan, too, had stored away something dead inside him. That is why his breath stank so insufferably.

FOUR

Have you seen a viper give birth? A pity, if you haven't! How are you then to experience the way in which fear and curiosity and revulsion rush into your spine all at once? I have been in the zoology lab only once. I shouldn't have! But I was that age. Body and soul did not take each other into account back then. One had no sense of the political and spiritual dimensions of fear.

Sriram was a lecturer in the college. 'Can you show me the lab?' I asked him one day. It sounded like a joke to him first. Later, he invited me himself. It was May, and a Saturday. I crossed the railway tracks and reached the college. The campus was full of pendula ashoka and gulmohar trees. The zoology lab was on the left as you passed the college office, rather isolated. My legs grew heavy when I entered it. My heart beat hard out of anxiety. The blue-coloured windows were shut. But light filtered in through the ventilators and the cracks between the aged wooden frames and the windowpanes which could not be fully shut. The rosewood shelves bore glass jars – they glinted. They contained all sorts of creatures – from a shark, a dolphin, to a seahorse, an octopus, and a human foetus – all suspended beyond decay. I was looking for the viper and its progeny. A viper and eighteen

37

baby vipers. They were all in a large jar. The nineteenth one had only half emerged from its mother's body, still sheathed in white skin.

My eyes were filled with darkness. Sriram put his hand on my shoulder. He slowly drew back the strands of my hair, stroked my ears. It felt creepy, like a snake gliding on my skin. That creature which was killed during childbirth was on my mind, after all. The head of the mother was crushed. She had been killed by a blow to her head. The babies were drowned in a chemical solution. Would those who had no pity for the young of another kind be merciful to their own children? I did not have the courage to take another look at that creature that had not finished giving birth when it died. There might have been more babies inside. They must have lain in wait for birth, swathed in white skin. I thought I was choking. Tears pricked my eyelids.

Sriram did not ask why I wanted to see the lab, neither did I tell him. My father had been a student here. So was my sister. Sriram as well. Acchan was the chief guest at the silver jubilee celebrations of the college. He rode there in our Contessa car and stepped into the celebrations like the hero in superstar movies of a later time, resplendent in the wide-gold-bordered mundu, sandal-coloured silk shirt, Rolex watch, and carrying a Sheaffer pen. Chechi was a first-year BSc student there at the time. The college authorities greeted Acchan with rows of young women carrying lit lamps and the college band striking up a welcome song. When he stood up to make his speech, the auditorium fell silent.

'Even if I die, my memories are safe in this college,' he said. 'I have left memories sealed in the zoology lab of this college. Go and take a look for yourself! The formalin jar which contains the viper and its babies – who do you think caught it? Who do you think caught, killed, and stuffed the mongoose family, the ant eater, the civet cat, and the monitor lizard that you find there? It was me. Such are the ways in which this Sivaprasad took shape.'

His voice rang in the silent auditorium. Chechi had goosebumps; she was, after all, the tender-hearted sort. It was on that day that I came to know that our father was the first student to pass the Sixth Form exam in those parts and that after the exam, he worked at a local toddy shop keeping accounts from six in the evening until midnight. When the customers were numerous, he also doubled up as a server. Acchan wiped his eyes as he recounted this. He also studied in the middle of all this work. And was able to come first in every exam, with first-class marks. The day he joined BSc here, the head of the department, Alexander Sir, took him under his wing. He was appointed assistant to the attender in the lab. Acchan brought the frogs and cockroaches for the practical classes. He would search for them in the fields the whole night; he would sell the large frogs in the toddy shop and the small ones to the lab. He also revealed that when he was a student in the Medical College, he had also worked to find dead bodies for the anatomy training.

It was when he joined the Medical College that he wore pants for the first time. It was Alexander Sir who got him the fabric and paid the tailor. Acchan's voice broke when he said that, his words faltered. My sister burst out crying. Her friends had to bring her back home. I was home; it was the study-leave time just before the final exams. My studies were interrupted because I was busy comforting Chechi and making her laugh. But I had decided that I would go see the lab myself. Just to find out if the story about the viper was indeed true. I did not tell Sriram any of this. And in any case, it isn't necessary to tell lovers more than what they need to know.

~

The glass jar in the trunk reminded me of all this. I thought it would startle Amma. But no! She straightened her glasses, took a good look, and yawned. 'Don't you have anything to say?' I asked her peevishly.

'Why are you opening this old, condemned stuff?' was her reply.

'But didn't you tell me that I ought to begin from Acchan's life?' I pressed on.

'I suggested that you investigate for the sake of investigation. Not for the sake of blubbering at the sight of random stuff.'

'But whose child is this?'

'Not mine for sure.'

'Amme, wasn't Acchan a medical student? Maybe this was a dead newborn that was preserved owing to academic interest...'

'Yeah, yeah, very intense it was, the academic interest ... Wasn't that the reason why your father dropped out of the course without passing?'

'So then, what are we to think of this?'

'That we should report this to the police. The rule is that if you discover a crime, you should report it to the police.'

'Do you suspect a crime, Amme?'

'What else! Who does not know that it is a crime to keep the body of a human infant in your house?'

'But then, why would Acchan store it away?'

'Maybe he was scared to dispose of it.'

'Scared? Why?'

'Maybe he couldn't find the right time or opportunity. He became immobile rather unexpectedly, didn't he?'

'What should we do now?'

'Just one thing, let the police know.'

'And then what happens?'

'They can make suspects of you and me. And arrest us too.'

'Best! That's all we lack right now.'

'No one will know if we don't report this. Except our consciences.'

'Aiyo, will I land up in the police station for this?'

'No. Right now, the murder attempt on you is all over the news. If that's followed by news that the dead body of an infant was found here...'

'What will we do if that happens, Amme?'

'We'll find a way...'

After two hours, Venukkuttan Chettan's car arrived. He once helped out around the house – lending a hand with chopping the firewood, watering the coconut saplings, and shopping for the household. Later he became rich and powerful. His son and daughter had done exceedingly well, becoming IAS and IPS officers, respectively; it was all over the papers.

Venukkuttan Chettan examined the box and the jar. Then spoke with his daughter Aswathy Venu IPS. In less than an hour, two policemen and the sub-inspector came from the local police station. They took away the jar for further investigation. They confirmed that only old ledgers and notebooks remained in the box. They took our statements too.

At night, when Amma was sitting on the cane chair, I went up to her. I sat down and leaned my head on her knees. The crickets were making their petulant sounds. Amma ran her fingers through my hair, her mind elsewhere. After some time, she asked, 'What is happening with your investigation?'

'It hasn't begun yet.' I sighed.

'I am sure ... he had kept it aside to bury it or get rid of it somehow ... at a later time.' Amma said that to no one in particular. I froze right there; I knew she was right. Subsequently, this is the conversation that unfolded:

'Amme, was this box already there in Vasanthaalayam? I don't remember seeing it.'

'I recall that four such boxes were built to keep the collection money safe. Only this was brought back to the house from the hotel after the attack ... Who knows what happened to the others. Maybe they were sold or given away...'

'You never checked what was in it?'

'How was I to? Every single day, something was going haywire! When I had the time, the key was missing. And then we began to use it like a table and quite forgot that it was a box!'

'Hard to believe!'

'Who thought one would have to make you believe!'

'But to think that no one had even opened to check such a big box!'

'You sound like it was I who put it in that box!'

'Okay, not you, then who?'

'Your father had learned to preserve snakes and fish and so on when he was a college student.'

'Is that the same as preserving a full-grown foetus, almost an infant?'

'The human being is a creature too.'

'The cardboard box in which we found it was sealed. Doesn't that mean that it was sent to him from somewhere?'

'Can't it be that your father sealed it himself?'

'How long has this box been at our house?

'Twenty-four years! For twenty-four years this corpse has been in our house without our knowing…'

'Without anyone to weep, even!'

'What's the use of weeping after death?'

'I have never seen you cry, Amma.'

'Are you upset because of that?'

'No, not that … I am just curious to know if you have ever wept.'

'At a certain age, everyone cries.'

'Have you cried thinking of me?'

'Once some tears did leap out involuntarily.'

'When?'

'When you went missing … after the third day…'

'Me…?'

'I remember. It was wartime, on the borders. It was on the day after a soldier of ours was captured by Pakistan.'

I stiffened. It was a bit like getting an unexpected blow on the back of my head. My body curled up like the viper whose head had been crushed while it was giving birth. I held my breath, trying hard to hide the thumping of my heart. My body burned up first, grew sweaty, and then became very cold.

'Where did you go that day? To Shanti's?'

Amma did not sound anxious at all. I swallowed. My name is Satyapriya. I will not speak untruths. Especially to my mother.

Amma was referring to the day I went to see the zoology lab. That day, I had sex with Sriram. Not because I felt lust for him, not because I wanted any sex. I was sorry for him. Also guilty, because I had hurt him earlier. Even after years, the old wounds continued to bleed in his eyes. I thought that it would heal if I submitted to him. Besides, I, too, was a wreck those days. I needed something to draw my attention away. The soul of that viper-mother bit me hard and shook me in its fangs. The body yearned to somehow push out the mind which was proving just too much for it. If it was to be sex, let it be so, I decided.

It was a room with a high ceiling. The walls were whitewashed, the floor coarsely cemented. There were cobwebs everywhere. He laid me down on the bare floor in front of a rosewood shelf on which skulls were arranged; no one could make out if they were of women or men. The stench of his sweat was as bad as it had been earlier. Inside a glass case to the left was displayed a chart in which the evolutionary path from dinosaurs to birds was illustrated – I tried to memorize it. I counted the bars of the four windows I could see in front three times over; pinpointed the location of the spider visible on the cobweb that shone in the light streaming in through the half-closed window. Sriram undressed me and then himself. Suddenly, we heard the sound of anklets in the hallway. His body jolted and began to tremble. He clung to me. The sound of the anklets reached the door. There were sounds of knocking and attempts to open the door. Then we heard the feet move away. Maybe out of fear, he came too soon. When we no longer heard the sound of the anklets, Sriram sighed in relief. But suddenly, the window right in front of us was pulled open from outside. The daylight fell upon our naked bodies. In the window appeared a sindoor-clad forehead and eyes lined with kohl. Then someone started to bang on the door of the lab.

Sriram jumped up, pulled his clothes on, and opened the door. I could not even get up. The young woman who stormed into the room was beautiful. It wasn't long after her wedding; this was evident from the undiminished lustre of her jewellery. She kicked me and spat on my face. 'Could you find only my husband to cure your rot?' she flared. 'I'll kill you!' she screamed, and Sriram dragged her away. I heard some pushing and shoving and then a bursting into tears and loud wailing. The door slammed shut. I heard the bolt being pushed into place. The sounds outside ceased. I somehow closed the window, somehow dressed myself. Then I tried to open the door. I had not known that he was married. I also did not know that the door was firmly bolted. I sat there, utterly petrified, for a long while, without even the strength to wipe off that woman's spittle from my face. I wanted to die and kill at the same time. Maybe that's how it feels if your head is smashed when you are giving birth. The hurt will be everywhere, and you'll die squirming in agony.

Day turned to dusk and then to night. I thought that he would return and set me free. But no. Rodents began to run around the shadowy room. I was gripped with a sudden wish to see my mother, or at least hear her voice. Those days there were no mobile phones, of course. The souls of the snakes writhed about as shadows and frightened me. Whenever I tried to sleep, the ghosts of the monitor lizards and mongooses and cockroaches woke me up. That was a night I thought would never end. His cum between my legs, her spittle on my face. I felt disgusted with myself. I wanted to throw up the whole of my own self.

~

Is the meaning of what I have said hitherto clear now? That there was a glass jar inside me, just like the one we found inside Acchan's box. It was this jar that my assassin shattered. That is the grave injury he caused me. The memories that one had not buried out of the fear that someone may find out, broke free when the glass splintered. All of it was horrible, stinking. Besides, the stench of formalin. Through the day, formalin swirled around me like the sea itself, making frothy waves. The foetus floated on that sea. It had become like wax, steeped in the solution for so long. It was male; a tiny penis was visible between the wizened little legs. The transparent eyelids looked like Gandhi's spectacles. The face of a fakir in deep meditation. That, too, a totally naked fakir.

I began to sear in memories of Samir. 'I want a boy,' I remembered him whisper to me as we lay on the narrow wooden plank in the tree house, which creaked at our slightest movements, concealed by leaves atop a tall mahogany tree in the forests of Niyamgiri. I was dissolving in love. And therefore, at that time, it did not matter – it could have been a boy or a girl, Kerala plantains or elephant foot yam.

When we got dressed again and were sipping coffee, I asked Samir, 'But why a boy?'

'Simple – a man can feel only a boy child to be his own. The girl won't belong to him.' He said this as he wiped his body with a cloth soaked in the water stored in a corner of the tree house. After he put on his dark green shirt and trousers, he held me close. 'The girl belongs to the man she loves. For example, aren't you mine?'

'Is that so?'

I laughed. His face fell. Even the tiniest rejection felt unbearable to him. For him, love and submission were one and the same. He believed that if love vanished, fear must take its place. Fear was his weapon, war his obsession. He had studied the war that happened during those three days I had disappeared. 'The war that changed the future of the nation,' he described it thus. That war was important for me too. It turned my future too. In any case, that's what wars are. It is the ones that don't fight in wars themselves who are always defeated.

Samir believed and argued that all wars stoke hatred and that hatred in turn stokes fear, and that the strength of those who wish to rule is precisely the fear that others feel about them. I did not believe that one could rule by instilling fear. But there was one thing that I was convinced of. And that is, love is a lot like fear. You have to experience it creeping up the spine, like fear. Like metal pots and pans in a kitchen aflame, you too melt, flow, and turn into some other shape. Whenever

I melted in love, I changed so much; I became so unlike myself. I have not regretted it. Nor have I yearned to return to my older self. The old me was a heart with a bullet hole in it. As it thrashed about, it spilled blood. The old me was the viper that died taking a blow to its head in the middle of labour. Even when half-dead, it was still bringing forth dreams.

I was able to understand Samir only later. He was right. The Indian man needs someone he can call his own. Only a boy child can be that. Because without that maleness, he cannot continue across generations. That is why he thirsts for a boy. That foetus, which was meditating in the jar, was some man's heir, to whom he would have passed on his memory, experience, convictions, and faith. Was Acchan that man? If yes, why did he seal it in a jar? And if not, why did he keep it for nearly a quarter of a century?

I was exhausted. I tried to recollect the grey face of that near-infant. But however much I tried, only Gandhiji's face came back to me. Did that foetus resemble my father? Or Chechi, or me? Did my father kill his mother, smash her head as she was giving birth to him? Did she escape death? Was my mother's inference that the person who stabbed him was a woman correct? Who could that woman be? Did she appoint my assassin, or was she the assassin herself?

Wait before deciding hastily that a woman will not start such a thing after a full twenty-four years. Have you seen the face of a snake giving birth? Have you experienced the terrible sweltering, searing, smouldering sensation when even a drop of formalin falls upon a wound? Have you ever been hit on the back of your head with a piece of wood with nails stuck on it? A pity, if your answer is no! How will you then understand the infinite revenge of serpents that are killed by blows to their heads while struggling to give birth?

FIVE

The sixteenth-day ceremony after Acchan's death fell on a Sunday. That was when I saw a two-thousand-rupee note for the first time. This was the real significance of that day. It was Venukkuttan Chettan who got hold of it after hours of standing in a queue in front of a bank. I felt guilty about troubling him, and to hide it, I made a snide remark, something like, 'Tough times! That we can't get our own hard-earned money in cash!' Paramarth, who was hanging around where I stood, overheard it. Paramarth was our neighbour Sarada Chechi's grandson. 'Even the prime minister's mother is standing in a queue,' he snorted. 'Why can't you do it for a little while for the sake of the country?' The enormous knowledge that this tenth-standard student seemed to have on just about everything shut me up. He launched into a lecture on the two-thousand-rupee note. It came fitted with a micro-chip in it, he said; therefore, from now on, no one would be able to steal currency notes in the country. I quickly handed the note back to Venukkuttan Chettan. Yeah, keep it, and let the government snoop on you! All I wanted in the forty-fourth year of my life was freedom and peace of mind. Those I did not have in my best years, all because of currency notes, money. I was not going to waste either freedom or peace just for a currency note, and no meant no.

The ceremony and the feast that followed did not go smoothly. I was exhausted. For days on end, sleep eluded me because whenever I began to doze, the sound of a bullet shattering glass would rip through my stupor. Ramakrishna Pillai, clad in his gold-bordered mundu and a silk shirt, and Rajendran Nair, in a ColorPlus shirt and a mundu from Karalkada, took charge of the ceremony as representatives of the upper-caste community to which Acchan belonged. They looked even more energetic and confident than they had been at my father's younger brother's funeral two years back – their presence and that sense of authority worried me. They kept a respectable distance from my mother's relatives. The secretary of the caste association to which Acchan's family belonged, a streak of sandal paste on his forehead with a touch of sindoor in the middle, was bustling around, the ceremonial red silk tied around his waist. But it was with a sullen face that he announced that it was time to make the bali offerings to the departed soul. I was the only one to respond.

'No men?' he grimaced. Both of Acchan's nephews and his younger brother's sons had refused earlier. 'It's not the practice in our caste for daughters to offer bali,' murmured Acchan's sister. At that, my mother's oldest brother, my valyamaaman, fumed, 'All right, then why not get your own son to do it, as is the custom among you?' Rajendran Nair and Ramakrishna Pillai intervened. It was like Samir had said – any kind of war is but a ruse to perpetuate the primacy of some. The crowd had split into two groups and were arguing. Finally, Amma came over to the veranda and spoke loudly to me so that everyone else could hear:

'If this ceremony is for the peace of the departed soul, then, Satye, offer your father a rice ball with a pinch of sesame seeds. But if it is to satisfy the pretensions of the living, then go get the nephews, whoever.'

No one uttered a word after that. Venukkuttan Chettan gestured to me. I was quick. I poured a bucketful of water over my head and went over in wet and dripping clothes to offer the bali. As the Karayogam official instructed, I half kneeled on the floor. Then I mixed the unhusked rice, poured a little water on it, and scattered the sesame seeds and flowers over it. My hands trembled when I thought that Acchan would eat this, unseen by us. The love that I had never showed when he was alive now melted and flowed through my eyes as tears. I feared that the bali-rice might be too salty. Acchan was very finicky about salt in his food. I offered the bali, weeping. Then calmed myself and took out the leaf with the offering to the south side of the house. There were crows on the aanjhili tree near the wall, on the poovarasu tree as well. I called to them, clapping my wet palms. They did not move. The only time Acchan called me by my name was just before his death. Only then did he reveal that he was concerned about me. It was that belief that made me feel that he would accept my offering. But was that glimmer of affection just a sign of his brain becoming fragmented? My confidence was shattered. As it happens when I feel rejected, all the lights in my heart went out at the same time. It became dark everywhere.

My luck that a raven – a bali-crow – flew down. A big one – not a common sight. It swallowed a whole rice ball in a single peck. Then it bent its neck and threw a look at me and all of us, and finished all the rice in no time. Only a tulsi flower was left on the leaf. 'Ah! The father has accepted the daughter's offering, ate well before he left!' some woman exclaimed. I lost control. I had never served Acchan a meal when he was alive. Never went up to him when he ate, never asked if he needed anything. Like banned currency notes, we had invalidated each other. And now, here he was, for a rice ball offered by his daughter. Just to remind her of the love she never got, that which she never gave, to wound her thus. I sobbed aloud. A few others sobbed along. People from the oppressor castes in India are gratified by the sight of tears. The same sight makes those from the oppressed castes burst with emotion. That raven was truly helpful. It saved Amma's face and the dignity of her caste! If it had not turned up, then they would have established that Acchan's soul

was seething because of wounded caste pride. Are you not aware
of the role the eagles and the ravens play in regulating our social
lives? Valyamaami, Valyamaaman's wife, put her hand around my
shoulders to take me away into the house. On our way, I glanced
at Amma. She was standing there, unfazed. I held her in my arms
and pressed my face on her shoulder. She flung my arms away. 'Stop
making a show, Satye,' she snapped, 'go, change,' and turned to greet
a mourner who had just come in.

I remembered an occasion on which she had indeed been distressed.
That was when she had stood in front of Acchan's hotel room. But
even then, she had not wept – she had been a bit shaken, that was all.
And that, too, for Appooppan's sake. Amma knew well how we would
find Acchan. That is, she had seen him in a similar state before. I have
never been sure if she had cried then. Because I did not see her cry
even when Appooppan died.

~

Appooppan's death was unexpected. Seeing Acchan so depraved in the
hotel room had broken him. Back home, he suddenly aged, became
despondent. He lived for just another Onam. In December that year,
he died. When Uncle Latif came to tell us about his death, Chechi
was at home.

'What is it, Latif Anna? All of a sudden?' Amma frowned.

'You must come home. Muthalaali asked.'

'Can't it wait till Sunday?'

'That ... I've brought the car ... Can't you come right now?'

Amma stared at him.

'Where should we come? To the house or to the hospital?'

Uncle Latif stood there quietly, tongue-tied. Amma did not ask
anything more. She went in, packed her clothes in the big travel bag,
or 'airbag' as it was called in those days. 'Why are we packing so many
clothes?' Chechi asked. 'We may have to stay there for longer than
usual,' Amma said. She told Chechi to pack our clothes too. She told

her to get in the car, called the hostel and told them to send me home,
left instructions for Laalamma and Venukkuttan Chettan. She was
silent till they reached the main road, and then asked:

'Anna, tell me, is Acchan alive or gone?'

Uncle Latif did not answer. When the car reached the little chapel
from where it turned to the family home, she exclaimed:

'He's gone!'

The car had barely stopped when she opened the door, leapt out,
and ran in, said Chechi later. On the veranda lay Appooppan's body,
covered with a white shroud. She went up to him, gazed intently for
a few moments, pressed her forehead on his feet, then going close to
his face, she kissed his forehead and sat beside him, by the side of his
head. She began to recite the *Adhyatma Ramayanam*. She could recite
by heart traditional Hindu classics, such as the *Adhyatma Ramayanam*,
as well as many modern classics, such as Narayana Guru's *Atmopadesha
Shatakam*, Kumaran Asan's *Chintavishtayaaya Seeta, Nalini* and
Karuna, and Changampuzha's *Ramanan*.

I reached after two or three hours. I saw the black flags and cars
stretching from the bus stop and so knew what had happened. I fell
on Appooppan's body, banged my head on the floor, and wept aloud.
Amma was then reciting: '*Sundaram Raamachandram paramaananda
mandiraamindradi vrindaaraka vrinda…*' Chechi got up, came to me,
and helped me up. We hugged each other and wept. It was dark inside
and outside. Our last refuge was now lost. We weep when someone
dies because we can't figure out how to live without that person – that's
a selfish motive. Amma was not selfish at all. So she did not weep.
When she reached the line where Rama asks his brother if their father
was well and if he suffered the pangs of separation from his beloved
son, now exiled, she stopped as though she'd forgotten the next line.
Her sweet voice that had resounded in the air until then, stopped all
of a sudden. A terrible silence enveloped us. I thought she was going
to cry. But after sitting still and silent for about an hour, she began to
recite the rest of Rama's query, which was about what his father had
wanted to convey to Lakshman and him.

Acchan was in Madras then. When he heard of Appooppan's passing, he took a flight back. He arrived clad in a safari suit and dark glasses, carrying a leather briefcase and looking like the hero from Singapore played by Prem Nazir in a movie produced by Nityavasantham Productions. Everyone greeted him with respect. He sat on the sofa crossing his legs, playing the blue blood. He called to Amma, issued instructions. She played the ideal wife, responding to him and greeting the mourners.

Appooppan's death affected me the most. I kept going to his grave. I had the premonition that this was the beginning of a great fall. I was beset by a thousand worries: Is Acchan going to marry the film actress Rajani? Will he bring her to our home? How will Amma respond? Will she allow her in as a co-wife like in some movies? Or kick her out, like in others? How will we, his daughters, react to her? Won't we have to call her 'Amma' too? The prospect of having to call someone other than my mother 'Amma' at the age of nineteen riled me. I'll kill them both – I threatened Appooppan's soul. You? His soul laughed. I shrank inwardly. 'Appoopa, what are we to do?' I asked, looking at the tender coconut that was placed on the side of the grave where the head would have been. 'What will I do? What will Chechi and Amma do?' Seeing the tumult in the heart of one who had spent merely nineteen years on the earth that had been witnessing births and deaths since three and a half billion years, the weeds shook with laughter. They had been cleared when the yard was spruced up just a few months back, for Onam. They had grown back now.

It was the moment of return to Vasanthaalayam that I really feared. It was called Vasanthaalayam after my mother, Vasantham, and meant 'Vasantham's Home'. It stood beside a lake, on the property that Appooppan had bought from the profits of a successful movie that they had made after Acchan joined his firm. Pleased by the young man's abilities, Appooppan had gone to meet him at his house with a carload of gifts. The scene that met his eyes there was pathetic. A thatched hut for a house, the very abode of want. Yet Acchan's mother insisted on calling Appooppan a degrading caste name. The gifts he took for them were accepted only after water was sprinkled on them. Acchan was embarrassed. Appooppan consoled him. On his way back, Appooppan saw the lake and was enchanted by its beauty. That was a den of the upper-castes. Probably because his ego as a rich lower-caste man was hurt, Appooppan sought to buy a traditional four-wing naalukettu house there. The owner asked for two thousand five hundred rupees, but Appoopan did not haggle. Within a month it was bought, then renovated. Later, when Amma threatened to commit suicide if she was not allowed to marry Acchan, he agreed on the condition that they live permanently in Vasanthaalayam!

'Why did I then repair the Koyikkal family home and add a bathroom and toilet there?' Acchan sulked.

'Your mother and siblings live there, don't they?' retorted Appooppan. 'Good, that was needed.'

'I got the house painted and tiled and the floor cemented so that Vasantham can stay there!'

'Vasantham will stay only in Vasanthaalayam.'

'But before that, for a few days at least...'

'Please don't take offence. But I am not happy with her sleeping in that house for even a few days.'

'The only thing we lack is wealth...'

'What's the use of wealth when a woman won't be respected in her husband's house?'

Acchan looked dazed. Appooppan continued:

'Each moment she stays there, and each moment I am there for a visit, we will be made to remember our caste.'

'No one in my family will treat Vasantham...'

'Yes, true, it may not bite, but why thrust your hand into a cobra's lair?'

Appooppan's persistence won. When they announced the marriage, Acchan's mother, Koyikkal Sarojini Amma, beat her breast and wailed. 'It was just cheap brass,' she lamented about her son. 'But I thought it was a pot of gold!' Acchan's brother-in-law mocked him – 'The low-caste Kochootty Panikkan's bum-holder!' His younger brother said that he was lowly, that he'd pick up anyone's turds if paid well. But unable to resist the pull of the thousand-rupee notes that my grandfather held out to them, the entire Koyikkal family attended the wedding. They avoided the housewarming, though. There was no one at Vasanthaalayam to greet the new bride – no mother-in-law, no sisters-in-law. It was the next-door neighbour, a lady who had come to see the bride and groom, who lit the bronze lamp, performed the *aratham uzhiyal*, and took the bride in. By the time I was born, she had moved away. Appooppan bought her house and compound, but he concealed that until his death. In his will he mentioned that the Kaavil Padinjhaatathil house near Vasanthaalayam should be donated to a temple there, a sacred grove. That took everyone by surprise.

The will was read on the forty-first day – the day after the final death ritual. It was a simple will. The *Vasanthakairali* magazine, Nityavasantham Productions, the Vasanthamaalika Hotel and the ten-acre beachside property on which these stood, as well as the lakeside Vasanthaalayam house and its two and a half acre grounds were to go to our mother. The cashew factories, cardamom estate, and the Vasantha Panchami mansion which he had built were willed to his oldest son. Vasantha Exports, Vasantha Prawns Factory, and the town house Vasantholsavam were to be given to his younger son. The house near Vasanthaalayam was gifted to the temple.

The next day proved to be unforgettable. The period of pollution over, we got ready to return to Vasanthaalayam. But the car headed to Acchan's house, the Koyikkal Veedu. He snarled at Amma, 'Let's see if you can live here for a couple of days!' He left us there. Amma's face became as pale as death. She held Chechi and me close to her and stood under the tamarind tree there. I remembered the story of Vasanthaalayam becoming our home, so I knew why he had done this. But Chechi was the coddled firstborn; she whined, 'Why are we here, Amme?'

'The Soviet Union has collapsed,' said Amma, with her typical sarcasm.

'So?'

Chechi flew into a rage. Amma was angry too.

'Don't you have any common sense, Sive? What comes if socialism goes?'

Chechi was too vexed to speak. As the daughter of a mother who had graduated in political science, I could answer, though I knew little. 'Capitalism,' I said.

'That is – caste, religion, money power, muscle power...' Amma sighed.

'What has that to do with this?' Chechi was almost shedding tears of rage.

'They've had to bow down to a lower-caste man until now – to your grandfather. The sores from that are going to get worse now.'

Only then did Chechi see. 'Oh, in that case, let us leave right away.' She hurried us. But Amma did not budge.

'We will live here,' she said. 'A father's sins seek out the children. That is the law of the world. Your father's will too. Watch out for them.'

~

When I was immersing Acchan's ashes in the river, all this spewed to the surface of my mind. As I came up from the water with folded hands, I saw someone on the opposite bank and was gripped with fear. He's pointing a gun at me, I thought! Though my uncles and neighbours were present, I felt terribly scared. I could not help looking back frequently when we came away. We should have found out who that was, I was dismayed. It was certain that from now on, I was going to seek him all the time; I was going to be continually haunted by the delusion that I saw him everywhere. When everyone left, my panic became acute. I sought Amma. She was in the bedroom, sorting out the papers in the drawer of the nightstand. I went to the back of her chair and laid my head on her shoulder. Soon, this was the conversation that happened between us:

'I was remembering … Amme.'

'Uh?'

'The day Acchan left us at Koyikkal.'

'Uh?'

'Didn't you say that day that Acchan's sins will seek us out?'

'That is male dominance.'

'Was that term around then?'

'The term came later, but the sense was already present.'

'What a day it was … the three of us sleeping on the sofa in the inner courtyard…'

'Yes, and they must have washed it the very next day!'

'There's a question that's troubled me since that day. Why did you hang back there so long, Amma? You had money, you were educated, you had Appooppan's support…'

'Kaanthan shathano kulsithano visheshaal
Shaanthan mahaansalkrithano satheenaam
Shanthaatmnaa daivathamennavannam
Chinthaadiyaal Sambrathamaivapoojyan.'

So that was it: Satidharma. No matter what the husband may be like, good or bad, you have to worship him as god.

'Such foolishness, and you, Amme?'

'Weren't we a generation which grew up seeing movies like *Savitri Satyavan*, *Adhyapika*, *Navalokam*, and so on? The idea those days was that a woman could have only one man in her life. That love was for marriage, the family. We prayed for a chance to sacrifice, to give up ourselves.'

'And what did that bring?'

'After a while, I realized that it was a mistake, but decided that I would not leave him. How would I have faced my father otherwise?

Marrying your father was completely my choice. My ego did not permit me to admit the mistake. And besides, it was the people around us who actually controlled us! Nothing was easy without a nod from them! But I had indeed thought that I'll leave after my Acchan passed. Especially when our firms were collapsing. But it was on that very day that he was stabbed. Then I found it hard to leave a wounded and disabled person by the wayside. After all, he was your father.'

I had no words. Amma continued to rearrange the files. A crow flew down on the breadfruit tree outside the window and began to call. The same one which ate the bali-rice, I imagined. Suddenly, a strange thought came to me. What about that full-grown foetus inside that glass jar? Shouldn't someone offer it bali-rice? What if it was Acchan's son? The son who should have offered him bali-rice? My breath stopped when I pictured Acchan shoving the slimy, tender body into the jar. I was trying frantically to love Acchan after his death. But for that, I would have to immerse into the water the ashes of countless memories about him.

Amma took out a diary from the drawer. Then she selected some papers from the bundles she had reorganized earlier, pinned them together, and placed them inside it. I saw a couple of five-hundred-rupee notes peeping out of the diary's jacket. I reached out and took the diary.

'Why are you keeping these notes? They can't be exchanged any more.'

'One of those is an old five-hundred-rupee note. There's Gandhiji's face on it. This was the first of those – people called it "Gandhi".'

'Now they are just pieces of paper. What is the use of demonetized notes?'

'Let them be. Maybe they'll be monetized again?'

'No government will do that. They'll just print new ones.'

'The new notes are politics. The old ones, history.'

Amma took the diary back and locked it in the drawer. Then she turned towards me and looked me in the face.

'Ah, aren't you going back? Don't you have to join work?'

'How am I to go leaving you all alone here?'

'Don't worry about me. I am healthy, I feel all right.'

'But don't we need to take some precautions in any case?'

'Seventy per cent of the currency notes in this country were taken off without any precaution! And so what? Didn't we get used to it?'

'No, Amme … over there, I'll be…' I told her the truth. Her face turned serious.

'No way. I must live alone. Only then can I leave in peace.'

'Leave? Where for?'

'I'd want to go somewhere too, right?'

'What for?'

'The prime minister of this country just said that he might leave as a fakir with a beggar's bag. Did anyone ask where he was going to go?'

My patience was wearing thin. You have pushed me into the midst of an abyss, and now you are leaving without turning a hair – I fretted. But it was no use. I had to go alone, because there was a phone call from the police inspector in Bangalore.

'Madam, you must come to the station at once.'

'What is it, Sir?'

'We have taken someone into custody. You must come immediately for the identification.'

My body grew red-hot, like a gun when it fires. Then it cooled, and froze. Death, in a way, is the body pulling a trigger. The life within is discharged that way. The fear of death is an ironsmith's foundry. It smelts the hardest of hearts. As time passes, the personality changes. No one can stay the same; they all turn and tumble as many selves. The socialist becomes a capitalist, the capitalist will become a communalist, the communalist will become a terrorist, the terrorist will become a spiritualist, the spiritualist will become a corporate.

I was worried about how I would turn and tumble. What would I do if the government decided to add to the Constitution new clauses that ordered all young women below fifty to marry and all married women to take an oath that their husbands would not suffer any inconvenience from them, and those who did not heed these clauses should be shot to death? Would I thrust my hand into the lair of the black cobra? Would I search for infants stuffed into glass jars in my husband's box? Much better to die from an assassin's bullet.

The following day, throughout the bus journey, I did not sleep. Even then, I turned around sharply in the middle feeling the cold steel nozzle at the back of my neck. And when I managed to doze off, I saw a foetus with round spectacles suspended inside a glass jar trying to tell me something, and large bubbles rising up in the liquid, shining, like drops of mercury. I squirmed with unease. I could have died instead of Chechi, I blamed myself. In the end, seeing that I had no other way out, I began to steel myself for an encounter with my prospective killer. It was painful to know that such a person existed, someone who wanted me dead, someone who was intolerant of me making my way peacefully without harming anyone, without taking much space, staying close to the world's sidewalks. I thought of how I must behave with him. Feared that I might turn teary. Must call him 'brother', I decided. I tried to imagine how he would respond to that.

He was a man, after all. He'd just be madder facing a woman. His heart would burst with the insane desire to cut me down – just like my heart. Like my heart which throbbed in pain, with the pus from the sores of all the wounds I had suffered until then.

SIX

It was on the day of Vishu when we found out that our well was poisoned. That was the year after Appooppan's passing. Chechi and I were preparing for our exams. But Acchan kept insisting that we should go to Koyikkal. We used to go there twice a year, for Onam and Vishu. Both were black days. The tension would begin the moment we'd step into that house. Acchan, his mother, his sisters and younger brother would start – poking at their own sores, washing their dirty linen in the open. They would make snide remarks about Amma's caste. There would be rude talk, dramatic breast-beating. Even violent gestures and murder threats. Chechi would feel thoroughly humiliated, she'd weep; I would become furious, and Amma would be completely silent. In the midst of all this, there would be a feast. By evening, Chechi and I would be back at Vasanthaalayam, worn out with all the sobbing.

That Vishu, Amma did not go to Koyikkal. Instead, she went to her father's house. Venukkuttan Chettan and his family had gone to the Guruvayur temple. Vasanthaalayam was locked the whole day.

The day was anyway important, because Acchan's drink that day was not Scotch whisky. He had the habit of stowing away a bottle of liquor mixed with water under his car seat. He would keep sipping from it, and that would leave a peculiar odour inside the vehicle.

That day, it wasn't the usual smell and it troubled me. I caught this new smell and looked at Chechi. She was leaning by the side of the open window, lost in her own world. Her nose caught only the scent of romance.

This time, Acchan was sloshed even before we reached the Koyikkal house. He got into a massive argument with his youngest sister's husband – an utterly detestable man whom we used to call Bhasi Maaman. 'Lakshmi,' Bhasi Maaman announced to his wife, 'your MBBS-failed doctor-brother is here!'

'Yes, the miser who wouldn't spare five paise for my fees is talking now!' Acchan shot back.

'Ah! That's why he took to washing that low-caste Kochootty Panikkan's bum and drinking that water,' he goaded.

Unable to find a biting retort this time, Acchan called him all sorts of names. Then his younger brother made his entrance, and they confronted each other. Further, their mother – our grandmother, Sarojini Amma, known as Koyikkal Amma – sauntered in at regular intervals and added fuel to the fight as though afraid that the firestorm would die down. However, she continued to play the loving grandmother to us. From time to time, she shouted, 'Sudhe, Sume, Unni, take these children inside, give them something to drink.'

That day, too, we could not finish our Vishu lunch. Weeping out of fear and shame, we ate what we could, and finally, when it was time to go back, scrambled into the car. Ulahannan Maaman started the car. Acchan fell asleep even before we passed the manjaadi tree in the mud road outside the house. Unable to bear the stench inside the car, I stuck my nose out through the open window. Chechi was busy acting the female lead in an imaginary romantic movie. The moment we reached home, I leapt out and gulped down some fresh air. Laalamma was bustling down the path. Seeing us, she hurried to open the house. Ulahannan Maaman helped Acchan inside the house and then to lie him down. Then Amma, too, returned in a taxi. What had happened to all the cars at our family home? I was perturbed. Amma stepped inside the house, opened her bag and took out two hundred-rupee notes – the old bluish notes.

'I'll make up next month, Ulahannan,' she told him. 'Take this now.'

'But Vasantha Chechi, will I still have a job here next month?' His voice quivered with emotion. That is when we got to know: Acchan was selling our car and had already taken an advance on it. Even Amma was startled. 'Please don't tell him that I told you!' he begged.

'But what was the urgency?' Amma asked, worried.

'Everything is lost!' he wept.

Chechi grabbed my hand and held it tight. My heart broke at the thought of losing our Contessa. What else remained to feel proud about Acchan? I was dumbfounded.

Amma recovered quickly. 'Have your coffee, Ulahannan,' she said. 'There is a solution to everything.' Laalamma brought the coffee. He sipped it once, but spat it out hard. 'Terribly sour,' he said uneasily. I tasted it – I spat it out too, unable to bear the sharp, biting taste. My throat and tongue burned. Amma tasted it and was convinced. We compared the water that was stored in the kitchen with the water that was freshly drawn from the well. The coffee was made with the freshly drawn water. We found that the well water was sour, it stank. The hubbub that followed was comparable to the one that occurred when the house had caught fire. Gopi Maaman and Valsala Maami came over. Someone brought a pushcart. All the large tubs and large copper vessels in the house were wheeled to Gopi Maaman's house, filled, and brought back.

By the time it was all over, night had fallen. Amma sat on the step of the open inner courtyard, her head lowered in her cupped palms. Chechi and I sat on either side of her.

'Why is Acchan selling the car?' I addressed the question to no one in particular.

'We will know only after he has sold everything,' Chechi said crossly.

'What if it is to buy another one?' I tried to comfort her.

'But then would Ulahannan Maaman cry?' she retorted.

Amma did not raise her head. Chechi rested her head on her shoulder. 'You two could let me have a moment of peace!' she snapped at us. Her face was pale. My courage dimmed completely. To think of Amma losing courage when we had lost Appooppan – what would we do? The question drained me totally. I was smothered by darkness.

'Amma, are you upset that the car is sold?' Chechi asked. Amma looked at her, infuriated.

'Sive, to ride a car you have to first stay alive. How is one to have a sip of water in this house safely? That someone has poisoned our well is not something to be taken lightly, is it?'

'Poison!' Chechi's eyes bulged.

'Yes, poison! The difference in taste – it was not there this morning? How did it happen?'

I was shocked, dumbstruck. It was hard to believe. 'Who? Why?' Chechi screamed. Amma covered her mouth. 'Stop screaming, no one should know that we suspect it.'

She got up, opened the front door, and began to walk in the garden. We went to her. A hot wind blew from the lake. The flowers from the trees floated down lazily. The gandharajan and pavizhamalli flowers swayed.

'Shall we tell Valyamaaman and Kochumaaman?' Chechi asked. Amma turned.

'Siva and Satya, there's something that you need to see and understand as soon as you can. The fact that we have no one but ourselves now.'

Amma continued without anger or pain: 'Appooppan is gone. We are all now different families. Don't expect people to come together to help anyone. It is true that we were all born from the same womb and are of the same blood. But the thread that bound us has broken. We are all free now. Freedom means relying on oneself. No one has time to take care of another. That is, there is no one now to call when we have a problem.'

We were completely stupefied. Something had happened in the family home, I could make out, but I did not have the pluck to ask Amma about it. However, she never went to her family home for Onam or Vishu ever again. When her brothers came for occasional visits, she was not as warm as before.

'What will we do now?' I asked anxiously.

'We have to get the water tested. Tomorrow itself. Day after is an Easter holiday.'

We did not sleep that night. After the day we stumbled on Rajani in the hotel room, Amma had moved into our bedroom. I have never seen her sleep deeply. That night, I, too, slept very lightly. Acchan, alone, slept like a log. He woke up as usual. Chechi was deputed to report to him the poisoning of our well. He was reading the papers sitting in the easy chair in the front room. Chechi took him his special black coffee, put the cup on the teapoy, and waited there hesitatingly. 'Uh?' he grunted irritably.

'There's something wrong with the well water...'

She sounded scared.

'Uh?'

'It tastes different.'

'So?'

'We must get it tested.'

'Who said?'

'Amma...'

'Tell her to run to her dead old duffer Kochootty!' He growled. My sister, being romantic, was also prone to fly into a rage. She was furious. I tried to pull her back gently. She swatted my hand away and moved ahead.

'There's not even water for drinking in the house...' Her voice was choked with sobs.

'Oh, go and drink your own piss, you little...' Acchan shouted. I pulled her back even more firmly. But it was useless. Chechi was all aflame.

'Now we know who poisoned the well!'

Acchan jumped up and slapped her hard. Her face, and even her body, were thrown sideways. Drops of blood flew from her nose and fell on her clothes. I was terrified; I tried to pull her back. But she did not bother to wipe off the blood and continued to glare at him with her large eyes. They faced each other in fury. He raised his hand again. At that moment, I forgot myself.

'Don't you touch her!' I raised my finger at him.

'What will you do?' He boiled over with rage.

'I'll piss and make you drink it in your coffee.'

I gnashed my teeth. Acchan was speechless, stunned. His face changed colour as though it had been slapped. This time Chechi was pulling me away. When we reached the kitchen, we hugged each other and burst into tears. Amma stood there like a stone, she had heard it all. Acchan flung the newspaper away, went into the bathroom, and bathed in the water that had been stored there for all of us. Then he put on his fancy clothes, took his briefcase, and got ready to leave. Ulahannan Maaman arrived. When the car disappeared, Amma changed her clothes, searched out an umbrella, and took a sample of the bad water in a bottle. Because we never had to walk in the sun or rain, umbrellas were irrelevant in our house, and so this one was really old and partly broken. For Chechi and me, it was as though the sky had fallen on our heads. The umbrella seemed to represent our indignity. The state it was in, it would soon leave us soaked in the unrelenting downpours that awaited us in the days ahead.

It was late when Amma returned. Chechi and I were sitting on the outer step of the east-facing room waiting for her. It was a completely windless day. In the summer heat, the surface of the lake shone like a sheet of glass. Amma was sweaty and exhausted when she arrived. We ran to her anxiously with questions.

'It is acid. The water has been poisoned. It will have to be purified. The well will have to be cleaned. We'll have very little water for three days. No use sulking or moaning,' she said.

Dismayed and helpless, we looked at each other. Amma washed, ate, went to my study desk, took out a pen and a sheet of paper, and started writing. We peeped at it from either side.

> *To the respected Sub-Inspector Sri Dinakaran Pillai,*
>
> *It has been found that our well water has been polluted with a substance suspected to be acid. Since there is reason to believe that this was deliberate, I humbly request you to kindly conduct an investigation into this matter and catch the criminal.*
>
> *Thanking you,*
>
> *Yours sincerely,*
>
> *Vasanthalakshmi Amma P.K.*

As we stared, our mouths agape, Amma asked Chechi to change her clothes.

'What for?' she asked.

'To go to the police station and submit this. If you want, you can take Venukkuttan with you.'

'Me? To the police station? I can't!' She burst out.

I tried to still my trembling heart. Amma stared at her hard. Her face was growing redder. I intervened then and accepted the task, and left for the police station with Venukkuttan Chettan.

~

That was a quarter of a century in the past. Whenever I had to go to the police station again, I grew restive. I feared that this may be history repeating itself. Then, too, there was an invisible killer hovering around. Then, too, the small notes were valuable. Then, too, the party in power in the country had sought to revise the ground rules of the exercise of power by passing the new economic policy. Money is a strange thing indeed, no doubt. A weapon that is at once political, social and psychological. Without exchange, who, what, would survive? Is there any dialectical materialism that will fly above it? Or any *vishishta advaita* that is of greater consequence?

There was one difference, though – this time my journey to the police station was to meet the killer face to face. My heart beat like a drum on my way there. But when I neared the building, which was a dirty rose-pink, my courage drained away. The rainwater drain, which ran around the parapet of the building like a headdress, ruined the image of a police station I bore in my mind. And the money plants growing on the pillars. At a time when we were drowning in debt, Chechi had planted several of them indoors. In the morning she would touch their leaves, fold her hands, and pray. After she died, Amma threw them all away. Now, they grew everywhere – in the garden, the inner courtyard, on the trees – turning our yard into a jungle.

The taxi driver Sunil was someone I knew. I asked him to wait and walked in, stumbling a bit on the way. They led me to a room with a large signboard that read 'Inspector of Police'. The inspector's name was Anurup Shetty. Cropped hair and a smooth face endowed him with a babyish charm. His voice was gentle too. 'Were you on leave?', 'Heard that your father passed?', 'Is your mother all alone back home?', 'You are Aswathy Ma'am's family friend, aren't you?' … It was evident that he had done his homework. But to what extent? I became alert.

'Ma'am, we have been enquiring, and have found someone. Not sure if he is the culprit. You will have to identify him.'

The woman constable who had come with the SI to take my statement led me inside. There were two cells there. There was an emaciated fellow in one of them; I was to take a look at him. He was sitting on the floor. He frowned as soon as he saw me. It was clear that he recognized me. But I did not. He was not half as tall or stout as the assailant who rode the bike. He was the product of a malnourished pregnancy for sure; neither was he well nourished in his childhood.

I could not call him 'brother' – probably 'son'. My heart melted. I turned away, my head lowered.

When I went back to the inspector's room, he was speaking with the SI who had recorded my statement. Seeing me, the SI abruptly ended the conversation and went out. I told the inspector that the person in the lockup was not the man.

'That makes it complicated, Ma'am,' Inspector Shetty said. 'We have to conclude from this that there is another person involved. This boy has admitted to mapping you.'

After this, Inspector Anurup Shetty and I exchanged the following words:

'Did he confess to shooting me?'

'The plan was to stab you. To sneak into your house on the ninth. But then demonetization was announced. This poor fellow had five bundles of one-thousand-rupee notes. He panicked. You should thank our PM. People are talking only of those who died because of demonetization. There are many who lived because of it – like you, Ma'am!'

'Any act will benefit someone or the other.'

'Is it so trivial? People have revealed black money worth 6,739 crore!'

'With that, it became white!'

'Those who did that have no way to escape! They are all going to get caught.'

'Is that why a certain family in Mumbai just revealed two lakh crore they didn't apparently have?'

The inspector had no answer, so he took another track.

'Why, Ma'am, is there something that you have not revealed to the police?'

I did not like his wise-guy attitude.

'Yes,' I said nonchalantly. I saw a streak of lightning in his eyes. I told him about the phone call that I had received in the bus and my father's last words. His face flushed.

'That phone call, that's a serious threat. But why didn't you report it immediately to the police?'

'I thought I'll report it after I return.'

'That was foolish, Ma'am.'

'I understand that only now.'

'Ah! But why didn't you report it at least in the days that followed?'

'My father died the day I reached.'

'The murderer must have contacted your father too, isn't it, Ma'am? That's why he warned you.'

'Maybe.'

'That means, he is a Malayali.'

'But the person who called me spoke to me in Odiya.'

'So what? Is it not possible now to plan a murder here sitting in any other corner of the world? Not just murder, any crime?'

'Say, he called my father. But does that make him a Malayali?'

'There are two reasons to think that he is: first, the bike he used had a Kerala registration. That's clear from the statement of the person who saved you – Mrityunjoy Sen. Secondly, your father warned you that you may be killed. That someone who has been paralysed for twenty-five years should say that – there *has* to be a link.'

'Inspector, what if someone from Odisha called my father and, like you said, spoke to him?'

'No, no one like that called him.'

'How are you sure?'

'Your parents don't own mobile phones. Their landline had not received any calls. There's of course the postal service – but no letter had been delivered there. By any reckoning, the message must have been delivered personally. In short, it was told to your father without your mother's knowledge.'

I realized he had done a much greater amount of homework than I thought. I was a bit fazed. As though noticing it, he smiled.

'Be it the complainants, be it the culprits, no one reveals everything. So we have to do our homework.'

'And what else have you discovered?'

'Ma'am, please don't be offended. This is our job, isn't it?'

'In that case, you must have also done your homework about that boy in the lockup? Why does he wish to kill me?'

'He is just a hired murderer. Just a tool.'

'In whose hands?'

'To know that, we have to nab the middleman who hired him. We'll get him today or tomorrow.'

'Is that a Malayali?'

'A Goan. This fellow is from around here.'

'But Inspector, I am certain that this is not the boy who attacked me.'

'Yes, Mrityunjoy Sen also said that. He said that the attacker looked above thirty-five. Five feet ten inches tall and well built.'

I had nothing to say. The inspector, Mrityunjoy, the conspirator, the middleman, the actual enemy – all of them – were they plotting against me? I felt nervous, my mouth dried up. The inspector seemed to have sensed that. He rang the bell and the woman constable who was there earlier brought two paper cups of water. I drank both.

'One of them fired a bullet, the other planned a stabbing. What is one to read from this?' My voice was hoarse.

'Look Ma'am, there are two possibilities before us. First, that the two represent two different missions. Or both were sent by the same person.'

Pressing his elbows on the table, Inspector Shetty leaned forward. His eyes shone like the points of rapiers.

'If it is just one person planning both, it makes it easier for us. But if they are different, then…'

'Then?'

'We will have to question you, Ma'am.'

I liked that glint in his eyes. It reminded me of Samir. I took a good look at him. Leaning back in his chair, he, too, returned my look.

The kindness on his face wore off like make-up is wiped off the face of an actor exiting the stage. I regained my confidence.

'Sir, I do believe the two are different. I think you should proceed with that hypothesis.'

The inspector grew alert.

'Any clue?'

'None so far.'

'If so, who from Odisha would be likely to assault you, Ma'am?'

I smiled at him.

'Ah, that means you haven't done your homework well enough!'

The inspector's cheeks flushed. He smiled to cover up the embarrassment. I smiled too.

'Okay, then I will do my homework better. And let us meet after.'

'Any time.'

'One more thing, Ma'am. Please don't stay on your own again. It is not safe.'

'I am alone. My life must be lived that way.'

'I mean, can you stay with someone for a few days?'

'What for? To put them at risk too? I am alone, Inspector. That is my strength.'

'So you are determined to give us as much trouble as you can?'

'The truth gives everyone trouble.'

'Is that why you were named Satyapriya – the lover of truth?'

Both of us laughed. I then remembered the boy in the lockup. 'What is his name?' I asked.

'Kripesh,' said the inspector.

'What an excellent name for a hired killer!' We laughed again.

'Will you file a case against him?' I asked.

'Since he has not committed the crime, we can't. We will get a written declaration from some relative or friend after convincing them that the police have not harmed him. That is the practice.'

'Did he give you anyone's address, of anyone around here?'

'Yes, he said that the owner of Moorthy's Fruit Stall in front of the metro station here is a distant relative. We have summoned Moorthy Prasad.'

'Let me know if no one turns up?'

'Why, do you want to take his responsibility, Ma'am?'

'Yes.'

The inspector smiled. I got up to leave. He held the half-door open for me, accompanied me till the grille door at the main entrance. And then when, as I stepped out, I turned to say goodbye, without any provocation, he asked, 'Ma'am, you have seen much in life, haven't you?'

His question jolted me. Tears rushed to my eyes. I did not reply, just dashed to the waiting car. It was really sunny, but I shivered. I feared that the glass jar that I had lain in until now had broken. The memory of going to a police station the first time, returned.

~

That police station functioned out of a rented house. There was a big tamarind tree in front of it. Everywhere, the kammunist paccha weeds thrived. An Ambassador car and a lorry, caught heaven only knew how long back for ferrying hooch, lay in the yard, tumbledown and covered with kaakkapoo vines. Venukkuttan Chettan introduced me to the policeman at the door. Sub-Inspector Dinakaran Pillai was going out somewhere. He recognized me. He took the complaint from me, read it, signed it, and handed it over to the policeman. He said that he had to be somewhere and that he would come home tomorrow. Then he got into the jeep in a hurry and left. I followed Venukkuttan Chettan. When we were waiting to cross the road, an Ambassador taxi braked in front of us. Acchan stepped out of the front seat. His gait was unsteady, his hair was messy, and his silk shirt crumpled, its buttons open. In the back seat of the taxi sat his regular drinking companions – an engineer and an iron merchant. He rolled his eyes at Venukkuttan Chettan and asked what he was doing there. I was still trying to adjust to the reality that we did not have the Contessa any more, still numb from it. When he repeated the question, I told him about the complaint. His face flushed angrily. He aimed a tight slap at my face and dragged me back to the police station. He demanded that the police return the complaint. The policemen told him they needed the SI's permission to do so. Feeling insulted, he dragged me to the car, thrust me into the back seat and ordered the driver to take us to Dinakaran Pillai's residence.

I sat in the back with my cheek smarting and heart on fire. Venukkuttan Chettan still stood by the roadside. The car passed him. Tears fell on my matchbox-blue skirt with prints of yellow flowers on it. The two men in the backseat added fuel to the fire. They pressed my shoulders and held me close as though to comfort me. As dusk fell, the car raced through the alleys to Dinakaran Pillai's house. Upon reaching there, they were told that he had left for Ernakulam. To drown the disappointment, they stopped at three bars on the way back. When Acchan came out of the first bar, I, who was sitting by the window, was pushed to the middle of the seat. 'Stop the car, I want to get out!' I screamed. Acchan kept abusing me in his drunken stupor. As I continued to sit there, I crumbled, slowly. Then, bit by bit, my voice died. It was ten in the night when we reached home. Venukkuttan Chettan had told Amma that Acchan had taken me away. Chechi and Amma were waiting anxiously at the gate.

Though the taxi had stopped, I did not get out. Had it been anyone else, they'd have been in tears. I did not weep. Instead, I made them bawl. The two men on either side of me, old enough to be my father, screamed loudly. One of them squirmed in pain inside the taxi, the other leapt out of it. I straightened my skirt and blouse, and got out when Acchan, completely inebriated, was trying to count the bluish hundred-rupee notes to pay the taxi fare. I ignored Chechi who came towards me, went straight to the bathroom, rubbed my hands and body hard with soap and Dettol. But bits of black skin and blood were stuck under my nails. I dug them out with a safety pin. For days later, I felt revolted when I ate with my hand.

~

The poisoner was never found. Acchan did not allow him to be found. Even if he had, he would not have been found. I sat in the taxi thinking about Inspector Shetty's question, if I had seen much in life. I was not seeing, experiencing, I was either melting, turning into thin air, or freezing. Sometimes burning inside, falling apart outside, in others, turning into ice inwardly and bursting into flames outwardly.

My taxi was like a mere grain of salt in the sea of the countless vehicles waiting at the traffic signal. I broke out in a sweat despite the air conditioning. My lips tasted the salt of my tears, or sweat. I tried to distract myself by thinking of Kripesh. He had planned to kill me, but it was not for himself. It was for a middleman, and the middleman himself was doing it for someone else. Someone invisible wanted to see me dead. Who was that? Whoever it was, it was no easy task for him. I had lived through, experienced, many deaths. It wouldn't be easy for the inspector to do his homework about my past. I had lived so many lives.

As I sat in the taxi, a sour taste filled my mouth. What was the name of the acid that was thrown into our well? Formic acid? What was the name of Sriram's wife? Sitalakshmi? What was the name of the engineer who was in the car that day, the one who had to be hospitalized because the wound on his balls had turned into a nasty abscess? Leelavallabhan?

I asked the driver to take me to the M.G. Road metro station. That Kripesh – I wanted him.

SEVEN

Kripesh looked meek. He disbelieved me. I tried to figure him out. The way he sat down, his walk, his movements. Didn't I have to do that if I needed to know ahead of time when he would pull out the dagger from the pocket of his faded jeans? I did not think that he was strong enough to stab fatally. Or that I would die of it. That was of course my fear. But what if I was paralysed instead of dead? What if Amma had to care for me like she had had to care for Acchan?

~

Acchan was stabbed in a January. On Republic Day. He had taken the last bus back and was walking towards the house.

We did not get another car after selling the Contessa. For a while, he came back home in a taxi; then, for a while, he did not come home at all. None of this affected us. Amma had a fixed deposit in the South Indian Bank. She had kept aside the money from selling the milk from our cows and the coconuts that grew on the trees in our yard, and the presents Appooppan had made her for Onam and Vishu. The interest from this paid for my hostel expenses and Chechi's travel expenses – she had joined a software firm in Ernakulam. But our visits to town and shopping for Onam ended.

Still, Onam that year was unforgettable. For the last time, Acchan arrived in a taxi. The stench of cheap liquor and the reek of sweat filled the courtyard and the house. He gobbled down supper and went to bed without a word. In the morning, he woke up early and walked around the yard. When Amma laid breakfast on the table and called out 'Sive, breakfast is ready,' he came without a separate invitation, and ate. Seeing his face in the daylight, even my heart throbbed in pain. The man was so rosy and healthy-looking once; he'd flitted everywhere with a powdered face, dark glasses, and Brut perfume. Now he looked like a dried-up piece of kokum. We sat down to eat after he had finished. For the first time, he came and sat beside us. And announced the news officially:

'We're suffering losses…'

None of us responded. Acchan continued: 'It's not like old times. You need superstars to make a movie click. And you've to make a thousand offerings for that…'

His voice failed. Amma was totally silent. She finished her breakfast and got up; waited for us to finish, then cleared the plates; then came back, washed her hands and her mouth, and headed towards the front room, very slowly. Acchan went after her. Chechi and I looked at each other. It was clear that something was about to happen. Chechi's eyes glinted like the lake before rain. I tried to stop trembling. We washed our hands quickly and ran over to the front room. But we were not brave enough to go in, so we hung back in the veranda.

'The share market … it failed…' His voice sounded gentler. I feared that Amma would melt and give in. But that did not happen. Her response was impassive: 'Money and some people are like that. They betray you without any notice.'

He had no reply. Amma continued: 'It's just that you haven't experienced it. Never mind. "If you train yourself, then even bitterness will be truly sweet".' She quoted the line from a poem.

'The five acres on which our hotel stands have been attached…' Acchan's voice was now very feeble.

'A month ago, right? I got to know of it then. Valyannan told me.'

Amma let out a short laugh. Chechi shuddered. I feared that she would have a heart attack and so clung to her. That was not because I was feeling brave. But who else did we have except each other to cling to? Our hands were frozen, but our palms felt clammy with sweat. The sea we had seen in town thrashed about inside me. Vasanthamaalika collapsed, piece by piece. The large curving signboard, the golden letters, the glass-windowed storeys – all of it was erased. Chechi's eyes overflowed.

'Let's ask your brother – your valyannan – for a loan? We'll pay it back.'

'Yet another debt? What for?'

'What's the meaning of that?' Acchan's voice rose now. 'That I am a good-for-nothing?'

Amma laughed again. Acchan lost control.

'Laughing? Laughing at the news that all is lost? No wonder! Everything is lost because of your arrogance. Woman, you ought to be humble! You lack humility, you forgot your roots! That's what you are suffering for.'

He stormed out of the room. Seeing us standing there, he grew angrier. Chechi moved a step back, scared, missed the step, and fell into the inner courtyard. I did not move, nor did I lower my gaze. I stood there, leaning against the pillar. The blood drained from Acchan's face. The hand he had raised to hit us fell. His head bowed, he went off, took a bath, sent Venukkuttan Chettan to fetch a taxi, and left.

When he was gone, we both ran to Amma and sat on either side of her. She drew us to her and held us close. It was not common for her to express affection after we were past childhood. Chechi burst out crying. I struggled not to. Laalamma ran to us asking what had happened. 'The children, Laalamme, the children,' said Amma. She sounded piteous. Laalamma beat her breast and wailed. I suppressed a sob. It lay trapped sideways, like a piece of metal inside my chest.

Not a month had passed but we lost the magazine *Vasanthakairali*, the press, and the two acres on which it stood. I was in the hostel. One day, I was stepping out to go to class when Chechi called and told me the news, almost screaming in despair. I could not help weeping either. Some holidays – Gandhi Jayanti, followed by the Puja break – were approaching. I lied that my grandmother was very ill and rushed home. Chechi was waiting for me at the gate. We threw ourselves into each other's arms and sobbed loudly. Amma heard the commotion and came to check. Startled at first, she soon regained composure and then laughed out loud. She pulled us close to her, and throwing her arms around our shoulders, walked, like Gandhiji, towards our house. 'Why are you crying while your mother is alive? Let the five acres or the two acres go! We will get it all back,' she comforted us. 'Let us repay all the debts!' she challenged. 'I'll show you what your mother is. My parents started from a tiny shop. That'll do for me too.' Amma sat with us on the steps outside the front door. Sitting on either side of her, we stuck to her. 'What will you do, Amma?' Chechi asked, still in tears.

'I'll sell five cents of this land and start a fancy store,' she said. 'We'll get glass bangles from Firozabad, black metal from Delhi, terracotta ornaments from Calcutta, lac bangles from Jaipur—' Pausing, she threw us the mischievous look that used to amuse us so when she entertained us as children. 'You'll have to help too. I can't do it alone. Siva will have to select the products, Satya will have to haggle!'

Chechi wiped her tears and laughed. Her childlike nature that persisted so long in her made me laugh too. Seeing me laugh, Amma laughed as well. For some time, all of us laughed. Have you ever laughed after your tears have completely drained you? That is true laughter. Your swollen eyelids will feel sore, the reddened nose will become wetter still, the huge weight that sat inside your chest like a large wooden granary will melt like a crystal of salt in the massive wave of laughter. Unwilling to concede defeat in the tug-o'-war with laughter, sorrow will still tug at your heartstrings. But if your mother is near you, laughter will surely win. We will all rise feeling light at heart, wiping our eyes and noses. After a brief interval, the tears will leap up again. They will drag us across the line like in a game of kabaddi. Until that happens, we could feel weightless enough to fly over the house and the inner courtyard and the door and the carved pillar in the front and the lake on which the cranes would alight.

I will not forget that day too. It was the day since when Acchan began to come home every day – the day since when he had no place in the town to go to, that is. I had finished my studies for the day and was about to go to bed. Shutting the west-side window, I saw something glow at the edge of our yard. Till then, Acchan always came back in a taxi which he'd hire; it would start honking before turning into our lane and its wheels would screech over the gravel in our front yard. He always arrived escorted by such sounds. How to imagine, then, that he would creep in through the west-side entrance in the dead of night, like a thief? Chechi had fallen asleep, weeping; Amma was reading K. Surendran's new novel *Guru*. I called them and woke up Laalamma. As we watched anxiously from the window, Acchan stepped into the light from between the shadows of the sappotta and moovandan mango trees. I was not really amazed about the fact that this figure stealing into his own house was my father. What appalled me was that he had come walking. One more nail had been driven into the coffin, I guessed. Chechi wept again. Amma sighed again.

Have I told you the story of the Contessa's arrival? It was a night of celebration. Acchan had bought it from Madras, for 95,000 rupees. Two cars escorted it. On the way, they stopped at all the bars and houses of friends. There was a mighty pandemonium – the drunken singing and the noise woke up the neighbours. The cows mooed in fright, the fowls scattered. When it stopped, a whole bunch of men – some ten or twelve of them, including the film actor Sridhar and the production controller Rajasekharan – jumped out of the cars like ants from a tin of sugar. I was twelve then; my legs ached from running between the front of the house and the kitchen carrying jugs of water. Venukkuttan Chettan did not go home that night; instead,

Radha Chechi came over. Ulahannan Maaman, too, did not go home. He changed his uniform for a kaili and banian top, hung the white trousers and shirt from a nail in the kitchen veranda, and took over the cooking. On the open firepits set up on the north of the yard, chicken and crab and prawns were cooked in bronze vessels. In the kitchen, Laalamma cooked the tapioca, Radha Chechi made the chapattis, Amma cut the salad. The revelry lasted till daybreak. The next morning, our uncles and Appooppan came to take a look at the car. The day after, we went to Koyikkal in the new car. To stop the children who had run up to dirty the car, Ulahannan Maaman kept watch wielding a stick. Our trips to Koyikkal for Onam and Vishu were made in this car. We never went anywhere else in it, though, or for that matter, never went anywhere with Acchan. The Contessa was stylish, so was Acchan. But each time he zoomed off in the car, I resented it. I did not want an Acchan who leaned back in the car stylishly in his silk shirt and gold-bordered mundu. I wanted him to walk with us on the green village paths covered with kalampetty and karuka plants, on which the thumba bloomed and the kakkappoo vines spread. I wanted him to tell us stories as we walked. Our Acchan was incapable of doing all this, and I never forgave him for it.

So I truly enjoyed the day he crept back at night like a thief, and all the days on which he left by the bus in the morning and came back by the last bus at night. But I continued to be under the impression that Nityavasantham Productions and the three acres around it were still ours. That November, the stock market crashed. For days after, Acchan did not step out of the house. He lay on the bed, pressing his face down into the pillow, weeping. To hide his swollen eyelids, he wore his dark glasses even inside the house. That show of courage, too, ended that December. Acchan's Muslim friend who handled his shares was killed in communal violence. Acchan howled and wailed that day: 'Vasantham! We are finished! What will we do?' And soon, Nityavasantham Productions and the three acres vanished as well. I came to know about this disaster the day before Republic Day;

I bunked classes and rushed home. But I could not return to college the day after. Because on the night of 26 January, Acchan was stabbed.

That's how Acchan's 'route map' was revealed. He would get off the bus at Court Junction. Then he would take the long route through a number of bylanes to reach our house. He would get into the revenue land walking through the narrow path between the granite walls of Meledeth Soman Sir's property. He would cross the pullanjhi thickets, the njaaval tree and the wild Ixora bushes, to reach the Punnakals' coconut garden, which was overgrown with false-button weeds. From there, you could enter our yard – there was just some barbed wire which you would need to slide under. I was astonished thinking how he could have slid under the barbed wire. It was only much later that I learned that human beings will do anything to shore up their false pride – crawl, roll, whatever.

Acchan fell in the Punnakal family's coconut garden. He sustained fourteen wounds, like the holes one makes in a jackfruit to see if it is ripe enough. But even then, he did not utter a sound. He would have died, bleeding. But that night, when Peter Sir, a retired official of the rural development department, on his way out of the toilet after taking a shit, noticed a light in the distance, he felt something was wrong. So he woke his son, and they went over. They found an electric torch, its light on, which had fallen from Acchan's hand. And they found him a few paces away, lying on the ground, covered in blood. They raised an alarm and soon people gathered. They carried him to our house. Laalamma and Chechi shrieked. Amma looked faint and sat down heavily on the floor. I stared at Acchan's blood-soaked body, completely taken aback.

It was chaos. In minutes, the house and the premises were full of people. The crowd followed us to the hospital too. Amma could barely find space to sit in the car. The two of us and Laalamma were left at home. Then, for many days, there was a parade of different stories, explanations. One claimed that Acchan was stabbed in a burglary he had attempted, a second that Acchan had been carrying on with Peter

Sir's daughter-in-law and so Peter Sir had stabbed him. Another said that this wasn't true – Acchan had run into someone sneaking out of Peter Sir's house and got stabbed when he tried to stop him. The Marwari moneylenders sent someone to finish him off, said others. There were also stories about SI Dinakaran Pillai's sleuthing abilities, about how he followed a trail of ants to the pullanjhi thickets where the knife, the assault weapon, was found. All these were trumped-up tales. There's just one difference between a true story and a trumped-up one: in the former, the wick of truth burns steady; in the latter, it dies.

~

There was just one story that could make my flesh burn and fester – that of the person who tried to kill Acchan. But it was never told. Some stories are like the foetus in the glass jar. They will not be heard. The true story of who tried to kill Acchan and why was stored away in some glass jar, drowned in formalin. So no one found out who it was or why. The biggest tragedy in life would be to be murdered without knowing why. I, therefore, had to know, and that's why I sought out Kripesh. I had just one weapon before him – complete honesty. He had never known it, and so was disarmed by it.

The first hurdle was to get him out of the lockup. Sunil had to drive around a lot to locate Moorthy's Fruit Stall near the metro station. It was a tiny shop near one selling eyewear under a large multi-storeyed hotel; it looked like a mass of small parasitic plants on a large tree. Moorthy Prasad was a sixty-year-old man, tall, thin, with sunken cheeks, and his hair, brows and whiskers painted an astonishing black. On his right wrist, he wore red and yellow threads. In all, an interesting-looking person.

'Are these fruits safe to eat? No pesticides in them?'

'Me? Sprinkle pesticide? I am a Hindu, Madam, don't forget.'

'Trade has only one religion, Sir, and that is profit.'

'Where do you come from?'

'I am an Indian.'

'Which state?'

'Does it matter? Aren't all Indians, Indians?'

'But there must be some place where you were born and raised?'

'Kerala.'

'Ah! There! So you are a communist!'

'Why, are there only communists in Kerala?'

'We could both gain time if you buy whatever you were planning to buy – if you were planning, of course.'

'So you do have an eye for gain!'

'Gaining time means one can recite "Rama-Rama" some more.'

'No matter how much we recite, won't we all have to go when Yama arrives?'

I bought a bunch of black grapes, a couple of large guavas and some dragon fruit. He weighed it all and asked me for 420 rupees. I gazed around and found a fruit cart close by. Pointing to it, I said, 'Look, it is much cheaper there.'

'But isn't he a Muslim?'

'So?'

'Will any decent Hindu buy from a Muslim?'

'Why not?'

'They are only bothered about making money!'

'Like Kripesh?'

He stared at me shocked, as though he had been slapped.

'When it comes to money, there's no Hindu, no Muslim, no Christian. You'll kill if the money is good, right?' I asked him, drawing up as much sarcasm as I could. His face blanched.

'Have you seen the cell where they have locked up Kripesh? Full of mosquitoes! Hope they are all Hindu!'

His face had turned yellow now.

'Madam, are you from the police?'

His voice had grown extremely faint.

'Do only policemen go to the police station?'

'Then you must be a journalist...'

'The issue is not who I am. You have to go right now to the police station, write a declaration and get the boy out. Or you are going to get into trouble.'

He looked flustered.

'But ... that...'

'Getting him out is going to be really important for your survival!'

'Madam, someone has misled you...'

'Mr Moorthy Prasad, do you think that a woman like me would come here to talk without good reason?'

'Madam, he had asked me to change some old notes for him ... Otherwise, I have nothing to do with his business.'

'There's this tricky thing about notes. The stains pass from the hands of the one who gives them to the hands of the one who take them!'

'I swear on God, I don't know where he got them from!'

'I'll tell you – it was payment to finish off a woman.'

'Which woman?'

'A woman named Satyapriya.'

'Who's that?'

'That's me.'

The way he jumped in shock! I really wished Chechi was with me. How she would have laughed! The force of it! It would have bent even the Purple Line of the metro! Anyway, Moorthy Prasad went with me to the police station and got Kripesh out. As per my instructions, he got him to sit in the back seat and he climbed in the front. When the car turned the bend in the road, it stopped, and I, too, got in. The boy shuddered. He turned in anger towards Moorthy Prasad and shouted, 'Stop the car!' Moorthy Prasad calmed him down. I called the restaurant in the housing colony and ordered vegetable biryani and chicken sookha for four people. We collected the parcel on the way, and I invited the driver and the two of them in. We ate together and chatted for a bit about things happening in the world. When we were done, I asked Sunil to drop Moorthy Prasad at his shop.

Kripesh, too, got up to leave. I called him into the kitchen. He was reluctant but came over. I handed him the sharpest kitchen knife I had. He shrank a bit. Helplessness filled his gaunt eyes. I could read in them the voids he had faced as a child. I put my hand on his shoulder. He flinched. I did not give up. I ran my fingers through his hair, held him, and pressed my lips against his forehead. My heart melted into salt water and flowed as tears through my eyes. They fell on his cheeks and wet his shirt. He was almost my height. So I heard his heart beat hard. Maybe it was always that way. What else to expect from the child of a burglar who was beaten to death by people? To make a made-up story sound real, you just need tears, not the repeated thrusts of the blade, as when you try to see whether the jackfruit is ripe or not. A teardrop, from the heart, that is all. That's enough to make anyone believe. The tears will spread on their flesh like sparks of fire, sear it. The searing pain is at the very core of their willingness to believe.

'Where are you going? Do you have a place to stay?' I asked. He squirmed. Clearly, he felt small.

'Do you have a bed? Someone to give you food? Anyone to ask where you'd been when you return? If you have, then you may leave.'

He looked even more forlorn.

'If not, you can stay here. Before you kill me, you can learn what sort of a person I am. I will live only until then, after all? Let us live here happily till then. I will take care of you like my own son.'

I caressed his head and kissed his forehead again. My father had never kissed me like that. His father, too, would not have kissed him that way. My eyes filled again. He too wept.

'Cobra Nagu…' he said. 'Cobra Nagu gave me the job. Gave me five lakh for it.' His voice quavered. I was stunned for a second.

'Do you have his phone number?'

'He always calls me; I don't call him.'

'Look, you have to show him to me … I'll give you any sum you want.'

'No, no need. I'll tell you if he calls.' He wiped his nose.

'Okay, in that case, you can stay here and be my bodyguard.'

He smiled. His sunken eyes shone with affection.

'Let me go now. I need to find a house. I have a little brother. Have to educate him. That's why I…' His voice broke. 'I'll call you once I get home,' he promised.

I bid him goodbye and went in, securing the doors and windows. Suddenly, I felt all alone and miserable. It is not easy to see a killer face to face. Especially at forty-four, it will drain you. I fell into the bed without even changing my clothes and slept like the dead until morning. I awoke hearing the phone ring. It was Amma. We spoke thus:

'I waited for your call. You didn't pick up when I rang you.'

'Isn't that why I asked you to come with me?'

'It was a mistake to have set out with your father. I don't want to repeat the mistake!'

'I was thinking of the day Acchan was attacked. But who? Who could it have been?'

'Whoever it was, they had no idea about how to stab someone.'

'Is that why Acchan looked like someone had torn out his flesh?'

'That was no credit to the attacker. It was because the dagger was shaped like an "S".'

'An "S"-shaped dagger? Twenty-four years back?'

'It was a peculiar dagger for sure. They say that the shape makes sure that it would pierce through an elephant's hide as though it were a banana! That sharp. Some producer in Madras had given it to him.'

'Maybe not a producer, must be Rajani.'

'When he got it, Rajani was probably not even born!'

'Ugh! What a thing to make a present of.'

'S for Sivaprasad…'

'S for Satyapriya, S for Sivapriya,' I finished what Amma was about to say. She ended the call abruptly. That was because I mentioned Chechi. I kicked myself for forgetting.

It was past seven now. I got ready for office. Found my identity card, booked the office cab, locked the house and waited in the sit-out. But it was the police car, not the office vehicle that came. Inspector Anurup Shetty got out. I greeted him and pointed to the cane chair in the sit-out. He stood leaning on the half-wall, a rolled-up newspaper in one hand. Tapping the half-wall with the newspaper, he smiled with some difficulty. We exchanged the following words:

'Good morning, Ma'am … I came now because it's an emergency … You must either move out or get someone to stay with you. Or request police protection.'

'What happened?'

'You brought Kripesh here yesterday, right?'

'Yes, what happened? Is he okay?'

'Ma'am, your case is growing more complicated by the day.'

He opened the newspaper and showed me an inner page. The top headline was about the suicide of an MLA's driver who had exchanged an enormous sum in old notes for the MLA. Below was the news, 'Extortionist Cobra Nagu shot dead in Goa'.

My eyes popped out of my head. A monstrous tremor shot up from my stomach and got stuck in my throat, choking me.

'Look, we know that Nagu hired Kripesh, but who hired Nagu? Only Nagu could have told us that. Now he's dead. The only way we could have found out no longer exists. Your enemy is extremely powerful. It all feels like a made-up tale to me.'

I struggled to answer him. Swami Mahipal Shah Baba's face came to my mind. 'Cut-out murder' – that was the name of this kind of crime. I couldn't start telling those stories, it would last forever. They were not trumped-up tales that lacked the weight of truth; they were true stories that weighed down on the flesh and branded it.

I don't know if you've noticed the resemblance between stories and currency notes. Murder is the process by which the victim's right to the truth is rendered void by the killer. With this, truth becomes the murderer's monopoly. Isn't that why so many murders go unsolved? I was lucky in that regard. I had of course not yet died. My right on the truth was intact. Was someone trying to invalidate it by killing me? Who? Which of my truths was making him insecure? To know that, I had to find his true story. And to find that, I had to find my own true story.

EIGHT

I did not share the term 'cut-out murder' with the inspector. It would have been trouble if I did. From whom, when, why did I learn it – I would have had to tell him all this. And it would have been his homework to find out the rest. I had just one clue for him. It was a shloka:

Samam pashyan hi sarvatra
samavasthitameeshwaram.
Na hinastyatmanaatmaanam
tato yaati paraam gatim.

That is, 'For someone who sees God as equally present everywhere and in everything, that he is subjected to violence, or he commits violence, is not relevant. Besides, he gains the ultimate release in Moksha through it.'

But I did not reveal to him even this clue. What was the guarantee that he would grasp it? Wouldn't he have had to study the Bhagavad Gita to do so? And even if he had, would he not have had to imbibe its inner meaning? I remember Chechi when I say this. She always found Sanatana values very complicated. If the rightful heir to the throne was the eldest son of the oldest man in the family, surely Dhritarashtra's eldest son was entitled to it? That was her question. Especially after Pandu, his younger brother, had abdicated his right to the throne and left the kingdom for an ascetic life in the forest with his wives? She was also never convinced by the argument that 'murder is a crime, but murder during war is spiritual merit'. She once even held me by the throat, asking me about the Mahabharata war. If it was such a great war waged out of a sense of duty, why did the paramatma wage it directly instead of making the poor jeevatma do all the killing, she asked. I wriggled out, saying, 'Ede, maybe the paramatma can't get a thrill out of getting it done directly.' But there was this thing: she had a crush on Arjuna. Whenever in the Gita class Madhavan Nair Sir said, '*Arjuna uvaacha…*' she would smile mischievously, holding back within herself a veritable ocean of true ananda.

But I! I had the ultimate revelation after the first two classes. The thing was simple: we are all jeevatmas. The jeevatma is a small chip, or piece of the paramatma. Therefore, the jeevatma neither takes birth nor does it die. Death is an illusion. The body to the jeevatma is just what a frock or a skirt is to us. If the body gets old and worn like an old skirt, it will throw it away and get a new one. The jeevatma needs neither petticoats nor panties. All we do is the paramatma's doing. But on the grounds that we don't do well enough, it makes us do karma again and again, like the extra work we do as punishment for poorly done homework. If it is good enough, the paramatma frees us from the bondage of karma. In short, all these are the deeds of the paramatma. And it is the paramatma that decides if the deeds are right or wrong. The poor jeevatma ends up getting beaten and writing the imposition!

I was indebted to Acchan for all of this. He sponsored those classes. 'The Maplas have Bible classes and the Kaakkas have their madrasas – only our people are in contempt of their own religion,' Madhavan Nair Sir complained to Acchan one day. 'Ah, let's set that right,' said Acchan. 'You take the lead, Saar, I'll do what's necessary.' He promised thus, but Amma was not pleased. No one asked her for permission, though. Within two weeks, Gita classes began to be offered at a small house near the lake. Acchan inaugurated them. On the weekends, Chechi and I went there with our neighbour Nisha Chechi. They always served sweet payasam after the class. When the news of the class spread, more students began to turn up. After one year, there were two batches. Before a class began, we would recite 'Hiranmayena paatrena...' raucously, and when it ended, 'Om sahanavavatu...' That was actually pretty tough. Because it was recited after the sweet brown jaggery payasam had already been served on green vatta leaves and laid in front of our seats.

I was just six then. That was the time Acchan was making the blockbuster family drama *Kutumbamanu Swargam*. Acchan was my hero at that age. I tried every trick to please him. This interest in the Gita was one of those. I gave it my everything and learned it by heart. In two years, I was one of the two children who could recite the whole of the Gita from memory. The prizes were given away by Acchan. That day, he patted me on the shoulder. I was in heaven – almost. The second prize went to a fifteen-year-old; he later became a communist. He was jailed for premeditated murder around the time we lost our house. In sum, he put into practice what he learned at the Gita class. I couldn't do that, but I did not forget any of it. So even at the very last meeting with Mahipal Shah Baba, I could recall perfectly all the shlokas I had memorized sitting on the breezy veranda of the lakeside house.

That meeting was in his private room. I had gone there to bid goodbye. My heart was in a tumult from anger and despair, yet all five senses were dull and passive. It was a thatched building with glass windows. I was angry enough to set it on fire. But Amma had no one else but me – that thought always held me down, it taught me self-control. Mahipal Shah sat on a dhurrie laid over a grass mat on the floor and was examining some files kept on a low table, his elbows resting on it. I entered and called out to him; he raised his head. His alluring eyes bore into my heart. It had swollen like a balloon ready to burst, but now the air leaked out. So it did not explode.

'I am leaving,' I said weakly. 'Decided?' he asked. 'Yes,' I replied. His face grew wan. Because he had renounced the world, he expressed anger through sorrow. I tried to be as indifferent as I could to what I sensed and felt. He sat in the sukhasana position for a short while, drawing his breath in and fixing his eyes on his upturned, interlaced palms, which rested on his lap. That was the first of the tricks of his trade, seeking time to hide what was going on inside him. It always shakes you up a bit. Taking that chance, he'll throw the sand into your eyes. Then knock you down, climb on your chest, and hit your eyes or nose forcefully to subdue you.

I was not wrong in my estimate. Without opening his eyes, he recited: '... *tulya priyaapriyo dhirah, tulya nindaatma samstutih...*' My heart stirred. Our relationship had started with that shloka. But who knew him like me? No matter how tightly you may shut the door, the fumes that linger will betray the fact that the hearth was still smouldering. Likewise, who knows better than me, the twinge of the yearning for vengeance in his voice? So I pretended not to hear, not to grasp. I feigned extreme humility:

'Great One, is not *samam pashyan hi sarvatra* ... more fitting for this occasion?'

He flushed, unable to find a quick retort. He could only recite from memory. He was ashamed of himself, so feared a direct confrontation. Ah, is there anything dearer to people than their own masks? He sighed sadly. Tried thus to distract me.

Thinking back, it feels like a joke. Fate lurking around. I was offered a teaching job in the MBA campus placement. It was in Tamil Nadu. At the time, I was trying to run away from the hellish memory of the zoology lab, and so accepted it. The owner of the institute was quite like my father, a nouveau riche. He was struck with the anxiety over saving the true Hindu national culture, the essence of Arsha Bharata. A month after I joined the institute, he conducted the Integrating Arsha Samskara summit, which lasted a week. Mahipal Shah Baba was one of the twenty-five leading speakers who participated in it.

Until then, I had neither heard nor seen him. But the large crowds that started gathering since morning amazed me. His appearance was memorable. He wore a piercingly white kurta-pyjama set and a saffron-coloured shawl with 'Om' printed all over it and stepped on to the dais with folded hands. He had a stunning stage presence. People were enraptured. He spoke on 'Bhagavad Gita as a Management Treatise'. His voice was more striking than his looks. His head was hairless and shiny. The greying hair behind his ears was thick. His beard was white and well trimmed. He had pinkish cheeks and charming doe eyes. Even I was crushing on him. But it was Saturday, and Amma would call me at five every Saturday. No man was so attractive that I'd forgo that. So I got up in the middle of his talk and went outside. I called Amma, and we chatted for some time. Then, leisurely, I went back in.

Mahipal Shah was interpreting that very shloka when I re-entered the auditorium. It meant this: 'He who is beyond desire, who is not stirred by the natures of things, who knows that these natures are essentially changeable and therefore remains unmoved by them, he who stays indifferent to pleasure and pain, treats alike gold and a clod of earth, the dear and the hateful, who treats honour and insult, friend and foe alike, and renounces all enterprise of embodied creatures, he rises above the three gunas.' As I stepped back in, Mahipal Shah paused. All of a sudden, he roared, 'Stop!' The audience was taken by surprise. He pointed at me.

'There! That lady! … Madam, please stop! I want a word with you!'

This was unexpected. I was a bit rattled. The audience was oddly silent for a moment and then began to murmur. His voice rose again.

'I am speaking to you! Hear me, this is a very pious gathering. Because these honourable people are here not to enjoy a dance or a musical performance. They have set aside all their urgent business to listen to the Bhagavad Gita, which is the essence of a religion that is the greatest in the world. No one forced them to come here. They came because they wished to come. Because the Gita is not just some common book. It is the distilled essence of the Upanishads. All the answers to modern man's troubles are in it. It is clear that you have no interest in it. If so, why are you here in the first place? Once you have decided to come, then you must show respect. That is not disrespect to me, but to a great culture. That is the civilization that runs through our veins. Unfortunately, only our own fellow-believers have no knowledge of the strengths of their own faith. They are slumbering. I cannot help but ask, would you have the guts to go to a place where the Koran or the Bible are discussed clad in jeans and shirt and with messy, unkempt hair? Will you dare to flit in and out as you please?'

That really shook me. The owner of the institute, who was sitting on the dais, rolled his eyes as though he were preparing to dismiss me then and there. The principal ran to me from somewhere. I withdrew, ready to leave. But Mahipal Shah was in no mood to spare me.

'Ah, so you are leaving? How can we let you go like that? Anyway, since you came back, Madam, please enlighten us. Tell us what you know about the Gita. I would really like to know. Someone please give her a mic?'

The audience started murmuring loudly now. A volunteer came over with a mic. Mahipal Shah continued:

'What did the Lord say? *Pravittim cha nivrittim cha janaa na vidurasura*…! What does that mean? People who are evil, like the asura, cannot discern activity and inactivity, they will be unclean, they will not even know the acharam. And without custom (or ritual or observance), there will be no culture. And without culture, we will not exist … Let that be, Madam, we are all ignorant people. Please be merciful and share your knowledge with us, poor ignorant folk!'

Okay, my job is a goner, I gathered. Besides, in those days, I had not achieved much self-restraint. The smouldering coals that had lain under the ashes within me flared up. I took up the mic, looked him in the eye, and here's the exchange that followed:

'Not just the Gita, no book should be mechanically followed; it is absolutely useless. There's just a single message in the Gita – that there is no such thing as the Other. I have only so much knowledge.'

'So you claim that there is no special good from studying the Gita?'

'Before I answer that, can you please tell me about the circumstance under which you came to study the Gita?'

'What a question!' He laughed derisively. 'My guru handed me this book during the biggest crisis of my life and assured me, read it, all your problems will be solved. That's how I came to study the Gita!'

'That is, you studied it under the expectation that you will derive some benefit from it. And having derived some benefit, you now teach it. But in all the eighteen chapters of the Gita, the Lord says, expect not the fruits of labour!'

'How sad! You are such a slow-witted person!'

'Yes, this country is made up of many slow-witted people like me. There's much that we don't understand. For example, in the Sankhya Yoga, it says "*Klaibyam maa sma gamah partha…*" That is, do not partake in the languor and inactivity of the eunuch. Of someone neither male nor female. God, who declares that He alone is at the heart of all creation, is the fount of all knowledge, makes all memory possible, that it is He who makes and keeps and destroys all of creation – that same God tells one of his creations not to be like another that He himself made! What is the logic of this?'

'Madam, I did not know that you knew so much! But do not forget something. You are able to openly ask this and say so much only because you are a Hindu. Do you have the guts to criticize the Koran or the Bible?'

'Why should I do that? Let those who believe in the Koran and the Bible criticize those texts!'

'All right, leave it. Suppose you were a Christian or a Muslim. Would you dare to criticize your sacred books?'

'Do you mean to say that the freedom to ask a question is munificence on the part of the religion? That asking a question is actually perverted freedom?'

'No, no, no, beti … let me call you that. You are after all just old enough to be my daughter or little sister.'

'But you are a scholar of the Gita. Someone who has known the *paramatma tatva*, how can he see another creation of the Divine as male or female or friend or foe, above or below him in social standing?'

I did not ask these questions expecting any response. I knew the answers to them. I asked them just for a thrill. Even jeevatmas deserve a thrill, now and then.

Mahipal Shah rose from his seat. He reminded me that if people like me served the Hindu faith and Bharat Mata, then this country would be the greatest in the world. This was the strength of the Hindu, he declared. 'No matter who or how the Hindu may be, they will shine from within! Jai Bharat Mata!' Many from the audience echoed his slogan.

These were his usual tricks. Picking on some poor duffer in the middle of his talk, reducing them to dust, and through that, making the rest of the audience feel that they were somehow better. And, precisely in this way, bringing all of them to their knees – spiritually. But it didn't work with me. He had to conceal his embarrassment, and he played the generous soul. So he came down from the stage, walked up to me, took off the saffron shawl that he was wearing and wrapped it around my shoulders, and in a final flourish, folded his hands in salutation to me. The shawl gave off a lovely scent. 'Very pleasant,' I said. 'What perfume is this?' He, who was waiting for me to bow down and touch his feet, was unsettled yet again.

After the talk, he summoned me again and invited me to his ashram in north India. 'In what capacity? As an ascetic? Or a renouncer?' I questioned. 'As an ascetic, I would have to engage in activity with no desire for its fruits; as a renouncer, I would have to give up the fruits of my labour.' His hooded beautiful eyes glinted.

Within days, I received an appointment letter as the HR manager of the Mahipala Cosmetics Company. A salary of 35,000 rupees, something a jeevatma could hardly resist those days. Mahipal Shah Baba lived in a large campus built over many hectares in the suburbs of the capital city. It included his stately ashram and a vast industrial estate on which several factories were run. It accepted me into its fold like the sea takes in a grain of salt. Money is a great narcotic. Power is even more enticing. But the illusion of having won a battle is greater than either. Like money, victory, too, is but an illusion of the soul.

Now, having heard me this far, many of you are probably already drawing a picture of two bodies wrapped around each other, rolling on the silken sheets of a bed somewhere inside the ashram. That's natural. After all, the stories of many ascetics that you have heard would lead you there. But Mahipal Shah was different. His abode was a mud hut thatched with grass. He slept on a grass mat on the bare floor without even a pillow. There was nothing romantic in his room except the softly swaying white silk curtains and his languorous eyes.

But there was something: whenever he looked at me, his eyes were lit with desire. That radiance was of the kind that I had always sought in a man's eyes. He looked deep into my eyes and recited shlokas in his resonant voice. Each time, it faltered, helpless. I enjoyed his vulnerability. His faltering voice made me want to take his face into my palms and press my lips on his eyelids. But those were days when the jeevatma did not find it thrilling enough. All my ecstasies had vanished. They had all died inside the lab, festering slowly in the formalin, and seething in pain. The soul, the Gita says, leaves the worn body in death, just like humans cast aside worn garments for new ones. But my body was not worn. In a strange reverse order, it was my soul that had decayed, not my body.

What I mean is simple. Our relationship was not physical. I knew nothing about his home or family. My workplace was just opposite the vast yard of the ashram which was like a green umbrella beneath which deer and peacocks roamed – in the Mahipala Industrial Complex. The ashram was generally empty. The 'Rama-Rama' chant could be heard there all the time, as it flowed everywhere from hidden speakers. Mahipal Shah had vowed that he would make 'a King out of the Caretaker', so was busy with election work. He held Gita sessions all over the country, from Kashmir to Kanyakumari, and his visits to the ashram were quite rare. But whenever he did come, after he met visitors, he would summon me. I refused to call him Swami or Baba. He called me 'Satyaji', I called him 'Shahji'. When there were no VIP visitors, we had meals together. I mocked him. I criticized him. Do not think I was feeding my ego in this way. I felt terribly insecure. Relationships have always plunged me into deep sadness, like Arjuna before the battle of Kurukshetra. The heaven promised to those who died in battle, and the hell of the defeated – scared me alike.

There was an artificial stream right behind his hut. On some evenings we sat by it, talking. He would speak for barely five or ten minutes and fall asleep even as he was laughing – flat on his back. Ten or fifteen minutes of very deep sleep. He would snore crudely, and sometimes drool too. That's how I learned that even those who know the ultimate secrets of the jeevatmas also snored and drooled! The tricks the paramatma plays.

It wasn't that he was free of the desire for the fruits of karma. I learned that when, a year later, Anjali Agarwal came to the ashram. It was she who first told me about 'cut-out murders'. She arrived at eleven in the morning one day. Mahipal Shah was gearing up for an eighteen-day lecture series on the Gita abroad. I had prepared an outline of it. Anjali arrived when I was reading it out to him. At thirty-two, she was a real head-turner. She rushed in. Her eyes were welling, and her cheek was bluish, as though she had been slapped. She opened the big suitcase that she had brought with her and flung it in his face. Bundles of thousand-rupee notes that the government of the time had printed flew everywhere and fell on the writing desk and the floor. Mahipal's face darkened. I knew only then that he was capable of such fury. He leapt and held her by the throat. I gaped in horror. But he reclaimed his temper soon enough as he requested me to wait outside for a few moments. I was petrified but managed to get out. My eyes stayed fixed on the white-coloured Warli art on the mud walls as I stood leaning against the door of the thatched hut. I could hear her scream and wail inside:

'No, no, no, I *don't* want to hear you out! He *will not* occupy that chair, no matter what anyone says. This is my vow! No matter what even you say, Baba!'

Mahipal Shah said something; I did not catch it. Then I heard her say clearly: 'Then why don't you get me cut out?'

Cut out? I didn't get it. The expression stuck. I knew that it had nothing to do with the cut-outs of cine actors and things like that. I listened, my heart throbbing. He was counselling her, non-stop. She wept. And then calmed down. After some time, he called me in.

'Satyaji, this is Anjali. She has some issues. She'll be here for a few days. Please let her stay in your cottage? You must think of her as your older sister. I really don't trust anyone else...'

'Older sister' – Chechi – that pierced me like a sharp arrow. He had done it deliberately. This is what I am telling you – never tell men more than what they must know. I had told him a little more than necessary about Chechi; that was a mistake. Then, how was one to say no to accommodating another person in a cottage with two large bedrooms and a kitchen?

Anjali stayed with me for two months. She came home with me for the puja break and stayed in our tiny house which was not air-conditioned and lacked any other luxury. But she got ready to leave on the second day after our return. She pretended to be happy. Things at home were normal now, she let me know. 'You lost your older sister. I am leaving so that I will not lose my younger sister.'

'When will we meet again?' I turned a bit emotional. She placed her hands on my shoulders; her tears flowed. They were straight from her heart, and they singed me.

'We will not meet again,' she managed to say. 'I am a cut-out...'

'What's...?'

'You will soon find out.'

She kissed me on both my cheeks. 'Call me sometime,' I reminded her. She sobbed. I never heard from her afterwards. It was Diwali the following week. Mahipal Shah invited me to a meal. His mirth and vitality seemed contrived. We had tea by the stream, and he lay on the grass in the savasana, when I asked, in a completely normal way, what this 'cut-out' was.

'Cut out – as a picture or a murder?' he asked with the vagueness of someone falling into sleep.

'Murder…' I suppressed a shiver. He looked at me with half-closed eyes.

'Oh, that's simple. Suppose I decide to kill you, Satyaji. Isn't it risky to do it myself? So I have to hire someone. Say, I tell my secretary Balbhushan. Balbhushan will find someone he knows will do it. That guy will entrust it to someone in his group. And it will get subcontracted six or seven times over, until someone actually does the killing.'

'But won't you have to pay all these people?'

'That's not a problem. The main thing is the cover-up. Like I said, if Balbhushan killed you, Satyaji, the police will catch him. Now, what if he decides, some day, to reveal my name? I will be finished!' He yawned. 'But if we have subcontracted it six or seven times, then maybe the eighth guy will complete the task. In some cases, we cut this very guy out. Suppose we don't have the time. And suppose the police have nabbed him. Now we will cut out the seventh guy. So that the thread is cut. So that the investigation will never lead to the real killer. In some cases, instead of the killers, the witnesses are finished off. All that depends on the case, the context.'

He slept off soon, snoring. I sat there, my very bones rattling. Thereafter, I felt no peace until I found Anjali. I should not have done that – because she was killed, very cruelly murdered. She was a 'cut-out'. How furtive the world has always been to an Indian woman, I learned.

Cobra Nagu was also a 'cut-out'. Did Mahipal Shah have a hand in it? Did he harbour enmity towards a trivial being like me? He never forgave lesser beings, that much I knew. But he had never sought me after I left the ashram. After sixteen long years, now I wanted to see him, his enchanting face, wanted to hear his seductive voice. What if I never saw him again? Only if Chechi were alive! She would have surely fallen for him. She would have refused to imagine him as the killer. She would have torn me apart asking, 'Why would he wait for sixteen years to kill you?' That's a relevant question. Why should a killer wait for sixteen years for a 'cut-out murder'?

Ah, who knows! Maybe some jeevatmas find their thrill in a long wait.

NINE

Kripesh and Nagu ceased to exist. The very next day, my job, too, ceased to exist. Tough luck, huh? But that's what happened. I had gone to rejoin my office. Shantanu, the manager, did not look at me but asked me to go meet the HR general manager, Rakhi Gupta. I should have guessed then and there. But Rakhi Madam was on leave. I went to the supermarket from office and bought some essential stuff. Cleaned up the house, set the kitchen right, slept a bit. By around five in the evening, I went over to Sandeepa Sen's house and chatted with her for some time. Came back, made myself some rice gruel and drank it, called Amma, and then went to bed.

The next day I reached the office early and went straight to Rakhi Madam's cabin. The moment she saw me, she said that there was some bad news. Someone from Advaita had sent the CEO a message. Since some controversies likely to erupt in the context of the murder attempt could cast a shadow on the company, I was to be paid the compensation specified in the contract and be relieved of all responsibilities immediately. That did shake me a bit. This job, I had loved it. But what to do except depart when it is time? I took a piece of paper from Madam's desk and, without wasting any time, wrote my resignation letter. Bid goodbye to my co-workers and threw a little farewell party at a nearby restaurant. After the formal relieving procedures were over, I returned home by three.

The compensation amount arrived in my account by evening itself. That it was a very large sum disturbed me. The banks were aflush with funds at that time. So much money, in my name. A person's true nature comes out under two circumstances: first, when they receive a windfall, and second, when they lose everything. My father was unnerved in both circumstances. My mother was just the opposite. When we lost all our wealth, my sister wilted and dried and became intensely superstitious. I, however, was merely vexed at it, like it were a lover who had dumped me. Whenever money came to me, I felt suffocated, as though I were wearing a tight blouse.

I remember getting the Upper Secondary School scholarship and feeling that way. Appooppan took me to the District Educational Officer's office; Chechi and Amma came with us. Nine hundred rupees was a big sum back then. I had planned to buy a sari for Amma, a dress for Chechi, and clothes for Appooppan and Koyikkal Amma, and for Laalamma and Venukkuttan Chettan as well, but somehow my spirits fell when I received the money. An inexplicably low mood came over me. Appooppan bought all that I chose so I didn't have to spend anything, but even then, I felt awful.

Appooppan stayed with us that night. I took him his black coffee the next morning when he was walking in our garden, relaxed, the chutti-printed torthu-towel on his shoulder, taking in the breeze from the lake. 'Why have you been so sad since the time you got your prize money, my child?' he asked.

I could have lied. But whenever I felt that it was harder to speak the truth than to lie, I always chose the former. So I told him, 'I don't know why, Appooppa … I have had no peace since I got that cash. I feel terrible at the thought of spending it.'

Appooppan laughed heartily. His coffee almost spilled. He offered me many an advice that day. Money is meant to be spent, he said. No one is going to become rich just by being tight-fisted. To become rich, you need not be brainy, but you must be diligent. Only those who are diligent in how they spend will be wealthy. And those who exercise diligence about who to spend on, will be happy. It is hard to balance the two all the time. Without money, there can be no happiness, and without happiness, you won't hold on to your wealth. But there is one thing one needs to remember. Never think that you can buy respect. Money will be unhappy and leave.

'Can we buy love?'

'Love is a form of respect, isn't it?'

That was true, and I was convinced of it later, after Acchan was attacked. He had flung around cash, in bundles, in his prime, buying love and respect. Later, all those ties littered our lives like the chewed-up sugarcane waste, shreds of balloons, burst, deflated, and bangle pieces left on temple grounds on days following a festival. Our lives became a waste bin.

Acchan was first taken to the Taluk Hospital. The doctor there, Dr Janardanan, assured us that he would be fine. He was a member of Acchan's drinking gang. Acchan was admitted there for two days. I returned to the hostel and college. Things, however, grew worse; Dr Janardanan then moved Acchan to a private hospital in town. Acchan spent two and a half months there. Amma was mostly there, and Venukkuttan Chettan and Radha Chechi stayed with her. She came home only to withdraw her fixed deposit. Money was falling short and Chechi and Laalamma were alone at home; so I vacated my hostel room and returned home in March itself.

My exams were in April. Acchan was still in hospital. Something happened on the last day of the exams. When I returned home, I saw two cars outside. One belonged to the famous moneylender from town, Xavier Panakkal, owner of the private financial firm Vyakulamata. The other was of the film producer Sreedharan Nair, whom I had often seen with Acchan. I invited them in. Panakkal's stocky frame filled the sofa. His thickly powdered face grew damp with sweat in the hot wind blowing in from the lake.

'Sivaprasad owed me some money...' he began. I froze. Such a moment was yet to arrive, but it was never expected.

'Acchan is hospitalized ... Amma is with him...' I fumbled for words.

'We know. That's why we didn't trouble you until now. But it's a life-and-death situation for us...'

'Without Acchan coming back...' I could not finish. Suddenly, Sreedharan Nair, who was wearing a three-layered gold chain around his neck and a gold bracelet on his wrist, barked: 'What if your father never comes back? Don't we need our money? Do you need to be told that he's never going to get up again? He's barely alive, just to fill the pockets of the owner of the hospital! That, too, after having blown up all the borrowed cash!'

I was struck dumb. When you are penniless, you lose both – your money and your voice.

'Don't make us come again,' they said, before storming out. I wept, and so did Chechi when she returned home after work. We felt helpless, not knowing whether to let Amma know or not. But we did not have to hide the news for long. The next day, the doctor in the private hospital in town suggested that we take Acchan to the Apollo Hospital in Madras. This meant that we needed money. Amma came back home to arrange it. We were shocked to see her. She had become thin and gaunt. Large, dark lakes circled her eyes; her cheeks were hollows and her shoulder blades stuck out. Chechi let out a loud cry and hugged her. It affected Amma a bit, but she pushed her back, chiding, 'You are grown up now! Isn't it time to stop cooing like this?' Chechi only hugged her tighter. 'Oh, don't take all the dirt from the hospital for yourself, leave some for Satya!' Amma said. That made Chechi smile through her tears. I tried to smile too, but tears pooled in my eyes.

After taking a bath, Amma came into the dining room and drank up the rice gruel and lentils hungrily. Want entered our house through the kitchen. It was weeks since we had bought any fish or vegetables.

She had barely finished when Xavier Panakkal and two others strode in. 'Where is your mother?' they asked. 'Inside,' I could barely answer. They marched in without a tinge of doubt, pulled up chairs near Amma and sat down. One of them asked for water. When Chechi brought him a glass, he pinched her on the cheek and remarked, 'You're a pretty one! You could be in the movies!' I had begun to quake by then. Amma got up and said, 'Please go to the front room, Sir. I will be there in a moment.' When she went in, Xavier Panakkal looked at me. 'Why are you so scared, dearie? Am I a tiger or something?' he joked and tried to hold me by the shoulder. I pressed my back hard against the bedroom door. Amma, who had come into the front of the room after washing her hands, looked at me disapprovingly.

'Move aside, girl!' she almost roared. 'Haven't you learned to take care of yourself yet?'

The blood drained from the man's face. Amma turned to smile at him almost deferentially.

'Don't take offence, Sir. People are of many kinds, aren't they? Most belong to the sort that thinks that if a husband is in debt to them, then they are allowed to finger the wife and daughters. These kids don't know anything about such fellows.'

His face grew dark.

'Uh! If the money isn't coming back, then yes, they may get fingered. Should have given it a thought before borrowing.'

'Was there such a contract when the money was borrowed?'

'Don't yap so much. Just return the cash. I'll leave at once.'

'How much do we owe you?'

'Four, and the interest.'

'How much is the interest?'

'Ten per cent.'

'Isn't that too much? I don't have…'

'That you should have thought of when you took the money.'

'If you'd asked me when you gave him the sum, I'd have told you.'

'I have the cheques and the promissory note.'

'Oh, really? Then please go, get it from him.'

'I thought you're a well-born woman, that's why I kept my tongue. I know how to get back my money!'

'I'll return the money with three per cent interest. If it is a deal, keep the cheques and promissory notes ready on Saturday morning, ten.'

She looked at the clock.

'It's eight-thirty now. Late. I suppose you are leaving, Sir?'

'No, I am not going until I get my cash!'

Amma pressed her hand on her hip and glared at him. Then she turned to me and said, 'Dear, just call this uncle's wife and tell him that he's going to be staying with us and that we're letting him return only after the money we owe him is paid back. Go, find his number from Acchan's diary...'

'Sister, don't you play those games with us...'

'I told you. Saturday, 10 a.m. Don't say that you can't find the cheque, that you misplaced the promissory note, when I hand you over the cash.'

Chechi and I shook like leaves; we clung to each other. Amma slammed the door after the men, marched into the bedroom, fell on Chechi's bed, and was snoring in a few minutes. We did not know what to do. For some time, we sat in the front room and blamed our mother's brothers, cursed our father, worried about our mother. We were two completely defenceless creatures in this big world, petrified with fear and shame, staring into what seemed to be pitch-black darkness ahead. Even the breeze blowing from the side of the lake was searing hot. We mumbled our fears to each other for a while and then we cried, giving up. Chechi hugged me and tried to console me, 'Vaave, don't cry.' I hugged her back and comforted her, saying, 'Akke, don't cry.' We fell asleep on the sofa. After a while, I woke hearing something fall to the floor. The sound came from our parents' bedroom. Amma had taken out our grandmother's gold and laid it all out on the bed. She set aside two waist chains and put the rest into a cloth bag. Seeing me, she held them out to me.

'Here, take these, this is all I can give you. Ten sovereigns of gold each.'

I just stared.

'Wear them. No one should know. They will help in a crisis.'

I remember Amma's face from that moment. She looked determined. As though everything was clearly thought out, as though she had been expecting it all. The next day, her brothers and their wives arrived. There was no tea, no chit-chat. Amma brought out the cloth bag with the gold in it. My kochumaaman, the younger of the two uncles, had brought scales; the gold was carefully weighed and valued. Four lakh, he announced, handing her the piece of paper on which he had made the calculations. Those days, a gold sovereign cost 4500 rupees. Amma went inside, telephoned someone, and handed the piece of paper back to Kochumaaman.

'Mathew Tharakan Jewellery offered four and a half lakh rupees. That suits me better.'

The faces of our uncles and aunts turned sour. 'If you were out to make a profit, why did you call us here?'

'It's Amma's gold. I just wanted to offer it to you first.'

'We can only give you what we can afford!'

'That's good. I can give you the gold for that price.'

'Oho, so you are trying to bargain with your own brothers?'

'But none of my brothers suggested that I should not sell it, and that they would help me instead?'

'You got the most from Acchan!'

'Isn't this bargaining too?'

'What are we to do if your husband threw away everything?'

'What could I do when he did that?'

'That's your negligence...'

'All right, I'll sell these to Mathew Tharakan.'

'Who's this Tharakan? You'll sell to some vague Mapla but not to your own brothers! What obstinacy!'

'Valyanna, no, I am not obstinate at all! Have to take him to Apollo ... Before we go, the bill in this hospital has to be paid ... the debts too ... I need the money.'

'How long are you going to treat him?'

'As long as I can.'

'Are you aware that aside from this, your husband has debt worth eleven lakh more?'

'I see that my brothers have worked hard to find that out.'

'How do you plan to repay it?'

'I'll sell the house and the land ... what else to do?'

Her brothers looked at each other.

'Any one of you can take it ... Twelve lakh in all.'

'The land value here is less than that.'

'This is the value of my land. I am valuing it.'

'If so, can't you just sell his share of the Koyikkal land? That belongs to these kids too?'

'It'll fetch only a pittance.'

So the house and the grounds were sold for twelve lakh. My kochumaaman's brother-in-law bought it. The whole amount was to be paid in six months. He made an advance of two lakh and gave Amma twenty cheques of fifty thousand each. He handed over the money and took back the cheques a few times. But Acchan's treatment lasted far longer than we had expected. The payments became unsteady. Money against two cheques was not paid at all. Amma tried to ask, and Uncle broke ties with her. We had to vacate the house before the registration. There was no time or money to find another house. We decided to go to Koyikkal. Not because we wished to, but there was no other way.

~

Losing one's house actually brings an advantage. The experience of loss ceases to bother you after that. So losing my job was not painful at all. I lay in bed, stretched my limbs. Silently thanked the CEO that

I did not have to rush out in the morning and limp back tired to the bone at night. I slept like the dead.

It was past five when I woke. The golden dagger-tips of the setting sun still pierced the sit-out and the porch. I made myself a cup of coffee, went to the sit-out, pulled a cane chair near the money-plant vines, and parked myself there. Sipping the coffee, I looked out into the street lazily. A police car headed towards the SI's house and two cars and a tempo went in the opposite direction.

The memory of the man on the bike began to stir in me then. The comings and goings of not just money but also of death can bring out the real you. It is impossible not to die, but you have to be diligent about what and who you die for. Was it all real? An office vehicle stopping, the gate creaking open, the bike rolling down noiselessly and spraying bullets – was it all a figment of my imagination? Just then, a bike rolled down the street. I thought I was hallucinating. I blinked just to make sure. The bike was real. A man sat on it, wearing a helmet and dark glasses, observing the premises, speaking on a mobile phone all the while, or pretending to do so. I was hiding behind the shade of the money-plant climber, so he did not see me. He took off the glasses and peered closely into my house. I shrank back, falling on my knees, tucking myself away between the wall and the chair. He put the phone back into his pocket and lingered there for a moment, absorbed in some thought. Then the SP's beaconed car came up. The biker rode away. I sat rooted to the ground, covered in a cold sweat. The wall I was leaning against was wet now. I panted as though I had been running for hours.

Because it was him. The man who had sprayed bullets on me on 16 November. Acchan was right. It was not mistaken identity. He was hell-bent on killing me.

But why?

TEN

Why?

That's the question that can make or break a detective. Nothing else is worth the trouble unless it is answered. It is the reason behind the act that makes it a crime or an act of justice. It is not enough to discover who did it or how. We need to discover why it was done. Three questions are always at the core of the investigation of a crime: who, how, why. In my case, the 'how' was not relevant, as I had not been murdered yet. There was no answer to the question 'who' either. There was more than one potential killer. Only the 'why' was obscure; it alone let me climb further down into the heart of the crime.

But it is never easy to answer the 'why'. Unlike the who and the how questions, this cannot have a precise answer. For example, my sister was like a butterfly, flitting from flower to flower. Why? Now, how to answer that satisfactorily?

It was true even if it cannot be explained. She danced in the air from blossom to blossom. But a strong wind could break her wings. They would be wounded easily, by a random pinch. On such occasions, she would lose her confidence and pride and turn into a lowly cricket. She would cry all night and irritate me. In the beginning, I cried with her and railed against the lizard and chameleon and bird and wind that hurt her. Then, gradually, I discovered the truth. Her wings were like the house gecko's tail – the moment she saw the next male flower, they sprang back. It was not easy to come to terms with this truth. The answer to the question 'why' would be necessary for this. We never came across such characters in the stories we read or the movies we saw. I fought with her when she gave someone a love letter she'd written earlier, merely changing the name of the recipient. I scolded her, snatched the letter, tore it to bits. But in time, I stopped asking why. It was unnecessary. Each one has their reasons and their ways.

So I did not pay much attention when she began to fixate on a batchmate of hers. She was an MSc student then. Physics was her main subject; he was in the zoology batch. His father disappeared during the Iran–Iraq war. Amma showed her the news and the photo, and that was enough to touch her. Two new wings, besides the two she already possessed, sprouted then and there. The five-thousand-square-foot home they had started building on the site of their old house that they had demolished was not yet complete. He lived in a rented house along with his mother, his grandmother who suffered from a kidney ailment, and his two sisters. He was waiting for his father to send him money for his grandmother's next dialysis. These details were enough to make Chechi weep and melt. At that time, she already had two beaus. One was her teacher; the other, the conductor of the Gopalakrishnan bus in which she went to college. The teacher was Muslim and the conductor, Christian. That weekend, she came to see me in the hostel. She had told Amma that she was visiting a friend. On her finger was a brass ring, the Virgin Mother's image on it. The conductor had got the ring from Velamkanni. And she also had on some new perfume, from the teacher, whose relative working in the Gulf had gifted it to him. She made me go out with her, and we got into a bus. I was thoroughly puzzled, but as usual, I relented at her tears. She won, and we went to that boy's place.

Some journeys never end; this was one of those. It took us a full three hours to reach our destination. A remote village with just a tiny shack for a shop and an even smaller tea shop. A few people hung about there. All of them jumped out to take a good look at the two of us who were wearing town-clothes – Chechi a salwar-kameez, and me a midi-skirt and blouse. My hair was cropped too. 'Everyone is staring at us! What do we do!' She grew nervous. That was no surprise: she always dived into the water but could never swim. All she could do was thrash about in the middle, and then I would have to dive in to rescue her. 'Let's go back then.' I gritted my teeth. 'No, no please, we've come so far...' she begged and pleaded. And so, I became the martyr. I went up to the crowd that was staring at us and asked about the house of Sadasivan Nair who had gone missing in Iraq. That provoked a volley of questions: 'Where are you from?', 'Why are you here?', 'Where is your house?', 'What's your family name?', 'What's your father's name?', 'What's your caste?', and so on. Having answered all of them suitably, I received instructions, and we were soon on our way.

That was a beautiful village. The hedges on either side seemed covered with green satin. We were on a dirt path, very uneven, with too many holes. On either side were verdant homestead gardens filled with very large trees. I walked on briskly, cursing Chechi, and she followed me with difficulty, trying to pacify me.

It was only after my feet were bruised, being rubbed against the skin of my slippers, that we reached the boy's house. A half-built house with foundations and walls of laterite. Next to it was a small tin shed, where the family stayed. His sister shouted, 'Two girls have come to meet Aniyankunhu!' Aniyankunhu, who came out with no shirt on and just a kaili-cloth tied around his waist, ran off on all four feet seeing Chechi. She, too, blushed and drew tiny circles on the sand with her big toe, overflowing with amorous excitement.

Following this, his mother came out. It fell upon me to answer her questions too. 'We were hereabouts and thought we'd drop by,' I said. The first thing she asked me was my father's name. When I said

'Sivaprasad', she wanted to know what our caste was. I mentioned my mother's caste. She hummed, went back inside. We very clearly heard her say, 'Manikkutty, don't bother to get out the cups. The glasses that we keep outside the kitchen will do.' Chechi blanched. My pride was hurt. Aniyankunhu came back clothed, leaned on the wall, and mumbled words that made no sense. I began to hurry to leave before Manikkutty brought the tea. But it was his mother who brought it. Chechi looked at me, mortified. 'Sit down, have some tea,' she tried to sound generous. I continued to stand outside the house as I said to her, 'No, we don't eat from the houses of people of your caste.' Her face darkened. 'Why?' she asked. 'What if you serve us tea in unwashed glasses?' I said. Mother and son stiffened. I grabbed Chechi and got out of there.

The return journey was one to be remembered. Chechi was offended; she felt that I had insulted her and her loved ones on purpose. Somehow, we managed to reach the bus stop. The next bus to town was only at five. I was seized with worry: they closed the hostel gates at six. Someone told us that there were buses to town on a route some two and a half kilometres away. We would have to walk it. It was a sweltering noon. My eyes were clouded with anger and hunger. We walked there feeling horribly hungry the whole way. A bus that went to the town arrived and we jumped in. It was one that took a very long route. Chechi got off in the middle and took another bus home. The one I was in took four and a half hours to reach town, and by the time I reached the hostel, the gates were closed. No latecomers would be let in without meeting the warden. She called Acchan and told him that his daughter had gone out at nine in the morning and had come back just then. Acchan was in town at the time. In fifteen minutes, the Contessa was at the hostel gate. I was cross-examined in the warden's room. Acchan slapped me hard on the face, dragged me to the car, and kept abusing Amma and me until we reached home.

When the car stopped, he yanked me out and threw me on the ground before Amma. 'If the mother jumps over the fence, the daughter will leap over the wall,' he taunted. Amma nearly pulled out the flesh from my wrist, asking, 'Did I send you to college for this?' I tried hard to suppress my sobs and went to our room. Chechi was lying on the bed, relaxed, following a bath and supper, reading a copy of the *Pauradhwani* magazine. I pounced on her, dug my nails into her fair-skinned hands, bit her, clobbered her, kicked her. She screamed. Amma came rushing in hearing us; she slapped us hard on our wrists and thighs, leaving reddish marks on them. Unable to bear my anger and sheer frustration, I wept out loud. Chechi felt terribly guilty. She bent down at my feet, placed her head on them, and begged, 'Please forgive me, vaave.' After some time, I relented and said that I forgave her. She gave me a kiss, but I still complained that I alone had been slapped. She then dug into her bag and drew out five one-hundred-rupee notes, her secret savings, and gave them to me – one for each slap. That compensation erased my tears, and I smiled. We hugged each other and made fun of Aniyankunhu and his mother.

But it did not end there. It must have been some two weeks later, after I went back to the hostel. On a Friday evening when I was chatting with friends in my room, the warden summoned me. The warden, the matron, the assistant warden, and Acchan besides were waiting for me in the warden's room. I was suddenly inert, lost. He glowered at me. In his hand he held an envelope and letter. He held the letter out to me to read. It was from the boy whose house we had gone to. He thanked me for having gone all the way to meet him and apologized for his mother's behaviour. He wanted to see me again and expected a reply. I lost my tongue. Acchan ordered me to pack a bag. I do not remember how I managed to do that and get into the car. I felt numb, except my limbs trembled as though I had fever. Behind my ribcage, my heart spun like a crazy top.

Acchan did not utter a word until we reached home. As soon as he sent Ulahannan Maaman off, he came to our room, hands clasped behind his back. I was alone in the room, sitting on the bed. If I told the truth, both of us would get beaten. If I did not, I alone would. So

I decided that I wouldn't mention her. Acchan pulled out his belt and the first lash fell. Then the rest followed, left and right. The leather was very smooth, but the sensation that it aroused on the body when it landed hard on it is hard to describe. It grew teeth wherever it fell, and had a hot, searing sting as well. Chechi, who returned to our room after her bath, let out a loud scream and got between us. I lost my balance and fell. Acchan was still frenzied, and he continued to whip us. Chechi tried to cover me, I had to struggle hard to push her away. And then, at the slightest chance, I grabbed the edge of the belt. We began to pull from either side. I pushed Chechi away and stood up straight, looking straight into Acchan's eyes. For a moment, he was weakened. Taking advantage of that moment, I snatched the belt away and threw it to Chechi. She grabbed it and ran out. Acchan lunged hard at my throat and gripped it hard. My eyes were bulging, and yet I faced him unflinchingly.

'Better to kill me…' I snarled even as I tried to get my breath back. 'If not, I'll go out and tell the whole world…'

His hands eased.

'Yes, get out, you bastard! Go, scream…!'

' … this Sivaprasad is a hypocrite! A man who got my friend pregnant…!' I shouted as loudly as I could.

He let me go and stood there, shaking. Chechi screamed again, asking him to spare me. He kicked her aside and strode out. I rubbed my throat and sat on the floor. The whip-scar ran on Chechi's face, from cheek to cheek. My body was covered in lash marks.

Have you ever felt the mind and body singe and sting at the same time? A pity if you have not. It is like being thrown into a firepit. The body burns to ashes. The mind, however, smoulders like raw flesh. When the fire spreads inside and outside, the body takes leave of the soul, intelligence flees the brain, the beating quits the heart. We do not exist in those moments. Nothing remains, other than the blinding fumes that pierce your eyes and tear them out. You feel nothing but the unbearable agony from the sting of poisonous wasps, or the unendurable suffocation from your head being forced into a bucket of water and held down there.

Amma had gone to a funeral at a neighbour's house. She returned after it was all over. Laalamma and Chechi greeted her with loud lamentations. Amma heard them without betraying a tinge of emotion. She then came into the bedroom. I was still cooped up on the ground where I had fallen. She examined the scars on my face and arms. Her face flushed. She got up quickly and went straight to Acchan who was sitting in the west-facing veranda sipping his drink. Chechi was weeping as she held me close. The window was open, and I could hear my parents talk.

'Why did you thrash her?' Amma asked.

'Ask her.'

'The one who thrashes knows more than the one who is thrashed?'

'Where do you think she sneaked off to from the hostel a couple of weeks back? To hang around with some fellow! She rode a bus for two or three hours to reach his house!'

'So? At what age should she be hanging around if not now?'

'Ha! Wonderful! Let her muck around and get knocked up. And Mama will take care of the birthing and the baby!'

'Well, we haven't been taking care of the birthing of the girls who've been knocked up here, have we? We just get rid of the bother, don't we? That's what your friend, that doctor, Janardanan, is for!'

'Chee!' Acchan snorted. 'Indeed! You … cheap … bastard!'

'I surely need not remind a former medical student that babies need to be fathered?'

Acchan hurled something to the floor.

'You are behind all this! You are training your daughters to be whores!'

'But it is their father who's showing them that whores can have more respect than wives!'

Some other things fell on the floor and broke. Chechi and I hugged each other tightly. I could hear her heart thump; she could hear my heart beat so hard, it sounded like a rock hitting another. 'Five hundred won't do for what I suffered today,' I whispered, trying to make her smile. 'I'll need at least a thousand.' 'Go away, you, Shylock, you…' she hugged me again. I licked her cheek. She fell on me, laughing. My back, all scarred, hurt. After a while, Amma called us and asked us what this was all about. Chechi fell at her feet and confessed, saying that she had wanted to go purely out of sympathy. Amma was amused and angry at the same time. 'You, Satya, you're the one who encourages all her crazy ideas…' Amma tutted and raised her hand at me in jest. To Chechi, she said, 'Next time you are overcome with sympathy, let me know. I'll take you.' All of us laughed.

But there was no end to Chechi's 'sympathies'. My ordeal did not end either. Two weeks after I returned to the hostel, I was on my way back after class one evening when there he was, under a tree near the gate – that fellow. I walked on pretending not to see him, but he followed. Helpless, I turned around.

'I came to know of the trouble you faced because of me, Satyapriya. I am sorry.'

'Who told you?' I asked him, feeling insulted.

'Sivapriya.'

'What did Sivapriya say?'

'That she came along only because you insisted…'

I went blank.

'No ordinary young woman would have the heart or mind to do such a thing. She'd need a big heart, a very big one.'

My very big heart was beating faster than it could bear, out of sheer rage.

'I'll never write to you again. I'll come over whenever I can.'

'What for?'

'Please! This is like waking someone who was sleeping and telling him that there's no supper! You offered something … now don't say you didn't…'

His eyes welled. I continued to feel bemused.

That was a Tuesday. I couldn't wait for Friday to come. The moment I reached home, I sprang on Chechi and scratched and bit her all over. 'Want to see me dead, uh! Want to see the smoke from my pyre?' I raved loudly.

'Vaave, please, in a moment of weakness I told him...' she begged me.

The story was actually fun. This fellow met her in the college veranda, and they were talking when her teacher-lover turned up there. He was suspicious and began to question them, and so she made up a story – in that moment of weakness – that her younger sister insisted on going to this chap's house and that she was the one to take her. 'How does your sister know?' the teacher-lover asked. Then came the next story, about the news item and how her sister had wept, reading it. She upped things, really – telling them that Satya was so fond of her father that she couldn't sleep without eating a ball of rice each day from his plate, and she would get very upset when she heard that someone's father was in danger.

Later she admitted that she had given the fellow a gold chain. 'Satya told me to give it to you for your grandmother's dialysis,' she told him. It was like a bolt of lightning had hit me. 'What's your problem? It was for a good thing, wasn't it? What's the problem with him thinking that it's your chain?' And then she declared, 'You'd know if you had such problems!'

And so it was. The chap came over to my college every week. That, too, after his classes were over, running after the bus, riding it for a whole hour. He'd reach sweaty and tired and wait for me outside. Each time, I wanted to just blurt out the truth and be done. But how? How to tell him such an unpleasant truth? I remembered his mother when I saw him. The dirty glasses in which she had brought us tea. I vowed to tell him the truth the following week. But when I saw his exhausted face again, I failed. I quarrelled with Chechi.

'What's wrong with him, huh?' she huffed. 'You-are-so-unromantic!' she scorned. 'Never mind, he'll mind his own business after the course is over!' she said, trying to comfort me.

But he did not give up. He kept coming regularly. When I was down with chickenpox, he came to meet me at home. He spent time with me, and then, when he was about to leave, he threw me a lovelorn look. I seethed inwardly. Because just a few days before, another man had trampled my life and left it a wreck. I was badly thrown. How could my sister's friend's romantic overtures not irritate me then? I tried to escape, but he pursued me relentlessly. One day, when he brought some glass bangles for me, I lost my cool. He thought it all right to take my wrist and put them on it; I pulled it away in anger. My arm hit his face. The bangles fell on the floor and broke. '*Do not* repeat this!' I growled. He perceived it as a slap. I remember him standing, weak and distraught. He glanced around to check if anyone had witnessed it. And then he walked out hastily, head bowed.

I saw him years later. On the day my sister died. Like a lizard that had grown back its tail, he came back. He regrew the relationship from where it had been severed. I was sinking into a bottomless sea; even a lizard's tail looked like a lifeline. But it was a mistake.

I did not mention his name – that was on purpose. Any story must have some suspense! But you must have guessed – yes, Sriram S. Nair. Why did I remember him now? Because the killer reappeared.

∼

Once I gained a measure of calm, I ran to Sandeepa Sen's house. Mrityunjoy was home. He called Inspector Anurup Shetty. Mrityunjoy tried to follow the assailant on his own bike. By eight at night, the inspector came over. The CCTV footage from the nearby houses between four and six in the evening was collected and the images of bike riders in it were culled out and examined. I identified the killer at 5.08 p.m. Inspector Shetty became excited.

'Ma'am, we'll get him! But please listen to me. It's not safe here...'

'But I will die when it is fated anyway.'

'Don't be silly! If you are killed in this house, I am answerable! Especially when Aswathy Ma'am has been enquiring about this directly from Kerala.'

'What do you want me to do?'

'Please write down the names of people who may have a motive to kill you. Have you seen anyone who resembles this man ever? Was there someone in Odisha who would want to endanger you? You are not telling us about them.'

'My brain is frozen. Please give me some more time.' I rubbed my forehead and entreated.

'Yes, do take your time, but please give us as much information as you can. This is a request.'

He left. Sandeepa Sen and Mrityunjoy were very worried, but they tried to comfort me. They insisted that I stay with them for a few days. Sandeepa laid out a bed for me in her room. While we talked, Mrityunjoy made dinner. Bengalis generally insist on a pet name, and he had one – Joyo. Sandeepa's pet name was Sona. Joyo's luchis and curry looked delicious. We sat down to dinner talking about the attacker who dared to appear in broad daylight.

'Satya, think – why would someone want to kill you?' Sandeepa asked.

'I am seeking answers to three questions – who, why, how. My investigation will be over when I find them.' I smiled.

'Interesting – those three questions are the core of democracy as well,' Sandeepa remarked.

'Ma, no theory, please. Who are your enemies, Auntie? That's what we need to know,' Joyo chipped in.

'Many. But none of them are foolish enough to do it directly.'

'That may be just a feeling. There are many who are pretty high up in life but are satisfied only if they do it by themselves.'

'Joyo, are you on Facebook?' He opened FB on his phone and held it out to me. With my left hand, I searched for 'Sriram Sadasivan', and opened his page. No matter what anyone says, social media has many uses. It is like liquor – it goes to your head quickly. Once high, the attention and acceptance of others is the psychological need of the intoxicated. And to get that, they will talk endlessly, make a lot of fuss. In the process, they will let out all sorts of facts about their life, secrets even. Now, for example, I found out through his post that Sriram was in town right then, as a speaker at the Malayali Association, practically next door to where I was staying.

Joyo became anxious all of a sudden. 'Auntie,' he said, 'look at this?'

He showed me a photo. After he became a full-time politician, Sriram always wore a mundu and a shirt. But this photo was from a tour of Europe or some such place. He wore pants, a jacket and a cap. I recognized the jacket and cap – the killer had worn similar ones. They seemed to resemble each other too.

'Who's this man?' Sandeepa asked, anxiously.

'He was my lover for a short while,' I said, reaching for another luchi. Sandeepa and Joyo looked at each other.

'But why? Why would he want to kill you, Satya?'

I became a little unnerved. The victim should never answer the question why. It is dangerous for her. Because any honest answer can be used to accuse her of abetment. The killer, too, would then be a victim, a victim who could not help but commit the murder. So I defused her question with another: 'Why would he want to, yes. So much time has passed!'

ELEVEN

Have you ever shat and pissed in your clothes after you crossed infancy? That too in the presence of strangers? A pity if you haven't. For that means you have no experience of the ups and downs of the share market that is the middle class – full of scams around honour and respect. If you don't know what the loss of bowel control in adulthood is, then you have no idea what it is like to be in the middle of these scams. I have known it. That is why the demonetization exercise made me nervous. My fear was not about the possible disruption of exchange. Exchange, of course, will continue unimpeded. But if currency notes disappear, their place may be taken by human bodies. To know what that's like, you have to survive that situation.

~

I have experienced it. The day I went to the lab. Don't ask which one – I have already told you about it – the lab Sriram had locked me in. Why did you trust him, you may ask. There was no reason not to – not on that day.

The day my sister died. I had forgotten him. In between, I briefly recalled his mother, her dirty glass tumblers. Other than that, I could

123

recollect only two things about him – his dislike of Saddam Hussein and his rage at the Mandal Commission recommendations. But I was battling life, and neither of these mattered to me much. At the time, he was a tall, bony chap, with Bata slippers and the long sleeves of his cheap cotton shirt folded up. When he reappeared on that day, he wore an expensive Van Heusen shirt, fancy shoes, and an expression of triumph. I did not recognize him and told him so truthfully. His face changed colour. 'Sriram,' he introduced himself. 'I was in college with Sivapriya. You have come to my house.' But when I did recognize him, someone pulled me away for something urgent. I was handling everything alone, speaking to everyone who came and went. What happened, they were asking. I had to tell them about how she died. Each time the tears overwhelmed me. In between, I ran to our room, sat there alone, and wept. Her scent still filled the room. There lay her white nightgown – blue flowers printed on it – that she had taken off that morning, half on the bed and half on the ground. The towel she had wrapped around her wet hair after her morning bath, which had been flung on the clothes-stand, still lay there crumpled. The clothes in the laundry basket still bore her sweaty scent. That morning, too, she had set the alarm for five. When it rang, yet again she pulled the blanket over her head and snuggled into bed until half past six and then hurried out of the bed moaning loudly that she was late. 'You alone are responsible for this,' she said accusingly, scratching and pinching me. I was still in bed when she came out of the bathroom, shook the water from her wet hair on my face, and pulled out my white kameez and churidar with purple flowers on it, upsetting the neat pile of the freshly washed and ironed clothes in the almirah. I jumped up and protested. She hugged me and kissed my cheek. No matter how much I tried to wipe it off with my tears, the pain from the moist warmth of the kiss lingered, refusing to dissolve.

That night, Sriram was the last person to bid us goodbye. He was also the first to come the next morning. I was waking Amma up and getting her to drink some black coffee when he arrived in his new

Maruti 800. I introduced him to Amma. She remembered him and enquired after his father. Sadasivan Nair, his father, had been jailed during the Iran–Iraq war. He came back after two years. Sriram had sold the house that his father had begun to build before the war and used the money to get himself a lecturer's job in a college. When Nair returned, he bought land, and built a new house with the amount he received in compensation. He got his girls married too. 'But Satya, how could you forget me?' Sriram grumbled. He came every day. Helped without us asking. He accompanied me to deal with the insurance companies and with the death certificate.

I was diffident; even he. I was an MBA student then. He called me regularly and visited me at the hostel too. He vowed that he still loved me. I found it hard to push him away decisively. Every time I saw him, I saw those dirty glass tumblers, and my children suffering in his house like Chechi and me. My rational mind warned me that a man like him was not likely to love a woman such as I. But I had changed. My mind was battered enough to feel empathy with a young man shattered by my sister's lack of discretion. I was like a vessel that the cook had left on the fire and forgotten about. The curry in it boiled, thickened, then started burning, finally blackened, turned into soot, and then the vessel glowered red, changed shape, tapered and appeared funnel-like. Misshapen now, unable to be what I used to be, I floundered. Sometimes I lost control. Or hallucinated. Or plunged into depression. Blubbered. Acted strange. That's why the day my MBA exams got over I said that I wanted to see that lab. I was hardly normal. He sensed that, and that was the reason why he invited me there.

Have you ever been locked up? Knowing that you were trapped there deliberately, cheated? With no one to hear you even if you screamed? For two whole days and two nights? If not, then you have indeed missed out, because you have not known the sweetest experience in all of life. It is very interesting. Every second feels like an age. Every moment you will expect the person who locked you in to turn up. Discover with disbelief that it is night. Break into pieces in the knowledge that he did not turn up even the next day. Hate him, and at the same time, pray hard for him to come back. After the first shock, you will feel a scorching heat all over. And then the thirst. You'll first check to see if the washbasin inside the lab works. First, your hand will feel sore and then become blistered trying to twist open the rusted tap. Soon the thirst will launch a full-scale attack, and you will be besieged by your own tears. And then, the hunger, and afterwards, the urge to pee. By and by, it will be dark. The rats and cockroaches will begin to move in the room. You'll sit on a bench, lift your feet off the floor, put them up on it – and weep. And doze off. The next morning, the sunlight will filter in through the ventilators. The urge to shit and piss will become unbearable. You'll pace the room, hoping that he will appear any moment. You may even fear that he would have injured himself in an accident. And you will inflate the consequences of that possibility and become more and more frightened.

The second day, too, was about to end. I was half-dead. My mind was lost. My body began to move on its own. I walked to a corner involuntarily and peed. The urine collected on the cement floor. It stank unbearably. I began to be revolted by myself. But even then, with one half of my mind I still hoped that he would come and release me. But no, the door was opened only the next day, at eleven o'clock. A teacher and an attender opened it. I was shaking with fever and lay flat on the bench. When they entered, I shuddered awake and got up. 'Who, what?' they asked, and all the piss and shit that I had managed to hold inside until then just gushed out. They yelled, raising an alarm. My body and soul seemed to be parting ways. I was like a corpse now.

What happened after that? I do not like to remember. They called others. The principal arrived. The degree students who had come for their exams gathered. The stench was appalling; they all held their noses and shrank away. In each of those moments, I killed myself over and over again. They sent me to a toilet nearby. Someone gave me a piece of soap and a bottle of Dettol. The toilet was filthy. I dipped the broken, mouldy mug in the water collected in a dirty bucket, washed my clothes, my body, and came out dripping wet. The police arrived then. A retired sub-inspector, two constables, male and female. They questioned me. I was all hunched up and my head was lowered. They took me in a jeep. Don't ask me what happened next – that must be told at length. I cannot but return to Sriram now. That, of course, is the climax of this story.

It was past three-thirty when I got away from the police. I went straight to Sriram's rented house. It was not hard to find. It was already getting dark. There was no one at home, except an elderly woman, their help. She was talkative and happy to have me there. 'Saar and the mistress have gone out to the matinee show. They'll be back soon,' she said. Something searing hot touched me and I broke into blisters from within. Where had they been the past two days, I asked cautiously. There was some lovers' tiff two days back, she said. Then Saar begged her to forgive him. And she did, and now they are merry as ever. The next day they went to a friend's house for dinner ... She was describing the scene when Sriram arrived on his bike, his wife riding pillion and hugging him from behind. Seeing me there, he was struck dumb. I went out to them, pulled off my shoe and hit him hard on the cheek with it. 'This is for your wife!' I yelled. He lost his balance and almost fell down. Then I hit his other cheek hard with the shoe. 'This is for me!' His wife tried to stop me. I twisted her arm off, pulled her close to me, and glared at her. 'First, your husband has always been a nuisance to me, then and now. I hate even the stink of his sweat! It was just pity – pity at the way he kept following me around and smelling my bottom...' Her eyes popped out. I could see shame spread all over her face. 'Who wants this filthy prick?' I spat hard. 'You can keep him!'

~

That need not have been. But wasn't I young and hot-headed? Joyo was at least six or seven years younger than I had been at that time, and that is why I stopped him. But he still went away saying, 'Don't worry, Auntie!' My heart struggled, like fire on a soggy piece of paper. It grew worse when he was late. Sandeepa was immersed in her reading and note-writing. The strands of her hair shone like gold threads in the light of the table lamp. Her face was statuesque.

'Joyo's late,' I tried to remind her many times. 'He'll be back, Satya,' she kept reassuring me. 'You can go to bed.' When it was midnight, I lost my patience and made her call him. But his phone was switched off. Now, even Sandeepa was worried. I called Inspector Shetty who picked up sleepily but perked up when he realized that it was me. 'I'll find out,' he promised.

Not at peace, I followed Joyo mentally. I saw him speed on the road from Domlur to Koramangala, passing St John's Hospital, to reach the airport, forty kilometres away from the city. I saw him storm into the five-star place where Sriram was staying and confront him. I saw them come to fisticuffs; I even heard vertebrae being crushed. My head spun, and I gulped down several glasses of water. I felt the need to pee many times.

Inspector Shetty called at around two o'clock. What we feared had come true. Joyo had indeed been in danger. He was found unconscious by the road in the military area. I was too afraid to even look at Sandeepa. She sat motionless for a few moments, face buried in her hands. She did not speak or cry. Unable to bear the silence, I put my hand on her shoulder. She hugged me.

On our way to the CMI Hospital, she drove. I tried to mutter something like an apology, but my voice failed. She spoke then.

'That's okay, Satya, probably just an accident.'

'I somehow can't believe that.'

'You are a habitual pessimist, aren't you?'

'I am a habitual truth teller!'

She chuckled. I thought I was going to cry. It was a good thing that I had never grown close to them though we had been neighbours for two whole years, living just across the road from each other. Else I'd have started to love them from two years back. I was rather contemptuous of Joyo – with his haircut that looked like a trimmed arbour – and used to call him 'freak-boy' in secret. But how bravely did he save me from the bullets! And with such compassion did Sandeepa receive me! What for? No answer! Love without reason. It always destroyed my peace. Like for murder, both love and money need reasons. Motives. In my opinion, the latter are trickier than murder. Both must have a real motive; otherwise, you do feel rather scared.

Sriram was in love with my wealth. He believed Chechi's stories because he wanted to believe them. He came in search of me because he thought I was rich. Can real love be possible for someone raised in a home where caste interferes with even the way tea is served? The poor man, I didn't see it then. How could I? All the books and movies we'd read told us that men were grand beings, imposing, masterful. Who knew that they did not know how to love without reason? That they would fall to bits in the face of death and want and the rejection of 'just a girl'.

Joyo wasn't like that. Though he was beaten up badly and exhausted, he hadn't given up. 'Auntie, they are two,' he leapt up to tell me, like a victor. I grabbed his hand and burst into tears. Mother and son had to work hard to console me. But whenever I saw him, tears gathered in my chest. Don't ask me why. I have no answer.

I was waiting at the cash counter of the hospital when Inspector Shetty came up. I did not recognize him because he was in jeans and a kurta; he looked like a student, a poet, a lover.

'Is it going to be a digital payment?' he asked, smiling pleasantly.

'Isn't that love for the nation?' I asked.

'Anyway, good that you paid the bill! He got beaten up because of you!' He chuckled in that innocent-looking way.

'Is that what you've found out from all the homework you've done this far?'

His smile became even more radiant.

'I've also discovered that there are two Malayalis stalking you.'

'Can't you be open with me, Inspector Sir?'

'If you aren't open with us, how can we be open with you?'

'What do you want to know? Please ask.'

'I can't just ask you here,' he said.

The day Joyo was discharged, Inspector Shetty came to Sandeepa's house. The policewoman who had come on the first day to take my statement was accompanying him. He spoke with Joyo first.

'Why did you go out that late, Mrityunjoy?'

'I saw someone who looked similar to the guy who tried to shoot Auntie.'

'If so, why didn't you call the police?'

'I wanted to make sure that it was the same man.'

'And did you manage to do so?'

'No. I am more confused now.'

'Tell me clearly from the start, Mrityunjoy. Where did you go from here?'

'To the airport.'

'Why there?'

'Because he was staying at a hotel close to the airport?'

'Did you meet him there?'

'No, he had left at four in the evening.'

'And then?'

'I called my friend who works at the airport.'

'What for?'

'To find out if he was on any flight out.'

'And?'

'I learned that he had a ticket.'

'And?'

'I went straight to the airport.'

'Why?'

'To meet him when he reached the airport.'

'But you did not reach the airport, Mrityunjoy?'

'No. On the way, I actually saw the shooter.'

'Who...?'

'The man who shot Auntie and got away.'

'Where did you see him? And why didn't you report it to the police right then?'

'But I ought to have been sure it was him! I followed him. He made me go around the airport in circles.'

'Then?'

'After we passed the Military Zone, he disappeared into the dark. I went after him. Then, near the spot where they are building the elevated corridor, a black cloth fell over my head – it was as large as a sheet, or a dhoti. My sight was cut off. Then I was beaten up; they almost broke my leg with an iron rod. Luckily, it is not that bad.'

'Oh, I will have to register a case.'

'Please do.' Joyo smiled.

'And what did you learn from getting thrashed like this?'

'I don't know if there's any connection between the Sriram Sadasivan whom Auntie mentioned and the shooter. But I don't think there is.'

'How are you sure? You didn't see the guy properly.'

'Sriram Sadasivan had boarded the flight by then.'

'Who told you?'

'My friend at the airport.'

Inspector Shetty seemed lost in thought. He took the cup of tea Sandeepa held out, had a sip, and leaned back.

'Anything more?' Joyo asked. The inspector flashed his childlike smile, finished his tea, and then asked, 'I just have one last question, Joyo. Why are you letting yourself get beaten up? Risking your life like this?'

'People are standing in bank queues and dying. Why?'

The inspector's face grew dark.

'I am asking you why are you putting yourself in danger like this for a woman you have no relationship with?'

Joyo smiled.

'My mother says that people around the world share around ninety-nine per cent of each other's DNA! Who isn't related to whom?'

I suspected that this gave Inspector Shetty a shock. It sure gave me
a shock.

'Oh, so people who think like this are still around?'

'They were always around.'

Inspector Shetty frowned. Then he called me, and he and I had the
following exchange:

'Who is Sriram Sadasivan?'

'A politician from Kerala. He was a college lecturer before. My
sister's collegemate. I knew him some seventeen years back.'

'What's his motive to kill you, Ma'am?'

'His wife left him because of me.'

'Oh?'

'He lost his job because I made a complaint.'

'Uh! What did he do to you for you to feel so vengeful?'

The inspector sounded outraged. I fell back a bit. I wondered if I
should tell him the story of how my body performed the function of
currency notes when we did not have the currency notes that Circle
Inspector Dinakaran Pillai had demanded. I did not. The memory
of that fifty-year-old body with a yeasty stench was not something
I cherished.

What I wanted was to know about him – about the killer who was
orbiting me all the time.

TWELVE

The night before you finally leave the home that you love, that is indeed a hard, hard night. A thousand things that you may have used, or were using, or were never likely to use – they all burst into anguished wails in your face. You will have to decide which ones to abandon. The place that each chipped or rumbling thing had in your life will be revealed. Your mind will cling to them to take back the times long gone. Every nail on the walls will awaken your nostalgia. You'll feel for every hidden brick in the walls. You'll feel possessive about even the rats and civet cats running in the loft above the yellowish ceiling of wild jack wood. You'll fear that the house lizards on the ceiling, the chameleons that fooled you in the garden, and the skink that sneaked into the inner courtyard will miss you. Having to leave the house you were born and raised in is not losing a house, it is losing your soul's nest. The long fingers of grass that held translucent dewdrops for your eyes, greenish spiders which left you in awe spinning whole palaces of gossamer webs overnight, chameleons that hid their eggs in the pit covered with tapioca leaves, the sunbirds that nested routinely on the henna shrub, the pupas that did headstands on hibiscus leaves, the kingfishers, tree pies, magpies, yellow warblers, owls … the day I found out that the new owner had torn the house down, divided it into plots, built villas, and sold them, I picked up quarrels with everyone. I lay in the hostel room and wept endlessly.

But on the night before we vacated the house, I did not weep. What was the use weeping? Amma, too, did not weep. Acchan and Chechi did. Laalamma, Venukkuttan Chettan, Radha Chechi, their daughter Achu – Aswathy – who was just three or four then – all of them wept. Acchan didn't just weep, he bawled, unbearably, rolling his head, blubbering. Chechi would weep, then pause, then the sobs would build up again, and then break out. She lay face down on the bed. We would comfort her, and she would get up and wipe her tears. But soon, she would lose control again.

In the middle of all this, Chechi, Venukkuttan Chettan, Radha Chechi and I somehow packed everything. The clothes and books were in wooden boxes and sacks. Amma supervised everything. My dilemma was about what to take and what to leave behind. I did not want to leave anything behind; each object looked like a treasure in itself, a bridge to the past. A rusty geometry box from school, a pencil stub, school notebooks, an old question paper, much-read children's books…

When the packing was over, it was late. The rooms were filled with dust and cobwebs and pieces of paper, cloth and coir. Laalamma, Amma and Radha Chechi swept it all up. Amma burned the pile of litter. I still remember how she stood motionless, watching it burn, eyes fixed on the surging flames. Chechi and I sat on the outer veranda of the kitchen. The red of the flames played on Amma's face. Will she break down into tears, I worried. She stood there still, like in a strange stupor. By the morning, all traces of our presence would be removed from the house. The kitchen, the storeroom and the pantry, which had been rebuilt after the fire, would look empty and unfamiliar. Acchan would be all that would be left of the old stuff there. The front room would be filled with boxes, sacks, suitcases.

When Laalamma, Radha Chechi and Venukkuttan Chettan went off to get some rest, Amma came into the inner courtyard and sat there. We followed her. It was dimly lit – only the light from the front room filtering into the courtyard. Chechi rested her head on Amma's lap. She was still sobbing softly. Amma caressed her head gently. The sky was overcast. The cold breeze from the lake blew hard before daybreak. She held me close and began to recite a poem. It was beautiful.

'The lightning strikes the proud, tall coconut palm, the
   blood-red coals smoulder,
Rivers and canals hold hands and rush headlong calling to
   the sea
Ah, my heart, here am I tonight, like a man bereft of home
   and hearth...'

'You can't let go of poetry even now?' Chechi complained.

'Poetry is to be recited when you are sad,' Amma said, 'not when you are happy.'

'What will we do now?' Chechi whimpered.

'We will live...' Amma sighed. 'As happily as we can...'

'Happily!' Chechi sniffled.

Amma's voice faltered a bit. 'You are all that I have. Do not fail me.'

That was a request she made. It made me numb. Chechi started at it. Amma's tone while making this request had shaken us. We could not see her face in the dim light. She held us closer still.

'We are passing through a hard phase. Please don't be weak. If you give up, I will not survive...'

Her choked voice made me feel tight in the chest. Chechi could not stop her tears.

'Not every human being enjoys every blessing throughout their lives. There'll always be some lack or another – of money or love or health ... Right now, we are all alive. That's all.'

In the darkness, her words were as sharp as the tips of daggers.

'We are going to Koyikkal. We will forever be refugees there, or less. Know that well before we go. Once we are there, don't complain about what they say or do. We have no money; they do. Your father has the right to live there until he dies. We too are going to hang in there on the strength of that right. But we cannot live there forever pawning our dignity. We will have to move. Until then you have to learn to endure. There may even be people there who'll try to grope or grab you. You need to learn how to keep them in their places. Do not expect me to shelter you under my wings all the time.'

'Amme, how are we going to live?' My voice quivered.

'It will be hard, but we will survive.' Her voice was firm.

'Siva has a job, but she doesn't earn enough to feed a family. Till she steadies herself, you can't go to college, Satya.'

I went cold.

'No, she must!' Chechi leapt up. 'She must. I will send her to college.'

'Your salary isn't large enough even for you,' Amma persisted, pulling her down. 'Then how can it be enough to send her to college? Sive, you find a better-paying job first, then we will see. Let her study privately till then. I cannot handle caring for Acchan and the kitchen and other work all by myself.'

Something like a whiff of warm breeze left my body then. Must have been a bird. One which nested in me.

'Where we are headed won't be like this place at all ... we will not have any of the comforts we enjoyed here. We might not have a clean room, even. But our faces should stay bright. Face all adversity with a smile! Neither of you should feel ashamed of our poverty. The moment you feel it, we would have failed.'

'But Amma, all this while we...'

'All this while we lived in comfort, didn't we, Sive?' Amma's voice rose. 'Just think, what if we were born in Palestine? People in the refugee camps there that were started when I was born are still trapped. But why go to Palestine? Just go to the houses that the government has built for the poor, in the One-lakh Housing Scheme colonies. The people there are the ones who, over generations, have cooked and cleaned and built houses for others. How do they live? What right do we have to complain? Did we earn the comforts that we enjoyed? It was my father's work. He gave me a share out of charity! I have not earned a paisa of it. Your father threw it all away. Everyone faces need and distress some time in their lives. There's no escape...'

'Amma, won't people make fun of us?' Chechi was still snivelling.

'They might. You just have to laugh back at them. We should be able to laugh at our own lives.' Amma smiled mildly.

'It's so easy for you to philosophize, Amma!' Chechi grumbled.

'This is all I have now, Sive – this "philosophy". This "philosophy" that nothing can wipe the smile off my face. Take it if you want. If not, then you can leave – you have been given an education good enough for you to find a job. Go and find yourself a good job somewhere. You don't have to come back to us. We won't force you to carry a share of this shame that's upon us.'

Chechi still tried to say something, but failed and rested her head on Amma's shoulder. Amma ran her fingers through her hair.

'I've told you – don't fail me.'

'Nnoo...' Chechi whimpered again.

'Mark my words, Amme, we will have a new house in two years—' She choked, trying to hold back her tears.

'It's good to be determined...'

'If there's any life left inside me, I'll do it.' She took up the challenge again. Amma pulled her close and kissed her on the forehead, a slight smile playing on her lips. She held me close too. We both burst out weeping and fell into Amma's lap. She sat there, unmoving. What a night it was! Shuddering and scared, we clung to our mother. And then she told us: 'Sive, Satye, there's another thing you should always remember. Wealth and happiness – no one will want to have anything to do with those who don't have both. Who wants to take over the debts or sorrows of another?'

I remembered those words when Inspector Shetty questioned me. Wealth or happiness – you have to possess at least one for others to need you. Shetty was not wearing his police uniform. He came pretending to visit Joyo but stepped into my house. I had finished my washing, taken a shower, and was on my way to Sandeepa's with the elayada I had made for Joyo with rice flour, coconut and jaggery, in a banana leaf. The inspector sat on the balustrade of the veranda and ate an elayada. We then had the following conversation:

'You people are strange,' he said. 'I find it hard to understand you.'

'For example?'

'For example, why did Mrityunjoy play the detective without letting the police know?'

'He didn't feel like doing it maybe.'

'I don't see why.'

'Inspector, people have their own reasons.'

'There's a system in place here, isn't there?'

'Is there?'

'Whatever you say, it was wrong not to inform me.'

'If he had waited to do so, then would he have confronted the shooter? Is it not clear now that he is in the city?'

'But then he has disappeared again. He is not to be found on any of the CCTV cameras on the main roads.'

'That means that he used the side roads.'

'That means that he knows the city well.'

'That means he's someone who knows a road without CCTV cameras when he sees one.'

'Ma'am, why do you always speak so negatively?'

'Inspector Sir, I am not being negative. I am just trying to remind you of another possibility.'

'Yes, agreed. Come … let's go.'

He crumpled the banana leaf from which he had eaten the ada and threw it aside. I followed him. He put his hands on the gate and took a look around. Then he looked at me again.

'I made some enquiries about this Sriram. He went back that very day. His phone records also do not indicate that he came anywhere here. Do you have a reason to think that he may have hired a killer?'

'Yes, two. First – the speech that he made back home the day after I was attacked. Two, his nature – if wounded, he lies in wait for an opportunity...'

'He married again. And is also well settled. He has been growing in politics every single day. I don't think that he will jeopardize all this by taking revenge on you.'

'Inspector, I don't know whether he will kill me or not. But he is the first on the list of the five people most likely to do so.'

'What do you mean?'

'Chronologically ... he is the first to have had a motive to attack me.'

'Who is the second?'

I hesitated a bit. Inspector Shetty fixed his gaze on me. I was not sure if I should answer.

'Swami Mahipal Shah Baba?' he asked with a mischievous smile. My face blanched.

'Inspector, you have done your homework!' I tried to joke. His smile broadened.

'You were the most influential person in that ashram. Then you fought and left. Why?'

'I just felt bored,' I said without flinching.

'Was that the only reason?'

'Is there a reason to think that there was something else?'

The inspector looked as though he were trying to make up his mind about whether to tell me or not. Then, in an effort to revive his faded smile, he said, 'Ma'am, Cobra Nagu – he was hired by someone from the ashram.'

I shuddered briefly.

'I traced all the calls to his phone. One was from the ashram.'

I sat there, wide-eyed. I was starting to tremble. The inspector hadn't finished.

'I traced all the calls from that number. Two of those went to another shooter, and they were made after Nagu's death. And after this, the number has not been used at all.'

'That is, someone else has been given the task, right?' My palms went cold.

'Not sure. But it has confused us more. Sriram, Mahipal Shah – which of these men hired the first shooter? If it was Mahipal Shah, why did he give this task to Cobra Nagu? If it is Sriram, why is he risking his future in politics? And besides, please consider the fact that the shooter spoke in Odiya!'

That felled me. I held on to the gate for support. Sandeepa was standing in her porch. I wanted to run over and hide behind her.

'Ma'am, please open up – who are the three others on that list?'

'Besides the person my father mentioned – Prabhudev Maheswari, Samir Sayyid...'

Shetty looked me disbelievingly. 'Samir Sayyid...?!'

'Yes.'

He was astounded. It was fun to watch. It amused me, and I stopped trembling. It is not just the rich and the happy who are in high demand; people also need those with secrets.

THIRTEEN

When we finally left our home, the sky was overcast. The lake was still and looked like a green carpet left out to dry. It was I who locked the door. Suddenly, the house turned into a nest of darkness. The empty cowshed and the September lily creeper that had blossomed on it pricked my eyes and brought tears. When the key turned in the lock, someone ripped out a tree from my heart. Its roots had run deep in there. The flesh scattered; something pulled hard at the veins and ruptured them. The tree fell in my heart, hitting its head there in lamentation. I feared I would die of a broken heart before the journey was over. The only other time I suffered such agony was when I left Samir Sayyid. I felt the pain of an uprooting in my heart shoot through my bloodstream, I felt my bones crumble like wood. At every step, the bone fragments pierced my flesh and tested my endurance. In each breath the poisonous fumes choked me. The pain left me hanging between life and death.

When we set out for Koyikkal, our tears could have formed a whole lake by themselves. The neighbours came to see us off. They sighed. Many cried. It was indeed a pitiful sight – a paralysed father, a mother, two daughters, many bags. The bigger things were sent off in a lorry. They included Acchan's wooden box. Unknown to us, the formalin-filled jar and the meditating foetus came along too. When I split with Samir, such a child was inside me too. When it thrust out its limbs, fragments from my bones and veins were seized by pain.

But whether it is fortune or love, it must occasionally vanish. Only then do we realize its true value. Value is that which someone else confers on us. Until that point, my value as a person and the value of my fortune were intermingled, like milk and water; they could not be separated. Once the money vanished, they separated. The formula to calculate the value of people was also revealed to me – it was the same as the one used to calculate velocity. That is, $V = S/T$. Only that V is value, S is what you are owed, and T is what you owe. The speed of a moving object changes. So velocity is always relative. It's the same with the value of people. The technique to increase velocity involves reining in time. With human beings, the trick is to increase utility. The day we reached Koyikkal after our home was sold, our value plummeted like the share value of ACC Cement after the securities scam. There was nothing to be surprised about. An invalid, his incomeless wife, and two grown daughters – when an object returns to where it began, surely its velocity falls to zero?

The first day was amusing. We had taken a taxi there. The furniture which had been sent ahead was scattered all over the front yard, in the open. The dogs, who were chained to the trees, were barking non-stop, for hours, it seemed. No one came out to receive us. Amma paid the taxi, lowered the wheelchair that was strapped to the luggage carrier above, seated Acchan on it, and took our bags. And still, no one came out to greet us. Acchan in his wheelchair, behind him Amma, standing, holding his chair; the two of us – Chechi and I – on either side, clutching plastic bags ... I cannot forget the look which the four of us shared in that moment. Tears streamed from Acchan's eyes. For some travellers, to return to the starting point is devastation. Their velocity sinks into inertia then. It will become impulse exerted on mass. Chechi sank to the ground in the veranda, like a corpse. Amma busied herself with moving the boxes and bags to the side. In the midst of that, she

said, 'Nobody's heard all this stuff being unloaded, or the car come …
Go take a look?'

Chechi and I looked at each other.

'Go on, knock on the door,' urged Amma. I hung back a bit. She grew impatient.

'All right, I'll do it.'

In my mind, Amma's value was enormous. I could not bear to see it fall. So I went to the north-side door and knocked. It was a door with four panels, two above and two below. The upper panels were open. I reached out, pulled aside the wooden bolt and stepped in. There was no one around. The east-side door that led to our kochappachi's room was locked. The house was as silent as a graveyard. My heart sank. My limbs grew weak. In a way, when your value falls, you get closer to death. I went into the kitchen. There, on a wooden bench, sat Koyikkal Amma. She wore a loose green blouse on which lay a dirty whitish upper cloth, and around her waist was a mundu on which were mud and vegetable stains. She was focused on chopping elephant yam. I held on to the kitchen-door frame and called her. She did not lift her head, merely threw me a sidelong glance.

'Oh, so … you have come…'

'Yes, it's been a long time,' I grumbled.

'Ah, I did not hear.'

She continued to chop the yam dedicatedly. The yam must have been priceless at that moment, especially when compared with refugees. I did not know what to do then, so I waited at the door, uncertain about whether I could step into the kitchen. They were strict about caste at Koyikkal. It was the first time that I saw the kitchen where no low caste had ever stepped in. All its four corners were covered in cobwebs blackened with soot. The hearth looked as black as a coal mine. The floor was almost covered in twigs and dried coconut fronds for the hearth. A hairy caterpillar, the type that gives you an itch, was making its way out of these. I watched it move. Its velocity was low. A tiny drop of a wave trapped on the cement floor. The way its body quivered, it reminded me of the sea. Though the yam Koyikkal Amma was chopping was as capable as the caterpillar of causing an itch, the value of the caterpillar was definitely lower. In every probability, the caterpillar and I shared the same value. That is the reason why we were both ignored equally.

'Acchan is outside…' I said.

'The fellow used to be able to walk and run about well when he was taken from here. You've brought him back here in a wheelchair!'

Koyikkal Amma picked up another piece of yam to chop. The yam was itself having a hard time. Its flesh was growing pinkish-black from the itch.

'Where shall we take Acchan?'

Koyikkal Amma straightened the upper cloth on her shoulder and looked at me.

'Nobody's home today. They've locked all the rooms. I am here by myself, and I can't hear well either. Do something, use the chaippu outside. You'll have to clean it up.' The chaippu was, for the most part, a storage room, with a low ceiling; it was also the place where the lesser mortals in the family had to stay.

Koyikkal Amma devoted herself to the yam again. I ran out, tongue itching, wiping my tears hurriedly. Amma had wheeled Acchan to the shade of the mango tree.

'What happened?' she asked without looking at me.

'Kochappachi's not at home today … Koyikkal Amma is busy chopping yam.'

'Poor yam!' Amma laughed.

'She says that they have locked all the inner rooms.'

'That's a wise thing to do these days.'

'She told us to go and settle down in the chaippu outside.'

'All right, the shed it is, or the cowshed, whatever they please.'

'But we will have to clean it.'

'Wash it clean.'

Amma laughed again. Acchan covered his face with both hands. His body shook as though he was sobbing. Chechi, too, blubbered. Amma paid no attention to her and headed to the shed through the eastern side of the house. I followed her.

I had never seen the back of the Koyikkal house. The chaippu was on the south side. On the west, close to the boundary of the yard, was the bathroom. Though I had slept in the house one night, I had never seen the inside of the house. I was allowed only until the open courtyard. Chechi had wanted to see it so badly. But she could not, not while she was alive. I had to wait until Koyikkal Amma died. When everyone crowded around the east-side room where they had lain her, I too slipped in. When I prostrated on the ground at the feet of her corpse, I touched her toes. Then, making my way through the crowd, I entered the puja room. From there, I went to the south-side room, and from there to the west-side room, in which there were two large granaries. Its doors opened towards the shed and into another room. I went towards the open courtyard through the side of the shed, and to the kitchen, the outer room where the grinding stones were kept. I walked over to the veranda on the north and saw the drumstick tree, the pepper vines and the areca palms leaning over the tiles of its roof. Then I returned to the inner courtyard through the kitchen and into Koyikkal Amma's room, where there was a third granary and a rice box. There was no one there; I sat on her cot and then lay on it for some time. For the first time I took in my father's mother's scent. I was the one fated to be the last to know about everything. Koyikkal Amma smelled of dhanwantaram oil and turpentine. When they called the women to bathe her, I got up. And that was when I drew water again from the well with sixty-eight steps and saw their bathroom.

When we came to live at Koyikkal, though, we stayed in the shed. It had two rooms, a side-room opening on to the yard, and a veranda. In the beginning, it was a real mess. They had stored sawn timber inside. I helped to carry the planks out. They were extremely heavy.

Termites had pasted on all of them the maps of their own territories. Both rooms were littered with rat-bitten cloth and paper, and soil and cobwebs. The rats ran off. The house lizards rolled their eyes as if throwing us a challenge. Like women evicted from their homes, pregnant spiders rolled up their webs and hurried out.

Venukkuttan Chettan, Radha Chechi, and Laalamma who had followed us in a bus arrived just then. Hearing that we had moved here, some neighbours and relatives as well as some old retainers came to see us. Some of Amma's caste-kin also helped. All of us got together and washed the rooms clean. Laalamma set up a couple of hearths in the back of the rooms and quickly cooked some rice gruel and curry. Someone got some lime, and the rooms were whitewashed. The house looked liveable now, as fresh as starched, crisply ironed clothes. One of the rooms was set aside for Acchan, and the other for us. The gas stove was placed on a table laid in a corner of the side-room and a temporary kitchen was set up.

Guests kept coming till late into the night. When every single one of them left, the water separated from the milk. Relatives piled sympathy upon us and, on their way out, visited Koyikkal Amma. 'In the end they've landed at a heap at your feet, iccheyi! This is proof that there is God!' they smirked.

A week later, our kochappachi, her husband, and their son made their appearance. Meanwhile, we had had a bathroom with an asbestos roof built next to Acchan's room and also a small kitchen next to the open room and settled in. Seeing how pretty and respectable our little house looked, caused them envy. Amma had chosen for the house only the nice-looking furniture that suited it. Chechi had pulled out and brought over the climbing vine full of blue flowers and the wild jasmine creeper, on which, mistaking the creeper for the sky, stars blossomed. Together, they turned the lowly shed into a beautiful bower.

On the very first day, Amma sold off four almirahs and a meal-safe. Seeing our things strewn all over the yard, the wife of our mother's brother, Valsala Maami, had asked what we would do with them.

'They are goods to be sold, Chechi,' Amma said coolly. 'I have offers. There's no space to keep them all in this tiny house. Why leave them here and there to be damaged?'

'How much did they offer you for this almirah?'

'How much would you offer, Chechi?'

Valsala Maami looked a bit discomfited.

'If it is you, I'll give it for thirty thousand ... but please pay me upfront. I can't afford to wait until tomorrow for the whole amount.'

'I will ... but isn't the price a bit too high...?'

'Chechi, please ask people who know about furniture. My father bought it from a palace. Can't you see the fine woodwork? If you like it, take it now because it will be gone in less than two days. They offered fifty. But I don't want to be running after them.'

When she went away, I rolled my eyes at Amma.

'Why did you lie to her, Amma?'

'I didn't!'

'You told her that you had offers for these things!'

'No, no, I had fixed the offers myself!'

The next day, that almirah was sold for thirty thousand rupees. It was a rosewood almirah with ivory work on the sides; it had been bought from the old palace of a royal consort. The new owners took it in a handcart. Overcome with grief, Chechi went in, fell face down on the cot, and wept. I, however, felt a sense of relief. It was terrible to see things that were part of my life lying orphaned, exposed to the rain and the sun. It was on that day that I wondered about the fate of the almirahs and cots that refugees left behind when they fled their homes. What was done with all the wooden furniture used by the Hindus who came to India from Pakistan, and the Muslims who went there from India? The furniture on which they slept, sat, wrote, and read? Did the Nazis who stole from the Jews they sent to the gas chambers feel any prick of conscience when they saw their things? How did the Jews who occupied the houses of Palestinians evicted to form Israel handle the latter's belongings?

The large chest of drawers with brass work on it and a lock, which we used to call the manichitrathaazhu, and all the other big pieces of furniture were sold off. The massive bookshelves and books were donated to the local library. Amma did not sell the wooden box and the smaller wooden shelves. The box suited the shed-turned-house quite well. It was ideal to keep Acchan's medicines and drinking water on next to his bed. Our aunt complained loudly that her brother had not given her any of the furniture he had promised her. Amma sat reading the papers in the veranda pretending as though she had heard nothing. That was when Medha Patkar was arrested for leading the Narmada Bachao Andolan. There was a feature on adivasis who were losing their land for the dam site. I read only half of it and began to feel suffocated. I looked only once at the photograph of people moving with their belongings. Caterpillars on the cement floor. Moving very slowly. Valueless. People who could never return.

~

When the inspector asked about Samir Sayyid, all this swept back into my mind. That is because the first time Samir and I had met was during an eviction. Back then, I was working in Advaita. The adivasis who had been evicted were agitating. I was a favourite of Prabhudev Maheswari, and so, part of the negotiating team. I fought hard not to remember the last few nights at Vasanthaalayam. Prabhudev spoke at length about the social welfare measures that the company had undertaken for the adivasis. These measures, he claimed, would change the face of the nation. The GDP would shoot up. Every adivasi would be assured of a job. 'Stop!' I wanted to snap at him. A person's greatest wealth is the land in which they are rooted. If that is snatched away from you, then what is the use of having any amount of money? But my voice would just not rise. I hated myself. 'Does anyone know of the benefits you will receive if the company is allowed to set up operations here?' Prabhudev threw them a challenge. And Samir Sayyid got up from among the audience.

'We have calculated the benefits from your company,' he said. 'It is the same equation we were taught in our physics class at school – the equation to calculate velocity.'

All eyes were on him.

'V = your profits; S = our poverty; T = our protest.'

That sounded great. I felt thrilled. I hadn't moved an inch and yet my heart had reached its highest velocity. I didn't share these memories with the inspector. He never asked. This is how our conversation went:

'This is shocking, Ma'am. What is your connection with Samir Sayyid?'

'I was in love with him.'

'What do you mean?'

'Yes, I mean I was once in love with him.'

'He is a criminal the police are looking for. Did you not know that?'

'I know that there are cases against him. Isn't it for the court to decide if he's a criminal or not?'

'Yes, but he has killed many.'

'Even if that's true, his killings won't be equal to even a thousandth of the murders that our rulers have committed.'

'Ma'am, I just lost all my respect for you. How are you able to love a criminal? I will have to arrest you!'

'Is falling in love with a criminal a crime?'

'This is no joke.'

'Love is never a joke.'

'Bullshit. Instead of handing him over to the police, you hid him. Isn't that a crime?'

'Where did I hide him?'

'Where did you meet with him, then?'

'In the forest. He had a tree house.'

'Where?'

'Any policeman there could point it out to you.'

The inspector's charming face looked shaken.

'All right, let that be ... Weren't you clearly aware of who Samir Sayyid really was?'

'Inspector, no one can know what another really is.'

'You are not on good terms now?'

'We parted.'

'Is that why you suspect him?'

'Once love is lost, then one must begin to fear, Inspector.'

'If so, you could have informed us about him?'

'What for?'

'Don't you know about the bounty on his head?'

'Would you ever forgive me if I betrayed love for a reward, Inspector?'

He could not find a retort. I laughed out loud. He was really angry.

'Ma'am, I give up. I am not sharp enough to handle you. I'll call Aswathy Ma'am and tell her to hand this case over to someone else. Look, if we are to investigate a case, the person who complains must tell us the truth. The whole truth.'

He walked off in a huff. The woman constable threw me a smile and followed him. I sat down again in the shade of the money plant on the porch. The price on Samir's head was in my mind then. Besides the government, Advaita, too, had declared a reward for information about him. Taken together, a crore. The amount that the stockbroker in the share market – that had destroyed Acchan – had allegedly paid the prime minister at that time. It was brought in a suitcase, they said. There were only hundred-rupee notes in circulation in the country then. A thousand bundles of hundred-rupee notes! The poor prime minister must have had a hard time counting it.

I tried to calculate the number of hundred-rupee notes in thousand bundles. You may feel irritated – someone's after her to take her life and here she is wasting her time! Also, because I was not lifting the suspense by telling the investigating officer everything I knew. But no one can discover another's truth fully. For instance, what happened to the money that the stockbroker had stolen back then? Where is the report of the committee set up to find it? What does all this show? Just one thing – suppose I rip open my chest, pull out my heart, and put it on a table in front of you. Suppose I cut it open and show you what's in it. Would that guarantee that you'll nab my assailant at once? No. Because the assailant is no ordinary man. He is smarter than the inspector. But to me, he was just a piece of elephant yam. It made me itch, but so what? Was I not Koyikkal Amma's grandchild? I chopped up my words with precision. I made sure the inspector itched more than me.

This is not mere bravado. I proved it that night. I went to bed in Sandeepa's room. Around two o'clock, I heard a sound – of iron scraping iron. Sandeepa was asleep. Joyo, too, was sleeping in the next room. I did not turn on the light. I crept out of the room. Alone in the dark, I heard the sound again from the floor above. Fear crawled all over me like an itchy caterpillar, my hair stood on end.

Have you ever tried to go where your killer was standing? Have you climbed the steps to where he was, with feet that feel as though iron weights were hanging from them? A pity if you haven't, since if you haven't, then you can never appreciate the black humour in drawing a black leather jacket, helmet, dark glasses, and boots on the image of the God of Death, seated on a buffalo, holding a mace in one hand and the noose of time in another. Even the stirring of a leaf will sound like the killer's footsteps and the flapping of a bat's wings will sound like the pull of a trigger. But what would be his value when you encounter him face to face? To calculate that, my experiences would have to be divided by his experiences. My truth would have to be deducted from his.

FOURTEEN

This is what happened that night: death arrived like a dark shadow.
It tried to break the lock. I heard it scratch on the door. Joyo's room
had doors facing the west and the north – the latter opened on to
the balcony. I opened the west-side door and, through it, moved
northwards noiselessly, my back against the wall. Though there was
a large weeping fig tree outside and a jackfruit tree that leaned over
on to the street, as well as the purple wreath vine that climbed up to
the balcony forming a tangled mass there, a small portion of the light
from the street still fell there. He was crouching, but still reached the
handle of the door. The helmet and the jacket made him look gigantic.
He was examining his work under the light of a pen torch, and I saw
his gloves too. I moved slowly until I reached beneath the electrical
switches on the wall. When his cutter worked on the wood, dust rose.
I sneezed loudly.

At that, the pathetic man not only started but he actually screamed.
I heard things fall. Like on cue, I switched the lights on. He saw me
and was shocked. Good God! Chechi should have been around! How
she would have laughed! Even I found it hard to suppress a laugh. He
scampered anxiously there like a trapped rat, even tried to leap over the
balcony. A killer he may be, but clearly, he had neither determination

nor courage in the face of danger. That's natural, of course. He wasn't born of my mother's womb!

I grabbed him. He struggled to free himself. He was more than I could handle. His jacket kept slipping from my fingers. Pushing me off somehow, he pulled out a pistol. But maybe out of sheer nervousness, it slipped out of his hand and fell. I leapt on him and clung hard to his back. He shook me off forcefully. I hit the wall hard. He then turned around and our eyes met. I saw the fear in his eyes. He was panting like a dog. He was clearly in a dilemma, but soon seemed to have arrived at a decision. Then, like a creature that freezes its prey with a stare, he glared at me. His hand went inside his jacket and pulled something out from his waist. I gathered courage, controlled my trembling and asked, 'Hey, brother, will it be done at least tonight?' He appeared feeble now. 'This has been dragging for so long … it's annoying!'

He looked even more listless. Suddenly, the lights came on in the garden and the porch. Sandeepa's screams 'Satya! Satya!' shook the air. The killer completely lost his presence of mind, he looked around frantically. Just as suddenly, the lights in Joyo's room came on and his door was flung open. Whatever the killer had pulled out of his waist fell down. In sheer desperation, he jumped on to the parapet, and in a mere second, could be seen on the outer wall. Before Sandeepa could ask what had happened, we heard him start the motorbike and zoom off. She caught a glimpse of the speeding bike. I sat on the floor, all crouched up. Sandeepa fell on her knees and hugged me. 'Did he hurt you?' she asked anxiously. Then, without waiting for a reply, she ran to call the police. I did not have the energy to stand up. Around me lay the instruments he had left behind. His cutter, two wires that went to the main switch in the car porch, the leather pouch that he had taken out from his waist … I reached out and picked it up. I thought it was a pistol. I felt good about the killer who had kept aside two pistols exclusively for me. He had realized that I would need more than one firearm! I opened the pouch. But inside it, there was no pistol – there was a dagger.

In an hour's time, Inspector Shetty, the policemen and the woman constable arrived. Her name was Mukta. Shetty was not smiling. When he turned to look at me, his face seemed to be filled with frustration – the frustration that men feel towards women who will not reveal their secrets to them. He examined the cutter and the wires, took photos of the sawed-out lock. The police combed the premises using powerful torches. The pistol was found caught in the tangle of the flowering vine. A constable climbed up the jackfruit tree and used a kerchief to retrieve it. Then the fingerprint experts also came.

I went up to Joyo. He invited me to sit beside him. Sandeepa too came up, drew a chair, and sat down. They were both terrified. I felt guilty. I tried to find words to apologize to them. I realized it was time for me to leave them.

By then, Inspector Shetty and Constable Mukta had come over. I got up respectfully. But ignoring me completely, he spoke with Sandeepa.

'Sandeepa Ma'am, tell me, what happened?'

'Someone tried to steal into the house.'

'Did you see him?'

'Not clearly, just like a flash.'

'Where was he?'

'On the balcony.'

'And you?'

'Near the north-side door.'

'Can you please describe him?'

'He is a tall man, six feet at least, big built. He had a helmet on and a black jacket. He was holding something in his hand.'

'What was it?'

'I did not see. When he saw me, he leapt on to the parapet and then we heard the bike start. I was scared that he had hurt Satya. I was too upset.'

'Okay. When you opened the door, were the lights of the balcony switched on?'

'Yes.'

'Do you usually leave them on?'

'No. We usually switch them off. Satya had switched them off last night and closed the door.'

'Are you sure she had?'

'My room is right below. If there is light above, we would know. When I went to bed, it was totally dark.'

'Were you alone in your bedroom?'

'No, Satya was there too.'

'Did she move here?'

'She comes over to sleep. She does go to the other house during the day. It was I who persuaded her to sleep here.'

'Okay, okay. What woke you up?'

'I sometimes wake up in the middle of the night. I heard the leaves of a tree rustle. When I looked around, I didn't find Satya. And the lights in the balcony were on. They had been switched off when I went to bed.'

'So, there were no lights when you went to bed, but you found them on there.'

'Yes.'

'And Satyapriya Ma'am was there too.'

'I turned on the lights,' I intervened. The inspector looked at me sternly.

'Speak when I ask you to.'

'Sorry.'

'It's okay. Sandeepa Ma'am, tell me, did you go to the bank or withdraw money yesterday?'

'I did but couldn't get any money. There were no notes left. Just wasted a day's leave.'

'The government is printing new ones.'

'What's the use of printing three lakh crore notes in place of fourteen lakh crore notes?'

'So what's the guarantee that this was not an attempted burglary?'

'I've been staying here since the past ten years. We have not had a single such incident.'

'You mean?'

'That this man came in search of Satya.'

'Okay, Satyapriya Ma'am, can we talk now?' He turned towards me, and this is the conversation we had:

'Satyapriya Ma'am, what happened last night?'

'At around two, I heard a grating noise.'

'Did you wake up hearing it, or heard it when you were lying awake?'

'I woke up hearing it.'

'Did you look at the clock immediately after?'

'Yes.'

'Why? Any particular reason?'

'I did it naturally.'

'Do you always look at the clock when you wake up at night?'

'Yes, it is a habit.'

'Was there any light in the room then?'

'No.'

'Then how did you see the time so correctly.'

'The dial is iridium. It glows in the dark.'

He fixed me in a glance.

'Okay. You woke up, saw the time, and then?'

'I got up, realized that the sound was coming from upstairs, and then…'

'Wait. You heard a sound. You claim that there have been many attempts on your life. In that case, wouldn't it have been appropriate to wake someone else and take them with you?'

'What for? So that they get shot instead of me?'

He could not say anything to that. His face grew a bit sullen. He did not like my jokes. He preferred my secrets. That my refusal to share them irked him was no surprise. That's how women's secrets are. They trouble men who are not in the least connected to them. They will writhe and struggle deep inside until they discover them. Like schoolkids denied candy, they will pull long faces. After some time, the distaste will turn into hatred. And serious enmity. I readily dismissed Shetty's hatred, but did not tell him that. The poor chap, it would only crush him more. I smiled sympathetically. He pretended not to notice.

'That means, you were sure that he would shoot.'

'I expect it all the time.'

'All right. Tell me the rest.'

'I reached the room. I realized that someone was trying to saw open the lock.'

'Wait, wait, how did you see? Was there a light?'

'There was a street lamp. I saw his shadow on the window under its light. He was using a pen torch to examine the lock.'

'Can you describe the shadow?'

'He was on his knees. He had a helmet on.'

'Why didn't you call the police?'

'It just didn't occur to me.'

'Why?'

'My nerves were too strung at that moment.'

Joyo laughed at that. The inspector's face grew darker still.

'Why, do you find all of this a great joke?'

'I can't think of a more scientific answer to that question of yours!'

'You'll pay a big price for this attitude!'

'To whom?'

The inspector turned away angrily.

'Yes, what happened then?'

I described the rest of the episode. When I mentioned how I opened the west-facing door, he intervened furiously. 'Stop! Are you trying to play with people? Is this a game? When some man is trying to break in, you open the door and step out? When did you become so brave?'

'For people who have nothing to lose, what's the use of fear, Inspector?'

He rubbed his hands together.

'Look, Ma'am, I find it hard to believe your words and actions.'

'When I make myself the measure of others, I can't bring myself to believe them either.'

'What do you mean?'

He did not hide his rage. I too got up. All my patience was gone too.

'Inspector Sir, you have to investigate to find out whether my words match my actions or not. Not to find out why I did not act as you think was appropriate in a certain circumstance.'

He cooled down at that, contemplated for a few seconds, and then his pleasing, childlike smile returned.

'Relax, Ma'am, relax. Look at it from my side, please. I have been after this case for days now. I've been patrolling this area for several nights, including this one. But there's not been a single clue. To find a clue, I need your help. And you just won't help.'

His tact only riled me further.

'Inspector Sir, please look at it from my side. You want to close this case, not find the truth. What guarantee do I have that my statements will not be used against me?'

'You can trust me.'

'Why should I trust you when you don't trust me?'

This time, the inspector was disarmed.

'Ma'am, we both want to nab the assailant, don't we? How can we do that without your cooperation...?'

'How would you have pursued the killer if he had actually murdered me?'

'See,' he said, turning to Sandeepa for help, 'this is her problem. If only she would open up, we could have solved this case easily.'

Sandeepa smiled. 'Even the government these days isn't transparent, Inspector.'

'What do you mean, Sandeepa Ma'am?'

'I mean, we don't even know whose idea this note ban was?'

'Don't you have anything else to talk about except the note ban? Citizens need not know everything. The government knows what is best.' He lost his cool and turned to me. 'I just don't know at what wretched moment this was loaded on me! Ma'am, I am asking you again, please tell me the truth.'

'Inspector, my name is Satyapriya, and I speak only the truth. I may not tell you the whole truth, but never a lie.'

'At certain moments, a half-truth is worse than a lie. What is the problem with revealing the whole truth?'

'I don't trust you, Inspector.'

'We'll have to file a criminal case against you.'

'Is not being able to trust someone a criminal offence in this country?'

My eyes grew dull with rage. Joyo held out his hand and took mine into it, telling me to relax. I shrank, feeling weak and helpless.

'Inspector, please, she is in shock. Let her rest a bit. Can we continue later?' Sandeepa raised her voice. The sun had come up. I did not bother to see him off. I continued to sit next to Joyo. He still held my right hand.

~

The inspector who had gone off now came back and called my name gently. I got up and went to him.

'You should not be irritated. The truth is, I like you and respect you. I want this case to end in your favour, I swear.'

'What for?' I snapped in annoyance.

'You are someone who has suffered much. You deserve peace and love for at least the rest of your life.'

That was unexpected. My eyes reddened and welled. He then asked: 'The man who attacked you today – have you seen him before?'

'Twice. He is the one who shot at me.'

I wiped my eyes. The inspector stood there with his mouth agape.

'Then why didn't you tell us?'

'Did you even let me?'

Inspector Shetty picked up his cap, pressed it, and put it back on his head. He was lost in thought.

'I think that this is the man Acchan had warned me against.'

'Why do you think so?'

'My mind tells me so.'

Inspector Shetty looked at me closely. Then, as though a thought had struck him, he touched his cap and smiled the innocent smile at me again. Without uttering a word more, he went away.

My answer was the truth. But it was not the complete truth. I did not tell him about the leather pouch that had fallen from the killer's waist when Sandeepa had entered the balcony. I did not show them the dagger that had been in it. It was in my hand when I followed her downstairs. I hid it in the large vase with the artificial flowers kept at the bottom of the staircase. I did not want to hand it over to the police. Because it is the sellers who decide even the value of notes. And can one say more about the value of a secret? I will decide it. I am, after all, its seller.

Because that dagger was the one that Acchan used to carry. The one that was used to stab him from behind and on the sides, the one that had torn through his flesh. Above all, the tip of which was shaped like an S. I felt tears pricking my eyes. I knew the pain now, of the dagger's tip tearing through my flesh. It bore in, like when used to check the ripeness of a jackfruit.

– S for Sivaprasad.

– S for Sivapriya.

– S for Satyapriya.

FIFTEEN

Have you ever sought a loan from a loan shark? Have you ever waited in his veranda with eyes dimming and a parched throat, wiping your sweat, ready to pay ten or fifteen rupees as interest for a hundred? Have you ever experienced the way in which his lips curve into a smile, his mouth offers small talk, and all the while his eyes are sharpening a knife? A pity if you haven't, for then you can never be a true citizen of India! Without depending on creditors, without making sense of the politics of the money that they extract from you and lock away, how will you participate in 'Make in India'? How will you calculate the per capita income? Creditors and debtors are eternal truths, the laws of the world. It is their exchanges that make the world go round. Every single financial transaction is politics.

Today, such things sound like a joke to me. Back then, they did not. My head had no value, it was never counted. That day, it was like a balloon tied to a body.

~

It was the month of Dhanu. The day had barely dawned. The sky was overcast, as though a massive storm was approaching. But like when it drizzles, the ground was barely wet. It wasn't raining, really – it was my eyes. The thunder and lightning were in my breast.

Seven months had passed since we began our refugee existence. The memories of Vasanthaalayam, *Vasanthakairali* and Vasanthamaalika had not yet faded – people wouldn't let us forget. They believed that it was their duty to remind us. Although it was us who had gone broke, it was them who felt the pain. They would start gleaning our memories meticulously, like grains of rice that a sheaf of paddy leaves behind, starting from the time when money was abundant in our house. At first, I ached from within. Struggled not to weep. It was painful to be comforted, 'Never mind, dear, the good times will come again…' How much could one bear?

Koyikkal Amma was the most honest of them all. Waking early in the morning and washing her face and feet, she would stand facing the rising sun reverentially, with folded hands. She would raise her joined palms above her head so high that her wrinkled tummy beneath her loose blouse would be visible. 'Bhagavaane, please do not make anyone suffer like this for their vanity,' she would entreat loudly. No one would have woken up in her house at that hour. But she would turn around as if she had heard someone stir inside, and call out, 'Hey, you children, do not be vain. It is not for the good. Please learn a lesson from the proof lying right in front of you…! You win only if your feet are on the ground…'

Our aunt's husband Bhasi Maaman was fond of drama. Sometimes he would come over with his kaili-cloth hitched up, barely covering his privates, while rubbing the few hairs left on his naked chest. He would stand in the doorway and observe Acchan. 'Did you eat anything, are your bowels okay? Did you take your medicine?' he would ask, and then crack a joke to himself, 'Aah! Why should I ask? Never passed the exam but he's still a doctor!' and then laugh by himself.

Sometimes he'd rush up as though there was some terrible emergency.

'Vasantham, just come over for a moment. Remember, long back, there was that woman who wrote a horrible story in *Vasanthakairali*? What was that dame's name?'

'I don't remember, Bhasi Chetta.'

'Something like Sumatikkutty or Madhavikkutty?'

'I haven't heard that she wrote a "horrible story"!'

'By "horrible" I meant ... don't you get it?'

'I don't get many things now like I used to, Bhasi Chetta...'

On other days he would come over with a decidedly downcast expression.

'Vasantham, today I passed by our Vasanthamaalika, you know, and it is overgrown with weeds ... a forest almost! I felt totally mortified...'

'That's hardly a bad thing, Bhasi Chetta. People will get more oxygen!'

If Bhasi Maaman tarried there for longer than usual, our aunt would swing into action. 'Ah, Chetta, you are here! Amma is calling you, come quick!' Then she would go into my father's room. There, she would touch and shake everything that had been cleaned earlier to check for dust. 'Oh, look at him! How he's fallen,' she would moan. 'If you didn't want him, Vasantham, you should have given him to us to look after ... Why did you hand him over to the butchers?...' She'd try every trick to provoke Amma. That was my cue to step on stage. I would start fussing about things that were missing. Amma would scold me, and we would keep at it until she withdrew.

But somehow, those days were happy. We realized that only later. Happiness is so like wealth. When you have it, you want more. When you don't, you pine for the little you had. It is so difficult to earn either. And so easy to destroy.

That was the third month of our refugee existence. One day, a Benz and an Ambassador swooped into the Koyikkal yard and braked hard. A middle-aged man stepped out of the Benz. He wore two heavy gold chains around his neck, several gold bracelets on his wrists,

and navaratna rings on his fingers. Out of the other car emerged a
few toughs. The guests strolled into our house and seated themselves
without seeking anybody's approval. Amma was just done with cleaning
up Acchan's shit. She had cleaned his bedpan and commode, wiped
his back with hot water, and applied some talcum powder. Seeing the
guests, she ran to take a shower, telling me to give Acchan the coffee
in the flask. As I was doing so, she came out wearing a crisply ironed
cotton sari, her wet hair wrapped in a towel. She applied kohl in her
eyes and sindoor on her forehead. She presented herself to the guests
with poise. To others, poise was an idea. To her, it was habit. Though
I was feeding Acchan his coffee, my mind was out there. Acchan was
curious about the guests. I'd have told him if he had asked, but his
pride wouldn't let him. And I was sure not to tell without him asking.

The middle-aged man was rather loud. He spoke in Tamil.

'Amma,' he began, 'I am coming from Kodambakkam. My name is
Muthukrishna Gounder. Your husband, when he came there last year,
took a loan from me. He has not repaid it yet. I've come for that. If
you give us the cash, we could leave soon. I'll have to, however, sit right
here till I get my money...'

Amma's voice was not audible for a few minutes. My blood ran
cold. Quickly, I calculated what was left to sell. She must have asked
him the loan amount. I heard just his reply:

'Three and a half lakh.'

It was silent again. Amma said something. His voice rose. Instead
of the polite tone, it rang with sarcasm.

'Am I the reason for that?'

'No, Saar ... but...'

'Look ... here is your cheque. *You* tell us now!'

His voice changed again, and now became pitiless. Actually,
chameleons imitate some human beings.

'My ... my cheque?' Amma was stunned.

'Your husband gave it to me. So it must be yours?'

'But I … this…'

'I don't know any of that. Go ask your husband!'

My hand went limp. I stopped feeding Acchan coffee, but he had already stopped drinking it. The last spoonful fell on his white mundu and left a stain. Amma came in like a walking corpse. Her face was almost as black as Koyikkal Amma's hearth.

'You heard them?' Amma struggled for words. Acchan turned his face towards the wall. 'What am I to do?'

He turned his head to one side. He was weeping. Amma stood by the bed, looking at him. Meanwhile, the Gounder lost patience. He came in without asking.

'Why, Saar, you didn't tell your wife about it? This is why I told you, I won't give you the money without telling your wife and kids. Why did you lie to me, Saar?'

Amma stepped in between them.

'I don't have three and a half lakh rupees to give you. I'll give you what I have. You'll have to give us time to repay the rest.'

'More time? Sister, no, no … this is business. We have just one rule. Kindness can't replace money. Nothing can replace money.'

'All right then, Saar, please wait. Let me go to the bank and bring what I have there.'

It was barely nine in the morning. Amma called me into the other room. She wanted the waist chain. I took it off and handed it to her. Amma's forehead and neck were drenched with sweat. She took it from me without emotion. When I took off my gold chain of nearly three-fourth sovereigns of gold and my earrings worth half a sovereign and handed them to her, she gave me a grateful look. She almost went out with the wet towel around her hair. I removed it. She tied up her wet hair mechanically. Then closing her eyes, collected herself for a few moments, and then sighed. Her eyes were not wet even then. But her chest heaved. And her face – it looked like a red-hot silver vessel which had been left too long on the fire. Her kohl had spread, mixed with the sweat on her face, and her eyes were bloodshot. I looked at her with brimming eyes.

'They will try to provoke you. Do not let them.'

'What will they do, Amme?'

'What will they do? They might file a case, might not.'

I hugged her in sheer fright.

'If they would have gone to court, it would've been all right. We would have earned some time. But as far as I can see, they are not that sort. If they were, they wouldn't have brought those thugs here.'

'What will they do? Kill?' I became tense.

'It would have been simpler if they were just murderers.'

I froze. Amma stepped out. The Gounder got up.

'You can go in my car...'

'No, Saar, this is a village. If I get into your big car, people will notice. I have to live here! Just let the people who have come with you accompany me.'

Amma picked up her bag and walked ahead briskly, with dignity. Our aunt and her daughter Suma came running then. Acchan's younger brother and our cousin Unni were in the yard next to ours. They asked Amma something and she replied. Amma walked on boldly. The burly young men in T-shirts and jeans walked swinging their iron-kada-clad arms behind her, like baby goats following their mother. Soon, Amma's umbrella disappeared beyond the lane and the mud walls.

With a heavy heart, I went back to Acchan's room. He lay with his eyes closed. The very sight of him made me grit my teeth. There he lay, uprooting everything we had. It infuriated me. I regretted being born as his daughter. When he began to squirm, I pushed the bedpan under him. When I went out to clean it, I found the Gounder and his minions taking a tour of the yard. When it was noon, he bought lunch for them. They pulled chairs into the shade of the mango tree and ate heartily.

Acchan did not ask for lunch. I did not offer either. Amma was getting late; I grew weaker. Finally, by three o'clock, she returned with her neck and ears bare. Chechi came back with her, eyes red, face overcast, soaked in sweat. Her neck and ears were bare too.

But though Amma had swept up all that she could, we could pay back only one and a half lakh rupees that day. The Gounder gave back only one of the cheques. He said that he would give back the other when we paid the rest. The time we were allowed was two months. Amma made Chechi get a loan and Radha Chechi cash her chit savings and repaid another lakh. The Gounder gave us another month to pay off the remaining amount and showed up promptly at the end of the month. We did not have the money ready. He gave us two more weeks. We did not have the money even then. Amma asked for more time, and he allowed it. We thought that he would be back in two weeks, but he showed up only after a month. I was alone in the house. Chechi had left to catch the 6.30 a.m. train. Acchan's body was badly swollen as he could not pass urine, and so Amma had been with him at the Taluk Hospital for the past two days.

Suddenly, a whole bunch of vehicles arrived. A large group of men alighted. I could only gawk. One of the men came up to me and asked, 'Where is your mother?' 'In the hospital,' I blurted. He turned back without a word and clapped his hands hard. The young men inside the larger vehicle brought out a generator and a chainsaw and went towards the large aanjhili tree located to the west of the yard. I ran to the house, knocked hard, trying to rouse everyone. Koyikkal Amma, Kochappachi and Kochacchan woke up. Kochacchan and Bhasi Maaman ran up to stop the men, but two of the thugs broke down the west-side door of the house and smashed some windows. My kochappachi and Koyikkal Amma began to hurl abuses at me. They heaped insults on my mother, her family, their caste. I listened silently. Then I went to the man and asked him, 'Look, you have given us so much time. Can't you give me two and a half hours more?'

'What for?' he asked in Tamil.

'To get the cash.'

'How?'

'I don't know. But you'll get it.'

I went in, changed my clothes, locked the house, and walked off. My feet felt heavy as though weights hung from them. I did not know where I was going. Who would give me, a twenty-one-year-old, so much money? I had no clue. But I stumbled on. Everyone shares the pride of the wealthy, but no one will share the pauper's shame.

That was the day when I met the moneylender for the first time. I was to meet many of that tribe in the following two and a half years. The science of wealth is interesting. It is not science or maths, as many think. It is an understanding. One that may or may not be mutual. In that sense, it is like a story. Like a certain understanding exists between the writer and a reader, there is an understanding between a giver and a taker. A story becomes a story only when passed from one to another. What is it until then? Where is it? It is just a fantasy. Like smoke or a snowflake. Money becomes money only when it moves from one hand to another. Otherwise, what is it? Just paper, or some metal. How amazing!

But there's something. The usurer knows nothing of this philosophy. Even if he does know, he does not value it. To him the currency note is like what a jackfruit is to a tree. Actually, a jackfruit is not just a fruit. For the jackfruit, it is a project – a plan to produce several hundreds of jackfruit trees in the world and thus take over the earth.

~

My would-be killer was a wicked man. He did not kill me. Instead, he threw me into the inspector's hands. He kept me alive but killed me in life. I was roasted live slowly on the coals of memory, on the searing pan of fear. When I locked the house preparing to return home, I was tired. I did not want to stay on there and create more trouble for Sandeepa and Joyo. Everyone has invisible roots that run deep in the soil. A piece of the money plant, thrown anywhere, will still grow fine white roots. Human beings, too, are like that. That is why

I never settled down anywhere. Whenever I began to feel a sense of belonging anywhere, I remembered the last night we spent at our home Vasanthaalayam. Some memories are as useful as the schoolmaster's cane. Just raise it once, and the memory of the agony of canings you have suffered will awaken. When our home was lost, it was not just my roots that were torn up. My desire to put down new ones also died. Wealth and happiness wiped out in a single stroke! Not at all surprising that no one needed me. It was this conversation with Inspector Shetty that brought back all these memories:

'We'll miss you for sure if you go back home, Ma'am,' he said. 'Of course, aren't we – my team and I – used to lying in wait at your doorstep because of some trouble or the other?'

'I'll miss your questions. That's become a habit too.'

'Oh, we will miss you. When we were coming here, Mukta said she's never met such a humorous complainant ever.'

'Never mind, I'll be back if I am still alive!'

'I, too, pray that you stay safe. But I can't guarantee that. The person who's after you is no ordinary criminal. And there is more than one hostile person…'

'But Inspector Sir, right now there's just one person. It's the same person who shot me three times, who surveyed the premises of my house, who attacked Joyo, who tried to break into Sandeepa's house. You may have your doubts. I have none.'

'Agreed, Ma'am. But there's a mystery surrounding him. Why does he try to kill you? What is your relation to him? None. So it's clear, he's an instrument. Not the power behind. That's what I am trying to find out.'

'This is like the government getting rid of black money! Banned the notes. Printed new ones. People died waiting in queues. But black money is still alive and kicking!'

'Give me fifty days, Ma'am! Then you can do whatever you wish with me.'

'I wonder if I am going to be alive that long!'

'Look, Ma'am, this is a complicated case. You refuse to reveal any information. Isn't it something that I have got this far?'

'This far?'

'That is, the owner of the pistol…'

My heart stopped. I leaned forward.

'You found the owner?'

He smiled and got up.

'Sorry … I cannot reveal more at this stage of the investigation. But let me give you a tiny clue. Its licence is in a woman's name.'

I was really shocked now.

'A Malayali woman?'

'No, Odiya. I can tell you her name – Mitali.'

I was struck dumb.

'Who's that? Do you know her?'

He frowned. My face went pale. I tried to recall the woman's face. She had been ill since the time I first met her.

'I know – you will not speak up, so I found out on my own. She is Prabhudev Maheswari's wife.'

I bent my head, closed my eyes, sat still for a moment. Then I faced him.

'What else did you discover?'

'Many things. You don't have to know all of it now. You'll be told when it's time.'

'Nothing I should know?'

He looked at me closely. His eyes glinted.

'For now, go home, Ma'am. Be with your mother, relax. But be vigilant. The old mistake – don't make it again.'

'What mistake?'

'Like approaching a usurer for a loan!'

I keeled over all the more inside. It was clear that he had dug up much.

'Oh…' I tried to hold myself up, 'I thought you were going to tell me not to fall in love or something…'

'That, too – it's going to be a mistake if you fall for someone like Abhilash again.'

I was in pieces now. Wordless and numb, even dizzy. He said something more, bid goodbye, and left. I continued to feel dizzy. Have you ever trusted someone blindly? Have you loved them forgetting the whole world? Have you seen them as your support in times of sheer helplessness? Have you gone to his house begging for a loan? Has he ever sold you to a man old enough to be your father when you defaulted on the interest payments? A pity if you haven't experienced all this, for then, you are deficient. Because you have not studied the economics of per capita agony. You have not submitted yourself to rebuilding the Nation. Another thing: Getting murdered without being told why is actually better than becoming aware of all this.

SIXTEEN

Inspector Shetty was pure evil. In a single stroke he had flung open so many graves – of my happiness, loves, beliefs. Graves in which you bury your loves should never be opened. The awful stench! Argh! No surprise, actually. Those corpses don't rot so quickly. They decay bit by bit. The vaults never empty. The odour never leaves.

Do you get it? Do you know why I have gone for such a dramatic opening? It is a warm-up exercise to tell you about Abhilash. For how long can I postpone it? Yes, I needed some preparation. It wasn't demonetization, was it, to be rolled out just like that? It was a criminal investigation. Like handling acid or poison. Or touching patients with hepatitis or smallpox. You have to be vaccinated, wear gloves, be safe.

That doesn't mean that I hated Abhilash fiercely. I no longer felt anything of that sort. Why should one feel any antipathy towards a mud statue that had dissolved in the rain? My hatred was entirely towards my own foolishness. Towards my futile affection. You may wonder if love is a well that never fills up once it dries. Fair enough. But in my case, it was not well water; it was lava. That lay scorched and melting within. That which seared all that it touched when it erupted. That which became hard as rock when it cooled. Ah, what is to be gained by describing all that in such detail?

Whatever be it, he entered my life with an explosion. I was a second-year pre-degree student then, just out of high school, barely sixteen. Back then we went to college straight out of the tenth standard. One day, the long bell in college which signalled danger, rang when we were in class. All of us ran out. When some of us arrived at the college gate, we found a crowd there, barring our way. The police were thrashing them. We gathered in the garden near the office block and watched. Then, someone jumped past the half-wall and the bushes and landed in front of us. My attention was drawn to his perfectly white rubber slippers, as though they had been bought just then. His feet, too, looked soft and fresh. He stood in front of us, his back to us, swinging back and forth. His hands were tied behind his back. In his left hand, he held a bottle, a piece of wet cloth covering its mouth, in his right, he held a cigarette lighter. I gaped as he used the lighter to set fire to the cloth and, before we could blink, he had flung the bottle over the wall forcefully. Then, he swerved sharply and, pushing us aside rudely, fled. Shanti, Sreekala and I fell down. In the melee, I was not able to catch a glimpse of the bottle. But we heard the explosion and the screams. And saw the fire. While helping people up, I saw the pure white slippers lying on the ground. I picked them up by their blue straps. Then we, all of us, turned around and ran towards the library.

The librarian was closing the windows and doors of the library. So I did not see the police beat up the students, drag them away. That was the first student protest I ever witnessed. Because it was before the fire in the house, the poison in our well, and the sale of the house, I enjoyed it. All the yellow bulbs in the library came on at the same time. Now that it was no longer dark inside, I could see that the library was full. Looking for a place to sit, I went into the reading room. There he was, sitting at the extreme end of a long table, his head buried in an *Economic and Political Weekly*. Who knows what was in my heart. A butterfly, a bird, or just a cockroach, trying to attract a mate emitting pheromones. Its wings began to flutter, I felt a strange throbbing in my fingertips. I went behind him and dropped the slippers I had been carrying, rather noisily. He started, and then, noticing the slippers, his face first lit up and then went pale. I looked at him and he took a good look at me. In the yellowish gleam, his face shone as though it were gold-plated.

There was just one word to describe him: neat. Everything about him was white, clean. He was like a living ad for a soap solution, and I was in love with him for five whole years. Never once in those years did I see his hair unkempt or his face unshaven. His nails, clothes – everything – were always spotless. His father, too, was like that. Crisp white khaddar shirt and mundu without a crease or a spot of dirt, powdered smooth chubby face. No wrinkle, no filth, no sweat, never fatigued.

There's a connection between these – neatness and wealth. Both require a great deal of calculation. Those who are extremely rich are exceptionally neat too; they have time for everything. They don't run after buses, they don't hog on their food. You will find hidden blackboards in their eyes and chests, in which they do calculations we cannot see. They are like pythons. They lie in wait patiently. Embrace you without getting muddied. Kiss you without wetting their lips. When they squeeze you to death, they make sure that they stay clean. They first break your bones. What's left then, except the job of swallowing you? That, too, they will do oh-so neatly. Without you touching their gullet, without retching, leaving no trace.

The mess that day lasted for an hour. The protesters were removed. The library opened again. We all got out. He pushed through the crowd and came to me. He touched my fingertips. I did not pull back my hand. He ran his fingers gently over my palm. And then pressed it. We gazed at each other and smiled. My body tingled with pleasure. My heart felt wonderfully light. I pressed his hand too. In the crowd, we held hands. I fell in love. Was I not young? Wasn't this enough to fall in love at that age? At that age, you don't really fall in love with another; it is yourself you fall in love with. You adore yourself. Love at that age is just the submissiveness you feel towards another who adores you. That was the trouble with that love. You just looked for excuses to make it go on. Everything looked so rosy, golden. But it was just those yellow bulbs, and one didn't notice that. Nothing to be surprised about. People's histories are determined by the money that they have or don't have. That applied to my love too.

It was all smooth to start with. He had been waiting for someone like me. I too was, for someone like him. The letters, the meetings on weekends, the coffees at restaurants, and if we could manage it, a movie. The handholding, the kisses in the dark movie theatre, cuddles without creases on our clothes. I was then the owner of Vasanthamaalika, Nityavasantham and *Vasanthakairali*. Of great value to him. In the third year, he told his family. That was before Appooppan passed. I went to the single-storeyed house painted in blue with the grille window in the front, which was just next to the small office building with the sign 'Gold Loans Available' on it. His parents and family welcomed me as though I were a princess. They competed with each other to be nice to me. Even relatives and neighbours came. That day, I went to his room. It was a small room. On the wall near the table, our passport-sized photos were pasted side by side. He embraced me lightly. Kissed me on the nape of my neck and made me ticklish. I took him for the adventurous sort. Of course, I was young then, knew nothing of the world. I did not know that what I thought was daring was actually a shrewd move, one he could wriggle out of later without getting caught.

~

The day Muthukrishna Gounder's henchmen arrived to chop the tree down, as I trudged on with unending tears in my eyes, he was my hope. My only refuge. But even then, I had no idea who to beg for the money. On the way, my eyes fell on the board of a pawnshop, and suddenly I remembered his father. I just couldn't decide where to go –

to the college, or to his house. The money would be with his father, so I took the bus to his house.

It was his father who opened the door. His face turned sullen when he saw me. He called his son rather blandly. He had been woken up from sleep, but when Abhilash appeared, his hair, as usual, was perfect. His face looked dour too. Seeing him, I could hardly hold back my tears. His mother and sisters peeped out. I told him everything. In the end, putting aside my shame, I asked him, 'Can you please get us a loan from your father?' He looked like he had bitten some poisoned fruit, but he went inside to his father. They came out together. The father's face looked even more sullen. He sounded severe.

'Do you know how hard it is to make a lakh of rupees, girl?' That was the first question. I shrank at it. My eyes overflowed with tears.

'Suppose I give it to you. The interest is five per cent a month. How are you going to pay it back?'

'My sister has a job...' I choked.

'Job...? What sort of job...? What's her pay like?'

'She's on a year's training now ... she will be promoted after that. She'll get ten thousand a month.'

'Really? What job is that?'

'Software programmer.'

'Is that true, eda?' he asked, turning to his son. Abhilash nodded. Then his father considered the arrangement.

'Okay, then I will give you the money. But you have to give me a cheque and a promissory note.'

'I don't have a cheque.'

'You have to get it.'

'Uncle, I need the money now. If I don't get it, I'll die!'

'Girl, you can live or die! Your old man who fucked up everything doesn't care. So why should I?'

If he'd slapped me on my face, that would have been better. I looked at Abhilash. He went into an inner room. Much as I tried, I just could not control my tears. My legs just wanted to run out, get away from there. But the thought of the Gounder stopped me. After some time, Abhilash's mother came to the door and called his father over. He went. I was alone, again. Minutes passed. I got up to leave, my heart breaking. But then Abhilash's father returned.

'All right – are you sure that you will open an account tomorrow and bring over the cheque?'

'Yes.'

'A cheque from your sister will do.'

'I will bring it.'

'But you'll have to sign this,' he said, holding out a stamp paper. I signed it with my eyes shut. He let out a mocking laugh, went inside, and returned with ten bundles of hundred-rupee notes.

'I have taken a month's interest. I never give such a large amount to a single person. This is because this boy's mother insisted. But there's one thing … if you fail to pay the interest…'

'No … I will,' I whispered, not believing myself. I took the money and made my way out. Abhilash went inside, changed his clothes, combed his hair nicely and came along. We walked side by side, in silence. He did not look at me. I could not bring myself to look at him either. As we walked thus, love hung limp in my heart like a snapped elastic string. He asked just one question. 'Are you scared to carry so much money, Satyapriya?'

The bus arrived. I got a seat by the window. When it left, I turned around to take a last look at him. He looked handsomer than ever. The vim and vitality of his twenty-four years filled me with a sense of inferiority, as if I had become unfit for him. He would wait there until the bus vanished from his sight, I hoped. But no, when the bus started, he, too, began to walk back. Like an unwanted puppy shoved into a sack and put on a train by its owner, I had been bundled into the bus. When I reached home, I was like a walking corpse. At the age of twenty-one, my life was stripped of all meaning. I took it all out on the Gounder. I insisted on a full receipt; he made a fuss for the missing five thousand. Obscenities in two languages rang out in the front yard of the Koyikkal house that day. I pulled out my slipper. He caught hold of my hair. In the end, the neighbours came rushing in. Someone started negotiating. At last, he gave in, and the matter was settled. Two people signed as witnesses.

When he left, our aunt and uncle swooped in. 'Get out today!' they ordered. 'What will you do if we won't?' I screamed back. By the time Chechi returned, I was almost dead from weeping and wailing. I had gashed my arm and thigh with a knife, inspired by the answer to the riddle 'How can you make a line look smaller without erasing it?'. I had hoped it would ease the bigger of my many torments. Chechi hugged me and wept. The next day, we went to the bank and opened an account. I went to Abhilash's house with the cheque leaf she had signed. His father opened the door, asked me what it was. I pulled out the cheque leaf and gave it to him. He examined it, said it was fine, and shut the door.

That day, as I stood at the bus stop, I did not weep. The eruption of the other day had ceased, the lava had emptied itself. My swollen eyelids felt sore. My body ached so badly, I could not even cry. Amma and Acchan came back that evening. When she heard the story of my approaching a moneylender, she flew off the handle. 'Who told you to get into debt?' she thundered, pinching the flesh off my wrist. 'What was your problem if they cut down that tree? Who is this moneylender? How do you know him?' I had not told her about Abhilash. 'A girlfriend of mine told me about him,' was all I said now. Amma rebuked me some more, and I cried again.

How to describe the days that followed? The horrible anxiety about the one lakh. We needed five thousand for the interest; Chechi's stipend was just 4,500 a month. My head broiled when I tried to juggle Acchan's treatment and our household expenses. But even then, for the first three months, I borrowed from Venukkuttan Chettan and Gopi Maaman and paid him. In the fourth month, Chechi caught pneumonia and had to rest for two whole months. She lost her job.

The interest could not be paid. Then, after six months, Abhilash sent a letter. It was curt in tone.

> *Dear Satyapriya, I hope that you are well. It's the third month now since you failed to pay the interest on the sum you borrowed from my father. You know without me telling you that our family lives on such interest. I am writing to you after being summoned and scolded by my father several times. Please pay back the sum at once. If not, like you, even I will be left without a home.*
>
> *With hope,*
> *Abhilash*

I did not show the letter to anyone. Acchan was in a pathetic state. Amma was struggling to make ends meet at home. On many days, we drank just rice gruel with crushed chillies. My heart broke seeing my sister's bloodless, weak face. On those days I wanted to die. And finish off the others with some poison.

~

Inspector Shetty had dug up this grave. How could I not have collapsed? After I sent my things away, I handed the keys back to my landlord and went to Sandeepa's once more as if to say goodbye. I held Joyo close and kissed his forehead. He promised to come to Kerala to see me once he was better. 'If I am around,' I joked. Actually, I had not gone to their place to bid them goodbye. I needed to retrieve the dagger. I had hidden it very smartly. First in my handbag, and then in the check-in bag.

All the flights were delayed because of the cyclone in Chennai. But none of that bothered me. My mind was a void. I pictured my return, my mother's reaction. My monthly income had ceased. But that didn't worry me either because the compensation was quite generous. Then, of course, our prime minister was promising each of us fifteen lakh! My real problem was about how I'd spend my time. Oh – then I remembered – there was this big job that awaited me! A big one – the one Amma had spoken about – the detective's job. The job of digging out the man who was out to kill me. Now, I had the weapon to find him. And the guts to use it.

However, despite that, I wept when I was in the plane. A feeling of insecurity assailed me. The experiences of the future frightened me. Those of the past, even more. Was my history to be determined by money alone? Or by love too? The love Amma had for Acchan, the love Acchan bore towards Rajani, my love for Abhilash, the love Sriram had for me, the love I had for Samir, the love Prabhudev had for me, the love Mitali had for Prabhudev, the love Anjali had for Jagan, the love Mahipal Shah had for me...

If so, what about the history of my would-be killer? What must have determined that? Love or money? If it was love, then whose was it? If it was money, then whose was it?

SEVENTEEN

Being in debt to a usurer is an interesting experience. Like walking on quicksand. Pull the left foot out, your right foot will sink right in. In the end, both your legs will fail. You can't find a foothold in the deep, wet sand. Then the body will start to sink. You'll hang on in your mind somehow until the sand reaches your neck. There's the split-second when it will rise above your neck, in which you'll struggle for your life like never before. It's the moment in which you give birth to another you. You'll think that it will all be over soon. But no. You can't escape choosing one of the two you-s. The old one, or the one that's just born. It's tough, because, after all, both the you-s are you. Surely, the void from the loss of one will inevitably be felt by the other?

Every time, I gave birth to another me in indescribable pain and struggle. I let the newly-born me live and the older me die. The new me acquired new debts. First, it was a lakh. I racked my brains to find a way to pay it back. Dreamt of many solutions. The thing about dreams – it's funny. Some of them come true right then, some later, some never. There are some dreams that return after a long time giving the impression that they are going to come true right then. For example, I had a dream back then – in 1994 – that the government was going to gift every citizen one lakh rupees. But it did not come true then; I did not even hope that it ever would. But when I heard that everyone would receive fifteen lakh rupees, I was thrilled with joy. Ultimately, no one got any money, but it was like we all got it – it was a feeling, that in some mythical bank, somewhere, fifteen lakh rupees were waiting for me! Ah, anyway, money is just a faith, your belief. But you can't replace money with faith. Faith has no currency, no bank. It is in the air, though, controlling the exchange of both wealth and love. Impossible to wrap your head around!

~

It was at the age of twenty-two that I saw a hundred thousand dreams. I seethed and burned inwardly then. No matter who it is you might borrow from, never borrow from a lover. If you do, it's the end of his love and your dignity. I did not reply to Abhilash's letter asking me to repay the loan. What was I to write? An unpaid debt is like slow-burning grain husk – those who have seen husk and those who have lit it would know. It keeps seething. The brown turns a smouldering red. The heat may not spread out until the end. The colour may not be visible. The coals quivered slowly inside me, glowering all the while. I was engulfed in heat and smoke all the time. On the outside, I was turning into soot.

And if the fire showed any signs of dying, there was someone who blew on it and brought it back to life. The real fun started after the Gounder left. Washed clothes began to disappear from the clothes line outside the house. Vessels and kitchen implements began to be filched through the window. One morning we found that the rattan seats of the two chairs in the veranda – the only chairs in the house – had been ripped to pieces. Someone had peed on the cushions. The stink of aged urine hung all over the place. We began to hear footsteps outside the house at midnight. On some days we found footprints under the ventilator. When such things happen, anger begins to simmer first; a crazy urge to wreck everything comes next; and finally, there's the flaming desire to kill the whole fucking lot. Then, the fear begins to surface. And the tears. A certain foreboding becomes a constant presence. As though an assassin were after you.

It is amidst this mess that Abhilash entered. Not as a lover, but a creditor, to get his money back, when he did not receive a reply to his letter. I had a bad headache and was resting when he came. I jumped up when I heard him call my name. I had expected his father, not him. I had not taken a bath, nor even washed my face or changed – I looked completely dishevelled in my old nightgown, with its top button gone. Seeing him in the veranda, where the old chairs lay supine, the torn cushions failing to cover their nakedness, I felt faint. He sat on the half-wall. I ran to Amma, in fright. She was in Acchan's room, darning a much-worn underskirt. I panted as I asked her, 'Do we have any tea powder?' She answered me with a single piercing look. I went to the veranda, struggling inwardly. He did not look at me. I stood there, unable to breathe. The light from the morning sun fell on his well-groomed hair. He looked handsomer still. That was my weakness – I saw beauty in all that I could never hope to claim, and I yearned for them all. Beauty is just a belief too. It, too, has no currency, no reserves. But definitely, it has exchange value. Not everywhere, though – only in some places, under specific circumstances.

'I got into this because I trusted you, Satyapriya.' That was the first thing he said.

Later, whenever I evaluated that moment, I felt respect for him. The lover meets his beloved. She stands there in a soiled nightgown, hair piled up messily on her head, eyes puffy and worn. The house is so pathetic, there is not even a chair to sit on. She has not even had a cup of tea that morning. There is no tea or coffee there. They don't get milk. And that day, they did not even have rice to cook. During such a time, how delightful, his opening statement! 'I got into this because I trusted you, Satyapriya.'

But I did not sense the poetic intensity of that statement then. You need a minimum amount of self-confidence, too, to appreciate poetry.

My voice refused to come out. A big rock was stuck in my throat, too big to spit out or swallow.

'You could've at least paid the interest on time.' He sounded irritated. I did not know what to say; the knowledge that Amma was listening left me tormented.

'Will it do to just remain silent? Don't you have something to say?' My eyes overflowed with tears. It was then that he raised his head to look at me. I felt the pitilessness of his look cut through me. My legs felt weak. A pyre burned inside my chest, and I could hear the bones split apart.

'Next time, Acchan will come in person.' His voice was drier still.

'Chechi is sick and bedridden...' I made an effort to answer.

'When will the money be paid back? Just tell me that!'

'I don't know, Abhilash...'

'Then what the hell were you thinking when you took the money?'

The words scalded me. I writhed in sheer agony. Only his face resembled that of the Abhilash of the past. His voice was that of Sreedharan Nair and Xavier Panakkal. I could see the watermarks of heartlessness in his pupils. 'One lakh fifteen thousand', 'One lakh fifteen thousand' – every blink of his eye seemed to repeat.

'I will return the money for sure ... somehow ... But I have no idea how,' I said, trembling. It was so painful, like my very heart was being torn out. And it was about the fact that I was worth exactly that sum to him. Was I not a fool those days? Didn't I think then that our love was like the gold reserves of the Reserve Bank? That it was beyond market forces?

'I can think of a way...' he said. 'I'll introduce you to someone, and you can get me the amount from him for now.'

'That would mean?'

'The debt passes into another's hands. That's all.'

'Will he give me the money?'

'If you have a cheque and a promissory note ... Just make sure that the interest is paid regularly.'

'Can't we beg your father for some more time?'

'My elder sister's marriage has been fixed. It could be badly affected.'

There was nothing more to discuss. He told me to be at the hostel the next morning. I agreed. When he left, I went back to my bed. Amma came and sat next to me.

'What's going on between you two?' she asked.

I did not answer.

'Whatever your relationship is – end it now.'

I think I was on my periods, so I suddenly felt that Amma was responsible for all of this. That this happened because Amma tolerated all of Acchan's filth. She was sluggish, careless, imprudent. Never questioned Acchan, never tried to restrain him, never tried to find a job and make a living to stand on her own two feet. And here she was, trying to offer advice. I lost my cool.

'He's the one who gave me the money to pay the Gounder!'

'You should not have taken it.'

'What if I hadn't?'

'Gounder may have chopped down a couple of trees. Maybe all the trees. The Koyikkal family should bear it. It was my father who got them out of debt and saved this house from recovery proceedings! It's clearly mentioned in the partition deed too. We could have taken back this house if we had filed a case.'

My anger knew no bounds now.

'Oh, so typical of you, Amma. When it is over, you'll say such things and more! When that Gounder was making such a fuss here that day, why didn't you say this? Will the Koyikkal people let us live here if their trees were taken away in such a way? You did not hear their cuss-words that day! I was the only one who did.'

'They would've made a fuss till the trees were chopped down. But if it happened, they would have just suffered it. But now, things are going to be harder. They'll smoke us out. They'll make sure that no one else tries to cut a tree.'

I froze as though she had slapped me.

'It was I who asked the Gounder to go and chop down a tree.' Amma spoke these words dispassionately, but I was shattered.

'When?'

'I phoned him on the way to the hospital. Just thought that it would be better if it happened in our absence.'

'Why didn't you tell me, Amma?'

'I did not think that you needed to know. And never dreamt that you'd take on the job of repaying him!'

'He didn't tell me either.'

'Why should he, when you agreed to get him cash?'

I wanted to go and hang myself. And die slowly just to punish myself.

'Now we are deeper in debt. Never mind.'

Amma ran her hand on my head gently. My world whirled. Everybody had betrayed me, I thought. That was my age back then, wasn't it? When you actually think that the world revolves around you? I began to bang my head on the cot, wailing loudly. Amma did not try to stop me or comfort me; she just watched.

'Well, what's over is over! No point weeping about it. Life is like a maths exam. No matter how careful you may be, some steps in the calculation go wrong,' she said.

'What do you suggest I do, Amma?'

'Either we wait till we make that amount...'

'Aiyo, no! I promised to return it!'

'If so, let me ask my brothers.'

My mind sank. Seeing her going down on her knees before them was unthinkable.

'What if they don't give it?'

'I'll ask again...'

'Amma, do you want to lose face in front of them?'

'Those in need have no dignity, no propriety.'

I sat up, wiped my eyes. I pictured her walk to our uncles' houses, sheltered by the open umbrella. Her standing at their gates, the sweat streaming, the local folk staring at her, her weeping inwardly as she stepped into the front yard of her family home, my uncle's wife, son and daughter-in-law ignoring her, my younger uncle shouting at her, her returning without a trace of the humiliation on her face...

'We need a lakh and fifteen thousand to pay off the debt. Do you think Valyamaaman or Kochumaaman will give it to us?' I began to argue again.

'We may get fifty, perhaps.'

'Valyamaaman will call up Kochumaaman and ask him – and we may get twenty-five – or say, they gave us fifty. What will that serve?' I asked adamantly. 'Fifty to be paid to Abhilash's father. Fifty to Valyamaaman ... or twenty-five each to Valyamaaman and Kochumaaman. Three creditors instead of one. And then?' I continued.

Amma looked at me. She had no answer.

'Finding a loan shark is better!' I exclaimed.

'Satye, don't fall into a trap for nothing, please.'

'Amme, let's say they give us nothing. Should we not live after that? Or shall we kill ourselves?' I asked.

Amma looked stumped. My reasons were simple. After all, wasn't it Amma who had taught us never to borrow money from a relative? If you do, the relationship will be lost, the money too. So, no, let us not do it. We were utterly wasted. But we could not die for that reason. We would live.

Amma sighed. 'I have only you two. If anything happens to you, my life is meaningless...'

At that moment, I imitated her confidence.

'Shouldn't we live even if you don't, Amma?'

She looked jolted and her face turned red. Then she smiled.

'Yes, just never forget that.'

That is how I went to Abhilash's college the next day. I wore a rather plain-looking churidar-kameez set, my hair was tied up carelessly, and I had not put on a bindi, nor used kohl. I just could not bring myself to. Abhilash took me on his bike to his hostel room. There, he tried to grab me and kiss me. I pulled away. The days when his touch gave me thrills of pleasure were long gone. His well-combed hair and stiffly starched white shirt repelled me now. I threw him a disgusted look.

'Uh? What's that look, girl?' he crooned lustfully, stroking the back of my neck. I was young. But age is not a barrier to recognize the faithlessness of men. I moved back. He pulled me closer even more forcefully. It was dangerous to annoy him, and so I said, 'Your shirt – it's going to get crumpled.'

He took off his shirt. He did, in fact, have a very attractive body. The hair on his chest, the blue veins on his neck, his sculpted back – he was sexy. He tried to force it on me. My state then! Abhilash was someone for whom I had felt a boundless desire for a long time. And now, in this moment, I hungered endlessly for his loving presence. But when he actually touched me, my body singed. My heart was scorched. I remembered the way he had dragged his feet when he was seeing me off at the bus stand that day. The sentences from his letter after we failed to pay his father the interest appeared before my eyes. I figured that all he wanted to do was use my body before getting his money back through another loan. If I were in his place, if I were a man, what would I have done, I asked myself. I would have held my beloved close. I would have whispered, 'Don't cry, I am here.' Rage gathered in me, enough to blow him to bits. He did not sense that and began to caress me. His fingers trembled. Probably the trembling of a twenty-four-year-old attempting sex for the first time. I grabbed his mundu and pulled it off. The brief he wore under it was soiled, a dirty brown. He tried to hold me close and rubbed his lips against my neck. Though I raised my face for him to kiss me, I jerked it back as though reflexively. He was taken aback.

'The way your mouth stinks, Abhilash!' My hand flew to cover my nostrils. His face blanched.

'Really!'

He raised his palm, blew into it, and sniffed.

'Shall I wash my mouth?' he asked helplessly.

'Try…' I said indifferently.

'Or should I brush?'

'That'll be better.'

The fool ran off. When he came back, I held out the shirt to him. He pulled on his underwear, and holding the shirt in his hands, looked at me, puzzled.

'You don't clean your teeth, Abhilash?' I asked, pulling myself away from him. He looked befuddled.

'I should…' he mumbled. His desire had evaporated. He combed his hair and powdered his face. When we came out of the room, I was relieved that I had escaped without injury. When I rode pillion on his bike, my thoughts were solely about money and interest payments. I calmed myself down. One had to live, somehow. Loans had to be taken till Chechi steadied herself, I had to complete my education, the bills had to be paid at home. But before everything else, the debt to the lover had to be paid.

Abhilash took me to a residential area. The bike stopped in front of a two-storeyed building with a signboard that read 'St Anthony's Chits and Funds'. I had two cheque leaves with me. Abhilash had brought a ten-rupee stamp paper. Seeing us, a pot-bellied man who looked at least five years older than Acchan came out. For as long as I live, I will not forget the heavy gold chains that peeped out of the gap between the buttons on his jubbah, and the gold bracelet on his wrist. He surveyed me from top to toe and smiled. 'Sivaprasad Saar's daughter, uh?' he asked. 'How much do you need?'

'A lakh and a half,' I muttered.

'Will that do?' he asked.

I was amazed when he called his secretary and asked him to bring over the cash. He took the cheques and the promissory note. He gave me fifteen bundles of hundred-rupee notes. I handed over twelve right there to Abhilash. The rest I put inside a plastic cover in my bag. The moneylender then invited us to lunch. 'Oh, I won't be able to have lunch in peace if I don't offer lunch to Sivaprasad Saar's daughter!'

he declared, and I felt gratified. He took us to a guest house behind the building and played an eager host. On the slab in the dining room lay many fresh banana leaves. He himself chose the best one, carefully sliced off its stem and laid it on the table before me. The staff there brought fried pearl-spot fish and chilli chicken. It was a long time since I had eaten so many curries. It made me feel tearful. And guilty that I was eating without Amma and Chechi. The huge pearl-spot, bigger than both my hands put together, reminded me of Vasanthaalayam. That is the problem with memories. They are not like currency notes. No matter how much you ban them, they will still return. You will struggle, not knowing what to do with them. The only relief is that there's no law against keeping them. No limits on numbers or value. No fine to pay for excess stock.

Abhilash finished his meal earlier than me, washed his hands, and disappeared into the next room. The jubbah-man served me again and again. I was stuffed. I felt sleepy while I washed my hands and mouth. The jubbah-man called me into the room nearby. My eyes searched for Abhilash. Probably because I'd eaten after having stayed hungry for so long, I thought, sleep was getting the better of me. My body and I parted. I saw the man run his hands over my body, but my body did not sense it. I saw him undress me, but I doubted if those clothes were mine. I stopped him. He grabbed my hand and twisted it, snarling, 'Fucking hussy! Agreed to it, took the cash, and now you are playing!'

The truth was that his mouth stank too. Bits of chicken and fish were stuck in the crevices of his teeth and decaying. I was barely conscious, but I still noticed it when he opened his mouth. I began to slip out of consciousness, becoming sightless like the smoke from a heap of slow-burning sawdust. I wanted to keep burning and spreading for some more time. The important thing was not to lose consciousness completely. I thought of Amma and Chechi. Wondered how I would face Amma when I got back. 'Mustn't you live even if Acchan and Amma aren't around?' someone inside me snorted. I tried to stand up straight. It was hard. Don't you see now that the simile of the quicksand I used before came from this experience? Before this moment, I had never been in one, never had I experienced feet sinking. But, of course, you don't need prior experience in this. Neither is there any need to experience it multiple times. Once is enough. Just once.

But really, whoever invented this lending-for-interest practice is a real boss. How plain and boring my life would have been without it! I wonder who invented it – cis-man, cis-woman, trans-man, trans-woman – who? Probably a cis-woman. Like me. Who knew that a debt can't be repaid with just the principal. But then, what is gender when it comes to money and interest? Only currency notes are without gender. It would have been troublesome if they were gendered: notes and coins you couldn't use while you were menstruating would have been invented and the hundi boxes in temples would have suffered.

That reminds me – as I sat on Abhilash's bike, which fell into all the potholes on the road, I had started bleeding. That very minute, I gave birth to a new me and killed off the old one. It's an interesting experience. I am grateful to the assassin determined to finish me off. Between this experience and being killed, there was just one difference. The assassin would have killed me right then, and I would have returned only in another birth.

~

Are you asking what happened that made me want to describe all this so closely? I was going home from the airport in a taxi. Night had almost fallen. The vehicle moved slowly through the traffic, like it was dragging itself over mud. There was a bike behind my taxi, and he was riding it. The same helmet, same jacket, same gloves, the same hefty figure…!

My assassin.

EIGHTEEN

Even if it is death, if it pursued you all the time, you'd get bored. You'd want to wave it off saying, 'Fuck off!' Maybe my assassin wasn't aware of this. Or was he just playing the fool? Who knows. People have no clue about themselves; then how would they be aware of others? I was eager to get the right moment with him. So we stopped at a restaurant and I insisted that the driver join me. We ate masala dosas and drank coffee. What if the assassin followed me there? I had decided how to confront him. I would go right up and say, 'Hey, buddy, hope things are good?' I'd provoke him by remarking aloud, 'You are a duffer, just a pozhan, right, allede?' But he was actually a duffer. He had already wasted so many chances. He could have easily planted a bomb in my car when we were inside the restaurant. But maybe the poor soul did not have a bomb. Or maybe he didn't trust a bomb enough. People can't trust each other, so how are they to trust a bomb?

When we got into the car again, I did not bother to scan the surroundings. He was somewhere around, I was sure. But after some time, my curiosity got the better of me. I turned to look, but there were only cars behind us. Then, after some more time, I turned to look again. This time I saw a motorbike winding its way through the rows of cars. I felt relieved. He was right behind me. It was actually something that gave me a sense of security. In such things as husbands and assassins, it is ideal to have one. It helps keep others from trying their luck – no nasty competition.

I peered hard to catch a glimpse of his face. He had a helmet on, but it was the highway, and our drivers generally never dim the lights of their vehicles. So I clearly saw his bulging eyes a couple of times. They looked familiar but I couldn't recollect where I'd seen them earlier. Probably on his face? Then I stopped turning around and peering out. Who had the time to get obsessed with the likes of him?

It was a beautiful night. Gradually, the traffic on the highway grew lighter. In the sky, grey clouds seemed to be on a chase. On either side of the road, the leaves of the Sheemakonna trees glistened like silver. 'Hey, Rajesh,' I asked the driver, 'don't we have any music?' He played a CD. The song 'Nin maniyarayile nirmalashayyayile…' wafted around. The reference to the bridal chamber, the cot and the coverlet made me quite sleepy.

As the night grew, the darkness became dense, and the road looked like the highway to death. That's the thing about death. It is not always the bluish-red bank of a river. Sometimes it may be a mountain, yellow in colour. Or a road on which the light and shadows fall intermittently. I tried to close my eyes and rest, but started awake, seeing a road coated with blood. I turned around to look and found the assassin following us. It was a relief – it seemed certain that he would attack me on the way. How, I tried to guess. By ramming his bike into the car? Or by stopping us in a deserted corner, ordering me out, and shooting me? Ah, who knew? What was the use of knowing, though? Wouldn't the story end with that?

The vehicle moved into the town. I woke up. My body tingled with pleasure. My home town! I craned my neck out to spot the small road that led to the beach. A wave of sorrow assailed me. I tried to convince myself that the curved signboard with carved gold letters that read 'Hotel Vasanthamaalika' would still be there. The sea breeze caused the cells in my body to sway like casuarina trees. Like the dead, perhaps the assets we lose have souls too. They may be wandering in search of their old owners. But lost assets are quite like banned notes. We are entitled to neither. Both are of no value to us. Both leave behind painful memories.

Then something happened. Our car was turning on to a side road from a fairly deserted junction when a woman clad in a cheap shiny sari jumped in the way. Rajesh braked hard and the car screeched to a stop. He shuddered in fright, and then, in a fit of anger, rolled down the window and shouted at her, 'You daughter of a whore, are you trying to kill yourself because you can't get fucked enough…!' The woman shouted back at him with equal fury, 'Oh, you and your car are too tiny for that!' I saw her face glower in the headlights. But it was only after a moment that I recognized her. Nisha Chechi!

Lowering my side of the window, I called out, 'Nisha Chechi!' My voice took her by surprise – she was confused. She peered hard into the car.

'Don't you recognize me?' I asked. It took a couple of moments for her to realize who I was.

'Satyamole?' she asked.

'If you're going home, come, get in!' I invited her.

'No, not now. You go home, dear.'

She turned away sharply and strode off to the other side of the road. Rajesh started the vehicle. 'She's of the wrong sort, Madam,' he said.

'Wrong sort? What do you mean?'

'She's into that sort of business.'

'What sort of business?'

'Madam, are you so naïve? She's just a prostitute … a proper slut.'

'How do you know, Rajesh?'

'I used to drive my car around these parts before I moved to the airport side … I know her from back then.'

'But how does she become the wrong sort for that?'

'What else would a woman who sells her body be? A saint?'

'If so, what about Reliance? Birla? They also sell something or the other, right?'

'But is selling one's body the same as that?'

'Selling – it's all the same, isn't it?'

'No good woman will sell her body. If she has to do it, she'd rather kill herself.'

'Is money so bad?'

'For a woman, her body is sacred, pure.'

'And for a man?'

He turned around to look at me. 'You are a feminist, aren't you, Madam?'

'That's not important. Tell me, isn't the body sacred for the man?'

'Okay, will you sell your body even if you are in dire straits, Madam?'

'Five crore ... no, maybe say two ... or one and a half ... or, okay, one crore ... that should do!'

The man squirmed as though he had been poked with a red-hot rod. I suppressed a laugh and continued: 'Actually, Rajesh, I don't need any money at all. Only that the man who buys me should have a body that's pure and sacred.'

I saw his discoloured face in the mirror. He was silent for some time. My words had probably irked him. I wasn't surprised – men usually are furious when they have no repartee. After some time, he asked, 'Madam, how do you know her?' He wanted to change the subject. I did not respond. It was not at all necessary to answer the questions of a fellow whose body wasn't sacred. And I was exhausted – exhausted enough to forget my assassin.

We reached home. Amma was waiting in the veranda. I got my luggage out, paid the taxi, and lowered my sacred body into the chair there. Amma was locking the gate. I noticed only then that there was a large gandharajan shrub in full bloom in our garden; a vellaal tree with a jasmine vine coiling around it. From the sacred bodies of the mango

and aatha trees hung huge leaves of money plants. When Amma came
back to the veranda, I hugged her.

'I am back, Amme!'

She stroked my back with one hand.

'Just like her father! No, don't give me a moment of peace!' She
laughed.

'No...'

I laughed, too, but was uneasy inside. Was my coming here a
mistake? I tried to remember where we had lost the assassin on the
road. I had not seen him after we turned into town. Had he been
following me through some side road? Would he try to break in here
too, like he broke into Sandeepa's house? Would he hurt Amma? The
thought burned me from inside. After a shower, I drank my glass of
milk and lay down beside Amma, hugging her.

'I saw Nisha Chechi today.'

My words spilled out despite myself.

'The poor thing...' Amma sighed. Something was pressing hard
inside me. I hid my face in the small of Amma's back. Not sure whether
I was asleep or awake, but I saw Acchan. His spotless mundu with
the broad brocade border and silk shirt gleamed. The scent of Brut
invaded the place. He stepped out of the car with his brown leather
suitcase. Nisha Chechi and I were playing akku on the north side of
the yard. Ulahannan Maaman parked the car in the car shed. Acchan
stood there watching us. Seeing him, we stopped, and held hands. 'You
are Velayudhan's girl, aren't you?' he asked. 'Yes,' said Nisha Chechi.
Acchan then took out a hundred-rupee note from his pocket and gave
it to her. Her eyes widened in surprise. She took the note, her face
shining with the sudden happiness. I didn't like it that he had offered
it only to her. 'From now on, you can live here,' he said. Nisha Chechi
and I looked at each other; we felt elated.

Ulahannan Maaman handed Acchan the car keys. Acchan went
inside. Nisha Chechi and I ran behind Ulahannan Maaman's bicycle
through the alley for some distance, then came back and continued

our game. 'What will you do with the money?' I asked. 'I'll get our house a coat of concrete!' 'I'll make Acchan give you more,' I promised. Not that I had such influence on him; I just wanted to make his generosity look like mine too. We were in the middle of our game when Acchan arrived and asked Nisha Chechi, 'Do you want to be in the movies?' She smiled her charming smile. Then Acchan sent Laalamma off to do some shopping and asked me to go take a shower and light the evening lamp. I was so eager to please him, I ran off to the bathroom. When, after taking a shower, I came out, I did not find him or Nisha Chechi anywhere. I lit the bronze lamp carefully and recited my prayers quickly.

Darkness was falling. I went up to the gate and peeped out. There was no one around. I went over to the cowshed. Only the cows seemed restive. The unusual quiet and emptiness made me feel scared. Even the breeze from the lake was soundless. The trees sighed quietly. From the front of the house I went towards its northern part, opened the latch of the pantry door and entered the kitchen silently. From somewhere inside came a strange, distorted sound, like the muffled scream of a chicken when Ulahannan Maaman would wring its neck. Acchan came out of the storeroom on the side of the kitchen. He did not see me. He wound his mundu tightly around his waist and went into the house.

I went to the door of the storeroom. It was dark inside. I leaned over and switched the lights on. I saw Nisha Chechi on the floor, naked. For the first time, I saw her barely formed breasts, and her crotch on which the fuzz was only beginning to form. I was stunned, I had turned to stone. She lay there like a half-wrung, half-plucked chicken, or one half eaten by a civet cat. There was blood on her face, her neck, and between her legs. I peed from sheer fright.

I ran to the front of the house. It was dark there. I sank to the ground, panting. My small body shook from fear, it tingled all over. I did not know why but I began to weep. Then Acchan arrived there with his sacred, pure body, all washed, and turned on the lights. Seeing me seated on the sofa, shivering, my face between bent knees, he asked, 'Ah, you were here! Where is Nisha? Did she go home?' He came over and sat near me. I was usually so proud and delighted when Acchan would speak to me. But that day, I drew back sharply. 'What is it, my dear?' he asked. Even back then, I had the ability to detect insincerity in love. I glowered at him. 'What happened?' he asked again, holding my chin to lift my face. I felt as though my sacred body had been defiled by his touch, so I slapped his hand away. I scratched him all over. He shook his hand in pain and slapped me hard. I leapt on him and bit him hard. He eased.

'You are not my father!' I almost roared. 'I don't want you!'

Acchan looked shattered. 'My dear…' he called to me, frightened. That was a terrible moment. How old was I then? Eight or nine? Whatever may have been the number, it was good enough to decide that I did not need Acchan. I had made up my mind.

'I am not your daughter…!' I screamed again. 'Do not call me that!'

I broke into loud sobs. In my throat were a thousand birds with their necks wrung, wailing together. My bony ribcage heaved up and down like a tiny wooden canoe caught in a massive storm at sea, rising, falling, turning, rolling, drowning in the lashing waters. Acchan stared at me, utterly scared. I threw looks of loathing and disgust at him and ran to Nisha Chechi, still crying loudly. I called to her amidst my unending sobs.

She was sitting up, as though she had just risen from sleep. Very slowly, she dressed herself. All she had was a yellowed petticoat, a faded shirt with a frayed collar, and a worn half-skirt torn here and there. After putting them on, she stood up gingerly. The hundred-rupee note lay crumpled on the floor. She bent down with effort and picked it up. Then she put it in my hand gently. How old was she then? Twelve or thirteen? The age one begins to sense that no one gives you a currency note for nothing. She did not look at me. Just lurched towards the door and out. It was since that day that my body learned how to freeze.

It began to shiver like a bunch of leaves. I shut myself in my room and wept. All of a sudden, I had grown up.

Amma and Chechi took another week to return. I stayed inside my room that whole week, like a sick hen. I hid that hundred-rupee note in my Gita class notebook. A few days later, when Acchan was not in the house, Nisha Chechi sneaked back into our yard to meet me again. I went out to see her, my legs sinking, my heart weighed down with guilt. She stood there, unmoving, her eyes on me. My eyes welled when I saw her lips bruised black, and the wound on her neck swollen and filled with pus.

'Our father's hurt … his foot was hurt with the hoe…' she said. She sounded different. Like a bird with a broken neck.

'Can you give me that hundred-rupee note?'

I felt a bolt of lightning shoot through me. Then I ran back into the room to get the note. I gave it to her, and as she took it, a dead smile appeared on her bruised lips.

'Don't tell Siva or Amma, okay?' she begged me.

I could not hold back my sobs. She held out to me the palm on which we had applied henna together, just days back.

'If you tell them, I will kill myself.'

My heart throbbing with pain, I put my own henna-reddened right palm on hers and promised, 'On my mother…'

She walked away with her legs slightly apart.

～

Don't you understand now – each currency note imprints by its presence key moments in our histories? But will things be resolved if all the hundred-rupee notes are banned? Will I get my old Nisha Chechi back? Can we play tag together on the way to the Gita class? Can we gather the twigs and take aim together at the ripe fruit on the branches of the njaaval tree in the yard at the Gita class? Can we go searching for sundew plants on the lakeshore? Can we go pick the purple-coloured kalambetti flowers and the funnel-like yellow kaakkappoo on cool November days? Can we swing merrily on Onam gorging on the chips and fries snuck inside our petticoats? Nisha Chechi's house had just two rooms with laterite walls. I don't remember if hundred rupees was enough to give it a coat of concrete. But when I remembered the price she had to pay for that bloodstained, crumpled hundred-rupee note, what I paid for the fifteen bundles of hundred-rupee notes seemed trivial.

Then it struck me that the assassin had vanished at the sight of Nisha Chechi. I sat up. My heart pounded. Are they connected, I wondered. I had no time to soak myself in old tales. I had to find the assassin. Or he would finish me. When I was on my way home, I had actually thought it would be really easy. The 'S'-shaped dagger was my weapon too. But what do people really know about themselves or others? My chest heaved like it had when I was nine years old. Inside me, numberless birds cried in agony, their necks broken. I lay on the seat of the fast-moving car while the song 'Nin maniyarayile...' played in the background. A young girl of twelve or thirteen crossed the road gingerly, her legs slightly apart, holding a bloodstained hundred-rupee note. Acchan, with his silk shirt, his mundu with the broad gold brocade border, the Brut perfume ... snarled, 'You daughter of a whore, you haven't got fucked enough...?' I leapt out of the car and hugged Nisha Chechi close. 'Hey, dude, are you well?' I asked. A dagger pierced my back. Like someone trying to find out if a jackfruit was ripe enough, it tore into my flesh and turned hard.

After years, I had a good, long cry. Cried *bheshaa*, as we used to say.

NINETEEN

A criminal investigation has something in common with the lottery. If you don't believe me, just think about the detective movies or novels you have read. In all of them, there's definitely a stroke of luck that the detective enjoys: a major clue that comes their way. I, too, had one: that 'S'-shaped dagger. Was it wrong of me not to have handed it over to the police? Maybe. I am not someone who's done only the right things all my life – neither have I seen anyone in my life do so. But there's this too, that I have not done every wrong thing that I could possibly have. I just brought the dagger back with me. When I was storing away the things that I'd brought back from my rented house in Bangalore, I removed the dagger from the leather sheath and took a good look at it. My hands trembled. That was to be expected. After all, didn't my father wear it for many years on his waist? Wasn't it stained with his blood?

It was half a century old. I found that hard to believe, but what did I know about the durability of iron? The only scrap I knew of was my own heart. It could, however, change unpredictably – into iron or brass or pure gold or soft, fresh butter. How to compare it with a dagger? The dagger was a neat thing for sure, with its brass-covered hilt. At first sight, it could pass off for an object of art. But the striking

thing was how sharp that 'S' was. I touched the blade. How cold! How
smooth! Like frozen oil, almost. My fingers slid down the edge of the
blade and stopped at the extreme edge of the 'S'. Beautiful and lethal –
the 'S'. When I checked both sides, I found lettering on the hilt. I took
a close look at it. On one side was *'Satyam Shivam Sundaram'*, on the
other, *'Satyameva Jayate'*. The 'S' of 'Satyam', 'Shivam' and 'Sundaram'
matched the shape of the dagger's arch. I felt a thrill. This was not
an ordinary dagger. It was the key to secrets. Was it actually a key,
I wondered, just longer than usual? Which lock opened with this
extraordinarily sharp key? Something lit up in my brain. There was
a secret to my father naming me 'Satya'. My name was related to this
dagger and the person who gifted it to Acchan. I froze and melted at
the same time. I was rapturous. Also terrified.

Just then, Amma came into the room. I did not try to hide the
dagger; she did not frown upon seeing it. 'Uh! That dagger?' she asked.
'Acchan's,' she said, taking it, and ran her fingers lovingly over its blade.
'So, this is its shape!' And we got talking.

'Amma, how are you sure that this is the same dagger?'

'It was exactly like this one.'

'Maybe the person who made that one also made a replica?'

'It was made just for Acchan.'

'How do you know?'

'Don't you remember the emblem of Nityavasantham? Blossoming
branches, it was. With "Nityavasantham Productions" carved in the
middle? And *"Satyameva Jayate"* above it. The lettering was made of
tiny flowers.'

'And what about *"Satyam Shivam Sundaram"*?'

'That's the first movie your father produced.'

'But isn't it a Hindi film?'

'Yes, but *"Satyam Shivam Sundaram"* is a philosophical idea, and
Indians all over are familiar with it – so that phrase has appeared
in stories and movies everywhere. A movie by that name from
Nityavasantham Productions was released in 1962.'

'Back then, Nityavasantham was under Appooppan, wasn't it?'

'No, the production house was your father's idea. He started it.'

'And Acchan wrote "*Satyameva Jayate*" on the banner?'

'Yes, all of it. My father just invested the money.'

'But it was a hit, right?'

'Not just this one, all his early movies were big hits. He had a golden touch those days.'

'Who directed it?'

'Your father himself.'

'Really?'

'He quarrelled with the director and then took over.'

'Did he use his real name as a director?'

'No, he called himself Satyan.'

'Why that name?'

'It was his pen-name.'

'Really?'

'He used it from when he began writing in *Vasanthakairali*.'

'Any reason why he preferred it?'

'Maybe he had one.'

'You don't know of it, Amma?'

'I just know that he had some reason.'

'How do you know that?'

'That was his pen-name, and then he retained it as director.'

'Was it he who named me Satya?'

'No, I did.'

'Why?'

'Well, when I figured out that the man who took the name Satyan was himself the very den of untruths, I named my baby Satyapriya.'

'Did he oppose you?'

'He was a bit rattled. His face went pale.'

'And he said nothing?'

'He asked me why I had chosen that name.'

'And what did you say?'

'When I got pregnant for the first time, he wanted to call our baby Satya if it was a girl, or Satyaprasad if it was a boy.'

'See? Acchan was very fond of the truth, satyam!'

'Yeah, yeah!'

'And why didn't you name Chechi Satya?'

'That's because she was named by your grandfather. I had told him that I wanted to call her Siva! And those days, your father wouldn't oppose him.'

'You were in love with him!' I said.

She recited:

> 'The coil of a deadly serpent
> Would seem but an air-filled pillow
> To the man asleep, the fool!'

'Tell me,' I continued, 'what made you fall in love with him?'

'The name Satyan.'

'And back then, Acchan was quite a looker?'

'Yes, that was important.'

'And a high-caste man?'

'Yes, that too.'

'Were you proud that you married a high-caste man, Amma?'

'I thought that we had gone beyond caste in our love.'

'Wasn't it so?'

'It is the nature of people's needs that shapes the way they fall in love. Some find money important, some find confidence most important, and others just want to have some fun…'

'And what about you?'

'The uplift of the soul! The desire to be wedded to a literary genius! To spend the rest of my life reciting poetry!'

'Was Acchan really a literary genius?'

'He was a good seller.'

'Was he a good doctor?'

'He's never treated me.'

'I have never heard you exchange loving words!'

'The love ended before you were born.'

'Was it still alive when Chechi was born?'

Amma looked jolted. She got up quickly and turned away sharply. I realized my folly then. After some time, I followed her to the front veranda, carrying the dagger with me. She was busy solving the sudoku puzzle in the newspaper.

She lifted her head and seeing me, gave me an enquiring look. 'Uh?'

'Amma, since when did Acchan have this dagger?' I asked.

'Since we got married.'

'But you got married after his first movie, right?'

'We got married in 1966. *Satyam Shivam Sundaram* was in 1962. Maybe he had it since then.'

'What was that movie about?'

'It was about a Nair youth falling in love with a low-caste woman.'

'And?'

'His family comes to know, and they oppose it. He goes to her, weeps, pleads with her. She then agrees to step back, telling him tearfully that she did not wish to become a hurdle in his life's path. His family shoos her away. But he is immersed in guilt and goes in search of her. In the end, they meet, but by then she is married and the mother of two.'

'And?'

'She brings him tea. Asks him, "Will you drink the tea made by us?" He takes the cup. Holds her children close, kisses them. Then he wishes her the very best and goes away.'

'What a story!'

'That movie had a song – the one which goes:

Ethra daaridryamundaayirikkilum
Enthellaam doshangal undaayirikkilum
Ethra viroopanaanennu vanneedilum
Kanthanoraale sharanamullu…

'So, no matter how poor or flawed or ugly he may be, there can be only one husband in your life, and he alone can be your refuge! The female lover sings it the first time, and in the end, the male protagonist.'

'Did you like the movie, Amma?'

'I cried so much seeing it back then!'

'It makes me want to cry too.'

'Don't make fun of it! There was another song in it:

> *Maadavalappile pichakavallikku*
> *Maalikathoppile kilimarathodu*
> *Moham thonni vyamoham thonni…*

'All about how a jasmine vine in a poor man's yard yearned for a tree in the palace garden.'

'Oof!'

' … and she yearned to embrace it, and shower it with fresh white blooms, and make its branches her kingdom…'

'Wah!'

' … But how? Were not the creeper and the tree parted by the wall? The palace and the hut were separated for so long by the wall!

> *Engane pakshe, engane kilimaram*
> *Maalikamuttathaaippoyille?*
> *Madavum Maalikakkettumore mathil*
> *kkettinaal pande pirinjhathalle?'*

'Okay, so what did the poet mean? Money or caste?'

'Aren't both the same?'

'But Appooppan who was low caste had more money than Acchan?'

'How many such people do you know?'

'Is that why we don't see low-caste heroes in movies?'

'Your grandfather wanted to make one on the lower-caste millionaire Alummoottil Channaar.'

'And why didn't he?'

'Because your father didn't think the film would succeed.'

'All right. So Amma, you're saying that Acchan had this dagger long before your marriage?'

'It seems that way.'

'Who might have given it to him?'

'He told me then that some film producer from Madras had given it to him. But that may not be true.'

'Who might have actually given him this dagger?'

Amma looked at me closely.

'I don't know, Satya. I have lived with him for around fifty years, but I really know little about him.'

'Aren't you ashamed to say that, Amma?'

'Yes, indeed, now I am ashamed of it. But I did not feel like that back then. But from where did you get this dagger?'

'I'll tell you about that later. I first need to know if this was Acchan's.'

'I have seen it just once. And noticed just the "S" shape. Yes, it was the same shape.'

'How do you think this reached me?'

Amma threw me a searching look. 'The blade that was used to attack Acchan was produced in court by the police. It was kept in the police locker and later auctioned when the case was dismissed. I am certain that you didn't bid for it.'

'How are you sure?'

'It was auctioned in 1999.'

I went goggle-eyed.

'How did you know that?'

Amma completed another sudoku column and smiled sarcastically.

'How do people get to know of things? I found out!'

'But why did you try to find out about the dagger?'

'One of those days, your father told me – you know how little he spoke – Vasantham, I need your help. Please find out where that dagger used to stab me is now. This was the man who had hardly spoken anything beyond "water" or "hungry" or "coffee" or "medicine". When he spoke so much, I felt sorry for him and found this out through Venukkuttan. It had been auctioned a few months earlier.'

I sat there frozen. Amma was such a skilled knife-thrower. How effortlessly had she thrown that sharp knife right into the centre of my heart!

'If you found out so much, you would have found out who bought it too?'

'S.P. Yadav, Tiger Hill, Dras, Ladakh.'

My mouth fell open.

'Didn't you see? That was the soldier who was awarded the Param Vir Chakra that year!'

'He won the auction?'

'Satya, don't be such a fool! That was a false address. No one cross-checked it then.'

That left me slack-jawed. Amma got up and went inside. I picked up the newspaper feeling light in the head. She had solved the sudoku. I wrestled with the sudoku in my head.

- Acchan's movie – *Satyam Shivam Sundaram*.
- Nityavasantham's banner – *Satyameva Jayate*.
- The name Acchan wanted to give his firstborn – Satya.
- The dagger was auctioned after the war of 1999.
- Chechi was killed in an accident the same year.
- Sriram returned to my life the same year.
- I was trapped in the lab the same year.

After the war, the share market jumped 1,500 points. We could sell the shares that Chechi had bought at a huge profit. Not just the share market, but people's patriotism too reached an all-time high. The caretaker government at the Centre, now incarnate as the protector of the nation at Kargil, became a success, and my life took a big turn too.

Have you ever tried to solve the past like a sudoku puzzle? If not, what a loss! What other means would you have to attain self-knowledge? You'd have realized that life is but a deployment of fixed numbers in fixed columns. You'd see that every figure has its own unique financial value. But there's this thing: Sometimes, two kinds of answers land you in a dilemma. You may have to choose any one. It is not as easy to choose between two truths as it is to choose between two falsehoods. Truths are balloons that can never be fully filled. They are vessels which leak all the time, which can never be full. They are riddled with holes. Some of those holes are so small you can't even see them.

The assassin did not pay me a visit after I returned to my home town. But Inspector Shetty called, and we chatted thus:

'Are you well, Ma'am? No cyclones there?'

'Not yet. But possible.'

'You have forgotten us all?'

'You won't let me forget, will you?'

'Didn't want to! But you don't cooperate enough!'

'What did I do?'

'You could have handed over that thing to us?'

'What thing?'

'The "S"-shaped thing!'

You can guess – my throat suddenly became dry.

'Ma'am, I really don't know why you are so hell-bent on inviting risk!'

'That's a habit of mine,' I replied, and put the phone down, looking as though I had swallowed a spear.

Have you ever had to choose between two dangers? A pity, if you never have had to! It only means that you have never had a chance to measure your inner courage. How simple it is! Close your eyes, imagine that these dangers are currency notes, and run your fingers on them. Choose the one that feels rougher. The advantage of doing so is that if you wrap a python around your shoulders, you will need to fear neither the cobra nor the krait, nor any other venomous reptile! You need to know how to slip out of the python's grip. There's a way – just tickle it. Can it laugh and swallow you at the same time? The poor thing! It, too, would have to choose between the two: either the prey, or the laugh. It can't do both!

TWENTY

Inspector Shetty called again. I was feeling low. How could I not? On one side, there was the cyclone battering us, on the other there was the Biennale. There was unaccounted cash on one side, the currency drought on the other. I was reluctant to talk. That's probably why he asked if I was at a funeral. It irked me, and so I snapped, 'Yes, a house with two down already and two more to go!' He chuckled. 'Ah,' he said, 'you are in a bad mood! Why don't you go out and relax instead of staying cooped up inside?' That only made me angrier. You need cash to go out. The restrictions on how much you could withdraw from ATMs were still on. The papers said that you were allowed to withdraw twenty thousand a week, but who believed the papers any more? It was better to go and find out for yourself. What if you didn't get any money? And what if you got a two-thousand-rupee note? That would be like getting a coconut that cannot be unhusked! Useless, that is. The trouble I had running around the airport with one of those trying to get a coffee!

But I did not tell the inspector any of this. This story was happening at a time in India during which it was pretty unsafe to open your mind to anyone. Especially for freedom-loving women like me.

Even otherwise, you could see only strained faces all around you. How would it be if the entire country was afflicted with piles, ready to burst? No one would utter a word, then, for sure. There would be no street-corner oratory, no announcements, no explanatory public meetings. It was as if people had realized that it was safer to stay quiet and stay put. Just two denominations of the Indian currency were withdrawn, and peace filled the country. Imagine, then, how peaceful it would have been if all the currency notes had been withdrawn! That's why I say – just withdraw all kinds of money, not just notes. If money itself ends, so will all the problems in this world. But who listens?

'What are you up to?' the inspector asked me twice. He was being shrewd. I did not answer. Actually, I was involved in a debate with Sarada Chechi's grandson Paramarth. He was lecturing me on the economic progress of the nation. He showed me a picture of the skylane in Gujarat shaped like the number 8. He told me that they were going to build such skylanes all over the country. The offer to turn in black money and receive half the amount as clean cash was all over the news. I asked him if that was ethical; he didn't like my question. Patriots do not suspect their government, he warned me. He vowed that the prime minister had set up cameras in each and every bank and no one with unaccountable cash would be able to escape. I was in no mood to relent. I reminded him that the prime minister himself had admitted that it was the honest folk who were waiting endlessly in queues for their money. Why do you need cameras in front of banks where the honest folk queued up? I should not have asked him. He did not like the counter-questions. He lost his cool. 'If you can't trust our PM, why don't you pack up and leave for Pakistan, you stupid female?' His love for the nation was that intense. It has always amazed me. When I was his age, the country for me was just the part of it in which I lived. But for him, the nation was the reason to even stay alive. How lofty! I felt inferior before him. But don't think that I am a separatist or an urban Naxal. It is true that once my heart had melted in love with a Maoist who was also a Kashmiri. Also true that once we lay in bed entwined like snakes, telling each other really funny jokes. But did that mean that I would share all his beliefs? Sex is one thing, belief another. And belief is one thing, the business of living life another.

Inspector Shetty was a good man. A true-blue patriot for sure. It would make no difference at all if you replaced his first name, Anurup, with Paramarth. Just that he was a little more compassionate than the latter. A teeny bit, that is. If not, he would not have said 'You are someone who has suffered much'. I did, however, suspect that that compassion was just towards me and not others. Not just to Satyapriya, even, but to a woman of my sartorial habits, employment, and so on. What if my clothes were shabby, I had no job, and no income? What if I lacked the confidence to meet each of his questions with sharp repartee? You need a law to expose not just the sources of people's incomes but also the sources of their pity. It wouldn't be a bad thing to ban some denominations of pity too. There would be no black money, no black marketing there. Such thoughts must have disturbed Inspector Shetty, too, sometimes. He must have wondered who my sharp retorts were aimed at – him, the male race in general, or the police force. Maybe that's the reason why he kept examining me closely. My next conversation with the inspector unfolded like this:

'Ma'am, can't you ask for police protection?' he asked.

'This is a small village. Everyone knows everyone else. Police protection makes no difference here.'

'Do you mean to say that, therefore, there will be no murder attempts on you?'

'Do you mean to say that there will be no such attempt if the police protected me, Inspector Sir?'

'The possibility will surely be low.'

'How long will I have to live like that?'

'Until we find your attacker.'

'If he's going to keep low as long as you offer protection, then how will you catch him?'

'We are tracing him.'

'Since so long!'

'That's because you don't cooperate enough!'

'What more should I do?'

'Did you ever give us any support?'

'What more am I to offer you in support, tell me?'

'You did not tell us that you found the dagger!'

'What if I didn't? Someone else has anyway?'

'Just remember that what you hide, we will surely find.'

'Inspector, I am forty-four years old. If you will be able to find the attacker only if I tell you every single incident that has happened on every single day of my life, then please don't bother.'

'Ma'am, we don't have the time to listen to it all. We're asking you to share just the incidents relevant to this case.'

'I have shared to the extent your questions have allowed.'

'What the hell have you told us? You mentioned that you suspected five people. But not why you suspected them.'

'Why should I?'

'How then are we to complete the story?'

'I didn't know that you were such a fan of storytelling! I'll order you a copy of *The World's Greatest Short Stories*!'

'What for? Your story is far bigger than any of those…'

'But how are you so sure that an untold story is a big one?'

'It's easy to guess.'

'If policemen begin to guess things, how can anyone expect any justice in this country?'

'Not surprising that someone who is in love with a Kashmiri Muslim Maoist speaks this way!'

'Correction – not "someone who is in love", but "someone who was in love" – these are not the same.'

'Okay. "Someone who was in love" until two years ago.'

'So?'

'You were in love once. Search hard, and you'll surely find a pinch or two of that feeling.'

'But what if there's nothing left to search?'

'Nothing's left? Are you sure?'

'I burned it all. And threw the ashes into the sea.'

'You are cruel!'

'Is it cruel to cremate a dead person and immerse their ashes in the sea?'

'What happened that you hated him so?'

'There was no hatred. Is it hatred that makes you cremate a dead one?'

'What was the real reason behind your parting?'

'He was not honest.'

He laughed out loud. 'Great! You expected an anti-national to be honest!'

'He claimed to be a true patriot.'

'Those who kill soldiers and the police can never be patriots.'

'Wouldn't it be more correct to say those who kill their fellow-citizens?'

'I am not interested in your theories. There will be no end to them. Tell me why you split with Samir Sayyid.'

'I told you. Because of his dishonesty.'

'Didn't you already know that he was a Maoist?'

'I did not know that in the beginning.'

'You mean you didn't do any background checks?'

'You mean check his Aadhaar card, passport, school leaving certificate...'

'Not to that extent, but some minimum background check about a loved one?'

'Telephone call list? Or an enquiry at the local police station?'

'All right, you didn't know his background. What if you did? Would you have fallen in love with him?'

'I would have anyway. But I would not have revealed it to him.'

'When did you get to know about his background?'

'After two or three years.'

'But you continued to be in love?'

'Is love something that you can withdraw one fine morning, like the five-hundred-rupee note?'

'Ma'am, you are testing my patience.'

He banged the phone down. I felt relieved, but also sad that my kind of humour made neither Inspector Shetty nor Paramarth laugh. I stepped out into the garden and walked around. The thick money-plant vines climbed the mango trees like fat pythons curling around the branches. The python of memory wrapping itself on the branch of forgetfulness uncurled itself on me in golden spots. It was my pet, so it did not scare me, and I loved it. But it was, after all, a python. Its way of loving was to squeeze hard, to squeeze the breath out of you. In love it could even swallow you whole, digest you into its flesh and blood. In a way it was fun, though almost deathlike in the pain you suffered.

Inspector Shetty called again.

'Sorry for the trouble. I'm just doing my job.'

'The truth is that it would have been better to die that day from the gunshot.'

'I sincerely want to prevent that. That's why I keep asking you.'

'It's been a long time since I met someone sincere. Go on, ask away.'

'Look, can't you hand over the dagger to us?'

'Why should I? I found it!'

'Ma'am, it is an important turning point in this case.'

'Yes, but that's already evident!'

'Why do you say that?'

'Find out for yourself?'

'I did. I have indeed found out several things. This dagger was used to stab your father.'

'Bright boy!'

'Don't poke fun at me! I traced the person who bought it in the auction.'

'You mean S.P. Yadav, Tiger Hills, Dras?'

'That's a false address.'

'But you have to admit – the guy who bought it was a patriot!'

'That dagger – someone waited for it to be auctioned. Bought it with a false address. What for?'

'What is your conclusion, Inspector?'

'See, some criminals exhibit certain obsessions. Like wanting to use the same weapon again. I think the one targeting you is the same person who attacked your father.'

'Yes, but no, too, perhaps.'

'Anyway, he seems determined to use it to finish you off.'

'I don't think so. He used a pistol the first time. And the second time too.'

'Why did he bring the dagger then? Maybe he wanted to shoot you first and then stab you.'

'Tell me, how did you get to know about the dagger?'

'Aswathy Ma'am told me.'

'Oh…!'

I was disappointed. He wasn't as smart as I'd thought.

'Is there any connection between this dagger and Samir Sayyid?' he asked.

'Not to my knowledge.'

'Then get this: there is a connection.'

'What connection?'

My heart trembled. He laughed aloud.

'Ma'am, shouldn't I, too, have some secrets?'

'Yes, everyone should have their secrets.'

I tried to get a grip on my breath. After the call was over, I went looking for Amma. She was in the dining room, speaking to Paramarth. There was a half-drunk cup of tea and the banana leaf of an eaten ada in front of him. He looked sulky. Amma went to the kitchen, and I followed her.

'Amma, you called Aswathy?' I asked.

'She called me.'

'Why didn't you tell me?'

'Did you ever tell me about Samir Sayyid?'

She poured tea into a glass and held it out to me with a plateful of ada and then went away. Stunned, I gulped down the hot tea and scalded my throat.

But what was this minor scalding anyway? I pitied Inspector Shetty. If he had been born to my mother, he would have known how to question me. He would have asked me to describe the day I saw Samir for the first time. Also how I'd met him for the second and the last time. Oh, if only he had asked! I would have described the last time in such detail. Because, as I told you earlier, that memory was my pet python. Golden in colour. Its body covered in large, golden-coloured markings. Heavy, but smooth and cool.

It was in Bhubaneswar. I had gone to Hotel Swasti Park with Aseema to a meeting of Ahmadiyyah Muslims. They had declared that no jihadi or extremist would be allowed in and promised a discussion on women's safety and progressive thinking. The conference hall was full. I took a seat among the veiled women. The other side of the hall was men-only. There were speakers from all faiths on the dais. One of them was on the hit list of Hindu extremists. Another was a woman writer whose life had been threatened by several fatwas. They all spoke of how repressive religion was and condemned extremism and separatism. Then began the question hour. A young woman in a burqa stood up and asked a long question. I don't remember what she asked, but it was another famous writer who replied:

'Child, we know about all that you mentioned from the media. But you must understand: Muslims in India are safer than Muslims in any other country in the world.'

It was then that he stood up. Six feet tall, lithe, firm body. His locks fell carelessly on his forehead.

'Mohammedji, a correction.' He raised his voice. 'Not "Muslims in India". It is "Muslims who are Indians".'

I sat there unmoving, electrified. I recognized him. My heart pounded, and I could barely hear anything else but his voice. The deep truth in it felled me. After some time, I saw him step out. I ran after him, not even telling Aseema. He turned around and looked at me with a tinge of suspicion.

'Hello!'

'I am Satyapriya, a Hindu who is an Indian.' I held out my hand.

'Hello!' He smiled and took it. 'Samir Sayyid. A Muslim who is a Kashmiri.'

I kept his hand in mine. We walked into the street, hand in hand. We walked till Sachivalaya Marg through Nandankanan Road. His hand was smooth, cool and strong. Like a python curled on a branch. I picked it off the branch and wrapped it around my neck. It strangled me. The truth was that I, too, was a python. I, too, wrapped myself tightly around him, suffocating him. Hindu or Muslim, a python is a python. What happens when two pythons coil their bodies around each other fiercely? What can possibly happen? After a while, they will tire. And then slip off each other. That's natural. But there's one thing: the pain of separation will be unbearable. It's better to die, one would think.

I was soaked in sweat by the time I finished the tea. I came out to the veranda, pulled a chair, sat down. Paramarth glanced at me suspiciously.

'Who were you talking about?'

'A friend.'

The acerbity in his tone amused me.

'What's his name?'

'Samir.'

'Muslim?'

'Yes.'

'What's your connection with a Muslim?'

'Yeah, there's something.'

I liked the confoundment on his face. It was hard not to laugh. I went off to my room to hide it, buried my face in the pillow, and chuckled. Paramarth was keen to know how I was related to that Muslim. I was keen to piece out the connection between that dagger and Samir. Only two people could tell me that – either Inspector Shetty, or Samir himself. I pictured meeting him again. Detective work was fun indeed. My hands tingled. How long it had been since I had taken the python off the branch and put it around my neck. My python, I miss you, boy!

TWENTY-ONE

I think the police, too, were hell-bent on doing something, else why did Inspector Shetty hurry to Odisha immediately after? He sent me a message: 'Ma'am, I am on my way to Bhubaneswar.' It shattered my peace. What was his intention? Avid interest in a murder attempt, that, too, of a Malayali? One possible answer was, of course, Aswathy's pressure. I tried to believe that. But it was not easy. Something felt wrong. Aswathy had never spoken with me directly about this. I went to bed feeling acutely uneasy. And barely had I closed my eyes when a terrible nightmare descended upon me. That I was stabbed with the 'S'-shaped dagger! I leapt awake in fright. I saw Amma lying next to me, watching me intently.

'What a terrible dream!' I sighed and moved up close to her. She ran her fingers through my hair.

'Everyone dies some day. Why are you so afraid?' she asked.

'How can I not be? You passed around the information that I had the dagger!'

'Shouldn't you have told the police?'

'But telling people that I have the dagger puts my life in further danger, don't you know?'

'Tell me, these days, aren't all lives endangered?'

'I just cannot make sense of your mind, Amma. What is it made of?'

'They say that some kinds of stones are made from my mind!'

'Aren't you a mother, Amma?'

'Will I cease to be a citizen or an individual because of that?'

'Tell me the truth – you know him, don't you?'

'Know who?'

'The man who's out to kill me?'

'Tell me his name. Let me see if I know him.'

'You know perfectly well that I don't know his name.'

'Just tell me his address or native place!'

'You enjoy irritating me, don't you?'

'Show me his picture, then.'

'Even I haven't had a good look at him!'

'Then how am I to say if I know him or not?'

'But you have some idea about who he is!'

'Smart girl! I am proud of your sleuthing skills!'

'Are you teasing me?'

'Never. It's true – I do have a feeling about who he may be.'

'Then why didn't you tell me?'

'Because I wasn't sure enough to tell you about it.'

'Can you be a bit more clear?'

'He's related to your father.'

'In what way?'

'Through a woman he had some relationship with.'

'Weren't there many women who fit that description?'

'I mean some kind of emotional connection – not sexual.'

'Love?'

'Submissiveness. Or dependence.'

'That is, a woman Acchan had some sort of dependence on?'

'That's what I feel.'

'Would she have given him this dagger?'

'Think about it, it feels like a possibility.'

'Is such a dagger available in the market?'

'No. I am certain this was custom-made.'

'So, made exclusively for Acchan. For what? His own protection, or to threaten someone?'

'Can't it also be to murder someone?'

'What do you mean?'

'I just meant that there could be reasons we aren't aware of.'

'So, Amma, according to you, the story of this dagger has to do with the mysterious relationship between Acchan and an unknown woman.'

'Yes, one that began in 1962, or before.'

'Because that's the year in which he directed *Satyam Shivam Sundaram*.'

'The word "satyam" was crucial in that relationship.'

'In which relationship is that word not crucial – the truth.'

'We can't be sure right now what's crucial here: the word "satyam", or the name "Satya"!'

'Inspector Anurup Shetty thinks that the dagger is following me!'

'Maybe. Do you believe that this attacker waited till the note ban to attack you?'

'I most certainly don't.'

'He was after you since long.'

'If so, he must have pursued Chechi too?'

All of a sudden, Amma fell silent.

'Go to bed,' she said. I hugged her and lay down again.

'Amma, please tell me. Was Chechi's death a murder?'

She did not answer. I heard her swallow something.

'Amme, please...' I begged her, my voice breaking.

But she did not say anything. She could have just said a 'yes' or a 'no', but she did not. After a few seconds, though, she let out a sigh.

'It all began to go wrong after that foolishness...'

'What foolishness?'

'With all that ... wrist-cutting that day ... Was it not foolishness?'

That question then fell on my head like a bolt of lightning. When Appooppan had objected to her marrying Acchan, Amma had slit her wrists – she was referring to that. But there was a meaning which she did not intend. It was that which shattered me. What if a two-wheeler rides over your chest at full speed? That was the pain I felt. How could I fall asleep after that? Was Amma trying to say without really saying that I was responsible for Chechi's death? I am the one who raised that python of usurer's debts. So we were spared the cobra, the krait and the viper. So? What was the use of that?

Being in debt is a state of mind. It reduces your humanity. In my experience, it is not merely an exchange of cash. Someone gives you money in the form of currency notes. In return, they expect you to gift them a share of your dignity. It is not granted any value. The one who lends you money expects you to be grateful and submissive too. Even if you were to repay the entire amount, which lender would give up the expectation of surrender? You may return the borrowed sum, but you will never get back the dignity you pawned. What you give up is lost forever. Actually, it is quite intriguing when you think about it later. But back then, it was not. The only consolation those days was that when I was running around trying to find the money to pay off the interest, even Indonesia, Korea and Thailand were running around to find loans. Sometimes, we, too, are like nations. But whether it is a nation or just Satyapriya, loans are never offered to meet actual needs; they are offered as per one's capacity to repay. And besides, once you are indebted, you may get grabbed, even if the creditor is the World Bank. You'll be dictated, too, on everything – from raising taxes to lowering subsidies to opening markets.

The owner of St Anthony's Chit Funds, Thomachan, to whom Abhilash had abandoned me, was just that sort. He gave me the cash and then fed me curry laced with drugs. I began to feel dopey. He took me to a bedroom. Took out a purse from the pocket of his jubbah and put it on the table. Took off his watch and put it next to the purse. Took off his jubbah, hung it carefully on a shirt hanger on the wall. And then stripped the mundu off his waist, folded it neatly, and hung it up on another hanger. He had to make sure that it was not crumpled; after all, he had to get back to his office and his calculations! I was barely conscious. My wakefulness waned and wavered, like a dying flame in an oil lamp. I was too afraid to even inhale a big gulp of air. What if the flame died? What if I sank into the darkness? St Anthony's Thomachan laid me face up like a corpse on the post-mortem table. My soul watched it with interest. It was moving back and forth on a swing, seated next to Nisha Chechi. When it peered at him from above, the moneylender's eyes and nose and mouth seemed to be quivering. I felt sorry for him. He thought he was very smart. A heavy, gold link-chain was crawling on his pot belly; a long, gold 'kamala' chain was glinting on his hairy chest; the bracelet on his wrist, rings on his fingers – oh, the man was a pot of gold, a golden boy. And his mind, a rubber balloon. He slipped out of his underwear and caressed his tool. He pulled my hand to it and made me touch it. I wanted to cry, but even for that, you need energy, don't you? My consciousness was hanging on some ninth-floor balcony, ready to crash any moment. I held on to its edge and kept hanging with all the strength I could muster.

'My father's two friends...' I began to talk, ignoring my slurring tongue, 'nice fellows. One day we went on a trip. They took my hand like this and put it on...'

'You saucy bitch!' He smiled coarsely. 'And what happened...?'

'One fellow's penis was fractured ... the other's balls got infected.'

Thomachan let out an ugly screech.

'The fellow with the rotting balls died.'

I tried hard to hold on to him though my fingers were slipping off. Not sure why, but the man leapt away. The poor chap was only that big. A scared puss. I felt a mighty wave of pity. The pitiful lowlife, he had money – that was all he had. He knew nothing else, nothing of the world, nothing of life. I decided that I would share with him all I knew. My tongue still slurred but I gave him some advice:

'Uncle, there are two kinds of men in this world. One, men whom women will love even if they are broke. Two, men whom no woman would even turn to look at if they are broke. Uncle, you belong to the second type. If you don't have money, no woman would ever love you. But don't you worry, Uncle. For the time being, you have money. As long as that is there, some women will spread their legs for you. So you should make sure never to lose your money! If that happens, you'll be worse than a mangy cur. See what happened to my father? So many buzzed around him when he had money? And now?'

'Enough…'

He turned away and started to put on his clothes. But I was in no mood to stop.

'I will atone for my father's sins, Uncle! Do you have daughters? If you do, that's a stroke of luck! They will atone for your sins. I'll teach them how to. Introduce me to them, just do it!'

He wrapped his mundu around his waist and wore the jubbah. Didn't I tell you? He'd been sleeping with women whom he paid; otherwise, he was harmless, weak. Came loose easily when I referred to his 'daughters'. I sat up. That too was fun. Like sitting on a mat on top of a rising wave in the sea. I kept swaying.

'Uncle, come, sit near me…' I called to him in an enticing way.

'Get up…' he ordered, impatiently. 'Put your clothes on!'

'No, no, no…' I complained. 'I don't want to clothe myself. Why do we need so much cloth? Bras and panties and slips and salwars and kameezes and dupattas … what's the use of tying it all up, Uncle? Whatever we do, we'll fall for a guy like Abhilash, and he'll pimp us to guys like you!'

I stood up, whirled around. Fell on the cot, laughed like mad, rolled on it. He dragged me to the bathroom, opened the shower, made me stand under it, and left. Menstrual blood flowed between my legs. I wanted to cry then, thinking about Abhilash. The poor fellow, he had died pathetically. Committed suicide right in front of me, pathetically. My one and only lover – dead, expired! I hit my head on the wall – how was I to bear it, who did I have now, I cried. Must go straight to his house after I get out of here, I decided. Must comfort his bloodsucking moneylender of a father. I could feel the sadness of a father whose son was dead. I would console him. I would soak up his sorrow.

Then I saw the shaving razor on the bathroom stand. Without thinking too much, I took out the blade and slit my wrists. I sat on the floor and hugged my bent knees, like I used to as a kid when I'd take a shower. The grey floor turned bloody. That was fun, too, like bathing in blood instead of water. Red, everywhere. Like sitting on a red flag laid out on the floor.

I regained consciousness in hospital. Chechi, Venukkuttan Chettan and Radha Chechi were by my side. The police had filed a case of attempted suicide. Venukkuttan Chettan pleaded with someone and managed to get me out. The way my sister burst into tears that day! I cried too. The glass frame of my self-respect had shattered into a thousand pieces. The shards pierced every pore; it became a sore. 'What happened to your wrists?' Amma asked. 'Just a suicide attempt,' I told her. She did not believe me. Everyone loves a lie. The truth has no logical core. Lies, however, can always be logical. Human beings want to be rational. And reason is what you get used to hearing.

Let all that be. These are not theories that I should be serving now, because we've been talking of an unfortunate woman whose lover had just expired, about her response. There was no reason or logic to it. What logic was there to find in death? If dead, then dispose well. Hold the sixteenth-day ceremony. How long can you delay that?

On Friday, I called Abhilash's hostel. Made sure that he was at home. I prepared myself to visit him on Saturday morning. Fished out an expensive dress bought a long time ago, wore it. Used some kohl, wore a bindi, tied up my hair nicely. I told Amma and Chechi that I had to attend classes at the tutorial college. No questions were asked because I had privately registered for an MA course in Malayalam. I went straight to Abhilash's home. His father opened the door. I stepped in, pulled a chair with an air of freedom, sat down. His father threw a distasteful look at me.

'Why are you here?' he asked me.

'I want to fuck you, Uncle!' I declared. 'I am horny just thinking of you … can't get over you… I don't want Abhilash, I crave you!'

He blanched. I bounded up, went over, and kissed him on the cheek. The fool shivered at first and then held me close. We embraced. In his chair first, and then on the sofa in his office. We rolled on it. Abhilash came into the room. He saw what he needed to see. I got what I wanted. I came out roaring with laughter. I laughed all the way back on the bus.

But it is true that, afterwards, I did weep for a long time. But never did I regret that laughter. For that is how my story became even more eventful. That's why Abhilash was driven by the desire for revenge. He took aim at my sister. She hid it all from me. And then, one day, she left me all alone in a pitch-dark tunnel and took off by herself.

Let Inspector Shetty come back, I thought, sighing. *If* he comes back, that is. I must share this theory with him: 'Inspector Sir, death is like wealth. No one sees it coming. But everyone knows when it leaves.'

Wealth, death, wealth, death – how they rhyme!

TWENTY-TWO

Even if it is for just one day, I want to become the prime minister. Just to privatize currency notes. What fun it would be! Thereon, not just the government but the citizens too would be allowed to print currency notes. Just about anyone would be able to print notes on their own reserve of gold. They could even use their own images and seals! What economic downturn could one complain of then? You'd be allowed only to spend money printed on your reserve, printed by yourself! Would there be tax evasion? No! What about black money or corruption? None at all! But then, there's one thing – it would be difficult to demonetize. To ban someone's notes, that very person would have to be banned first! How to delegitimize people? By finishing them off? Or shutting them up in prison? The easy way out would be to change the person's name. For example, wouldn't it do to simply change the name that I had been known by until that day – 'Satyapriya', that is – to 'Asatyapriya'? That would delegitimize me totally, wouldn't it?

When Chechi changed her name, this was what happened. All she did was add Acchan's caste name. With this, the old Sivapriya was delegitimized. Sivapriya became a higher-level Sivapriya. I learned of it when her passport arrived. I stared at it till my eyeballs nearly popped out. She snatched it from my hand. 'Don't look too long,' she teased. 'The light bulbs in your eyes will fuse!' 'Who are you to change your name? An airport?' Did you get it? Sorry, if you didn't, because it had to do with the year. 1995. The burqa and purdah were becoming more and more popular. The Kolkata airport had become Netaji Subhash Chandra Bose International Airport and Bombay had become Mumbai. The Sahar International Airport was renamed Chhatrapati Shivaji International Airport and Connaught Place was called Rajiv Chowk. The Outer Circle became Indira Chowk. There's no escape once this pride in the past becomes endemic, in individuals or in governments. The bus will run backwards for sure. The next stop will be Caste. Then the Ancient Scriptures. Then Darkness. Haven't you heard, 'the treacherous darkness, of a kind…'

The truth is that it is not the name that changes in a renaming – but something else. Imagine Ahmedabad being renamed Karnavati, or Hyderabad, Bhagyanagar. Is it that simple? That's what happened with Chechi too. Her name changed, but so did her caste. Her future and her consciousness changed. But was it her fault? Wasn't it I who made her get a passport?

That was a decision we had thought about. Not really seeking a route to easy money. Actually, we were seeking an easy route to dignity. It was a few days after I slit my wrists. The wounds had not healed; actually, my veins were infected. Seated on roots that protruded at the bottom of the jackfruit tree near the shed, which was our home, I scanned my life. I counted our debts. Ten thousand as interest to St Anthony's Thomachan; Chechi's salary, just around five thousand. Acchan had been missing his medicines since quite some time then. On some days, our meals consisted of just some black coffee and peanuts. Imagine, then, a young woman, under such circumstances, thinking of debt. A bandicoot would be gnawing at her heart, probably. Have you seen a bandicoot's tunnel? It is really something! A bandicoot is skilled at creating a complete underground tunnel network. Enter one tunnel, and it would have built fifty exit tunnels. If you smoke out one of those, you'll see the fumes billowing out from all four sides, and the bandicoot will leap out of, maybe, the tunnel on the south-east! What would it be like if a bandicoot kept on digging tunnels while the existing tunnels were being smoked out? The smoke would keep swelling inside our breast. The bandicoot would continue digging, paying no heed to us. With the same ease with which it cuts out spreading roots, it would chew up the nerves and blood vessels. You would break out in a cold sweat, even if you remained still. But your nostrils would be filled with the steam from something boiling somewhere within.

I could see our chaippu from there. On the clothes line at the back of the kitchen, my parents' clothes had been hung to dry. I wanted to hang myself with the straps of Amma's worn yellow bra. My eyes bore into the tattered underskirt. Amma came out of the kitchen and watered the greens with the dish water. I saw the hole in her much-used yellow slipper and, through it, fell into a bottomless chasm. The throbbing pain from the infected sore on my wrist spread all over my body. I questioned myself: is this what my mother deserves? She was so bony now, her cheeks sunken, eyes fallen in their sockets. Amma gathered the clothes, folded them, and took them in. I kept my eyes on her. My blood boiled. Hot tears fell. But has anyone won a war with tears? I turned practical. Here's how my mind worked:

That is, all you need to make money is a bit of reckless courage. The sort that lets you leap without a safety net. My father did not have it. He used my grandfather as his safety net. One day, my grandfather was no more. And Acchan landed hard on the ground, right on his back. There's a lesson one needs to learn from it. No safety net is eternal. But that doesn't mean you should, therefore, never jump. It is possible that you'll break your back. So be sure to keep a walking stick with which you'll be able to lift yourself up again. I decided to jump, and I needed a walking stick. Chechi was to be that to me. Who else but her?

That was the beginning of globalization. Even a walking stick had a neoliberal existence then. Nothing was like what it appeared. My debts were around a lakh and a half then. All I had was thirty thousand rupees. In the days that followed, I went to the local library, scoured the papers for numbers of visa agents, called them all, and shortlisted three. They all wanted ten to fifteen lakh rupees as commission. I asked for addresses of their clients. One of them gave me two. Over two weeks, I went to their houses and also sought out others who had migrated. In the end, I found three software engineers who had migrated, and spoke with them about the chances of working in the UAE. One of the visa agents took pity and agreed to provide a visa for five lakh. I bargained with him and brought it down to three.

Was this not to be a reckless leap? What was there to fear? The next day I went to Vyakulamata Bankers. Remember Xavier Panakkal? Acchan's old creditor who came to Vasanthaalayam to get his money? Even if it is a snake, the known one is better than the unknown; it will be less venomous. He did not recognize me – so changed I was, grown so much. And I wore a silk salwar-kameez that wasn't faded yet. I was also wearing a necklace and a bracelet of the latest fashion, on which I had spent ten of the thirty thousand rupees I had; I had had my hair set at a beauty parlour. I rejected the image of the daughter of the paralytic pauper stuck in a shed in the Koyikkal family home; retrieved that of the daughter of Sivaprasad, the film producer, editor and hotel owner. I can tell you from my experience that everything about wealth is just an impression. Abundance, prosperity, glitter, pomp, eminence, elitism – all of it. If we decide that we possess it, we will. If not, we won't.

'Don't you remember me, Uncle?' I asked, walking in like a familiar face. He was surprised. I told him that we had decided to revive Acchan's business and that we needed money for it. A total of twenty lakh. We had sixteen and a half and were looking for three and a half more. 'Ah, kid,' he said, slightly amazed. 'But do you have anything to offer as security?' he asked, even more amazed. 'Yes Uncle,' I replied. 'Land. We can offer you land.' He agreed.

I had in mind the land Venukkuttan Chettan had bought in Kakkanad with the money Amma had given them. I went to

Venukkuttan Chettan's house; he made no objections, and readily gave me the deeds. In three months, Chechi got her visa. This thing, economics, is a game – a game of dice between reality and the imagination. A kind of conjurer's trick. If you are alert, you may observe the feather hidden in the shirtsleeve or the coin stuck on the back of the palm. Only when we gain that level of alertness can we escape. What can one say – except that we need vigilance, more vigilance. And that is in short supply.

Anyway, I pulled out the visa and offer letter from my frayed shirtsleeve that evening and waved them in front of my family. Amma's eyes bulged in surprise. We shared the following thoughts afterwards:

'Satya, this is a risky game.'

'All games are like that, Amme.'

'You are throwing your own life into the ring!'

'It's you who read me the tale of the hat seller and the monkeys. To get back his hats from the monkeys, the hat seller had to throw at them his own hat.'

'What if you lose both?'

'I'll get a few hats from somewhere else and throw them again!'

Amma lowered her head and was silent for a few moments. Then she said: 'Now, besides the lakh and a half, we have to pay back another three and a half!'

'Amme, in business, there is no such thing as debt, there's only capital.'

'How are we going to get rid of this, my dear?'

'With profit.'

Amma fell quiet and just stared at me.

'Very brave indeed!'

'Would that be more reckless than your decision to marry Acchan?'

She did not ask me anything more. We kept it all a secret. No one at Koyikkal knew. By that time, we were hardly on talking terms and our interactions were limited to petty quarrels. Chechi even packed her bags elsewhere – in Venukkuttan Chettan's house – and left for the airport from there. He borrowed a friend's car and drove us himself. Radha Chechi and Aswathy too came with us.

Before she left for Venukkuttan Chettan's house, Chechi hugged Amma and wept. 'Persia-bound lady! And in tears?' Amma teased her.

'You don't love me, Amma!' she complained.

I was the one who was tearful. I ached like a mother who had to abandon her daughter. Only in that moment did I realize that I loved Chechi like my own child, my little girl. We lay hugging each other on the cot that Amma had gifted Venukkuttan Chettan. 'Chechi, Chechi...' my heart howled. I was an orphan now. I feared that if I took my eyes off her, she would fall into some danger. I cautioned her many times that there would be many good-looking Arab men around and that she should not flirt with them. She laughed through her tears promising to marry only 'an Indian and a Malayali'. How could I have even guessed that she had my ex in mind? She was probably feeling guilty, and so, cried some more. I tried to make jokes and comfort her. 'After a year we expect to see you with a big suitcase, dark glasses, and a silk sarong with large yellow sunflowers printed on it! Get a big music player, let us shatter the eardrums of the Koyikkal folks! Flood the place with Chinese silk saris and full skirts!' She should have laughed at such words, but she didn't. How could she? With a python around her neck, how could she?

She was to work with an American company. She was paid six thousand dirhams a month. The exchange rate was nine and a half rupees per dirham. The following month onwards, she began to send us money: thirty-six thousand per month, for six months. Even after paying St Anthony's ten thousand and Vyakulamata twenty-three thousand as interest, we had two and a half thousand. It was enough those days. Only that we could afford just rice gruel. But we ate three times a day.

When it looked like we could finally stretch our backs a bit, came the next explosion – on the pretext that I had polluted the well when I was menstruating. They covered the well and put a lock on it. We had to carry water back from a house in the distance. My shoulders were strained and calloused from carrying the water. But within a week, Kochappachi got a boundary wall built around the house with a gate in it and put a lock on that too. We couldn't get out of the yard into the alley to go fetch water. I had to jump over the gate with the water pot, fill it, then bring it back, hand it to Amma over the gate, and jump back in.

One day, my father's younger brother paid us a visit. He was distressed to see the locked well and the gate. He tried to reason with my aunt and her husband but failed. 'Why don't the three of you come and stay at my place?' he suggested. The upper storey of their house was vacant. He said that we could stay there. Amma was reluctant. I was eager, though. I had had enough of jumping over the gate!

'Amme, after all, Kochacchan's invited us. Let's move there?' I asked.

'No, let's complain to the police that our mobility and access to water have been taken away.'

'You are so simple, Amma! You know perfectly well that Bhasi Maaman will just bribe the police and put an end to the matter!'

'Then we'll go to court.'

'Indeed! We are sitting on a pile of money! No problem paying the lawyer!'

'It's not wise to move, Satye. Don't forget, we have the right to stay here until your father's death.'

'Is your plan to stay here until then, Amme?'

'I think it's wiser to stick on for the time being.'

'I feel the opposite. We must move soonest...'

'Where to?'

'Kochacchan's house.'

'That's a foolish mistake. Do you think Soman's invitation was sincere? It's most probably a conspiracy – his sister and he are in on it together. They want us out, and that very moment, they will demolish this chaippu.'

'Will Kochacchan wilfully take the burden on his head?'

'They'll make things so difficult for us there, we'll be smoked out.'

I thought she was right. But before a week was over, when I was away at the tutorial college for my classes, Bhasi Maaman and my aunt attacked Amma and Acchan. They forced their way into the house, smashed our things, pushed Acchan off the cot. Bhasi Maaman grabbed Amma and tried to disrobe her. When I returned in the evening, Amma was packing our things.

'Okay, in that case, I am not going to move!' I brimmed over with anger and hurt. 'I want to see what the hell they will do!'

'No, Satya – a woman who watches her husband disrobe another woman – that's a dangerous type … capable of anything.'

My blood boiled. 'You've given up so easily, Amma!'

'A small withdrawal to avoid a massive defeat, that's all.'

My hands tingled; I wanted to burn down the Koyikkal house. But what could I do? I was helpless from carrying huge debts that hung from my limbs like heavy rocks. And from carrying Amma who carried my paralysed father on her head.

The next day, we moved to my kochacchan's house. It was on the north-side boundary of the Koyikkal family house, a newer building with a concrete roof. We were moved to the half-finished second floor, which they had planned to rent out. We had to climb up the spiral staircase made of iron outside. We had to carry water up too. There was a hall that included a small room, a cooking area, a dining space and a bathroom – that was all. The very first day there I realized how comfortable we had been in the shed. It was much easier to get water leaping over the gate.

Acchan's and Amma's cots had to be placed in the same room which included the cooking area. Our things had to be stuffed in the tiny space. The fumes from the cooking fire choked Acchan. It was awfully hot all day. My back nearly broke carrying water up the spiral staircase. I began to worry when Amma climbed down the staircase to wash our clothes and hang them to dry. The instructions we received grew by the day: switch the lights off by nine at night; make sure that the water does not spill while carrying it up … And, when Amma took our soiled clothes down to wash each day, they began to add their underclothes and nightgowns and lungis to her pile. I would be reading something, and a bunch of commands would follow: 'Satya, run to the shop and get a kilo of sugar!'; 'Go soak some tamarind seeds for the cow!' … Two weeks passed. One night, I hung on somehow until my parents were asleep. Then I sat up on the mat in the middle of that tiny room and pressed my face on my bent knees. I did not intend to cry. Amma had instructed that I should always look happy and that was on my mind. But as I sat there, it happened by chance, like the way my feet sometimes slipped on the way up with two buckets of water on the winding staircase. The water spilled. My knees were soaked. Then Amma came and sat beside me in the dark. She held me close.

'All this want and trouble will end,' she whispered. 'My darling girl, please don't let your spirits fall with all this…'

I leaned on her and struggled to control my sobs.

'Don't you worry. I'll go to our family home tomorrow, to my brothers.'

'What for?' I asked, wiping my eyes and nose on my nightgown.

'I'll go fall at their feet.'

I felt a blade pierce my heart.

'In that case, we could have done that long back, couldn't we?'

'The poor have to act like the defeated if they want to win!'

Oh, that night. Amma and I in the dark, alone. From the other room, Acchan's laboured breathing. A dreadful heat was cooking us from within. Outside, the sombre cries of owls and night-birds. It was just murkiness, everywhere. A treacherous murkiness.

But anyway, Amma was saved the trip to her brothers' homes. They came over. Her oldest brother accused her of selling him poor-quality gold and claimed that it was not their mother's. The middle brother complained that the sale of our house was a loss and that he had to lose face before his brother-in-law. Amma listened to all of it quietly. She leaned on the cot on which Acchan lay, with his legs covered with a thin sheet, in that room that stank of Dettol and phenyl. My heart laboured and I could not bear to look at her in that crumpled and unstarched sari, her sunken cheeks, neck-bones sticking out. She raised her haggard eyes in between to look at her siblings and saw only contempt there.

'Are you studying anything now, eh?'

That was my mother's oldest brother who once climbed trees when I told him to do so, and played elephant with me, going down on all fours for me to ride, delighting in my laughter. His question dripped with disdain.

'No. I am trying to get a job.'

'What job?'

'Domestic work – in the Gulf.'

'Excellent! To shame everyone in the family, uh!'

'Won't it be worse if we die starving here?'

'Oh, look at her! She's being sarcastic! Girl, if you are starving now, am I responsible for that? Or is it because of my brother? It's all because of this one bugger, your father. Who did our father give all his wealth to? Who got Vasanthamaalika and Nityavasantham? Did this woman suggest back then – let my brothers have a share in this wealth too?'

'Why say this now, Valyanna?' Amma asked. 'You should have raised it when our acchan was alive.'

'Why should I have? You should have known. But when have you been considerate to us? You were so full of yourself even as a one-year-old! Do you know, Acchan got me a Hero pen when you were that age? You threw a tantrum to take it from me and then broke it!'

'I seek your forgiveness for this terrible sin committed at the age of one.'

'Anna, not just to you,' Amma's middle brother began, 'what all has she done to me? How many beatings has she got me from Amma, such a horrible sneak she was!'

'I ask for your forgiveness too, Kochanna.'

'Indeed! Who needs your apology! Just leave us alone at least now, that's all we want!'

'Satye,' Amma turned to me, 'go inside, and study.'

When I turned around to go in, I heard her tell them: 'I'll be grateful if you closed the door on your way out, Annanmaare. I have to wash this man's clothes.'

She gathered up the clothes and went downstairs. I stepped into the small room. For some time, it was very quiet. When I came out, Acchan was alone. Tears were flowing from the corners of his eyes. I felt nothing. But I wiped them anyway, gave him a sip of water, and turned the table fan towards him. He lay with his eyes closed. His bony chest rose and fell. His form and face had changed totally. Someone must study the link between wealth and a man's physical height. When he became a pauper, Acchan shrivelled. He was always curled up, a small person now.

I told you, the year was 1995. There were many STD and ISD booths then. I called Chechi. I lost it when I heard her voice on the other side. I whimpered. 'Find a house on rent right now,' she ordered. I went to Venukkuttan Chettan. He looked everywhere and found a few. I liked two of those. Especially a house that a college lecturer had put on sale, called 'Ponmana Illam'. We took it on rent and moved in. After some time, Chechi bought it and renamed it 'Vasanthaalayam'. It was when we went to register the sale that we discovered that she had changed her own name – to 'Sivapriya Abhilash'. I was stunned. As usual, she hugged me, cooing 'Sorry! Sorry!', vowed that she had meant to surprise me. The imp! She did not reveal the true surprise then – but it was hardly a surprise; it was a shock.

Why say anything more? I alone was unable to change my name. So nothing about me changed. I would think about the changed names sometimes. Did they stay the same? Or were they changed by the new governments in power? The truth is that I always felt a niggling fear that governments would take for themselves the power to name citizens, just like they hold the power to print currency notes. It's just a

matter of setting up a department to approve or reject names. Just make
a poet who's a politician the minister-in-charge and entrust the duty
to a literature-crazy IAS officer. The taluk and village officers in every
constituency would be responsible for giving names to people. What
name would they give me? Asreekarapriya, as in 'Inauspiciouspriya'?
Or Mithyapriya, as in 'Falsehoodpriya'? But that wasn't the thing
that bothered me. I was really concerned about whether changing my
name from 'Satyapriya' to 'Falsehoodpriya' would also mean that all my
truths would instantly be converted to falsehoods too. If my old name
was banned and a new one was still pending, would I remain? Would
I exist? Would I still be a citizen?

~

I was stirred so badly that day that all this surfaced – because of the
exchange with Inspector Shetty. I called him when Amma went to
meet Venukkuttan Chettan. He was in Bhubaneswar.

'What news?' I asked him.

'A lot,' he said, sounding amused. 'Tell me what you wish to know,
and I will tell you.'

I wanted news about Samir but did not have the strength to utter
his name. Therefore, I just asked, 'Any idea who bought that dagger in
the auction?'

'Ma'am, do you know someone called Jivesh Kumar?'

'No.'

'A man by that name used to work in S.P. Yadav's Delhi home.'

'Did he buy it?'

'That's what we suspect.'

'The Yadavs don't know his address?'

'He left them, found another job.'

'Where did he go?'

'No idea. But they did run into him once afterwards. He was driving
a taxi – but wasn't dressed like a Hindu any more.'

'Which means?'

'That he had converted.'

'Then his name would have changed too?'

'Yes, that's understood. His name was George then.'

'Where is he now?'

'I found out through a friend. He discovered the place this fellow was renting and also the church where he preached. They said that he quarrelled with them, packed up, and left. When they saw him last, he had a long beard and a round cap, and was cutting shawarma at a restaurant!'

'So, he converted again?'

'Yes, his name now is Akbar Ali Muhammed.'

'And? Where is he now?'

'That's the fun thing. According to our sources he reconverted to the Hindu faith in a temple in Karnataka.'

'He could've tried a few more religions!'

'But that's not his aim, is it?'

'Then?'

'Ma'am, he's changing identities. A religious affiliation is an identity. What better way to wipe out an existing identity?'

I was dazed. My brain was flooded with a blinding light. Inspector Shetty was talking about my would-be killer. He wasn't just changing his name but also his faith. And that marked his citizenship too.

~

Even if it's just for a day, let me become the prime minister! I'd then ban people's names here and replace them with registration numbers. What fun that would be! One citizen, one number. The numbers will be unique to each individual. What would we need Aadhaar for, then? Why would we need a Citizens' Register? Second names indicating caste or faith?

TWENTY-THREE

There ought to be an assassin if this is to feel like a life. Someone you'd be waiting for. Now you'll ask – then why not just fall in love with someone and keep waiting for them? Naturally. The unsuitability of lovers is their predictability. If a lover is a firecracker, the assassin is a landmine. Where is he hiding? When will he explode? That suspense – that's the assassin's plus point. Without suspense, what would life be?

Anyway, I had plenty of it for sure. There was no sign of my assassin. But my thoughts were all about him. Even small noises scared me; silence, though, was worse. I imagined menacing footsteps at night. Losing patience, I sometimes opened the windows and examined the yard under the light of a powerful torch. Where the fuck was this man! A fellow who'd chased me right until I reached this town? He had totally disappeared after I reached home. What could be the reason? I was almost crackling and burning inside from all the apprehension and anxiety, enough to make me want to scream. Of course, there was no one but my mother to hear me out, but she had long declared my agitated jabber as invalid as the demonetized notes. But I had to share it with someone, so I went to her with two cups of coffee. She was reclining on the easy chair in the veranda, waiting for the newspaper boy. It was pleasantly cool. The sky was a fine blue; in general, the greenery seemed to be thriving. She was pleased with that cup of coffee. I sat on the floor, leaning against the pillar. We sipped the coffee and got talking.

'I have no peace at all, Amma…'

'Not just you, nobody in this world…'

'A joke for you! I am almost dead frightened!'

'Fear, happiness and sorrow are all a part of this life.'

'Yeah, you can proclaim that. The assaulter's not after you.'

'Actually, he could have finished me off very easily. Wasn't I all alone here?'

'Why doesn't he try to kill you, Amme?'

'I can only think that he has nothing to gain from killing me.'

'How come he doesn't hate you?'

'Maybe, in his judgement, I don't count?'

'Or maybe because you are old…'

'Who the hell's old, huh?'

'Me, of course.'

'Uh, forty-four isn't old.'

'My friends' daughters are all getting married!'

'Now *that* should have been banned before the notes!'

'Is he married – the chap who's out to finish me?'

'If he were, would he have the time to prowl around you like now?'

'But he's been after me since just a few days.'

'Maybe he's sick of his wife. Or maybe he's divorced.'

'Amma, don't test my patience!'

'Or maybe someone in his family fell ill? That makes you pretty immobile, right, somebody in the family falling ill? Like, how long it took me to just pay Venukkuttan a visit?'

'What news there? You didn't tell me.'

'They are well. Just worried that Aswathy doesn't want to marry.'

'Why doesn't she want to marry?'

'Why didn't you want to marry?'

'Because I couldn't find the right guy!'

'That could be her reason too.'

'But no nice men in the IPS?'

'Not good enough for her maybe.'

'Was she home?'

'That's the reason I went there.'

'Anything special?'

'She came down to meet me.'

'What for?'

'To talk about your case.'

'And why wasn't I told about this?'

'Maybe it isn't yet time to talk to you.'

'What did she ask?'

'Some things about you.'

'And what did you say?'

'Things that I know.'

'For example?'

'For example, she asked why you never married.'

'And what did you tell her?'

'I told her that I was happy you hadn't.'

'Are you a mother, Amma?'

'A mother isn't just a mother.'

'Okay, agreed. What else did she ask?'

'About people close to you.'

'And what did you say?'

'That I did not know.'

'Did you not ask her anything?'

'I asked if they had any news about the guy who's after you.'

'Do they?'

'They found his bike.'

'Uh?'

The cup slid from my fingers, the coffee splashed on my clothes.

'H ... how?'

'They located it through some CCTV cameras.'

'Only the bike? Not the person?'

'He escaped.'

'Was it registered in his name?'

'No, it was stolen.'

'That's why he went missing!'

'He was in a hospital!'

'And?'

'His bike hit a car.'

'Aiyo! Is that true, Amme?'

'That's what the police said. Don't know if it's true.'

'He's in a hospital now?'

'He escaped as soon as he regained consciousness.'

'Really?'

'I told you. That's the police's version.'

'Amma, you sound like you don't trust Aswathy.'

'She's in an official position. You can expect sincerity only minus that fact!'

'What else did she tell you?'

'When he disappeared from the hospital, the police got suspicious and checked the vehicle. The number plate was false.'

'But how did the police know it was him?'

'They checked CCTV footage and found out that he was following the car you were in!'

'And now they don't know where he is?'

'No, but when they checked the bag that he left behind in the bike, they found a SIM card. Registered in Odisha. When they traced it, they found that he'd been running a shop in front of the Muniguda railway station for some years.'

'And yet, they don't know his name?'

'The SIM is in someone else's name. He was just using it.'

'Why didn't he, then, kill me when I was in Odisha?'

'That you'll have to ask Samir Sayyid.'

'Wha…?'

'Samir Sayyid. Why, haven't you heard that name?'

'Umm…'

'Who is he?'

'Someone I know.'

'What does he do?'

'Teaches in Delhi, he said.'

'Aren't you sure?'

'I have never seen a certificate.'

'Why, can't he be trusted without seeing one?'

'I used to trust him.'

'Is he from Odisha?'

'No, from Kashmir, he said.'

'What are Kashmiris doing in Odisha?'

'He used to organize the adivasis there against the Advaita Company.'

'If protests were his thing, he could've stayed in Kashmir?'

'No, he'd come to Odisha with a friend – and stayed back there.'

'Why? He liked the place too much?'

'No. The police took his friend. And he was found as a corpse.'

'So the job in Delhi?'

'Lost.'

'That's how he became a Maoist, right?'

'Everybody made him one!'

'Like our old Malayalam communist play – remember? *You Made Me a Communist*!'

'Communist then is Maoist now!'

'And why didn't you become one too?'

'Oh really! And then I would be hiding and starving in the forests and getting bitten by leeches … and then finally the police's guns…'

'The police won't shoot you straight, they shoot from the back.'

'Big joke, uh?'

'You're the big joke, aren't you? Maoist, Kashmiri, and an assassin in between.'

'All of it is your fault, Amme. The day you cut open your wrists because Appooppan didn't let you...'

Amma found herself cornered but did not give up. She recited:

> 'Women in this town
> Turn to smouldering ash, their inner lives
> Seething in unrequited love.'

'That's all right. But what's the connection between Samir and the guy who's out to kill me?'

'Aswathy says that he was one of Samir's chief contacts.'

'I can't believe that.'

'Anyway, he has been after you for quite some time.'

'I wonder if it is so hard to finish off a woman like me.'

'Your time hasn't come yet!'

'The other day you said that he was taking revenge on Acchan. He should have been after Acchan then, right?'

'Your Acchan was bedridden, wasn't he? And maybe he thought that the better revenge would be to kill his children.'

'Amme, if someone's revenge can be had only if they kill the enemy's children, what kind of hatred is that? Where does it come from?'

'What do you think?'

'That Acchan must have hurt their children, or killed them even.'

'Possible.'

'But from his age, that doesn't seem very plausible...'

The newspaper boy's horn sounded then, and Amma ran. For her, listening to my worries was not as important as the pleasure of reading the papers. So I went off to make some breakfast. I prepared some coconut chutney and took the idli batter out of the fridge. Soon, the idlis were getting steamed, but in reality, the steam was billowing within me. My heart felt like it was getting cooked in hot steam. If only the killer would just kill me, I wished. Dying seemed much better than living in a state of fear. I was ready to die; I didn't think it to be worse than my present predicament.

Just imagine, what a strange joke it was! A man goes out on a mission to kill a woman; he ends up in an accident. The poor man, what a stroke of bad luck. The thought he might die made me feel a little low. My story would end then. Stories are meant to continue. A story that does not offer another beginning is not a good one. Human beings are like that too. When a woman dies, her story should not end. Instead, a new story should begin. If not, her life would be futile. We, who believe her – our lives, too, would be useless.

I also considered the possibility that the assassin may not really be adamant about murdering me. Acchan was dead, after all. He probably wants me to go mad. That's not going to work, I told myself. He can't do it. Even Samir could not. I had loved him so, but no. The question, however, was – what was Samir's connection with my would-be killer? Did Samir know that he was aiming for me? Did Samir help him? Or was he really using Samir? For him, Samir was probably just a bridge to reach me. Ah, who knows? There was something for sure. Else, what was the meaning of Inspector Shetty's claim that there was some connection between the dagger with the curved edge and Samir? I felt hot, cooked. The steam seemed to be emanating from all over me. I was a cooked piece of meat. To calm myself, I called Inspector Shetty. My conversation with him went thus:

'Inspector Sir, how's the investigation going?'

'I am enjoying this case, Ma'am. Retrieving your life through the paths that you walked.'

'And what have you retrieved so far?'

'Little things. A red kurta, a CD player, music CDs, a watch with an image of Mao…'

'So the woodcutter's ended up sweeping the dry leaves?'

'The tree's life story isn't in the wood but in the leaves.'

'I pray that a mighty wind blows.'

'The wind reads the leaves as it blows.'

'Has the policeman become a poet upon reaching a forest?'

'How can I not become one in this tree house? Is it not the nest of love?'

That shook me a bit.

'Are you there, then?'

'Yes, right here – in your secret hideout.'

'Didn't you find anything other than the kurta, the watch and the other stuff?'

'Two lakh rupees too.'

'Lucky!'

'What luck? These are worthless demonetized notes! The dry leaves are worth more.'

'Like my love!'

'Yes, serves them right for not depositing them in a bank and stowing them away in a tree house!'

'The tree house was their trusted bank at that time.'

'Only that the banker shut the bank down and went off to Kashmir.'

My heart grew steadily dim, and then the darkness fell. If Samir had disappeared into Kashmir, then how to find him? I wanted to cry. I remembered the tree house. The expanse of green below. The smokestacks of Advaita in the far distance. The emaciated teenagers cooking rice and dal in large vessels in the deep-forest camp. I saw the local people protest against Advaita. Some of them lay dead in the forest. My head ached. That map terrified me. It was like a picture of my own life. On one side, the creditors, on the other, lovers. On one side, parents, and on the other, the past…! That place should have been named after me. And I, after it.

After a long time, I took my heart out and examined it casually. The poor thing, it looked like a lion torn apart by many hyenas. Its skin scratched out, flesh loose, scrawny, with its bones showing; worm-eaten, with flies buzzing around it. I could hear only a faint heartbeat. That was of the suspense that kept it going always, then and now.

TWENTY-FOUR

Moving to a rented house was a great relief. I even wondered if the new house wasn't too big. Two rooms, a living area, a large hall, and a big kitchen, besides which were a storeroom and work area. Good god, big enough to play football in! I could not sleep that night. I did not know if this was just a dream or reality. What if I woke up and it was all just a dream?

But the relief was momentary. In two weeks, the accountant from St Anthony's came looking for me. He said that we had to repay the loan at once. I did not know where to find such a big sum. Would we have to leave this house too, I panicked. We were given two weeks' time. They would produce the cheque in the bank after two weeks. If it bounced, they would file a complaint for cheating. I feared that Amma might overhear us. So I said yes, served him tea, and sent him off.

That was a Monday. I decked myself up, set off. Wore an old silk sari of Amma's and a black blouse. Tied up my hair properly, put on some make-up. Amma came into the room and asked, 'You are no longer scared of getting into debt, are you?'

'Oh, even whole nations are desperate to get into debt these days!'

'Who's going to lend you a lakh and a half?'

'I won't ask for such a big sum – just ten or fifteen thousand. It's easier to repay the principal and interest together then.'

'From how many creditors? Many?'

'Yes, many.'

'You don't go – let me.'

'What's the difference, Amma? Between you going and me going?'

'A lot.'

'Just one. If you go, I have to stay back to take care of Acchan. That's inconvenient for Acchan and me. Better you stay here, and I go out and beg. Besides, they won't give you the money. You need a lot of self-confidence to borrow money.'

'How come you are so full of self-confidence?'

'Born out of experience!'

I hid a sigh that was born from the memory of my blood flowing on the floor of Thomachan's bathroom. Blood that flowed from between my legs and from my wrists. Blood that you could not tell apart when it coalesced. Actually, it rid me of my disgust for blood. It was that self-confidence that sent me to St Anthony's now. I was sure that we could postpone the deadline to later. But things seemed to go awry when I reached the office. Something didn't smell right – people were milling about in the yard. I thought they were waiting for the lots to be taken. But the grille was locked. I asked someone if the office wasn't open yet. 'Did you come for the chit money?' he asked. His eyes were welling. 'The bastard's gone. The chit company's busted!'

My immediate feeling was one of peace. Of joy that he would not bug me for his money. But the memory of his family surfaced. I found his address, went straight there. The gate which was locked from inside had been kicked aside. The glass windows were smashed. A jeep parked there had been vandalized, its tyres ripped apart and windows broken. I rang the bell. No one came. I went behind the house and sat in the work area of the kitchen. After some time, a woman opened the door from the kitchen. She had come out to throw away some dish water. She jumped upon seeing me.

'I want to see the master's wife,' I said. My silk sari and youth helped. Though a little suspicious, she invited me in.

The family was on the upper floor. They were huddled together on a large cot, exhausted from weeping. His girls were about my age; the son was barely five. He sat playing with his abacus and telling himself stories. They started up seeing me. 'Please don't get up,' I said. I could not help but be gentle. The wife burst into tears. He had been lured into bad investments – goat, teak, manchiyam deals. Those fell through. He'd gone missing since the past ten days, no one seemed to know where he was. I caressed the head of the little one who stuck his finger into a nostril and stared at me with his large eyes wide open. I tried to recall their father's face. But I had hardly seen his face! It was his pot belly and hips that I had seen. And the kamala chain around his neck that kept rolling and the heavy, gold link-chain that kept twisting around to the front. And yes, the gold bracelet. There was the silk jubbah on a hanger in the room, probably the same old one.

When I came out of the house, I was drained. Who wouldn't be? My throat was parched from the unrelenting sun. The tarred road in front of me lay nearly melting from the heat. Have you ever been on an empty road in the blazing sun, alone? Seen the mirage, which you learn about in school? Have you ever walked towards it soaked in sweat, throat all dry, quickening your pace bit by bit? Have you experienced the sheer helplessness of noticing that no matter how much you quicken your step, the mirage moves further and further away? A pity, if you haven't! How will you then learn that life is like a bluish-red onion with its unending layers? But these layers are the onion's wealth. Its politics is about getting acidic juice into your eyes. Therefore, the sting that brings tears to your eyes is its ideology. Our tears are its message.

I walked on aimlessly that day. The road was lined on both sides with upper-class homes with lawns and fountains. Some had more than one gate, and many walls. That the poor build houses close together, and the rich, with walls separating them, is the world's biggest joke. Wealth creates several outer layers, like around onions; fills them with acid. That's actually out of sheer helplessness. Not just poverty, wealth, too, disarms people.

I needed cash. I had to play the risky game to find it. Confidence is your main asset when you play that game. I chose the house with the leafiest yard. 'Joseph Mathew', the nameplate said. In the height of assuredness, I put together this script: I will ring the bell, someone will answer. Is this Lina's house, I will ask. You're at the wrong house, they will answer. Then I will ask who they are. And thus, meet them. It's an emergency, I will tell them. I came for a loan. They will tell me where to get it. So simple!

But how did it actually play out? Just looking at the face of the middle-aged man who opened the door, my poise broke down. I began to sob. 'What happened, girl?' he asked, astonished. He called his wife. A woman in a white, embroidered nightgown came out. I traced my steps back, weeping. But she stopped me, and insisted that I come in. They fed me. Rice and pulissery, and thoran of cabbage, fish curry. She went to the kitchen and fried a cutlet. Before lunch, they prayed together; their eyes welled. Their prayer over, they wiped their eyes and cracked a few jokes. They asked me nothing. I was struck dumb, nearly. I ate only the cutlet, decorated with onion rings. And got ready to leave as soon as they had returned from washing their hands.

'But you can't leave – without telling us why you came?' the man insisted. I found it hard to face this man with grey hair, a beard, and kind eyes.

'Appacha, I came to the wrong house…' I told him, feeling abashed.

He held me by the shoulder and made me sit on their sofa. 'Why were you crying?' he asked. 'You need money?'

I panicked and leapt up. At that moment, I could not think of anything more shameful than asking them for cash.

'How much?'

I swallowed.

'But you don't know me at all, Appacha!'

'No need to be friends to help another. But let's get to know you anyway – what is your name? Where are you from?'

'My name is Satyapriya. My father's name is Sivaprasad. My mother is Vasanthalakshmi. My father used to own a hotel and a publication in town. He is now a paralytic patient.'

'The daughter of the film producer Sivaprasad?'

'It's all gone.'

'That's not uncommon in life. Yes, things disappear, then they appear, and disappear again. None of this belongs to us. Not even our children. The Lord gives and takes back all.'

'Have you ever been a businessman, Appacha?'

'Ever been? That's all I've ever been! My very life is a business!'

'What sort of business?'

'Many kinds. The last was onion wholesale.'

'How was it? Profitable?'

His wife – her curly hair, tied up, which had barely greyed near her temples – chuckled. I could not make out what her laughter meant, but it definitely hid something.

'Profitable? There's no business more deadly than the onion business!'

'You purchase it directly?'

'From farmers, and resell it here.'

'Is it big money?'

'You can make big money before the elections for sure.'

'Why is that?'

'It is how it is. The jackpot was in 1984. There was a jump in prices. That year, the opposition leaders speaking in the campaign meetings were greeted with garlands of onions! I built this house that year.'

'My grandfather was a businessman too. I never heard him mention onions.'

'You need to learn something about politics for that.'

'You don't do it any more?'

'Not any more.'

'Why?'

'I used to get the goods from Maharashtra. The fellows from whom I used to buy are all gone.'

'Gone? Where?'

'Dead.'

'How?'

'Some poisoned themselves. Some hanged themselves. Some threw themselves in front of trains ... Poison, in most cases.'

'Aiyo!'

'What to say? That's life. Like an onion. Very hard to peel. You'll weep. And when you remove all the layers, what's left?' He sighed, then got up and went inside. I sat there motionless. He came back with two bundles of cash, of hundred- and fifty-rupee notes.

'I have only so much now.' He put them into my hands. 'This is our own money, which we kept for ourselves. Aren't we both old now? We might have needed it.'

I was overcome. My hands shook.

'So much cash ... and you don't even know me.'

'Money belongs to nobody permanently. Today in my hands, tomorrow in yours, and the next day, in somebody else's.'

'I will return it when you need it, Appacha.'

'Hey, please, no need! We don't need much of it. We have enough.'

I had nothing to say. They came up to the gate to bid me goodbye. When, after walking for some time, I turned to look, they were still there. My heart melted and all its impurities were washed away. Not because I had found some money, but because I had a chance to feel grateful. The true debt human beings incur is of gratitude. Debt that can never be repaid.

My next hurdle was to convert that fifteen thousand to a lakh and fifty thousand. I went to the reading room of the local library, scanned the papers. Not to read the news, of course. Why read the news that ought to be read? Those are about things that you experience! Why read news that you need not read? It will only confuse you. For example, the news about the arrival of the Internet was on page one.

The advertisement about Saubhagya Chit Funds, which let you claim the whole amount once you paid the first chit instalment, was on page five. Which of the two was more important to me who paid a sum of thirty thousand every month as interest? Who cared about the Internet? Saubhagya was more important to me.

I did not have to go to the town. Saubhagya was in a new building in the village: four bus stops later, right on the roadside – a room on the top floor. It was run by a Gulf-returnee, Rajasekhar. Curly hair, too strong a perfume, and lots of face powder. Full-sleeved checked shirt tucked into pants. I sat upright on the chair, with confidence. He didn't like it, so I crossed my legs too.

'It's true that you need to pay just a single instalment. But let me warn you in advance: if you fail to pay the interest, it becomes a flat rate. Ten per cent. Also, we take twenty-five per cent of any amount when the sum you take is above twenty thousand. The monthly payment must be in before the fifth of the month. If you're late, I'll send the cheque to the bank. Don't bitch and moan then.'

'That is, if I invest in four chits, you'll take one.'

'If it's fifty thousand, I'll take only eleven thousand five hundred.'

'But what if I join one for a lakh and fifty?'

'Take all three in the second month? Not possible, sister!'

'If I am really your sister then don't take the twenty-five per cent!'

'Girl, you are my sister's age, that's why I called you that.'

'Not "girl". Satyapriya. That's my name.'

'Okay, Satyapriya Madam. Not possible to give the same person three chit amounts. It's not safe.'

'Thanks for the advance warning. I am leaving.'

'That's up to you. I didn't invite you here. But there has to be some decency. What if you disappear with the three chit amounts?'

'What if you disappear with the cash I pay back over three or four months?'

'If I am Araikkal Ramakrishnan's son, I won't do it.'

'That is, you won't do it only if you are Araikkal Ramakrishnan's son?'

'Mind your words…!'

'You're the one who said that you won't disappear if you are the son of…'

'So? You'll insult my father?'

'Mr Rajasekhar, I am not here to discuss paternity. I need a sum of one lakh fifty thousand. I have to repay Thomachan of St Anthony's Chit Funds. He is missing after his Chit Fund collapsed. He's not going to ask me under the circumstances, but I am insistent that I repay the sum. Tomorrow if your chit fund collapses, I will do the same. You'll get your money back. Let us proceed if you can give me the sum for all three. If you can't, then fine.'

That was unexpected. His face went red. He dithered. Thought for a few minutes. Then he said, 'I need your name and address. What is your occupation? I need your employer's permission to attach your salary.'

'I am not working. My sister is abroad, and she sends money every month. But I need one lakh fifty thousand rupees.'

'Are there no older people at home?'

'I am twenty-two.'

'No, your mother or father?'

'My father is paralysed. He has only my mother to care for him.'

'What did he use to do?'

'He was a businessman. Was ruined.'

'What business?'

'Vasanthamaalika Hotel, Nityavasantham Productions, *Vasanthakairali* weekly…'

'Sivaprasad Sir's…?'

'Yes.'

'My god! … Why didn't you tell me this earlier? I used to be the receptionist in your hotel!'

I liked that. In my hotel? One and a half years had wiped out the memories of the hotel and the movies and the weekly. He told me that he remembered seeing me as a child. In my memory, I'd been to

Vasanthamaalika only a few times. I did not remember anyone there except the receptionist to whom Amma had given a hundred-rupee note. And that, too, only because that day was so crazy. Rajasekhar suddenly became very humble. He described how he had joined the hotel after passing matriculation and how, after four years, Acchan had got him a visa to work abroad. He had worked in the Gulf countries for twenty years – first in the UAE, then in Muscat. Then returned home and started this chit fund.

Anyway, everything was for the good that day. He agreed to give me the money. Reduced the interest to fifteen per cent. I gave him a cheque and a promissory note. In a fortnight, I received one lakh twenty-seven thousand and five hundred rupees. Putting together the sum I owed them, I returned to Thomachan's house. His wife called the accountant; he brought my papers. I gave her the cash, took the papers, and got out. But since I'd gone there, how could I not visit Joseph Mathew? I went to his house. It looked different – things seemed to have changed in two weeks. The gate was locked. The front yard had not been swept, it was covered with dry leaves. As I stood there not knowing what to do, a middle-aged security guard peeped at me. 'Is there no one home?' I asked him.

'Oh, so you didn't know?' he asked.

'No, what happened?'

'It was in the papers…'

'What?'

'They killed themselves.'

'Who?'

'The husband and wife.'

A bolt of lightning shot through my body. The ground beneath my feet shook.

'They had kids, both girls. The two sons-in-law were fleecing him. In the end, his business ended up in a loss. And those two refused to help. They sold everything. This house was going to be recovered too.

On the day they were supposed to be evicted, in the morning, the two of them ... It was pesticide.'

He added: 'There's one thing – they were good planners! Had left thirty-five thousand rupees on the table, for the funeral.'

∼

There's a reason why I am recalling and describing all this after so many years. I was going through my old account books. I had written down the sum I owed Joseph Mathew – the fifteen thousand.

> *Went to the office of St Anthony's. The Chit Fund is closed. Went to Thomachan's house. Saw his wife and kids. Their situation was pitiful. Got out of there, troubled, not knowing who to ask. Stepped into a random house I saw. The house of a Joseph Mathew. It was a miracle. That man, who knew nothing about me, gave me fifteen thousand rupees (bundles of 100 and 50).*
>
> *Sum given by Joseph Mathew: 15,000.00*
>
> *Registration fee for three chits at Saubhagya: 750.00*
>
> *Monthly payment: 15,000.00*

Why did I check all this? Because Inspector Shetty sent a WhatsApp message. Amma was visiting Gracie Chechi because it was Laalamma's memorial day. Inspector Shetty sent me an image of a bag. I thought it must be a mistake, but then he sent an image of a small purse, with an old passport-sized photo of mine in its pocket. Suddenly, I remembered and recognized the bag. It was the bag that I had lost when I stepped on to a bus on my way back from the bank. It contained the entire sum that Chechi had sent as a draft that month. That is, the interest that had to be paid to Vyakulamata and Saubhagya.

'Can you tell me when you lost the bag?' Inspector Shetty asked. That's how I began to look through these old account books. '*1996 August 2 – My bag has been stolen. The interest payment to Vyakulamata and Saubhagya has been interrupted.*' I found that lamentation and called Inspector Shetty. 'Where did you get the bag and purse from?' I asked him.

'You are a bright one, Ma'am. Guess?'

'From S.P. Yadav's house?'

'Wow! You're great! But no, not from there. From the house in Karnataka where our man stayed as a paying guest. He forgot a cloth bag. The people there kept it. This bag was in it.' He laughed heartily. 'I am running around in Bhubaneswar for nothing. He's right there, in your place. He is Malayali. And besides, he's known you from 1996 or earlier.'

I could say nothing. The detective in me was making notes.

1996 August – My bag is stolen.

1996 October – Vyakulamata and Saubhagya both ask me
    to return their money.

1996 October – They both come to our house, make a
    scene.

1996 November – I go to the houses of people I barely
    know, asking for loans.

1996 December – Rajasekhar of Saubhagya summons me
    to his office.

I sat there, feeling dull. I have told you already – my life, those days, was exactly an onion. Bluish-red. Not a fruit, nor a tuber, just a collection of skins, layers. Have you ever had the experience of someone peeling your life like it were an onion? Known how it is to have all that you tucked away inside the smooth external layers torn out, one by one? Have you felt the pain of seeing tears flow like blood, eyes burn like they were being scratched out? A pity, if you haven't. Because then you are quite incapable of feeling what my assassin was doing to me at the time. How would you ever understand, then, that the onion was not a mere metaphor now?

TWENTY-FIVE

Life is the art of deflecting attention. It is a mess. Is there any way out of that? No! Today's solution is tomorrow's problem. That is, there's just one way to solve a problem in life: create another problem. When a child comes bawling for a toy, grab his hand, break it. Then the toy problem is solved for three months. Or, divide a problem into sub-problems. Take, for instance, the note ban. One-thousand- and five-hundred-rupee notes disappeared. That, too, overnight. There were folks who asked what the hurry was and why these two were banned together. Idiots. If they banned just the five-hundred-rupee notes, then we would have girded our loins and raised hell, asking if the thousand-rupee note was a bastard or something, to be banned by itself. If the five-hundred-rupee ones were banned, then we would surely have rolled up our sleeves and snapped, 'Did the five-hundred-rupee notes fall through the roof, or were they actually printed by the government?' Finishing off both in a single blow ended both problems. How did they end? With morons pushing and shoving in queues. Banks were destroyed, some people had dizzy spells, others had heart attacks, some others committed suicide. What did we learn? That in order to solve 'national' issues, you must turn them into innumerable 'local' events. That is, turn the rock formation into heaps of granite metal, turn the jungle into piles of firewood.

I am saying this in the light of my own experience. My life was once like this. Something or the other would keep happening every day. Each day would feel like a minute, and each month, like a day. If it was an argument with St Anthony's on one day, it would be a quarrel with Saubhagya the next. The day after, my money would get stolen; and then, Acchan would develop an allergy to his medicines. When that day passed, the motor in our well would malfunction and then the timetable for the MA exam would arrive. The next day, Saubhagya would present my cheque in the bank, the following day, St Anthony's would send a notice, and on the subsequent day, Chechi would come home on leave. Life was a riot! No chance of boredom. That's why I say: To solve one problem, create another. Or divide it into many smaller problems.

That is, back then, I would get out of the house every morning, bathed, decked, and wearing freshly ironed clothes. Only the white mundu gets a seat on the mat! Your clothes should not be soiled, your face, not in the least! The biggest problem those days was of shoes coming apart. Women's shoes, after all. Walk five kilometres, and their lifespan ends. I'd be in a silk salwar-kameez, all done up with eye shadow and lipstick, and climbing the stairs when suddenly – my slipper would have come apart! There! Confidence gone! And then the earth could cease to rotate around the sun and start rotating around the slipper. The challenge of asking for a loan, of not getting it – all that would become minor. The slipper, only the slipper, would be *the* issue. But you could get another slipper and there the problem would end. But a new one would begin. Rao goes, Vajpayee enters. Vajpayee goes, Deve Gowda arrives. When he exits, Gujral arrives. If Gujral leaves, then Vajpayee will come again. When the new one enters, people sigh in the realization that the earlier one was so much better. That's the crux of it.

The truth is that I did not think that Rajasekhar of Saubhagya would file a case. There's a connection that links lender and borrower, like a marital tie. There will be many disagreements, but there will still be a common minimum – the commitment to the system. And so, both sides will try and endure it until they start fearing each other.

My bag was stolen in August. I defaulted on both interest payments. From the amount Chechi sent the next month, I repaid the whole amount due at Saubhagya. Then the payments due at Vyakulamata accumulated. So next month, I made that payment. That made the debt accumulate at Saubhagya. I took the rest of Chechi's money and some that I had borrowed from my classmate in the MA class, Aisha, and invested it in the Japan Life Magnetic Bed scheme. That was in the hope that I could recoup the cash that had been stolen. But it was useless – the mattresses simply gathered dust at home. What more is there to say – Xavier Panakkal of Vyakulamata soon arrived at our doorstep. Amma got to know only then that I was in debt to him. Like from when I was a child, she pinched my arm so hard that the flesh nearly came off. Before Vyakulamata left, Saubhagya arrived. The very basis of economics is that two creditors of the same debtor do not meet. But my times were hard. Both gripped me by the throat. On the third day, Saubhagya's lawyer sent me a notice. Anyone else would have collapsed, but I was glad. The problem of one and a half lakh was over. Now I had to find the three and a half lakh. But then the notice from Vyakulamata arrived. The cheque for three and a half lakh had bounced. The outstanding debt and principal had to be repaid, or the security, Venukkuttan Chettan's property, would be recovered. I would not blame him. I had after all secured that loan with a hundred lies! Didn't it all collapse right before my eyes? This is why I never lie. We do tell so many lies to others, but we resent it when others lie to us.

Those were interesting times. I hardly slept, and was always fatigued. My eyes would be burning, twitching with unease; my eyelids would not close. Soon, something would begin to boil inside my head. Like the massive pot set on a huge open hearth to cook rice gruel for the workers in my grandfather's paddy fields long back. I could even hear the crackling of the firewood burning. My brain was boiling, brimming over. In between, someone would stir it. I could even catch the scent of the new paddy getting cooked. There was pain too. No cooking is possible without some pain, after all, is it? Will the grains of paddy boiling in the pot fail to recollect the coolness and the breeze of the open fields? The crabs in their holes in the ridges, poking their heads out? The white herons, in deep meditation? The manathukanni fish…? The boiling grains will try not to think of all that, but they won't be able to help it. They will remember. Imagine a grain of paddy sitting in the dark, its face pressed on its bent knees. She, who had not seen life. She, who by the age of twenty-four had been slow-cooked and turned soft and mushy, like payasam. She, who desperately wanted to make sure that Amma, who was asleep in the next room, did not wake up. She would keep remembering Appooppan, and the times she spent with him. When they drove around town in his Benz car. That was in some other age, when she did not know want for anything. Back then, she could not imagine the fire in one's belly when one had to beg for the money that was then in somebody else's pocket. She could not understand the sharp tug in the chest when the question of how to repay it arose.

In the midst of those memories, I would grow weak. My heart would wince, desperately wishing to be with Chechi again. I just wanted her near me, I just wanted to hear her voice. Who else did I have? To put my trust in, to quarrel with? To scold, to accuse?

But even then, when she returned and stepped into the house, my mind was empty. She had not let us know of her plans. I had gone to town trying to find a loan again. No one who had any connection with Saubhagya or Vyakulamata would give me any. But I managed to find fifty thousand from one, and a lakh from another. Both were new 'blade' financiers. I had to wait for a week to get the cash. The interest was seven per cent. That was some relief but not enough for sure. I came back feeling thoroughly harried, took a shower, and

Amma served me lunch. I was nearly done eating when I noticed a young woman in a red silk sari open our gate and enter. The ball of rice got stuck in my throat. I had to struggle to convince myself that this was Chechi. She stepped into the house; Amma ran up and hugged her, laughing in delight. I was as still as a statue. It felt as though it wasn't a ball of rice but a huge mountain that I had swallowed. It lay suspended inside my chest. She kissed Amma and came up to me slowly. She held me, but not as firmly as she used to. I froze. It simply did not feel like her. She had changed very much. She was sparkling now, and looked beautiful in the flaming red silk sari. The glow on her cheeks and the redness on her lips were extraordinary. For the first time in my life, I felt wary of her. She took a tour of the house. 'We could have found a better one,' she said, sounding disappointed.

I tried to finish my meal. Amma came close and looked at me searchingly. 'What happened?' she asked. I shook my head to say 'nothing', my eyes welling. Afterwards, when I went to my room, I found the almirah flung wide open. Chechi had pulled out all the clothes, and the ones that I had folded and stacked inside had fallen all around; some were on the floor, some on the bed. She had undraped her sari and flung it on the bed. When I picked it up to fold it, her shoulder bag, which was lying under it, fell to the floor. The zip was open. Her passport and boarding pass had fallen out. I saw that she had boarded from Dubai at 11 a.m. Three days earlier.

I folded her sari, closed the bag, and went out into the veranda. She took a shower and soon came there with a towel around her wet hair, with cups of coffee and plantain fries for us both. I took the coffee, and we began to talk.

'Why're you mood-off, vaave?'

'Tired ... I was in town.'

'For what?'

'I'll tell you. When did you start?'

'Early this morning...'

'How did you come from the airport?'

'A colleague was with me…'

'Male or female?'

'Female…' (She sighed.)

'What's her name?'

'Uh … Anita. Didn't I tell you last time on the phone?'

'What's this trip for? So sudden?'

'I got a visa to work in another company. Just thought I'd make a quick trip before moving.'

'Is there something wrong with the present company?'

'No, this new one offers better pay … and they'll promote me too.'

'That's good…'

I too sighed. How I wished she had given me a hug and kissed me! If only she would ask me, 'Vaave, what's wrong?' – I turned more and more romantic. But we were not in the Romantic Seventies; we were in the Practical Nineties.

'I have arranged to pay off five lakh. We should be able to settle all our debts with that sum, right?' She put it so simply, as she took a bite of the plantain fry.

'No way!' I was astonished. She started.

'What! That won't do?'

I began to feel weak.

'There were some problems…'

'I want to see the accounts. Now!' She jumped up. I was dismayed. I had never seen this side of her. I went in and brought the diary in which I wrote the accounts. I was tottering, nearly. She checked the calculations. She began to ask me about a fifty here or a fifteen there. My accounts were not merely numbers, they were annotations which always mentioned the context and spelt out the meanings.

'So my earnings of a whole month – gone! Right?'

I was on the brink of tears.

'I had come out of the bank and was getting into the bus. Someone snatched it.'

'And you didn't complain to the police?'

'No...'

'Why?'

'I just wasn't brave enough then, to tell the truth.'

'Oho! So you just threw away fifty thousand rupees!'

'Akke, please, don't speak so thoughtlessly.'

'I can't have anything to think about any more. Never thought that you'd do this to me!'

'What did I do?'

'You should have at least thought – she's slaving in the desert to earn it!'

I grew faint. Tears flowed. I could not utter a word. Her voice rose. Amma heard it and came over.

'Look,' Chechi said, 'I sent you two lakh and a quarter in the first six months. Then fifty thousand each month. I have the accounts. Around a total of five and a half lakh. For what?'

'Amma,' she continued, turning to her, 'look, we still have to repay eight lakh eighty thousand rupees.'

'I am responsible for the eighty thousand,' I admitted.

'What about the rest?'

'Don't I have to manage things here?'

'What manage? My foot! By taking a loan on an interest of ten rupees to pay back a loan with an interest of five rupees?'

'All right, you can manage things from now on...'

'She turns a debt of five lakh into a burden of ten lakh and then tells me to handle it all...'

'I'll take care of it. You don't have to send any more money.'

'If I don't, how are you going to repay it?'

'That you don't have to bother about.'

'If that is the case, you could have repaid it all by now, without letting me know of it?'

'My apologies for everything so far.'

I turned around and went back to my room. I could hear Chechi grumble on. Then Amma's voice rose.

'Sive ... she's borne huge debts since she was just twenty-one. It is she who went out to beg for loans. That's because she didn't want us to grovel. She could well have looked away, stayed put. Then I would have surely had to try! Even now, to hold my hand out to a stranger for anything makes my flesh creep. When I think of how she bears it, my heart breaks. Do you know how long it's been since she slept properly? Her face is so pale – it's been ages since it looked bright!'

A wave of tears surged and crashed against the walls of my throat. I fell on the bed face down so as not to break into pieces.

'Please don't try to justify her, Amma. How dare she play around with eighty thousand, a loan, and on such frauds as the Japan beds? It's all because I sent the money, is it not?'

'The poor thing, she was probably looking for an easier way to repay the debts. She's also lost money in a money chain. There are all sorts of people who try to make an easy buck. Some are greedy, others are just unbelievably desperate.' Amma's voice faltered.

'Oh ... you don't know what she's been up to ... God, my skin crawls!'

This time Amma lost her cool.

'If you are so ashamed, Siva, you need not live here. You are the Gulf lady, you have nothing to fear. You have a name, status. From now on, we won't have a single paisa from you.'

'How are you going to carry on, then?' Chechi began to back off.

'That you need not know.'

Amma came into my room. She bolted the door, came over to where I lay, and sat beside me. Chechi kept banging on the door, calling us. Amma lay her fingers on my head and caressed me. I lost control and broke into loud sobs. She pulled me up and held me close. My sobs began to wane after some time. Amma wiped my face with the edge of her sari and pulled me close to her chest.

'Siva is now over twenty-eight. At this age, young women become a bit selfish. She probably wants a family and a world of her own,' Amma said. 'Let her go…'

I swallowed a whimper.

'Let her go…' Amma repeated.

'You, too, will feel it one day. Amma will never stand in your way.'

'Only if I feel!'

'You must tell me when you do. Don't repress it and then explode!'

I could not help smiling. Amma smoothed my hair again and planted a kiss on my forehead.

'I have not really cuddled you much as a baby. You were born when my life was at its worst. That wasn't a bad thing, it seems … You are stronger than your sister.'

Any other mother would have broken down at least then. But my mother got up and left smiling. I, too, got out of bed weeping and smiling. Chechi came to me. She made peace. I gave in.

~

I remembered all this – again – because of Inspector Shetty. It was all because I called him.

'Have you moved to Odisha? Swept away by the case?'

'I returned this morning. But you were right, Ma'am – this is the most thrilling case I've handled. I should thank you.'

'But I am getting bored. There's no news of him! No idea why he's out to kill me. Is it so hard to sniff out someone these days?'

'That feeling is justified. But this man is the most intelligent criminal I have seen in recent times. He's wiped off his footprints wherever we have traced him to. But we've had a stroke of luck – a picture of his, from 2011!'

'His photo?'

'Not sure. See if you can identify him?'

'I have not seen his face.'

'See if there's any overall resemblance, at least? It was taken on a mobile phone by one of his neighbours.'

'Send it to me then. But what's the use, without a solid lead?'

'We do have a lead. We recovered an envelope from his rented room. There's a name on it – S. Prakash. The crucial thing is that the postmark is from a Kerala post office, a Malayalam place name. I sent it to Aswathy Ma'am. Will send it to you too.'

The inspector sent me S. Prakash's photo and an image of the postmark on the envelope. I could not really recognize him as my assassin. But it shook me – because the face was a familiar one. I recalled exactly who it was after a couple of moments. It was the face of the man who'd worked as Prabhudev Maheswari's personal driver! I was excited. The question about the connection between my pursuer and Samir Sayyid had now shifted – to another question: about the connection between my pursuer and Prabhudev Maheswari. And that shifted to another one – about the connection between my pursuer and Abhilash. That's because the postmark on the envelope was from Abhilash's village.

Back then, Chechi had returned in a hurry to register her marriage with Abhilash. She fought with me to conceal the guilt. When we made up, she handed me a plastic carry bag full of money. Five lakh rupees. A bank loan, she said. That was a lie. She had a loan of fifteen lakh, not five. Ten, she had given Abhilash. That came to light only when he married another woman.

Debts are like problems in life. To solve one, you create another. Love is like that, too. To get over one, you find another. After all, all this is the art of deflecting one's attention. To rule is to deflect people's attention from one protest to another. To live is to deflect one's attention from one wound to another. And death, deflecting one's attention from one life to another.

TWENTY-SIX

That morning, I was woken up by Paramarth. There was a new declaration that day. People who had deposited more than two lakh in bank accounts were going to be investigated! I had a large compensation amount in mine. My hope was to live the rest of my life on it. Good Lord, was that hope going to be busted? I rubbed my eyes and looked at him.

'Hindu women should not sleep late,' he chided. I sat up hastily, joined my palms, and recited '*Karaagre vasate lakshmi...*' and '*Samudravasane devi...*' before touching the ground in obeisance. His face relaxed a bit. Then I raised my voice and recited '*Brahmaswaroopamudaye...*' to his face and escaped into the bathroom. I stayed there for as long as I could, but when I came out, he was still around. Amma and he were talking and sipping tea. My tea was waiting for me. With no other way out, I pulled a chair and joined them. Losing no time, he asked me, 'How much money do you have in your account?'

I was a bit embarrassed. 'Less than two lakh,' I assured him. He then began questioning me.

'Do you pay your taxes?'

'Yes, every year.'

'If not, someone's going to visit you.'

'Let them. I'll send them off with some tea.'

'All that was long back. Now these visitors won't be satisfied with some tea.'

'The ones who just found a thousand crore in a raid?'

'They found the money, right? What if it were the former guys?'

'But this means that black money is still alive and kicking!'

'The finance minister has requested for another fifteen days.'

'The same one who said that they didn't know when all the money would get printed again!'

'The country needs digital transactions. That's why the government has chosen this measure, with so much foresight.'

'Yes, even the folk dead from waiting in queues for their hard-earned money agree.'

'Stop the nonsense. Only thirty people died in the queues. The rest committed suicide.'

'Your grouse is that only a few people died?'

'When a grand scheme has to be implemented, we all have to make some sacrifices!'

'Yes. That's the job of people who are starving.'

'Have you ever fed any of those starving people? Look at how you keep accusing others!'

'Governments are elected so that no one starves in the country.'

He leapt up.

'You are a communist. I know.'

'The communists say that I am a Maoist.'

'Can't you get lost? Go to Pakistan! The menace!'

'Who the hell are you to tell me to leave my country?'

This time he raised his hand to hit me. The tea spilled. He then decided against it.

'Go, whore yourself. It's better than this.'

'Better than what?'

I laughed. He almost lost control. His eyes blazed. He was a thin, pale fellow, didn't look his age. But he tried to stick out his chest as

much as he could. His anger made for an amusing sight. The teenage
fuzz on his face quivered. His eyes welled with rage.

Amma got up, went inside. I drank my tea as though nothing had
happened. Amma came out with a kitchen cloth. 'Son,' she called him.
He was waiting for that motherly affirmation, it seemed. But what she
said was, 'Wipe that spilled tea, please?' He shrank from it and tried to
leave. But Amma was firm: 'You may go only after you wipe the table
clean.' He decided to defy her. 'All right, leave the place dirty and go,
but don't step into the house again.' He turned back from the door and
wiped the table clean. Then Amma handed him the cup and told him
to wash it. He stomped into the kitchen, almost in tears, barely held
the cup under the tap, and returned as fast as he had gone in. Then,
hitching up his saffron-coloured mundu, he thrust his chest out the
best he could, and stormed out.

'He's terribly worried about you.'

'About my love jihad, isn't it?'

'The poor fellow! Small-minded in the extreme.'

Amma went back in. I sat there for some more time. 'Go, whore
yourself!' His voice resounded in my ears.

Let me tell you a truth now. I paid off the debt to Saubhagya doing
just that – selling my body. Reading this, some of you will decide, ah,
paid sex! Congratulations! Why do you need any more documents to
prove your Indian citizenship? But, sorry. I didn't mean paid sex. Yes, I
did sell my body. More clearly, I sold an organ – to name it, my kidney.
I got a good price.

Today it may seem trivial. But this was 1997. Salt was forty rupees a
kilo, and onion, seventy-five! There was a huge outcry. The thing about
salt was interesting. Two years before raising the price, the government
banned rock salt. Yes, our rock salt. The same stuff we used to store
in the wooden jar in the soot-coated old kitchens. But isn't it a fact
that everything that the government does is for our good? Citizens
consuming plain old rock salt falling prey to goitre! How could the
government bear it? 'Indeed, company-made salt has more iodine than

the sea-made one?' Amma was sceptical. I tried to tell her that the salt brought to the market in sacks and sold in the open was full of germs. 'These bodies of ours are the places in which the ancestors of those germs lived full lives, died and disappeared!' she retorted. Don't think that I was arguing out of sheer love for the government. Just that I liked the shiny white salt powder sold in packets more than the rock salt crystals in sacks packed in paper. And, the honeymoon with liberalization was in full swing too. There was a lot of confusion those days – people took whiteness for cleanliness.

It was at that time that I sold my kidney for six lakh. I had joined a distance education course in Communicative English before I completed my MA in Malayalam. Every semester, there used to be contact classes for two weeks. My centre was Chennai and I stayed in a house as a paying guest. My roommate was a nurse from Kattappana, Karuna Abraham. She was struggling to find one lakh rupees to pay an agent for recruitment to the UK. She told me about a female patient from Mumbai – filthy rich, but likely to die because she needed a kidney from a donor with B Negative blood. What a pity, her blood group wasn't B Negative. 'Give me a good price, and I am ready!' I joked. We laughed. But have you noticed? None of our jokes are really jokes. Most of them are disguised positions. Some are secret confessions. And others, bloodless murders. The rest are usually plain manipulations – only that the manipulated are not necessarily others, but even oneself. My joke was a warming-up of sorts. Because the burden of my debt to Saubhagya smouldered inside me those days. Whenever it flared up, I struggled to conceal the flames so that others would not notice. So I pondered the matter the whole of that night, and the very next morning, asked Karuna the number of days a kidney donor needed to be hospitalized. She started, not noticing that I was serious. Of course I was. In times of globalization, what do people need – kidneys, or the means to purchase them? Money is God, of course! I convinced her of that, and she finally agreed.

That evening, someone came to see me. A middle-aged man, forty or forty-five perhaps. His cheeks had gone red in the heat of the Chennai summer. He was handsome, barring his eyes. Not that they were ugly – just that they looked as though engaged in some constant and never-ending calculation. So, his face was perpetually drawn. You'd think that he had pulled a chessboard on your face and was moving the pawns on it with his eyes. He was the HR manager of some prominent firm in Mumbai. Big firms, crafty moves – who was I before him? Just a woman ready to cut off a piece of her body and put it up for sale. We began to talk.

'Sister Karuna Abraham sent me here.'

'I gathered.'

'Satyapriyaji, you are ready to donate your kidney, aren't you?'

'If you will pay six lakh.'

'I am ready to pay ten.'

'Six will do.'

'Your business skills are poor…'

'You need not just skills but ethics too?'

'In business, ethics has to do with profits.'

'This is playing with one's life. I can take only a calculated risk.'

'You have a way with words, Satyapriyaji!'

'That's different from having the right answers, isn't it?'

'All right. When do you need the money?'

'When all the tests are done, and I am okayed.'

'Cash or cheque?'

'Cash.'

'According to the law, only a close friend or relative can be a kidney donor.'

'So what?'

'You are fearless beyond your age!'

'Isn't age a state of mind, Sir?'

'But aren't you afraid of the law?'

'You are rich. Will the law touch you?'

'All right, let that go. Has your family agreed to this?'

'I am not selling you any of their kidneys.'

'No family in India will leave such decisions to a young girl.'

'Do you not see now that that is untrue?'

'But won't your family be upset if they get to know?'

'You have to make sure that this remains a secret.'

'My view is that you should speak with your family.'

'So you are not interested in saving your wife's life, Sir?'

His face, the Roman nose, his ears – all looked like they were on fire. He departed saying we should meet again in the hospital. I passed all the medical tests. My kidney was just like me, born in the fire, tenacious. I received the six lakh that very day. I gave one lakh to Karuna – she was shocked, and wept. 'Don't worry, only one's sold,' I joked again. It was not just a joke of course – just warming up, manipulation.

The surgery was on the second day after the contact classes. I was admitted the day before.

Whenever I thought of it, it always made me sad. I was young back then, after all? I remembered Chechi and Amma, even doubted my decision, worried about turning back at the last moment. Some journeys you cannot turn back from. You cannot decide against moving ahead. I became a corpse consumed by the flames on an unseen pyre. My bones cracked, the stink of the burning flesh spread inside me. The hollow was filled with soot and ashes. No one suspected. I lay flat in front of them, a woman greedy for money.

Karuna undressed me and shaved me. Her tears fell on my stomach and thighs a few times. She made me wear a green surgical gown. It was a room with white walls. On three sides, there were screens; behind my head was a wall. I could hear someone walk in the space between the beds, the purr of the air conditioning, and the clang of items made of steel. It was a moment of utmost loneliness. All of a sudden, I was gripped with a fear about my body. I felt a rush of tender affection towards my kidneys, which were innocently cleaning my blood still. I wanted to pee. My chest ached. I feared that I may die during the surgery. How would that feel? Maybe instantly, like a light bulb fusing? Or would my mind, like a bird picking up twigs, quickly gather some treasured memories, and fly off? Would it wander in the sky, homeless, and see Amma and Chechi and Acchan? Would they be able to see me?

That was actually a kind of death. The 'I' who existed until then, died. It was not only a spiritual demise but also a physical one. Like I lost my home, I lost my body. I trembled, thinking what it would be like if my body had to be taken home, with no forewarning at all. I threw my left arm on my face, shut my eyes tight. My tears flowed through the corners of my eyes. Prabhudev came up to me then – and saw my reddened eyes, my teary face. I felt foolish. He went out. Before long, an army of doctors appeared. They examined me again and gave me courage. Two nurses stood on guard all the time. The surgery went off superbly. I got the money, lost my kidney. Lost my kidney, and gained, instead, a crescent that ran from below my right breast to my navel.

It was from then that I acquired this nervousness about whether the body would be treated as a sign of wealth. What if in the times ahead, money couldn't be turned into wealth? If it couldn't be used as a medium of exchange, what good was it? It would merely pile up in our pockets and almirahs and banks and maybe rot, stink. If such a time came, then we could survive only with two assets – our bodies and our freedom. Truly, is there any exchange in life that does not involve the full or partial transfer of these two? It is like an indirect tax. We don't try to separate the prices into direct and indirect components. And if we do, we lose sleep.

Anyway, my kidney was lost. There was terrible pain. For four days, I was sedated. Karuna took leave and sat by me, nursing me. Then I stayed for three weeks in Chennai. It was Karuna who took me home; she stayed with me the day we reached. The day after she left, I went to Saubhagya, bargained with Rajasekhar, repaid the sum of three lakh, and settled the debt. From the remaining amount, I gifted Venukkuttan

Chettan one lakh, lying to him that I had won a lottery. The other one lakh I deposited in my account. When the entire debt was finally paid off, I felt very empty and rather uneasy that there was nothing left to do. I stayed in bed all day, feeling lethargic, long enough for Amma to ask me numerous times why I was so exhausted.

When I went to Chennai two months later to write my exams, I had become somewhat stouter. The woman who had received my kidney was still in Chennai. She had been asking for me. The day before my exam, she visited me, a mask covering her nose and mouth. She was beautiful, but frail and sad. She brought me many presents, thanked me over and over again. She gave me her phone number and her husband's visiting card, and reminded me countless times to call her.

But do not forget one thing. All exchanges are a game of sorts. One pawn moved up, another moved down. The relationship is all about knowing the other side's moves in advance. I did not desire to have any further connection with them. I faulted myself for having sold my body. I thought that I had debased myself beyond anything a human being could endure. It was just stupid – what is wrong, really, in selling something that one can spare and another needs desperately? Especially if it could save a life? And remember, it was the heyday of liberalization. You may have to sell all, the spirit of the times declared. You'll have to buy too. Take a loan when you need it. If you are poor, you will sell what you have. What was there to be ashamed of in that? Weren't governments selling their gold reserves? Just like that, I sold my reserve kidney! I held high my per capita false pride. That was all. But that was not apparent to me then. For a long time, I gave up tea and milk and bread. Did not wear a sari if I could help it, and if I did, did not pleat it at the shoulder. I had to hide the crescent scar. Then, in time, it faded. I forgot the pain, my very conception of dignity and shame changed. And then, one day, I remembered her, when I left Mahipal Shah Baba's ashram. And thus chose one of the two indignities – the one that was smaller. I chose between the two businesses – the one less likely to end up in loss.

The story of my calling her is interesting. The old number had changed. I dug up her husband's visiting card. Called his Mumbai office. The woman who answered the call told me that he had left the firm, but she gave me his personal mobile number. I called him and we spoke.

'Sir, I not sure if you remember me...'

'Satyapriyaji – am I right?'

'How did you know?'

'I did expect you to call some day.'

'My apologies for not calling earlier.'

'They say that it's better late than never!'

'I thought you had forgotten me.'

'How can one forget someone who settles for six when offered ten?'

'That's to do with my poor business skills!'

'No. Your high ethics.'

'I am wary of those who offer money.'

'But you needed it badly then.'

'I was in a crisis then.'

'I thank God for putting you through such a crisis then, Satyapriyaji.'

'Is Madam doing well?'

'Your kidney is very sturdy!'

'Great to know.'

'All right, I know that you would not have called if it wasn't something serious.'

'I am in a crisis again.'

'You need money?'

'No, a job.'

'What's the time now? Eleven-thirty. If you can reach before noon, then join today itself.'

'Are you joking?'

'Okay, then, tomorrow morning?'

'Are you serious?'

'I have to behave with the seriousness that befits my position, Satyapriyaji!'

'And what position is that?'

'Have you heard about Advaita?'

'The multinational firm?'

'Yes, we have a factory and refinery in Odisha. I am the personnel administrator and marketing manager there. Tell me which division you'd prefer to work in. And we'll place you there.'

Now you see who that was? Yes, that was Prabhudev Maheswari. Now do you also see what selling your body actually means? And why I worry about a time when there will be no currency notes, and bodies will be used instead? My poor business skills. The failing that was a result of my ignorance about business ethics as essentially wedded to profit. I went wrong in two ways with that relationship. My first mistake was to mix a business deal with personal concerns. The second was to bring in my personal feelings instead of limiting myself to an official involvement. What's the point of feeling sad about it now? Nothing! But I still had to recount all of it. For Inspector Shetty. He was no longer trying to investigate my case; he was writing my biography and getting me to write my autobiography.

~

'Ma'am, please don't feel bad that I am asking this openly: your relationship with Prabhudev Maheswari wasn't merely an official one, was it?' Anurup Shetty asked.

'Your question isn't clear.'

'Was there an illicit relationship between you two – please don't be angry at the question.'

'No, never.'

'That means?'

'That is, after the past two years, I have ceased to feel angry at stupid questions.'

'All right. What was the nature of your relationship?'

'It was a complex one.'

'But it still can be named?'

'It was not one which could be given a single name.'

'That's it. Your relationship was more than what normally exists between a superior officer and a subordinate.'

'It was not just that.'

'What does that mean? It was romantic?'

'No.'

'Physical?'

'No, not that either.'

'But Mitali was suspicious.'

'Yes.'

'She says that you and Prabhudev interacted intimately.'

'We worked in the same office.'

'But you travelled together.'

'All those were official trips.'

'It's the secretary who accompanies the boss on official trips. You weren't that.'

'I was his assistant manager.'

'Are you arguing that you had no other kind of relationship with him?'

'Aren't arguing and answering questions entirely different?'

'So you claim that Prabhudev never made romantic proposals to you?'

'He did not make any such proposals.'

'Which would indicate that he made other kinds of proposals…?'

'He asked me to marry him.'

'There! This is what I was asking you all this while!'

'All this while you were asking if we had an illicit relationship, a romantic relationship, a physical relationship, and if he had made romantic proposals to me.'

'My dear Ma'am, I bow to you, you are impossible!'

'May you prosper!'

'So, he proposed marriage to you – let us suppose. Also, that you refused. Then why is Mitali so full of enmity towards you?'

'Did she tell you that?'

'Didn't I tell you? The gun that your assailant used was registered in her name!'

'Maybe Prabhudev gave it to him?'

'That man is still deeply in love with you.'

'Did he tell you that?'

'What was the need? When I uttered your name, he blushed to his ear-tips.'

'Inspector, have you solved many cases with this face-recognition science?'

'Don't be sarcastic, Ma'am.'

'Maybe he was feeling hot. That's reason enough to turn red.'

'Ma'am please, stop joking. What do you infer from this? If he's not in love with you, does he harbour vengeance? If so, for what?'

'Inspector, are you writing my biography or investigating a crime?'

'Don't make fun of it, Ma'am. The two are related. That gun was given to the assassin by Mitali herself. She is really furious about your relationship with Prabhudev. She suspects that you continue to encourage him even after leaving your job there.'

'Why? For what?'

'Prabhudev hired a detective agency to watch you.'

'Does that mean he is in love with me?'

'If not, why would he have wanted to marry you?'

'What is the connection between marriage and love?' I laughed.

Inspector Shetty was irritated; he murmured something and hung up. I sat quietly for some more time and laughed to myself. Prabhudev, hiring a detective to spy on me! For love – indeed! His marriage proposal was surely not for love. What was it for then? Sex? My body? What was left to cut out in this body? A liver? In which all the dirt produced by my body would be deposited?

No. He was taking aim at my freedom. From the very beginning it made him uneasy. I would not be a pawn in his game. That dented his pride. These rich folk! But I felt pained by the fact that this had affected Mitali. I sympathized with her. She lived bothered constantly by the

feeling that she did not deserve this man as her husband. He was, for
her, the most precious gem in the whole world. The poor thing, did
she even have a whiff of the science of gemmology? Her husband was
a fine piece of glass, would have sparkled like a diamond if light were
to fall on it at a proper angle. But a piece of glass is just that, after all.
Poor Mitali. How long she carried on thrusting that worthless piece of
glass into her breast instead of flinging it into some waste bin!

But why blame her? I, too, have done the same, with many different
broken bits of glass.

The need of the hour, though, was not to count the number of glass
pieces; it was to identify the assailant. I called Inspector Shetty again.
He answered me with a rude 'What?'.

'Did you not find out how Mitali met this S. Prakash after all this?'
I sounded harsh too.

'He was a driver at Advaita for three years. In the fourth year, he
became Prabhudev's personal driver.'

'How?'

'You should have asked that question first.'

'Please tell me, Inspector Sir.'

'It was S. Prakash who informed Prabhudev about your affair with
Samir Sayyid.'

All of a sudden, my voice dropped.

'That's how he became Prabhudev's trusted man.'

'And how did he become Samir Sayyid's man?'

'Won't it be easier for you to ask him that directly?'

'Won't I have to go to Kashmir for that?'

'No, he has come to Kerala, in search of you perhaps.'

This time it was I who hung up. This Anurup Shetty was no mean
player. He had managed to get not just Prabhudev but also me red-
faced. I lay face down on my bed, trying to control my pounding heart,
and slept off. In the evening, Amma came to me with a packet. 'This
came by courier,' she said.

It was a green bag, with a plastic wrapping. Still half-asleep, I took it and opened it. There was a transparent plastic bag inside; a white kurta embroidered with red thread fell out of it. Not just any kurta, a Kashmiri one. My hair stood on end. I tried to hide the way in which I blushed from head to toe. This Anurup Shetty was formidable. He was right. Samir Sayyid was in Kerala. I looked at the address: Kashmiri Designs, Fort Kochi.

It was on that very same day that the finance minister declared that the withdrawn currency notes would not be fully replaced. That applied to my romance too. But I was delighted at the prospect of meeting one of my former lovers. Especially someone who knew my assassin face to face. There was also some suspense and fear. What would be exchanged in that meeting, fully or partially? The body, or freedom? Life, or death? Article 14, or Article 370?

TWENTY-SEVEN

I should never have seen Samir Sayyid, never fallen in love with him. But I did see him, fall in love with him. We walked hand in hand on Sachivalaya Marg the first day. Then we met every evening. Walked in the parks until late – sometimes in Buddha Jayanti Park, sometimes in Gandhi Park. Six months later, I set off with him to spend a night together. I don't remember anything about it. The journey itself was a kind of sleepwalking. When I opened my eyes, I saw him beside me, asleep, his face pressed on my left shoulder. His fair skin was marked with numerous scratches, ridges, stitch-marks, calluses. I smoothed his hair gently. He opened his eyes. I turned to my side and lay facing him. He ran his finger on my belly, over the scar on it.

'What's this?'

'The price of my body.'

'That means?'

'Sold my kidney.'

'Really?'

'I am the lover of truth – Satyapriya.'

I ran my finger over the scar that ran across his ribs.

'What's this?'

'The price of freedom.'

284

'That means?'

'The BSF's autograph.'

'I didn't get you.'

'My place isn't like yours. There, right from when you wake up until you go to bed, you need identity cards. Sometimes even after you sleep. No use claiming that it is the land of our forefathers…'

'Tell me, what happened?'

'I was an engineering student then. One day, I had to drop a relative at the railway station early in the morning. I was on my way back, the BSF pulled me up.'

'For what?'

'That's what I asked them.'

'How old were you then?'

'Twenty-two.'

'You weren't carrying your identity card?'

'They didn't ask. They took me straight to an open ground.'

'For what?'

'I had no idea then. There were several Gypsy SUVs there. Then I realized, there was an identification parade going on.'

'I am totally confused, Samir.'

'That is, our place is full of informers. They help catch terrorists.'

'But you weren't one?'

'You don't have to be. Sometimes, there would be stone-throwing against the army. Then all the men in the area would be summoned for identification parades. That's announced in the mosques. We all have to go to the open grounds to be paraded in front of the informers. An informer will be seated in a jeep with his face covered and only his eyes would be visible. When we cross them, if they identify you, they'll blow a horn.'

'Yes, but you weren't a terrorist?'

'You don't have to be! The informer has to wriggle out somehow. He can get away only if he identifies a significant number of people.

So he may pick at random. He, too, might have been picked up the same way, so why should he feel merciful?'

'Good god! And then?'

'One of them blew a horn seeing me.'

'But you were innocent!'

'Satya, it is easy to allege a crime. Very difficult to prove innocence.'

'And?'

'Over four whole hours, they crushed me to a pulp…'

'I don't want to hear…'

'No, it is fun. You must. They do it in many different ways. With the butt of the gun, for example … here, below the neck. You'll feel like your heart stopped.'

'Enough, Samir!'

'Some stroke of luck, they let me go that day. That's why I reached home even though with broken ribs. My nephew's body was recovered from the border. They claimed that he was shot while trying to cross over.'

'How can people who haven't committed a single crime be punished like this?'

'Not one, we have committed two. Being born Kashmiri first. Being born Muslim next.'

'But what about the Kashmiri Pandits, then?'

'What wrong did I do to the Pandits? How did my family wrong them?'

'Are not the Kashmiri Pandits asking exactly the same question of the Kashmiri Muslims?'

'Is it not those who wronged the Pandits who deserve punishment? What is the use of butchering Kashmiri Muslims who have nothing to do with it?'

'Don't the Pandits deserve justice?'

'Will the injustice suffered by someone be remedied by doing the very same to another?'

'Then how to make sure that the Pandits get justice?'

'Their lives must be improved, that is justice.'

'Oh, you sound like no Muslim in Kashmir lives peacefully!'

'Maybe there are. I don't know.'

'I can't believe any of this!'

'That's better for you.'

'How do you manage to live there?'

'You'll understand that only if you try living there.'

'Aren't you going to go back there?'

'Yes, I want to. No one will have peace until they can freely return to and live in the land of their birth.'

'Then why did you move to Delhi?'

'My Abbajaan wants at least one of his sons alive.'

'And your siblings?'

'Both are dead. I had two brothers.'

'How?'

'We recovered the body of one. The other's still not been traced. It's been seven – no, eight – years.'

'Was that too the army's doing?'

'One of them died in an explosion. No, that was not set off by the army.'

'Who is at home now?'

'My mother and my older brother's wife.'

'All alone?'

'They are not afraid.'

'Samir...'

I touched him, feeling really scared. He looked at me with eyes still as ice.

'There are many stories. Do you want to hear?'

'No, I can't.'

Tears pooled in my eyes; they brimmed. He kissed me. I melted like snow. This is the reason why I don't fall in love. I am just impossible when I'm in love. It's like being trapped in an avalanche – once you get into it, then there's no you, no me, no love. Samir was lucky. He escaped.

On second thoughts, it was for the best that our love came asunder, flowed, and emptied itself. What all trouble it could have caused. All that I needed in life, after a mountain of troubles, was a lover who was a Maoist! And a Kashmiri to top it!

Still, the landslide is an experience, a sensation. I felt it twice on my way to Fort Kochi.

Have you gone to meet a former lover? When there was evidence that he was a friend of the person out to murder you, your assassin-in-waiting? A pity, if you haven't! You've lost the spiciest moment of your life. The chilli spray and tear gas of the BSF are nothing compared to it. The broiling sensation won't be on your tongue but in your eyes. It will enter your blood through your throat. It is quite a feeling. But it is said, isn't it, that past lovers and banned currency notes are alike? They are useless, and it is dangerous to keep them beyond a point.

~

I took a bus to Ernakulam. A low-floor bus, air-conditioned, with music playing. I asked the conductor for directions to get to Fort Kochi. Take the boat, he suggested. I liked it because it was such a long time since I had got on a boat. I took an auto to Marine Drive. It was crowded in the boat. The expanse of the lake dazzled the eyes in the morning sun. The glitter deflected your attention away from the dirt accumulated in it. The lake made me remember Vasanthaalayam and the lake beside it. Every lake has its own rhythm. This rhythm was of fear. I searched for my assailant. This would have been a truly excellent chance for him to finish me off. Where was the sad chap now? Thinking from his point of view, I felt sorry. How long it had been since he set out to kill me. I was the victim, the one to be snuffed out. He probably had his own reasons. Anyway, he had been following me wherever I went. Since 1999, when Chechi died. Where was he until then? Was he in Delhi, playing Hindu, Muslim, Christian? Or was he following

Chechi? Did he pursue her in the Gulf? When this thought struck me, my heart swayed. It beat tenderly. I imagined that she was beside me, to my left. Her absence frustrated me no end. When she disappeared, our conversations too stopped. I don't know if you have noticed, really, but you become alone not when people disappear from your life, but when these dialogues between you end. 'We' or 'I' actually refers to such dialogues. If there's no one to listen and respond to what we have to say, we're finished. And then, there's just one way out – setting up a dialogue with oneself.

I got down at Fort Kochi and glanced around. Don't think that I knew the place – I did not. It was kind of empty – there were a few tourists. The atmosphere was generally glum. I saw a shop that sold chains and earrings and such stuff, entered it, looked around a bit, and chatted with a young chap who was minding the shop. 'Are there fewer tourists now?' I asked him. 'Yes,' he said, 'after the note ban.' I asked him about the shop named Kashmiri Designs. He told me that it was near the synagogue. I found the shop but there was no one there. I went in. There were many short white kurtas on hangers and short tops, gently swaying in the breeze. They were pretty. I looked for Samir but was scared to utter his name.

A young man, some thirty or forty years old, came running in from somewhere. He was not fair and pink like most Kashmiris. But I was sure that he was a Kashmiri. Because he had the same look in his eyes – still as ice. The same expression, like he was carrying a mountain of snow on his head. I took out the kurta from my bag.

'I want one like this…' I said to him in Hindi. He looked at it, picked up the phone and called someone. He spoke in a language unfamiliar to me. He told me to sit. I sat down. I felt alone, so I engaged in the following exchange with him:

'What is your name?'

'Farhan.'

'Are you from Kashmir?'

'Yes.'

'How long is it since you came here?'

'Eight years…'

'Is this your own shop?'

'My older brother's. He was the first to come. Then I did.'

'Straight to Kerala?'

'No, I was first in Mumbai, then in Bangalore, and now here I am.'

'Out of these two, where would you like to settle down?'

'A Kashmiri has to always bear a tag wherever he goes, Madam – that of a Kashmiri. As long as that is there, we will not be accepted as normal human beings anywhere in India.' He smiled bitterly.

I regretted that loose talk. Then a young boy, around seventeen years old, came in. He had what seemed like a large callus over one eye. He asked me to follow him. I bid goodbye to Farhan and went with him. The young boy walked beside me leisurely. He was not paying attention to me. He murmured something to himself. 'Who are you talking to?' I asked him in Hindi.

'Me?' He looked at me, amazed.

'I thought you were saying something.'

'It's that way back home.'

'How?'

'People talk to themselves.'

'Everyone?'

'Some people just count.'

'Why?'

'I don't know.'

My heart melted. I put my hand on his shoulder. He turned his face away from me. I saw the mark above his eye clearly.

'How did you get this?'

'Pellet wound. When I was a baby.'

'Pellet?'

'When the army fired.'

'How did you get wounded?'

'Ummijaan was at the window holding me, about to close it. The room was just on the side of the road. There was firing, from the other side. The glass pane of our window shattered. Ummijaan lost one eye.'

My mouth fell shut. I did not need to know so much. I was not prepared for it. But he had only begun.

'The protest would begin after the Friday prayer, and the firing. The tear gas too. The tear gas was what I was scared of. I'd cough and cough! My throat would bleed.'

I felt as though innumerable pieces of broken glass had pierced my throat. I looked at his face. The same look – still as ice. I shuddered inwardly. Who would not, if they saw a seventeen-year-old this way?

'Where are we going?' I tried to change the subject.

'Don't you want to see Samir Chacha?'

'Is Samir your uncle?'

'He is Abbajaan's classmate.'

'Where does he work?'

'He's a teacher. In Delhi.'

'What are you doing here?'

'Working.'

'Not studying?'

'Ummi is very unwell.'

'And your Abba?'

'He disappeared.'

'Disappeared?'

'Went out to work one morning, never returned.'

'You did not try to look for him?'

He laughed. I felt like my eyes had been hit with pepper spray. We had reached a two-storeyed house. He stopped, pointed to the upper floor. I went up quickly. On my way, when I turned to look, he was going back. He was counting on his fingers, his lips were moving. I writhed under a huge mountain of snow. This thing, nationalism, isn't what you think it is. It is terribly heavy. It crushes your ribcage. Makes every pore bleed. Anyone would scream in sheer agony. I shouldn't have met Samir, loved him, come back seeking him; I should never have seen that lad. There's no use saying all this, however. It was on such occasions that my would-be murderer became relevant. If only he had finished me with a single bullet, a single stab. Peace of mind is more important than life itself. It's okay to be dead – it's just the absence of life. If you have no peace of mind, then it's better not to be alive at all.

I pressed the bell only after he disappeared from my sight. Have you never, not once, set out in search of your old lover? Never stood on his doorstep after pressing the bell? A pity if you haven't, for then you've missed something, really. You have not experienced the most expectant of moments in your life. But there's something – that moment is unique. Not sure if you have noticed, but experiences are like the banned one-thousand-rupee notes. They are worthless when you want to drink a cup of tea, but you can display them like museum pieces. You can bargain and auction them too. Experiences are like that. By themselves they may be worthless, but their memory has value. Do you know what? The only thing that money can't buy, really, is memory.

The door opened. Samir stood in the doorway, looking at me intently. He wore a grey cap and a sandal-coloured long kurta. His beard was well trimmed. His moustache was turning salt-and-pepper. The heat had reddened his cheeks and ears a little. The same eyes, like ice. The same neck, scarred by shattered glass – I began to feel a tenderness. He held out his hands to me. I took them. It is true, I had rejected him. And knew that he had something to do with my assassin. But my body both melted and froze at his touch; it brimmed over and shimmered and rippled; it became a lake and a river. He said something indistinctly. I grew numb, then.

Have you ever loved a Kashmiri? You would have then known the real meaning of self-sacrifice. He will never be able to love you from the bottom of his heart. How can he? Some three or four decades ago, didn't the state storm into his home, crush his body, pluck out his soul, rip it apart, fling it violently on the ground, and then grind it underfoot into non-existence?

My body began to glow and darken in a fearful rhythm. I pulled my hands away. He rubbed his hands together. I felt that something from my hands had got stuck on to his. Maybe it was nationality. Or patriotism.

Anyway, I did not waste time and asked him what I had to.

'Samir, why are you trying to kill me?'

He did not take even a moment to reply. It was a question:

'Satya, why did you betray me?'

TWENTY-EIGHT

Seated in that dormitory full of bunk beds, I studied him for changes in the past two years. He had greyed. There were bags under his eyes. Tall icy peaks had grown in his eyes. His cheeks were now sunburnt, and the skin on his neck was loose and hanging. For a moment I lost my sense of time. I went back to being that old me. That woman who used to tremble with delight at the sight of him. Let me give you a bit of advice from my experience. You must go seek old lovers sometime, talk to them; there's no better way of re-experiencing early youth. It is fun. Like eating the Bombay Mittai you ate long back. Who does not like to savour the old sweets? Who does not like to go visit old haunts?

In truth, all love is jihad. So do not look for profit in love. And vice versa. They are mutually repellent. But I can say in the light of lived experience that after some time, money will get into love. Then the latter will begin to be led by the former. It happened with Samir too. He was human – and is it not a fact that deep pockets make a human? If not, what is the difference between a human being and an animal? I could not forgive him. I did not expect it from him – that was my fault. When each romance failed, I dreamt of a better, flawless romance. How was that to be? Only the lover changed, the romance was the same. Because humans are humans everywhere, in Kashmir

294

or Kerala. It doesn't matter what their faith is. Truly, humans have just one faith – and that is the religion of lucre. Just one beloved – power.

But I have to admit for sure – I have never loved anyone else the way I loved him. He had a special place in my heart. A Muslim, to begin with, and a Kashmiri, to top it. I had never seen a Kashmiri in person before I met him. I had seen them only on TV. They were faces covered with scarves. Either killers or the killed. It was only when I met Samir that I knew that that land, too, had paddy fields and snakes and birds. Now and then, I would ask him about his childhood. That was not to learn about Kashmir but about him. I don't know if you have noticed but, to know men, one must ask them about their childhood. Samir loved to talk about his boyhood. The ice in his eyes would melt then. He told me about their wooden house in Anantnag. It's not like we think. In Kashmir, too, little children hear the sounds of the vessels from the kitchen while half-asleep in bed. They, too, hear hens clucking and cows mooing as they wander off to graze. The room of his window opened on to a lane that separated the paddy fields from the houses. He could overhear snatches of the chatter of passers-by, the sounds of children playing cricket in the fields, the voices of women returning after gathering firewood from the forest. I would ask him only about the times before 1990. He had good memories only of those years.

He sat continuing to gaze at me intently. Our eyes locked into one another's like hooks; they tugged at each other. I felt both tears and laughter jostling inside me. Some alpha men can be like this at some moments – like youngsters, teenage boys. Let me give you some advice from my life: seek out your old lovers, talk to them, and you will learn who you were back then. But be sure not to expect too much. Be ready to be shocked and disappointed. Because it is quite likely that they may not have moved on much from where we bid them goodbye. They must have sent down roots there and now there may be termite heaps on those roots and hollows on the trunk. In their eyes, moving on – travel – is a crime, so our journey back may provoke them. But do not be provoked yourself. Don't hate. After all, there's no record of a woman drowning herself twice in the same man.

'Samir, so far I have not betrayed you. But I will, now.'

'Who has not betrayed the Kashmiris?'

'Then why did you come here?'

'Kashmir is an integral part of India, is it not?'

'I thought we were a woman and a man who completed each other.'

'We are from two worlds, which do not meet at all.'

'Is that what you learned from Maoism?'

'Satya, haven't you given up this urge to argue?'

'I am asking you about a doubt and you call it an argument?'

'I am not someone who became a Maoist and then started to work for adivasis. I started working with adivasis and then became one.'

'All right. Just tell me what exactly is the philosophy that you believe in. Just that.'

'Let's discuss that another time.'

'What if I am killed before that?'

'I am likely to be killed before you. But just because of that, we cannot forget priorities.'

'My priority is whether I'll be killed or not. What's yours?'

'Look, Satya, I am not just a lover.'

'No, not "just a lover" – you are no lover at all. How can one who wants to kill be a lover?'

'I am committed to my politics, the movement I am a part of.'

'What responsibility have you been fulfilling until now?'

'We have no other way but to eliminate those who betray us.'

'Who's this "we"? Kashmiris?'

'I meant the Maoists here.'

'Confusion! Confusion!'

'Don't mock me. I tried to blend in here. It did not work. I wish to go back.'

'That's good.'

'I must thank you. You're the one who taught me that I will be a Kashmiri forever.'

'How?'

'Satya, what is your relationship with Prabhudev Maheswari?'

'The answer can be exact only if the question is clear.'

'Were you not in love?'

'Were we?'

'That's the news I got.'

'You received such news. And you decided to kill me. Is that how I should understand the situation?'

'Satya, how could I bear it – you falling for such a man?'

'That is, you hired a killer just out of jealousy?'

'There was an element of that too.'

'What else was there?'

'You asked me about Golla's encounter killing – where did you get that information from?'

'Was it not the truth?'

'You got to know of it from Prabhudev Maheswari.'

'Also from the police, maybe?'

'If it were after the encounter, that would be true.'

'That is, only you and Prabhudev Maheswari knew that there would be an encounter, right? That means, the two of you planned it and had the police execute it?'

'Since when did you begin to lean so much towards Golla and the Maoists?'

'The day I found out that you were a Maoist we had come to an understanding. Do you remember what it was?'

'People agree to so many such things when they're in love!'

'So then are you a cheap man who will pretend to be romantic and make false promises for a kiss or some sex?'

'What understanding have I violated? Then and now, after Kashmir, you are all that I have.'

'Leave that be. You had agreed on two things: first, you will not kill anyone or assist in any killing; second, I will not act in violation of the law of the land.'

'When did I induce you to violate the law?'

'The moment you cooperated in betraying a comrade and causing his death, you violated both.'

'You take Prabhudev's words for holy scriptures! Tell me the truth – who did you love deeply? Me or Prabhudev?'

'Why should you be doubtful? Prabhudev, of course!'

'Satya, we may never meet again. So tell me the truth at least now. Did you not love me?'

'If you cannot sense my love without me telling you, better not sense it at all.'

'The evenings we walked about hand in hand, the rendezvous in the tree house … was it all a lie?'

'When you are acting, you need to do that and more.'

'Satya, we are people who lead the riskiest of lives … to take one step forward we may have to take many steps backwards.'

'What does that mean, walking "backwards"? Killing? Participating in murderous conspiracy?'

'It's not what you think.'

'I thought that you were fighting to help the adivasis preserve their free life and their large mountain tract and forests for some more time. I was wrong.'

'We have been declared internal enemies of the Indian state. They have the entire Indian army to kill us. Look, I could be killed even here in an encounter. I know that. Many of us know it. But I cannot prevent even that. Please understand.'

'Did you come here to die?'

'People are dying in queues before banks. Easy way out.'

'What, then, are you aiming at?'

'To bid goodbye to you.'

'What happens to the struggle for Kashmir, then?'

'There are others who will continue it.'

'Or are you leaving because you have made enough money?' I rolled my eyes at him. He shook his head and stood up.

At some stages of romance, you stop being compassionate. Especially when your lover falls in your eyes. Don't think that I had any pleasure in this. His words and looks pierced me like pellets. Did you not notice, he did not deny his role in the conspiracy to kill me? What if one of the assailant's efforts had borne fruit? I would not have been here at all! But did this bother him? No. He didn't care if I lived or died. Let me give you some advice from my own life: go in search of old lovers sometime so that you know how much the principal in your romance was and how much the interest. Just do not expect much profit. Sheer luck if there are no losses! Because there's no history of any romance recouping the investment in full.

I looked around for him. He was in the kitchen, making tea.

'How long have you been here?' I asked, leaning on the door.

'Three days.'

'When will you return?'

'Today itself.'

'Tell me the truth – why did you come here?'

'To see you.'

'It makes me suspicious to think that you came here to meet a woman who you thought was in love with Prabhudev!'

'I have a tiny corner somewhere in your heart.'

'In the waste bin!' I laughed.

He pretended not to hear. He poured the tea into the mugs silently and held out one to me.

'Have you poisoned this, Samir?'

'If you are so wary, why did you come to meet me here?'

'I need to know something.'

'Yes, you'll come only if there is something!'

'You used to have a helper, near the Muniguda railway station. A tea-shop owner? What was his name?'

'Isn't it easier to ask Prabhudev?'

'Oh, we have so many other things to share when we meet!'

'Just count this among those things?'

'If you don't have the guts to tell me, fine, I am leaving.'

'Don't go away angry! Sit down – what if we never meet again?'

I sat down again. He gazed at me, unblinking. I have always been wary of men especially when they begin to coo and coddle. Who knows what they are planning? He swallowed a mouthful of tea and started to turn the mug in his hand.

'He told me that his name was Akbar.'

'That means he had another name?'

'Yes, Prakash Das.'

'When did you meet him? Before us or after?'

'A couple of months after we met.'

'Where is he from?'

'I thought he was from Odisha. Spoke Bengali, Odiya and Hindi quite well.'

'How did you meet him?'

'We didn't meet formally, just got used to seeing each other. He came to the forest to look for medicinal plants.'

'How did he become Prabhudev's driver?'

'Won't Prabhudev tell you if you ask?'

'Samir, aren't you ashamed to be so jealous?'

'Why should I be jealous?'

'Because he stole your love.'

'Oh, I'll find a thousand others, don't worry.'

'Where? I can't see a single one!'

'I am not interested any more at my age.'

'Forget it! Don't I know you?'

He moved a little, his eyes moved. It was certain that he would fall into my arms if I barely held out my hand. But I, too, might have done the same. I held myself back and sipped my tea; then raised my eyes again towards him.

'Samir, if you want to kill me, why not do so by your own hand?'

He jerked mildly. Then he turned the mug in his hand and smiled at me.

'Why should I kill you?'

'I don't know.'

'I have no desire at all to kill you.'

'Then who's so keen to kill me?'

'Prabhudev. Who else?'

'What would he gain from it?'

'He's hooked. Helplessly.'

'Nonsense!'

I felt amused. He rose, came up to me. My heart skipped a beat again; I was on the alert. But I concealed it and looked at him. He sat beside me and put his hand on my shoulder. Took the mug from my hand, put it away. Was he going to wring my neck or kiss my lips, that was the question. I told you – at the time this story happened, romance involved more risk than the share market. The body would cave in, your freedom would vanish. The sole comfort was that the prices of petrol and acid were going through the roof. He cradled my face in his hands and looked into my eyes deeply.

'Satya, tell me, did you not love me?'

I felt a thrill, but also sorry for him. Maoist, indeed!

'I did, once.' I gently pushed his hands away and told him the truth. His face fell.

'Who do you love now?'

'You were the last of my loves. Wasn't it a massive failure?'

My voice faltered at this moment. It made me feel foolish. Here's a piece of advice from an experienced person: Do not think of your former lover as an individual, a human being, but as a magic mirror that shows you the old you. In Samir's eyes, I saw the me of 2003. The same thick tresses, the pimply face, the undying thirst for love. It is fun, in a way. To know that this was the old me. I suppose he, too, sought the old him in my eyes. He was my hero then, and I was ready to die for him. That was, after all, my problem. In love, I lost all my senses, my brains, every organ in my body. Just one remained, the heart. It stirred and swayed tirelessly like a river in the season of storms shattering its shores. In the beginning, I only knew that he was a Maoist sympathizer. But I was shaken when, in the vehicle in which we were travelling together, I saw some of the weapons stolen in the Maoist raid on the Indian Army's arms depot. He admitted to being a part of the organization but vowed that he had never been part of any violent action. It was a tremendous shock, but I just could not leave him.

A clock struck somewhere. Suddenly Amma called me on my new mobile phone. I answered it. I saw Samir grow alert all at once. It was amusing to see that. I started speaking to Amma.

'You didn't go to Venukkuttan's house?' she asked.

'I am just doing the rounds.'

'Oh ... okay.'

'I will be back in an hour or so.'

'All right.'

'Why did you call me, Amma?'

'They're now saying that if you want to exchange old notes worth more than five thousand, you have to provide an explanation.'

'What's wrong with that? It's for the nation, after all?'

'Two bank officials will question you.'

'Why are you so scared of that?'

'We should be afraid of anyone who asks us for explanations and refuses to explain themselves to us.'

'Never mind, you'll gradually get used to it. Did you call to tell me this, Amma?'

'If you see Samir Sayyid by any chance, please tell him that the news on TV says that the police have information that he is in Ernakulam.'

That left me deflated. I hung up and let out a sigh.

'What happened? Anything wrong?'

Samir's eyes were fixed on me. 'Huh! Amma is hard to deal with!' I tried to smile.

'What is it?'

'She told me, if I see Samir Sayyid, I am to tell him that the TV is announcing his presence in Ernakulam.'

A slow smile lit up his face.

'Hmm. You are definitely your mother's daughter, Satya.'

I sat there for a while, not knowing what to do.

'Samir, do these traders here know who you are?'

I grabbed his hand. He slipped his fingers into mine. My palm grew cold.

'No, they don't, and I won't make trouble for them.'

'Then who will you trouble?'

'You, of course.'

He got up. I had to get up too.

'Satyapriya, it is a greater crime to be speaking to a Maoist in a closed room than being a Maoist.'

'And that, too, over a cup of tea.' I tried to make it lighter. The moments flew. But what new information had they received? I pressed my fingers into his hand.

'Samir, before you go, a last question. Where is this Akbar, alias Prakash Das?'

He smiled at me. The frozen waters in his eyes gleamed.

'I won't tell you now.'

'Then when?'

'When we meet next.'

'But you said we may never meet.'

'We should leave a reason to meet again, shouldn't we?'

I asked him nothing further after that. I loosened my fingers. He was expecting a kiss – oh, these lovers! I pressed my lips against his cheek and looked into his eyes. I saw the old me in them. She who was electrified by his touch. She who would have died, had a single one of the killer's bullets hit me.

'Samir, the police will arrive soon,' I whispered.

'I know. I am waiting for them,' he whispered back.

For a moment, I was taken aback – these men, who knows what they think. I picked up my bag and climbed down the staircase slowly. An AC tourist bus with an OD33 number plate was parked in the alley. Men in floral shirts and colourful hats but with police boots on had surrounded the house. I went back the way I had come, as though nothing had happened. The boy who murmured to himself came running screaming, 'Samir Chacha, Samir Chacha...' I stopped him, caught his arm, and turned him away, firmly.

'Quiet! Those men are police!' I told him. He started hard and looked at me.

'But for what?'

'There's a case against your Samir Chacha!' I told him.

Don't think this gave me any pleasure. How could it? He was standing there, staring at me, his eyes locked into mine. The eyes of a youngster who'd seen people disappear from his life, one after the other. His eyes were not filled with frozen waters, they were filled with death. He seemed rooted to the ground. I walked ahead. The soul had come apart from my body. My body was now just my legs, my eyes were dimmed with tears. This is my advice from what I have suffered: Visit your old lovers sometime, spend some time with them, and when you part, you will feel the distance that you have travelled. But remember: You cannot return unscathed. Fear not, though. A man cannot kill a woman twice, there's never been such a precedent.

I had betrayed Samir Sayyid. My priority was not the former lover but the present killer. If he could betray his comrade, I could betray my old lover, I decided. The law took its course, and love, its own path. After all, there's never been evidence for love where profits mattered most. But why did Samir Sayyid come to Ernakulam and see me? That's the twist in this tale of mystery. But to reach that point, I needed many more journeys.

TWENTY-NINE

Is there something called 'black justice' – like 'black money'? That question haunted me that day. I don't have to tell you which day. The day I parted from Samir Sayyid. It was a terrible night. Romance and money are sure to leave people who trust them in tears, at least once. But that night, my tears were of a different kind. It felt like someone was hurling an unhusked coconut at my chest. Each time, something inside broke and crumbled and the pieces pierced the flesh. The body was just a bag of bone shards. I know how hard it was to drag that bag and reach home. I climbed into my bed as soon as I could get back to my room. Amma brought me some tea. I drank it and vomited at once. My stomach was empty; I hadn't eaten anything since breakfast. I kept vomiting. Amma gave me ginger juice in honey; that didn't help either. I writhed on the cot and wept aloud. Amma called Sarada Chechi, who called a doctor. They gave me the medicine that the doctor suggested. I threw that up too. At that, Amma drew back, scrutinized me, and pinched me hard on the arm like in the old times. It was agonizing, as though both my skin and flesh had been pulled out together. Like in my childhood, she rolled her eyes, gnashed her teeth, and narrowed her lips menacingly. I was shaken. I screamed from pure pain and collapsed on the bed. Anyway, the vomiting ceased.

When I awoke, it was dark. I could hear Amma's breathing. Its rise and fall made me uneasy. How would it feel to keep repeating the lines 'And thus I fall, I fall relentlessly / into the deep, the bottomless deep'? Her breath seemed to have the same rhythm. This is what happens when you study poetry early in life. The government should have banned it like they banned the currency notes. In fact, poetry is more fatal than black money. It is impossible to predict how, where, when, who will stash it away. And which terrorist might seize it as a weapon.

I got up gingerly. I simply could not lie down any longer. I did not feel brave enough to walk around the room. What if Amma woke up and started asking questions? So I went to the adjoining room. Have you ever noticed? Every house wakes up at night. The walls whisper to each other then. Who can guess what all the roof tells the floor? What the veranda whispers to the kitchen, the windows to the doors? Only they know the real stories of their inhabitants. I thought that the walls of the kitchen were bitching about me to the walls of the open side-room. They were taking me apart, peeling me like an onion. It hurt badly. Very slowly, I went over to Acchan's room. The windows of that room let in the radiance of the street lights the best they could. Acchan's scent still hung there. It was hard for me to believe that he did not exist any more. That was natural. I could not forget him. The spot where his wheelchair once stood was where one expected to see him. As long as that memory remained, he could not die. That's why I say, human beings are wiped out not by death but by forgetfulness.

That night, I stood all by myself in the middle of Acchan's room. I felt the heat leaving my body. A shadow moved in the mirror on the almirah near the window. Acchan used to get ready after his bath in front of that mirror. He used Brylcreem on his wet hair and the red round comb to carefully do his hair. Once he perfected his hair, he would use Lacto Calamine on his face, followed by Pond's talcum powder. He would then put on a perfectly ironed silk shirt and pants or wrap a gold-bordered mundu around his waist. Everywhere he went, the scent of the Brut perfume followed.

During his trips to Madras, Acchan wore safari suits. He always took a flight there. On his way to the airport, he always had a white handkerchief folded in a triangle in his breast pocket. I used to be delighted by it. I used to feel so proud; as a child I adored him. But once I lost that feeling, I began to detest not just the safari suit but even those who wore them. That's why Prabhudev Maheswari repelled me so. He always walked about in a suit as though to make it proclaim, 'I am a very important person, be respectful to me!' My father was the same. Whenever Prabhudev wore a new suit, it was totally unnecessary, but I still tried to picture his wardrobe and count his innumerable clothes, feeling irked.

That does not mean that I had actually seen his wardrobe. The only one I had seen was my father's. Samir's wardrobe was in a single backpack, and it contained things I'd bought him. Acchan had 260 shirts, 170 pairs of trousers, and 370 mundus. He had nearly a hundred suits. They served Amma well in the last days of his treatment at the hospital in Chennai. When it looked like it would be impossible for us to pay the hospital bills, Amma called Venukkuttan Chettan and asked him to pack all of them and send them to Chennai. My mother was adept at finding a way when there was none. When Acchan was undergoing dialysis at the hospital, she went searching for the suit rental places on Sterling Road – only she would think of that. Only she could drive hard bargains over well-tailored, sparely used suits made of expensive cloth. She sold them all and made a tidy profit. The silk shirts and the trousers. Later I heard how she sold them, standing by the wayside, bargaining. When we learned of it, Chechi and I wept inconsolably. But there was little shame in it actually. Selling and buying are fundamental rights. Some people sell knowledge, others, medicines. Some sell kidneys, others, the space of their wombs. Yet others sell new shirts, and some others, used ones. What's there to cry over this? Should we not be laughing bitterly? If this was our plight, then what to say about the vast majority out there.

I was reminded of it all when I opened Acchan's almirah in the darkness. The scent of clothes ironed long ago assailed my nostrils. When I groped inside, my fingers brushed against a few gold-bordered mundus neatly folded and stacked on the top shelves. When I touched them, I wanted to see my father. I was doubtful if, were we to meet again, he'd be the same. He had been melted slowly in death's furnace, and maybe, he was a much better father now? The question of how death might change people began to bother me. What would happen to me if the killer appeared now and ended my life with a bullet or a dagger? Like consciousness being shut down by pressing a switch and removing the bulb? Or like deflating a tyre? If it were like putting a piece of sugarcane into a juice machine and extracting the syrup, then there was some hope. One could then be sure that what came out was sweet juice. But what if it were like sowing the seed of the varikka jackfruit? There was no guarantee that a varikka jackfruit tree would spring from it; it could well be another, less favoured, variety.

I lay down on Acchan's cot. It was covered with dust; no one had slept on it for the past couple of months. As I lay there, it seemed to me that Acchan had come to me. But it was only the light – followed by Amma. I blinked. Amma was standing at the door, her long hair untied, eyes popping, nearly.

'Satye, you gave me a scare!'

'Why, Amma? Did you think someone killed me?'

She sighed, came up to me, and sat on the cot. Her hair, fallen loose, touched the bed. I felt a great rush of love for her.

'Amme, if he kills me, you'll put away all my things, won't you?'

Amma got up and started to go away. I caught her arm.

'Don't go. I have something to tell you.'

She sat down again. I caressed her hair lovingly. She looked at me carefully.

'Is it about Samir Sayyid?'

'Did Aswathy tell you anything, Amma?'

'Venukkuttan told me.'

'What did he tell you?'

'That you told the inspector about going to meet him.'

'Did I do something wrong?'

'In the eyes of the law, what you did is right.'

'Are you upset that I did not tell you in advance?'

'No, you are an adult woman. You can do what you think is right. You don't have to tell me, and I don't have to know about your actions, as long as they don't affect me.'

'Then why did you call me to tell me of the news about him?'

'That he was arrested was enough to make you throw up all day for one whole day. What if they had killed him in your presence? You'd have thrown up your stomach and intestines as well.'

'Hey, am I such a weakling, Amma?'

'Everyone has someone in their lives whose value is beyond measure ... He was that to you.'

'He wasn't who I thought he was.'

'He has every right to be different from what you thought him to be.'

'But he could well have been what I wanted him to be.'

'No one is obliged to be what others want them to be.'

'So it is impossible to find someone like that?'

'If you recognize that it is indeed impossible, half your problem will be solved!'

'What about the other half?'

'For that you will have to realize that you are not the person you think you are!'

'Amme, will they harm Samir?'

'That depends on how he deals with them.'

'That means?'

'If he reveals secrets and cooperates with the police, they may release him.'

'If he resists?'

'They may kill him.'

'That boy will never forgive me.'

'Which boy?'

'The boy who calls him chacha. Samir was his father's friend. His father has been missing for years.'

'Why didn't you just bring him with you?'

'Great! Here I am with no idea about when I am going to disappear myself and I should bring that child home?'

'This will end if we catch the guy with the pistol, won't it?'

'But he is still at large!'

'You already have so many leads – just try putting them together, you might find something.'

'Amma, finding a criminal isn't like reading a detective story!'

'There's a story behind how every criminal in the world ended up as a criminal. Find it, and the crime is unravelled.'

'But which story can we fully read, comprehend?'

'We can read as much as we can? Let us fill in the blanks, then, guessing.'

'Okay. Then why don't you fill in the blanks from whatever we have now?'

'What all do we know now?'

'Just about three or four things. One, the assailant is somehow connected to Acchan. Two, he has been following me for years. Three, he had some dealings with Samir Sayyid and Prabhudev Maheswari. Four, there is a possibility that he is connected with Abhilash too.'

He was connected with Chechi's death, too, I should have said that, but I did not because it would have made Amma withdraw into herself. So I swallowed it.

'His connection with Samir and Prabhudev had probably to do with his stalking you.'

'What do you mean?'

'The police should have nabbed him by now.'

'But they say they can't.'

'We can't believe everything the police say.'

'Aswathy at least must be telling us the truth?'

'No one is obliged to tell another the truth.'

'So what do we do now?'

'We must wait.'

'For what? My murder?'

Amma got up. I was lying on my side. She turned and threw me a look.

'For him to come.'

When Amma left, I stretched out on the bed and surveyed the room. I saw Acchan's large wooden box. Its broken lock beckoned me. I went over to it and opened the lid. The tattered old papers and the dust that had accumulated on them made me sneeze. The silverfish scrambled off to hide. I closed the lid, went back to the cot, sat on it. The thought of the hidden assassin worried me. I switched off the lights, went to Amma's room and lay down next to her. You'll probably understand that on such a night, one would simply not fall asleep easily. I tossed and turned. Something seemed to swell inside me, like steam in a pressure cooker. It was stifling. I just wanted to release the steam, like a pressure cooker would. But even the pressure cooker cannot remove its own weight. So I tried to deflect my thoughts. I wanted some suspense, an essential resource for a detective. I made some for myself – easy for a woman with a stalker with murderous intentions. I vowed to myself that I would find him. It made me feel better, more confident that I would find him. I did have more information than I'd told Amma. For example, this man had been Prabhudev's personal driver. Actually, I should have met Prabhudev or Mitali, not Samir.

I gave the thought of meeting Prabhudev Maheswari serious consideration. Then I heard the silverfish gnawing. Do they gnaw so loudly, I wondered. *Krrrrr … krrr …* it sounded. The noise was really close. Amma leapt up and shouted, 'Who's that!' The sound stopped. Amma switched on the lights. I rubbed my eyes and looked at her.

She was standing by the window. The wood around the latch on top of one windowpane had been cut clean with a handsaw; the wood around the latch at the bottom was almost sawn off.

Strange fumes emanated from my body. I grew clammy with sweat. Peed a bit. Amma ran her fingers over the rim of the hole on the windowsill and stood there, looking thoughtful. Something that she had said earlier appeared like a huge silverfish in the corner of my mind and began to gnaw at it – all criminals have a story. I saw through my eyes grown dim the one latch completely sawn out and the other one half sawn. It became clear to me that somewhere in my stalker-killer's story, I was present. Not just me, but also Acchan and that 'S'-shaped dagger. Because the shape in which the wooden frame of the windowpane had been sawn off to remove the latch was an S.

A light bulb went on in my head. I was in his story; and if that were so, he was in mine too. Maybe as a character, or a prop, or maybe as someone irrelevant. Anyway, one of the characters in my story was the bridge to who he was. For the time being, it was not Samir but Prabhudev Maheswari. While Amma was busy calling Aswathy, I opened my computer and booked an air ticket to Bhubaneswar. Maybe, after many years, the government would ask me why I booked a ticket at such an unearthly hour. But for the rest of that night, I slept peacefully.

By the way, is there any history of a killer cutting open a window two times on the same night with an 'S'-shaped dagger?

THIRTY

Have you ever imagined your life to be a path, and then tried to walk back on it? Right until the very spot at which you chose the very path you are presently on? Finding the exact place, the crossroads, have you lingered there for a moment with a sigh? A pity, if you haven't. Since, then, you have missed one of life's greatest moments! I have known it many a time. After 16 November 2016, this day was the decisive moment – on which I became a full-time crime investigator. I stepped from the gallery on to the field, from the audience to the stage.

Not that anything extraordinary happened that day. Venukkuttan Chettan and Radha Chechi arrived before dawn. Amma took them to see the vandalized window. I had packed my check-in baggage. So there was no need for special announcements; nor did anyone ask. The atmosphere was tense. I saw that the police may follow. The flight was at ten-fifty at night. There was plenty of time. I checked my hand baggage and then went over to chat with them. In such situations, my sense of humour comes alive. I make people laugh with a vengeance.

By nine in the morning, the police came. Their work got over quickly, earlier than expected. Some neighbours visited us. I set out after lunch. Amma had agreed to stay with Venukkuttan Chettan until I returned. Relieved, I dozed off in the car until we reached the town.

Before I reached the airport, I did some shopping for Aseema, Laina and Mitali. The flight was via Bangalore. We reached Bangalore at midnight; the connecting flight was at six-thirty in the morning. I killed time somehow. Not that I did not try to catch some sleep. But when I closed my eyes, I saw Samir.

I reached Bhubaneswar at eight-thirty. 'Good!' said Amma when I called her. I should have brought her along too, I thought then. She had not travelled much. The truth is that the 'S'-shaped dagger had pierced her spine, it was she who became immobile afterwards. As I waited for my bags, a sudden thought forced its way through my mind – was it that the person who stabbed Acchan actually harboured a grouse against Amma? The thought made me squirm inwardly. This was the trouble with me – unnecessary thoughts, tripping me over and over again. It would even make me forget that I was in Bhubaneswar to trace my assassin-in-waiting. This trip was crucial, but may not necessarily turn out to be a fruitful one. It would not be easy to face Prabhudev Maheswari and Mitali – both were tough nuts to crack. And I was clueless, like a dog setting out for the market.

But I perked up when I got into the taxi. I saw the city. The cities you leave are like the people you've come away from. They appear unfamiliar in a second encounter. I was relieved only when the driver opened the driver's door and spat on the road – only the face of the city had changed. I leaned back on the seat and let my eyes wander over it affectionately. It was the wedding season again and so the decorative stands decked with pleated chiffon saris of ugly pinks and greens and yellows were all over the place. As we moved through Vidyut Marg, a small wave of sadness lashed my mind. To forget it, I fixed my eyes on black hoardings outside that read 'The Pride of Bhubaneswar'. It announced the Femina Miss India Finale on 5 March. I kept murmuring to myself the slogan 'My State, My Story'. The sight of the police headquarters and the Central Stadium troubled me. A thornbush tugged at my heart at the sight of the Botanical Garden. It left a gash and scratch marks. They burned.

Aseema's flat had been repainted. The new shade was bluish-red. It pierced the eye like a massive two-thousand-rupee note held vertically. I paid the taxi and was getting my luggage out when Aseema came down to meet me. We hugged and kissed and shared happy complaints, teary-eyed. Her fifth-floor flat was home to me. Even then, I lost my sense of direction when we alighted there from the lift. I recognized it only from the bell that I had gifted her, which served as a doorbell. I rang it playfully. Laina opened the door, holding a Class 10 textbook. 'Ah, the bell is celebrating its owner's arrival!' she teased. We hugged and kissed, but I felt a certain distance. That was not her fault, it was mine. In my mind she would always be three years old. That was her age when Fasal threw them out. It took many years for the pools of detachment and impassivity that had formed in her little eyes to evaporate. I used to make her laugh, read her stories, play with her. Children get over things soon, after all, don't they? They grow up quickly. The trouble comes only after.

I occupied my usual room, which I always loved for its windows, light, and its two balconies. I had a quick shower. Aseema set out breakfast, Laina helped her. I ate the luchis and ghugni and Laina brought over an omelette and a glass of strong, hot tea. Then she went back to her studies. Aseema and I were now alone. We began to talk.

'Satya, the old man seems to have forgotten everything and settled down. Why are you here now? To dig up the mess?'

'He has forgotten nothing.'

'Isn't that worse?'

'My dear, now I have to choose between two dangers.'

'But sometimes I feel sorry for him. After you left, he started losing his temper with everyone.'

'What did you learn from it?'

'That you did leave him badly hurt.'

'Any child who plays with a knife will get hurt.'

'If you know that it is a child, don't give it a knife!'

'Did I know that he was but a child?'

'Don't you know that people who sit in high places are just children?'

'I didn't know that he was such a small kid.'

'Did you really give him any hope?'

'Hope? What hope?'

'Why is he so full of revenge towards you?'

'Because he was my superior officer.'

'What does that mean?'

'Superior officers can put up with anything – except insubordination.'

'Oh, your dumb definitions! Wasn't this something that you said about lovers sometime back?'

'In any relationship, one of the two will be the superior officer. And will demand submissiveness from the other.'

'Which of us is that?'

'Whichever of us demands submission from the other, of course.'

'Ah! Not enough that I made luchis and ghugni for breakfast and her favourite fish curry with fried mustard...'

'The attitude that demands submission in return for a salary or kindness or friendship – as a kind of indirect tax – that's what I call the superior-officer mindset.'

'I won't blame him even if he stabbed you to death!'

'If you want, I can give you the coolest dagger.'

'Then who'll eat my fish curry?'

'Yes – why would you need two weapons to kill one person?'

We burst out laughing. Aseema took the breakfast dishes back to the kitchen to wash. I was always lazy about washing my plates soon after a meal. So she took mine too. I sipped the cup of tea with pleasure. She returned and sat down beside me.

'Satya, have you decided to meet him?'

'Not sure if he'll agree.'

'You will meet him in office?'

'Most probably, I won't be allowed into the house.'

'It's going to be difficult even in the office.'

'I just need to see him when he gets out of the car and walks towards the office.'

'He's the CEO now. Two thousand staff members work under him. He's in Chhattisgarh three days a week and at the company's global HQ at least once a month. Who knows where he is today.'

'If you don't know that, why are you in the HR there?'

'Aiyo, I am just an assistant GM. To know the CEO's schedule, I will have to be at least a senior GM.'

'That's an exaggeration.'

'No chance of finding out today, for sure.'

'I'll wait.'

'How long?'

'Till I find a return ticket for three thousand.'

'So your plan is to stick around this house until then?'

'If you aren't game, I'll find another place.'

'I am!'

'Me too.'

We both laughed. After chatting for some more time, Aseema left for work. I decided to rest the whole day. My head rocked like a cradle from long sleeplessness. I dragged myself to the bed and fell asleep, nearly blacking out. Only when Aseema returned from work at five-thirty in the evening and woke me up, did I get up. I was not fully awake even then. She helped me reach the washbasin and I splashed water on my face reluctantly. She made me a cup of strong tea. My senses grew sharper as I drank it.

'Is the CEO in town?' I asked.

'In Spain.'

'Did he go alone?'

'I think so. The travel agent said that only one ticket had been booked.'

'Good girl. And you claimed that it was impossible to find out.'

'This much is possible to find out. But I can't say when he'll come to office.'

'How to find out his comings and goings?'

'Let me see.'

'We can, if you try.'

'How can I refuse you?'

We smiled at each other. I have always felt extremely secure by Aseema's side. Poor thing, she too was so like me. So much had she suffered in life! At the time I met her, she bore on her body the scars and burn marks left behind by her husband's violence. When I arrived here first, she was only a neighbour. She and Fasal and his mother were in the flat above mine. Laina was a baby then. One day, I found a rattle on my balcony and went up to return it. Aseema pulled her headscarf close and opened the door. I held out the rattle, she took it, closed the door. She did not even smile. I noticed a bluish scar above her left eye. I had with me some Arnica cream – Mitali's gift to me when I bruised my hand in their house. I took it upstairs. It was Aseema who opened the door. I held it out, asked her to use it on the bruise. She looked shattered; she stared at me. Later, she told me that it was the first time since her Papa and Mummy had passed away that someone had been kind to her. Her fingers trembled as she took the cream. She tried to smile but her eyes were full of tears. I pretended not to notice and ran back.

The next evening, she came over. The rattle had fallen on my balcony that day too. I gave it to her. Then it fell every day, and I returned it promptly. She came every day. One day I asked her about her education. She was the daughter of professionals – her father had been an engineer working in the Gulf countries and her mother a doctor. She had studied in Delhi for her degree in Business Studies and then in London for a postgraduation in Business Management. I was stricken when I realized that this woman was now standing in front of me with the bruise from an aluminium vessel flung at her face and the scar from her hand being burned on the gas stove. She had been an only child. While she was preparing to move to Princeton for a PhD, her parents died in a car crash. She returned to India with the dead bodies of her parents. She lost control of her life after. Everything was taken over by her father's younger brother, her chacha. Fasal was his wife's nephew. Her chacha fixed the marriage. Before she even saw his face properly, she was married to him. Fasal treated her like an enemy – because of her education. And of course, the knowledge that the marriage would have been totally impossible if her parents were not dead. He raped her on the wedding night and on several nights afterwards. He beat her from dawn to dusk. At first, she put up a fight. Left their home and went back to her uncle's house. But he drove her back. In the middle of it all, she became pregnant. The childbirth affected her womb. It was a girl, and seeing that there was no chance of having a boy ever, Fasal became a demon. And she was on the brink of insanity.

That was the time we were recruiting in the Human Resources department at Advaita. I asked Aseema to apply. She was not bold enough. I kept tempting her, giving her pep talks, threatening her. In the end, she sent an application. I had to sneak her into the interview. I waited outside holding her baby. She got the job. There was a veritable earthquake in her house. Fasal beat her to a pulp and was ready to kill the baby. That night, she took refuge in my flat with her child. The next day, he and his mother intensified their attack. I thought that she might give in. That's what happens usually. But she didn't. Fasal began to behave violently. I called Mitali. The police reached in ten minutes and dragged Fasal away. He came back after two weeks, a bag of bones. The next day, when we opened our door, we found her things and those of her child piled up at our doorstep like a heap of trash. He, along with his family, had moved. Apparently, he remarried the next month. He had squandered most of her wealth, and some of it was stolen by that uncle of hers. She fought three whole years to reclaim the rest, while she stayed with me. Laina grew up as my daughter too. When she moved to her own flat, I was prouder. I had a room there, and it was to be mine always.

The only thing that had changed since I left last time was the flame creeper on the balcony. It had grown lush and flowered profusely.

The balcony was now covered with orange-coloured blooms. It was really cold. The wind blew gently. I tried to imagine what a petal being blown away would feel. Would my soul feel that way in death? It would be suspended in the air for a little while, blown around for some time, and then it would descend slowly to the stillness of the earth – I felt it in my body. Mine would be a flower with a petal lost. The other one was, of course, in Mitali's body. Even if I died, my kidney would continue to protect another body.

The trip to Bhubaneswar was an impulsive decision. But it was a good one. First of all, there was some relief from the stress. When Aseema left for work and Laina for school, I would be alone at home. I would have enough time to rest and think. Sitting on that balcony with a cup of tea or coffee brought back clarity and perspective. There was just one thing that bothered me. Memories of Samir. The road on which we had walked together the first day, hand in hand, was right in front of my eyes. I could still feel the warmth of his palm in mine. Were the veins of love on my palm? Anyway, I had melted in love for two men whose hands I had held. When Abhilash had held my hand, I had thrilled with pleasure. I had been aroused with admiration at the coolness with which he flung a petrol bomb at a police vehicle, run into the library, and pretended to be buried in his reading. I was wrong to think that he was led by idealism; no, it was the love for power that drove him. I was just a step in his complicated arithmetic of power. I realized that only later, and how much did I rue that error of mine.

Samir, however, was different. He had held my hand firmly only because it had excited him as much as his hand had excited me. I never regretted him. He was my mate, my perfect mate. I did not really know him; nor did he know me. But how we celebrated each other! Like elephants in a forest, we walked ten and twenty kilometres. In circles, straight ahead, covered with sweat, panting, sitting down at wayside eateries for pani puris and chai, and then walking again ... The very memory made my body quiver with delight. No man had affected me so. Everything for him was a source of delight. And love. There is a connection between love and joy, you may have noticed. If there is love, then there is joy. And vice versa. The way he used to wait for me when he returned from his trips. The sparkle in his eyes when he saw me. That smile – the corners of his mouth curling up. Those were the joys of love. But an occasional note ban may benefit love too. What other means do we have to find out if our lovers are fake notes or not? Remember, though, be it currency notes or romance, demonetizing is a pain. It is costly, and new notes have to be printed for sure. ATMs have to be recalibrated, the cash trays have to be replaced. Useless expenses, all of it. Many continue to stick to the familiar, keep on 'adjusting', because of these burdensome tasks.

Are you bored with my endless chatter about love and money? I apologize. The impact of a demonetization – of a love's currency – is still unabated in me, that's why. Give me time until fifty. If I continue with this blather even after that, you may roast me alive. But until then, I need to mumble about it. Because, for me, this crime investigation was a quest to recover the ultimate Truth. And that Truth was a kind of Love. It was eclipsed by a shining golden disc, of wealth or revenge – the *hiranmayena paatrena*...

My Truth was the sum of the many journeys I embarked on to discover it.

THIRTY-ONE

When I first came to Bhubaneswar, I was twenty-eight. It was a tricky age. The loneliness begins to weigh down upon you. Thoughts of death appear. The body craves for a loving touch, the heart, for love. But it still stays wary of human beings.

Mitali came in person to pick me up from the railway station like I was a valued guest. She made me stay with her for nearly a week, during which she taught me that, in a relationship, the one who is richer is the superior officer. She stayed in that position for the entire duration of my stay there. She decided what I should do, found a dwelling for me. She rejected my choice of an apartment – it was called Trishna Manor. She liked 'Suchismita' better, so I had to change my preference. But remember what my condition was then? Hard cash, just hard cash, was Supreme Deity to me. Poverty scared me now. I was terrified of returning to the world of Vyakulamata and Saubhagya and St Anthony's with a single kidney in my body.

It was when I stayed with her that I learned what it was to be really wealthy in India. Wasn't anything like I'd seen until then, for sure. Vasanthaalayam, Nityavasantham, *Vasanthakairali* – none of this was wealth. Wealth lay with people like Mitali. She called it 'C.R.' – short, actually, for 'crore' – that struck me only after some time. Silver plates,

322

golden vessels, and blocks of solid gold, countless bank lockers – to me, her life resembled a fable, a piece of fiction. Two sisters, a brother. The brother squeezed the very life-breath out of them, octopus-like. He was their nemesis. My life, too, changed because of him. On the third night of my stay there, I was woken rudely by screams. Prabhudev was beating up Mitali! How could I ignore that? I went over and got in the middle, got slapped too. I lost my cool, grabbed the stick he was using, and pushed him hard. He was stunned! The poor fool had staged this show thinking no one would give it back to him in the same coin. I grabbed his collar and, staring hard into his eyes, snarled, 'Not enough to have fair skin and a high-flying family and a palace! You need goodness, goodness of the heart, do you understand?' He just stood there, looking gobsmacked.

Mitali did not like it. She was, of course, a *Bharatiya naari.* 'It's my husband, he can hit me!' she exclaimed, bursting into tears. But I was in no mood to let go, was I? My rage grew even fiercer. I challenged him. That was not really necessary. The roots of the super-rich run very deep into the ground. It is better not to see what they do down there. It's enough to derive pleasure from the tree trunk and branches, flowers and fruits. You can eat the fruits, too, maybe. Sleep in the tree's shade. But do not dig. If you do, there will be no tree left. Only networking and trading beyond your imagination. Only an ecosystem inhabited by bandicoots and worms.

After that confrontation, I came to my senses. And remembered that he was the superior officer. How was I to go to the office now? How could I stay in that house? Better to clear out immediately sometimes. Just let things take their course, be prepared for whatever may come. I prepared to leave. Then someone knocked at my door. I opened it. Wife and husband stood there, united now. When they saw that I was about to leave, they stopped me.

'Satyapriya, I apologize for everything that has happened. Please forget it all, please don't go away.'

'I had a very different idea of you,' I said. 'I never thought that you were a wife-beater.'

'No, no, Satya, it was not his fault. The fault was mine – truly. If your mother gives away a large sum of money to someone without seeking your father's permission, how would your father respond?'

'If my mother sets her mind on something, no one, and not just my father, can stop her.'

'Really?'

'It was my mother who managed our finances in our worst days. And after that, it was my sister and I. No one asked my father for anything.'

'Oh! But that is not how things are in our families.'

'Educated people should move with the times.'

'Shouldn't women in our families always respect the head of the household in our culture?'

'Mitali Didi, families should rest on mutual respect.'

'My family is everything to me.'

'What greatness is there in a family that rests on the foundations of falsehood?'

'Mitali, I think Satya is a feminist.'

'Prabhudev Sir, it does not matter who I am. My problem is with you believing firmly what you did is right.'

'Mitali sometimes understands only the language of a stick.'

'What language do you understand, you who accepted as a wife a woman who knows only the language of the stick? That of the stick itself? Or of your wife's bank account?'

Wife and husband looked petrified. I went back to getting ready to leave. But Prabhudev begged me not to go. Ultimately, I gave in, but never forgave him. Nor could I think of him as my superior officer after that. Later, a few weeks after I joined the office, we talked.

'You are still angry with me, Satya?'

'Anger? Towards a highly civilized person like you?'

'Are you being sarcastic?'

'No, no. Arsha Bharata culture demands that the husband should beat his wife at least thrice a day.'

'I had told her a number of times that she was not to give any money to that asshole.'

'True. Mitali Didi is not human, is she? She is just your pet animal!'

'Satya, you are complicating things unnecessarily.'

'If I respond that it is not I who's complicating things, then that may be contrary to Arsha Bharata culture.'

'I don't want to argue.'

'I did not argue – I was assenting to all that you said.'

'All right … How's the promotion appraisal going?'

'It is ready.'

'We need a new pro forma. Can't be just the same things that we asked last time.'

'Shall we ask about wife-beating?'

'You are crossing your limits.'

'Will you beat me, too, Sir?'

'You may please go.'

After half an hour, he called me to his office.

'Satya, actually, you are making me uncomfortable.'

'I am ready to resign, Sir.'

'Why do you have to poke me each time like this?'

'Didn't you notice why, Sir? I am trying to condition myself!'

Actually, I was in a rage. My heart boiled; my blood vessels swelled from the blood turning into vapour. But only later did I see that it was I who played the superior officer there. It was a fun game, like playing with a dagger. You'll poke yourself sometimes, and get a scratch, a gash, now and then. The most important element of this game is that you create in the other a sense of guilt and inferiority. Your superior officer should feel guilty, sorry – his head must be lowered in shame or guilt. And you should push it down if he does try to raise it. But you should not do that by challenging him directly. You must stand before him looking meek; you should deal with him going down on your knees, as though you are submitting to his authority. Prabhudev Maheswari could only deal with me physically, but I was able to deal with him psychologically. That is why he was so vengeful towards me. I knew it, and he knew that I knew it too.

To think of it, he was in a bad spot. Mitali had spies everywhere who kept an eye on him. She told me that he hired sex workers on his trips abroad. I thought it unforgivable. I looked through his bills and observed that all the rooms he'd stayed in were double occupancy. The wickedness in me stirred. I called three hotels he had stayed in and asked for the detailed bills, and found out that each time, he had had women with him. In Thailand, he had three guests in his room, one for each day of the stay. I was angry. There was no reason to be angry, but back then, I was young and stupid.

A meeting at the company headquarters was fixed for the next day. The manager who was to travel with him was on sick leave. Prabhudev asked me to be the substitute. I refused. He was taken aback.

'Satyapriya, this is a golden opportunity. You can climb at least two steps in your career.'

'I am not brave enough to travel with you.'

'What does that mean?'

'How can I travel with someone who buys sex?'

He blanched.

'Stop that nonsense!'

I went back to his room with copies of the bills of his hotel stays. I had written the names of his female companions on them. What could be more insulting than this for a superior officer? Yes, I should not have done that. But what can I say, I have made so many such mistakes! He called me in the evening.

'Satyapriya, this is a serious allegation.'

'It's not an allegation. There's evidence.'

'Are you trying to blackmail me?'

'I don't want to accompany you. How can that be blackmailing?'

'What's the meaning of that? Are you a sex worker?'

'I am afraid you'll think that.'

'I gave you this job.'

'But I don't feel brave enough to come with you.'

'What a pain in the...'

'... ass?'

'Satyapriya, this is serious. Just because someone spread a stupid...'

'I found it out for myself.'

'You mean you were spying on me?'

'That is being done by people in your family already.'

'Who? Mitali?'

'That you should find out for yourself.'

'What the hell is your problem?'

'I have heard a lot about people who buy sex during their travels abroad. I do not wish to accompany such a person. That's it.'

Prabhudev sat in his chair looking shell-shocked. I went back to my seat, thought it over, wrote a letter of resignation, and went back to his room. He was in the washroom. When he came out, his face was flushed, eyes reddened. He had been weeping, I thought. That agitated me a bit. I held out the letter. He stared at it for a few moments and gestured to me to leave. I took my bag and went home. No sooner had I pushed the door and entered the house than I burst into tears. I wept for some time, thought about my next step. Should I stay on in Bhubaneswar, or not? I should move, I decided. Those days, Mumbai was a paradise for MBAs. I decided to move there and try my luck. Then someone rang the bell. I opened the door and saw Prabhudev Maheswari waiting at my doorstep. He came in and handed me my resignation letter, torn in half. He lowered himself into a chair, and after a few moments of silence, asked, 'Tell me, how have I wronged you, Satyapriya?'

I had no answer. Indeed, I thought of it just then. Yes, what wrong had he done me? That he gave me a job as soon as I asked? That he let me stay in his house? That he gave me an opportunity to go abroad? He had beaten his wife – that was his only fault. The Domestic Violence

Act did not exist in those days. But I could not forgive him. I told him that, openly. He looked at me, eyes open wide, amazed.

'I didn't beat you, did I? It was my wife I struck, isn't that true?'

'A man who strikes his wife will strike any woman. And a man who does not will also not raise his hand against any other woman. That is a mindset.'

'Should I not punish when I see a wrong?'

'Only the state can have that power.'

'You are complicating things unnecessarily.'

'That's why I have decided to resign. The complication I am causing you will end that way.'

'End? It will only become worse. Do you think Mitali is going to stay quiet?'

'I will convince Didi that my father's health is worse than before and that my mother wants me home.'

'Convince me as well. I have never harmed you in any way. I have not forced you into anything illegal or immoral. I just offered you a chance to travel abroad. That was my only fault.'

'Sir, this is not your fault, it is mine. I had placed you on a high pedestal, and I see that I was wrong.'

'Satya, I am a man, and my body has its needs.'

'I did not realize that you were someone who paid to fulfil those needs.'

'What's wrong with that? I love my family, I take care of them, I give them all that they need.'

'If my husband spoke to me like this, that would be the end of the marriage.'

'I admit to all my faults. I apologize. But you should not leave now, Satya. It will take a big toll, personally and professionally. I beg you.'

I began to feel weaker.

'It's going to be bad not just for me but also for you. I am telling you, like an older brother. A job change in your career now is no good at all. You worked for hardly a year at Mahipala. Now you're leaving this place after barely four months. Please wait till you can find a better opportunity.'

'What if you take revenge on me?'

'You know how to keep me in line, don't you?'

I smiled. He too.

'You are like a member of our family. I cannot let you leave like this.'

I was now totally disarmed.

'This Saturday is Amita's birthday. You are invited. Do come?'

I agreed. Are you convinced about Prabhudev's HR management skills now? He had such command over tactics and tact, both. His negotiation skills always amazed me. And that his family was the only place where they did not work had also puzzled me.

I went to Amita's birthday party. She was Prabhudev and Mitali's elder daughter. I met Pritiranjan there.

'Oh, so you are Didi's new adviser?' he smirked.

'Oh, so you are her wastrel of a brother?' I retorted.

First, he was taken by surprise. Thereafter, he gave up.

'Who told you?'

'People here. In one voice.'

'Tell those people to get lost.'

'You'd have found it easier to say that if you were sitting on your father's pile of wealth; but if that wealth was made from your own sweat and tears, you'd be more careful.'

He turned sharply and marched off. I took a glass of wine and settled down in a quiet corner. Prabhudev came over with a whisky.

'What did he say?'

'Oh, nothing, this and that.'

'Don't let him close.'

'Prabhudev Sir, isn't there anyone in your family who can be allowed to come close?'

'That's a good one,' he said, trying to smile. I liked him at that moment. He had stopped playing the superior-officer game; he had acknowledged my dominant position. He continued that way for a long time. He changed again, however, during the 2G scam judgment. It was a great blow to Mitali's family. But the politics that he played in the whole affair made him dominant in that family. He began to exercise power, and even I had no respite now. That's why I am telling you: each and every one of the despicable acts of those who ruled us in particular times has affected me directly. Prabhudev tried to tie my hands. He made me his assistant, made sure that I was on my toes, behind him all twenty-four hours, and, at the same time, tried to make Mitali suspicious about our relationship.

One day, she invited me over. As we were chatting, she asked if she could have my phone. I gave it to her. She called a few people and went into the toilet while speaking to them. She checked my phone sitting there. It had some messages that Prabhudev had sent. Her eyes were teary and red when she came out. 'My head aches,' she said, avoiding me.

When I reached home, I received a message from her. 'Why did you do this to me?' it said. I became anxious and called her back, but she did not pick up. I went over, then, to see her. She refused the meeting. I grew even more worried. Then, she exploded. My pride was hurt. In the end, I had to seek Prabhudev's help.

'Never mind, Satya,' he reassured me. 'Mitali is paranoid, a bit.'

'But why does she suspect me? For no reason?'

'Who knows?' Then, after a moment, he said, 'It's partly my fault too. I called her "Satya" a couple of times unwittingly.'

'What was wrong with that?'

'I called her by that name at the wrong moments…'

I blushed. He came up to me and put his hand on my shoulder.

'Her suspicions aren't off the mark, Satya. You have stolen her husband's heart completely. Which woman would suffer that?'

I felt listless. Slowly, it dawned on me – he had been manipulating Mitali. And me as well. I did not see the reason for it then. Now I do. Is it possible to control any human being without manipulating them?

After all, this whole world stays in place essentially through mutual manipulations.

~

A year and a half ago, when I finally left Bhubaneswar, I had decided that I'd never go back. But Prabhudev made me go back. Either he or Mitali. It could be a trap. I longed to fall into it. Because Prabhudev was an important step in my investigation. I needed to step on him to reach another – my assassin, and his connection with Samir.

I made a plan to meet Prabhudev. Aseema managed to sneak out the details from his appointment diary. He returned from Spain on Friday. On Saturday, at seven-thirty in the evening, there was a Christmas eve dinner at the Blue Flower Lagoon. Four people who had come from the company's office in Britain were his guests, along with their families.

I checked in at the Blue Flower Lagoon. Just twenty-five thousand per night! Money, after all, is impermanent – just a flow, comes and goes. But life? I waited in the restaurant from seven o'clock onwards. It was certain that his superiors, those Britishers, were sticklers for time. Surely, he would arrive before time to keep them in good spirits? Just as I had thought – he came in half an hour early. I went up to him. He started.

'Hello, Prabhudevji, I hope you are well?' I asked.

He stared at me.

'I need to know two things: tell me at once. That's best for us both.'

He looked at me, caught completely off guard.

'First, the real name and address of S. Prakash. Second, your connection with Samir Sayyid.'

I looked at the clock in the hall.

'It is 7.02 now. I'll wait until 7.07.'

That was it. Be terse when you speak to former superior officers. One or two sentences, with as much information as they can carry.

I returned to my table. But there was someone else sitting there. I thought he had made a mistake. I was wrong. A couple of days back, the PM had warned us that it was no breeze that was blowing here but a veritable storm, and that all criminals would be caught red-handed. That came true! At least I was caught, red-handed. The person who was sitting at my table smiled and waved, and then held out his hand. That was truly a blow in the dark. Know who it was? Any guesses?

THIRTY-TWO

It was Inspector Anurup Shetty, nattily dressed in a suit. His hair was nicely groomed. He wore an attractive perfume and seemed elated. But I? You can well guess what my state was. Until then, I had been a feather on some bird's body. Not sure which bird, though. Anyway, it felt like the bird had been plucked off me. Facing him thus, completely out of the blue, I felt disarmed and naked. In such instances, however, a certain on-the-spot spunk has often saved me. On its strength, I pulled a chair and sat opposite him. But I did not have the spirit to look at him or speak. I had to return to Prabhudev in five minutes too. So the only thing I could ask the inspector was when he had arrived. My good fortune, the waiter brought the menu just then. I excused myself, got up, and went towards Prabhudev.

Three important exchanges happened that evening. The first one was with Prabhudev. It began like this:

'Prabhudevji, the five minutes are over.'

'How are you connected with that policeman, Satya?'

'My first question – the name and address of your former driver.'

'Is he your latest lover?'

'Second question – what's the connection between Samir Sayyid and you?'

'Sorry, Satya, I should not have interfered in your personal matters.'

'My first question – the name and address of your former driver.'

'I will tell you – give me some time. I am very upset.'

'My first question…'

'Okay, enough. His name is Prakash, that's what he said.'

'Full name?'

'Who asks the full name of a driver?'

'Didn't you get his address?'

'It was cleared by HR.'

'You were the HR manager?'

'C'mon, Satya, he was a contract worker, not on our payroll.'

'Did the HR manager make him his personal driver?'

'My personal driver was Debashish. His younger brother joined the Maoists, so he had to be dismissed.'

'You – who had been close to the Maoist Samir Sayyid – you were scared of a poor villager?'

'Satya, when you are part of a corporate company, you network a lot!'

'Was Samir Sayyid bought thus?'

'He was fixed on Kashmir. He saw his life's work there.'

'Not clear.'

'The company had to have him go back.'

'So?'

'We made a deal. He was to return. We would pay.'

'Did he agree?'

'When his land and house are on fire, any man would.'

'You men and your politics! So, tell me, what or who was behind Golla's death?'

'He had enemies among his own.'

'I want to know whether Samir sought your help first or whether you approached him.'

'I did.'

'What was the power play behind it?'

'I told you, corporate…'

'Your negotiator was the driver Prakash, right?'

'In a way…'

'But there were many drivers here. Why him?'

'He was referred to me by Ramesh Mohanty, the IG of Police.'

'How were they connected?'

'He said that he was the IG's driver.'

'When did you call him last?'

'Not after you left.'

'Why?'

'I am going to be frank – no reason to hide anything. I called him to find out about you. After Samir and you parted, I hired a professional detective; and then I did not need him any more.'

'And what did the detective discover?'

'That you live by yourself and that you have no relationships.'

'Yes, that's because I caught gonorrhoea and so couldn't have sex for some time.'

'Go…?'

'A sexually transmitted disease that women get.'

'Don't make fun of me, Satya.'

'Will any woman reveal her gonorrhoea to just tease a man?'

'You have not been able to forget Samir even now, am I right?'

'That's none of your business.'

'I know that you are waiting for him, even now.'

'Prabhudevji, your guests will arrive soon, so please give me his phone number, and proceed?'

'This is the address that I have.' He took out one of his visiting cards, opened his WhatsApp, and copied the address on to the back of the card. He held it out to me. Just then, the glass doors opened and the Britishers walked in. I got up. 'See you later,' I said, and walked back to my table. As soon as I sat down, Inspector Shetty snatched the card from my hand. Before I could stop him, he had read it. He smiled that cute childlike smile.

'But this is the old address, Ma'am…'

Having no reply, I gulped down the water from the glass. He pushed the card towards me, then leaned back and smiled broadly.

'Are you pissed with me, Ma'am?'

'What for?'

'For incarnating in this form here like this?'

'The gods do not give notice when they incarnate to destroy evil!'

'I took up this mission precisely to chat with you like this. I do miss our chats!'

I did not ask him which mission. This was a policeman, he wouldn't tell you, that was sure. I never trusted the police, never told them all. Not because I was guilty of anything, but you know what the police are like. They are skilled at turning a goat into a dog and a dog into an elephant – that's the police for you. At the first chance, I got up and went back to my room. I wanted to be alone, to douse the steam building inside my head, to see things clearly. The next blow in the dark came right then. I opened the door and tried to place the key in its holder – but there was another key there. I could see the light from the bedroom lamp. I went in – and got a shock.

In the room were three or four men, and a woman, reclining on the bed, her head on the pillow propped up behind. It was Mitali; I took a moment to recognize her. She threw me a hostile grin. I remained where I was for a few seconds, shocked. Who thought such things were possible? Five people trespassing on a room in a five-star hotel! Then I shook like a leaf. Don't ask how someone who claimed to be free of the fear of death shook so. When do human beings feel fear? When they can't figure out something well enough, when they don't know what is about to happen.

I thought of my options as I stood there. She may kill me, I thought. What was the difference between death by her hand and death by the assassin's? Death was a trifle to me. The second was torture. I would have to suffer pain. If needed, I could suffer anything. But the third one scared me. Gang rape. I could deal with one, but a group? I did not know what to do because I lacked the experience. I decided to face it, whatever it was, and my courage returned. I smiled at my potential rapists and asked them if they needed tea or beer. Then pulled up a chair and sat down facing Mitali. She glared at me vengefully. The second conversation of that evening followed.

'Why, you did not expect me here?'

'No.'

'You thought I would not know when you'd come to Bhubaneswar?'

'I was going to come over to meet you. Glad that you came here.'

'No need for that smarty-pants talk. I got to know the moment you landed.'

'I am gratified.'

'I knew that you'd be meeting my husband here.'

'I did not.'

'I wanted to catch you two red-handed today.'

'You caught us many times anyway?'

'Every time you slipped away with some excuse or another. This time you are trapped.'

'My dear Mitali Didi, please believe me. I have no interest in your husband at all.'

'Your lover probably taught you to say this!'

'I have absolutely nothing to do with your husband. I don't need him. I have said this multiple times. I am saying it again.'

'Lie! Fucking lie! I have the full record of everywhere you and Prabhudev have stayed together.'

'We stayed in separate rooms!'

'My husband is your slave.'

'I do not believe in slavery.'

'I can give you any amount of money. Leave my husband.'

'You are talking to a woman who sold her kidney for some money. I did not need to sell it for money, really.'

'That's what I can't understand. Why did you sell your kidney?'

'That's because I can't bear the stink of the sweat of men like your husband.'

She began to weep.

'How I loved you once, Satya! Like my own younger sister! Why did you do this to me? If you wanted a man, there were so many out there. Why did you ruin my life?'

She sat there looking despondent, holding her head in her hands. I had encountered this state of hers many times. She needed no response, no evidence. She would weep, accuse me of trying to steal the sindoor on her forehead and the mangalsutra around her neck, threaten to kill herself; that day, too, she began to complain and beat her breast. I began to feel bored. Leaping up, I yelled, 'Stop!' The four young men lunged forward.

'There is a limit to my endurance. I was not in love with your husband. I loved Samir Sayyid, and he is still my lover!'

'Lie! Lie! You are lying!' she screamed again. It was painful to hear; her cries were heart-rending. I knew her anguish. People cry like that not out of love but from the lack of trust. That's why Amma was able to hang on and not burst into tears when we caught Acchan in the act with that actress Rajani. Amma was confident, but not everyone possesses that quality. Who else knows that better than me? Love someone – realize that he does not need your love – the strongest of hearts would be wounded. Burn like it was doused with chilli-paste. After some time, the burned parts will get infected, pus will form, it will start to stink. That's a terrible stink, really. You begin to seek out its source, and you'll do so till it dawns on you that it is coming out of your own heart. Because I am the intelligent sort, I saw this early on, went on to heal quickly. But Mitali was a fool. And, of course, there was her elitist ego on top of it. Her subconscious worked hard to dump all the blame on a woman of a class lower than her – me. In reality, she was hurting herself, making herself weep. I got up, went to her, held her close, and tried to comfort her, 'Please don't cry, Didi, am I not your little sister?' She broke into sobs again and tried to push me away. I held her firmly, and her protests began to subside. She rested her head on my chest and sobbed softly. My eyes grew misty too. The sight of an ailing person, writhing in agony, would make anyone's eyes moist, wouldn't it?

Her sobs echoed in the hotel room. The young men waited impatiently for a command. Then the doorbell rang, and she jumped. There was expectation in her eyes. Her face flushed, paranoid.

'There! He's come! Didn't I tell you? He doesn't know that I am here. I knew he'd come here. He left home dressed like a dandy just to spend the night with you!'

My face turned pale. My heart beat hard. Did Prabhudev come up here to meet me? I was terrified of the possibility. Great, then! I cursed the moment I left home. Mitali's bodyguard opened the door. But it was Inspector Shetty who came in.

'What's happening here?' he asked. 'A conference?'

He pulled up a chair and sat down.

'She and I are two bodies and one heart,' I said.

Mitali's face turned yellow; relief and disappointment flashed alternately on her face. Lack of confidence is not a crime, but it can be fatal. Not just to her, but to others as well.

'Is there a penalty for intruding into another person's hotel room?' I asked him.

'No, if it is the owner of this hotel, like Mitaliji.'

Only then did I remember – her family owned this hotel. She got up. Her bodyguards followed. When they left, I let out a huge sigh of relief and thanked Inspector Shetty.

'I thought something was wrong because you were taking so much time to get back – I was waiting,' he said.

'Thank you, Inspector Sir,' I replied. 'You have finally done me a good turn!'

'You have misunderstood me, Ma'am.'

'Isn't that because you have never given me a chance to understand you?'

'It's because you don't try.'

'If so, tell me, why are you following me?'

'Because I need to. To investigate this very important case.'

'Now that Samir Sayyid has been nabbed, aren't you done with it?'

'My interest will remain till we catch your assassin.'

'What is your interest in this?'

'It's got into my bones. No other case has been so challenging.'

'Are there no other cases to solve in your station?'

'I am on a long leave.'

My eyes popped. My heart quavered. Something felt terribly wrong. There was a time bomb under my feet, someone had placed it there.

'Let's go to the restaurant. The food must have arrived.'

'I am not hungry.'

'Please, just give me some company?'

'That's not my job.'

'Okay, goodnight, then. But before that, here's a little gift.' He pulled out a small notepad from his pocket, tore out a sheet of paper, scribbled something on it, and then held it out to me.

'The address used by S. Prakash in his former life.'

I felt an electric surge passing through my body. I looked at the address anxiously.

'S. Prakash, Contract Labourer, Despatch Section, Mahipala Cosmetics, Faridabad.'

I wanted to laugh and cry at the same time. It was confirmed again – that his story and mine were the same. When Inspector Shetty left, I closed the door securely. The pillow was wet – with Mitali's tears. I too felt tears prick my eyes. The tears of the feather that believed it was a bird, believing the lies that the breeze told. Tears, thinking of the distance that was yet to be covered. A really sad, strange bout of tears. You must try shedding such copious tears, at least once in your life. Else, how would you know the market value of the heart's feelings?

It's better not to describe my sleep that night. I tossed and turned. Dozed, but woke up with a start. Then I walked around the room until it was daybreak. Before dawn, Inspector Shetty called. That was the third conversation.

'Inspector Sir, were you analysing my case sleeplessly?'

'I was thinking about you. And through that, analysing your case.'

'It's been quite some time since you started.'

'I haven't counted the days.'

'It began the week after the note ban.'

'They haven't even finished counting the notes!'

'But the government has published fifty-nine notifications!'

'Isn't that easy, Ma'am? Can you compare a crime investigation with it?'

'No, that involves many questions and answers.'

'What are you doing for Christmas, Ma'am?'

'Make a guess?'

'I don't have the nerve to go about making guesses about you, Ma'am! You have proved many of my predictions wrong!'

'The truth is I have not decided.'

'Then let me suggest something.'

'That I should be quiet and good?'

'No. Go meet Mitali, talk to her.'

'What's your interest in that?'

'Catching your assassin, of course.'

'Never, the police are not likely to take such close interest in a case like this.'

'If you are killed, will the media spare us, Ma'am?'

'What's their interest in me?'

'Samir Sayyid, Prabhudev Maheswari, Mahipal Shah Baba ... and maybe even Sriram from back home ... Dig up ten generations of these men, and they can fill their pages for at least a month!'

'But there is no evidence that my assassin was hired by any of these men!'

'If you ask me thus, then the only evidence is against Mitali.'

'There's just one way to get it: blackmail.'

'Ma'am, you are a sensation! How are you going to blackmail her?'

'Can't you help me, Inspector Sir?'

'Good god! Asking the police to assist in blackmailing someone?'

'You help only the government?'

'Our job is to obey the government.'

'Government means the people of this country. That means, the police belong to them.'

'I'll give you a clue. Your assassin came to Odisha from Mahipala.'

'But it was I who told you of that!'

'There's one thing that you did not tell me – that Mitali knew him from then.'

'How?'

'He was a witness in a criminal case involving her brother Pritiranjan.'

'What case?'

'A murder case.'

'Murder? Whose?'

'Pritiranjan's friend Pranab.'

'Tell me more.'

'Pranab and Pritiranjan were friends. Pritiranjan had an affair with Pranab's wife Subrata. Pranab got to know about it; Pritiranjan killed him. Cut his head off. Threw the headless torso into the Mahanadi. Someone informed the police about having witnessed four or five men murdering another in a car. His name was S. Prakash.'

I began to tremble. My body shook whenever I heard that name.

'And then?'

'The police filed a case. But the witness could not identify Pritiranjan. Then someone else owned up to the crime.'

'That is, the witness pulled a trick. In return, Mitali rewarded him.'

'That's the plausible guess. But Prabhudev does not know about this.'

'Naturally. Since it was about her brother, she must have kept it away from him.'

'Happy marriage!'

'Where is that woman, Pranab's wife?'

'She disappeared. To be exact, around the time you joined Advaita.'

'Does she have children?'

'No. They weren't married for long.'

'Doesn't her family know?'

'They filed a missing persons complaint. The enquiry did not yield fruit.'

'Thank you.'

'For what?'

'For speaking with me for so long so early in the morning.'

'Ma'am, there is something I need to know.'

'Ask me…'

'Who in your life have you loved sincerely?'

'When I love, I love all the objects of my love with the same sincerity.'

'See, you never give me a precise reply to any question!'

'Let me ask you a question. How much profit has the country made from the note ban?'

'Why do you keep irritating me forever with references to the note ban? Forget it! Tell me, what is your next step?'

'What would you have done if you were in my place, Inspector?'

'That's a good question. I would have told the police everything a long time ago!'

'So you know well that I will not tell you everything. Why do you irritate me then with that demand?'

I pretended to be angry and ended the call. But in my mind, I thanked Inspector Shetty. Enough information at the right time – what greater help could someone give? A person's private property is not composed of merely wealth, there are also truths. Earning truths is so much harder than earning money! I began planning to seize truths from Mitali. Seizing the truths – that is what a crime investigation is.

THIRTY-THREE

Human beings live not on money or food alone. They live on trust: without trust, any exchange – of love or wealth or whatever – is immoral. That's what makes you think – the sheer guts of the government to wipe out nearly eighty-six per cent of the entire currency circulating in the country on the eighth day of a month, at eight o'clock at night! That's called trust. The trust the government had in the people. The trust the people had in the government! I have seen such deep and enduring trust only between Mitali and Prabhudev. Prabhudev did not doubt for even a moment that Mitali would leave the family irrespective of whether he kicked her or wiped his feet on her. Mitali believed firmly that no matter how much he trampled her underfoot, he would still come home without fail. I was just a currency note passing between them. I was like wealth – sometimes Mitali's to possess, at others, Prabhudev's.

But when does any currency note belong to someone exclusively? Which currency note has served just one? And it was then that they decided to demonetize me. What were they to gain from it? Nothing, except loss. I went to sleep weeping, woke up, paced that large suite, and asked myself – why, why did Mitali have to demonetize me?

I showered, dressed quickly. Then I called an Uber and went to Prabhudev's house. The security guard started to ask me questions, but luckily at that moment, the gardener Madhab Dada came in. I was the only one to call him by his name followed by a 'dada'. Everyone else called him 'maali' – meaning, gardener. I used to give him new clothes not only on Deepavali but also on Eid and Christmas. Madhab Dada opened the gate for me.

The house was the same. It had had a new coat of paint, and the garden, too, had new plants. Jayanti Didi opened the door. Her face lit up when she saw me. We exchanged greetings. I did not bother to wait but went straight up to Mitali and Prabhudev's bedroom. I did enjoy that freedom once. I knocked on the door once. When I heard 'yes' from inside, I went in. Prabhudev was reclining on the bed and reading a newspaper. Mitali was on her way out of the bathroom. She was wearing a red satin knee-length nightgown. Even without make-up, her face looked like it was covered with rose-paste. Seeing me, both husband and wife started alike. I sat down on a chair. And we talked.

'Prabhudevji, Mitaliji, I beg your pardon for this terrible intrusion. But I had no other way to meet you both together.'

'Chee! Out! Out of my house!' Mitali screamed.

'Mitaliji, I don't intend to stay, or stay long. Just two minutes. I have one request. If you wish to murder me, why do you trouble others? Why can't you do it yourself? I prefer to die by your hand.'

'Huh! Kill a third-rate bitch like you? And go to jail for it? Am I mad?'

'Rich people like you will never go to prison. Did Pritiranjanji go to jail for Pranab's murder? The witness turned unfavourable, the case was dismissed. So simple!'

Mitali looked deflated. I thanked Inspector Shetty in my mind. I then turned to Prabhudev.

'Prabhudevji, now I regret it. If I had taken up the offer and become your keep, I would not have had to suffer all this. But I couldn't – this woman seemed too much like an older sister to me. I could not help seeing a brother-in-law in you.'

In that moment, my tears stopped me from saying anything more. That was because I remembered my own sister, and Abhilash, when I uttered the word 'brother-in-law'. Suddenly, in that moment, I became a despondent child. I lay in the room in Vasanthaalayam, under its yellow-coloured ceiling. She lay beside me, hugging me. I was resting my bony legs on her. 'Vaave, don't cry, sleep, sleep, sleep,' she whispered. Somewhere in the house, Acchan and Amma were quarrelling. I covered my face with my hands and wept. It must have been the tears that had collected in my heart the night before. My eyes burned. My whimpers rose higher and higher.

'Why are you crying? I don't want to see your deceitful bawling...' Mitali murmured.

As my sobs grew stronger, her voice grew fainter. Prabhudev went out of the room. The sight of my tears always rendered him weak. After some time, Mitali came to me and said, 'Enough of crying. Stop.' She sounded milder. I got up and hugged her close. It was easy. I just had to think that she was Chechi.

I pressed my face against her smooth, rosy shoulder and continued to cry. My tears soaked her red nightie and shoulder. She held me to her bosom. I trusted her. I have always trusted people. Human beings are living currency notes. The price that we may have inscribed on them and the price that they would have inscribed on themselves may be different, that is all. In the days ahead, the fate of all currency notes is that they will be demonetized at some point of time. It would be pointless claiming at that moment that the government printed them, that they bear Gandhiji's image, or that the Governor of the Reserve Bank signed them. There will be no one to listen. No one will answer any of your questions.

My tears abated. I wiped my tears and moved away, and got back to what I had been trying to say.

'Didi, if my death will bring you peace, I will die this moment.'

'Who said that you must die?'

'Why did you send that Prakash to kill me?'

'I did not tell him to kill you, only to give you a fright.'

'But he killed off Pranab and Subrata for you?'

'Pranab who? Subrata who?'

'Didi, the Karnataka police have evidence!'

'What do they have to do with this?'

'Prakash tried to kill me in Karnataka. That is why they are investigating this case.'

'I have nothing to fear.'

'But Pritiranjan has much to fear.'

'Oh, the poor boy – someone framed him.'

'The evidence implies the reverse, Didi! I came here only to let you know!'

'What evidence?'

'They have a pistol registered in your name. How did that happen?'

She went red in the face, appalled, as though someone had disrobed her.

'Didi, you have insulted me so much! You told everyone that I tried to seduce your husband. You destroyed me to an extent that I can never find a husband, ever.'

'But you were faithless!'

'What proof do you have of that?'

'I saw the messages on your phone!'

'What messages did you see? We are all human, are we not? Don't we joke in our SMSs? Write lightly, playfully? Haven't I sent such messages to you too?'

'I don't want to listen to you. Would you have sent such messages if it were to your own brother-in-law? What is the meaning of sending a message that reads "Let me feed you, let me feed you till you are full"?'

'The problem with all writing is that you'll pick up only that which you want from it!'

'Are you claiming that you had no such relationship with him?'

'How many times should I swear on that? Why should I fall in love with a man twenty years older than me? For pleasure?'

'For his wealth, his status!'

'Nonsense! In that case, I would have owned at least one apartment in this city? I have lived here for at least ten or twelve years. What did I have when I left? Except the remainder of my salary, not a single paisa did I have. I'll show you my passbook.'

'I am not smart enough to win an argument with you.'

'That means you have no data or evidence against me, Didi.'

'But my husband has admitted that he was interested in you.'

'Did he admit to having a relationship?'

'What is the difference between the two?'

'How can it be my fault that someone gets interested in me? Do you have any evidence that I encouraged it? That I let it grow into a relationship?'

'Satya, I had a lot of affection for you.'

'I value that love much more than Prabhudevji's affection.'

'How can you prove that?'

'By having come here risking my life. To tell you that you are in danger over Subrata's death.'

'What am I to do about it?'

'Give me Prakash's address, I will take care of the rest.'

'I met him at Mahipal Shah Baba's ashram.'

'I did not know that you were his devotee.'

'I visited all the ashrams I could when I was ill.'

'But only I gave you the kidney.'

'Not free of cost – it was for a large sum of money.'

'Okay, I'll return the sum with interest. Will you give the kidney back to me?'

'That is impossible, isn't it?'

'Didi, I am not saying that you should be grateful. But please don't be ungrateful. God will never forgive you.'

'Don't curse me.'

'I won't, but God will. Have you had the slightest peace of mind after you began to hate me? Do your children have any peace?'

'If you keep cursing, how would we ever be at peace?'

'I did not curse you, but however rich you may be, you get as much as you give.'

'What do you want now, really? His address? I don't have it. He never stays anywhere for long. Whenever he needs something, he calls.'

'How did you meet him?'

'I met the baba in Mumbai. Then we went to his ashram. He was the caretaker of the cottage we stayed in. That is how I met him.'

'How did he land up here?'

'I got to know that he was the witness in Pritiranjan's case. I went to see him.'

'He must have told you that he did not know that Pritiranjan is your brother.'

'Yes, that's what he said.'

'Good. And then?'

'Pritiranjan insisted that we give him a job here.'

'But how did the IG Ramesh Mohanty come to recommend him?'

'You know Prabhudevji. He refused to hire him. So I got Mohanty to recommend him.'

'He's finished off many people for you, hasn't he, Didi?'

'What are you saying?'

'Did you give him the pistol just to kill Subrata?'

'I have not given anyone a pistol.'

'Then it must be Pritiranjan. What if the media gets hold of this? I have just one worry. What if the media concocts connections between me and your husband who kills poor people for corporate gains as part of this mess? I wouldn't want to even stay alive, then!'

'Satya, stop spreading tales!'

'That inspector's going to come again.'

'The Karnataka police? I'll deal with them.'

'Didi, it isn't as easy to deal with them as it is with Prabhudevji.'

'Mind your own business!'

'Sorry! If I was overstepping the line, my apologies. But before I leave, please check my bag to make sure that I am not sneaking out that horribly boring old man, your husband.'

'Don't hurt me unnecessarily, Satya.'

'You can send a killer after me, Didi. You can also spread rumours that I am trying to steal away your great wife-beater of a husband! And I don't have the right to utter a single word?' I pouted.

~

She served me breakfast. We talked a lot. This game – of manipulation – was fun too. I reminded her of Prabhudev's faults, each and every one of them, through every statement I made, and made some calculations while I was at it. S. Prakash was a cool one. Joining his footprints, you got a whole map. The information about him was like small change. You needed patience to count all of it. It was hard to turn the sum to paper money.

Amusing it was, when I stepped out! Prabhudev was sitting in the veranda near the dining room. He had overheard everything, the poor man. I was ashamed to meet his eyes that were succumbing to age. The dye he had used until now had turned his hair a dirty yellow. The wounds he bore on his chest, I saw in his misty eyes. Sad. Wonder if you have noticed, but in life, from time to time, you may have to 'demonetize' some people. Questions and answers were not fashionable back then. Governments could do anything, not citizens. At least I should respect democratic courtesy, I thought, and so I whispered to him, 'Sorry, I had no other way.' He smiled a heart-rending smile. Later, I would think of his face in that moment on countless occasions. That's what people's faces will look like when they get 'demonetized'. Some of you may ask, can't we just print notes to fill the gap created by the invalidated notes? That is your ignorance.

Because what was invalidated was not just bits of paper with numbers printed on them, after all – was it? It was trust, my dear brother, trust!

But the question remained: What was Mitali to gain from demonetizing me? If one believed that she had wanted Prakash only to scare me off, one would think that this was trivial. Especially when it was evident that S. Prakash had been after me to finish me off for a pretty long time. That, too, is your ignorance. It's because you don't know Mahipal Shah Baba. Nothing happens in the world without his knowledge. Especially Pritiranjan's case, Subrata's disappearance. What's your next step, I asked myself. I am a smart one, am I not? Will I reveal it? That, too, to myself? I have only proven false my own predictions.

THIRTY-FOUR

In truth, human beings get exchanged exactly like currency notes. From the pockets of one government to those of another. From the purse of one relationship to that of another. From the locker of one ideology to another. Your head reels thinking about it. These are all worldly truths. Injustice is everywhere. From toothbrushes to sanitary napkins, everything is a symbol of something else. Messages – each one of them. One could not pretend to not have noticed. And if I tried doing that, my mother was sure to remind me of it.

It happened that evening too, the day after I went to Mitali's house. I had checked out of the hotel and reached Aseema's house. She was at work and Laina was attending tuitions. I was thinking of making myself a cup of tea when Amma called. The following conversation happened between us:

'How's your investigation going?'

'It's on.'

'No clues yet?'

'Half a clue.'

'That's not bad.'

'What's the good of half a clue?'

'Half a clue is half knowledge!'

'Like one half of a currency note?'

'During the times of the British, all currency notes would be cut in half soon after printing.'

'What for?'

'The first half would be sent first, and then the second. The two would be joined together only later.'

'What an idea!'

'Just to make sure no one stole them! They were printed in Britain.'

'Why did they give up on this idea?'

'Counterfeiting. Each half-note began to have two or three matching pieces.'

'What are you trying to say, Amma?'

'If you have one half, it is not hard to complete it.'

'The half-piece I have is not that of a note. I have one-half of the truth.'

'Isn't that easier to complete?'

'Everything is easy for you, Amma.'

'Everything is trivial to me.'

'Then why haven't you solved this mystery yet?'

'That's your task, not mine.'

'Did you call to tell me this?'

'No, I wanted to ask when you will return.'

'I have one more trip to make.'

'To that Swami's ashram?'

'How did you know?'

'If you decide to turn back on your path, you'll have to walk all the way back.'

'I am scared, Amma.'

'Why?'

'This is like entering a labyrinth. Every path leads to other paths.'

'The poor chap who's after you – how much more baffled he must have been.'

'Leave it. Where are you now, Amma?'

'At home.'

'Alone?'

'Paramarth comes over to stay at night.'

'What does he say?'

'He's learning a song.'

'He sings…?'

'This is the song:

Pakaram naam veettende
Thalayarinjhu koottende?
Vairikal than chuduchora
Kudukudaa kudikkende?

'That's what he's singing these days … Revenge, more revenge. The thirst to drink the warm blood of foes…'

'Amme…!'

'I tried to teach him the romantic, lyrical, "*Aaru vaanguminnaaru vaangumee, aaaramathinte romaancham?*"'

'And?'

'Before I reached "romaancham", he was already asking me about the author.'

'So he has not studied this poem?'

'When I told him that the author is Changampuzha, he immediately asked me if he was a Hindu or a Muslim.'

'And what did you tell him?'

'Oh, what was I to say? I just wanted to hear your voice then.'

'Uh! So some maternal love was indeed awakened in you that way!'

'Verily! Paramartham! Like his very name!'

We laughed. I made my tea reciting the gory lines from Paramarth's song. It sounded cool. I went to the balcony reciting the lines about drinking blood and gulping it down. I felt good. The world was beautiful. Anything not seized in a hurry is beautiful. That's what I liked about Bhubaneswar. Wide roads, unhurried people, an attitude that one would be ready to worry about things when they happened. Like the go-pita that walked sluggishly on the tiled path below. By the way, I call a bull 'go-pita', to match 'go-mata'. What might be on its mind, I wondered. How was it seeing this world? Then I saw its body quiver, and the cow dung squirt out from its backside. It was watery, almost like water flowing out of the water tanker. The poor thing had diarrhoea. Its bony body showed signs of starvation. It raised its eyes and looked at me. 'Can you please just kill me,' it seemed to be asking. My heart melted. It did not have a handy assassin, the sad creature. On such occasions, I remembered my own assassin gratefully. No, he was not an assassin, he was a saviour. Yes, a saviour.

No one could walk that way without stepping on the dung sprinkled all around by the Progenitor. The cars speeding by splattered it on passers-by, making amusing patterns on their clothes. Only one, a man with multicoloured threads around his wrist, speaking intently into his cell phone, walked by confidently stepping on it, leaving the prints of his designer shoes on the footpath. He's lucky, I thought – look at him cleansing the path on which he walks! I watched him walk from up there, holding my empty mug. He crossed the road and disappeared. I counted the footprints – for some five minutes – and the doorbell rang. I'd thought it was Aseema, but there was no one there. I caught the scent of rotting cow dung. There was no one in the hall; the designer-shoe prints had stretched out of the lift until the door and then back to the lift. Just then, I noticed something near my feet. A long, white envelope. I picked it up, thinking it must be for Aseema. But the words written on it with a black sketch pen said: 'To Satyapriya'. My eyes popped out. I felt a cold shiver spread over me; I felt weak. Those shoe-prints seemed to be sneering at me.

I closed the door, ran to the balcony, and searched for the shoe-prints on the footpath below. It was not clear if they were the same as the ones in our hall outside. I could not make them out distinctly. My heart pumped the blood hard into my body. The go-pita had collapsed in the middle of the road. From the way its neck was twisted, it was obviously dead. To be honest, I was frightened. I ran back in, came to the dining table, and opened the envelope with clammy and trembling fingers. It contained a folded rectangular piece of paper. When I opened it, another piece of paper fell out of it. It was one-half of a demonetized thousand-rupee note.

A kind of silence engulfed me. Even the falling flowers of the flame vine seemed to be pounding the floor. I was too scared to get up or even move my leg. The shadows moved in the kitchen. I felt that there was someone in Laina's room and mine. Outside, the daylight had withdrawn completely. I was drenched in sweat. The part of the envelope I touched got soaked. I was at a loss about what to do. My head felt engorged with smoke. It would have been good to lie down, but for that I should be able to get up from where I sat and walk to my room. Then I thought of something else. What if the person who sent me this was watching me? Watching my nervousness and fatigue? Laughing at it? That brought back some spunk in me. Let him not derive pleasure from my unease. I wiped my face, placed the note and the paper back inside the envelope, and called Inspector Shetty.

'Inspector Sir, are you back in Bangalore?'

'No. My flight is tomorrow, at night.'

'I'd like to see you before you leave.'

'I am in Cuttack now.'

'Someone is tapping my phone.'

'How do you know?'

'The person doing so let me know.'

'Can you tell me in detail?'

'I had spoken with my mother a little while back. She told me about how in British India currency notes used to be cut in half.'

'So mother and daughter have only such topics to discuss?'

'When the call was over, someone rang the doorbell. I found just an envelope out there.'

'You did not see the courier?'

'No, but I have a hunch.'

'All right. What was in it? Did you open it?'

'Yes, a folded piece of paper. When I unfolded it, there was an old thousand-rupee note in it.'

'Oh, how to change it now?'

'That's impossible. There's just half of the note.'

'Wait, how long was the time gap between your conversation and this?'

'The time you'd need to make a cup of tea and drink it.'

'Okay, Ma'am, let's talk in person. I'll come over tomorrow morning.'

The call ended. I was still frozen. The doorbell sounded again, and I nearly peed in fright. Collecting myself, I picked up the envelope, kept it safely in the inner pocket of my bag, went to the door dragging my legs that felt very heavy, and opened it. It was Aseema. I sighed in relief.

'Who the hell dirtied the floor—' she complained, and came in asking, 'Has Laina gone to her tuition class?' Seeing my face, though, she frowned and asked, 'You look drawn. Why, what is it?'

'Don't know ... not feeling well.' My voice fell.

'Ah! I have just the cure,' she said.

'I was waiting for you.'

'I got all his details.'

'Really?'

'From his joining date. You'll have to find out where he was before, though.'

'Let's see what we have?'

'Will give it to you. I need a strong cup of tea!'

I ran to make it and brought back two mugfuls. Aseema changed and came back with a brown envelope. I snatched it from her. There was a copy of a joining form from Advaita in it – a Contract Labourer Authentication Form. On the right side was the applicant's photo. I shook like a leaf once more. Straight hair, combed to the right. Sharply defined eyebrows and moustache. Large, slightly slanted eyes. The face looked familiar; surely, I had seen him many times. But earlier, I never had the time to scrutinize it like I was doing now. Of course, when you travel with the general manager, you'd definitely not scan his driver's face, would you? I picked up my phone and compared this image with the one Inspector Shetty had sent me. It was clearly the same person. The file photo, however, was clearer. I quickly took a photo of the form and then read its contents. It had been filled with a firm and well-formed hand.

> NAME: S. Prakash
>
> NATIONALITY: Indian
>
> RELIGION: Hindu
>
> PRESENT ADDRESS: 237, Biju Patnaik Vihar, Raiguda
>
> PERMANENT ADDRESS: 'Sarada Bhavanam', Thekkeparambil, Kerala
>
> PREVIOUS EMPLOYMENT: Driver, Mahipala Cosmetics, Faridabad, Delhi
>
> REFERENCES: 1. Ramesh Mohanty IPS, State Police Headquarters
>
> 2. Swami Mahipal Shah Baba, Mahipala Ashram, Faridabad, Delhi

He had signed it. A copy of the joining order was pinned on the form.

> S. Prakash is hereby appointed a driver on contract in the HR department. His salary will be 2500 rupees a month. The contract is for two years. With satisfactory performance, it could be extended by another two years. The final decision regarding the extension of the contract will be left to the sole discretion of the Company. Neither work performance nor the length of service may be the criterion for extension.

'Drivers and loading labourers sign a payslip to receive their pay, so no bank details are available,' said Aseema.

'But we don't have his full name or educational qualifications?'

'Who takes those details while hiring contract workers?'

I drank my tea hastily and began to pace the room. Name: S. Prakash. Religion: Hindu. According to Inspector Shetty, he was first Jivesh Kumar, then he became George, and later, Akbar Ali Muhammed. Then he reconverted to the Hindu faith. What was his new name? S. Prakash? Or Jivesh Kumar? Was Jivesh Kumar an assumed name? My mind boggled. I went back, sat down on the chair, and covered my face with both hands, trying to hide in the darkness there.

'Don't worry.' Aseema touched my hands lovingly. 'Let us try...'

'... try what?'

'Let us try asking this Ramesh Mohanty? He's the IG now.'

I sat up straight.

'Will he speak openly?'

'His brother is a classmate of Ambarish Naik, from our office.'

'Will you ask him?'

'No, my dear – I am not risking my job. You will have to find a way.'

'Your help with this file was absolutely priceless.'

'Satya, let me tell you, Prabhudev harbours deep enmity towards you. He is hurt, and the wound runs deep. Even if you have to give away all, never give anyone hope, my dear!'

'Hope has to come from within our own minds. Not out of calculations about the profits we may make!' I said, while searching the travel website. I found a ticket to Delhi, an Indigo flight, at seven thousand rupees, at four twenty-five in the evening the next day. It would reach Delhi at 7 p.m. I had to find a hotel room. The New Year rush had not yet started. Leela Ambience had a room for seven thousand per night. Fifteen thousand more, gone. Never mind. Money comes and goes. It's life that's important.

Laina came back after her tuition class. We went to Narula's for dinner. Laina loved the food there. It was past nine-thirty when we finished dinner and stepped out. While we waited for the Ola cab, Amma called.

'Satye, where are you?'

'What is it, Amma?'

'Just to know, nothing more.'

'You have Paramarth there with you, right?'

'Yes.'

'Have to pick up the rest of that song of his ... After I come.'

'He is at it! Lighting fires of hell and wanting to burn all of life!

> *Narakathee koluthenam*
> *Jeevanaaya jeevanellaam*
> *Pizhutheduthu karikkenam...*'

'Good god!'

'There's a call for tearing out the wombs of the women who brought the enemies, etc., as the song ends...'

'Amma, will you stop? I have just had dinner. This makes me want to throw up!'

'That's nothing. I've been vomiting two or three times every day.'

'Can't you go to Venukkuttan Chettan's house and stay with them?'

'Paramarth won't let me. He believes that well-born women should not sleep under another's roof.'

'Did you call to tell me this?'

'No.' She sounded a bit low.

'Satye, someone came here a little while ago.'

My heart began to thump loudly.

'It was Paramarth who opened the door. He didn't see anyone.'

I summoned my voice with difficulty.

'Was there an envelope there?'

'Uh!! How did you know?'

'Was it for you or for me?'

'For you.'

'Did you open it?'

'Paramarth insisted that mothers should open all letters that daughters receive, but I did not.'

'Don't open it.'

'Why?'

'I'll tell you when I am back there. Please keep it safe.'

'Shall I give it to Aswathy?'

'Only when I tell you.'

I was almost lurching in fright when the call ended. Luckily, the Ola cab arrived then.

'Who was that?' Aseema asked.

'Amma,' I answered.

Aseema talked while in the cab, but I hardly heard her. I was seeing the dung-smeared designer-shoe prints in our front yard, a white envelope at our doorstep, and inside it, the other half of the note. One zero and a half, and the smiling image of Gandhiji. Gandhiji's smile was his message. But the message that the two halves of a single note conveyed – what was it? Maybe *'Eneedukaarkkum ithu thaan gathi'* – be warned, this fate can befall anyone? Or, *'Onnallee naamayee sahodararallee'* – are we not one, brothers to each other?

THIRTY-FIVE

The meeting with the IG of Police Ramesh Mohanty was a bit foolhardy. I am not sure if it helped or hurt. But it definitely added to the suspense. He was neither handsome nor ugly; plain hard-heartedness alone was writ on his face. The weight and clout of a rank radiates in the body language of the person who occupies it. I have met only one policeman who looked and sounded humble in my life, and that was Inspector Anurup Shetty. I used to wonder at how he managed it. What I could make out from my interaction with him was this: Among those who wear khaki uniforms, there are readers too. They see each of us as a story. They too fear, stay anxious, that we may cheat them with made-up tales. The IG surveyed me from top to bottom. I did have a striking personality, doubtless. He probably guessed that someone like me would not be peddling a meaningless story. As it happens, I had just one story to offer, an endlessly long one, with many sub-stories. It's impossible to pull free once I start. Unaware of that, the IG tried to study me. My face looked like it belonged to someone who knew him inside and out. Let me offer this advice from what I learned in life: do not act meek, nice, with those in power. It makes them suspicious. So as soon as I sat down facing him, I showed him the photo of Prakash I had in my mobile phone. He recognized him at first glance.

'Why are you looking for this person now?'

'Prabhudev Maheswari told me that you had recommended him for the job, Sir?'

'Yes, I was the ASP then. He was my personal driver for some time.'

'The ASP would have a driver from the department?'

'This was for the car that my family used.'

'You hired someone who literally had no real name or address?'

'Someone very close to me recommended him. He applied for the job at Prabhudev's just two weeks later. I recommended him. That was better for him I thought – a permanent job, some perks. I haven't seen him since he left.'

'But I have heard that you were very close to him, Sir.'

'Who told you?'

'I am like a younger sister to Prabhudevji's wife.'

'What did she tell you?'

'That you are very valued.'

'What was the context in which she said that?'

'If I remember right, it was about the killing of a Maoist.'

'Which Maoist?'

'I forgot the name.'

'All right. See you again later.'

'Sir, are you avoiding me?'

'Hey, no. You asked me a question. I gave you my answer.'

'You're the one who also nabbed Samir Sayyid?'

He looked directly at me. I smiled at him.

'Samir Sayyid who?'

'The Maoist.'

'See, I am not a part of that force.'

'But I have heard that it was you who negotiated on behalf of the company...'

His face hardened, eyes narrowed – they bore into me. I liked it because it was proof that this King of Beasts was now confused.

The look was one of suspicion – that even a grasshopper's hop could be an expression of contempt. Before it faded, I dealt the next blow.

'… and also that your link was actually this S. Prakash.'

His face now turned pale. That made me more confident.

'I know that you know him well, Sir. When he calls, please tell him that I came to meet you, seeking him.'

I got up, folded my palms in salutation, and walked out of the room without looking back. He was already looking shaken. I knew that even without turning back to look. It is fun to live like a mere grasshopper. You can't be so easily swatted by large hands. Our smallness is our strength.

~

After this, I headed straight to the hotel Inspector Shetty was putting up in. We went to the restaurant there and ordered a coffee. Inspector Shetty wanted the cover and the half-note. He took them with his handkerchief, examined them, and took photos. And we talked thus:

'Ma'am, may I take these with me? We may find fingerprints.'

'Not now.'

'When, then?'

'When I have the other half of this note.'

'That means?'

'The person who sent this cannot be sending the other half as well?'

'Is that necessary?'

'As far as this person is concerned, it is.'

'Why do you say that, Ma'am?'

'He sent this to prove that he's tapping my phone. So he'll surely send the other half too.'

'You are right.'

'I will find him before you do, Inspector Sir!'

'Why should there be a competition between us on this?'

'What interest do the police have in an individual like me?'

'In such matters there is no "individual" before the police, only deeds.'

'And what have you found out about this deed?'

'Many things, for sure. His name, his trajectory.'

'You got his vehicle, but still couldn't get him?'

'He surely has the support of someone powerful. I am certain.'

'We'll be certain only after the smoke rises from my pyre!'

'You'll live a hundred years, Ma'am. I guarantee that.'

'I feel like I am going to be killed in a month's time.'

'Why, Ma'am?'

'Within a month, any day.'

'Don't scare me!'

'I am going to meet Mahipal Shah Baba.'

'How did you fall out with him?'

'Aren't we all human? How do we move ahead in life without slipping and falling out?'

'Don't be so pessimistic, Ma'am.'

'I am just being realistic. I am just out of a meeting with the IG, Mohanty.'

'Oh, my! Are you out of your mind, Ma'am?'

'I have had enough of this cat-and-mouse game.'

'You have ruined everything!'

'There's fun in that!'

'What did you tell the IG?'

'I poked him.'

'You are really crazy.'

'Is that a crime?'

'Ma'am, you are really crossing the limit.'

'Inspector Shetty, today I will separate the wheat from the chaff!'

'How?'

'The IG will warn him. He will come in search of me today.'

'Ma'am, it's the police who'll come looking for you today.'

'What for?'

'Don't I know you? You must have played up yourself before him!'

'Is that a crime?'

'Don't test my patience, Ma'am.'

'All right, I am leaving.'

'Wait, what time is your flight?'

'Four in the afternoon.'

'Change it if possible?'

'Leave later?'

'No, earlier.'

'Why?'

'They have reason to arrest you and keep you in custody for a few days.'

'Custody?'

'Yes.'

'My assassin will be mortified.'

'Only if he is outside the prison.'

'That means?'

'Nothing. Please believe me. Leave on the first available flight.'

'I am going to Delhi.'

'Anywhere. But escape as soon as you can.'

I did not argue further with him. I thought about what I must do. Aseema rang me then.

'Where are you, Satya?'

'I met the IG. Now thinking of doing some shopping.'

'I got a call from the office.'

'For what?'

'Asking where you are.'

'And what did you say?'

'That you are leaving by the four o'clock flight this afternoon.'

'Good.'

'What is the matter?'

'Matter? Nothing at all? I met the IG. Discussed things with him.'

'Did you have a row?'

'No. I wasn't irked. But I don't know if he's irked.'

'Oh, I am done with you!'

'Me too!'

I laughed. After the call, I looked at Inspector Shetty. He was looking at me intently. He appeared really anxious, and that set me at ease. I felt a rush of affection towards him. This always weakened me, so I gathered myself. His expression turned into a hopeful one.

'What have you decided?'

'Come what may, I am not going to run away.'

I strode out arrogantly. Inspector Shetty said something sadly or angrily – and he then went towards the reception, spoke briefly to the receptionist, and headed for the lift. I sat in the car, checked the flights to Kolkata. There was one at twelve-forty. The check-in had not closed yet, so I got a ticket online. Then I bought another ticket from Kolkata to Delhi. I was the last passenger at the check-in counter. I caught my breath only after I had safely boarded. On the flight, I removed my SIM card and flushed it down the toilet.

I had to run to catch my connecting flight from Kolkata to Delhi. As soon as I snapped on the seat belt, sleep overpowered me. I had never made such risky moves. I had feared that the IG would catch me from Kolkata airport or later, from Delhi. Luckily, nothing happened. Still, I did not take a prepaid taxi but the metro – the Orange Line till Shivaji Stadium. It was a pain, lugging my bags in and out. But I managed to do it, find a seat. It was a fairly busy time. I let my eyes wander on the passengers. Then, the person who had been standing just in front of me moved forward and the person sitting in the seat opposite mine came into view. A man, with his right hand on his knee. He moved, lifted his right hand, and scratched his beard. It was then that I saw his face, close up, clearly, very clearly…!

I have never claimed to be fearless. My limbs trembled and my body emitted heat and cold simultaneously.

Have you ever looked unblinkingly at your assassin? At how his heart beats when he dozes, how his shoulders slump? At how his head tilts involuntarily until you think that it's going to topple? A pity, if you haven't. Then what on the earth have you experienced in this life? But there's this thing: he will not have any mercy for you. Do not try to play yourself up before him. Know that his hand is the lion's paw that swats the grasshopper out of this world. You know who this man is, don't you?

Who else?

My assassin: S. Prakash.

THIRTY-SIX

What happens when you see your own nemesis, your killer, right in front of you? Your brain turns into a non-performing asset, the world smoulders a bluish-red. I shivered, perspired.

I had two options. Option A: Acknowledge his presence. He may shoot, then. Or stab. Or strangle. True, this was a public space. But it was full of middle-class and upper-middle-class folk who'd just turn away at the sight of violence. Or just close their eyes. Option B: Pretend not to notice him. There's art in that, poetry too. You can pretend to be oblivious of him, yet keep observing him. At the time of this story, power lay in the ability to watch people. Watching without the other's knowledge is art. Watching them after letting them know of it is politics.

I took out my handkerchief and wiped my face and neck. I don't remember when we reached Shivaji Stadium; I got out, somehow climbed on to the escalator, and reached the exit. I did not see him; actually, not just him, I saw no one. My eyes were filled with a bluish-red smoke. Soon, though, I did see him, at the exit. His head was covered with the hood of the sweater, and he seemed engrossed in his cell phone. The night was growing darker. The cold was getting severe too. He and I alone stood motionless while people and vehicles flowed past us. My blood pressure shot up. In such a circumstance, there are two options:

Option A: Run away. Option B: Face him.

Run? Till where could I run? I walked towards him. That was a great moment. I reached up close. 'Prakash,' I called him. He drew back a step, looked stunned. I observed his face. Was the photo Aseema showed me an old one? Or had he doctored it in some way? Was this the face that I had seen at Advaita? It was hard to decide. Because it was night, and the lights in the metro, dazzling. And he wore day-and-night goggles. On top of that, the bluish-red smoke in my eyes. I did not see anything new. His lips, mostly invisible in between his beard and moustache, quivered faintly.

'Prakash, do you not recognize me?' I struggled to find my voice. He stiffened. Remained silent. 'What is this, as if you do not know me at all?'

I could hear my heart race. My fear was that he may hear it. I smiled, to mask my fear. It was not easy. I faltered but got it all right. Then, when I managed to finally smile properly, it grew wider. He drew back again. The poor man looked frightened. It amused me. This beefy exterior was just a show. Inside, he was a scared, trembling kid. That's why he always chose the night and shade. He feared the light. The courage of a killer is actually this small – I can say that from experience. They catch you unawares, shoot you in the forehead, stab you in the back, wring your neck. But they'll be scared of facing you, looking into your eyes. God, after all, will not shower a human being with courage of all sorts. Either it will be the courage to win, or the audacity to cheat. Either the bravery to fail, or the nerve to kill. Either the pluck to love, or the daring to take one's own life. I had the mettle to fail and to be killed. So I found the guts to speak up too.

'Prakash, here I am. Why not finish me off right now?' I asked him.

Inspector Shetty was right. I did puff myself up a little too much. My ardour returned. The fatigue and stress of the long journey evaporated. I was dying to address him like an old friend, say something like 'Hey aliya, let's go have a drink!' But my tongue slipped, and instead of 'aliya', as in 'dude', I used 'aniya', that stood for younger brother! 'Hey aniya...' I said, 'hold this suitcase for a moment!' I pushed it towards him. He was clearly baffled. Maybe he thought that there was a bomb inside the suitcase? The poor man! This is why they say that it is the killer who is usually more scared for his life. Anyway, he vanished in the blink of an eye – scooted. How long had he been after me, and lo and behold, I had appeared right in front of him, within easy reach. So what! The golden opportunity was knocked flat on the ground. I stood there looking like a fool. It was then that a taxi stopped beside me. The driver was a burly Sikh man – he had to barely bend for his red-turbaned head to reach the passenger-seat window.

'Faridabad,' I said.

He stopped the vehicle by the side of the road, got out, and took my bags. 'Seven hundred and fifty...' I began to bargain. He complained. 'Will you drop me there safely?' I asked. 'Madamji, the moment you step inside this car, your life is my responsibility,' he declared, placing his hand on his expansive chest. 'What if someone tries to kill me?' I asked again. 'In my car?' He rolled his eyes. That was one lovely person.

After I got into the car, we chatted some more. I was sleepy, and also really hungry. As the car moved ahead, the lights on the road began to push their way inside from all sides. It was a Delhi road, after all. A desert it was, each car but a grain of sand. I thought about S. Prakash, the night he shot at me. It was around forty days since it had happened, but it felt as though an age had passed. Time is, anyway, a feeling. So is love. So is intoxication. Even life is but a feeling. Only the assassin is not.

When I saw him, I first shook with fear. But when he disappeared, I began to feel worried. Many questions arose in my mind. Where did he disappear? Where did he get on to the metro from? From the airport? Had he been in my flight? Or was he on some other flight, and waiting for me? How was he able to know about my travel plans?

Was he the one who left the half-note at Aseema's doorstep? If so, who did it back home? Was he able to tap my phone by himself? Was he not just an instrument of someone powerful enough to do all this? I saw his face in my mind's eye. I felt pity bubble up in me. The poor man, I did not like to see him as a contract killer. There was no beauty, no art, in it. He should kill me for himself – that's what I liked. Only that felt thrilling.

We reached the gates of the ashram. It was eleven forty-five. It was terribly cold. I got off with my bags in front of the huge gates that were closed. I paid the driver a hundred more than what he demanded as his fare. He thanked me and left. I was left alone on a deserted road with a shoulder bag and two suitcases. I went towards the glass cabin in which the security guard was usually seated. He was asleep, with his head on the desk, in the dimly lit cabin. I woke him up, he switched the lights on. The surly young man stared at me. Then, for a whole hour, we wrangled. He blankly refused to open the gate; he had to have orders from above to do so. No way, a woman could not be let in without such orders. 'Call your chief,' I ordered. He refused. He was a young man, just thirty or so. Maybe married for seven or eight years – the age at which being the head of the family goes to your head. So you'd want everyone to dance to your tune, like your wife and kids. Who doesn't like others to be in fear of them? But I was plucky for sure. I had the pluck to speak and to fail. I did not back off. Finally, he called his chief. He came in half an hour, accompanied by another man. The chief was muscular and looked like a bouncer in a bar. Around forty he must have been. You know it. That's the age at which you become a know-it-all. We began to exchange words.

'Madamji, please do not test our patience. Please leave and come back in the morning.'

'With these suitcases? In this cold? I won't be alive to return tomorrow!'

'That you should have thought about before setting out.'

'That's my mistake. Then don't open the gate. I will sit here until morning.'

'It is not proper for a woman to be sitting in front of the ashram all night. We will not allow it.'

'What if I sit on the other side of the road?'

'This is an ashram, Madamji, a sacred place. We cannot allow it to be polluted!'

'How can the ashram's purity be affected if I, an Indian citizen, in a country in which free movement on public roads is a fundamental right, sit or stand on a road?'

'Look, we do not want to talk much with you. You must leave immediately.'

'I want to reach the sacred abode of the great seer and divine Swami Mahipal Shah Baba. I have left behind everything to touch his lotus feet with my forehead. I will not return without achieving my goal!'

'Are you mad? There are rules and codes in this ashram. You are not allowed to come uninvited in the dead of night! What do you think this is? A wayside inn for anyone to come in when they please?'

'The whole world, O Great One, is a wayside inn for orphaned souls.'

'This woman is crazy, Gangadhar. Let us go inside. Her body's going to lie in some thicket to be eaten by a fox.'

'If that happens, then please tell the whole world that it is you who gifted the foxes in the wild out there the body of the woman who came seeking refuge to Mahipala Ashram at midnight!'

'Madamji, our women – women of our families – do not speak like this.'

'Securityji, even the men in our families do not shoo away a woman seeking refuge at night and then happily declare, "Oh, the fox is so lucky!"'

'Madamji, is it fair to drag yourself here at midnight and demand entry? Think about it yourself!'

'Where else do you expect me to go? The ashram is a place of refuge, isn't it? Am I to go to Parliament or what?'

'Aren't you an educated person? Why are you arguing with us? We are only employees. We are allowed to let in only people with appointments. Visitors are allowed in only from ten in the morning to five in the evening.'

'Securityji, I am someone who stayed here for years together. I came here on that faith. I just need a phone call.'

'Then why are you not calling?'

'I lost my phone. If I had it, do you think I would be standing here and hearing you scold me like this?'

'Okay, Madamji, I will give you my phone. Call whosoever you like. Anyone who has the power to order us to open the gate.'

'All right, then call Mahipal Shah Baba.'

'Ah, Madamji! Are you making fun of us?'

'All right, don't. Then call Balbhushan Jha.'

'Can we call someone a little lower in rank?'

'Please call Balbhushan Jha. I will not speak with anyone lower. Dial his number from your hotline. Is it still 100?'

The man looked rattled. He called someone and said something. After some time, the hotline rang. The chief went inside and picked up the phone. Then he called me and said respectfully, 'Madamji, *aap baat kijiye.*' I took the receiver through the window of the glass cabin.

'Balbhushan speaking.'

'Balbhushan Dada, Satyapriya here…'

'Satya…?'

' … priya. You must remember me!'

'Bhagwan Mahadev! Satyapriya?'

'Don't you believe me?'

'How long it has been since you called, Satya!'

'Sixteen years!'

'What is this? With no notice at all?'

'I will explain in detail. But do you intend to kill me tonight? Standing in the cold?'

'Oh no, for sure. Just hand the phone to Sukhcharan.'

I did that. He kept saying, '*Ji haan, bilkul.*' After a few minutes, both the men came out and took my bags. '*Aayiye*, Madamji', he invited me courteously.

I stepped into that expansive compound once more. The tiny speakers hidden in the grass began to chant 'Sri Rama, Ramaa, Sri Ramaa, Ramaa, Ramaa...' A freezing sensation began to creep up my body. My blood pressure began to rise. I remembered the day I had walked out of the ashram through the same path. The path was the same – only the tiles had changed. The flowering trees planted on either side had grown and were rubbing each other's cheeks now. Now there were cast-iron bowers between the trees. The bunches of flowers growing on the flame vines seemed to be of a saffron shade. One heard the chanting of Rama's name back then too, but its tone had changed now. It was mild then. Sixteen years later, it felt more like a warning of sorts. They took me to that old cottage where I had stayed with Anjali Didi. Mahipal Shah Baba's principal secretary Balbhushan Jha was waiting for me there. My heart began to pound again at the sight of him. Will my body lie in the thickets and be dragged around by wild animals? I was afraid.

'Satya beti, welcome back!' Balbhushan Jha embraced me warmly. I expected a knife to enter my back, and the agony of it. But that did not happen. He opened the door of the cottage. Sukhcharan and Gangadhar carried my suitcases inside. When they went out, I went in.

'My old room...' I murmured, looking around.

'The same old room, the same old Balbhushan Jha!' He let out a big-belly laugh.

He had aged a bit. The hair on the back of his bald head had greyed completely. The belly bulged some more. The skin formed heavy folds on his face and neck. I looked into his eyes. Revenge? Fear? Alertness? But what I saw in them was something else – fatigue. Maybe from lack of sleep. Or age. The poor man. I could find just a single metaphor to describe the man – that of the thick, black rubber band that village kids once used to keep their schoolbooks together while going to school, and otherwise, as a sling to shoot stones with. A rubber band that had flung stone after stone and lost its elasticity, bit by bit. He looked it – very long, tired, loose.

The old sofas in the cottage had been changed. These were foreign-made, it seemed. He lowered himself comfortably on a single-seater sofa. I went into my old bedroom. There was a new cot and mattress there, in the same spot as before. The wardrobes were the same; the bed sheets were still blue. I took my suitcases in, took a quick wash, and came back. I found Dada making coffee in the kitchen.

'No one stays in this cottage now?' I asked him when I took the cup he offered.

'Very rarely. Only some VVIPs.'

'So I am a VVIP, right?'

'You are a host, Satya, not a guest, don't you know?'

'That is news for me, Dada!'

'How sad! When will you realize it? Satya, this is where you belong. There's not a single day that Swamiji hasn't mentioned you since you left. When he picks up a file, prepares for a talk, answers letters … Few have influenced him as you have. No one could come as close to him as you did. Swamiji gets irritated by their failings, but you know, he doesn't get angry. Just sighs – if only Satya stayed…! Ah, but tell me, have you eaten anything? Are you hungry? Shall I wake the cooks up? Or I have some noodles, shall I just cook some for you?'

I agreed to the noodles. He selected a pan with care and prepared the noodles. I watched him boil water, break the noodle cakes into it, add the masala powder, and stir them in the water. I ate them with relish along with some pickle. Then we both went back to the drawing room.

The conversation that happened between us that day was somewhat like this:

'Hah! All right now! What news of you, beti? Hope your mother is well at home?'

'You could say that…'

'Your father's passing was unexpected, wasn't it?'

'You hear all about me here?'

'Sure. You are on my radar always, Satya beti!'

'Okay, then tell me, Dada, why have I come here?'

'I hope you have come to stay here for good!'

'I may not go back, you think?'

'That's for you to decide, dear.'

'Do you not understand the meaning of my question, Dada? Will I live long enough to go back?'

'There can be no threat to your life here.'

'How are you sure?'

'That's my guarantee.'

'So it wasn't you who sent S. Prakash after me?'

'S. Prakash who?'

'Dada, I am only happy to die by your hand. That's because I love you sincerely.'

'Satya, I hope you understand me. There is absolutely no threat to your life or body or wealth while you are here.'

'What about my soul?'

'I am uneducated. What do I know of the soul?'

'Let us leave the soul. Who is S. Prakash and why is he after me?'

'Satya, it is two in the morning. My head is reeling. I have to take a pill and go to bed.'

'What pill, Dada?'

'Sleeping pill.'

'I need some too. Haven't slept for a long time now.'

'Even you suffer from sleeplessness?'

'The dead trouble me. They call to me.'

'Your didi?'

'Anjali Didi too…'

'Let me go. My head aches.'

'Where are you running away to, Dada?'

'Satya, please don't go prying into such things now. Please, it is my wish that not a hair on your head should be harmed when you are here. So I beg of you.'

'All right, then. Tell me, Dada, where is this Prakash now?'

'Satya, you haven't changed a bit! The same stubbornness. Look, your mother has only you. So heed my words. Stay here. The moment you step out, your life will be in danger.'

'But what for? Who am I? Just a grain of sand in this huge world! Why do people want to annihilate me?'

'Nothing happens in the world without Bhagwan's knowledge. He decides all.'

'I just want to know who S. Prakash is.'

'You can ask anything else. I will answer.'

'All right. Can you tell me where the wife of the man Pritiranjan killed is now?'

'Which Pritiranjan?'

'How many Pritiranjans do you know, Dada?'

'That real estate man from Odisha?'

'Will I ask you about lesser people?'

'He is a devotee of Swamiji.'

'That I know. Where is that woman, Subrata, now?'

'How would I know?'

'Did you not promise to tell me anything except about S. Prakash? Men should keep their word, shouldn't they, Dada?'

'My dear sister, are you determined to finish me off?'

'There's just one person who has the guts to touch even a strand of your hair, Dada!'

'And who is that?'

'Mahipal Shah Baba.'

'Now, don't blow me up into a huge thing. I am just a blade of grass.'

'There's a saying back home that for the skilled man, even a blade of grass is a weapon!'

'Becoming a weapon is not comfortable, my child, especially in one's old age.'

'You are not old, Dada, you have many more years left to send many more to heaven.'

'So now you are talking. Talking and turning me into the God of Death?'

'You must not have killed Subrata.'

'She is here.'

'In the ashram? I guessed as much.'

'Didn't I know you would?'

'In that case, tell me, how did you get to know at the ashram that Pritiranjan had murdered Subrata's husband Pranab?'

'He was on our radar since some time.'

'What for?'

'Swamiji wanted to open an ashram in Odisha.'

'I understand.'

'When the issue broke out, we helped him.'

'But you didn't set up an ashram there?'

'We didn't, because of the Maoist threat. Instead, we started one overseas. Now, enough for today. I need to sleep, or I won't get up tomorrow.'

'Just one more thing, Dada. Did S. Prakash trap Pritiranjan and inform you, or did he do it on orders from here?'

'Satya, I fear you. You are really here to see me burn on the pyre, are you?'

'I want the person who wants to see my body on a pyre to tell me this!'

'I vow upon Bhagwan – neither I nor Swamiji have done anything to harm you.'

'Then tell me the truth. Wasn't Pritiranjan brought here by S. Prakash?'

'Why are you biting my head off despite knowing all of it?'

'He brought Pritiranjan here, introduced him to Swamiji. Or did he introduce him first to you, Dada?'

'That is immaterial.'

'Then he was caught in a murder case.'

'Satya, in truth, I fear you.'

'Was it Prakash who planned and executed it?'

'You will have to ask him.'

'But he is not letting me!'

'Let me tell you the truth – in this world, you're the only one to share the same crooked intelligence he possesses.'

'Is that a compliment?'

'Beti, let me fall at your feet. May I please go to bed now?'

'No, I don't trust you, Dada. You will not be here tomorrow morning.'

'Are you going to kill me tonight itself?'

'Don't I know you well? You will leave the country this very night. And return after my pyre is ablaze.'

'What am I to tell this child? May Bhagwan forgive you.'

'There's just one more thing that I need to know. Who brought S. Prakash here?'

'He was here.'

'Please don't provoke me with lies, Dada.'

'My dear Satya, you know well that lakhs of devotees visit this place. When so many ants are gathered on the ground, how to know where a particular ant turned up from? That, too, ten or seventeen years ago?'

'Dada, do not belittle your ability to remember! He was here much before I arrived, am I right?'

'You left shortly after he arrived.'

'Can you say why you remember that?'

'Reason to remember? Why, there's nothing special. That's how memory is.' Dada got up. 'Please, Satya, I have to go get some sleep, see you tomorrow.'

'If I am right, you will disappear from this place right now.'

'In fear of you? Get lost, girl.'

I got up, opened my smaller suitcase, and took out the Ray-Ban glasses, the Kashmiri shawl, and the white silk kurta with red embroidery on it that I had bought for him.

'When you leave, wear this kurta and shawl, and these dark glasses.'

His face brightened. He took the gifts and looked at me tenderly. His eyes were filled with happiness and gratitude.

'Beti, in this world I have only you to give me gifts.'

'Don't you butter me up! I know where you hide the gifts your girlfriends bring...'

'Oh, those are old stories. I am an old man now. All of seventy-three.'

'Yes, yes...'

'No one can match your selection of gifts!'

'You know why? I choose them with love.'

'Of course, I know.'

Dada leaned over and planted a kiss on my forehead. I leaned on his shoulder. Tears pricked my eyelids. I saw them spread on his brown-coloured sweater. I loved the man. When I was an inmate here, I tried to find in him a father's affection. It was he who had arranged to kill me. Really, I did not understand people.

'Dada, my father never loved me. I saw you in his place. I love you so much!' My voice faltered. His body seemed to tremble once.

'Are you not my daughter?' His voice trembled too.

'Then why did you send Cobra Nagu to kill me? What loss would you suffer from my staying alive in this world?'

I looked straight into his eyes. His pale-skinned face flushed. The tears flowed out of my eyes. After a half-second, I saw his throat and cheeks quiver. Without uttering a word, he placed the woollen cap back on his head, took the shawl he had placed on the hanger earlier and wrapped it around himself, picked up the bag of gifts, and went out quickly. I watched that seventy-three-year-old man walk away on the tiled path. On either side of the path stood maruthi trees. Their branches, decked with yellow and violet blooms, grew over the path and covered it, the tips touching in an arc. My sleepless eyes were burning now; they were achy. Everything looked vague, smoky. Dada went past the cast-iron bowers on which the flame vines had grown. He faded away from sight. But on the yellow flowers lying on the ground in front of my cottage, his heavy footprints were visible. Like notes torn into two. Incomplete, partial. He had admitted, in theory, to the following facts:

- S. Prakash reached the ashram just before I joined it.
- Dada knew Prakash since then.
- Prakash brought Pritiranjan to the ashram.
- Prakash became a witness to the murder of Subrata's husband Pranab.
- Prakash played a key role in the killing.
- He saved Pritiranjan in court. Then using him, became Mitali's trusted man.
- Then, using Samir Sayyid, became Prabhudev's trusted man.

Why? Just to follow me. To observe me. His pleasure seemed to be in observing me, unobserved himself. He was an artist then. Later, he became a politician. From that day onwards, he made sure I knew that he was observing me.

Think of it, all of us have just two options:

Option A: Become an artist. Option B: Become a politician.

My aim was to follow the tracks of my would-be killer to trace his path. What I knew and what Dada told me ought to have been two halves of the same currency note. But that did not happen. One half did not fit the other. Something was amiss. That is, Balbhushan Dada remembered that Prakash had arrived at the ashram just before I left the place. He had not forgotten that even though sixteen years had passed. Why? The answers could be either of the two options:

Option A: He had an amazing memory.

Option B: There was an inseparable connection between Prakash's coming to the ashram and my leaving it.

THIRTY-SEVEN

Black money: the currency we pocket duping the law. White money: use the same currency and buy stuff, and hey presto! Just like human beings. One may look like a good person to me and an evil fellow to another. Another may be your saint, but my sinner. That is, notes become 'black' or 'white' depending on whose pocket they are in. Human beings are the same too. They, too, can be classified according to the powers that have pocketed them. We, too, are fated to move from one pocket to another. In sum: human beings can be either 'black' or 'white'. At times, they may be entirely 'black', in others, insanely 'white'.

What a philosophy! When it struck me first, I got goosebumps. And the more I thought about it, the more intense it grew. I thought of it first when I saw Mahipal Shah Baba. We were meeting after such a long time! I was feeling energized by the idli, sambar and filter coffee that had reached me in the morning. I wrapped around my body the shawl that he had gifted me at our very first meeting, locked the cottage, and stepped out. It was cold, calm, deserted. It felt pleasant to walk. The only irritant was the menacing tone of the chant 'Rama, Sri Ramaa, Ramaa…' I pretended not to hear it. In the distance, I saw Mahipal Shah Baba's office – the mud hut, thatched

383

with grass. The Warli paintings on its walls. The room threw a lasso around me and pulled me hard towards it. Should I go or not, I asked myself. Wasn't Baba an evil man? Who hired a hitman to kill me? But another thought surfaced in my mind, then: the value that his countless devotees assigned to him was not what I had assigned to him. That did not mean that he had changed, though. That is, a person's value is maya – mere illusion. You have to immerse yourself in maya to perform your karma. At the same time, you must be aware that maya is, after all, only maya.

I went straight to his office. Knocked briefly on the door and entered. He was sitting on the floor clad in his usual white kurta-pyjama. He was reading a file, one hand resting on the same old, low writing table in front of him. His shiny bald pate reflected the fan overhead. He did not raise his head, just his eyes – the same doe eyes. I saw a flash of lightning in them. He sat up straight, held out his arms, and called to me, 'Come, come!' His voice broke. Then he leaned on the pristine white, long pillow and looked directly at me, but not into my eyes. The same ruddy health of some sixteen years ago was still evident. His forehead and cheeks were unwrinkled. But the signs of the approaching old age hung all around his neck. The flesh on it had dried up; the veins on it bulged prominently. I lowered myself on the seat right in front of him. I was a bit nervous too. To cover it up, I recited:

'Na tvevaaham jaatu naasam na tvam neme janaadhipah.
Na chaiva na bhavishyaamah sarve vayamatah param.

'I have never been non-existent. Neither have you. These kings – they, too. Henceforth, none of us will be non-existent.'

Mahipal Shah Baba sighed. Sadness undulated in his eyes like sea-waves. He leaned a little further on his long pillow, smiled, and replied with these lines:

'Avyaktoyama chintyoyama vikaryoyamuchyate
Tasmadevam viditainam naanushochitumarhasi.'

The same alluring voice. Yes, like back then, his voice rendered his form irrelevant. But the warmth of old times was missing. I noticed that. We got talking.

'Satyaji, you still read the Gita!'

'Yes, but why is the soul referred to as "he"? Is the soul male?'

'"He" includes the female too.'

'Is it that the woman's soul is male?'

'The Supreme Soul that abides in all as the essential light is male.'

'Then, what is the difference between people who are cis and those who are trans?'

'How long has it been since we argued like this, Satyaji?'

'A doubt. Was Anjali Didi's soul male or female?'

'Which Anjali Didi?'

'Age has not withered your beauty. But has it affected your mind?'

'Don't make fun of this old man, Satyaji!'

'There was a woman named Anjali Agarwal. She's dead. Someone killed her.'

'Jaatasya hi dhruvo mrityurdhruvam janma mritasya cha, tasmaadaparihaaryerthe na tvam shochitumarhasi.'

'There's a saying in Malayalam about the same water nourishing the banana tree and the leafy vegetables that grow under it...'

'I didn't get you.'

'Death is inevitable for anyone who is born. The dead are sure to be reborn. Does it not mean that you should not be sad about things that cannot be resolved? The same shloka – to Anjali Didi whom you killed, and to me, whom you wanted to finish off using a hired killer? The same explanation?'

'What are you saying, Satyaji!'

'Let me make myself clear. You killed Anjali Didi. Now you have turned against me.'

'Satyaji, words are like arrows. Once they leave the tongue, they cannot be taken back.'

'Words never take anyone's life, Mahipal Shah Baba! But acts? Can they be undone, taken back?'

'You seem very uneasy, Satyaji.'

'Should I jump up and down in glee while being pursued by a killer?'

'No one is going to even pinch you here.'

'So you know that someone has been after me!'

'I knew only when you told me.'

'Don't you want to know who that is?'

'If you tell me, yes.'

'His name is S. Prakash. He was an inmate of this ashram.'

'Look, Satyaji – the sanyasi and God have no choice. They have to accept whoever comes, take whatever is given.'

'Sometimes they summon people, even drag them by the rope.'

'When we recognize some people's mission in life, we do help them to find their unique paths.'

'Was S. Prakash summoned, or did he come on his own?'

'Why should I summon him?'

'It is also possible to summon someone knowing their mission.'

'What mission?'

'That of despatching Anjali Didi to the City of Death?'

'Satyaji, Satyaji…!'

'And after that, that of despatching me to the same place?'

'Satyaji…'

'No use avoiding my questions. I know all.'

'Satyaji, it is impossible for even Bhagwan to convince someone who is determined not to believe.'

'If so, please call him here! Now.'

'Satyaji, stay here for some days. Let your mind calm down.'

'I need that man here for my mind to calm down.'

'Look, he can do nothing to you here.'

'What does that mean? That he will harm me if I leave?'

'It means only that nothing bad will happen to you here.'

'What is the guarantee that nothing wrong will happen to him here?'

'Satyaji, you are just blowing things up in your mind unnecessarily.'

He sounded harsh; his eyes were a shade of hostility. I felt harried. I did not need his love. He had given me more than enough of it. Back then, I used to enjoy the way his desire sneaked out of his eyes even when he tried hard to hide it. That was sixteen years back. Will any man receive any woman with the same romantic ardour after such a long gap? Only fools would be hopeful. In any case, my aim was not to immerse myself in his love; I wanted to find S. Prakash. I was a hunter leading my prey into a trap, making sure that it was following me. The Mahipala Ashram was merely a thicket on that path. All this was fine. But that romance that disappeared from the eyes of Mahipal Shah Baba! Where to find it again? In whose eyes would I see it again? Love, too, was like an arrow that had left its bow. Where to search for it? How to reclaim it?

I got up, and walked out without a word in farewell. Shut the door without turning to look. My cottage was a furlong away. I did not go there. Instead, I headed to the spring by which Mahipal Shah and I used to sit.

It was bitingly cold. But the sight of the maruthi, ashoka and gulmohar trees – which were mere saplings back then but had now grown into beautiful, tall trees, full of flowers – delighted me. On the ground, the fallen flowers formed a thick, colourful carpet. The bower beside the stream was bigger and more spacious than the other structures around. The flowers of the flame vine covered it with a saffron hue. The irritating chant of 'Sri Ramaa ... Raaamaaa...' was a nuisance there too. I sat down on the half-wall of the bower. My mind was both in tumult and tranquil. I sat there and looked at the path on which I had walked. The ashram looked like a painting. And then I contemplated the actual distance that I had covered in my life. The walking paths that twisted and turned appeared like the map of my life. The Mahipala Ashram was merely a wayside inn on a long journey from Vasanthaalayam. I tried to recall what my situation was when I arrived there seventeen years back. Those days, when I walked these paths, I used to throb in pain inwardly, as though I was half-cooked inside. Remembering that me now, the me from even before was reborn. The family home, the town, Appooppan's textile shop, the hotel Vasanthamaalika, Nityavasantham, *Vasanthakairali* ... I yearned to be back at Vasanthaalayam, lying near Chechi, who'd be on her stomach reading the soppy romance, *Kanneeraattile Thoni*, with my legs on her back while I read *The Count of Monte Cristo*. The cold wind stirred my tear glands and my eyes welled. One feels alone not in solitude but when happiness looks impossibly far. I covered my face with my hands and sobbed. Then I felt a hand on my shoulder. It was Mahipal Shah Baba.

Now, don't you see that he could simply not let me leave like that? His flawless face was a bit flushed, perhaps from the walking. I stared at him with eyes filled with tears. His doe eyes had relented somewhat, there was less anger in them now. I felt stubborn then, about making him love me again. I threw myself on his chest. That unique fragrance of his body pierced my nostrils, rushed to my brain, and spread through my nerves. It was made solely for him by a French perfumery. I was always captivated by it. I rolled my head on his chest and burst out weeping. He was taken aback at first. Maybe he wasn't sure if my tears were genuine. But he still touched my head gently with one hand. I quickly withdrew, wiped my tears, and began to move away from him. He stopped me, ordering me softly, 'Leave after all of those tears are shed, Satyaji.' He wrapped my shawl properly around my shoulders. I rubbed off my tears and looked at him crossly. He made me sit on the half-wall again, and then going over to the bench opposite, sat down there. I felt horribly depressed. It was a moment in which the past, the present and the future weighed down on me together. I buried my face in my hands and wept again. I could hear his serene voice:

*'Drishtvedam maanusham roopam tava saumyam janardana
Idaaneemasmi samvrittah sachetaah prakritim gatah.'*

I looked at him through my tears. He began to explain:

'Seeing Krishna's eternal and world-submerging form, the vishwaroopa, and terrified by the sight, Arjuna asks him to assume his comforting normal countenance. When Krishna assumes that form, Arjuna says, "Hey Janardana! My mind is tranquil at the sight of your familiar form, and I return to my natural state of mind."'

That left me enraged, but I still smiled.

'You think that this is the comforting form?'

'A woman's gentleness lies in her tears.'

'And what about the man's?'

'No, no, Satyaji, do not show your eternal form again!'

'That which asks questions – is that form the vishwaroopa?'

'Let that be. Tell me, why did you cry now?'

'Shahji, tell me, why was I summoned here?'

'Satyaji, surely you came of your own accord?'

'I am asking you about seventeen years back.'

'Oh, that! I just thought that you were meant to live in this ashram, Satyaji.'

'What was it? Romance? Lust?'

He crossed one leg over the other, leaned back, and threw me a look of authority. Then he laughed.

'Ha ha ha! The desire to see the comforting side!'

'That is, you wanted to see me as a woman, in a clichéd way.'

'There is a clichéd woman inside every woman.'

'And perhaps inside every man too?'

'Not inside a real man.'

I smiled mildly first, and then it grew wider and wider. And then I broke out into a loud laughter.

'Uh? Why are you laughing?'

'Nothing, O One Skilled in the Gita! I was just remembering the tricks you played to make me a clichéd woman!'

'When I saw you here today, I felt disturbed, Satyaji!'

'It was either hostility or vengeance that I saw in your eyes.'

'Is that why you cried?' He looked at me closely. I knew that he wanted the answer to it. So I ignored the question.

'But it has vanished now.'

'I have felt only affection towards you at all times, Satyaji.'

'Affection towards the clichéd woman?'

'Respect for the non-clichéd woman.'

'If so, tell me why you hired an assassin to kill me.'

It was good to observe Mahipal Shah Baba examine his hands and nails and let out a long laugh. He must have been about seventy, but his good looks were still deadly. I leaned forward.

'Did you send S. Prakash to Bhubaneswar to come after me?'

'Satyaji, please avoid asking such questions.'

'All right, I'll ask just one question, just one. I need an answer.'

'Ask. I'll try to respond.'

'Who killed Anjali Agarwal?'

He got up and began to make his way towards the stream. I barred his way. The wind lifted his shawl with 'Om' printed on it and the gold button on his pristine white kurta showed.

'Do you plan to go back from here, Satyaji?'

'I came to bid goodbye.'

'Where are you headed?'

'To death, where else?'

'That can only be God's will.'

'It is S. Prakash's will now.'

He fell silent. I moved a little more towards him, looking at his face.

'Before I die, I need to know two things. One, who killed Anjali Agarwal? Two, why does S. Prakash want to kill me?'

'Do not don your vishwaroopa form again, Satyaji.'

'All right, just tell me why Anjali Agarwal was killed.'

He sighed heavily.

'She was an eyewitness in a murder case.'

This time, I was thrown. He paid no notice and walked towards the stream. I ran after him.

'The murder of Swaroop Gupta?' I asked him in a trembling voice. He smiled; it made me feel very afraid. A cold shiver ran through my body.

Swaroop Gupta was a powerful politician who was probably a prime ministerial candidate. He was killed before the elections were announced. He had just returned home after a political rally. His wife was asleep, so he had not switched on the lights. But his wife woke up. She had been on medication since long for paranoia and depression. She sensed something move in the dark. Terrified, she pulled out a revolver from under her pillow and fired, again and again. By the time others rushed to the spot, he was dead. It was a .45 revolver, with thirteen bullets. All thirteen were found from his body. Photos of the wife screaming in terror and of her arrest and transfer to the hospital had been prominently flashed in all the newspapers the next day. She was acquitted in the case. Her name was Tanu.

But what was mysterious about this case? Why was the eyewitness to be killed? I remembered Anjali Didi telling me – 'I am a cut-out.' My brain lit up.

'So Gupta was not killed by his wife?' I asked, sounding anxious, hoarse. His greying eyebrows quivered for a moment. Then his gaze turned towards the distance. He smiled, at no one in particular.

'Satyaji, you are so smart!'

'Was it Anjali Didi?'

'She was only a witness.'

'So, who did it?'

'How am I to reveal it?'

'All right, then just tell me why it was done.'

'It is politics, isn't it? Why someone gets eliminated there is a non-question.'

'Were there any other witnesses besides Anjali Didi?

'Satyaji, you don't belong here, really. You should be in Scotland Yard!'

'So the two people in Gupta's bedroom were Anjali Didi and his killer?'

'Dear Satyaji, I will not reveal my admiration, because you will not believe it.'

'But there is a problem there. Anjali Didi and the killer in the bedroom, in the other rooms of the house, Gupta's children aged seventeen and twelve, and four helpers … How can it work?'

'You are right. It can't be. Then?'

'So the murder was not committed there.'

'You are a genius!'

'The murder was committed somewhere else. The wife was made to own up.'

Mahipal Shah Baba looked at me in amazement. His drooping eyes grew wide. It was only then that I noticed how wide his eyes really were. I felt a rush of pride. And fear, too.

'That was you, am I correct?' I asked, panting. He was shocked.

'What! Me? A killer? Oh Satyaji, you just ruined it after such a build-up!'

'Then who?'

'I don't kill even an ant with this hand of mine.'

' … *kollikkayatre ninakku rasamedo…*' I chanted in Malayalam. Yes, you revel in setting up murders.

'That means?' he asked.

'That's a famous line from my mother tongue Malayalam.'

'But no one has come so close to the truth so quickly.'

'My name is Satyapriya, is it not?'

'You have your answers now, Satyaji?'

'No. When moving a corpse riddled with bullets, the blood on the floor would have to be removed too?'

'That's easy. If the blood is on a carpet, then just take the carpet along.'

'There'll be a forensic examination?'

'Satyaji, the killer is a high-profile politician.'

'Who are you trying to fool? A high-profile politician will not touch even an ant with their own hands!'

'Satyaji, stop stabbing me this way!'

'Okay. Let's suppose that he did it himself. Then…' Another possibility struck me at that moment. My tongue froze. I had to struggle to find my voice. 'That killer is now dead, right?'

This time, Mahipal Shah Baba looked really shaken. He stared at me as though he could not believe his ears. His face blanched. I observed keenly the way this man, so adept at concealing his feelings, was struggling now. The suffocation I had experienced until then, vanished.

What have you learned from this? That all truths are actually very simple – if you have the evidence. You see now, I am really something. How easily did I take Mahipal Shah Baba apart? He tried to play smart. With me. This me.

'Oh, it is late,' he said. 'I have an appointment at twelve.'

He got up to leave.

He smiled, pulling the saffron-coloured shawl around him. His doe eyes drooped again. I looked at him with sympathy. The poor man used to weigh a hundred and fifty kilos, once. Now he looked wasted; he was probably down to some eighty-five kilos. How much would a soul that lugged around that eighty-five-kilo body weigh? How many ants would he have got killed after Anjali Agarwal? How much would they have weighed collectively? I sat there watching him walk away. Then I went straight to the administrative office. Balbhushan Dada was speaking to a young woman clad in a salwar-kameez, his new secretary. His face fell, seeing me. 'Why have you come?' he asked, sounding suspicious. I asked for a laptop. He asked the secretary to give me one. It came in two minutes. I took the Wi-Fi password and went back to my room with the laptop.

The facts were like the flowers that fell from the flame vines shaken by the wind. My task was to recreate the vine with them. Anjali Didi's angry exclamation 'No matter what anyone might say, he's not going to stay on that seat another time!' rang in my ears. I googled Swaroop Gupta and read the reports of his murder carefully. Jagannath Sinha, two-time minister in the union government, was his close relative and friend. He was quite likely to be the murderer. But he, too, was killed before long. What did that mean? Though Sinha had murdered Gupta, he was made to do so by someone else? Someone more 'high-profile' than Sinha?

Anjali Agarwal was killed after Sinha. That is, she knew who had made him do the deed. The real killer was someone close to Mahipal Shah Baba. That's why she came to meet him back then.

I searched Swaroop Gupta's name once more. I went through each link carefully. I first opened the link titled 'Archita who filed a case against Swaroop Gupta found dead'. My body froze. Archita was a model who apparently got pregnant by him. He had denied it as a political conspiracy against him. She killed herself in despair. The article had a few more lines: they said that Archita was the second daughter of Praveen and Sneha Agarwal. Their other daughters were Anjali and Anjana.

I sat there still, my body tingling from head to toe. A whole series of murders unfurled in front of me. I quickly collated what I knew:

- Archita was Anjali Agarwal's younger sister.
- Swaroop Gupta got rid of Archita.
- Gupta was killed by Sinha.
- Sinha was murdered by an unknown assassin.
- Anjali Agarwal, who tried to get rid of Sinha's unknown assassin, was killed by another hired by Mahipal Shah Baba.

My doubts, however, only flared up further. I needed to know:

- Did S. Prakash kill Anjali for Mahipal Shah Baba?
- How did he come to commit that murder?
- Was the murder a means to sneak into the ashram and keep an eye on me?
- Or, did Mahipal Shah Baba get me to join the ashram for his sake?
- If so, when was that? When he converted? Or sent a letter to someone in Abhilash's village?

This was now a difficult sudoku. The long chain of facts broke in the middle; a link was lost. I struggled to find it. It was like black money. Buried by someone. If hoarded, then black. If circulated outside, then white. Black money would always be new and crisp, whereas white money would always pass through several hands. So just by looking at a note you can tell if it is black or white. Truth, too, is like that: black, when hidden, but white when revealed.

But there were many ways to each truth. Archita was one path. That was closed by someone. Then there was Gupta. When he died, that way was closed too. Then Sinha and Anjali remained. Their deaths sealed those paths as well. Would Nature allow such a situation, where there were no ways at all? Total blockage? No, a path would stay open, somewhere. There would be efforts to block it. That is, there was the chance of another cut-out, even after sixteen or more years.

No. Not me. But someone I cherished – my own assassin!

I now faced the challenge of saving him, not allowing even a scratch on his soul. You know why? If he died as a cut-out, then the path to my truth would collapse for sure! Speaking of my truth, it was sometimes a deep black, or a lucent white, or for the rest of the time, an incomparable grey.

THIRTY-EIGHT

That night, I hallucinated again. That the sacrificial fire in the ashram was live and glowing. I even saw the shadows of the flames play on the walls of my room and on my bed. It was just a feeling, but isn't all the world just a feeling anyway? The shadows of the trees looked like those of people. I thought I saw people carrying on their heads and backs large sacks and bags and boxes. They threw all of it into the fire. Wads of currency notes fell out of them. Not just five-hundred and thousand-rupee notes but all the notes signed by the Reserve Bank governor. My heart ached. I knew how hard it was to earn some. Here they were burning them like wastepaper! Even my lone kidney writhed in pain. As I watched this scene unfold, Mahipal Shah Baba emerged from his grass-thatched mud cottage. The shadow of his shawl with the 'Om' print rose right up to the sky. He, too, held a suitcase. He dragged it, actually. It was an old, weather-beaten one, its zipper nearly gone, and wheels broken. Wads of notes fell from it too. He threw all of it, along with the suitcase, into the flames. 'Quit India!' he shouted. 'Black money, quit India!' all of them hollered. I could see only the furiously burning suitcase. It looked familiar. It once belonged to Anjali Agarwal.

Dreams are tricks that your subconscious plays on you. But a hallucination? That's a gag your consciousness pulls on you. Any kind of joke is a manipulation for sure. I got up, splashed water on my face several times. Opened the windows and looked outside. Made sure that the sacrificial fire and the crowd did not actually exist. But Anjali Agarwal's suitcase stayed right there. I saw her again, entering Mahipal Shah Baba's room, dragging it. How dignified she had looked! Her rage was such that it seemed as though the flames leaping up from within her were casting their tongues of radiance on her face. The poor woman, how much she concealed within! I felt indescribably sad about losing her. It had all been so soon, her coming and leaving. But had she really left? No! Some people are like that. If they come, they never leave. And if they do leave, they leave behind traces, feelings. My sister was the best example. Anjali was another. This is why I say – the indemnity that human beings enjoy lies in their secrets.

Anjali had left on 13 October. I waited for weeks but there was no news of her. I was scared. The Internet and computers were not so common those days. So I did not know how to look for her. I asked Balbhushan Dada and Mahipal Shah Baba about her again and again. Their replies were vague. How could I not become completely nervy then? I waited for an opportunity. Asked a DSP whom I'd met at the ashram for help. Pestered Balbhushan Dada, found her address, wrote letters to her. I even placed messages in the classified section of two English newspapers, saying 'Anjali Didi, I miss you!' Those were the times, after all. It was easy for human beings to disappear, and not easy to recover them.

The yearly celebration at the ashram was round the corner then. It wasn't as huge as it is now but was still quite an event. The President of India inaugurated it. Mahipal Shah Baba was being interviewed by Jayanti Banerjee, a reporter from a leading news agency. I was present there. After the interview, while we were all sipping tea, I asked her without any forewarning, 'Jayantiji, a friend of mine – she was also a devotee here – Anjali Agarwal – has gone missing. Can you please help us locate her?'

That gave Mahipal Shah a real jolt. Balbhushan Dada's face stiffened. Jayanti Banerjee looked at all three of us keenly through the gap above her reading glasses. We were all silent, and then Balbhushan Dada changed the subject. Mahipal Shah ended the meeting soon, and Jayanti Banerjee bid goodbye. Mahipal Shah got up and left the room without even looking at my face. He did not summon me or speak to me for days after. Balbhushan Dada scolded me for being so impetuous. Then it took barely one week. They cleared the wild areas around the ashram to expand Mahipala Cosmetics. The workers found a skeleton, apparently a woman's. Wild animals had eaten it; it was mostly decomposed. It was identified by the bag and purse that were found near it.

Some woman murdered by her lover – the employees of Mahipala were quick to decide. It was quite common in those parts. The assistant managers asked each other if she would have shrieked or wept when the lover turned killer. I listened, feeling uneasy. It was still too early for me to forget Abhilash or Sriram. I was just a rent sack stuffed with Abhilash, Sriram, Chechi, Vasanthaalayam, debt, wandering, kidney, pain, and so on. But when I watched the police arrive and people gather to haul the remains into the ambulance, I did not imagine in my wildest dreams that this was Anjali Didi's body. Only when I saw her photo in the next day's newspaper did I know. My head began to swim. My heart was rent with grief. That was my last day at Mahipala.

'Woman's body found among thickets' ran the newspaper headline. Also, 'Body almost fully devoured by wild animals'. See now? People don't die from daggers and pistols alone. See why the head of security, Sukhcharan Singh, warned me of the foxes prowling out there? Mahipala Enterprises owned many hectares of land, the campus extended to the far horizon. All gifted by a devotee from Mumbai. Years back, if you stood on the balcony of the office here, you would see rocks and denuded hills in the distance. The forests were anaemic but there were monkeys and peacocks, plenty of boar and porcupines. There were wolves and leopards, too, for sure. Then, naturally, there would be foxes too. Actually, the fox that Sukhcharan mentioned was a metaphor. Sixteen years later, the thought of the fox rattled me. I trembled. It was not easy to determine which kind of death was better: death by a bullet or a dagger, or by wild creatures. And it was not I who could decide that. But I placed my trust in the goodness of human beings. I dreamt, fully awake, that my assassin would respect democratic values and let me choose, as a citizen.

But dreams and reality are far apart. There was no guarantee that S. Prakash would display such courtesy. He did not show it to Anjali Didi. I believed that he killed her. In other words, he was the 'fox'. If I got killed inside the Mahipala campus, my body would be food for the fox or wolf. Who would know? Maybe Amma would try to find out. But how much could she do? So that night, what mattered was not how he would kill me. It was more important to know where he was. There was a thrill in meeting him at intermittent, unforeseen moments and addressing him directly. I tossed and turned in bed. Lay on my stomach and then on my back, somehow killing time until dawn.

At the sight of first light, I got up. Ignoring the cold, I took a bath, made myself a coffee. Fished out the SIM-less phone from my pocket, charged it, and put it back into my pocket. When the sweepers in heavy chadors began to appear outside, I stepped out and walked towards the compound to the east of the campus where the mess and the apartment blocks were. Now there were twenty towers of 250 flats each. Sixteen years ago, there were only ten towers. The cottages were for VVIPs, like me. VIPs stayed in the luxury apartments. IPs occupied two- or single-bedroom apartments. The middle-class were housed in less fancy apartments. The poorest devotees stayed in dormitories. If a person snuck into an apartment and lived there, it was quite like a fox prowling around in the jungle. No one would know; there would hardly be any trace.

I went to the security post and looked for Sukhcharan Singh. The man on duty called him. He hurried to me. Recognizing me now as someone dear to Balbhushan Jha, he was keen to make me happy. I chatted with him a bit, and then showed him Prakash's photo on my phone. I had only a faint hope, but he confirmed – '*Ji haan* – Jivesh – he used to be a security guard here. He comes for the monthly prayer and the sadbhavana prayer too. Madamji, please come to the auditorium in the evening. He will be there.' I felt like I had been lifted off the ground. In fact, this was a golden chance. I decided to make the best use of it. I returned to my room without losing a minute. Rested the whole day. Slept well.

The sadbhavana prayer was a weekly mass prayer. A huge ceremony. Whenever Mahipal Shah was in the ashram, he would present himself at the auditorium at six-thirty in the evening to preach from the Gita. He would offer his devotees a chance to touch his feet in prayer. Ordinary folk had to take an appointment for a darshan. Only ten thousand people were allowed in a day. Actually, it was a great musical show. Baba's Gita lessons, interspersed with chanting from the Gita, the darshan – all stretching until midnight.

I reached the auditorium by five-thirty. The sadbhavana auditorium had been rebuilt. I crossed four or five metal detectors and pat-downs to reach inside. The venue was adorned with marigolds and chrysanthemums, areca-tree blooms, and garlands of basil and ixora. A red carpet was laid up to the dais. Mahipal Shah came in looking quite regal. Balbhushan, clad in a spotless white kurta and pyjama, cleared the way for him. I had partaken in the prayer just once when I was a resident here. I did not go back despite Balbhushan's many requests. So when he saw me there now, he frowned. I covered my head with my dupatta and went over to him, looking as demure as I could, and took my place behind him. Mahipal Shah went up on the dais and sat down there. Balbhushan Dada withdrew into the console room behind. I followed him. My aim was to scan the faces of the audience on the TV screens lined up there. I found him in the fifth row, seventh seat. Yes, it was S. Prakash. I did not flinch for even a moment. When the Music Mojito, scheduled after the Gita teachings, began, I slipped away from beside Balbhushan and went to the door that opened on to the sixth row. I entered the hall behind S. Prakash and stood leaning on the wall right behind him. The next item of the programme was Gita Meditation. When the prayer songs began, S. Prakash rose. I hid behind the door. I followed him through the green room and the console room and observed him. The poor man, he had got up to relieve himself. I waited at the spot where one turned to go towards the ladies' toilets. When he came out, I stepped in his way.

'Hello, Mr Assassin,' I said, laughing.

The auditorium, the lights, the sound, this man in the brown woollen jacket ... all of it felt like the dream of a fully conscious mind. He jumped and stepped back, his eyes bulging and fixed on me. I saw his eyes. The pupils were dead. There were lines around his eyes. The sad wretch too must have seen much in life, it seemed certain.

'Do not try to run, you will surely be caught,' I said in a friendly tone. He looked around nervously.

'Want to come to my cottage?' I asked, without a trace of anger or hatred. He drew back some more.

'If you come, I'll make you a nice coffee. Once you feel less startled, you can finish your job too.'

He seemed to be sinking a bit into the ground.

'Let me tell you since we have come this far. I don't think that you will return alive from this place,' I added.

Suddenly, he turned sharply and looked around. I, too, turned my face towards the direction of his eyes, reflexively. That split-second was enough for him. By the time I turned my head, he had fled! I saw him run up the stairs in a flash. I gave chase but my path was blocked by devotees coming out after their darshan and going to the dining hall. So I decided to give up and let the fucker flee. Panting, I sat down on the black granite steps of the auditorium and caught my breath. Then I went to the security post near the main gate. Sukhcharan Singh was

on duty. I spoke with him for some time. He gave me some prasad –
rava kesari and ginger coffee. After some time, he asked me if I needed
to be escorted to the cottage, and I said yes. He came with me. The
walking path below the trees upon which so many beautiful colours
played, was unearthly indeed. Sukhcharan walked ahead, showing the
way. In between, he turned around and asked, 'Madamji, your home is
in Malayalam?'

'Keralam. Malayalam is our language.'

'Both are the same. Your family?'

'My mother.'

'Is she well?'

'I have not been able to call her since I came here, Sukhcharanji.'

'What happened, Madamji? No range?'

'Remember, I lost my SIM.'

'Oh, you didn't get another?'

'I would have to go out for that. I couldn't.'

'Madamji, I can give you mine. But you will have to top it up.'

I could do that, of course – didn't I have plenty of money? He took a
purse out of his pocket and gave me a SIM card and its number. I took
out the phone from my jeans pocket and inserted the card. Sukhcharan
topped it up from his phone. I handed him two five-hundred-rupee
notes and clearly, he was pleased. I called Amma. She picked up at the
first ring. We had a conversation then, and it went like this:

'Haven't I told you never to attend a call from an unknown number,
Vasanthalakshmi?'

'Satye, where have you been!'

'Were you afraid, Amme?'

'It was a horrible turmoil … inside.'

'Amme, do you get this jittery thinking about your daughter?'

'Satye, I am growing old.'

'Are you crying, Amme?'

'Not yet. Don't make me.'

'I had some trouble, Amme. Lost my phone.'

'Phone or SIM?'

'Yes, the SIM.'

'You know well that one can be traced even if they dump a SIM.'

'Now, don't you go telling everyone that!'

'You are in Delhi, aren't you?'

'How did you know?'

'I found out.'

'And you were still agitated?'

'It was difficult, till I heard your voice. Only that.'

'What news back home?'

'Nothing. Paramarth is keeping me company.'

'What about him? Teaching you new songs?'

'When he isn't singing songs, he's teaching me science.'

'For example?'

'For example, when you water the tulsi, it releases a flood of oxygen which energizes the brain.'

'Says who?'

'NASA.'

'But NASA is a space research organization!'

'If you tell him that, he'll call you names!'

'What's going to happen to him at this rate?'

'Ask what's going to happen to me!'

'This world is his too, Amma.'

'He believes that it is his alone.'

'Can't you talk to him? Correct him?'

'It's easier to catch the moon.'

'What happened to your optimism, Amma?'

'He took it apart!'

'Let me come back. We'll set it right.'

'Have you got your ticket?'

'Easy to get when you have money at hand.'

'What are you actually doing there?'

'Participating in the sadbhavana prayer here today.'

'When is your investigation going to get over?'

'Give me fifty days. If it doesn't end by then, you can burn me.'

'You want to send me to jail?'

'I haven't sent you even to a queue in front of a bank! And to jail?'

'He's around there, isn't he?'

'Who?'

'Who else? Your killer, that's who.'

'Amma, you are truly a boss!'

'Each one is a boss of some sort.'

'They don't remind others of that fact, though.'

'But he won't harm you there.'

'How do you know that?'

'Because the police are after you, and he knows it.'

'Are the police after me?'

'That's what Aswathy said.'

'Amma, someone is tapping our phone.'

'So what? I am not saying anything criminal.'

'Not that, the police…'

'That the people tapping the phone know for sure?'

I did not continue. The vigour I had gained from my recent discoveries left me. I felt drained of courage too. I did not even notice the blooming bowers on either side as Sukhcharan and I walked. 'Sukhcharanji, I need another favour from you,' I said to him. He was a little ahead of me, waiting. I went up to him.

'Tell me, Madamji…'

'I need to meet Jivesh immediately.'

'He is already in Jhaji's cottage, Madamji…' he told me simply.

I thought that the ground under me had parted. For some time, my ears, eyes, nose, nothing worked. But my feet moved on their own. Sukhcharan came up to my cottage and bid me goodbye. I waited till he disappeared from sight. I was left alone in the dark with the trees and the shadows. My heart pounded heavily inside my chest. I felt a terrible desire to take out the curved dagger from my bag, plunge it in my chest and turn it, as though checking a jackfruit for its ripeness.

Losing no time, I went to Balbhushan Jha's cottage. It was behind Mahipal Shah's cottage, from where one could see the hillocks in the distance. The neon lamps on top of the bowers there did not work but the path shone like gold owing to the lights at the ground level. I staggered up that way. My eyesight was dimming, and consciousness, sinking. Like when I saw Chechi's boarding pass, or when I found out that she and Abhilash were married, like when I was told of her death.

If you have forgotten, let me remind you again. I am a woman who has suffered much. I arrived, somehow, at the doorstep of Balbhushan Jha's cottage. I made up the steps to the cottage, tottering and lurching. The moment I stepped in its front yard, the sensor lights lit up and a bell rang inside. There must have been CCTVs or MRI or whatever. I jumped on the veranda before my image could be caught and pushed the door open.

There was light inside, people too. On a low stool, a bottle of expensive liquor and glasses. Plates full of fried or roasted things. Three men.

The first, Balbhushan Jha, clad in his pristine white kurta-pyjama and the sacred ashes on his forehead.

The second, S. Prakash, in his sandal-coloured kurta-pyjama and a shawl wrapped around his shoulders.

The third – and maybe I was hallucinating – but that was Anurup Shetty, in a blue sweater and jeans.

THIRTY-NINE

That day, I failed as a criminal investigator. A criminal investigator has no foes. She must be unemotional, detached. It is a form of asceticism. But at this crucial moment, I forgot precisely that. The three were seated still as statues there. I heard three sighs. It was Balbhushan Jha who awoke first. 'Come, come, Satya,' he called, 'come, sit here.' Then the other statues showed signs of life. Anurup Shetty busied himself with tasting something that was on the plate. S. Prakash looked the other way.

Actually, I should have walked in coolly then. There was space on the sofa Anurup was sitting on. I should have sat down and crossed one leg over the other. Should have snacked casually on the cashew nuts. Should have asked, 'All fine, guys?' The guys would have squirmed, their faces would have fallen, their minds would have been in a tumult. I really, fervently, wanted to do this. But what could I do? My legs wouldn't move, my voice refused to come out. That's the problem when you are splintered from within. From the outside, everything looks fixed and hanging together. We alone know what is going on inside.

And just that? No! A wail started rolling upwards from the lower part of my stomach. I began to hallucinate. Amma now stood in front of me. She was draped perfectly in a beautiful blue Binny silk sari with a black border. Her long hair had been tied up high in a bun. She wore chunky ear studs and a long chain with a red locket in which two swans gazed at each other. The large dot of sindoor on her forehead and the thin streak of the powder on the parting of her hair were both soaked in sweat. The place I stood transmogrified into Vasanthamaalika. She stood erect, head up, in Room No. 555 on the fifth floor. On the floor, women's underclothes lay scattered. She bent down and gathered them, put them into some unseen hands. Then she walked away, head high, towards the lift. Alighted from it smiling. Gifted a hundred- rupee note to the receptionist. It was a crumpled note, stained with blood. Nisha Chechi held it out to me. The blood that had dried on Nisha Chechi's bony body looked like grains of sindoor. Thomachan of St Anthony's took off his jubbah in front of me. My head spun. I nearly retched.

I managed to take a few steps. Though I feared that I might fall down, I was determined to hold myself up. I walked gingerly, like Nisha Chechi. The pain spread all over my body. My eyes were fixed on S. Prakash. I wasn't sure that it was him that I was seeing then. And I was not even sure that it was my eyes that saw him. Everything felt foggy around me; everything was merely a feeling. But I noticed that his hairline had receded. His paunch stuck out. I did not take my eyes off him. He was sitting with his head bowed. He might leap at me any moment, I reckoned – his posture indicated that. The coward's pose. Ready to attack when the prey's gaze falters. I held my gaze. I should have stayed in that pose, or walked out. Instead, I wanted to swagger and play the hero. That's where I went wrong. All of a sudden, I grabbed the bottle, poured its contents into my throat, and gulped down the liquid. My tongue was on fire. The liquid thundered down my gullet into my stomach. My blood turned into petrol, it boiled and burst into flames. A colossal tidal wave of anger swept inside me. I must break this bottle on the floor, pick up the broken half, and stab him in the heart like in the movies, I decided. Then the story

would end soon. But my aim was hardly to kill him, was it? It was
to know his story. So my tongue ached to tell a joke. Something that
would manipulate myself. I could find nothing. 'Sit down, sit down!'
Balbhushan Jha repeated weakly. I turned to Anurup Shetty.

'But should I sit down where my murder is being planned?'

A sound similar to that which escapes a strangled throat was heard.
He looked at me. A cry of pain writhed in my throat, like a living fish.
Its bony fins and tail bruised my throat and left it bleeding.

'Satya, this is a misunderstanding.' Balbhushan came up to me and
placed his hand on my shoulder.

'No, Dada, no, you should not say another word,' I burst out. 'To
think that I loved an evil man like you, like a father!'

'No, Satya, it's not like that. You speak without knowing the truth.
Please listen calmly … I was talking to him and…'

I refused to listen. His elaboration! I saw only S. Prakash. And the
more I saw him, the sorrier I felt. The miserable man had dark circles
around his eyes. His cheeks were puffy and sunken. He did not look
healthy. Or wealthy enough. The biggest lack was of self-confidence.
But there was one thing: he did not lack hatred. He was like a food
bowl that had been bitten completely out of shape by a lone Alsatian
pup. A killer needs to be just eliminated, not described. But I did not
need to take his life. I needed his secret. Until then, I would have great
sympathy for him. And once I found out? The sympathy might be
folded up and stored away. I was cutting him up in my mind. I will pull
his guts out. He will shrink with shame seeing the filth inside him. He
will either kill himself, or kill me.

My mouth burned. My throat smouldered. My head parted from
my body. It rolled on my throat like a football on a windy lawn.
Balbhushan offered me a glass of water. I swatted it away, grabbed
the bottle of water, and drank all of it quickly. '*Pakaram naam …
Thalayarinjhu kootten … than chuduchora … Kudukudaaaaa…*' I
chanted in my mind, as Paramarth's bloodthirsty song thrust itself up
there. I suddenly wanted to see Paramarth but couldn't recall his face.

When I tried to dig it up from memory, I felt that it was the same as Prakash's. I began to tire, I badly wanted to lie down. But I needed to boast and swagger first. How was I to go away otherwise? My tongue came loose now. I held down my conscious mind with the strength of gravity. I had nothing to say to these three. Anyway, what was the use? To wound human beings, especially males, the better instrument was the word, not the blade. I wanted to swig down some more booze, but controlled myself. What if I fell? Or my tongue failed? So I lost no time. I went up to S. Prakash. He looked at me apprehensively. The fear was writ large in his eyes, in the sunken, darkened sockets of his eyes. Everything that he had suffered until then filled them and brimmed over. His hair had been falling and the scalp was showing. Very soon, there would be just a thin row of strands left, like a fence. That would soon vanish too. And with it, his head would be bald, like the moon. I stretched out my hand and touched his head. 'Oh, you're already going bald,' I quipped. I pressed my hands on his cheeks. His eyes flew open, and I could feel his body tighten. But I raised his chin and looked into his eyes.

'Aniya – hey, my little brother,' I called him. 'Aniya, why not just finish me off now? Right now?'

Only after that sentence came out of my mouth did I realize what I had just babbled. My organs are also like me: disobedient. What if he decided to fulfil that wish of mine? I had not made any preparations to depart from this world. Hadn't even bid my mother goodbye. But my tongue continued to roll insolently. I continued to babble:

'Or these fuckers will kill you. You know what, Prakash? You will be cut out any moment by this Balbhushan Jha and this fake sanyasi Mahipal Shah. You know what a "cut-out" is? You probably don't. Ask this Anurup Shetty – or maybe no, he knows fucking nothing – you should ask this Balbhushan Jha. And come to my cottage. But stop this game today! I beseech you with folded hands. Please!'

I folded my palms in salutation. But my heart was throbbing in agony. A howl was gnawing at my throat like a rat attacking paper.

I was filled with longing for Chechi; once more her absence left me in agonizing pain. We become truly alone when there is no one to make us laugh. How I yearned to see her lovely face once more, just once. Death may not finish us; but the death of those who will never abandon us surely will. The thought that it may have been S. Prakash who took her from me made me shake with rage. The sympathy I'd felt for him until now vanished. That was my Waterloo as a criminal investigator. My right hand grabbed the liquor bottle and swung it hard. Its contents splattered on all who were seated. S. Prakash leapt up. I saw only that, and then a flash of lightning, on top of my skull. Has anyone smashed a glass bottle on your head? If not, a pity. Time goes glug-glug-glug for that one minute. And then, a total blackout. Your ears are filled with the sound of shattering glass. You wouldn't know that the bottle was broken; you'd think that its shards had scattered and fallen into your ears.

~

I woke up to water being sprinkled on my face. The doctor and nurses were cleaning my wound and applying antiseptics. There were no stitches. Balbhushan Jha and Anurup Shetty were mute witnesses. S. Prakash was nowhere to be seen. The medical staff left after telling me to contact them if I experienced nausea in the next twenty-four hours. The blow to the head was just a metaphor. In actual fact, you have to experience a metaphor to know it. It felt like a fifty-kilo weight had been tied above my neck. I thought my neck would break from it. Balbhushan summoned two women to clean up the room. While he was giving them instructions, I got up. I had received what I deserved. Then why wait? I tried to walk. Balbhushan and Anurup ran up and tried to support me. I ignored them and came out. The pain was such that I felt like my head was coming off in layers. In that moment, the agony intoxicated me. My steps, as I walked, were even more unsteady than when I had arrived. Anurup Shetty walked with me, he tried to help me. I did not stop him, I needed him. Not just till I reached the cottage but also after. Opening the door, I went in and sat on the sofa. He sat down opposite me. I did not look at him. I was too fatigued to open my eyes. But though still only half-conscious, I began to search for tickets for a flight back home on my phone. Anurup Shetty cleared his throat. 'Satyapriya Ma'am,' he called to me.

'Yes, tell me,' I responded, sounding very formal.

'Satyapriya Ma'am, you shouldn't be using the phone in this condition.'

'You've forgotten what our PM has said? The bank is in your thumb, your mobile phone is your wallet!'

'But your head will be worse…'

'Is that worse than treachery by those who one trusted?'

'Look, Ma'am, I have not betrayed you.'

'Maybe you betrayed yourself?'

'Please believe me. I went to Jha's cottage looking for Prakash.'

'Same pinch! Me too!'

'I was going to question him.'

'I never knew that police questioning was such fun!'

'Jha and he were having a drink.'

'When I saw you, even you were drinking with them.'

'With a criminal? Me?'

'What am I to say? Nowadays I can't trust even my own eyes!'

'Ma'am, there are some things that you haven't grasped.'

'Surely there are.'

'He is a Malayali.'

'We all seek just a single truth in this life, don't we?'

'I am not done. He suffers from severe mental illness.'

'Of course. Otherwise, why would he pursue me like this?'

'No, Ma'am. He has spent long periods in mental health institutions in Odisha and Kerala. I have proof of it.'

'That's cool. Now even if he kills me, you don't have to arrest him!'

'You mean to say that he's pretending to be mentally ill to avoid arrest?'

'No, he's avoiding arrest to pretend to be mentally ill.'

'It's actually you who's sick in the head. You hug him one moment and then try to clobber him with a glass bottle! Tell me the truth, why did you beg him to beat you up, literally!'

'When you don't have something, you beg for it. I did not find anyone who could break my skull. So I begged him to do it.'

'Ma'am, I am not interested in arguing with you. You have to either trust me, or I'll drop out of this case.'

'This you have been threatening me with for quite some time!'

'I am investigating this case out of my personal interest.'

'Is there some way to reduce that interest?'

'Ma'am, why is your tongue filled with such venom?'

'To survive, what else?'

'Why did you touch that Prakash, Ma'am?'

'I felt empathetic towards him. The poor man, does anyone know his sorrow?'

'Is that why you tried to break his head with that bottle?'

'I remembered my sister then! I suddenly felt suspicious – that she must have been killed by him!'

'She's been gone since the past seventeen years, right?'

'I have never believed that she's gone.'

'Were you so close to her?'

'We were two halves of the same soul.'

'And is that why your sister got married to the man you loved?'

'She was romantic. Would fall in love very easily.'

'But to fall in love with her younger sister's lover?'

'Abhilash and I weren't close any more.'

'Didn't you tell me that her death wasn't a murder?'

'That's what I believed.'

'Why do you think otherwise now?'

'"You, too, may be killed any moment..." – those were my father's last words ... Since then, I have doubted that it was a murder.'

'So you must have set out to check if your father was right?'

'I feel that he had a point for sure.'

'That means, you believe that S. Prakash harbours some deep hatred for your family!'

'What wrong have I done him for him to feel such acute hostility?'

'That's what even I need to know. All right. How long are you going to be here?'

'I have not decided.'

'Why did you wish to stay here?'

'To speak with S. Prakash.'

'You were going to speak with him while swinging a glass bottle at him?'

'I lost my control when I saw you – who ought to be arresting him and throwing him in jail, sitting beside him and sharing a drink.'

'I was making him come round.'

'And did you?'

'But you ruined it all, didn't you?'

'Inspector, I understand your limitations.'

In the middle of this conversation, I booked a ticket for a flight for two o'clock that afternoon for six thousand rupees. Setting the phone aside, I looked at Inspector Shetty. He tried to say something, but could not find the words. I took advantage of that interlude.

'Never mind, Inspector, I am ready to die. Sometimes I even think that I am already dead.'

'You are really mad.'

'You mean hallucinations? Or schizophrenia?'

'Is this the same phone? A different number?'

'You need to know that in order to tap this one too?'

'You think I am the one who's tapping your phone?'

'I did suspect that before.'

'And now?'

'I am certain.'

'Great god! I give up!' He hit his forehead with his palm.

The wound on my head ached badly. Sleep hung on my eyes. But I did not feel brave enough to sleep. What if once I fell into a deep slumber, he smashed the rest of my head? I now feared Anurup Shetty too. Since it was clear now that I knew all, what if he took over the task from S. Prakash? A police officer can easily wriggle out. It was painful to imagine the inspector killing me. But that was my problem. I wasn't bothered by the fact that I may be killed. Who was going to do it was my problem. Let S. Prakash do it if he so wished, but not Anurup Shetty. There was an unfairness to that. But can you live in this world without contributing to its injustice in some way? If you have two lovers, you are being unfair to one of them. I did feel guilty. Maybe to extricate myself from it, I fell asleep quickly.

When I opened my eyes, it was already light. Anurup had dozed off on the single-seater sofa opposite the bed. I got up with great difficulty. I seemed to be carrying a heavy sack on my neck. Having somehow managed to get to the bathroom, I brushed my teeth and washed my face, in a lot of pain. When I came back to my room, the inspector was still asleep. I went to the kitchen, made coffee for us both. He awoke only when I shook him awake. He wiped his face and mouth, and apologized numerous times. I showed him the way to the bathroom. He came back, took the coffee, and we sat facing each other, drinking the coffee. We had another conversation, which went like this:

'Does it still hurt, Ma'am?'

'What if it does?'

'You are always in that same mood, even the moment you wake up?'

'Also when I sleep.'

'A terrible birth, for sure.'

'You are right.'

'This nature of yours is why one can't say anything to you.'

'But you should have something new to say?'

'Don't you at least want to know if I have anything new to tell you?'

'I am listening – tell me?'

'Do you know his full name?'

'Prakash?'

'The full name.'

'S. Prakash.'

'Ma'am, his full name is Satyaprakash.'

That smashed me once again. The coffee cup fell on the floor, the liquid splashed on the sofa and the floor. My body began to shiver uncontrollably. Anurup was shaken too. He came over, bent down, and began to pick up the broken pieces of the cup. I could see nothing at all. I was experiencing the impact of another glass bottle coming down on the top of my head with full force. The chinking of broken glass rang in my ears.

– Satyaprakash.

– Satyapriya.

– *Satyameva Jayate.*

FORTY

'Ma'am, are you all right?' Inspector Shetty asked me. I stared at him vacantly. I tried to fix my gaze on his face but failed. My pupils slipped. I felt water fall on my face. This must be what the world looks like from inside a glass jar filled with formalin – I experienced it. Then I woke up. Saw Anurup Shetty clearly. His big eyes reminded me of Gandhi spectacles. He sprinkled some more water on my face from the mug that he held. I regained consciousness. 'Are you okay?' he asked again. 'Yes, I think so,' I replied. This provoked him. We talked.

'Why do you retort so sharply even when you faint?'

'Why do my answers feel like sharp retorts to you?'

'If these are your answers, then what are your retorts going to be like!'

'Aren't you certain that you won't be able to bear them?'

'Ma'am, with a nature like yours, I am surprised why you weren't finished off earlier!'

'Does that mean that you think my being murdered wouldn't be so bad?'

'Till I die, I will not let anyone kill you.'

'I am past the age at which one trusts men's promises.'

'You haven't met good men. That is it.'

416

'Inspector Sir, you are right. I have never seen a really good man. Can you show me one?'

'For that you must first become a good person.'

'I must first become good for men to become good?'

'I have no time to argue. Have a lot of work to finish. If you need any help from me, let me know.'

'I want to see Satyaprakash.'

'Haven't you had enough of him?'

'He's a dear one, isn't he? I can't have enough.'

'Dear one? How?'

'My father's son.'

'I thought that too.'

'That may be why my father tried to warn me.'

'True.'

'I think it is he who stabbed my father too.'

'Yes. Otherwise, he wouldn't have sought this dagger out.'

'Now all I need to know is whether his mother is alive.'

'Any guess who that might be?'

'You should be finding that out?'

'I am.'

Balbhushan Jha came in right then. I turned my face away from him sharply and went in. I packed quickly, booked an Uber. When I came out with my suitcases, Balbhushan Jha and Inspector Shetty were talking. I put the key of the cottage on the little stool.

'Balbhushanji, here's the key. You must check the place and see if I have taken away anything.'

'Beti, so I am no longer Dada to you?'

'Will dead bodies call their murderers such endearing names?'

'Please don't hurt me with such sharp words!'

'Those who wield knives to hurt others will be hurt by words!'

'Did you come to leave so soon?'

'If I stay any more, I'll not leave at all.'

'Beti, let me tell you, this is a terrible misunderstanding.'

'Everything is maya, is it not, Dada? What is there to misunderstand?'

I stepped out with my luggage and called Sukhcharan to send over an electric pickup cart. 'Aren't you meeting Baba before you leave?' Balbhushan Jha asked me, following me. I did not reply. I just wanted to escape as soon as I could. The taxi I had booked was waiting for me at the main gate. Sukhcharan brought the pickup cart and loaded my suitcases on it. I returned his SIM card and gave him some more money. He thanked me several times. Without losing any more time, I set out for the airport.

~

I breathed easy only after I checked in. Heading straight to the south Indian restaurant at the airport, I ate to my heart's content. Then went to my gate, found a seat, and eased myself into it. I could only think of Satyaprakash. It looked certain to me that he was my father's son. Maybe because that feeling had been present in my subconscious from the beginning. The thought gave me goosebumps. What if he had been born to my mother? Then we would have grown up playing together, he would have slept in the same cot as Chechi and I, we would have laughed and cried and got caned together. I wanted him to be my younger brother. I did not like older brothers. They were likely to be overbearing. But with younger brothers, you could exert power. My mind, filled with such thoughts, grew tender.

Boarding had begun for the Hyderabad flight. The passengers in the queue stood in a line, each a character in a separate story. The others, too, were travelling to complete their own stories, like me. If only all the characters in my story too would line up like this! This criminal investigation would then have become so easy! But my characters were not the sort who would reveal their stories on their own. I couldn't blame them. I was never like that ever, was I? And there is another thing – the core of a criminal investigation is not the investigation, it is the waiting. Waiting for the character who'd make available the last missing piece. I thought that this character was Satyaprakash's mother. I believed, futilely, that finding her would be the end of this story. I racked my brains to identify her. A woman who gave birth to my father's son and raised him. Did I know such a woman? My enthusiasm and thoughts both encountered an obstacle. What did I know about the women in my father's life? What, actually, did I know of him, even? He must have interacted with so many women about whom I knew nothing. What all places had he visited? In any case, who knew their father fully and completely? I cried a lot during the flight. The woman who sat near me was concerned. 'I lost a loved one,' I told her. Who, she asked. I should have said, 'Peace of mind', but I did not. A friend, I replied. Who can be a better friend than peace of mind?

It was past nine when I got home. Amma and Paramarth were waiting. 'Why are you so late?' Paramarth started. 'I had to hack down some foes on the way,' I told him. His face darkened. 'The big money in the Jan Dhan accounts will be caught soon,' he threatened me. 'Who's going to make up for the fifteen thousand crore lost from the people queuing up for fifty whole days?' I shot back. He hated questions, so he gnashed his teeth and stormed out. 'You're going to die by his hand,' Amma warned. 'Never mind. That way I'll be spared of his singing,' I joked. Then I called Anurup from Amma's phone. His phone was switched off. I went off to take a shower. Coming out, I noticed that our window had a new pane and bolt. I felt a little sad that the 'S' that Satyaprakash had etched on it had disappeared. Whatever, I preferred to die at his hand. He was sophisticated. Paramarth was just too crude.

Amma served me rice gruel; we ate together. When she went off to wash the plates, I called Anurup again. I could not reach him, so called Aseema and chatted with her for some time. Amma came back after locking the gate and the main doors, ready to go to bed. I hugged her and gave her a kiss. She looked at me carefully. 'How's Aseema doing?', 'How's her daughter?', 'What news at the ashram?' – she asked. Only once we had gone over all this did she ask, 'Who smashed your skull?' After this, the following conversation happened between us:

'What do you think?' I asked.

'It must have been him. The chap who's after you.'

'Do you know his name?'

'Prakash, or something like that?'

'Satyaprakash.'

Amma was silent for a moment.

'Did that startle you, Amma?'

'A little.'

'What do you make of it?'

'What did you think?'

'That he is my father's son.'

'Could be.'

'Could be? Just that? Not sure?'

'Isn't this a human affair? How can one be sure beyond a point?'

'Okay, for the sake of argument let us suppose that he is Acchan's son. If so, who's his mother?'

Amma sighed. 'I am not sure.'

'Don't you know how many lovers your husband had? A wife you call yourself!'

'But for that, the man should have been capable of love!'

'He could only rape?'

'Shouldn't he know the difference?'

She sighed again. Pulling back her hair, she lay down.

'Amme, could this be the same person who stabbed Acchan?'

Amma closed her eyes. 'That was someone else.'

'Who?'

She was silent. I waited with bated breath. She did not open her eyes. I shook her awake. 'Amme, tell me, please…'

'Nisha…'

That was unexpected. How would you feel if a searing coal fell into your eye? I saw Nisha Chechi walk bow-legged, in pain. That day appeared before my eyes. From that day onwards, we stopped playing hopscotch together. She stopped attending the Gita class. She never shook the njaaval tree in front of the Gita class so that I could gather the undamaged juicy black fruit. She did not come looking for cat-berries by the river, or search for the bulbul's nest.

~

I did not tell anyone what Acchan had done to her. Not even Chechi. Chechi was dumb, anyway. She went to the east-side wall many times to call Nisha Chechi to come and play with us. But she would not respond. One day, losing patience, she decided to head over. 'No, no,' I pleaded with her. She ran down the lane, slid down the slope and stopped in front of Nisha Chechi's house. It was a small house of two rooms, built with laterite. Nisha Chechi came out into the small veranda of exposed brick. I stood by the east-side wall, watching. Nisha Chechi's messed-up clothes and hair, and puffed-up, reddened face scared me. I was racked with sadness and fear. I did not fear her; I feared the terrible unease that she could now stir up inside me. I was helpless; after all, I was just a kid then. How could anyone bear so much at that age? How could one walk straight with that weight?

Chechi came back in a huff. Nisha Chechi's refusal irked her. She called her proud, ungrateful. If you speak with her again, I'll never speak to you, she threatened me. Chechi was actually very fond of her. They were in the same class in the government school. Nisha Chechi used to do her maths homework for her too. She was a good student in all subjects except English, in which she always failed. Only because of that, Chechi stood first in class. Nisha Chechi sought my help with English. When Chechi got to know of it, she kicked up a fuss. She's conspiring against her own sister's first rank – Chechi bawled. Amma intervened and helped Nisha Chechi attend a tuition class for English without Chechi's knowledge. She began to pass the English exams. But before she could outdo Chechi in class, my father failed her. That hundred-rupee note turned her into someone else. She stopped going to school. In between, her mother gave birth for the fifth time.

With this, she dropped out of school altogether. The infant died in its fourth month. The next month, her father was crushed under a pushcart. He survived, but his spine was seriously injured; he became bedridden. No one asked about her studies after that. No one saw her outside their house, either.

Nisha Chechi got her first monthlies five or six months later. That was a July. There was no school because of very heavy rain. The sky was dark, overcast since morning. Before noon, her mother came over shielding herself with a large leaf, asking for some clean cloth. My mother gave her a few laundered mundus and a packet of Carefree sanitary napkins. She had Laalamma make some sweetmeats and sent them over to Nisha Chechi's house in plastic jars. Chechi made a face when she saw that. 'Look at her face when you give someone anything!' said Amma, pinching her hard on the wrist.

The following month, Chechi, too, got her periods. There was a big celebration. Our grandfather, uncles and aunts arrived. Also my father's sisters, his brother and his wife. Basketfuls of sweetmeats piled up on the kitchen table, dining room, and the storeroom. My sister's neck and wrists shone with gold ornaments. Appooppan gave Amma five thousand rupees to buy Chechi gold jewellery. At that time, a gold sovereign cost some four hundred and fifty rupees. Amma took me along when she went to the jewellers in town. She bought Chechi a palaikka-style gold chain and four bangles. With the rest of the money, she got a three-quarters-sovereign kaashu necklace and a pair of small gold studs.

I was sent to fetch Nisha Chechi. My heart pounded. I was afraid to face her. But I still went. She came out. 'Amma is calling you,' I told her. Her face flushed. She caught hold of my arm and asked me, 'Did you tell her anything?' No, I vowed. In the end, she decided to come. We were as anxious as two criminals guilty of the same crime. She held my arm as she walked. Her palm was cold and clammy.

She would not even look at Amma's face; her eyes were fixed on the floor. 'We don't see you here these days? Why aren't you going to school?' Amma tried asking her. 'Don't give up school,' she advised, handing her a small magenta-coloured paper packet. Nisha Chechi was wearing two tiny pieces of dried-up coconut-frond stems in her ears. Amma replaced them with the small gold studs. She looked prettier when Amma made her wear the gold necklace. I watched with a mixture of envy and relief. But Nisha Chechi's eyes filled with tears. She thrust her face into her palms and burst into sobs. Amma laughed and asked her why she was crying, but she turned around and ran back to her house. I, too, was about to cry. I should have told Amma everything at least then. But at that moment, Laalamma came over to ask Amma about that day's lunch menu. My experience is – there's always a moment at which you get to reveal the truth. Make use of it immediately. No use crying when it's gone.

Then there is this truth: the older you grow, the less brave you are to speak the truth. Children grow up when they learn about sex. I grew up too early. Chechi took a few more months to catch up with me. I was in school that day. She had skipped school because of her periods. Amma was not at home that day too. Her sister-in-law's mother had been hospitalized. Amma had gone to pay her a visit. Chechi and Laalamma were alone at home. By noon, Acchan arrived from Madras. 'Where is Vasantham?' he asked, and he murmured angrily, 'Forever gallivanting in town!' He asked Chechi why she was not in school, and she told him of her tummy ache. 'Go and lie down,' he ordered her, and she went off meekly, scared. She drifted into sleep. When she awoke, it was evening, and the house was silent. There was no one in the kitchen. She heard some movement in our parents' bedroom. She pushed the door open and saw Acchan on the bed. And Nisha Chechi, like a tadpole on a dissection table. She was completely shattered.

By the time I returned from school, Chechi had screamed the place down. Acchan had left the house. Laalamma was not back yet. She banged her head on the wall and screamed, and swore, under her sobs, to kill Nisha Chechi. I felt a great relief. A truth that had to be hidden all the time, suffocated me. Chechi's anger was directed towards Nisha

Chechi, and mine, towards Acchan. Why did she come here again if he hurt her earlier, she asked. At that age, I had no answer. Anyway, from that day onwards, our hearts beat together, borne down upon by the same fear. We hid the same wound. I did not let her tell Amma. I could not inflict pain on her. I should not have kept it from her really. It is not the truth that hurts people, actually, it is the act of hiding it.

The next blow came during the time of my exams just before Christmas. I had been pacing our front yard while doing my revisions, and soon reached the east-side wall. There seemed to be some commotion in Nisha Chechi's house. I leaned over the wall to take a look. In the yard behind their hut, Nisha Chechi's mother was thrashing her. She took turns smacking her own head and then striking her daughter. Nisha Chechi stood still, head hung low. I could not make out anything, but someone whispered from within me that this had something to do with my father. It was impossible to concentrate, and so I came back into the house, took a shower, packed my schoolbag, ate dosa for breakfast, and was putting on my school uniform when I heard a huge hue and cry outside. A tongue of fire leapt up inside my chest. Chechi and I ran out to see what was going on. A crowd was pushing its way through the path beside our house. Some people were carrying Nisha Chechi's mother. She and her brothers Nishant and Neeraj were running after her, in tears. Later, Venukkuttan Chettan told us that she had tried to hang herself. I felt utterly crushed.

That day, we missed school. Neither did we go to Nisha Chechi's house. Two days later, I went near the wall and peeked over it. She saw me; she had been sitting in their veranda. She rose, came near the path, and called to me, 'Satyamole...' I was a bit perturbed, but went out to meet her, hesitantly. She looked around and made sure that no one was around. She was thirteen then. But her body was still bony; her cheeks were sunken. Her eyes looked older for her age, and there were dark circles around them.

'I have to tell you something.'

I looked at her, surprised.

'I am pregnant.'

'Preg…?' My mouth flew open.

'There's a baby in my tummy.'

I was struck dumb. My eyes popped out.

'Your father's…' Her voice broke.

'Go tell him … to do…'

'Wh … at?'

My eyes filled.

'Must get rid of it.' She sounded harsh now. Her eyes twitched like fish in a dried-up pond.

'Rid…?'

'It must be killed.'

I had begun to cry.

'Yes, of course! Should I raise it? Your fucking bastard of a father's child?'

I thought I would pee right there. My breath stopped. She lifted my face up by my chin. Her eyes bore into mine. I started to weep out of fright.

'Go tell that damned man, your father, to solve this.'

'Uh … umm.'

'Siva should not know.'

'Um … um…'

'Your … your mother too—' Her voice failed. 'If your mother gets to know about this…' Her voice sounded menacing now.

'I won't tell.'

'Siva shouldn't know either.'

'No.'

'Amma's sanjayanam rites are tomorrow. It must be solved at once.'

I ran back. Went straight into the bathroom. My pee just broke. I was crying. I did not know what 'preg…' was, and so I began to think how it would feel to have a baby inside my tummy. It would grow inside. Then tear open my belly and leap out. It would wail aloud, call me 'Amme…' It would suckle milk from my breast. I pictured such an infant in Nisha Chechi's hands. I almost died of fear imagining it.

'What happened to you?' Chechi and Amma asked. Headache, tummy ache, I mumbled. The real challenge was how to tell Acchan. I had stopped talking to him since a long time. He had begun to beat me hard for small failings, scolded me for the tiniest of things. On each of those occasions, I gritted my teeth and did not shed a single tear. I'd stare at him unwaveringly. I never called him 'Accha'. My tongue refused to. But that night, I lay awake waiting for Acchan's Contessa to return. I counted the seconds, my heart pounding, when the car arrived and the sound of Ulahannan Maaman's bicycle leaving was heard. I could not speak with him at night. So I woke up early next day, at five in the morning. I woke up Laalamma and had her make me some coffee. I waited till Acchan was up and coming down. When he finally did come down, he went over to the front room and sat there. 'Laalamme, coffee,' he called, picking up the newspaper and opening it. I went into the kitchen quickly and asked her for it. 'Why this new love for Acchan today?' she asked, pouring the coffee into a cup. I took it to Acchan. He threw me a sidelong glance, and seeing me, his face clouded. I looked around and made sure that no one was listening.

'I have something to tell you,' I said, reproducing the harshness from Nisha Chechi's voice in mine. He looked startled. 'Nisha Chechi is pregnant.'

He now looked numbed.

'It must be washed out, she said.'

Acchan's eyes nearly fell off.

'Her mother's sanjayanam is tomorrow. You have to do something quickly after it's over. Or else…'

He did not ask what would happen if he didn't do anything. If he had asked, I'd have no reply. And Nisha Chechi hadn't told me either. I saw the pride drain off his face. It gave me a cruel satisfaction. I ran into our room. Chechi was still asleep. I lay down and hugged her. She woke up, probably hearing my little heart thumping. 'What happened?'

she asked. 'Uh … uh…' was all I could say. She was a bit dumb, you know that. So she did not probe. Or suspect anything.

Acchan left in the morning, as usual. But he returned earlier than usual. Soon after, his friend Leelavallabhan and his wife paid us a visit. They had come over to invite Amma to accompany them to Guruvayur. Amma wasn't too keen on the temple visit. But they pressed her with many reasons. Finally, Acchan said, 'Siva and Vasantham will be coming.' Then let me take Satya along too, Amma suggested. 'No, don't take her. The rush will be too much for her.' I wanted to cry. I went to my room and sat, whimpering. Acchan followed me. He stood near the door and said, 'You are not going tomorrow. You have to be here. There's something urgent.'

My whimpering ceased. I perked up a bit. You know me. I am the one who felt slightly proud of the fact that there were many who would have liked to see me dead? I felt proud then too. Because Acchan's tone had in it a tinge of an entreaty. It delighted me. I, too, loved power, I liked controlling and frightening people. I avoided Amma the whole day. I knew that I was about to do something wrong. But I had to do it to save Nisha Chechi. And also to protect Amma. That night somehow passed. Amma and Chechi left before dawn. When they had gone, Acchan called me.

'Have to leave for town at seven,' he said. I was a bit confused. 'Get Nisha.'

My heart stopped. When it was light, I ran to her house. She was helping her bedridden father drink his coffee. I asked her to get ready to go to town. She said yes. When I came back, Acchan was telling Venukkuttan Chettan, 'Today I am taking Satya with me. Tell Laalamma to get breakfast ready.' I took a quick shower, put on a red frock with a yellow yoke and a yellow rose sewed into the middle of it. I combed my hair myself and tied it up in two ponytails on either side. I pressed a bindi on my forehead and lined my eyes with kohl. Don't think that I was doing this in some rush of joy. I just didn't know what I was doing. All I knew was that I did not want Nisha Chechi's

belly to swell. I loved her, and feared her even more. I was getting ready
to commit a murder for her sake and mine. Not by my hand. But it was
murder, and I was a party to it. At that age, I saw no other way.

At seven, a taxi arrived. Acchan and I set off. Nisha Chechi had
been waiting in the lane. She had got out of the house on the pretext
of going to the market. Those days, Dr Janardanan, Acchan's bosom
friend, was running a clinic in his wife's name in the town. The car
took us there. Acchan dropped me and Nisha Chechi there. He got
out of the taxi and gave us instructions without looking at us. See
the doctor, then go to the parking, get into the car. If you are hungry,
go to the restaurant and get something to eat, he said, thrusting two
hundred-rupee notes into my hand. I rolled them up in my fingers.
The truth is, I became a grown woman in the space of that single
day. Before turning ten, I had managed to wash out a womb! It was a
big responsibility. I managed it most efficiently. I held Nisha Chechi's
hand and took her to the receptionist. I spoke with the receptionist,
took Nisha Chechi to the doctor. The doctor asked me to wait in the
reception area. Time rolled on – 10 o'clock, 11 o'clock, 12 o'clock …
But all our lies were to flop. The second of my mother's brothers,
Kochumaaman, had brought along to the clinic a friend who had been
injured in a bike accident. I was sitting on the chair near the door; he
spotted me at once. He began to question me. I lost it. And on top of
that, Nisha Chechi came out just then; her steps fell awkwardly.

There was a veritable explosion at home that day. Amma has never
beaten me so hard since. And never have my parents quarrelled so
furiously, before or after.

~

The revelation that it was Nisha Chechi who had stabbed Acchan
hurled me into a dreadful turmoil. I could hardly believe it. Acchan was
stabbed ten years after the incident at the clinic. By then Nisha Chechi
was married twice. She had three children.

I grabbed Amma and began to shake her.

'Who told you that it was Nisha Chechi?'

'She herself,' said Amma, still half-asleep.

'When?'

'Three or four days back.'

'And why didn't you tell me?'

'Thought I'd wait till you returned.'

'And why did she tell you after so many years?'

'I asked.'

'How did you meet her?'

'She came here.'

'What for?'

'To see her daughter.'

'Is her daughter living nearby?'

'She came here. She meets her daughter here.'

'I don't get it.'

'I educated her daughter.'

'Oho! And I get to know this only now!'

'There's no reason to be telling everyone everything.'

I had no answer. I paced the room.

'What is her daughter doing now?'

'She is a nurse. She's found a job abroad.'

'What about the other children?'

'Satyapriya is a medical student. Lakshmipriya is a higher secondary student.'

'Satya…!'

'The eldest is called Sivapriya.'

'Are you educating the younger ones too?'

'All three grew up in the Mary Matha Poor Home. I paid for their upkeep.'

'Then why not just let them live with us?'

'Did you forget that there was a bedridden patient in this house?'

'If you suspected Nisha Chechi earlier, why didn't you ask, Amme?'

'We needed the information urgently only now, isn't it?'

'But who gave her the dagger?'

'I had no chance to ask her any of that. Just asked if she did it. She admitted it and ran away weeping.'

'What suspense!'

'What's a crime investigation without suspense!'

'Uhho! But still … from where did she get that dagger!'

'That we can ask her.'

'But when? Will she come by again?'

'If I call, surely. Any time.' Amma said that with confidence, turned over, and fell asleep. I sat up, losing sleep. Nisha Chechi was not Satyaprakash's mother, that was a relief. But now my peace of mind was half-gone. Did Acchan get her pregnant again without my knowledge? Did she go to Dr Janardanan again? Did she have to come out of the doctor's room with that awkward gait? As I sat there thinking, a fresh doubt struck me: the foetus in that glass jar – had it been torn out of Nisha Chechi's womb?

In truth, my investigation looked pretty much like the demonetization. There was the expectation of a jackpot. But a colossal loss was what one ended up with. No one tried to calculate the loss with any precision, so the loss was never captured exactly. But that did not wipe out the loss. Like a crime does not cease to be a crime just because the culprit is still at large. I kept sitting, dazed, and hallucinated about that foetus. It wore Gandhi spectacles, held a lathi, and was walking towards me.

FORTY-ONE

No truth is truth until such time as one is convinced by it. That is the curse of crime detection. A good example of it was the claim that it was Nisha Chechi who had stabbed Acchan. She made that claim herself. But I was not convinced. Which is better: an unconvincing truth or outright falsehood? Crime detection felt like a pain in the head that day. Not just figuratively. I was literally suffering from a headache ever since I had returned. The very next morning, therefore, I went to the hospital. Amma came with me. We took Harish's autorickshaw. I went to two ATMs and tried to withdraw money, but had no luck. In the end, we could withdraw some from the Gramin Bank – two two-thousand-rupee notes for Amma and me, respectively. This was a non-performing asset now, but it was still better than nothing. I opened both the notes. Gandhiji was printed on both.

The Taluk Hospital looked modernized now. This was the first time I had come here since Acchan got stabbed. Back then, the corridors here were full of patients, and many of them would be lying on the floor. The scent of pus was ubiquitous. It had all changed now. I liked the tiled rooms and the newly painted walls. The doctor in the casualty was a young woman, bespectacled and sporting short hair. She examined my wound very carefully. 'If you were married, I'd

have suspected that your husband had smashed a bottle on your head,'
she said. 'Oh, the bottle fated to land on one's head will find its aim,
husband or no husband!' I wisecracked. She broke into a smile.

The wound was a bit infected. She cleaned it, dressed it. Then, after
giving me an injection for the pain, she prescribed a week's medicine.
'Don't you want to see Nisha?' Amma asked. I had just wanted to go to
bed, but this suggestion perked me up immediately.

Nisha Chechi lived in a colony below the Pump House. I did
not know that she had shifted from the house near Vasanthaalayam.
Appooppan had rebuilt the old house for them. But her two brothers
sold it and divided the money between themselves. They threw her out.
The house in the colony wasn't hers either. It was leased out. Though
not even a kilometre from the main junction, it was still pretty rural.
It was a rough path, steep. Amma wasn't brave enough to go there. 'I'll
go spend some time with Laalamma's daughter. You talk,' she said. I
descended the slope alone. Found her house among the many huts
built all over.

It was not really possible to call it a 'house'. It was more a hovel
made of a few metal sheets hammered together. A black dog was tied
to a pillar; it did not even take notice of me. I stood there and called her.
She peeked from inside. She was wearing a soiled nightie. A smudged
towel was flung over her shoulder and her hair was carelessly tied up.
When I looked at her face, the lights inside me began to flicker and
die one by one. The thought that I was responsible for her plight now
gripped me hard. I could have saved her. How, I did not know. Not
knowing how was a crime – I felt it. My heart drowned in darkness.
Someone beat their head on its walls and wailed aloud.

'Satyamole! My god!' she came running. She hugged me close. We
went inside, and she found a red plastic chair for me; wiped it again
and again with that towel on her shoulder. The house was a heap
of dirty. I remembered her school textbooks. Amma used to get the
schoolbooks for both Chechi and her on the same day. They used to
sit together to cover them with brown paper. By the time of the exams

before the Onam break, Chechi's books would all be a mess. But Nisha Chechi's textbooks and notebooks would be as good as new. I saw her notes, written in a neat, well-shaped hand. The connection between people's wealth and their sense of cleanliness became apparent to me. Actually, it was between wealth and status; cleanliness was but a manifestation of status.

She brought me tea. I drank it greedily. Maybe because of the injection, I was very tired. 'Is there any food?' I asked. 'I just woke up, my dear. Let me make something right away,' she said, hurrying into the kitchen. I followed her and sat on the windowsill. She lit the rusty gas stove and boiled some water. I sipped the tea and looked around the house. Some utensils. A shelf that looked like it would crumble any moment. Cheap, shiny saris hung inside, on a clothes line. In a corner, undergarments, soiled and worn.

The pain in my head now trickled down into my chest and formed a pool. 'I did not know that you'd come ... You should have called ... Why did you have to come all this way ... I would have come over there...' she kept mumbling.

I kept feeling that I should not be bothered. She scraped some coconut, mixed it with jaggery and cumin, kneaded a dough from rice flour. Made sweet dumplings and steamed them. 'Will be ready now,' she reassured me. In between, I steered her towards a conversation. It went like this:

'Your children are all grown, Nisha Chechi?'

'My eldest girl is twenty-eight.'

'Amma said that she just finished the nursing course?'

'She learned the alphabet at eleven!'

'Why was that?'

'Who'd care for the little ones when her mother went out to whore?'

'What about your younger ones?'

'All three went to school late. The older one was admitted to the fourth standard; the middle one went to the first standard; and the youngest went to nursery school.'

'But they all have been doing well!'

'They know that it is the only means to escape.'

'Let's say that they inherited your brains.'

'It's not brains that you need to survive, you need to be brave!'

'I thought that you were married and settled!'

'How could that be? When the money that your grandfather gave us ran out, that man left me!'

'Appooppan gave you money?'

'Of course. How else could I get married?'

'And where is that man?'

'That son of a scoundrel was already married and had kids! When things went really bad – his abuse and beating and hurting the kids … I had just had enough. I eloped with the first lorry driver I found.'

'And was he a scoundrel too?'

'He gave me my third girl. But when I recovered from childbirth, he changed. He began to bring his friends over…'

'That the girls survived this – that was a stroke of good luck!'

'That was because of Vasanthamma. Her help.'

'Well, you should not be calling it help. It was compensation.'

'But what harm did she do to me to compensate for it?'

'Maybe not her, but her husband!'

'If wives have to compensate for the harm their husbands cause, then how much will I have to shell out! I married three times!'

'I just can't get out of this feeling of guilt, Chechi. I keep feeling that I am responsible for it.'

'Oh, that was my fate, what else?'

'I really thought that you had gone home when I went to take my shower that day…'

'He said, come on in. Who? My friends' father. The man everyone respected…'

'I don't want to hear, Chechi.'

'When I went in, he pulled out that dagger…'

'I had gone off to light the evening lamp … I heard nothing.'

'The screaming in rape is only in the movies. In real life, your tongue sinks.'

'Nisha Chechi, weren't you mad with me?'

'Is that why I named my girls after you sisters?'

'Couldn't you find better names, Chechi?' My eyes moistened.

'What's wrong with your names?'

'Why do you need the names of one who died an untimely, ill-starred death, and of another who's going to die the same way?'

'Ill-starred?'

'Don't you know that Chechi was murdered?'

'My god!'

'I may be killed any moment too.'

'By whom?'

'His name is Satyaprakash.'

'Who's that son of a bitch? Show him to me, I'll wrench his guts out!'

'Are you bold enough to do so, Chechi?'

'I am good enough to put a knife through him.'

'Did you really stab Acchan?'

'I told Vasanthamma when she asked.'

'I want to know more about it.'

'Ask. I'll tell you what I know.'

'Why didn't you tell Chechi about Acchan? You were great friends?'

'Isn't there a limit to friendship between the rich and the poor? I knew that Siva would be angry with me. And that's what happened.'

'Why did you come again to the house? Because Acchan made you come?'

'That wasn't the second time ... Your father would call me into the car while it stood in the lane. It happened many times inside the car too.'

'Couldn't you have resisted?'

'He was mentally ill. He did it not for pleasure. He wanted to frighten me.'

'Did he hurt you after the abortion too?'

'No. But I had grown up by then. He looked for kids to hurt.'

'I thought you would be happy after you got married.'

'I have never been happy after the age of twelve.'

'Is it you who stabbed Acchan, really?'

'If you ask if it was I, well – it was not the I of today.'

'What made you take such a step?'

'I was hired by someone. For ten thousand rupees.'

'Who was it?'

'A young man.'

'Can you tell me more?'

She checked the dumplings. They were not yet cooked. She continued:

'This was soon after I had my third child. This lorry driver would come and go, but not give me any money for the house. I had to raise my kids, didn't I? I would take the five o'clock bus to town, find one or two customers, return by the last bus. One day, when I was on my way back, there he was, your father, in the last bus.'

My chest heaved with shame.

'He did not talk to me on the first day. After two or three days, he came and sat next to me and asked, do you have any money? I had sixty rupees on me that day. I gave him fifty.'

My tongue had slumped, but she had just begun.

'Then it became regular. When I got off the bus, there he would be, waiting with a man, a client.'

I stared at Nisha Chechi, unable to utter a word. My father who left Vasanthaalayam every day in a silk shirt, gold-bordered mundu, doused in the Brut perfume, riding in a Contessa; the owner of Vasanthamaalika, of *Vasanthakairali*, of Nityavasantham Productions; son-in-law of the exporter, planter, real-estate contractor K. Panikkar – the pimp of the minor girl he had raped a few years back!

'I did not fear him any more. But still agreed. I thought of you. I knew that you had lost everything. I just thought, well, if this can get you some rice gruel, then so be it!'

Her words pierced every pore of my body. I sat there bleeding.

'But Satyamole, you rich people have no pity. When you get some money, you want more. And when you get some more, you want a lot more. He kept bringing more and more men. Once he brought four. My body isn't stone or wood to bear so much! The youngest was still at my breast, remember!'

I sat still, eyes closed. The headache which had eased a bit earlier, became much worse now.

'We quarrelled that day. That day, too, he brandished a dagger at me. That was in an old lodge in town. People came running at the din. He was among the crowd – that young man. They disarmed him, pulling away the dagger, and kicked him out. I cried. That young man consoled me; he brought me some country liquor to help me calm down.'

'Had you seen that young man earlier?'

'I had seen him sell peanuts at the bus stop. A thin fellow. He asked: "I'll give you ten thousand, can you kill that fucking bastard?" I agreed, in the state of mind I was in. He gave me two thousand five hundred as advance.'

'Were you scared, Chechi?'

'I went to town that morning all dressed up. Had second thoughts about it, but I needed the cash too. He came again that evening. I decided to go ahead with it.'

'Was his name Satyaprakash?'

'He said, "Call me Raju."'

'Did you know the time and route Acchan would take?'

'He knew. He told me when and where I'd find him. And that's where I grew up, of course. He took me there on his bicycle. Dropped it on the ground near the Samajam building. We got to the place where the Punnakals' coconut garden began going by Kumaran Saar's house and the puramboke plot…'

'What was really in your mind then?'

'Just the determination to kill.'

'Please tell me in detail, Chechi!'

'We saw your father's torch light up in the distance. He held my hand and asked if I was scared. No, I said. He then made me hold that dagger.'

'Stop, stop, which dagger?'

'He gave it to me.'

'The one that Acchan used to carry?'

'Ah … no idea.'

'No, Chechi … you told me that he had threatened you with a dagger earlier and the people at that lodge, which included this boy, had snatched it from him … Was this the same dagger?'

'My dear, it was night. He gave me a dagger and told me to stick it in hard.'

'All right. What happened then?'

'We crouched near the wild screw pine bushes. I was scared. But when your father drew close, this boy pulled my hand. I followed him. He grabbed your father from the back. I stabbed hard. I was really scared that I would hurt the boy. Your father turned around and kicked him. I then thrust the dagger in with all my strength. I stabbed him again and again … as many times as I had wanted to … since I was some ten or twelve…'

I sat motionless. I could see it all. The darkness, the torch, two people like shadows. How old would Nisha Chechi have been then? She was past an abortion and two marriages. She had given birth three times. Had seen many men by then.

'We ran then, got into the yard of the Samajam building, and hid there. We saw the crowd that ran that way and the ambulance. When the commotion was over, he paid me the rest. Seven thousand five hundred rupees. I left the place with the money that very night and headed to Velankanni.'

'Why Velankanni?'

'No particular reason. The first bus was to Thiruvananthapuram. I saw some people waiting to go to Velankanni from there. I tagged along.'

'And the children?'

'Could I leave them? I met a hawker from Kollam there. He was around fifty, and with a family back home. He was alone there. I hung back with him.'

'Then, when did you return?'

'I bumped into our Peter Saar at Velankanni once. He told me that Siva died. I also found out that no one suspected me in the stabbing case. At that time, the hawker had a heart attack, and his family came looking for him. They made a huge fuss, and I just left for home.'

'What about the hawker?'

'He passed away after six months.'

'Did you have any money when you came back here?'

'Just around two thousand rupees. I started selling vegetables. One day I met Venukkuttan Chettan at the market. The following day, Vasanthamma called me. Told me that the girls should be educated. I had had enough of lugging the three of them around. Vasanthamma told me to send them to the Mary Matha Poor Home. And the lorry driver chap found out that I was back. The older kids were not his – and they were grown ... I tell you, my dear, I don't trust this race called men at all!' She sighed and checked the dumplings again. I wiped my eyes.

My hunger and thirst had died. But when she served the dumplings, I could not refuse. I asked for a spoon; she found me one. I cut into a dumpling and put the piece into my mouth. It was tasty.

'Are you on your own, Chechi?' I asked while we were eating.

'Have had no one for the past five or six years.'

'I was stunned when I saw you in town that day!'

'Me too!'

'Chechi, have you seen that young chap who hired you somewhere in town again?'

'No, mole.'

I put the plate down and found Satyaprakash's photo in my phone and showed her.

'Is this that chap?'

'I can't remember. It was night, and I have never seen him in bright daylight. And it's been so long!'

'What was his grouse towards Acchan?'

'He just said that your father would destroy a lot of people if he stayed alive.'

'What did he do after you stabbed Acchan?'

'At the Samajam yard, we drew water from the well and washed our faces and hands. With the ambulance arriving at the spot of the incident, we figured that your father was being taken to the hospital. Would he have conked off, I asked. He did not reply. He was weeping as he pushed the bicycle.'

'Didn't you ask why?'

'I was crying too. So, no.'

'Didn't you see him again?'

'No. Early that morning, I'd bundled the kids off and left for Thiruvananthapuram.'

'Is there any way we could trace him?'

'This is all I know, my dear. I was not that smart at that age, back then.'

I ate the dumplings mechanically. Nisha Chechi's phone rang. It was Amma, waiting for me near the road. I finished eating quickly, washed my hand and prepared to leave. 'Come and stay with us, Chechi, please,' I told her. She smiled, helplessness writ all over her face. I made her accept the three thousand five hundred rupees I had in my purse. My head began to spin when I stepped out of her house. Clearly, the job of a detective did not suit me. It seemed to drown me in questions instead of leading me towards answers.

When I climbed into the autorickshaw, Amma reminded me to get a new SIM card. So we went to the BSNL office. After I got a new SIM card and came back, I saw Amma and Harish busy criticizing the state of things around. The fifteen thousand rupees that his mother-in-law had hidden away came out into the open with demonetization – Harish was telling that story with much merriment. 'Yeah, the black money of old crones must at least be dug out!' declared Amma with a laugh. I had neither the interest nor the energy to join them. I was on the verge of blacking out by the time we reached home. I took the medicines and went to bed. Amma shook me awake at lunchtime, but in vain. I fell back to sleep and awoke only at three, drank some gruel, took the medicines and slept off again. Then, at teatime, Amma woke me up yet again, made me drink some tea and eat a few pieces of rusk. She did not let me lie down after that, though, so I went and sat in our veranda. The SIM was active now. I dialled Anurup Shetty. He was still unreachable. My drowsiness evaporated. I was on high alert now; something had happened. I sat there holding the phone. Amma came up, and we exchanged these thoughts:

'Amma, that inspector is not reachable.'

'Where has he gone?'

'He said he'd be joining work the next day. But his phone is constantly switched off.'

'Maybe like you, he, too, threw away his SIM card?'

'Unlikely.'

'Don't you have his office number?'

'No, we always spoke on the mobile phone.'

'No way to find out?'

'I'll search the Internet.'

'You could ask that boy maybe?'

'Which boy?'

'The one who saved you. His name is Mrityunjoy, isn't it?'

My senses grew sharper. It was actually embarrassing to think that I hadn't called Sandeepa and Joyo even once in all these days. I dialled Joyo's number. He picked up at the first ring.

'Hellooo … remember me?' I tried to sound light.

'Auntie! Where were you?' He sounded eager. 'I called you so many times! Was just telling Amma today about coming to Kerala to seek you out!'

'Shall I book your tickets?'

'I'll do that. Why didn't you call for so long, Auntie?'

'It's been a mess every day, Joyo. I just couldn't call. Forgive me.'

I gave him a summary of all that had happened. He, too, was worried when I told him that Anurup Shetty was unreachable. He promised to find out and let me know. After some time, he called back.

'Auntie, the inspector has not rejoined duty.'

'How did you find out?'

'I called the station.'

'What did they say?'

'That he's on long leave.'

'For how long?'

'They said he'll join only a month later.'

'Mysterious.'

'Don't worry, Auntie. I'll search him out another way.' Joyo tried to reassure me, but I was not convinced. Something was wrong, my mind told me. Joyo passed the phone to Sandeepa, and we chatted for some time.

My mind was strained. Where had Inspector Shetty disappeared? Why had he gone on long leave? One could find out from Aswathy maybe. But I did not feel brave enough to call her. She had always maintained a safe distance from me. She would talk about even things that concerned solely me to Amma alone. I was always scared to face her – you know I had always been a den of secrets. At that moment, however, I remembered something else, and it excited me much. 'Amme! Amme!' I shrieked. She was on the phone with someone. She covered the mouth of the handset with her hand and chided me, 'Why are your screaming your lungs out!'

'Amme, where's that envelope? You didn't show it to me?'

'Which envelope?'

'The one that someone dropped here.'

'Please hold,' she said to the person on the other side and quickly went to her bedroom. She took the envelope out from under her pillow and threw it on the bed impatiently. I picked it up and opened it, trembling. Like the one in Bhubaneswar, this, too, had a white sheet of paper inside. I unfolded it and found one half of a thousand-rupee note. Something tore through my body – steam, or an icy wind, or electricity. I took out the half-note I had been given in Bhubaneswar and fitted it along this one. They made for a whole thousand-rupee note. One half was grimy, the other fresh. Gandhiji's image was on the latter.

No truth is truth until such time as one is convinced by it. That is the curse of crime detection. Especially when the individual truth lacks political conviction.

I looked closely. What I saw on the note was not Gandhiji's image. It was Godse's – but Godse with a bald head and round spectacles.

FORTY-TWO

That was an important day. The Supreme Court ruled on that day that religion and caste should not be evoked during elections. The verdict was on a petition filed in 1992. April 1992. The month in which our well was poisoned. Remember the time I went to the police station? Was it fate or just a coincidence that I went to Leelavallabhan's house on the very same day that this verdict was passed? Ah, who knows. Anyway, I had actually set out for somewhere else that day. It was only then that I found out that he lived around here and decided to pay them a visit. Not to see him, he had died years ago. That's the trouble with people. They have to die before there arises something we need from them. They leave something or the other unsettled. The biggest lesson I have learned from this crime investigation is that every person has their unique story, one only they can tell; but before they can tell it, they die. No journey is fruitless, though. It helps us discover something new about ourselves, and sometimes retrieve something old.

It all happened because of Paramarth. Following our visits to the doctor and to Nisha Chechi, I fell badly ill and was bedridden. First, it was because of the medicines, and second, because of a terrible internal battle. One day, Paramarth came over and told me that cows and buffaloes were going to receive Aadhaar cards. I was half-asleep and wasn't sure if he was there at all. Did he come here yesterday, I asked Amma, and she said that we had chatted for a long time. I was scared now. What if I had told him something that I should not have? In truth, there was nothing to be so scared of. He was a mere stripling, barely sixteen. Not a policeman or a judge or a family elder. It was, however, his innocence that scared me. There was something cruel about it. When I spoke to him, I could not help picturing him sitting in some dark room with that saffron-coloured mark on his forehead and many-coloured threads on his wrist, singing 'Pakaram naam veettende, thalayarinjhu koottende...' Therefore, I was forced to think twice or thrice before talking to him. Then something struck me: was the fake note that I had got been printed in some nearby press? I took a photo of the fake note and cropped the photo so that just the face on it remained. As expected, Paramarth turned up that evening. Amma and he would debate regularly. I waited in the inner room till they got into their argument. Amma offered him toasted bread. I slipped in between the two of them and led him into a conversation:

'Paramarth, didn't you say yesterday that cows are going to be given Aadhaar cards?'

'Health cards, not Aadhaar cards. The announcement will be made in a week's time.'

'Why not goats too?'

'The cow is the mother of all Hindus.'

'Gandhiji used to drink only goat milk.'

'I don't want to know.'

'Is it true that plastic currency notes of ten are being printed?'

'Why are you interested in all this?'

'Will Gandhiji's image be removed from the new notes?'

'The government will decide all that. Don't provoke me with such things.'

'Actually, I was waiting to ask you something else. Where can I find a printing press near here?'

'What for?'

'To get a book written by a friend printed.'

'What kind of book?'

'The title is *The Scientific Mysteries of Hindu Customs*.'

'If it is about Hindu customs, I'll speak with Binoyettan.'

'Which Binoy?'

'Binoyettan's uncle runs a printing press.'

'His father's younger brother is Rajendran Nair?'

'No, Krishnakumar Nair.'

'Oh, I know them. That Krishna Press and Printers?'

'No, Sriram Press and Printers.'

'Okay. Back in our time, they used to own a Krishna Press.'

'I know only the Sriram Press.'

'Okay, Sriram Press it is, then. Tell me where it is.'

He told me. I went there in Harish's autorickshaw.

The logo of the press was the 'Angry Hanuman' face. My religious sentiments were immediately hurt. Right since childhood, Hanuman had a special place in my heart. Who among those that have read the Ramayana can imagine a Hanuman who gnashes his teeth and rolls his eyes in hatred, when the Hanuman of the epic is one who brims over with fun and wicked teasing even when his tail is on fire? I wanted to ask Krishnakumar Nair that question, but when I saw him, my wish turned into vapour. His face seemed drawn into a perpetual frown; he had eyes that were suspicious of everyone. This man has never enjoyed any happiness in his life, I told myself. Therefore, his face seemed familiar, like I had seen it somewhere. His glance first fell on my feet, then on my jeans, and then on my shirt. When it reached my breasts, his face darkened. I could see that this was someone who'd insist that Bharatiya women wear Bharatiya clothes. If so, would he forgive my boyish hairdo? He met me with a scornful, mistrustful look. 'Where are you from?', 'Where is your home?', 'Why are you here?', 'Who told you about this press?' – his questions flew like arrows. My tongue tired of sending him answers. I could well imagine what he would have taken away from the epic, if he read it. My experience is this: Measure people not by their intelligence but by their imagination. Do not try to speak for long to people bereft of imagination. Plant a banana sapling instead of wasting your time on them. So I stopped trying to show off my wit and got to business. This was what we said:

'I want to print a book authored by a woman friend. I don't have a lot of money.'

'What kind of book?'

'A history book.'

'Bring me the manuscript. I can make a decision only after I read it.'

'All right. I would like to know how much it will cost.'

'What is the title of the book?'

'*Mahatma Gandhi to Nathuram Godse.*'

He thought about it.

'But why have you chosen this press?'

'This is her first book, and she doesn't know any publishers.'

'Anyway, let me read the book draft first.'

'Can't you give me an estimate of the cost without seeing the draft?'

'I need to see it first.'

'There's another reason why I chose this press.'

He became alert. I showed him the photo of the fake note in my phone.

'We want the cover to be like this. Was it printed here?'

'What if it was?'

'We would like to buy the copyright.'

His face now filled with pride. He pulled out a bunch of papers from inside a desk. My eyes nearly popped out. They were all notes, the same size as the one I was sent, cut into two. They were notices – invitations to the Balidan Diwas. I ought to have felt elated at that moment, but I felt the reverse. My blood rushed hard, surged. Fear made me feel weak. I felt more afraid of this small man in front of me than the assassin. He did not tell me who had drawn the face. I did

not press for more information. I took one of the notices, put it in my
purse, bid him goodbye and got out. Harish reversed the autorickshaw.
Then, all of a sudden, I remembered Leelavallabhan. But I could not
recall where he lived. So I went to the press again.

'Didn't a certain engineer Leelavallabhan live in this area?'

'Who's he to you? What's the matter?'

'I thought since I've come this far, might as well visit him.'

'But he's dead.'

'I want to meet his family.'

'How do you know him?'

'He was a family friend.'

'That means?'

'My father's friend.'

'Why do you want to go to your father's friend's house now?'

'To discuss a marriage proposal.'

I sensed that of all the ones I had uttered until then, this was the
only statement that Krishnakumar Nair approved of. He gave me the
directions. Then I thought I must get a bit smart.

'You have asked me so much, but you did not say anything about
yourself.'

'What is there to tell you about me?'

'Where do you live?'

'Hereabouts, somewhere.'

'Where in these parts?'

'You have to go some way.'

'That's rather precise, uh?'

'Ah, but what's the need?'

'Since your questions went almost as close as to smell out even my
family members' horoscopes, I need to ask you a few.'

'Nonsense! When did I ask for the horoscopes?'

'I meant figuratively! You almost reached there!'

'But I did not ask for them.'

'That's true.'

'Asking women for their horoscopes is not my culture. I am from a cultured family. This is not our culture. I have never asked any woman for such things, nor will I ever.'

'I see your game.'

'What game?'

'Avoiding my question about where you live.'

I thought he would take it as a joke. But instead, he flew into a rage. His face now resembled the Angry Hanuman. I quickly cleared out. This was what Paramarth would look like in the future, I thought. I wondered what made Krishnakumar Nair feel so insecure. Even on my way out I continued to worry about him and then I climbed into the autorickshaw.

The directions he had given to Leelavallabhan's house were wrong. I was saved because, luckily, Harish asked the way to the house while I bought a present for the family at a local supermarket.

I had gone to that house three times earlier. But my memory cleared up only when I reached the place. Back then, the long boundary wall beyond which you could see the yard from the main road had been painted white. Now it was an ugly, washed-out grey. I asked Harish to stop and went in alone. The gate was made of wood. The big mango tree just next to it spread its large canopy like a massive umbrella on the front yard. The light and the shade that played there made that old-style two-storey house look grand. On the wall next to the small sit-out with four cane chairs and a teapoy, there was a signboard that read: 'K. Leelavallabhan, Chief Engineer'. All the 'l's in the name had fallen off. The door was opened by his wife. Her grey head and eyebrows made her look older than her age. 'Who?' she asked. I introduced myself. She greeted me with unexpected warmth. Don't think that she overflowed with affection for me. The truth is her love was not for me, it was for her own past. The past is the most elaborate construct of the human imagination. You can't call it history. Because it is completely imagined.

Anyway, the layers of my memory came apart quickly. Its core came into view. I remembered the names of their daughters – Kavita and

Kalpana. Kavita was my age, Kalpana a couple of years younger. Luckily, they were both at home. When I heard that Kavita was a divorcee and Kalpana was unmarried, another wave of fear swept through my body. My sister was a divorcee, and I unmarried. Were these two women like us? I looked at Kalpana, anxious. Would someone take a shot at her, like at me? She was short-haired, like me; clad in a T-shirt and pyjamas. She had a defiant expression not common among women from around here. Maybe because she lived in Mumbai. She was an editor in a publishing company. Kavita was a schoolteacher. The dark circles around her eyes were wider than the shade cast by the mango tree in front of their house.

On the wall hung a large image of Leelavallabhan with a garland and serial bulbs around it. My memory of him did not actually match the image. Anyway, people's real faces and their images in the memories of others do not match. The showcase was of the type that was in fashion back then – when the house was built. I liked it. On it were statuettes of a herd of elephants on display. On the wall, a forest and a lake had been drawn, and so the display produced a three-dimensional visual effect. They took me back in time, immersed me in the delusion that I was taking back that time.

Leelavallabhan's wife brought acchappam, cake and tea. 'Stay for lunch,' she insisted. When I tried to wriggle out saying the autorickshaw was waiting, Kalpana said that she could drop me in their car. So I paid Harish and sent him away. Kalpana invited me to her room. I went past the dining room with large built-in cupboards for crockery, the large kitchen, and the bedrooms on either side, climbed the staircase, and reached her room on the first floor. Several of the photos she had taken were mounted on the wall. Every one of them was beautiful. I could not stop myself from expressing deep admiration. Then she pulled open a drawer, drew out a packet of cigarettes, took out one for herself and offered me another. I refused. It was amusing to watch her close her eyes when she brought the lighter close to light it and letting out a breath of relief after. I found her defiant look, confidence and mental strength admirable. She smoked, and we chatted thus.

'Can I call you Satya?'

'Only that.'

'Remember, you came here first for the housewarming?'

'Oh yes, I remember now.'

'That day, you, your sister and my sister got together and played hide-and-seek. You did not let me join you!'

'I apologize!'

'Apology accepted!'

We both laughed. Then she threw me a keen look.

'So?'

'What?'

'Why did you come?'

'I came to speak with your mother, Kalpana.'

'Don't bother with the full name – it is Kallu.'

'Suits you.'

'What do you want to ask her?'

'About my father.'

'That's interesting.'

'I know nothing about my father's past.'

'So you are doing some research?'

'Sort of.'

'What do you want to know?'

'If your dad had told your mum anything he knew about my dad.'

'What would my mum know of your dad which your mum doesn't?'

'Kallu – can I trust you?'

'Sure.'

'My father has a son. I need to find his mother.'

'What's this? A Malayalam movie script?'

'Because that son is out to kill me.'

'No way!'

'It's true.'

She stared at me. I began to like her more. Her bushy eyebrows and abundant eyelashes lent character to her face. A face that betrayed no anxieties, trouble or hypocrisy. It was a long time since I had seen such a face. I told her in brief about Satyaprakash.

'Isn't it easier to let the police find out?'

'They are investigating a crime that's not yet happened, after all. I heard that the inspector charged with the investigation has gone on leave.'

'Can ask Amma. But generally, Mallu men do not share their friends' dirty business with their wives.'

'Might as well ask?'

'Don't have high hopes.'

'Don't make me feel despondent!'

'No need. There's another way.'

She got up and opened a sliding door under a wall-shelf. There were numerous diaries stacked in several layers inside.

'If you browse through these, you may find something.'

'That's for sure.'

'But Amma won't let you take them. They are priceless treasures for us.'

'What to do then?'

'Either I'll WhatsApp images of the pages to you. Or we can go through them together.'

We laughed again. She blew rings of smoke into the air.

'When do you have to return, Kallu?'

'I am on leave. Amma's undergoing uterus surgery next week.'

'My dad came back here in 1961. Were they friends since then?'

'Let's ask Amma. Then we'll go through the diaries from the year they met. When did Uncle SP die?'

'SP?'

'My dad used to call your dad SP, Satya.'

'Oh. Acchan died this November.'

'My dad died in 1992.'

'I know.'

'It was a huge shock.'

'You were very young then?'

'Pre-degree, second year.'

'My father never showed any affection towards me.'

'My father was very affectionate – both of us were his very life.'

'Lucky!'

My blood began to race. It was hard for me to continue. I feared that my face might give me away. Didn't I say it is easier to speak the truth than to hide it? Her father's face rose up in my mind. He used to wear terylene shirts and trousers. Used to sweat like a pig. A kerchief of red or dark blue was always wrapped around his collar. Kallu did not resemble him. Both daughters resembled their mother alone. That was good; that made it easier for me to like them. Kallu stubbed her cigarette in the ashtray, went over to the easy chair near the window, and sat down. She leaned her head back and closed her eyes.

'Know something?' she asked without opening her eyes. 'Only when the children of a dead man declare that it was better that he died will his soul be set free … My father will never be free. Because even after all these years, I have not felt that it was better that he died…' She wiped off the tear that flowed past the edge of her eye. 'He died in great pain. His testicles were infected. It was from a scratch, from his nails. But he didn't consult a doctor early enough. In the end, it became septic. He just took some home remedies … His liver and kidney were soon affected. In the hospital, he kept crying for us … Kallumole, Kavimole … You were right, Satya. We were lucky girls. Acchan did not cry out for his mother or to god even in his last breath. It was our names that he repeated again and again…' Her eyes overflowed. I felt even more drained. 'I had an exam on the second day after he died. The truth was I could not even make my way to the college by myself. I realized this on that day. Until then, I would get ready in the morning, get into Acchan's car, he would take us right inside the college, he would kiss us both before we got out...' She hid her face in her hands and began to weep.

I seethed and simmered inwardly. Her weeping was truly heartbreaking. 'Don't cry, don't cry,' I went up to her and begged. She continued to sob. She hugged me, fell on my shoulder, and continued to sob, 'Acchan, Acchan...' What could I do? I stood still holding her close. She kept heaping praise on her father. He had fulfilled all his responsibilities before he died. Had deposited enough money for his daughters' education and their marriages, in separate accounts. He had left no bill unpaid until the month he passed away. Every time she fell in love, Kallu searched for the qualities of her father in her lover. None of her relationships lasted...

'Lucky girl, lucky girl...' was all I could say.

When she was able to finally control her sobs, she rose, wiped her face, and lit another cigarette. Her intensely romantic idea of family crushed me. What did I think she was? And what was she, really? Luckily, before we talked more, her mother came to call us for lunch. Hearing her footsteps, Kallu grabbed the ashtray and ran into the bathroom. I went with her mother to the dining room. Kalpana turned up a few minutes later. She and her mother served the food. Then, suddenly, her mother broke down.

'How happy he would have been if only he were here now!' She wiped her nose with the edge of her unstarched pink cotton sari.

'He was so fond of Sivaprasad Saar. "SP, SP" – he was always saying something or the other about him. Whenever they came, they would be sitting under the mango tree and having a fine time chatting and laughing! And your father was so fond of him. The way he would call to him – "Hey, Leelan..."'

'Were they friends when you were newly married, Auntie?' I asked.

'They were friends from the time he started working at *Vasanthakairali*. Leelan Chettan had not yet joined the Kerala State Electricity Board. I've heard that they first met at the Ravi Varma Club – that's what I remember.'

'Did you two get married after that?' Kallu asked as she served me another piece of fried fish.

'Oh, your parents came to our wedding, mole. They were newlyweds then, it must have been just four or five months after their wedding. I still remember Vasanthalakshmi in a bright red Kanchipuram silk sari, wearing a red-stone-studded necklace and red-stone tops on her ears ... She was the toast of the wedding, not the bride!'

'Does Satya's mum still have that lovely head of hair?' Kavita asked.

'Yes, she does,' I replied, proudly.

'I did not know when your business failed, my dear. My man was gone by then, wasn't he? Who thought he would leave me alone so soon? I was alone with these two. I am my mother's only daughter. My father died when I was three. I had to somehow get these two to safety!'

'We too suffered badly after.'

'I learned of it much later. Was totally unnerved by his death, worried what would happen to the girls if something happened to me. That's why Kavi was married off so soon ... Everyone thought it was a great match ... inhuman lot ... only we know what we suffered.'

'Why talk of it again, Amma? I am just so relieved that it is off our heads!' Kallu stepped in. She became really sentimental only when she talked about her father. Otherwise, she was pretty strong. Wonder if you have noticed – there's not a single person on this earth who isn't sentimental about something or the other. Also, there's no one alive who's sentimental about everything. If you're looking for a simile, then sentiments are like kidneys. You need at least one to stay alive. If you have two, at least one should work. But too much of it is a bother. You'll spend your whole life drinking water and peeing.

It was after dinner, when we came back to the drawing room, that I put the question point-blank to her.

'Auntie, in your knowledge, did my father have a relationship with any other woman?'

Kavita and her mother looked astonished. Kallu snapped her fingers.

'Goodness, to ask that...' Kallu's mother sounded awkward.

'Auntie, I came here to ask you this. Did you hear Kallu's father mention anything of that sort? That Acchan was close to some other woman?'

'My child, my man here was a true gentleman in such matters ... He was clean, pure gold. Then, of course, he used to occasionally have a drink or two. That, too, only with close friends, like SP Saar. On such days he'd be merry, singing and all ... So I never had reason to complain.'

'So you have not heard anything at all, right, Auntie?'

'No, my dear, I haven't. And my man here wouldn't lend his ear to such tales, too, remember.'

'I was hoping you would have a clue, Auntie.'

'He just told me one thing about SP Saar. That he gave up his medical studies because there was some trouble at college...'

'What trouble?' I sprang up, interested.

'I don't remember exactly. When he mentioned that SP Saar had once been a medical student, I asked him why he didn't complete his studies. Then he said ... a girl in the house where he had stayed died during delivery ... or something like that ... can't remember too well.'

My heart leapt up. My enthusiasm, which had been dormant since the past few days, was now resurrected. I felt something like intoxication.

It was Kallu who drove me home in their Alto. She had taken eight or ten diaries inside her cloth bag. Amma was delighted to see her. We chatted together for some time. It was a great relief for me to have someone like her to talk to. We went to my room and began to leaf through the diaries. They were full of tightly packed little notes, accounts, one-line statements like 'SP and I went to the club'. We did not find anything substantial, until finally, Kallu found a note in a diary from 1966:

'My first trip to Madras. A thousand thanks to SP who made my dream of meeting Sheela, Sarada, and K.R. Vijaya come true! For the first time, I stayed in a star hotel. Heavenly days!'

Date – 7 July 1966.

Following this, a second note from the next year's diary:

'The trip from Ooty to Madras was unforgettable. The only little snag was the accident at Kallakurichi and the unpleasantness that followed. But SP showed us that not even an eagle can fly above the power of money. Seven beautiful nights and days.'

Date – 2 February 1967.

I found the third note:

'How quickly the city of Madras grows! How it changes! My eyes popped seeing SP's new office. I helped resolve some issues with the wiring. People in Kerala still don't know SP's eminence well enough. When we returned, CE pulled a bit of a long face. I told SP. If he gets too sour, we'll get him transferred to Kozhikode, he promised.'

Date – 1 August 1968.

'In Madras again. Stayed in SP's new guest house. Tyagu's – Tyagarajan's – culinary skills will put women to shame.'

Date – 23 December 1970.

'Had to leave for Madras on SP's request. Travelled by air. So my very first flight was with SP. Things were pretty bad there. It looks possible to settle things for the time being. SP trusts Tyagu blindly. Hope the Tamilian won't betray him.'

Date – 15 September 1972.

The date gave me a shock! That was the time my mother was pregnant a second time. The time during which she read all those detective novels. The foetus in her womb was me. What was the great trouble that Acchan and Leelan settled together when I was in my mother's womb? Who could reveal it to me?

Kallu lit a cigarette as she went through the last diary. She found an envelope in it. I did not notice her open it. I was pacing the room with my BP shooting up, feeling pretty fervid. It was like two doors had suddenly opened out of the darkness. When my eyes turned to

her again, Kallu had shut the diary and slumped on the bed, her face
buried in her hands. I went near her.

'Huh?' I asked, absently. 'Thanks for these diaries, Kallu,' I told her.

'Have you got any answers to your questions, Satya?' She raised her
head and gave me a strange look.

'No, but I have two new questions now. If I can answer them, I am
certain the puzzle will fall into place,' I told her ardently.

'What questions?'

'One, why did my father give up his medical studies? Two, what was
the trouble that was settled on 15 September 1972?'

Kallu let out the smoke and stared at me. Then she made me sit
beside her on the bed.

'I too have a question for you, Satya.'

She took the envelope out, pulled out the letter, and handed it
to me.

I read it.

> *Leelan Chetta, I hope you have healed. Please make sure that it*
> *doesn't turn septic. The girl seems to have broken my dick! The doctor*
> *said that my penis is actually fractured. Peeing is unbearable – the*
> *pain! We MUST get her once we recover. No quarter because she*
> *is SP's daughter!! I'll crush the bitch! Yours, R.P.*

I felt myself diminish, turn bit by bit into dust.

'What's the meaning of this letter?' Kallu asked me.

The smoke from her cigarette wrapped itself around me. It was
menthol, with a light fragrance. But it burned me then. My eyes
smarted, my nose itched. I faced her with trepidation. Her eyes were
full. Those were the tears of one betrayed. My heart melted in guilt.

'Those were my nails,' I whispered. Kallu looked shell-shocked.
'Nails from the age of nineteen.'

My eyes filled too. I told the story of that April from twenty-
four years ago. About how I had gone to the police station and

to SI Dinakaran Pillai's house in the Ambassador. About how Leelavallabhan and the iron-goods-store owner R.P. had sat on either side of me. About how my breasts were crushed, and how I was forced to hold their erect penises. It was not easy, but telling the truth was easier than hiding it.

'My Acchan? My Acchan did this to you, Satya?' she asked, sounding choked. I nodded, with the same sense of suffocation. She sat there completely still. Her cigarette smouldered between her fingers. I took it and threw it on the floor. She hugged me, begged forgiveness on behalf of her father, implored me not to hate him. It took a lot of effort to console her. When Amma came in, Kallu got up still looking mortified, went to the bathroom and washed her face, and got ready so that we could leave. I followed her.

When we got into the car, she said, 'Good that Acchan died.' She tried to smile, but her lips curled in pain. The car sped off.

Her father had not died. I had killed him. Don't think that I enjoyed killing a father who had refused to die in his daughter's memory. I, too, was crying, in pain. Who will not weep at the memory of being forced to kill? Who will not wail aloud remembering that no one had helped to stop it? Who will not be shattered when they realize that the world had not protected them, shielded them, from becoming a killer?

The visit to Leelavallabhan's house had not been fruitless. Two things were achieved from it. One, Leelavallabhan's soul received salvation. Two, it seemed evident now that behind Acchan's abandoning his medical studies, there was a death. Not just a death, a post-partum death. But the biggest gain was something else – a big clue in my crime investigation.

But unfortunately, I did not recognize it.

FORTY-THREE

Have you ever tried sculpting? A pity, if you haven't, for then you have missed out something vital in life. If you haven't, you have not touched the truths of stone. To do so, you will have to chisel away everything that is not aligned with that truth. That is how a sculpture emerges. A criminal investigation is like that – in it, you carve out the truth. The difference is that the sculptor knows beforehand what the form of the truth is; their only job is to retrieve it. The criminal investigator does not possess that advantage. She will struggle, unable to discard a single chip of stone that comes off with each application of the chisel. After all, it is data, every bit of it. I had too much of it, and this made my work harder. It is like having many lovers. One may feel proud for being in such high demand, but truly, it is a pain. I learned that from Chechi's life. To carry on with several lovers, one needs a keen memory and sharp wits. It's like juggling four or five balls, like we used to do while playing with the small unripe coconuts that fell off a tree too young. You need excellent focus and a talent to consolidate your insights. When the data piles up in a criminal investigation, the same challenges arise.

Actually, the bother would have been reduced to a great extent if only Satyaprakash had been a bit more merciful. If only he would have told me why – just one word – why – he wanted to kill me. But he would not. If he was open to saying it, would he have not done so before shooting? That is, Satyaprakash seemed to have made sure when he was planning the murder that I should not know who he was. Why was that? To wreak vengeance? If so, did executing a murder without revealing the why or what of it give him a thrill? Ah! Who knows? Maybe some jeevatmas get a thrill from that kind of murder.

I examined all the clues that I had once more. I had many diaries from the firm I used to work in while in Bangalore. I turned one of those into a criminal investigation diary. I pulled together all the clues I had until then.

Discovered	To be discovered	Hypotheses
Satyaprakash seeks to kill me to take revenge on Acchan.	The exact reason.	Because he was denied the love and care a son deserved. Maybe living as an illegitimate child turned him thirsty for revenge.
The secrets will be unfurled when Satyaprakash's mother is identified.	Who is Satyaprakash's mother?	1. A woman Acchan had relations with when he was a medical student. 2. Some woman he exploited in his cinema-making days. 3. Neither (1) nor (2); a woman he met somewhere.
There is an unknown story behind Acchan's not continuing his medical studies.	The story: Has to be dug up from Acchan's ex-classmates.	The reason was the death of 'some girl'. One might suspect that she is somehow related to Satyaprakash.

Discovered	To be discovered	Hypotheses
Some trouble broke out in Madras in 1972 – the year I was born.	What was that? Who is Tyagu?	The settlement that Acchan and Leelavallabhan made might be related to Satyaprakash's mother.
The word 'satyam' had some significance in Acchan's life.	Was there someone named Satya in Acchan's life?	This may be related to Satyaprakash's mother and the dagger.

I felt like things were falling into place. It is anyway true that only when you write everything down can you really separate the grain and the chaff within. The truth was now close at hand. It lay with Satyaprakash's mother. Finding her would complete my sculpture.

Finding Satyaprakash's mother meant finding his address. The addresses that the police found were all fake. Suddenly, I craved to see him one more time. If Chechi were alive, she would have already set out in search of him. I imagined her dragging me into some bus, us alighting in some godforsaken village, and me pushing forward to ask the way to the place. My heart yearned to travel with her, laughing and quarrelling. All at once, my heart was steeped in loneliness. I bent my head towards the diary, sadly. Wiped off a tear that fell on the word 'satyam'. It was then that Amma came in dressed to go out.

'Are you crying?'

'Ah, just feeling a little down, Amme.'

'It is good to cry. You feel relieved.'

'Says the person who can't shed a tear.'

'I want to cry when I think of my inability to cry!'

'Big joke!'

'*Kathiravanude cherukiranavum kaamyamallee / Yatimaatramirul thingumandhakoopathil...*' she recited, asking if even a little sunray was not welcome in a well in which darkness throbbed.

'Ah, never mind – but where are you off to? Nice sari, bindi…?'

'Aswathy's coming, Venukkuttan was saying. She wants to see me. You want to come?'

'No, you go, Amma.'

'Can't you just speak to her once?'

'A police officer can summon me whenever she wants to.'

'But she's not investigating your case?'

'They say, "One Nation, One Police"!'

'What am I to tell her if she asks about the case?'

'Why do you have to tell her anything? They are the ones who ought to be telling us!'

'What if she asks about your Delhi trip?'

'When I went to Bhubaneswar first and then Delhi, a police officer was following me, like a shadow. Ask her where he is.'

'You seem angry with her.'

'Why should I be?'

'She probably wants you to go to her, discuss these matters.'

'If she'd bothered to call at least once, I'd have run to her now.'

'Maybe it isn't time yet.'

Before I could respond, Amma picked up the diary, flipped it open, and looked through what I'd written. A slight smile dawned on her lips. She straightened her spectacles and met my eyes. 'Detective Satyapriya!'

'Stop teasing me and hand over any clues that you may have!'

'You who are so smart – what trouble can you possibly have in solving the rest of the puzzle?'

'At least tell me the reason why Acchan gave up his medical studies?'

'He only told me that he gave them up because he had no money.'

'Did you think that was the truth, Amma?'

'At first, yes. Then, later, I began to have doubts.'

'Why?'

'My father had tried hard to persuade him to complete his studies, promising to support him.'

'Just that?'

'And when I got to know him, didn't I realize that he did lie a lot?'

'Why do you think he gave them up?'

'Back then I had thought that he must have failed in some subjects.'

'Did he even hint about facing any trouble during his MBBS?'

'No.'

'Did you ever go with him to Madras?'

'He never invited me.'

'And you never asked him?'

'My pride did not permit me to do so.'

'What about Appooppan?'

'As far as I know, only Valyannan has gone there.'

'When?'

'He used to go there in connection with his prawn export business. Many times. That was when your father was at the height of success.'

'And what did he tell you after those visits?'

'Nothing in particular.'

'But he must have said something about a Tyagu?'

'I don't remember. And I wasn't really keen to know either.'

'Why, Amma? Why were you so uninterested?'

'Oh, there was some problem or the other every day!'

'What problem?'

'Oh … if you ask me … things were always tense.'

'Tell me the truth, Amma. My feeling is that you know who Satyaprakash's mother may be.'

'You are right. But there's one small mistake. I don't know *about* his mother. I know *I* am not his mother.'

'Hard to believe that there are women who are absolutely clueless about their husbands' lovers.'

'There's one woman for sure.'

'You are keeping it from me deliberately.'

'Won't you miss the joy of discovery if I told you?'

'Okay, stick to your guns even if your daughter goes belly up!'

Amma's face went red. She tried to smile, but it was distorted. A hacksaw passed through my chest. I struggled, unable to take back what had escaped my tongue. She loosened and then retied her hair. She flipped through the diary again and two envelopes fell out. She opened one of them. It was the piece of the fake note that she had received. She stared hard at the man who'd disguised himself as Gandhi. The sadness on her face gave way to worry.

'What's this? Why have you kept it?'

'This is the envelope someone left at our doorstep.'

'And this one?' She opened the other envelope and took out the other half of the thousand-rupee note.

'God! If you keep this, you may be arrested!'

'What for?'

'If you insult the national currency, won't there be punishment?'

'I got this in the mail!'

'Satya, according to the law, we have to report this to the police!'

'I had shown Inspector Shetty one of these pieces. He had promised to investigate.'

'What about this, then?'

'You can give it to Aswathy if you want, Amma.'

'I'll definitely do that. I am not sure about the legal aspect of it.'

'Amme, this is the image printed on the Balidan day notice!'

'How do you know that?'

'I went to that press and saw that notice.'

'Good lord! No wonder they say that the more you live, the more the world turns upside down!'

'Leave all that be, please, Amma. Please help me!'

'If you can't help yourself, how can I?'

'All right, then. Please go and be back soon.'

'I decide when I go out and when I return. That's not your business.' Amma appeared vexed. She took the envelopes and left.

I went back to my case diary. First of all, I needed to find out the reason why Acchan dropped out of college. Everything, most probably, began there. I closed the diary and went over to the veranda. Amma stood there holding her purse, looking out at the road. Harish, the autorickshaw driver, was still on his way. I asked her about Acchan's classmates.

'I have not seen any of them.'

'Never heard the name of any classmate mentioned?'

'Our marriage was not one that involved any such light-hearted exchanges!'

'And you still said that it was love?'

'Love of those days, remember. I was dipping in the sea, offering the ritual libations to my deceased mother. He was doing the same, and I saw him come up from the water, weeping. That's how I saw him the first time. Then I saw him at our home. I would see him on my way back from college. I would look at him and he would return the look. On the last day of my degree exams, he came to my college and told me that he would like to marry me. Back then, love was just these things.'

'I find it hard to believe that you were such a fool, Amma.'

'Everyone will be fooled at some stage or another in their lives.'

'I need to find someone who studied with Acchan.'

'Someone from your Koyikkal Amma's biological father's side – Ramakrishnan – was a doctor at the same medical college your father attended back then…'

'Biological father's side?'

'She had two fathers?'

'How can someone have two fathers?'

'I mean her mother had two husbands.'

'At the same time?'

'Koyikkal Amma is the daughter from the first husband. The others are children from the second marriage.'

'Will Acchan's sister know where Dr Ramakrishnan is?'

'They'll definitely be in touch with relatives who have made it big!'

'Okay, in that case, why don't I make a trip to Koyikkal?'

'Neither you nor I need to take permission from each other. We are now past that age, aren't we?'

'Goodness, Amme!'

The autorickshaw arrived, and she left. I, too, wasted no time. I pulled on a kurta and a pair of jeans, and, as an afterthought, threw a stole around my neck. This place was full of the likes of the owner of the Sriram Press. It would not be surprising if my breasts hurt their masculinity or religious sentiments. I quickly locked the door, stepped out, and took the first autorickshaw that came by.

~

I was under the impression that I knew the way to Koyikkal. We used to visit the place twice every year, after all. It was a lovely ride then. The low walls on the sides of the road were a beautiful, lush green, covered with fresh moss. The trees in the yards on either side were tall and stately; they stretched out their branches to touch each other, or rubbed cheeks, with no thought at all about the castes of their owners or the distance between them. But I lost my way trying to find the house after so many years. The older houses were mostly gone, and new ones had mushroomed. With high walls and new lanes, the whole place had changed. I had to ask two people before I could locate the place. Despite that, I stood confused for some time in front of the house of Acchan's younger brother where we had stayed for a while. There were two houses in that yard now, and a small shop in the front. I was saved by the gate our aunt had had built to bring us to our knees back then. How was I to forget it? Hadn't I leapt over it several times with pots filled with water?

Only that gate and that house looked decrepit. The old kulamaavu tree that once stood near the gate was now gone. There was a wall that cut the yard into two now. The cowshed was now on the other side of the wall. The big moovandan mango tree and the varikka jackfruit tree had vanished. In place of the chaippu that we used to occupy, there

was a two-storey house. That, too, was hidden by an ugly wall. I could
not make out the direction from which one could approach the gate.
Noticing a compound wall behind the kitchen, I divined that there
must be a path beyond it. Anyway, the Koyikkal house was boxed in
on three sides for sure. Some hens were pecking and scratching the
ground in front of it. As soon as they sighted me, a fowl jumped on the
step near the gate and blocked my way. It looked a lot like Koyikkal
Amma! Maybe this was her soul in a hen's body, trying to stop me from
entering the property, thinking that I would demand my inheritance!
Since I wasn't sure if the prevalent order of caste would allow me to
step in or not, I waited outside. My aunt opened the door. The same
four-part door – the one I had pushed open when we came here as
refugees from Vasanthaalayam.

Kochappachi was clad in a shabby nightie. I don't think she was
wearing a bra. That I inferred from her hurried effort to cover her
chest with a smudged towel. Has not the poet sung, 'Ah! Even in death,
women will not forget honour'? But her face made me sad. It resembled
the dilapidated house. Feelings of inferiority and disappointment had
ploughed furrows on it. There had never been any love lost between
us, aunt and niece. Even then, the genes we shared cried out in my
blood. My heart grew tender. I wished to hold close that body which
had crossed seventy-five, wipe away the sorrow from her face, and fill
it with happiness. I wondered if, given the difference in our castes,
I could touch her.

Anyway, she recognized me. 'Who's this!' she exclaimed. 'So you
haven't forgotten the way to this house!'

I stood there, on the stone near the gate, and sought her permission.
'Can I come in, Appachi?'

'Why do you ask that?' she complained.

I entered the house and was assailed by the reek of urine. Bhasi
Maaman, her husband, called in a weak voice from the room that once
belonged to Koyikkal Amma, 'Lakshmi, who has come?' My heart
melted further. Who would say that this was that man who used to

bother us all the time in the chaippu, arriving there without a shirt on and his waistcloth under his navel, nearly coming off? I introduced myself. He seemed absolutely delighted. 'Lakshmi, please help me sit up,' he requested his wife. 'Aiyo, you've peed again!' she complained. 'Satye, please sit, let me change Maaman's clothes.'

I waited in the plastic chair in the side room. I was filled with a strange kind of cold isolation and fear. I saw clearly the asbestos sheet crumble; I even thought I heard the tiny bits fall to the ground. My state was like that of a soul reborn in a place besmirched by an evil death. Acchan had renovated the house so that he could marry Amma. He had also replaced the old cow-dung floor with concrete. When Appooppan came to meet his family, they were still living in a thatched house with cow-dung floors. There was a large granary in the vestibule of the old house then. When the floor was laid with concrete, Koyikkal Amma insisted that the east-side room be partitioned, and one part be turned into a small shrine. It was to make sure that those who entered that portion would not defile it. I reminded myself that I too was a child of this house. The thought of what I was denied vexed me. But wasn't Satyaprakash also another heir? His ire would be so much more, so many times more, than mine? I pictured Satyaprakash pursuing me here and killing me with his bullets. I writhed as though I had been shot.

I felt that the black spider that hung meditatively in a corner of the room like Vetal himself, the dirty lizard on the wall that looked like it had some skin disease, and the ants that were hurrying to get under the cupboard – all of them were souls of the members of this family, and that all of them were beckoning me to enter their world. I feared that any minute now they would abandon their disguises and walk about in their old bodies. Even otherwise, I imagined Koyikkal Amma walking this way slowly in her soiled mundu tied up right under her blouse and her shoulder-cloth stained with turmeric and chilli and mud. I had never seen her look at anyone directly. And never had I seen anyone else give the kind of sidelong glances she would give.

She was her mother's first husband's child; did her mother not love her enough? Was she left alone among her stepbrothers and stepsisters? Who taught her to look at the world only with sidelong glances? To offer only bitter words, words that stung? My heart became unsteady.

Kochappachi now called me inside, having changed her husband's clothes and covered him with a new blanket. Bhasi Maaman looked shrivelled and small as he lay curled up. His legs were barely any bigger than dried twigs. 'Satyamole, you look really young!' He stretched out his hands to me.

Back then, when he'd try to touch us that way, Chechi and I would run away. But now, I went over and held his hands. He held mine firmly. His tears flowed. 'You had to see me like this!' he wept. It was hard for me too.

'What to do, he's been like this since he became bedridden.' Kochappachi wiped his face with the towel on her shoulder. 'Tea or coffee?' she asked.

'Is that old granary still there in the north-side veranda?' I asked her.

'Oh no,' she said with a sigh. 'Taken away by the smart ones!'

When Koyikkal Amma died, there was a scramble for the property and the valuables. Of the three granaries inside the house, two were taken by Valyappachi, my father's older sister, and Kochacchan, his younger brother, respectively. The third, Bhasi Maaman sold. My cousins, Suma and Unni, Kochappachi's children, fought over the one on the north side. Unni had married a Christian girl, and had converted too. Bhasi Maaman, who took Suma's side, was attacked by Unni who whacked him with a hoe on the back. He was thrown from the inner room to the yard outside and fell on his back. His spine was injured. Unni filed a case against Suma and her husband. They, in turn, hired thugs to beat him up. Unni was the one who built the wall which ran right through the yard, cutting it in two. He lived on the other side.

'He won't let even the kids come this side,' Appachi said.

'He shouldn't step in here even for my death feast!' Bhasi Maaman cried.

The house was to go to Suma after Kochappachi's lifetime. But she could not even put a foot into the area. Whenever Suma and her husband came over, Unni and his wife would reach the nearby junction, ready for a showdown, so that they could not even enter the house. Suma's husband was a proud man. He proclaimed that he was not going to visit his wife's house again. Father-in-law and mother-in-law could go stay with them if they so wished. But how was Kochappachi to leave a house where there was a shrine to worship and lamps to light every day? Anyway, there was some trouble or the other for all the members of the family; some curse or the other. The reason behind this, Kochappachi thought, was our neglect of our family shrine. The annual worship at the Kaavu shrine was not being performed any more. The astrologers had warned us many times; it had been revealed in their consultations. Kochappachi was soldiering on on our behalf, taking care of the everyday worship at least. To hear that the self-sacrificing Kochappachi was living there, taking care of her husband and serving the rest of the family by lighting lamps in the family shrine for them, filled my eyes and my heart.

There was a reason why I had asked about the granary in the north-side veranda. The washed glass tumblers, meant to serve visitors who might have been of a lower caste, used to be kept on top of it. If used to serve tea to such persons, they would be washed not just to clean them but also to wash off the invisible taint – left by the touch of lower-caste lips. They were always inverted in order to retain the 'purity' restored to them by washing. My worry did not cease even after I heard the news of the granary disappearing. I followed Appachi. When I reached the kitchen door, I asked, 'May I come in?'

'What is this, Satya? Are you teasing me?' she asked me a bit crabbily.

A Hindu leader had recently made a pronouncement that non-Hindus, too, might be permitted to enter temples. When I heard Kochappachi say what she did, I experienced the same shock I'd felt when reading the pronouncement. I felt gratified to know that

Kochappachi had become a progressive. I was, however, keener to lead her into the discussion I desperately needed to have.

'How long it has been since I saw you both!' I said, trying to sound effusive.

'But you people don't come this side at all, do you?'

'You too did not try to find out about me, Kochappachi?'

'Aiyo, I had called when I heard that someone had shot you by mistake! After that we got to know that Kochaattan died.'

'He probably died from the shock of that news, Kochappachi!'

'But you escaped! That's because of my prayers! You won't believe it, but I still pray for all of you.'

'I believe you, Appachi.'

'Who was that? Did they catch him?'

'Far from it!'

'Ah, are you still in Bangalore, Satya?'

'Isn't Amma all alone? So I came back.'

'Aiyo! But what about the job there, then?'

'I'll look for something here. I am not leaving Amma alone here, for sure.'

'Can't she go there with you?'

'Amma should be willing to go, no? She won't.'

'Hope both your maamans are in touch?'

'Yes, we do see them now and then.'

'What about their children? All doing well?'

'Both their children are doctors.'

'You, too, should have been living like a queen!'

'Yes, yes, wasn't Acchan studying for the MBBS degree once?'

'He didn't have money to pay his fees for the first year, so I took off my minnalkkanni chain, two and three-quarter sovereigns it was, and pledged it with Soman Chettan of Vadikal house and gave him a hundred and fifteen rupees. Kochaattan put his hand on my head and vowed to buy me a five-sovereign necklace when he finished his studies...'

'Will anyone but you believe his word, Appachi?'

'But back then we all thought Kochaattan would become a doctor and all of us in this family would escape our misery!'

'Why didn't he complete the degree, Appachi?'

'He couldn't keep his head up among his classmates, that's why he came back.'

'Maybe because he failed an exam?'

'Failed? He failed? If that were the case, would someone have come here to persuade him to go back?'

'Who came?'

'Dr Reddy. He was Kochaattan's teacher. He found the house and came. The house had a thatched roof at the time. There wasn't even a good chair for him to sit on.'

'Some relative of Acchan's was also in the medical college then? Somebody from Koyikkal Amma's father's family?'

'Ramakrishnan Annan – he was the one who gave Reddy Saar our address.'

'Ramakrishnan Annan never came to visit?'

'He was in Madras for a long time, wasn't he? And when Kochaattan was in the college, after two years, Annan went off to London to study. He married there.'

'How is this Dr Ramakrishnan related to Acchan?'

'My mother was the daughter of my grandmother's first husband. His family was called Thuruthel. This grandfather, whom we called Thuruthel Appooppan, had a sister named Bharathi Amma. Ramakrishnan was her grandson, her son's son.'

'Why did Koyikkal Amma's parents drift away from each other?'

'When my mother was five, her father went away to meet Gandhiji. A few years later, by which time he returned with a lot of gifts for his wife and child, his wife was married again and had given birth a second time. He then left and never came back.'

'He did not marry again?'

'No. Amma, when she lost her mind, used to mumble that he was killed by Pulikkal Appooppan.'

'Who's that?'

'That was our grandmother's second husband. Our uncles Raghava Maaman, Govinda Maaman and Sreedhara Maaman were his sons.'

'Did Koyikkal Amma say nothing about this?'

'She thought it shameful.'

'Is there anyone left in the Thuruthel family?'

'No. Ramakrishnan Annan's father died before his mother. He was the only child. That house and property were all sold off some thirty years ago.'

My interest was snuffed out now. I told Kochappachi that the autorickshaw was waiting and that I had to leave. It was past evening. I had some five thousand rupees in my purse, withdrawn at two different times. I handed the money to Bhasi Maaman, who counted it, wept, and blessed me. Kochappachi came to the gate to see me off.

~

When I reached home that evening, Amma had not yet returned. I opened the gate in the headlight of the autorickshaw. I opened the door, switched on the lights inside and outside, and sat in the veranda. I opened a Facebook account and began to search for Dr Ramakrishnan. Found one in the end. Dr Ramakrishnan, Madras Medical College, 1952 batch. FRCS. Settled in Kochi, Meridian Villa. Without wasting any further time, I sent him a message.

> *Greetings, doctor! Are you the grandson of Thuruthel Bharathi Ammumma? My father's name is K. Sivaprasad. The family name is Koyikkal. I have heard that my father and you studied together at the Madras Medical College. Regards, Satyapriya.*

As I pressed 'send', my heard thumped with excitement and eagerness. Whatever the risks, the thrill of crime investigation is something else.

The sculptor knows what figurine will emerge from the block of stone. But in a criminal investigation, that's a thrilling mystery! Both the sculptor and the onlookers have to wait patiently to know what will reveal itself.

Right then, Amma's autorickshaw drew up near the gate. She pushed the gate open, came in, and turned to bolt it firmly. Something was clearly off. She ran up to the veranda and stepped inside. I stood up. Amma pulled me by my hand and took me inside the house. She locked the door from inside. Her hands were cold, she was trembling a little. I had never seen her so scared and drained. She struggled to find her voice. Just four words: 'Samir Sayyid has escaped.'

FORTY-FOUR

I shook from head to toe, struggled for breath as though caught in the whorl of a tornado. Have you ever experienced that? A pity, if you haven't, for then there is indeed much that you have missed. How would you know the suffocation from too much of air? Sometimes, that's a pleasurable experience, at others an agonizing one. I first experienced such suffocation with Samir. Sitting in the tree house on top of the mahogany at Niyamgiri. It was a strange and perilous wait. The leaves of the tree brushed against us as they shook hard. The tree house rocked so badly we thought it would be swept away any moment. When I held his hand firmly and let the wind take my body, it was like flying in an open aircraft. I did not think at all of a future without him. Had I known better, I wouldn't have become so engrossed in him. There is no point at all, thinking of such things now. A wind that's blown over and the love that's withered and fallen are alike. They never return. Even if they do, the old exhilaration would be missing. Never mind the loss of the exhilaration, what about happiness? Who will compensate for the loss of happiness?

I kept pacing aimlessly trying not to think too much or sink into a depressed mood. I ran to the bathroom frequently. A shower is a good remedy for such a mood. You feel revived by the cold water falling on top of your head. Do not read the papers or watch TV, though. For example, if you opened the papers in the morning and read 'Farmer gets two thousand-rupee notes without Gandhi's image from ATM', how would it feel? Like clambering up a slippery rock and getting slapped near the top, right? Yet again, I fell into the sea of gloom. It rocked me. I dreamt of my great-grandfather who had gone away to meet Gandhiji return with a basketful of gifts. What would their meeting have been like? What would my great-grandfather have told Gandhiji? Valyappooppan, too, was murdered. That memory made my blood go cold. That day, I shook with fear even when Amma went to take a shower. I sped about fastening the doors, checking the bolts on the windows. But my heart continued to thud, the blood in my veins pounded, my nerves swelled to the size of balloons. I wanted to pick up a knife and slash my arms quick and hard. The blood should leap out and flow furiously, fill the room. I should drown in it. But then, how would Samir kill me? What would Satyaprakash do? My fingers went crazy seeking a blade. Then Amma came into the room and asked what I wanted to eat. With that, the frenzy in my veins ceased. 'Note ban: Gains limited to fifty thousand crore only' – I noticed that in the newspaper only then. The government had hoped for ninety-five thousand crore. I felt deeply disappointed. We all had suffered all that had to be suffered. And dreamt a lot too. And then what? It ended up like my love affair.

As I read it, Amma came to me and sat down on the chair beside me. And we exchanged the following words:

'Why are you so quiet? Thinking of Samir Sayyid?'

'He will return only after he kills me, Amme.'

'Don't worry. Satyaprakash won't allow that.'

'Amme, aren't you afraid for me?'

'I am scared about Samir.'

'For what?'

'Usually, Maoists on the run from prison are killed in police encounters.'

'Please don't say such things with that inauspicious tongue of yours!'

'Otherwise, the police would not have let him out.'

'If they wanted to kill him, they could have done it inside the jail, too?'

'That's all a big trouble these days.'

'Is this Aswathy's view?'

'She said that since it is a high-security prison, there is no way that the police wouldn't know.'

'Did she call you over to tell you this?'

'She asked about you changing numbers.'

'What did you tell her?'

'I told her you suspected your phone was being tapped.'

'Did she ask you for the new number?'

'No, just asked to tell you to inform the police if Samir Sayyid tried to contact you.'

'If it is the police that have helped him escape, why should we inform the police?'

'The police force in Kerala and in other places are not the same. Nor is the politics the same.'

'So they want to catch him again?'

'Running from a court is like running on one leg. You can't run very far.'

'Don't scare me, Vasanthalakshmi.'

'What is the use of getting scared by the truth, Satyapriye?'

'Amme, what am I to do now? Will Samir forgive me?'

'Were you his first love?'

'Not likely.'

'Then it's not likely that he will forgive you.'

'Why is that?'

'The first lover is the guardian angel of one's confidence.'

'For women too?'

'That'll depend on one's own doings.'

'How cruel you are, Amma!'

'The truth must be very cruel.'

'Can't you make it sound kinder? Mix some compassion?'

'No matter how you put it, the truth is the truth.'

I grew weary. Amma took my hand.

'Don't be scared. We have to face anything that comes – what else to do?'

'Have I not suffered enough, Amme?' My voice failed. A tender look filled her eyes.

'*Sukhavum dukhavum anubhavakaalam poyaal samamiha* ... Pleasure and pain, beyond their times, feel alike...'

'But the pain does not seem to be ending at all.'

'Of course it will end. By the way, did you manage to trace Koyikkal Amma's relative?'

'I looked up a Dr Ramakrishnan on Facebook. Have sent him a message.'

'Tell me when he replies.'

'What for?'

'To send him a friend request.'

'Uh? Are you on FB?'

'It's been two months.'

God is especially generous with her who already takes on a lot. An abundance of shocks and wounds is her lot! I was left open-mouthed, engulfed by a wave of disappointment and fatigue. Anger and frustration overpowered me. I felt that my life was meaningless. The tidal waves of debilitating despair grew into a veritable tsunami. One man had shot at me several times; he was still out there, trying to kill me. One did not even know who he really was. He was sure to attack again, it could be any moment. And why was I clinging to life? For Amma alone. And she? Did she feel even a tinge of affection or gratitude? How easily she did things behind my back! I had been living with her and talking to her all this while without even knowing that she used an FB account! What deceit! This was exactly what my sister did to me too. And Sriram. And Mahipal Shah Baba, Prabhudev, and

even Samir. In other words, all the people in my life were structures of
the same build. The entrance with a low ceiling, the open spaces inside
the house so well polished that you would find it hard to figure out if
the floors were hard stone or glistening water, sheets of glass for the
walls. And each time, I hit my forehead, slipped and fell on the floor,
got wet. Mistook the floor for a puddle at times and felt foolish. Tried
to fly through the thin walls of glass and fell on the floor like a baby
bird, my brain scattered on the floor.

I went to my bedroom and lay down. It was then that I saw that
Dr Ramakrishnan had sent me a response.

> *Hello, Satyapriya! I am very happy to have received this message!
> Yes, I am indeed the grandson of Thuruthel Bharathi Amma, born
> to her son Vasudevan. I now live in Meridian Villa, in Ernakulam.
> Hope Sivaprasad and the family are doing well. Would like to
> know how you are. With love, Ramakrishnan.*

I stared at the letters for some time. Was Dr Ramakrishnan yet
another of the structures I just mentioned, I worried. But I still typed
a response.

> *Respected Doctor, my father passed away this November. He was
> bedridden since long. Now Amma and I live together. I would like
> to meet you. If you do not mind, may I please have your address,
> and can I come over?*

His reply was quick, and this is how our exchange went:

> *You are always welcome. I live by myself. If you let me know in
> advance, I can get lunch ready for you.*

> *Can I come tomorrow?*

> *Sure. Welcome from the bottom of my heart! When will you reach?
> What is your preference, Satya, vegetarian or non-vegetarian?
> Any allergies? Anyone coming with you?*

I'll reach by 11.30. No particular preferences in food. No allergies.
I will be alone.

Great. See you tomorrow.

The stuffy feeling from the fear inside me vanished. Life shone with meaning again. I searched for Dr Ramakrishnan's photos on FB. He had just a profile picture. In it, he had on a hat and dark glasses, so it was impossible to catch a likeness. His timeline was full of photos of birds. Wildlife photography was his retirement pastime, or so it seemed. That gladdened me. Someone like that, sharing our genes! That was reason enough to feel happy.

Hereafter, everything happened quickly. I told Amma of my travel plans. Called Harish, arranged for a taxi. He brought his friend Shafeeq along. 'You could have told Venukkuttan,' Amma suggested, but I did not show interest. The taxi arrived at eight the next morning. When I got ready and stepped out, Amma and Shafeeq were loading a whole bunch of poovan bananas and a varikka jackfruit. 'Won't that be a bit too much?' I was sceptical. 'He's Koyikkal Amma's blood! Make no mistake, he will love offerings.' Amma teased. 'Never judge a man by his relatives,' I declared. Anyway, we set out at eight-thirty. And reached at eleven-thirty sharp.

Dr Ramakrishnan's home was enchanting. The trees and the English fence made it seem as though a piece from a European city had been planted here. The home and its premises were full of flowers. The inner room was a single long hall. The doors and windows lay open. A soft tune, from a flute, played somewhere. Dr Ramakrishnan was reading, lying on the nook by a large French window that opened outwards. A thin, dark-skinned man, his head and moustache completely grey. 'Come in, come in, Madam Satyapriya,' he greeted me. He was much more in control than I thought. No sign of the weariness or wistfulness of someone who was over eighty was evident on his face. He was full of energy. When Shafeeq unloaded the gifts that Amma had sent and took them to the kitchen, he cried in joy like a child, 'Hey! Poovanpazham! Varikkacchakka! Irshad,' he called his help sounding quite effervescent, 'do you know how to make a pulinkari with banana stems? Or a thoran with the banana flower?' A slow-moving forty-year-old man in an apron peeped out from the kitchen, which was at the other end of the hall. 'Uncle, we have food to fill ten people already. These people will eat just a pinch or two, and let me warn you, you'll have to eat this stuff this whole week!' he threatened. In the end, they arrived at an agreement about the banana-stem pulinkari.

When Dr Ramakrishnan went to the kitchen, I headed to the door that opened towards the lake. Vasanthaalayam wafted into my memory. Two yellow butterflies that had come into the hall through some other door seemed to catch my scent and fly away. When the doctor came back with a glass of fruit juice, a bulbul flew in, sat on the table for a few moments, completed its observation, and flew away in a hurry as though it had to report what it had observed to someone. The doctor had brought over some green mango juice. I downed it in a single gulp. He sat down on the sofa, I sat on the chair opposite. We looked at each other. For some time, there was only the sound of the flute in the room. The knots of tension in my mind came undone. The following conversation took place between Dr Ramakrishnan and me:

'Do you know what music this is, Satyapriya?'

'Flute?'

'It is Native American music.'

'No wonder, I feel the peace of the wild.'

'That means that you are stressed.'

'Who is not stressed in these times?'

'Well, I am not. Neither is Irshad.'

'You mean, someone with a wife and kids, a householder, isn't stressed?'

'My wife died twenty years ago. Both sons are well settled. So what stress can I have? Irshad is divorced. No children. No stress!'

'Where does he come from?'

'We both belong to the forests! I met him first at Parambikulam. And the following year in Mullakodi. And in Sikkim, two years later. Then we decided to travel in life together.'

'Unbelievable, Doctor!'

'I am not Doctor – I am your senior uncle,' he said, 'your valyacchan.'

'How does one become a senior uncle – by deed or by birth?'

'Would have been by deed as well if your grandmother's father – my father's grand-uncle – had not set off to meet Gandhiji!'

'So Gandhiji is the reason why we never met!'

'Ha! Ha! Are you really of the Koyikkal family?'

'Never. My mother is a low-caste woman.'

'Good one! So tell me about yourself – what you do for a living, your family, children…'

'I am single. No children. I was working but resigned last month.'

'Why did you give up your job?'

'Amma is all alone.'

'Are you an only child, Satyapriya?'

'I had an older sister. In 1999, she died in…'

'I am sorry. Was she like you?'

'No, she was kinder than me.'

'Ha! Ha! Satyapriya's mother – she belongs to a business family, doesn't she?'

'She used to. Now the two of us live in a small house.'

'Anyway, this is a happy day. Glad to have met Sivaprasad's daughter!'

'Should have come over and met you earlier.'

'Why didn't you come?'

'I did not know that there was someone on Acchan's side of the family who built a house for himself and butterflies and birds!'

'Ha! Ha! You have a way with words! Where did you get that from? Not from your father for sure.'

'As far as I know, Acchan was never a good conversationalist.'

'Being a good conversationalist has nothing to do with skill; it is more about the ability to build trust and come close. You need a lithe tongue to impress strangers. To someone close, whom you trust, you speak from your heart.'

'Did Acchan never speak from his heart?'

'He was cordial. But see, we have been talking for barely ten minutes, and I already feel that I've known you since long! Your father was a very close relative of mine, and we shared a room too, but I never felt half as close to him. Neither he to me.'

'I thought he was a better man back then.'

'But he made it big, didn't he? Big-time businessman, film producer, publisher, whatnot…?'

'All of it was lost later.'

'I came to know about it all when I returned to Kerala.'

'When did you see him last, Valyaccha?'

'When my father passed away … I came to Kerala in 1970.'

'I wasn't born then.'

'Yes, right. My younger son was in the fourth grade at the time.'

'Acchan's golden age.'

'Yes, a king without a crown, he was – that's the right description.'

'Did you two meet? Chat long?'

'No, we didn't chat … He was too busy.'

'He avoided you, that means, right?'

He looked at me with an astonished expression and laughed out loud.

'Yes, you are right! I should have met you earlier, surely!'

'Why did he avoid you do you think?'

He looked at me intently for a few moments. Then, with a smile, he said, 'Aren't we all human? We all change with time.'

'Does Acchan's behaviour have any connection with the incident in Madras?'

'What incident in Madras?'

'Valyaccha, I am here to find out about that incident.'

'I knew from the start that you wouldn't seek out an old geezer past eighty-four without a good reason!'

'Let me tell you everything. There was an attempt made on my life.'

He flinched. I told him all that had happened, briefly. Dr Ramakrishnan looked completely appalled. His deep eyes moistened. I continued:

'The police have filed a case. They, too, believe that the culprit is someone closely connected with Acchan. I need to find out if Acchan has ever had a son from any of his relationships.'

He was utterly dumbfounded now. How I wished I could take a picture of him then. Didn't I have to keep some proof of having shocked such a senior gentleman, of having left him completely rattled?

'I know that there was a reason for Acchan giving up his medical studies. You know exactly what it was.'

He stayed silent and fixed his eyes on his palms.

'My dear, there are limits to what one can reveal of a father to his daughter.'

'Valyaccha, you are speaking to someone who was forced to know too much of what a daughter should never know about her father!'

'What is it that you wish to know? I'll tell you what I can remember.'

'I've heard a story that a young girl was found dead in Acchan's room. Is that true?'

His face fell. For a few moments, he was completely silent. His frail chest rose and fell rapidly.

'Not found dead.'

'Murdered?'

My heart stopped.

'Making a thirteen-year-old pregnant is murder in itself I suppose.'

'Please, can you tell me clearly?'

'I was back home after the first-year exams, and Sivaprasad came to see me. He said he wanted to study medicine and become a doctor. I told him what I knew about it. Then, whenever I came home for my vacation, he would come to see me. He was very humble. It was I who took the initiative, brought him the application form. He was a bright student. Great marks. So admission was easy.'

'Did he have money to pay the fees?'

'He spent lavishly. My family was financially better off than his, but I had barely enough for my expenses. He had a whole wardrobe, of some ten or twelve sets of trousers and shirts, back then.'

'I've heard that he worked and earned an income to pay for his studies.'

'Maybe. But it did not affect his studies. His teachers were very fond of him.'

'What about you, Valyaccha?'

'No, I wasn't, and that's the truth. He was a complex character. Extremely intelligent, hard-working too, but with a strange sense of inferiority. And he was not trustworthy at all. Never had any qualms about using another. He never admitted to any of his failings, would always blame others. Never heard of the word "self-criticism", I'd say.'

'You lived in the same house, didn't you?'

'A friend of mine, Vinodanand, and I found a house in Park Town. Sivaprasad joined us. One day, Vinodanand warned me, be careful. He had found Sivaprasad with a little girl, our neighbour, inside the house once when he had gone back home unexpectedly. She was just eleven or twelve. I found it hard to believe but I still asked Sivaprasad about it. He denied it, and I forgot all about it. Vinodanand completed his house surgery and left. I continued there. I was attempting the FRCS exam and was busy when, one day, our rented place was besieged by the neighbours. The child, our neighbour, was pregnant. To tell you the truth, it is distressing to recall that day even now. The neighbours beat us up. In the end, it was agreed that Sivaprasad would marry the girl. They took them to the nearby temple and got them married there. That very day I vacated the house. I saw him again when the girl died.'

I sat there, flabbergasted.

'He did not take her to a hospital, managed the delivery at home. Don't know if that was deliberate. Anyway, she died.'

'And that child?'

'It survived.'

My body went on the alert and trembled. My blood pressure shot up. The crucial turning point in the investigation! Have you ever gone through such a decisive moment in your life? Sought out a truth and discovered that what you had guessed and pictured in your mind was actually the truth? A pity, if you haven't, for then, you have not had the good fortune to enjoy a truly exquisite moment.

I was thinking of that infant. That was born into its father's hands in that rented place. How old must he have been then? Twenty-two, or -three.

'Did Acchan accept the child?'

'He slipped away after the child was born – never came to college again.'

'Which year was this?'

'The year before I left for Britain – 1957. I reached London in 1958.'

'Did you get to know anything about that infant?'

'No. I just know that it lived. The truth is, I didn't want to get mixed up in all this. I just thought about my own life. What if I got blamed in the end?'

'Born in 1957 – the child should be fifty-nine now!'

'If still alive.'

I felt weary again. Satyaprakash didn't look fifty-nine for sure. He was younger. I sat there, looking at the lake. In the afternoon sun, it appeared like a heap of broken glass. There were new hurdles in my path now. But I rummaged through Dr Ramakrishnan's memory once more.

'Valyaccha, where was Acchan after you left the rented house?'

'He lived there.'

'And the girl too?'

'I suppose so. Those days, it was not uncommon in those parts to get thirteen-year-old girls married.'

'And you never went back there?'

'I told you. When this girl died, I was on OP duty. Four or five people came looking for me. They pulled me into a bullock cart and took me there, like a thief.'

'And what did you see?'

'There was a pool of blood in the room. The girl's body was on a mat on the floor. The girl's grandmother was wiping the newborn's body. Sivaprasad was in a corner, with his head hung low.' He sighed deeply. 'The hubbub was such that someone called the police. I wanted to save myself – that was all. Luckily, the police let me off.'

'So you know nothing about the infant?'

'I had admitted the infant to the hospital. It was healthy, weighed two and a half kilos, I remember that.'

'Admitted just the baby?'

'No, no, there were relatives. They were Tamil people. They stay back to help and carry out responsibilities. Not like Malayalis, who turn their tails and run.'

'And Acchan?'

'I don't know. Didn't look for him. But the next day, some people barged into Dr Reddy's house looking for Sivaprasad. Dr Reddy called the police. It is then that we discovered that he had sneaked off.'

'And you didn't ask about the child after that?'

'I didn't have the guts.'

I listened anxiously. Then Irshad called him from the kitchen. He went over. Hearing the clatter of plates, I went too. They were serving lunch; I joined them. We invited Shafeeq to eat with us. The curries were tasty. After lunch, I returned to my seat near the French window. My heart rang with sorrow. Yet again, my life felt meaningless. Then, Irshad and Dr Ramakrishnan appeared with bowls of ice cream.

'We both were waiting for you.' A mischievous smile peeked out of Dr Ramakrishnan's grey moustache.

'This guy is looking for a bride.'

I took a good look at Irshad.

'I am ready,' I said, tasting a spoonful of the ice cream. Irshad blushed. Dr Ramakrishnan laughed gaily.

'Okay, then – I am ready too,' Irshad said.

'But I can't cook. You will have to cook for me too.'

'Oh, in any case, he doesn't let anyone into the kitchen.'

'Second condition – I will not ask for permission or consent for anything pertaining to my choices.'

'Don't – he gets stressed by that sort of thing!'

'Third, never say no to me.'

'Never.'

'The last and most important condition – the consent of my assassin.'

Dr Ramakrishnan laughed. He picked up the empty ice-cream bowls and carried them into the kitchen. Irshad took on me then.

'Have you ever been to the forest, Satyapriya?'

'I have even stayed in a tree house in a forest.'

'Alone?'

'No, my ex-lover was with me.'

Irshad seemed to be caught by surprise, but he hid it well.

'What was he doing in the forest?'

'He was a Maoist.'

This time he looked well and truly shocked.

'And where is he now?'

'I heard that he escaped from prison a couple of days back.'

Irshad looked even more shocked now. He took some time to resume the conversation.

'Will he come looking for you?'

'Not sure. I am waiting.'

'If he does not...' His look was now quite romantic.

'... let me know.'

I laughed. I watched with amusement his cheeks glow and his eyes grow droopy. Of course, that did not mean I was falling in love. Fall in love – good heavens! – when I was running holding my life in my hands? Anyhow, the escapee Samir Sayyid was the only one I could ever love. I had to get to the truth first – before I could fall in love with another. I was certain that he would come looking for me. Even the notes that the government had demonetized – ninety-seven per cent of those – had come back. So why wouldn't my lover? The story of my life would not be complete without his return.

Don't know if you have noticed but some romantic relationships are like curries set to boil. They lack some flavour. Until those flavours are added, stirred in, and the pot is taken off the stove, it remains a bother. As was with Samir – there was something left to be added. I simply could not turn off the stove without doing so. Until then, I had to put up with the smoky scent rising from the cooking pot.

I bid goodbye to Dr Ramakrishnan, albeit most reluctantly. Our eyes misted. He patted me affectionately.

'You bothered to come all the way here to meet me and found nothing of any value!'

'This was one of the best days in my whole life!'

I took my purse and turned to leave. Dr Ramakrishnan put his hand on my shoulder and came with me. Irshad followed him.

'But you didn't get what you wanted from me?'

'All this while I had thought that my would-be killer was the son my father had by that woman – actually, girl. I was wrong, I know now. That's a step forward!'

'How so?'

'We don't know if that infant lived or died. And the man who's trying to murder me can't possibly be fifty-nine.'

We stepped out into the porch. In the sunlight, the lake shone like a pure brocade sari splayed out. In the neighbour's yard, a young man was pruning the lantana bushes. It was then that Dr Ramakrishnan said: 'Let us suppose that the child lived. But even then, it could not be this assassin.'

'How are you so sure, Valyaccha?'

I turned around to face him. He gave me an affectionate look.

'Because it was a girl!'

There! Everything that I had built until then was smashed in a second! I was gobsmacked. Now, 'what next' was the question that loomed larger still. This is the trouble with crime investigation. You solve it like a maths problem, write all the steps down, and in the last step, discover that the steps were all wrong, and you have no time to start all over again…!

Shafeeq was reversing the car when Dr Ramakrishnan touched my shoulder again.

'Mole, wait, there's something else. May not be relevant, but still.'

I turned around again but without much hope.

'The girl Sivaprasad got pregnant…' – my ears pricked up – '… she was from a family of ironsmiths.'

That was like another blow to my head. Figuratively, of course. But when they fall in quick succession, what difference does it make whether the blows are literal or figurative? My eyes dimmed. My innards seem to be turning into vapour. I struggled for balance amid a terrifying tornado. It suffocated me, threatened to uproot me and fling me afar. But it was different from other storms. For example, it was a razor-edged wind that pierced right through. And it had a shape – the 'S' shape.

FORTY-FIVE

After my meeting with Dr Ramakrishnan, I put together another table: Table 2.

Discovered	Yet to be discovered	Hypotheses
Acchan's medical studies ended when that thirteen-year-old girl died in labour.	Details of the girl.	Her name was Satya.
The baby born to my father when he was twenty-three was a girl.	Is that girl alive today? If so, where is she?	Satyaprakash is somehow connected to her.
The dead girl belonged to a family of ironsmiths.	Did she make that dagger?	If not she, her relatives.
The word 'satyam' is decisive in Acchan's life.	The reason behind it.	The word connects the dead girl and Satyaprakash.

Discovered	Yet to be discovered	Hypotheses
Some troubling incident occurred in Acchan's guest house in 1972.	What was it?	It had to do with the daughter born to Acchan when he was a medical student. Or with some other woman.
The troubling incident of 1972 was settled with the help of Leelavallabhan.	Who will be able to supply more details?	Tyagu.
Tyagu was a servant in the guest house.	Who can help trace him?	Valyamaaman.

One thing was very clear. There were many more things that were yet to be discovered compared to what I had already discovered and the hypotheses I had framed. This was an extremely complex phase in my investigation. A narrative had taken shape. It lay inside me like a seven-week-old foetus. It had limbs but could not fold or bend them. It had a heart, liver, and even a navel, but no body. It had a brain but no head. Eyes, but the face was still incomplete. You could say that it was a human infant, but it was barely so. Nobody would believe you. So the narrative was taking shape, but it was not complete. For example, Acchan's life after he dropped out of MBBS. It was unknown. Where was he? In Tamil Nadu? Or in Kerala, or somewhere else, hiding? Who to ask?

But what troubled me was not Acchan's whereabouts during those three years. Also, not what he did then. I just wanted to know if he had fathered other children during that time. Given his track record, he was quite likely to have got other women pregnant. A girl of just twelve or thirteen. I tasted blood in my mouth, as though I had vomited it. Nisha Chechi's bony body rose before my eyes. When I turned the idea over and over in my head, I found myself wondering if the boy who hired Nisha Chechi to attack Acchan might not have been his son born around this time. I had at first thought he was Satyaprakash. But as Acchan's story unfolded, nothing remained stable.

I really missed Inspector Shetty then. Several days had passed since I had heard his voice. In these forty-four years of mine, many have betrayed me. But none matched his betrayal. Not even Samir Sayyid. Because of the reluctance to admit that betrayal, I felt vexed even with Amma. I felt like a kid sitting in an exam hall totally clueless about the answers, pain scoring my heart up and down with its pointy tip. I writhed inside, thought of my next step. What happened in that guest house in 1972? Finding that out was my priority. For that, I needed to find Tyagu. Valyamaaman was the only person I knew I could rely on, at that moment, to help me find him. I got ready in a hurry. Called Harish and fixed to go out in his autorickshaw. When I set out, Amma and Sarada Chechi were chatting. Amma looked at me questioningly. I pretended not to notice and climbed into the auto.

When the autorickshaw reached the main road, though, my courage began to ebb. Especially because the fact that I was going back to my mother's family homestead struck me. To go back there after we had lost all our wealth, I felt guilty. But what was the guilt for? Because we had lost the wealth that had been entrusted to us? Because I was no longer a relative that Valyamaaman and his family could proudly welcome? Because I had willingly embraced the loss of face that comes with poverty? Who knows! Maybe the guilt was from having mistakenly thought that human relationships were beyond wealth where, once, before the debts and the attachment of our properties, I sat on Valyamaaman's shoulder to watch the temple festival, when I slurped down the sweet aanjhili fruit that he deseeded and fed me lovingly, when he tickled me playfully with pieces of ice on my face or back. When we were children, Valyamaaman would make us laugh a lot. He delighted at seeing us laugh. Let me tell you from experience: do not trust the love people show for another's children. That lasts only as long as the promise that the children won't become a burden to them.

When we turned from the small chapel towards the house, my heart began to calm down. From there, Appooppan would lead the way with his silver-tipped walking stick. The balls of his feet were cracked. When he would sit feet up on the easy chair, between Chechi and I, we would attend to a foot each, cut his nails, apply Pond's cold cream on the soles and the balls of his feet, and tickle him. He would laugh, tenderly, lovingly. The sheer joy that he experienced when he looked at us was evident on his face, I remembered. 'All of this became mine after my Vasantham was born,' he used to say. 'Look after her well when she is old,' he would implore us. That felt like a memory from another life. The family home, the easy chair, the heaps of ripe coconut in the front yard, the dried-up ones separated from the good ones, the scent of paddy that filled the air during harvest, how Chechi and I used to compete while counting the bundles of paddy and writing down the numbers, workers threshing the paddy, their bodies swaying like graceful dancers. When Appooppan was buried, the soil fell over all this, burying it all. As we neared the family home, I trembled in terror, wondering if I'd see Appooppan's body in the white shroud lying on its open porch. The darkness that enveloped me that day had never really lifted. It remained, like the clouds in the sky, assuming various shapes in unpredictable corners.

The autorickshaw stopped at an impressively large, gated doorway. Harish told me that we'd reached. My mouth fell agape with surprise. The last time I had been here was when my cousin Kannan Chettan had had a daughter. That was a couple of months before Chechi's death. The family home had now been completely redone. In place of the old gate with griffins on either side, there was a regal gateway built big enough to house an elephant. The house itself had been rebuilt like the Kuthiramalika Palace in Thiruvananthapuram. It was still called Vasanthapanchami – the name was carved in gold letters. Even though they had removed her from their lives, Amma's brothers could not bring themselves to remove her name. The house that our younger uncle, Kochumaaman, inherited from Appooppan was called Vasantharamam. He had changed it to one closer to his wife's name – called it Indivaram or something like that. The month immediately following this, the four consignments sent to the USA came back, rejected, one by one. The astrologer said that changing the name had been inauspicious. So 'Indivaram' became 'Vasantharamam' again. But Valyamaaman did not do anything foolish; he was convinced that a name was really nothing. His son Dr Sarath Babu, his wife Dr Sindhu, and their daughter Sneha, who was a medical student, were all in Ernakulam. I had heard Amma mention that Valyamaaman's next mission was to purchase or build a large hospital complex for them.

I entered the house with a heavy heart. There were many SUVs parked out there – they bore the names of Valyamaaman's many businesses. Valyamaaman was having his breakfast. In the family home, for all meals, there were always more guests than family members. And the guests weren't often just guests; they were members of a durbar. It was the same when Appooppan held court here. There would be many to share the table. A police constable, a journalist, and the family lawyer would all be present. Valyamaaman was keen to preserve traditions. I was glad about that. Have you noticed – maybe you haven't – for some people who feel a lack in their soul, 'tradition' becomes an obsession?

When I entered the house, a young man with a sandal-paste kuri on his forehead began to question me. I introduced myself as Satyapriya, Vasanthalakshmi's daughter. He went in and returned at the same speed. This time he bore a happy grin bigger than the kuri that he wore on his forehead. Valyamaami hurried up behind him. 'What a surprise! Unexpected things happening! Today the crows are going to flip over in flight!' she said, sounding amiable and amused. Valyamaaman saw me, and for a few moments, his eyes remained fixed on me in surprise. I was quiet for some time. This is not the uncle on whose back I played elephant, I reminded myself. This man is the president of the powerful association of local merchants and industrialists.

'Mole, sit down,' Valyamaaman made an effort to be welcoming too. He introduced me to the others. 'My only sister's daughter.' The table was laid with several breakfast items. I served myself some appams and stew; my valyamaami and two women helpers served everyone else. The talk there was all about the finance minister's statement that 'There were no fake notes in the money that had returned to the banks'. Valyamaaman led the conversation. The police constable, the local hack and lawyer were all praise for the note ban. Money is piling in the banks, the monetary reserve is increasing. 'Did you have no trouble changing the currency, Maamma?' I asked. 'Goodness, before the decision was taken in Delhi didn't Babu Muthalaali have all the news?' the family lawyer jumped to comment. I had no further questions. I ate the appams in silence. They were absolutely delicious.

We got up one by one after finishing the breakfast, washed our hands. My uncle and his friends went to the room to the right of the hall where we were. When I was washing my hands, my aunt came over and invited me to go with her to the room on the left side of the main hall. I saw that the house had been reconstructed to include a large drawing room and a dining area to the left of the main entrance. This living-cum-dining area was for the family, Valyamaami clarified. When there was just one, it was a real bother. There was no place for the women in the house to gather in peace or have a meal together. Now it was better. Now when Kannan Chettan and Sindhu Chechi came, and also her friend, my aunt had a quieter place to welcome them. I shared her sense of relief. My only doubt was how she managed to keep such a huge house clean. A Nepali family was now living on the premises for the sole purpose of house-cleaning, she said. They were housed in a two-bedroom outhouse. I liked her living room and dining hall. I silently thanked the architect who had made these additions without ruining the original. Valyamaami brought me a bowl of sweet payasam, an offering from some temple, and advised me that when I returned to work, I should take Amma along, and get married as soon as possible.

The chit-chat over, I brought up my business. I'd like to see Valyamaaman, I said. She went to him, called him over. Valyamaaman arrived, looking quite grand in his white silk shirt with its sleeves rolled up and the gold-bordered mundu. He walked confidently, running his fingers over his protruding belly. In Appooppan's time, he used to stoop a bit. Then he was the sapling trying to grow under the shade of a massive tree. When that tree died, the smaller one grew faster, its core hardening, its confidence rising. But there is one thing: the confidence of others rattles us a little. It happened to me too. Nevertheless, are we human if we don't feel the urge to at least poke the confidence of others with a teeny needle? So when he came over and lay down on his side, like Vishnu in his ananthashayana pose, on the ornately carved wooden swing-cot right opposite where I sat, his right elbow resting on the round pillow covered in a silk fabric red in colour, I could not help myself. When he raised his head majestically and looked at me, I asked him, 'Valyammaama, do you still climb the aanjhili tree?'

That left him utterly puzzled. 'Aanjhili? What tree is that?' his surprised look seemed to ask. I felt an excitement. My poor aunt who did not understand our code was left muttering – 'What aanjhili? Wasn't the one on the north side chopped off two years after Acchan passed? All the three in the south-side yard were chopped down to plant rubber?' Then a woman called her from the kitchen, and she left. Valyamaaman's eyes were fixed on me. That made me even bolder.

'So you never plucked aanjhili fruits for your grandkid? How sad! I remember how often you used to climb the tree, pluck the fruits, put them all into a sack, and lower it carefully. When you squeezed one gently from both sides, the fruit would give way. You used to feed me the sweet flesh…'

Valyamaaman looked like someone had knocked the stuffing out of him now. He looked around, shifted, and smiled sheepishly. I continued:

'Even now when I see the aanjhili fruit, I remember you, Valyammaama.'

Valyamaaman gave up his sleeping-Vishnu pose and sat up, feet touching the ground. The swing-cot rocked on its own. The silk curtains hanging over the windows went 'isssh' as the wind blew. Valyamaaman did not take his eyes off me. I dealt with his look lovingly. Gradually, his face became calm. A sigh escaped him. When he looked at me again, affection shone from his eyes. This is the conversation we had that day:

'How long it's been since you came to meet your valyamaaman who fed you that fruit!'

'I did not think that you'd be pleased to see me.'

'That's your misunderstanding. My affection towards you has never waned. If I stepped away, it was because of your mother's arrogance. Just that.'

'I didn't know that you were capable of stepping away like that. It was a shattering experience, getting to know it.'

'Mole, you are in the dark. The truth isn't what your mother has told you. There are many things that she hasn't told you. My father gave her almost the whole of his wealth. And she ruined it all. And even when things had collapsed completely, did I not save her, making Mohan buy that house and the property?'

'I am grateful for that favour, Valyammaama.'

'I won't argue with you. Tell me what you want. Do you need any money?'

'Oh, don't worry, I did not come for money.'

'Why do you say that? I am only happy to give you anything that you need.'

'Never mind. Tell me, have you ever been to Acchan's guest house in Madras?'

'Why do you ask that?'

'Didn't you hear about the attempt made on my life?'

'That was a mistaken attempt, wasn't it?'

'No.'

'Uh?'

'No, it was not a mistaken attempt. The attacker has targeted me before and after.'

'And the police haven't yet caught that bastard?'

'It's a murder that failed. And that, too, outside Kerala. The police have their limitations.'

'Give me his details. We have our boys in town. We'll just get rid of him. No one will know.'

'I suspect that this assassin is Acchan's son.'

My uncle stared at me his mouth agape. Moments later, he let out a sigh. 'Yes, that's actually possible.'

'But I don't know with which woman.'

'It was your father – only god above can know!'

'So you knew that your brother-in-law was a wastrel…'

'Yes, I knew it. Mohan, too. And our father as well…'

'And you didn't do anything to help your sister?'

'We did all we could. But isn't there a point beyond which we can't interfere? And we had to think of you two as well…'

'All that's in the past. Now I need to know something.'

'Ask, my dear.'

'Valyammaama, have you been to Acchan's guest house?'

'Yes! Three or four times. All of it got sold back then. Such excellent, valuable property! A beautiful house on Sterling Road!'

'Who all were there when you visited the place?'

'A caretaker – that is all. I stayed there for three or four days each time, five or six times maybe.'

'Do you remember the caretaker's name?'

'Hmm. It was a Tamil man.'

'Tyagu?'

'I can't remember. It's been some forty years!'

'Was there no one else there?'

'If you ask me … uh … yes, there was a girl too. She helped in the kitchen.'

'A girl?'

'Yes, some ten or twelve years old. She wore a half-skirt.'

All of a sudden, I felt cold.

'Was she a helper there?'

'I can't remember ... he said it was the Tamil man's daughter. But...'

'But?'

'She was well dressed. With gold on her ears and neck. She looked like she was from a good family.'

'When all did you go there?'

'I went in '68, then in '70. Went there four or five times in '70. Then two times in '71. And in '72 also.'

'Was the girl still there in '72?'

'No, they said that she was married.'

'At what age?'

'Oh, there they marry girls off at a very young age – she must have been fourteen or so. The Tamil man said that she was married.'

'Have you ever been there when Acchan was present?'

'Yes, once.'

'And was this girl there then?'

'Yes, uh-huh! When you say that ... That girl was very free with your father. He was so warm to her – so much more than he was ever with the two of you!'

'My father?'

'Yes. I was stumped by that.'

'Do you know anything about this caretaker, Valyammaama?'

'When he sold the guest house, I'd told your father to send the caretaker over to us. He was such a fabulous cook! Chicken or prawns or crab...'

'And Acchan didn't agree?'

'He did say he'd ask. But later, he made excuses saying that he didn't have his address or number. That was a lie.'

'Why do you say that?'

'I saw him later, in another house in Madras. Can you guess whose?'

'Whose?'

'Of that cine actor, Rajani!'

I was jolted.

'Which year?'

'The year our father died.'

I sat there with an empty head. A clock ticked inside my brain. I rewound it to a time years back.

'Why did you go to Rajani's house, Valyammaama?'

He looked embarrassed.

'That was when a friend of mine made a movie. We went to ask for her dates.'

'Tell me the truth, Valyammaama.'

His face blanched.

'She was siphoning money from your father. I went there to give her a scare.'

'And was she scared?'

'That relationship did not last long.'

'Was the caretaker there?'

'When I reached the house, he was watering the plants in the garden. He was the one who opened the gate. When I asked, he told me that he was serving in that house then.'

'And his daughter?'

'Aiyo, I did not ask. That was not a moment for any light-hearted chats.'

'Thanks, Valyammaama, this has been very useful. I am very grateful!'

'Wait. You give me the details of that fellow – let me see?'

'If I had the details, would I bother you at all?'

He stood up. Suddenly, he looked aged. I called my aunt. She came running and asked in a huff, 'Are you leaving before lunch?' I calmed her down. Valyamaaman called his assistant, the sandal-paste kuri-clad youth. He came up quickly. Valyamaaman whispered something to him. He ran in and then back out to us at the same speed, carrying a packet. He handed it to Valyamaaman; Valyamaaman made me take it.

'Keep this.'

'What is this?'

'Some money. Go get yourself something that you like.'

My eyes filled. I gave it back to him.

'There was a time when I desperately needed money, Valyammaama … but not any more. I have more than enough now.'

'But it is money anyway? Your Valyammaama's giving you a gift, gladly. Take it.' Valyamaami encouraged me.

I looked at my uncle with overflowing eyes.

'There won't be money if they ban the notes.'

'Then go get some gold to keep.'

'You have already given me the greatest gifts you could possibly give your sister's child. Long back. Before you became this rich boss.'

'Oh, I have only given some trifles, when you came of age…'

'Valyammaama, you have taken me to the temple festival, remember? Got me strands of hair from the elephant's tail? Made me sit on the hobby horse? You have taken us to the beach and the hills too? To places where our father never took us? Bought us sweets and toys?'

Valyamaaman looked sad, wilted.

'You still remember everything…'

'Valyammaama, the biggest gift you can give a child is beautiful memories, isn't it?'

He stood looking at me sadly.

'If you want to give me something, don't give it as cash,' I consoled him.

'Then?' he asked.

'Give it to me in the form of aanjhili fruits!' I laughed. So did his assistant. But my uncle and aunt did not.

'I remember you whenever I see the aanjhili fruit. You separating the fruits, putting them into my mouth, waiting for me to spit out the seeds…' A seed got stuck in my throat. Two tears escaped my eyes. My aunt's eyes grew moist. My uncle held me close and burst into tears. I, too, nearly wept aloud. Then I pulled away his hands and ran out. I did not turn back to look. 'Come, Harish, let us leave,' I hurried him. I just wanted to get back home. Thinking about Acchan's caretaker ending up with Rajani set off a veritable jallikattu inside me.

I use the word 'jallikattu' on purpose. The jallikattu agitation – the protest against the ban on the traditional bull-taming sport in Tamil Nadu – broke out the next day.

The trip back was shorter. As soon as I had sent Harish away, I ran to my cot, threw myself on it, and wept. Amma came into my room, chiding me, 'How can you sleep like this!' I was vexed. I wiped my eyes, turned on my back, and looked at her. Amma readjusted her spectacles on her nose and prepared for battle. We had the following exchange:

'Where did you go?'

'Where did you go yesterday, Amma?'

'Why do you need to know? To sign the TA Bill?'

'You weren't back until nine at night. That's why I asked.'

'Is this place a ladies' hostel, to lock the gates at nine?'

'If you have a fall somewhere in your old age, I am the only one around!'

'Who knows who will have to care for whom!'

'Are you a mother, Mother?'

'A mother is a citizen, all right? A citizen.'

'The daughter's in agony, the mother plays the symphony.'

'Was it a crime that the mother thought that playing the symphony will reduce the daughter's agony?'

'Yes, please play your music, keep it up, please, until you get to see me dead, and that will give you peace.'

Amma came over and sat beside me. She stroked my hair tenderly, gently feeling my wound. She noticed the diary on the bed. She leaned over and took it. Opened it, read it carefully. Looked thoughtful. I got up, pressed my face on her shoulder.

'What do you think of my case diary, Amme?'

'That my daughter should have joined the CBI or the Interpol.'

'Teasing me?'

'No! You are clearly able to dig things up and analyse them.'

'Acchan gave up his medical studies because a girl of twelve or thirteen died during childbirth.'

'That is, you have another older sister.'

'If alive, she would be fifty-nine. A sister who'd be celebrating her sixtieth-year feast next year.'

'That is, when we got married, this child was seven.'

'If the child lived.'

'If she lived, who raised her, without a father and mother?'

'Dr Ramakrishnan knows nothing of it. The mother died in childbirth. The child was admitted to the hospital. Her mother's relatives were present. Later, when he checked, she had been discharged.'

'Dr Ramakrishnan told you this?'

'Yes, he is a very good man.'

'The very good man reveals all this now?'

'This was in 1957. He went abroad in 1958.'

'The Communist Party of India came to power in Kerala in 1957.'

'What's the connection?'

'It was that election that gave us the hope of a world without caste and religion. That was why I fell in love with your father and married him.'

'What are you trying to say, Amme?'

'That the elections of 1957 had an impact on my personal decisions.'

'I saw Valyammaama today.'

'Is that why you were all dressed up this morning?'

'Valyammaama has seen this caretaker at the guest house. He couldn't recall the name.'

Right then, a car's horn sounded at the gate. Amma got up hurriedly, muttering that someone had come. I grabbed her arm and said, 'You can go after this one last bit. The caretaker's daughter also apparently stayed at the guest house.'

Amma stopped abruptly and turned.

'How old was she?'

'Twelve or thirteen.'

Amma straightened her spectacles and looked at me.

'So the case that Leelavallabhan solved had to do with that.'

Amma pulled her arm away and went off. I sat there, numbed. A huge aanjhili seed was choking me. I swallowed it. It sprouted in my belly. Grew rapidly into a huge tree inside me, spreading around at great speed. Its invisible branches thrust their heads out, shattering my nerves and flinging them around violently. Its leaves grew larger. Have you ever experienced carrying within yourself a rapidly growing tree? Oh, a pity, if you haven't, for then you missed something big for sure, because then you haven't experienced the biggest circus act! But there's this advantage to carrying something like that inside you: you will never be alone. When you carry a forest inside, how can you be alone?

It was Valyamaaman's car that was honking at our gate. My poor dear uncle, he had taken much trouble to seek out aanjhili fruits for his niece! A government can only divest currency of its value, but its subjects could surely restore it – if not of currency, but of some other things. I am telling you the truth. I wept when I ripped open the fruit that my uncle sent me and savoured it bit by bit. Never did I weep like that again – wounded by sweetness.

FORTY-SIX

I bought a ticket for Chennai for Amma as well. I did not ask her beforehand if she wanted to go; just picked out four sets of saris and blouses from among her clothes and packed them myself. I called Shafeeq to take us to the airport; sneaked her suitcase into the car. Amma was told that we were going to town. She did not object. I made her wear a nice printed silk sari, made her do her hair up nicely. She looked ten years younger. Amma was excited. It was when the car passed the town without stopping anywhere that she smelt something fishy. 'Where are we going?' she asked. We talked thus:

'Does it matter? Your daughter's taking you.'

'I am past the age of setting out without knowing where!'

'Let's go to Chennai.'

That surprised her much. Her face gave away only the faintest trace of happiness. A short while later, she said, 'I also need to learn how to book a ticket online!'

'It's simple if you have an email address and an ATM card.' And then I poked her. 'Oh, you must already have email?'

She only smiled.

'Where are you going to travel booking an e-ticket, Amme?' asked Shafeeq.

'Before I die, I want to see the entire world.'

Amma opened the newspaper she was carrying. 'PAN made compulsory for bank accounts', 'Black money after demonetization 4,807 crore' – I read the headlines from the corner of my eye. Had I not proclaimed right then that unless all money is banned, black money cannot be prohibited? But then, would any government take seriously what ordinary folk like us say?

'Ah, the poor man!' Amma sighed in the middle of her reading.

'What's the matter?' I asked.

Amma read aloud:

Old notes cannot be exchanged

New Delhi: The RBI has turned down a son's demand that he should be permitted to exchange the currency notes that his father had saved before his death. The father passed away on 26 December. The family found the savings only after his death. It contained a hundred five-hundred-rupee notes.

'I saw a movie like that at a film festival,' said Shafeeq. 'Of children seeking the money their mother had saved up when East Germany collapsed. They find a whole cupboard full of notes, but they had all become worthless.'

'Therefore, never hide money. And if you do, tell others.' I tried to provoke Amma.

'Don't worry; I'll spend all that I have before I leave.'

'Please tell me in advance!'

'It was the fashion back in my day to leave a note when you eloped. I'll leave one – "I am leaving, dear daughter. Do not try to find me".'

'That won't do. You will have to throw your mobile phone into the back of a moving truck,' Shafeeq reminded. Amma laughed heartily. We had reached the airport by then.

I took out Amma's Aadhaar card. 'When did you steal all this?' she asked, with faux annoyance. 'From now on, I am going to keep all my things locked away!' All in all, it felt good. We checked in. 'I had to wait until seventy to get on a plane,' Amma said with a sigh. It was amusing to see how she took in the sights. She looked adoringly at the smart, well-groomed young people at the counters and terminals. 'How energetic and bold!' she said, with a touch of envy. The bookstore near the boarding gates excited her. 'So many books!' she said softly to herself in delight.

Her simple, absolute delight pained me, though. There was a time when she used to go out just to buy books. Had a lifetime membership in the public library, and was always taking pre-publication offers to buy books from booksellers. There used to be a gigantic bookcase at Vasanthaalayam. When the house was sold, she donated the books away to some library. I never saw her reading after Acchan became bedridden. I never bought a book in those times of trouble, when I was grappling with my debts. After I started to earn, I only thought of buying her clothes.

Amma chose *The Ivory Throne*, and I, *Walking with the Comrades*. Amma opened the book and took a long, deep breath, smelling it eagerly. The salesman laughed, amused, and it made her a bit shy. To hide it, she took the book I bought, opened it, and teased me: 'Hmm, so you haven't yet stopped walking!' 'Since when have you been on an ivory throne, Amma?' was my riposte.

I felt a certain lightness. One man was after me, to murder me. Another had reportedly escaped from prison. A third one who was investigating these events had disappeared. But these things felt least important now. Even the thought of the young girls whose minds and bodies my father had ripped apart, drifted away. Only Chechi I could not forget. Her absence troubled me. The third seat next to where we sat was empty. She should have been there. Amma was engrossed in the sights outside. She peeped through the window when we took off. In truth, I had convinced myself that taking care of Acchan as an invalid was Amma's duty and joy. Not just for one or two years, but for a full twenty-four. I felt very guilty. The sights, experiences, journeys, books that she had been denied for a quarter of a century ... My eyes grew misty. 'What is it?' Amma asked. And we had the following conversation:

'Nothing, I just realized how selfish I have been, Amme.'

'Okay. What is its latest manifestation?'

'You loved to travel. I never thought of it.'

'Isn't that an ancient form of selfishness? If you had children, they, too, would have felt the same guilt. And by then, you'd have reached the age in which it becomes hard to travel.'

'Amme, why didn't you tell me at least once – Satya, take care of your father, let me rest a bit?'

'I did not know that I could claim such rest as a right!'

'You are so smart, Amma, did you need to be told that?'

'It isn't about being smart. It is about conditioning. Conditioning that happens when you read and hear the same thing over and over again, meet the same people again and again. You get stuck with the idea that there's nothing beyond what you have seen and heard.'

'This is a stunning observation! How come you never mentioned it before?'

'I took notice of it only recently. When I started talking to Paramarth. When I wondered why he was the way he is. Really, there is a lot we can learn about ourselves from him.'

Amma looked out of the window again and then turned towards me. 'Look at the clouds! Like cotton mattresses laid out to dry without their covers!'

'Maybe Indra's wife Indrani is drying her mattresses!'

'Softly! Enough to make someone go nuts!'

'Since when have you been so scared?'

'Not scared. I don't want to hurt anyone's sentiments.'

'Really? Someone's sentiments will get hurt by this?'

'Some get hurt with much less. I always think of it when I speak with Paramarth.'

Food was served. 'Tell me the truth? What are you up to? Make the old crone wear a new silk sari and then dump her at Rameswaram or someplace?'

I laughed.

'What's the use? The old woman with the fat English book will be back home before me!'

'No, never! I'll take that as an opportunity!'

'What times! Can't trust even the woman who gave birth to you!'

'Well, you can't trust even the RBI governor. Those notes refused were signed by him!' Amma sighed. 'Just fifty thousand rupees. That man must have put it together with so much effort! And it would have helped his kids!'

'You've got to suffer some losses for the nation.'

'Tell me the truth, Satye, is that a warning for me? Where are we going? What hole are you going to push me into?'

'My dearest mother, I have dug no holes! I needed to go to Chennai. Last time when I landed in Bhubaneswar, I just felt that you could have come along too. So this time I booked you a ticket too. Did I even know that you were so wary of me?'

Amma adjusted her spectacles. Her face glowed with affection.

'Thank you. But this trip isn't a sightseeing one just for me, right? You want to look for Tyagu?'

'Vasanthalakshmi is shrewd!'

'Who needs to be shrewd for this? Just common sense will do.' Amma looked at me, tasting the madhura pongal in the food. 'Where have you located Tyagu presently?'

'I haven't traced him. Just a tiny lead is all I have.'

'And what's that lead I don't know of?'

'You know that lead, Amma. The cine actor Rajani.'

Amma stopped eating. She fixed me in a sharp look. 'I should come along with you to meet her?'

'No. What for? She lives on Sterling Road. Our room is at the Taj Coromandel – very close by. You can remain at the hotel. I'll visit her and be back soon.'

After finishing all the food, Amma folded the packets neatly on the food tray. 'Is searching high and low for Satyaprakash so vital for you?' she asked me. 'Shouldn't the police be doing it?'

'But who told you that I am searching for him?' I stopped eating and folded the packets; took the ones Amma had too. 'I am searching for Acchan's past.'

'Why?' Amma was irked, clearly. 'There may be things in the lives of parents that kids need not know. You'd understand if you had kids. What is the point of rummaging through the trash cans and scattering the rotten stuff all around?'

'I want to know why he wants to kill me.'

'Will he stop if you find out?' Her voice sounded tired. It pained me.

'No,' I said. She looked at me expectantly. 'Amme, did you notice something? He's been after me for over some seventeen years. But since 16 November last year, he's been attacking me directly. Even now, though, he needs to keep his cover – so that I don't get to know who he his and what his intention is.' She listened attentively. 'Therefore, I must know. If I find out and he realizes that I know, then he may not try to kill me any more.'

'Aswathy says that he will soon be nabbed by the police.'

'Oh indeed!'

'Why do you distrust her so? She grew up so close to us!'

'Trust has to be felt from within. Don't know why, but I don't feel it.' My voice sounded harsh. Amma fell silent.

We landed in Chennai at twelve-thirty. The jallikattu agitation was going on at the Marina Beach. There was a massive traffic jam. Amma sat in the car, looking around.

'Are you trying to trace the footsteps of your beloved, Vasanthalakshmi?' I asked.

'No, I am looking for my own footsteps,' she said. She gestured with her hand to the back. 'I sold his shirts on the roadside somewhere back there.'

That landed on my chest, it scalded me. I saw Amma standing there, on the street, which had suddenly turned into a sepia-tinted image, holding the shirts and calling out in Tamil, 'Come ... come ... Silk shirts, first-class silk shirts, just one hundred a piece...' The taste of blood hit my tongue – the blood from my heart. The roads we had travelled coiled around me and squeezed me tight, like the arms of an octopus. Wherever they touched, it burned, and the flesh liquefied. I pictured Acchan's first and last journeys here. The first time, as a student. Twelve sets of shirts and trousers. Then as a film producer. Thirty whole years of living lavishly. His last trip? To sell all his assets? Or to borrow from people he knew? And then I remembered our trips to this city. Amma sold shirts, I sold my kidney. The last trip was after that. I met Mitali that time.

I did not have the energy to think more, only felt impatient to reach the hotel. For Amma, this stay was new. Hearing the room tariff, she snapped a bit testily, 'Why spend so much?' 'Where should the owner of Vasanthamaalika be staying, then?' I pulled her leg. I had not chosen this multi-star hotel for the luxury; I had chosen it more for the safety. And I wanted to give Amma the best. That she was happy made me happy too. I noticed how she enjoyed the new sights and meeting new people, the way they talked ... I must take her on a tour of the country, I decided. By the time she washed and changed into a fresh sari, I had already taken one tour of India. Then it struck me – I could not make this wish come true just by myself. My mind fell into despair. A wound inside stung like it were doused with chillies. Would Satyaprakash let me take Amma on a few trips at least? He was somewhere, watching me all the time, I felt. He was going to leap at me when he got a chance, I feared.

After lunch, I relaxed a bit. Amma was still absorbed in the views outside the window. I got up at four-thirty, she was still sitting there.

I ordered filter coffee, got ready to leave. Amma lifted her head, looked at me.

'Want me to come?'

'No, it will be painful for you both.'

'Painful? For me? Those days are all gone. She may feel bad, though. The poor thing, so young she was…' Amma sighed.

That scene flashed past my mind's eye. When she struggled to cover herself before a whole group of people…

'I am so glad he's dead!' I spat out. 'Just think about it. If it were now, he would have been in jail, do you know?'

Amma smiled.

'Satya, men like your father never go to prison. They know how to cover up their crimes – even more than how to commit them.'

'But he was a paedophile, Amma! Your husband, my father, was a paedophile!'

'That was not something we had heard of back then. So many of my own friends were married at fourteen and sixteen! Getting married early, having a child early – used to be considered very positive.'

'Are you trying to justify him?'

'I am just saying that the state of knowledge and awareness was that poor.'

'But Acchan was surely a pervert? Attacking small girls repeatedly…'

'I am just saying that I did not know enough, and wasn't really aware…' Her face turned glum. I felt sorry. There was a limit to how much a daughter could ask her mother. But I had no other way. Who else could I talk to about this? Every bit of information about Acchan pierced my heart like an arrow. Half my blood froze. Almost half of my genes, charred. The eight-year-old who would look adoringly at Acchan, who yearned to catch a whiff of his Brut perfume, writhed in pain somewhere inside me. I wanted to hear something good about him, I wanted to say only good things about him. But, alas. He did not allow it. As long as he lived, he brought me nothing but shame. And after his death, imposed it tenfold on me.

I had Rajani's address. It was not hard to find. I called a cine magazine back home. They gave me the number of their Chennai reporter. He shared her address, number, and some details about her. That is how I came to know that when my father became a pauper, she married a co-actor. Then, when his career waned, she left him, became an industrialist's second wife. She had two girls, one from each of the men.

I booked an Ola cab for four hours and found the house on Sterling Road. The modern house of half a century back. Grand and old. The cab honked, and the security guard came out. He questioned me. I leaned back into the back seat of the car and said, 'I am here to interview her.' He called the house to ask. The gate opened. I reached the porch, and a young man of some eighteen or nineteen opened the door, invited me in. He offered me fruit juice. It was a mansion indeed. Luxury that aimed straight at your eye. I took out a diary from my bag, switched on the recorder on my phone. Rajani took another ten minutes to appear. Her footsteps on the staircase were, without a doubt, alluring. She looked stunning in a black sari with a yellow border, a matching yellow blouse, and a beautiful necklace. Her clothes had been yellow even the first time I saw her, I recalled. Maybe that was her favourite colour. Her hair was now straightened and coloured. From her look it was evident that she had expected more than one person. Seeing just me, she frowned. Her face fell. She was two years my junior, but her eyes shone with the strength of surviving fifty whole years. She was like me – someone who had been through a lot.

'The photographer hasn't arrived yet?' she asked, piqued.

'He will.' I said that without getting up or expressing awe in any way. That was not because I did not respect her. It was to actually rile her. My questions weren't the kind that could be asked meekly or tactfully.

'But your editor told me that it was to be a photo session?' Her voice turned abrasive.

'The interview was my idea.'

'All right, ask what you want to ask,' she commanded. I took a deep breath, crossed my legs and leaned back on the sofa, and without a tinge of mercy, asked, 'The gardener Tyagu, who used to work here – where is he now?'

She flushed. 'Is the interview about Tyagu?'

'Yes,' I said coolly.

'How is that relevant?'

'You'll soon see.'

Her patience had reached its limit. She got up.

'I don't want to speak with you. Let me ask your editor why they send such boorish people to conduct interviews!'

She pulled out her phone in anger, searched for the number. This amused me. The picture of a young girl grabbing a bed sheet desperately to cover herself rose in my mind. I kept sitting, unmoved; there was no rush. She dialled the number and pressed the phone to her ear. I told her: 'It is foolish to call the editor. They will publish my interview anyway. Then don't be mad. Remember, it is you who forced me to do this.'

She frowned and glared at me. And then her expression changed to one of worried surprise and alertness.

'You ... Where have I seen you before?' she asked.

'Call the editor, I'll tell him.'

She hung up. And glared at me again.

'Shall I describe the circumstances under which we met?'

I leaned back into the sofa some more.

'You were lying on a bed when we met. Those days, the kurta-pyjama set that used to be called "Punjabi dress" was in fashion. Yours was a yellow kurta, with large white-leaf prints on it. It was on the floor. Along with it were a black lace bra and pink nylon panties with a red rose sewn on it. My mother picked up all of these and handed them to you...'

The blood drained from her face. She was pale now, and clearly terrified. I liked that. Nisha Chechi's words came back to me – 'He did it not for pleasure. He wanted to frighten me.' I now knew the kind of pleasure he had experienced from terrorizing another. I found myself afraid of my own self now. Rajani could find the strength to open her mouth again only after some time.

'What do you want?' she asked.

'Satyapriya. That is my name. I am older than you – and also, have seen more of the world.'

'All right, what is it that you want?'

'Just two answers.'

'If it is money…' Her voice dried up.

'The money that you received from my father for sexually exploiting you?'

'What is it that you wish to know then?'

'I told you. Just two answers. First, to the question: Where is Tyagu now?'

She thought for a moment. 'Why do you need to know?'

'If you aren't inclined to answer, then all right. Let me ask the second question. The girl who used to live in Acchan's guest house – where is she now?'

She looked even more perplexed. 'Why do you need to know all this?'

'To protect you, of course. You are happy now. Your father used to have a tea shop on the Tamil Nadu border. My father went there to choose a location for his movie. You served him tea then. He liked you, he cast you as a child actor, and then as heroine. You who started from such a humble place, now live in this posh area of Chennai in a mansion worth crores. If these old tales begin spreading, it is you who'll suffer, not me.'

'Are you threatening me?'

'No, it is just some advice.'

She became rather ill at ease. Her fuddled look pleased me.

'Tyagu Annan died.'

'When?'

'Two or three years back. Brain tumour, it was.'

'What's the proof?'

'His wife and kids are still around.'

'Where?'

'His eldest son Shanmugha Selvan runs a vegetable store in the Koyambedu market. The eldest daughter Murugammal was a clerk in the Greater Chennai Corporation office. The second son is a chef in a TTDC hotel; I think his name is Palani Selvan. There was another daughter, Valliyammal – she's a schoolteacher in Valasaravakkam.'

I noted down all these details.

'And the girl from the guest house…?'

She looked even more befuddled, wondering whether to speak or not. I cut through her thoughts swiftly. 'Was that girl my father's daughter?'

She looked shocked, and that expression gave me a shock too. But even when I asked that question, I had expected a 'no' for an answer. I held on. She found her voice again only after a long pause.

'She … she became pregnant.'

'At what age?'

'I wasn't even born then. This came from Tyagu Annan.'

'What did he tell you?'

'That he had a daughter while he was a student. That she came and stayed in the guest house during her vacations.'

'Who made her pregnant?'

'It was a production office, too. So many people must have come and gone? These are cinema folk!'

'Did she give birth?'

'I don't know the details. Maybe Tyagu Annan's wife Maariammal would know.'

'How can I find out?'

'I have Shanmugha Selvan's number. Will share it.'

Rajani gave me a number. I found myself develop respect for her. Someone who maintained ties with a family that had worked for her. I got up to leave, put the phone and diary back into my bag, folded my hands in salutation.

'Many thanks, and my apologies for barging in like this.'

'Sit down please. Have some coffee?'

'No, your photoshoot must begin soon?'

'Stay till they come. Did you come alone?'

'My mother's with me.'

Her face changed colour again.

'Waiting in the car?'

'No, at the hotel. I'd asked her to come, but she felt it might be too much for you.'

Her eyes moistened.

'No other woman has shown me as much compassion. I have thought about your mother again and again. She thought of another woman's dignity even when she'd seen her husband in that situation with her own eyes ... I need to ask for her forgiveness...'

'Why should you? Aren't we bound to actually beg for your forgiveness? For the horrible cruelty my father subjected you to at that tender age?'

She laughed bitterly.

'Beg forgiveness of me? If you do so, so should the wards of countless others. And besides, my father has claimed the price of each moment I spent with your father.' She sighed. 'I hate these others more than your father! These people who gave birth to me, raised me. I was sent off to Madras to be with that man barely two months after I got my first period...' Her eyes glistened again. 'He ... it was in a moving car ... The driver was seeing it all in the rear-view mirror. That day, after your father fell asleep, that driver stopped the car and called me out. He made me climb on to the bonnet of the car...'

'Ulahannan Maaman...?' My eyes nearly popped out of my head. She found that very funny. Didn't I tell you that fear in someone else's eyes can be rather intoxicating?

'The next day, when we reached Madras, the director came to see me. I slept with him that day. The next day, the actors – two of them. On the third day, my Appa and Amma arrived. The boss – your father – gave him five bundles of one-hundred-rupee notes. Once he took those, he was never the Appa of the old.'

She sobbed, apologized, wiped her tears at the corners of her eyes carefully so that her kohl and make-up would not be smudged. But it wasn't easy. The tears broke free and flowed down her cheeks. When her sobs ended, something like the cooing of a pigeon remained in her throat.

'I was with a retired IAS officer when I heard that your father had been attacked – an old man of sixty-five. I kissed the old coot over and over again in delight. The fool thought he was being doused in affection! Anyway, besides what he gave Appa, he also gave me a bundle of hundreds. I thanked god many times that day. It was one of the happiest days I'd ever had...'

I prepared to leave. Dusk was falling. She accompanied me to the cab. After I climbed in, I said to her: 'Acchan passed away a couple of months back.'

She looked taken aback. She tried to say 'Oh I didn't know...' or something of that sort, but I didn't hear that too well. The poor thing, if it makes her glad, let it be so, I thought to myself. When the cab moved past the gate, I turned around to look at her. She was still there. I sighed heavily; felt drained enough to collapse. You may have noticed how some truths are so, so heavy. Especially those that have to do with wealth, love and death. So many such heavy truths hung from my heart. No wonder I felt depleted.

I reached the hotel yearning to lie down. And then Amma's 'surprise' hit me. I rang the bell, there was no answer. I used the key card, opened the door, went in. There was no one in the room! My heart pounded in fear. I called the reception at once to know if the guest in 2303 had left any message. No, they said, but they had seen her step out. I called her several times, but just could not reach her. I was gripped by a deadly fear and anxiety. Within ten minutes, I travelled from hell to heaven and back. And then, all of a sudden, she appeared! With a bunch of shopping bags. I was furious; I told her off, scolded her, reprimanded her. Then I broke down and asked, 'Amme, why did you give me such a scare? Make me so worried?' It was all a joke for her. Her reply was full of sarcasm: 'Oh, you haven't seen anything yet! So much is to come!'

Some time passed. Then, she came to me, ran her fingers gently through my hair, and asked playfully, 'Why is my daughter so glum? Look, I got bored. Wanted to take a walk. Am I a bird to be caged?' She tried to justify herself. The need to speak to her was entirely mine, not Amma's, so I let it go. We discussed my meeting with Rajani.

Amma had two questions.

1. Did you ask Rajani what that girl's name was?

2. Did you ask her if she knew Satyaprakash?

'Why should I ask?' I argued. 'There's no chance that she'd know.'

Then Amma pointed out to me a general principle: 'The questions we ask must not be those for which others may have sure answers. We must ask what we need to know. Never underestimate anyone.'

Amma lay down and fell asleep that instant. I stayed awake. Amma wasn't pointing to an axiom in crime investigation, really. It was a general truth, of human relationships. Amma lay on her side. Her palms were joined together and placed under her cheek. Her legs were slightly bent. I covered her with a blanket. As I sat there gazing at her face, I felt the agony of my heart being ripped open. What a life she had lived! Married a man who pretended to be in love with her just for her wealth; then lost it all. Suffered indignities, poverty, severe want. For a quarter of a century, cared for a bedridden man, cleaning up his piss and shit, washing him, feeding him. Not once had I asked her if she wanted a book, or if she wanted to travel. And, of course, I never asked if she needed a man's love. Nobody taught us that mothers, too, had a right to rest and love and travel.

Anyway, it was not too bad. One was saved of guilty feelings.

FORTY-SEVEN

When I set out to meet Shanmugha Selvan, Amma accompanied me. That name had made me imagine a handsome man of forty-five, but the real Shanmugha Selvan on his bike was well past sixty. Five and a half feet tall, weighing well above a hundred kilos. White shirt, white trousers. Sacred ash on his forehead. On his right wrist, several black and red threads of varied wear. Numerous chains on his neck, made of various materials – from gold to crystal. Our Ola cab followed his bike. It stopped in front of a five-storey building in a narrow lane that looked like a thousand-rupee note suspended vertically. There was hardly any gap between the road and the house; we could step into the house directly from the car. But that did not mean that the house had no gate or the small sacred platform with tulsi plants growing on it. At the iron gate, a Murugan resembling N.T. Rama Rao stood bearing in his hand a tiled spear. The peacock, his mount, was found encrusted in concrete on the fifth floor of the house.

He looked burly on the outside, but Shanmugha Selvan was childlike. He stepped down from the bike with his palms joined together in greeting, already. When Amma emerged from the cab, he lay down flat on the ground in obeisance. Amma was hugely embarrassed. It was as if a goddess had appeared there. Not knowing how to bless the devotee, Amma looked quite bewildered. She scanned the place discreetly to check if anyone was looking. Noticing that all the neighbours, who lived cheek by jowl in that closely packed area, were witnessing the drama, she turned even more sheepish. She helped him up, but Shanmugha Selvan's devotion was unaffected. She was escorted to the inside of the house, along with the junior goddess, myself.

It was a thousand-square-foot house. 'The house is small,' he explained as we were welcomed into the front room. 'But the four floors above have been rented out.' I liked his sofa set with the red velvet covering. There were framed photographs on all the walls. Amma was about to sit down, but it seemed like something on the wall had given her a shock. I looked in the direction of the wall and her shock proved infectious. The wall at the back was covered with Acchan's photos, framed and hanging. Black-and-white and colour photos, in equal numbers. The most prominent of these was one with Acchan posing with Sivaji Ganesan, Prem Nazir, and a fat Tamil man – a black-and-white image. The photos had garlands of blue electric series bulbs around them. Lotus-shaped neon bulbs were lit above each of the photos. The blue lights kept twinkling, one at a time, in a row, along each of the garlands, and the lotus bulbs shone benevolently on them all.

That sight moistened my eyes. I had never imagined that my father's memory would be mounted so high, anywhere. The Tamil man in the prominent photo was a smaller version of Shanmugha Selvan. That's Tyagu Annan, I guessed. The wall was like a guest book from Acchan's guest house. Photos instead of signatures. A photo museum.

Shanmugha Selvan went to the kitchen to call his wife. Her name was Sundari. Seeing us, she was beside herself with joy.

'Please sit down, Madam ... we have wished so long to meet you. We wanted to come to Kerala, see Producer Saar at least one time ... It didn't work out. We couldn't even get your address ... Producer Saar just vanished into thin air ... How sad it was for us. Now, seeing you, it is our good deeds that let us have this favour!' She laughed and wept.

Shanmugha Selvan went to the room on the left and called to someone, 'Come, Amma, please get up, she is here. Come, speak with her.' Maariammal, I guessed. I was right. She came out holding her son's arm for support, steps unsteady.

Maariammal was a small woman, old and wizened, with large toda-ear studs and studs on both sides of her nose. Her sari was draped in a way that her calves were visible. 'Producer Saar's wife? Where? Let me see her! Ah, our Producer Saar has passed!' she muttered as she came to meet us. Amma went close to her and held her hand. She frowned and peered at Amma. 'Abba! She is like Mahalakshmi! Goddess of Prosperity!' she exclaimed, clearly delighted by Amma. And to ward off the evil eye that her admiration evoked, she circled her hands around Amma's head and, cupping her palms, pressed her fingers against her temples. My short hair, shirt and jeans assuredly received little approval, it seemed. The family's focus was surely on Amma. Amma rose to the occasion. She got up, greeted the old lady with her palms joined, and made her sit next to her. 'When did you come? Ah, why, we couldn't even come and see Producer Saar once! We knew of his death only when Rajani Madam told us yesterday! Oh, you have just one daughter? What does she do? Not yet married?' The questions flowed. Amma answered them. In between, excellent filter coffee and slices of ripe mangoes were served. After the coffee, I came to our business.

'Shanmugha Anna, do you know why we have come to meet you?' I asked him in Tamil.

'Please speak in Malayalam. I can speak four languages.'

'All right, we came here...'

'Rajani Amma told me. You want to know about Producer Saar—'

'—Producer Saar is a great man!' Maariammal interrupted, weeping. Her Tamil was the purer one; she wept and beat her breast. 'He was not man, he was god! Lived with both his hands open, so generous! Never refused anything we asked! He would help just anyone! Never bothered about anyone's caste or faith or anything!

Just one small weakness – but is that a weakness? Men, after all? How
to blame? A weakness for women…! His friends took advantage of
that, sucked him dry … So he lost everything … My husband used to
say … those who get into cinema, they have a sun rising over them.
But for some, it becomes afternoon too soon and the sun sets too
early. For some, the afternoon lasts long. But the sun does set, that is
for sure. For Producer Saar, noon came too soon, and also sunset…'

'How did Tyagu Maama meet Producer Saar?' I cut into her flow.
That question made her even more enthusiastic.

'Producer Saar first came to Madras to study for the doctor exam.
There was a tea shop near where he stayed. My husband worked there.
Then he dropped the studies, went back, and returned as producer.
Saar came looking for my man – Tyagu, you come with me, he said.
My man ran to him, he was so fond of Producer Saar.' She wiped her
nose and eyes. 'He came back to Madras when I was pregnant with
Selvan. I was married at fifteen. I lost my first baby in the womb.
Then for seven years in a row, he went to Palani, climbed the hill,
prayed to Murugan … That is how he was born. He went to Palani
once every year for as long as he was alive.'

'Paatti, do you know why my father decided to give up studying?'
I asked.

'Some or other small problems…'

'Amma, tell them the truth. They know all…' Shanmugha Selvan
nudged her gently.

'I have heard that my father married a young girl then. And that
she died in childbirth. Do you know anything about it, Paatti?' I asked,
getting impatient.

'Yes, I have … but … how, when, I don't know…' Maariammal was
dithering.

'Didn't Tyagu Maama know that my father had a daughter?'

'Of course he did.'

'Do you know details about her? Name? Where she lives? How
much she studied? What she does now?'

'Child, I don't remember much since some days now...'

Amma leaned back in her chair and shot a glance at Selvan. He faltered like a schoolboy, leaning back further into the wall, sighing. Then he said, 'The child was named Satyaprabha.'

'And her mother's name?' Amma asked, summoning an imposing look.

'She died. It was my man who saved Producer Saar then.' Maariammal got back into the conversation fervently.

'This girl lived next door to Saar. Her mother had died giving birth to her second child. Her father then killed himself. It was their old grandmother who took care of her and her brother. She seduced poor Saar.'

'So she had a brother?' Amma asked.

'Yes, he was just four or five when she died.'

'Is he still alive?'

'Have not known anything about them after the guest house got sold.'

'Did he ever come to the guest house?' I asked.

'He did make a ruckus there once asking for his sister's girl.'

'Did you stay with Tyagu Maama in the guest house, Paatti?'

'No, no, we were in Alandur. It was Producer Saar who bought us this house. We came over here then.'

'How many years has it been since?' I asked Shanmugha Selvan.

'That was in 1973. After this incident.'

Amma intervened: 'Maariamma, tell us clearly, please. Producer Saar married Satyaprabha's mother. Satyaprabha was born. The mother died giving birth. What happened then? Who raised Satyaprabha?'

'Amma, what is this? These are men, no? They will put their feet in the mud when they see it and wash it clean when they find water. Don't have bad thoughts about Saar because of that. God gave him everything – brains, health, energy – in plenty. But also a weakness, like a hole in a new copper pot. That is all...'

'Yes, that is fine, Maariamma. But who brought up Satyaprabha after Saar stopped his studies and went back?'

'Her paatti and uncle, that is the mother's brother.'

'After Satyaprabha was born, Producer Saar ran away from here to his home. Then how did they meet again?'

'When the movie *Satyam Shivam Sundaram* was released, they saw him in a photo in some newspaper. Her paatti and uncle went to meet him, to ask him to pay for her upkeep.'

My mouth fell open. Amma, too, looked jolted.

'Producer Saar was a great man. He agreed to take care of the child. Put her in a big boarding school, educated her.'

'Have you seen her, Maariamma?'

'Yes, I have...' Shanmugha Selvan said. 'During school vacations, Saar brought the child to the guest house. Her grandmother stayed with her then.'

'Then how did she get pregnant?'

'That was her uncle – her bridegroom by custom among us Tamils – they liked each other. The old woman encouraged it.'

My hand flew to my forehead in despair; Amma looked stunned.

'When the child returned to the boarding school, the teachers there found out that she was pregnant. Producer Saar sent someone to fetch her. Her uncle got to know of it, and he went over to get her. It was a big fuss, a fight. Amid all the hullaballoo, the girl's grandmother hit her head hard somewhere and died.'

I could not muster the courage to look at Amma.

'It was very bad. The police came. My father called me at once. I admitted to the crime and went to jail...' Shanmugha Selvan said that with pride. I felt my skin peeling. I threw a glance at Amma out of the corner of my eye and saw her face ashen.

'I was in jail for two years. Producer Saar hired a good lawyer, got me out. He set me up this shop in the Koyambedu market.'

He tried to console us. But for some time, both of us were speechless.

'And what happened to Satyaprabha?' I asked, after a long spell of silence.

'She was married off.'

Amma and I looked at each other.

'And what happened to her uncle?'

'He was nowhere to be seen afterwards. We don't know if he is alive.'

'And what about her baby?'

'One of them died.'

We started violently.

'That means?'

'There were three babies. Like little rats. One died then. We don't know if the other two lived or died.'

'Where are they now?'

'Saar got them adopted.'

'Who took them?'

'Don't know. They were taken away on the very night they were born.'

'And Satyaprabha?'

'She was married off after six months.'

'Who married her?'

'Someone from Kerala.'

My body went cold.

'Any idea where she is in Kerala?'

'No...'

'Do you know who took the babies?'

'Madam, we don't know so much. I doubt if even Appa knew. Appa just obeyed whatever Saar told him. That was it.'

There was no use prolonging this meeting. I started to get up. Amma ran her eyes over the photos on the wall and asked that question then: 'Don't you have any photos of Satyaprabha?'

'Selva, look for the photos,' Maariammal ordered. He ordered his wife in turn, 'Sundari, get the album.' Sundariammal ran into

the house. We heard sounds of something being opened and closed
and something falling down. Soon, an old album was brought out.
Selvan opened it, began to search for Satyaprabha's photos. Unable
to contain my curiosity, I joined him in the exercise. In the end, we
found a picture of a ten-year-old girl, in a green puff-sleeved blouse
and skirt, peering curiously at the world, standing in the middle of an
old woman – also standing, upright – and Tyagu, who was, facing the
camera with his arms crossed.

'This is Satyaprabha,' Selvan said.

I took a good look. A whitish scar was beginning to spread over her
face in the photo, but she looked very familiar.

'You have just this snap?'

Amma took the album from me. There was another photo of hers,
from later. She was clad in a half-sari. Her hair was a mass of springy
curls, and she wore wreaths of kanakambaram flowers in it. On one
side of her stood Tyagu Maama, and on the other, a skinny young man
with a sallow face on which a thin moustache showed. His face was
not clear.

'Is this her uncle?' Amma asked.

'I think so, Madam,' said Selvan. 'I have not seen him.'

I took another look at the photo. How to locate the man with
this old image? Post it on Facebook? Or in the *Dinamalar*? My head
reeled. I considered the prospect of staying there for the day. It might
revive the old lady's memory and we may be able to extract more
information, I felt. Most of the people I knew were of that sort. They
could never recall all the relevant information at one go. It was like
trying to reconstruct an elephant in the mind's eye with one's eyes
closed – the trunk here, the tail there, finding each part one by one,
and then putting it all together. We must visit them again on the
way back from Mahabalipuram, I decided. When Maariammal and
Sundariammal would be by themselves. They might recall better in
Shanmugha Selvan's absence, it was certain. Don't know if you have

noticed, but the very presence of men often sets in motion a certain censoring. Like playing hide-and-seek in the headmaster's room. After all, a headmaster is a headmaster? That truth always bothers us. It controls our unconscious. I got up. Amma was still engrossed in the album. In the page with Satyaprabha's photo.

'May I please take this photo?' Amma asked. 'I will get a copy made and return it by tomorrow itself.'

'Yes, please, take everything you need. It is all yours, really,' replied Maariammal.

Meanwhile, Selvan brought a suitcase, the big one that Gulf returnees used to carry once. When it was placed on the low table and dusted, all of us were thrust into a veritable sneezing competition. 'Did you not dust it? Didn't I tell you they were coming?' Selvan scolded his wife. Sundariammal pulled the edge of her sari and wiped the suitcase clean. Maariammal chose a key from the bunch that hung from the edge of her sari. It was I who opened it. My heart throbbed at the thought that everywhere he went, my father seemed to have crammed things into a box and left it there. Who knew what foetus was going to leap out of this one! Fortunately, the only items in the box were a bunch of old photo albums. Ones with thick oil paper between the pages. Eleven in all. Exactly the same as the number of movies my father had produced.

'When the guest house was sold, Appa brought all this here. This sofa, dining table, and two large wooden almirahs were given to us by Saar back then. Many other smaller things too. Just take care of this box for me, he asked. When I repay my debts and come back to make my next movie, I will take it, he said. But he never came.' Selvan sighed. 'Appa would not let any of us even touch it. He dusted it now and then to keep it safe from termites and cockroaches. Even when he was nearing death, he reminded us to keep Producer Saar's box safe.'

I turned the pages of the albums greedily. My father was present in most of the photos. Each was from a particular movie he made. The seal on each said: 'Top Stills Studio'.

'Is this studio still working?' I asked Selvan.

'I don't know, Madam,' he said. 'In those days, photographers came along with Saar to take pictures. Appa was crazy about photos. He has made an appearance in almost all of Saar's movies.'

'Can we take this home?' I asked them, rather hesitantly.

'Why ask even?' Selvan said promptly. 'All this is yours.'

'He was God to us. All that you see here is his generosity. Our bodies are from the food he gave. He got Murugammal her job, sent Palani and Valli to college…'

We struggled to calm them down, and struggled even more to lug that huge suitcase. Selvan got a boy from the neighbourhood to help him lift it into the cab. Before we got into the cab, Selvan and Sundari fell at Amma's feet again. I invited them to our home in Kerala. Selvan was dealing with the losses from the note ban, he said. There were many pushcart vendors who used to take vegetables from him, sell them, and pay him on a daily basis. They had lost their income. But he was hopeful that since there would be no black money now, the future was going to be full of profits. 'Let the business stabilize,' he said, 'we will surely visit.'

~

We were silent while we sat inside the cab. I was hungry. But Amma did not let us stop the cab. As soon as we reached the hotel room, she opened the albums and began to look through them. 'These are stills from *Satyam Shivam Sundaram*! … Look, Miss Kumari is so lovely! … Do you know who this is? It is Ramu Kariat! … Hey, Vayalar! … Oh, here's Thikkurishi!' – Amma was in a state of high excitement. I did not respond. I was steeped in the fullness of presence – which is Absence. Emptiness. My mind felt vacant. My thoughts were tangled, like a ball of twine. I did not know where it started or ended. I kept muttering to myself: Satyapriya, Satyaprabha, Satyaprakash.

Is Satyaprakash Satyaprabha's uncle?

Or her son?

If so, does he have a brother?

My head felt smoggy. Then, all of a sudden, Amma almost screamed, 'Satye!' She had her finger on a black-and-white photo in an album that lay open on the low table. Her face showed shock and horror like never before. It was a photo of Satyaprabha. Her wedding, apparently. She had grown. Her body was glowing. She wore a silk sari with a golden zari border. Her curly locks were tamed with oil, plaited, and adorned with jasmine garlands. She wore wedding jewellery – a netti-chutti on her forehead, the odyaanam around her waist, golden hair-ornaments. But she looked like a guilty one, head bowed. By her side was a thin young man with hair grown long, hippie-style, up to his neck. His expression was like one who had just admitted to a crime someone else had committed. Amma's index finger brushed against his face in the photo. I looked again. I had seen him somewhere. But where? I thought hard.

'Do you recognize him?' Amma's voice sounded like she was being strangled.

'Very familiar…' I said.

'Dinakaran Pillai!' Amma whispered the name. 'The policeman Dinakaran Pillai!'

Shock, jolt, terror, suspense, alarm, fright, shudder – in a second, I understood all of these and their synonyms and multiple meanings. A shiver spread all over my body, from head to toe. Dinakaran Pillai's image rose up slowly in front of my eyes. Appooppan used to refer to him as 'PC 614'. He was later promoted as sub-inspector. We had heard then that Acchan was responsible for this advance in his career. I remembered how he would visit Acchan regularly. Acchan used to exercise a peculiar sort of freedom with him; also displayed an unusual sort of submission to him. He, in turn, put on show an exaggerated façade of civility before Acchan and seemed to exercise an unreasonable amount of influence over him. I realized why the fire at our house, the poison in our well, and the attack on my father went un-investigated.

I shook with fear. Steam rose from my body. My palms and inner thighs were drenched in sweat. Amma's eyes were still fixed on the album. She, too, was thrown off balance. But compared to my terror and horror, her shock was nothing. In fact, I should have rejoiced in that moment. I was preparing for a huge leap in my crime investigation. I was about to land in the front yard of Satyaprakash's house. But I had sprained my foot. I was thrown back into the past.

– Into the vehicle the police had forced me after I got out of the lab Sriram had locked me in.

– Into the police quarters in which the then Circle Inspector, Dinakaran Pillai, lived.

– Into that rickety house built by some public works contractor who had cheated on cement and steel.

– Into that bedroom to which he led me after sending the policemen away.

My tears rained on the album. Until then, Dinakaran Pillai had been just a policeman to me. A corrupt wretch. An evil man who, when he got the chance, tried to prey upon the daughter of the man to whom he had pawned his sense of self-respect once. But he was not just that, apparently. He was also my sister's husband. I thought then of my older sister Satyaprabha. She, who was already the mother of three infants at the time of my birth. She, who had to turn away from them and their father and marry someone else. I recalled her husband's body. When I saw him, he was a bulky, obese man. His thighs were covered in ugly, whitish fungal scabs. His sweat stank so much that one could faint from it. My heart was shattered when I realized that the nausea that I endured for just a day, my sister had to suffer all her life. My poor Valyechi – my older sister. She, who should have been laughing with me and Chechi. She, who should have been joking and quarrelling with us, getting high and going crazy on sisterly love. I wept in her memory.

Why? Can't a woman investigator of crime weep?

FORTY-EIGHT

Fucking crime investigation! It ruined my sleep, and by night, I started sneezing. And that grew into a cold and fever. With the trip to Mahabalipuram the next day, it worsened. Our return flight was on the following day. During the day, Amma went around town by herself. I warned her not to buy books. The suitcase with the albums weighed more than twenty kilos already. But she still bought Ambedkar's *Annihilation of Caste*. I was too weak to open my eyes or sit up. She managed to complete the web check-in and pay for extra baggage online with a little help from me. But on our way back, she, too, started sneezing. We both went to the hospital the next day. The medicine did not help, and Amma took to the bed.

That was unexpected. I had never seen Amma ill and bedridden. When the medication did not seem to be helping much, I began to worry. That seemed to cure my fever. I even forgot Satyaprakash. Amma was in delirium one whole night; she vomited non-stop, almost. I was terrified, even more than I had been on the night on which the assassin had shot at me. All my pride evaporated. I whimpered. Sarada Chechi put a piece of wet cloth on Amma's forehead and took advice from some doctor, who prescribed some pills. Harish got the medicines from a twenty-four-hour pharmacy. My eyes were swollen from crying, and I thought that my chest would explode any moment. I forgot the assassination attempt, the assassin, his mother, the 'S'-shaped dagger, Anurup Shetty, Samir Sayyid, even Dinakaran Pillai. I was now just an emotion, and it was not clear if it was fear or suspense.

Fortunately, Amma's fever abated the next day. But she was still exhausted. 'If it's going to be like this, how are we going to go on the all-India tour?' I fretted in between. 'I am done travelling with you!' was the reply. In the midst of all this, my investigation got shelved. While she was recovering, Amma finished *The Ivory Throne* and got into *Annihilation of Caste*. I could not muster the courage to move from her side. 'Won't give me a moment of peace,' she grumbled at times. One day, she, in fact, exploded. 'Stop sitting beside me all day like a broody hen and go get your crime investigation done, girl!' Actually, I was sick of it now. First of all, Satyaprakash seemed to have forgotten me. Besides, what all garbage emerged from the trash can as one probed deeper and deeper! My own sores – pus-filled, termite-ridden, rotten, stinking. Why should I continue? Why not find some other work?

But you won't believe it – a story half-heard is like a tiger that could only half-eat its prey. It will come back until it manages to eat all of it. My story, too, came in search of me, escorted by a statue of Gandhiji, complete with the round spectacles and the staff. This was what happened.

On the day we left for Chennai, Dr Ramakrishnan sent me a message on FB. I did not see it. He was in the Gir forests. While in Chennai I had been too busy to even check my face, leave alone Facebook. So he called me. I described Amma's fever to him. He came over in a red Maruti Baleno, accompanied by Irshad. They met Amma; we shared a meal of tapioca and hot sardine curry. I asked him about Gujarat. 'We were lucky,' Irshad said. 'We sighted an Asiatic lion. It's rare except in March.' It was then that Dr Ramakrishnan took out the gift – the Gandhi statue I mentioned before, complete with the round spectacles and the staff. That day was the eightieth anniversary of his first visit to Kerala. Amma was the one who remembered that. She, too, liked the gift. I put it in the glass showcase in our living room. 'I have wanted to visit Wardha since long,' said Dr Ramakrishnan.

'I'd like to go too,' I added.

'Naturally. We have some genes in common – that draw us towards Gandhi.'

'Upper-caste genes, Valyaccha?' I teased him.

'I feel that no Indian can resist a return to Gandhi. At some point in their lives.'

'But let us not be blind to his failures,' Irshad opposed him.

'Just because someone has failed, they don't become irrelevant,' Amma added to the debate. She had been reading Ambedkar and was enthused by what she read.

The day would have ended that way. But it did not. That other tiger got hungry, and it crept into the bushes where the soul it had left half-eaten, lay. All that went into a tiger became a part of it. The prey and predator would then seek the rest of the prey together. But when Dr Ramakrishnan invited me to go with him to town, I could not have imagined myself to be a part of my story seeking the rest of it. My only attraction was the pleasure of going around town with him. Irshad stayed with Amma. We set out.

~

'My dear child, since you left, I have been thinking about you all the time. You were in my mind when we were in Wardha too. Very strange. A daughter entering my life in my eighty-fourth year, telling me a story, and leaving!'

'In truth, we are our stories, Valyaccha.'

'But we don't know those stories!'

'That's because we don't seek them.'

'No one has taught us to seek our stories.'

'Because of that we end up not knowing ourselves, nor do we know others.'

'One reason for that is that we lack the humility to treat ourselves as characters in a story.'

'If that humility were common, the world would have been so much better a place!'

'True. I thought of that while at Wardha. There were two common characters in our stories, right?'

'Yes, Grandfather Thuruthel and my father.'

'Grandfather Thuruthel was my grandmother's brother.'

'I learned only the other day that my grandmother's mother had two husbands.'

'Oh, there is so much more that you are yet to learn! Leave that for now. What have you discovered about your father? Tell me only if you trust me.'

'There are limitations to how much a daughter can reveal about her father to someone past eighty, Valyaccha.'

He laughed, tilted his head towards me, and smiled affectionately. 'Your retorts!'

'Those are from my mother's genes.'

'I can see that. Just wondering how Sivaprasad could put up with her!'

'I ask her just the opposite. How could she put up with him?'

'No, no, I am certain that it was not your mother but Sivaprasad who must have struggled. Because people with a sense of humour can carry on with anyone. But for those who do not have it, every moment with a humorous person will be a torture.'

'She's a bright one, but Amma is a romantic. It was romanticism that felled her.'

'But it is good to see you both. A mother-daughter duo that never gives anyone a dull day!'

'You didn't tell us about your family, Valyaccha?'

'What to say? I went to London. Earned the FRCS. Went to the US, got another degree. Then returned to London, got married.'

'Was she Indian?'

'Yes. Malayali. From Kottayam. They had migrated to London. Her father was a medical man too. We met in London.' He sighed. 'We were very happy. We had it all. Good jobs, incomes, two wonderful little boys, a lovely home…'

'Made for each other?'

'That was what we thought. Until we both hit thirty-five. One day she came over to the hospital where I worked.'

I looked at him with concern.

'She didn't take the car, she had come by the Tube. Waited for me in the lobby. I came out, got my car. We drove back. When we neared the park near our house, she asked me to stop. Ramu, I need to talk, she said. She had been very moody since a few days, but she would often be like that, so I was not so worried.'

I became worried now.

'She told me – Ramu, I like you a lot, I love you too. I have no complaints about you at all. But I am not sexually satisfied. I miss the passion. I don't know what that would be – all I know is that I am not happy.'

I sat there, stumped.

'Satya, remember, this was around a half-century back. An Indian man, a Malayali, was not prepared for such a thing back then.'

'And then?' I asked.

'I was shattered. Is there someone else, I asked her. Yes, she said. Who is he, I asked. And she said…'

I was unsettled. Valyacchan was calm as he drove. We were crossing the sea bridge. A strong scent – of fish drying, or of ozone, whatever – pushed itself into the car. He continued:

'It was later that I found out. She had a close woman friend as a student in India. They had a relationship. At that time, in that age, it was a source of guilt. They parted then. Both of them married. Had children. This friend became a university teacher and came to the UK on a fellowship. The old girlfriends met again. And they realized their real needs…' He sighed heavily again.

'And?' I asked him, bursting with curiosity.

'We divorced, but stayed on two separate floors of the same building. That was typical of us Malayalis. To maintain the impression of still being a family – in the eyes of the children, society, family. Her friend completed her research and went back to India. After that, my wife – sorry, ex-wife – Rugmini decided to return to Kerala. But she fell ill with cancer. Her treatment lasted years; she was never able to go back. I was with her till her last.'

'You were both in the same house?'

'Yes, where else to go? But there's something, Satya. That changed me. Until then, I was just a careerist, wanting to conquer more and more. I was unfaithful to my wife, several times, when I went abroad. But the day my wife confessed to me that she was not happy with me sexually, my confidence and pride disappeared. I found it hard to face people. I drank day and night those days. And once got arrested for drunken driving. Rugmini got me out on bail. The next day she asked me, maybe I should not have told you the truth?' He smiled. 'That was "the moment" of my life. The moment in which someone who had been inside a pitch-dark cell all his life stepped out into the light. The light pierced my eyes – it was painful, you know. But gradually, my eyes adjusted to it. I asked myself – what did I want? To betray myself? Or accept the truth? Refuse the unpleasant truth? Or silence her? The harshness of the truth hurt me. But no matter how much you lie, the truth remains the truth. Like a foetus that can't be aborted. It will come out when the time is ripe. It is a biological reality.'

I was silent. What was I to say? I was trying to seek my story when this strange tale popped up. But let me tell you from my experience – stories can betray you. The woodcutter might mistake a tree to be a forest from its spread and verdure. He'll choose a trunk and start chopping. Only by the time his blood turns into sweat will he notice that what he had taken for a tree trunk was merely the root.

We had reached town. People grow old not when their hair turns grey but when they can't make out the roads. Memories troubled me.

Naturally, I remembered Chechi. Appooppan's silver-tipped walking stick, his starched and ironed jubbah and mundu, the fried rice at Hotel Sudarsan, chilli chicken at Supreme Bakers, movies at the theatres Grand-Prince, Archana-Aradhana … they squirmed up to the surface of my mind like the etta fish in the lake when you throw them rice. Dr Ramakrishnan's story was already gnawing into me. And on top of it, the pain from my broken past, like a severed bough. Truly, bygones should not be referred to as the past; they should be called spectral time. The past is after all time's spectre. That is why it acquires unearthly beauty, like the spectres of humans. Like the bloodsucking vampire, the Yakshi. It needs to lure the life force out of the living into some black palm-tree top, teach them a lesson, leaving behind just the teeth and nails.

'Have we reached the Collectorate Junction? There's a Vasanta Paurnami Auditorium somewhere here.' Dr Ramakrishnan spoke to himself.

I was in a daze, like a butterfly which had just broken out of its pupa. The town wasn't what I'd seen back in caterpillar times. It had changed from the very roots. The Vasanta Paurnami Auditorium was not alien to me. It belonged to my valyamaaman. All four of our cousins got married there. Amma did not attend those weddings. Chechi and I attended the first two. I went by myself to the other two. Chechi was not in the country for one. She had left the world itself for the last. All four were after our downfall. At the ones we attended, neither Chechi nor I were invited to step on to the dais to be with the rest of the family or introduced as relatives. I did not feel sad about that. Because it is not people or relationships that get invited to such events – is it not clothes, ornaments, high status and influence that do?

We found the auditorium soon, and also the lane that ran on its left, just before the one-way road started. On the post at the edge of the boundary wall, there was a flex board that announced the death of a handsome eighty-year-old man and a black flag of mourning. The picture was pasted just below the decorative bamboo that stood on the inside of the wall and reached right on to the road, on the wall, all through until the gate. There was another large flex board and black flag right in front of the gate. It was a large, beautiful house. The white pandal set up reached right up to the gate. The gate was open. A cardboard with a sign written with charcoal which said 'Parking' pointed to the adjoining yard. Seven or eight cars were already parked there. I realized that we were going to this house of bereavement only when Dr Ramakrishnan turned his car towards it. We got out of the car. We were walking towards the house when he put his hand on my shoulder and said, 'My child, the story I was sharing was not over.'

'We can get back to it when we go back home?'

'No. You will not experience it fully then.' He straightened his glasses and sighed. 'We are going to meet Nalini, my wife's soulmate.'

That took me by surprise. That is how any story must be. It should flare up and sear you at the start – and then slowly, constantly, scorch you, like slow-burning chaff. In the end, it must fell you with a single blow to the forehead. I was filled with eager anticipation now. Suspense, bordering on frenzy, filled me. But even then, I did not realize that I was walking back towards the rest of my own tale. From my experience, I can say that crime investigation and love and death are all alike. You just have to initiate it, and then it will carry you along with its force.

Dr Nalini Prabhakaran was a well-built, imposing woman. She was around my mother's age. She sat in the largest seat in her beautiful living room, with all the authority of the mistress of the place. She leapt up from the chair when she saw Dr Ramakrishnan. The imposing look melted away, and she fell on his shoulder and wept. He comforted her, led her to the chair, seated her on it. It was interesting to watch the two of them; there was absolutely no tension in their exchanges. 'When did you arrive?', 'How did you come?', 'Did you drive by yourself?', 'How's life in Kochi?', 'Couldn't you have remarried?', 'How do you manage by yourself?' – the chatter streamed endlessly.

She noticed me only later. 'My niece,' Dr Ramakrishnan introduced me. He asked her about her children. Of her two children, one was a doctor, she said. And her husband too. They were settled in Melbourne. The younger daughter was a professor at a university in the US. She got out of a failed marriage before she migrated; after that, she had better luck in marriage and tied the knot again. They were all doing well. To prove it, she called Gita and Sita. Gita appeared first – a stunningly beautiful fifty-year-old with short hair, in palazzos and kurta. She brought along a tray with cups of hot tea. Sita followed her – she wore a sleeveless frock, and her straightened and coloured hair was tied in a messy bun. Nalini called her affectionately, 'Come, baby, these are Rukkuma's husband and niece. Ramu, do you remember her? Sitalakshmi.'

'Have seen her once, in the UK...' Dr Ramakrishnan replied. I, however, shuddered. A windowpane of memory was flung open. A window, with a blue-coloured frame, almost coming apart. In the daylight, a hair-parting smeared heavily with red sindoor. Kohl-lined eyes. Jewellery which had not lost its newness. That outburst: 'Could you find only my husband to cure your rot?' I froze. I looked at her with clouded eyes. Sitalakshmi. Married then to Sriram. She, who had glittered with gold and the freshness of love. She, who had spat on my face.

My face must have gone pale, my eyes must have popped out of my head in fear, my body must have cowered with shame. Maybe because of the expression on my face, she looked closely at me. Her face lost colour too. 'You...' she said, pointing her finger at me. I reached out, took it. 'Yes, me,' I confessed. 'Oh my god!' She shook her head. And thus I went through the most sheepish moment of the whole of my life.

It was she who recovered first. 'Satyapriya, I didn't recognize you. You've changed a lot!' she said, astonished. I could not find words. She turned to her mother. 'Amme, did you recognize her?

This is Satyapriya ... Remember? She complained against Sriram...'
Dr Nalini's expression changed. I feared that she might burst out in
anger at me, but Sitalakshmi did not give her a chance. 'I was hugely
mad with you back then, but now I am so very grateful to you for
saving me, Satyapriya,' she mumbled. She insisted that I go with her
into the house. She took me to an upstairs room in that tastefully
decorated home. When we climbed the stairs, she made a video call to
her husband Ramsay and introduced me. He gave me a friendly wave
and said, 'Thank you for gifting me Zeeta!'

On the whole, it was like getting high on charas. A beautiful
moment in the history of my crime investigation. I wept, laughing.
I had never expected to meet her again. All the internal strife I had
suffered in the past few days just melted and flowed as tears from
my eyes. My heart felt light. I just couldn't get enough of seeing
Sitalakshmi. Her face, brimming with vitality. Dark, well-shaped
brows. Eyes lined with imported kohl, sharp and bright. Cheeks –
spotless, smooth, shining. Abundant tresses. Well-preserved beauty.
And above all, endless confidence. She was now many births beyond
the woman I had seen with Sriram.

'I have been seeking you since so many years, Satyapriya!' she said.

'Why?' I asked, wiping my nose and my eyes.

'To thank you, of course! What I am today is because of you. If you
hadn't saved me, I would have stayed in that mud pit thinking that it
was heaven itself. I had not even completed my master's. I would most
probably have had kids, and then it would have been their schooling
and tuition, and then him and his family lording over me. And in
between, he'd have had some other affair. I'd have been finished. It
would have been just too late. I wouldn't have had the time to study
and find a job. You saved me in the nick of time, Satyapriya!'

'But did I not put you through a lot of pain back then? I feel guilty.'

'Yes, it did hurt. My self-respect was shattered. Really, I would have
killed you then, Satyapriya. But afterwards, it began to dawn upon
me slowly. I realized it was not your fault. I went to Delhi and did a

master's degree. I did a PhD in the US. Met Allen and learned what a man's real passion for a woman is.'

'I always felt guilty for wrecking your life, Sitalakshmi.'

'The new can't be built without destroying the old.'

'Not everyone can do it.'

'True. My mother was a great support. Should the foot be chopped to fit the slipper or should we just find a slipper to fit the foot, she asked.'

'Lucky woman!'

'I misjudged you seriously at the time, Satyapriya. Cursed you plenty. Hated you.'

She smiled. I explained to her what had happened all those years ago – in four or five sentences. But that was enough to hit her hard. She shuddered. How I'd been trapped in the lab, how I'd peed and pooped ... Tears came to her eyes. I told her about what had happened with CI Dinakaran Pillai and we both wept. Once we had got a hold on ourselves again, she asked, 'Did Sriram ever try to contact you again, Satya?'

'I suspect that he's sent a contract killer after me.' I hinted at the attempt to kill me. She winced even more violently.

'God! Didn't you complain to the police?'

'It's being investigated.'

She thought for a bit. Then, as though remembering something, told me, 'If Sriram has a hand in it, surely that friend of his should know.'

'Which friend?'

'We'd been to see him several times after the wedding. He came over to our house many times too. He was the one who insisted that Sriram join politics. After I left him, he tried to mediate. He wanted me to fall at your feet and beg you to withdraw your complaint. He said that you'd back down if I looked sufficiently sorrowful. And then, he said, we could teach you a lesson.'

She tried to remember his name again.

'See, Satya, he was horribly angry with you. It wasn't anger in any simple sense – it was hatred, loathing, vengeance...'

'I don't know this person...'

'His house is in Thekkeparambil. We went there once. His father was a moneylender.'

You know me well, I have taken many blows. But this took the prize.

'Abhilash,' I whispered slowly.

'Yes, Abhilash,' she repeated the name.

As it happens on such occasions, my body oozed hot steam. An icy wind blew through my veins. I froze and sweated profusely all at the same time. All of a sudden, I wanted to pee. My brain felt like an empty bronze pot, my memory, an empty nest abandoned by the birds. I went totally blank. Thereafter, everything felt hazy.

We somehow reached home again. Dr Ramakrishnan and Irshad left soon afterwards. I gave Amma her medicines, food, chatted with her. She slept off.

Then I came out of my daze. Memories, emotions, thoughts, all came back, as hungry as ever. Like a tiger that had eaten up a huge prey that it had killed, I felt fulfilled.

FORTY-NINE

It was Leelavallabhan's daughter Kalpana who took me to Dinakaran Pillai's house. But I did not give her any hint about him or Satyaprabha. That it was she who took me there was also a coincidence. I can tell you – my experience is that you should not have too many dreams about journeys with any person. Journeys planned and money to be received are alike. Do not set much store by either. Both are worse than human beings.

The day after I met Sitalakshmi, Kallu called. 'Hey detective,' she said, 'I am bored. Can we go for a drive?' Even then, Dinakaran Pillai's house was not my destination. The toughest hurdles in the path of crime investigation lie in the last steps – the ninety-eighth and ninety-ninth steps. When you reach that far, the hundredth step seems within easy grasp. That is, all your questions will seem to have been answered. That is a trap you must be most wary of. There will always be some steps after the hundredth step for the end to be reached. That's my experience.

Kallu came by four o'clock. We drank the coffee Amma served us and chatted for a bit. Her mother was now resting after the surgery. 'I am dead bored at home,' she complained. 'Let's go take a round,' she suggested, and I agreed.

After I got into the car, she asked me where we should go. 'Wherever you want to,' I told her. 'Does the detective need to go somewhere in particular?' she asked in half-jest. It made me remember her father. I thought for a moment and told her, let's go to Planchod. That was where Dinakaran Pillai used to live. Just twelve kilometres away from my house.

We asked for directions on the way and finally reached Planchod. None of the autorickshaw drivers at the local junction seemed to have heard of Dinakaran Pillai. It was an old man, who ran a small tea shop that stood apart from the rest of the shops at the junction, who told us that Pillai had been away in Bangalore for the past ten or twelve years. My hopes dimmed a bit, but I did not give up. I asked about his relatives. They too seemed to have left. 'Only the old neighbours may know,' the man said. And so, we kept asking around, to make our way to the Thundikkal house. We met Rajamma, Dinakaran Pillai's neighbour. Our car and urban demeanour seemed to have made a favourable impression on her. She welcomed us.

'Are you from Dubai?' she asked. 'Has Anju sent something?' Anju was her granddaughter, married in Dubai.

When we mentioned Dinakaran Pillai, though, her face clouded. 'Oh, they are all big people now. Make money shamelessly, the money will cover the shame,' she sounded exceptionally forthright. That made things easy for us – we needed to just nudge her slightly. Countless stories lay in wait for hearers in that aged heart, nearly eighty years old. We had a long chat with her.

'My dear children, you don't know how miserable they used to be once … His mother Meenakshi … who doesn't know how she scraped and slaved away to feed them! There were four girls, you know, and this one boy. And ill-omened he was for sure. The fellow was just born, and in no time at all, his father, Raman Pillai Chettan, fell dead! We've had nothing but suffering. But then isn't the whole land suffering? Back then, who had any money? Still, we helped him as much as we could.

But does he remember even a little bit? Oh, leave him aside – did Meenakshi remember anything?'

'Where are his sisters?'

'When Raman Pillai Chettan died, Meenakshi took them to rich houses and made them servants there – and that too the houses of lowly Chovan-caste people, the Ezhavas, you know, and the Muslims! She was greedy for cash back then too. In the end, the eldest girl came back with a baby in her belly, I heard. Who knows? Ah, the boy managed to get to that rich man, the muthalaali. He saved him.'

'Which muthalaali?'

'The chap who made all those movies? Had a hotel and all. Sold everything, ruined it all. Threw it all away. Gave it all to stray women.'

'Sivaprasad?'

'Yes. Dinakaran licked his boots and somehow got into the police.'

'Was it so easy to get a job in the police?'

'Wasn't so hard in those days. He did not pass the ninth-class exam.'

'He became an SI without passing the tenth standard?'

'Oh, he wrote some exam later and passed. And Vanaja's father told me once that he went somewhere in north India and got himself a degree. And he was aflush with cash after the wedding! What is not possible in this land if you throw cash! Didn't he retire as DySP? Do you know where he is now? In Bangalore – he has a coffee estate. Two boys – both are engineers.'

'His wife is called Satyaprabha?'

'That is his first wife. Meenakshi and her daughters did have a merry dance with her money, didn't they?'

'Did it end in a divorce?'

'Divorce? What for? What do you need divorce for if you can throw the wife into some mental hospital?'

'Mental hospital?' I gasped. My breath caught.

'Wasn't it a long story, my dears? That was a little girl, and wasn't she already weeping when she stepped into the Thundikkal house?

To start with, she didn't want this relation. And on top of it, she was Tamil! The poor thing, fatherless, motherless, no one to care about her! Buried in cash! And with no one to bother if she lived or died! Do you know how beautiful she was? She shone like a gold sovereign! Vanaja's father took one look and said – Rajamme, something is not right.'

'What was the reason for marrying the Tamil girl?'

'That's what I was hinting at – some hanky-panky with that rich fellow. He had something to gain from it. What it was, we don't know. Until that wedding, Meenakshi had leaned on this house to survive. But after the wedding, she and her girls changed! She got her girls back from where they worked. And one fine morning, their miserable hovel was replaced by a concrete house, with bathrooms inside! The girls started wearing gold, they started to go to Madras to attend weddings…!'

'Ammachi, did you attend that wedding?'

'How could I? If they took us along, wouldn't we find out all about it? Just the girls and their mother went. They took a train … reached the next morning … and there was a van waiting there to take them to a lodge. Fifty rupees room rent, someone said – so expensive those days! Who paid? That rich man. There was a reception at the girl's house that evening; and the next morning, the wedding. They got into the train to come back that very evening. I saw the wedding party return early in the morning.'

'Didn't you head over to see the girl, Ammachi?'

'Didn't I? Of course, of course! Wasn't it I who lighted the lamp and handed it over to Meenakshi? What beauty – you wouldn't want to take your eyes off her! Her hair – oh, four hands could not hold it, so thick it was. Black, curly, waist-length. Tamil women's beauty – really something to behold! But what was the use? Wasn't she wailing like someone had died?'

'What was she saying while she cried?'

'Was this marriage with her consent? No, right? It was evident to anyone who had eyes. What a lovely child! And he? Okay, they say that looks don't matter for a man. But shouldn't the man have something that makes him worthy? How was this man worthy? The girl hollered all the time in English, you know? And oh, what kind of English! Even English madams can't speak like that!'

I sat there, totally flabbergasted.

'When we tried to make her hold the lamp that had been lighted and step into the house, she pulled away and began to run … like a young calf, screaming in Malayalam and Tamil and English, "Let me go, let me go!"'

'And Dinakaran Pillai?'

'My child, that was the day I saw his true nature! When she cried and wailed inside for some time, he rolled up his sleeves and went there with his mundu hitched up, and caught her by her throat and lifted her. Her legs dangled below, like she was being hanged to death!'

'And?'

'Only when everyone begged and pleaded did he loosen his grip. She collapsed like a jackfruit cut down from the tree! What was one to say, the new bride fell in a heap. I pleaded with Meenakshi, please take her to the hospital. But she didn't listen. They delayed it by two weeks, and then it was too late. She never got up. They would feed her medicine in the morning, and she would fall asleep. She would do whatever they asked her to – if they told her to drink the gruel, she would; if they asked her to spit, she would. Piss or shit, when they told her to. My child, it is so hard to recollect all those scenes!' Rajamma wiped her eyes and nose.

'We all tried to reason with them – tell her relatives to come and take her away. He wouldn't listen. And why? Wasn't money flowing to them from her account each month? That would stop if they sent her back. Slowly, they began to resent us going there. And so, they quarrelled with us for minor things. And that woman, that Meenakshi, she ordered me out of her yard! And I, no, no, never did I step in there again! But I told her – hey Meenakshi, you and your wenches are going to suffer, mark my words! And wasn't I right? Her oldest girl was hit by a vehicle and lay unconscious for four years. The second one died in a big accident when she was on her way back from the vidyarambham ritual of her grandkid. Didn't you read in the papers? Big accident! Seven people dead! The third married a miserable drunk and he frittered away everything they had and is now a squalid beggar. The fourth was a kind sort – she had some disease of the heart, and died. Meenakshi suffered a lot in the end.'

'And Satyaprabha?' I asked, trembling.

'Within a year, she went completely mad. They tied her hands up saying that she had begun to pick up her own poo. The knots were so tight, her wrists got infected, pus formed, there were worms and all ... Janamma, who lived around there, once said ... if you go near the window, the smell is so bad, like a dead rat rotting ... Then we saw them take her somewhere in a car. To the hospital, they said ... not to me, to Vanaja's father.'

'Which hospital?' It was Kallu who asked.

'I don't know, dear. To Kuthiravattam or Oolambaara, some mental place.'

'Is she still alive?' Kallu asked.

'Who knows? We didn't hear anything about her after that. He then became a sub-inspector, then a circle inspector. Who'd even ask?'

I can't recall how I managed to bid her goodbye. The moment I got into the car, I broke down. Like a large glass vessel that had crashed on the floor, I was reduced to fragments lying on the hard ground. That was how the easy day in my crime investigation story ended. This is why I say, do not have expectations from days and people. I shuddered again and again while inside the car. Bitterness bubbled in my mouth. I felt worms crawling all over me. I saw Chechi and Satyaprabha through my tears. My chechi, with her long, luxuriant hair; Satyaprabha, with her abundant curly locks. Satyaprabha was my oldest sister, someone I could not touch even once. One who never gave me a chance to love her. Which mental hospital did he condemn her to? I saw her come up after her wedding, screaming, please, please help me, let me go … was she crying even in the wedding pandal? What was her wedding like? Who gave her away? Acchan? Did he dare to look at her face as he did it?

She must have also wept the day before the wedding, even during the wedding. She must have sat in the train weeping. The train must have run to the rhythm of her sobs. Just fourteen, or fifteen, maybe. Just a girl, who'd given birth barely six months earlier. Did she cry in the memory of those three children? Or of their father? Were her breasts dry when she got married? Or did the milk collect inside, harden, turn her breasts into stone, blacken them like they were poisoned? Did he rape her on the wedding night?

I awoke from this daze only after a short while, when a strong scent filled the air. I was still in the car. Darkness fell. The car was parked on the roadside. Kallu was smoking a cigarette. She was almost done. I wiped my eyes and nose, felt discomfited, and apologized. She took one more puff at her cigarette, then put it out by pressing the butt into the car's ashtray and looked at me. 'Are you all right?' she asked. I tried to smile. 'Relax,' she said, patting my shoulder. I tried to relax. She started the car. In the car's headlights, the newly tarred village road shone like the surface of the lake at night.

'Now tell me. Who is this Satyaprabha?' Kallu asked. My voice refused to leave my throat.

'Your father's daughter, Satya?'

I nodded. She was looking intently at me, and sighed deeply.

'From the time I saw you, Satya, I have been wondering – how is it that you manage to carry such a load of experiences inside you? And still remain able to laugh and talk and joke?'

I was too weak to offer her a response. It felt like I'd swallowed an enormous iron ball or that a ton of weight had been loaded on to my chest. Kallu could see that and did not ask anything more. The drive back felt shorter. She parked the car in front of the gate, opened it before I could. I thought that she would leave as soon as she had dropped me home, but she took the car in. When I stepped out, she went back and closed the gate.

'I am going to stay for a bit,' she said before I could say anything. Inside, Amma sat reading *Annihilation of Caste*; she had left the TV on. When she saw me, she put the book down and got up. Let Kallu tell her if she wants to, I thought, and then went straight into my room to take a shower. I stood under the flowing water for a few minutes, then changed, and came out. Kallu was sitting on my bed and flipping the pages of a diary.

'Sorry, I took a look at this without your permission.'

'No problem,' I said. I pulled a chair and sat down opposite her. Amma brought us coffee. Kallu drank it gratefully. I put my cup on the low table beside the bed. Amma leaned on the chair and ran her fingers gently through my hair. I lifted my face to look at her reluctantly; but the moment my eyes met hers, the tears leapt out. I got up, hugged her.

'The mental hospital…' I mumbled, 'just fourteen or fifteen … just a kid, a kid…'

Amma held me close. I could not control my words, they kept flowing.

'Amme, she wept without end, and then she fell silent. They locked her up. Tied her arms. The knots were too tight … her wrists were infected, filled with pus and worms … How she must have hurt, Amme … If she had someone, someone who would have said, I am here for you, would this have happened? If Acchan had bothered to ask after her even once, would she have suffered thus? Isn't it impossible that Acchan did not know that they had thrown her into a mental hospital? Maybe he pretended not to know? Couldn't he have told us? Or killed her quickly, sparing her all that suffering? Amme, why did Acchan do this to her? When we were happy here, she was in a mental hospital in agony! What were you doing here, Amme? Why did you not try to find out, at least once, about the filthy things that the fellow you shared a home with was up to? Your father – the great Kochootty

Panikkar who would know if a leaf moved in this place – even he didn't make an effort! Or did he just remain silent even though he knew? She was no one to Appooppan, was she? So he thought, let her die in hell! Let her be non-existent! But she was still human, wasn't she? Was she not in pain? In fear? That too, in a mental hospital of those days. Oolampara or Kuthiravattam, or someplace we don't know of. How they must have tortured her there! They must have chained her, given her electric shocks. The poor thing, they must have slapped her when she screamed. She must have wailed, calling for her mother...'

Amma clapped her hands on my mouth. I just could not stop. I wriggled, writhed, as if to vomit out all the poison that I had swallowed. But suddenly, my voice stopped. For the first time in my forty-four years, I saw my mother sniff and break into sobs. Her eyes cried first, and then her lips. Her face became like that of a child. I stared, my eyes popping. She burst out crying loudly. Then, sitting on my bed, pressed her face against my chest and whimpered. I completely froze. Amma, who did not move when she heard that I had been shot at, who didn't weep even at Chechi's death. Amma, who did not weep when the house was set on fire, or when our well was poisoned, or when Acchan was stabbed, or when Appooppan died...

That day, watching her cry, I grasped that truth of life. It is not sorrow that reduces people to tears. It is helplessness, or a sense of loss. Or repentance. Amma wept for a long time that day, then fell asleep, tired and spent. I hugged her and fell asleep too. But that was not resting, it was a kind of escaping. Like one faints when faced with unbearable truth, the brain in flight. At night, I awoke having heard something. Amma was still asleep beside me, but her breath hummed: 'Ah, here I fall, I fall, into bottomless depths.' But there was light in the next room. I jumped up from the bed and went to the door.

Kallu was sitting on the sofa, about to light a cigarette. I realized only then that she had not gone home. She smiled at me. 'My last one,' she said, holding up the cigarette. I looked at the clock, feeling embarrassed. It was two in the morning! I apologized, washed my face, went up to her. She laughed. 'How was I to leave when mum and daughter just slept off without a word!' We spoke:

'You could have woken us up.'

'Let them sleep, I thought.'

'Didn't your mother call, Kallu?'

'Amma sleeps early since the surgery. I called Kavi, told her. She'll take care of Amma.'

'*Sshe*! But you must have been bored here, all alone.'

'Oh no, why? I did some detective work too.'

'What?'

'First, about what Rajamma told us about Dinakaran Pillai's appointment. Back then, they used to recruit to the Reserve Police on a district basis. Then, those recruited would be moved to the local police force as per their seniority. And if you passed the test and had some powerful recos, then you'd be promoted to an even higher position. Dinakaran Pillai was crooked; loaded too. No surprise that he retired as a senior officer.'

'And?'

'The second point is more important. In 1974, a woman was admitted to the mental hospital at Kuthiravattam. Her name was Satyaprabha. She was there until 1984.'

My heart beat hard. 'Was she discharged?'

'No one came to take her home, so they sent her to a home for the destitute.'

She got up, held me close.

'I know that you cannot take all of it in in a single day, Satya, but it is better to know the truth as soon as possible.'

I broke out in a cold sweat again. In the height of helplessness, I surrendered my body and its burdens to her. She smelt of menthol cigarettes and some perfume. When the scents combined, it reminded me of someone. She held me closer. An iron ball encrusted with sharp nails kept revolving inside my throat.

'She died there, right?' I asked.

'Yes.'

Kallu hugged me tight. The scent of someone dear, its memory, grew stronger. I pressed my face against her shoulder.

'But it was not a natural death…' Her voice trailed away. I jerked hard, lifted my head.

'Murder?'

'No…' She held me again. Caressed my head. In a soft voice, she said, 'It was suicide.'

I felt relieved for a moment, and then shocked, like the very sky had fallen. Suicide!

'She cut her veins,' Kallu whispered.

Something pierced my chest; an 'S'-shaped dagger sunk hard into it and twisted, as though to check the ripeness of a jackfruit. The genetic connection between Satyaprabha and me became evident then. Kallu sat me down on the bed and sat beside me. She eased my head on to her shoulder and comforted me. I caught the scent of her body; I knew it from before. You won't believe it, but it was the same scent as Chechi's. I won't ask if you have gone through such a thing, because even I don't know what it was. But there was something. Even then, I was clearly aware that it was fruitless to cry for the dead. No bird that flew away ever returned because someone howled their heart out. Didn't I tell you, people cry not out of sorrow but out of helplessness, loss and guilt? I cried again then. And laughed thinking about it all, again, and again.

Because Satyaprabha had killed herself in 1999. The same year that Sivapriya died. The same year that Satyapriya had a glimpse of Dinakaran Pillai's mouldy thighs. The year when there was war on the borders. The year when the dagger with which Acchan had been stabbed was auctioned…

How was one not to laugh even when each blood vessel in my chest was being cut oh-so slowly by a rusty, old iron chainsaw?

FIFTY

For what?

Why did Satyaprakash want to kill me? Everything started from that question. When I got to know about Satyaprabha, that question grew a thousand heads. More unbelievable than her birth was her death. Kallu was trying to say that she died of mental illness. I was not convinced. She decided to kill herself while in full possession of her mind, was what I kept feeling. But for what? At which moment did she take that decision? What was the incident that must have provoked her? After Kallu left, this alone stayed in my mind.

Was Satyaprakash Satyaprabha's son? It was this question that bothered me the most. The answer to it would be the vital pointer that would help me find answers to the other related questions. I decided to go in search of the house named 'Sarada Bhavanam, Thekkeparambil', Satyaprakash's permanent address as per the document he filled out when he joined Advaita. The police were expected to pursue this lead carefully, but Anurup just said that there was no such house at present. He sounded so negligent. So I wanted to find out for myself. My usual self would have been in a state of high excitement by now, but I felt afraid. I expected someone like Rajamma Chechi there too, and a blow worse than what she had delivered. Didn't my mind have to be strong

558

enough to take it? It needed time to heal. So I began to sweep the house and clean the toilets. My experience is that there is no better way to de-stress. I plunged blindly into it, swept and swabbed the whole house, and felt relieved. Amma came out after taking a bath. Her face and eyes were swollen. 'What happened?' she prodded. 'Is this Service Week, or something?' 'No,' I retorted cheekily, 'it is the Swachh Bharat Abhiyan.' We both tried to behave as though nothing had happened. Dialogue is an excellent way to get rid of depression and disconnect. We had the following dialogue that day:

'If you're doing this to feel better in your head, you'll have to sweep this whole country.'

'My investigation is stuck, Amme. No progress.'

'Ambedkar says that the progress of a land should be measured by the progress of its women. When you look at the country, is it surprising that you are stuck?'

'And how am I to progress, Matashri?'

'You must learn from your experience.'

'What did you learn hitherto?'

'That even those whom one sees every day, one's familiars, may have a life and a story that we do not know – this is what I learned.'

'What stories do you, Vasanthalakshmi, have, that are hidden from me?'

'Just one or two less than the stories I do not know about you, Satyapriya.'

'You are so smart, Amma, but you did not have the slightest suspicion about Dinakaran Pillai?'

'Satya, what if he married Satyaprabha without the knowledge that she was your Acchan's daughter?'

'Vasanthalakshmi has read not only many detective novels but also many popular novels, am I not right?'

'Is that not the only reason why I have suffered the father and the daughter this long?'

'Do you mean to say that Acchan could have dumped her on him via someone else?'

'Yes, and he must have found out the truth later.'

'The old woman we met told me that cash was flooding the house after he married her. So does that mean that Acchan was being blackmailed?'

'This happened, remember, when he was at the height of his fame. My father was at the height of his power too. It was not possible to blackmail him directly.'

'What do you mean, Amma?'

'There must have been an intermediary in this affair, Satye. Someone we have missed.'

That might be true, I felt. But I had no idea at all about who that could have been. I felt like I was immersed in a darkness with vague shadows shifting around me. Nothing was clear – but there was surely something. I went out, swept the yard, then took a shower, and felt quite exhausted afterwards. Amma served the idli and chutney. I ate up six idlis ravenously, two fried eggs as well. That was forgetting the lonely state of my kidney, but since some time now, such things had ceased to worry me at all. When you're running holding your life in your hands, what kidney, what diaphragm? The heavy meal made me sleepy. I slept until three that afternoon. I dreamt of Chechi. She came past the gate with three suitcases. I was standing on the veranda. She left the suitcases behind and rushed towards me. But though she ran, she could not reach me. I stayed quiet, trying not to hurry to her. Losing patience, I opened my eyes. I was like a traveller who'd fallen asleep on a train. I was to alight at a stop seventeen years back in time. But I woke up at a deserted and alien place. Who knew that my train would end its journey there? Who thought that Chechi would not be with me then?

She was not with me. I had kept a distance with her over money. She too. That, too, was because of money. But really, it was out of jealousy. Abhilash made his moves silently. I have, in this life, always forgiven those who hated me and wished me dead. Even towards Dinakaran Pillai, in the last reckoning, I had nothing but pity. But no, not towards Abhilash. Towards him I harboured neither compassion nor empathy. Not even sympathy. It was not necessary. He was like a hunter for whom every other living thing was either a prey or an enemy. He refused to evolve from that state. All around him were either steps for him to climb, or instruments, some of which he converted into weapons. He had no use for any empathy. He would have smiled, put his arm around my shoulder, and then thrust a blade deep into my chest. If possible, he would have dug out my liver, marinated it in salt and turmeric and pepper, and eaten it all by himself. And one thing was certain – while he did this, his shirt and dhoti would have remained spotless. No bloodstain or smell would have remained on his hands either.

What I meant to tell you was the way he turned Chechi into a weapon. This is why I always say – never tell a lover a word more than what he needs to know. I fell into the trap. He realized that Chechi was my weakness. And Chechi – she had told me about all the lovers in her life, but not a word did she utter about Abhilash. She tried to quarrel with me just to conceal his name. When I asked her to get a passport, he volunteered to help. When she was abroad, he'd visited her on a tourist visa, lived with her there. Naturally, she was forced to register a marriage. He made her return to take a loan of fifteen lakh rupees and an insurance policy for twenty-five lakh.

It is true that she was a romantic. But don't think that she was a fool. When she was working in a firm, she started her own business of importing computer parts, assembling them, and selling them. She made roaring profits, and that's how she made enough money to buy us the house we lived in. Only when the house was to be registered did I get to know that her name was now Sivapriya Abhilash. I was shaken when she began to nag me about my spending habits. Even then I did not suspect that her present husband was my former lover. But I felt drained. I had no response to offer to her jokes or suggestions.

This, she thought, was because I had learned the truth. We avoided each other. Following the registration of the new house, she stayed in the country for six days. The first day, after she came home, I went off to Venukkuttan Chettan's home and spent the day there. The second day, when she invited me to go with her to town, I turned her down saying that I had a lot to study. That night, she lost her cool. Amma was helping Acchan out of the wheelchair into his bed; I took that chance to serve myself some dinner. She rushed in and started the quarrel. Amma came in and asked us what the matter was.

'Do you have no eyes to see such things, Amme?' she exploded. 'I've been watching since the past two days. She won't speak a word to me. What wrong have I done to her? That I toil in the desert, turn my blood into sweat, and send you money? I am working so hard to take back all that we have lost. Not saying that you should cover me with compliments, but can't you at least stop acting as though I did something terrible?'

I did not say anything. Amma had added too much pepper in the fried fish. I ate in silence. It riled her.

'Just you wait! There'll come a time when you'll yearn to see me. My flight will crash in the sea while on my way back there. You will weep then.'

That made me speak up.

'Don't say such things, please? Who'll be left to take care of your husband, Chechi?'

Her rants stopped all of a sudden, as though they had been switched off. Amma looked dumbfounded.

'Husband? So you're married, then?'

'Oh, informal – gandharvam – Sivapriya Abhilash – how does it sound, Amme?' I said tauntingly. Chechi's tongue sank. Amma looked completely taken aback.

'Chechi is of our father's caste. The husband, too, I suppose?'

She marched back into her room. Amma sat down there and was motionless for a while. I washed my hands, set Amma's and Chechi's dinner plates on the table, and patted Amma on her shoulder.

'Are you sad, Vasanthalakshmi?'

Amma smiled from the corners of her mouth.

'Happy for sure. No more worries about organizing a wedding!'

I sighed deeply. In reality, I was pretty upset; the sense of loss only multiplied. I tried hard to come to terms with it, but it was not easy. Chechi had, after all, been half of me; I was an organ in her body. But really, I had no right to get angry with her. I had my secrets too. I had not told anyone that I had sold one of my kidneys. Maybe it was for the same reasons that she did not tell me that she had given away her heart. The poor thing, how could she tell me? Could she ever say: 'Vaave, I am in love with the man you loved'! Or, 'I married that dirty man who pimped you'?

It was good that she didn't tell me. In any case, my heart was already dead. It had stopped pushing the blood on and was rotting inside. My blood vessels were clogged with dried-up bluish blood. I was poisoned, from head to toe. I had an urge to bite others, murder everybody. You will not believe what all I did that day. Before Chechi awoke, I stuffed some clothes in a bag, made up some excuse to Amma, and set off – to the railway station, just like that. The Guwahati Express was arriving on Platform Number One, it was announced. I ran up to the counter and bought a ticket to Guwahati. The general compartment in the train was overflowing with people. The biryani bought from the pantry did not suit my tummy. I had to get off at Visakhapatnam. I was so weak, I could have died. Somehow, I managed to get on a train going south and reached Katpadi. From there, I caught the nine-thirty train to Thiruvananthapuram. By the time I reached home on the fourth day, my sister had left for the airport.

This was just before the MBA course began. I moved to the hostel when the classes began and went home only on second Saturdays. Chechi had stopped phoning me. The truth is, for humans, everything is a habit. Not just food and sleep but also loving and sharing. Just like the parrot in a cage and the fish in the aquarium that are fed at fixed hours, relationships too have a kind of biological clock. That's the story of the relationship between siblings, so what to say about romantic ones? But it may be a little different for a woman steeped in romance like my sister, someone who could see something beautiful in any man. While abroad, she again met her old flame from the Literacy Movement classes. It was his odd name, Brestan, which had made us laugh even amidst the high drama of our house catching fire. He was apparently delighted to come across her again. She discovered that he had been Abhilash's classmate.

It was around the same time that the arrears notice of the loan she had taken reached us. The sum was so large that Amma was terrified. When Chechi called, Amma questioned her, and she had only incoherent replies to offer. Amma called me home. I went to the bank. The total sum was fifteen lakh; the EMI was sixteen thousand a month. She was paying only five thousand a month. I asked the manager who her guarantors were. He gave me two addresses. One was of her admirer from college, the lecturer. The other was someone she knew from the company she used to work in at Ernakulam. There was a rule in those days that said that you could open an account in a certain branch of a bank only if introduced by someone who already had an account in the same branch. I asked who had introduced her. The bank gave me Abhilash's name and address. The truth hit me in the head that moment. I fainted in front of the manager.

Have you ever been in a state in which your soul died but your body still moved? A pity, if you haven't. It is something to regret! It is a great revelatory moment. You realize that you do not exist at all. That you never were, really. That you were just smoke or mist, ash or soot. The silver lining is that, with this, all your pride evaporates. Without existence, how can there be pride?

Chechi called Abhilash to talk to him about the loan arrears. He kept giving her some excuse or the other. Chechi was always fond of sharing sorrow; she told Brestan about it. The man took a special interest in the affair and called Abhilash – only to find out that he was getting married! That gave her a violent shock. As said before, I have always wondered why she was so fond of flitting from flower to flower. Having love affairs with many men at the same time was in her very nature – like the trunk to an elephant or the elongated neck to a giraffe. What one lover hid from her, another revealed. And yet another helped her to 'cross-check' the other guy.

However, when Abhilash let her down, she was devastated. She resigned from her job, sold her company, rushed back home, wailing and sobbing. It was a working day, and I had a class. I caught her scent early, in the corridor that led to the visitors' room. My heart writhed and my legs grew heavy. Chechi sat in the visitors' room, her face in her hands. My blood boiled and something ruptured inside of me. It was then that she raised her face towards mine. I looked only once, and my heart broke. I went to her, trembling. No sooner had I sat down beside her than she fell on me. Her body was so cold – even in her death, later, she'd feel warmer.

I took leave for the day and took her to my hostel room. She fell at my feet and broke into tears. I sat there unable to move, like a living corpse. The zeros in the fifteen lakh tumbled in my mind, and I counted them. And tried to figure out what else from my body I could sell. Prepared myself to return to the world of Vyakulamata and St Anthony's and Saubhagya. I would not abandon my sister like Abhilash. If I did, what guarantee remained that he would not pimp her to another Thomachan? Did she have the experience to deal with such Thomachans? 'We'll pay off the debt, don't cry,' I comforted her. It was then that she told me: 'It's not the money, Vaave. I have money.'

Ha! What great relief I felt! 'Why are you crying, then?' I asked her.

'Abhi is going to marry someone else.'

I was now rattled. My body shook a little.

'Who is this Abhi?'

'Forgive me. I wronged you!' She fell at my feet, rubbed her head on my foot. I felt utterly drained. I could fight anyone in this world, but how to fight her? Her face made my heart melt. Her beautiful face looked as if it were scorched. She had always borne great pride, even conceit, in her looks, complexion, manner, gait, our father's caste, and our former wealth. I used to tease her, criticize her, for it – fool, I'd say. But at that time, her staying a fool helped us. I softened, comforted her somehow. Made her wash her face, line her eyes with kohl, paste a bindi on her forehead, did her hair nicely, and gave her one of my good suit-and-churidar sets to wear. Her eyes were swollen, but she looked as pretty as ever. We went home to Amma.

Amma wasn't expecting her at all. She acted normal with Amma and Acchan, who were seated before the TV, and said chirpily, 'Amme, Accha, I am home! Got a transfer here!' When the taxi driver brought her suitcases inside, she paid him and gifted him some sweets. She took one of the suitcases to our parents' room and said, 'This is for you.' Then, she opened her handbag, took out a jeweller's box from it, took out a chain of gold beads from it, and put it on Amma's neck; held out two gold bangles to me. Then she pulled me into the inner room. Amma followed us. I was trying to crack a joke, but Amma stopped her from behind. I thought she was going to enquire about the debt, but she pulled off the gold chain and flung it on the floor.

'Go, give it to your husband! A wedding gift!' She did not sound angry, but asked, 'Was it really you I gave birth to, Sive?'

Chechi did not weep any more. That's why I say, to forget one blow, one merely needs a stronger one. Amma's was a terrible blow, and it fell on her most vulnerable spot. Chechi recovered her strength. He won't be spared, she swore. I, too, had no such intention. But what was more important was the debt of fifteen lakh. She was ready to pay it off, she had the money – but I dissuaded her. It was boring to settle the matter in that manner. So we went together to the bride Aruna's house. The taali-tying ceremony was over; it was being held at the Guruvayur temple. The rest of the ceremony was to be on the following day.

Really, after my visit to Sriram's house years ago, this was the one truly enjoyable trip we made together. We went and got ourselves dolled up in a beauty parlour. Chechi's long, luxuriant hair was shampooed and left open. She wore a dazzling red Kanchipuram sari with a red-stone-studded necklace with a large pendant. I, too, was in no mood to trim anything down. My hair was shoulder length at that time; the beautician set it in the simple kuli-pinnal style. We took a taxi there. At that time, Abhilash was a rising local leader of the community. His bride, Aruna, was the daughter of a state-level leader. We reached her house, a very extravagant place. A small pavilion covering the doorstep, and behind it, a mansion sprawled over an acre of land. The whole way was decorated with hangings and a massive pandal. But when we stepped out of the taxi, everyone noticed us. 'Who are they?' they asked each other. We were received very warmly. Abhilash was at his house. We met Aruna, handed her the wedding gift, asked her if Abhi hadn't told her about us. We clicked several snaps of us posing with Aruna on Chechi's Sony camera. When we were on our way out, we met Aruna's father and bid him goodbye specially. From there, we headed straight to Abhilash's house.

The old bus stop from where he had sent me away had become unrecognizable. The smaller houses that had once lined the lane leading to his house had all vanished. In their place was a large wall bearing a plaque with 'No Bills' written on it in letters that looked menacing. His was the third house located at the crook of the lane, where it turned to the left. There was a shop in the corner which bore a board with the words 'High-tech Computers'. Chechi nudged me; it was Abhilash's shop. The role my sister had played in the incomparable advances that a young man had secured delighted me. I congratulated her. 'Don't stab the corpse,' she replied. Can you imagine the amazement that Kuchela felt when he returned home from Dwaraka, to see a palace of gold in the place of his once humble hut? A pity, if you can't. I have. At Abhilash's house, then. The huge wall that we had noticed belonged to his house. It had turned into a luxurious mansion.

The bridegroom was chatting with visitors. His eyes fell upon us, and instantly, they turned lifeless. I went towards him enquiring in a loud voice, 'Hi, Abhi! All good? Oh, you have forgotten us, haven't you?' I tittered. I cried within, though. His fair, rosy, well-groomed face went red. I have told you: this man was a hunter. He had the presence of mind to hide in the thickets at the sight of an enemy, a focus that helped him leap on the prey the moment its look wavered. One who made sure that his hands were left as clean as possible after any such deed. I feared that Chechi might faint. I dragged her along with me, striding inside, and nearly shouting cheerily, 'Amme, Anjana Chechi!' His father and some guests were sitting in the dining room. I went up to him, patted him on the head, greeting him merrily. 'Uncle!' Everyone there, including him, looked stumped. Meanwhile, Abhilash hurried in, hitching up his mundu, ready for battle. He did not face me; he was sure that Chechi was the easier prey and moved towards her. Chechi was hiding behind me. Without further ado, I pulled out a bunch of photos, of them together in Dubai, and threw them on the table. That was a shocker, it was clear. Chechi's eyes overflowed.

'Are you trying to scare me, eh?' Abhilash came up to me, rolling up the sleeves of his shirt.

'Don't touch me, you'll dirty your hands!'

'Hey, trying to pick a fight, here in our home?' his sister cut in. 'Oh, these women are going to be the death of my brother!' I paid no attention.

'Your son has made my sister take a loan of fifteen lakh. It must be repaid by tomorrow,' I said turning to the father, as everyone there listened.

'I did not take fifteen…' Abhilash began.

'Fifteen.' I was firm. All of them were still, petrified. I held my sister close and stepped out. Near the door, we ran into Abhilash's mother, pressing herself into the wall and looking staggered. From the very beginning I had noticed a streak of goodness in her that did not match the family. I asked her a question: 'Amme, couldn't you simply have raised a crocodile instead?'

That day, Chechi wept copiously. I returned to the hostel. Abhilash called her on the landline and told her that he needed to meet her urgently. She called me, and I advised her to tell him to come over to my college. He arrived within two hours. I took him to the canteen and ordered tea for him. We sat on the opposite sides of a steel table. He looked handsomer still. Bright, rosy face, dark moustache, alluring eyes. Poor Chechi. She always fell for the fair and the shiny. Maybe because it was the first night of his marriage, he looked sleepy, but not embarrassed. This was our conversation:

'So you are out to ruin my life, aren't you, Satya?'

'Of course!'

'Poor Aruna – what did she do to you?'

'True! Poor Aruna – what did she do to you?'

'Do you think that the relationship between me and Sivapriya will work? Can I ever come to your house? How could I carry on as Sivapriya's husband in your constant presence, Satya?'

'Why not? Are you not the son I could never have?'

'Satye, I will repay the loan.'

'That sounds like you're doing us a favour!'

'I mean, I have no legal obligation.'

'The husband has no obligation regarding his wife's loans, right?'

His face flushed. 'There's no evidence that she's my wife…'

'You speak, perhaps, confident in that you have destroyed evidence of the registration of your marriage?'

'I didn't marry her at all. What's there to destroy?' he replied, not looking into my eyes.

My blood stirred, but I did not lose my temper. Instead, I said, 'Abhilash, I am telling you out of the love I once had for you. Please meet a competent psychologist soonest. Because you are showing psychopathic tendencies. They can't be cured, but can surely be controlled.'

I thought that he would hit me. But he, too, controlled himself. I made myself even more gentle.

'Please think of poor Aruna, at least.'

He kept glaring at me.

'I'll take care of Aruna,' he said. 'But don't think that I am going to pay the loan in full. I don't have the money.'

'That's okay, I'll ask Aruna's father.'

'Look, there's no need to drag others into this…'

'Since you dragged Chechi into something that was between you and me, I'll drag your father-in-law, even though he's rather heavy, into this.'

'You started this! You started the romance, the debt … and then you made your way into my home and to my father … in front of my eyes.'

'But didn't you pimp me to a man older than your father? So I thought that if I satisfy the sexual wants of men of that age, you'll be pleased!'

He gnashed his teeth; his face turned a fiery red. He almost got up to leave, but sat down again, controlling himself. He took out a plastic cover from the black-coloured bag that he was carrying and put it on the table.

'One lakh twenty thousand.'

'How ironical! Wasn't it for this sum that you pimped me back then?' He looked a bit crestfallen, but I continued, ignoring it. 'This is the arrears to date. To be paid to the bank. Abhilash, you will repay the loan that you took. Not Chechi or me.'

'What if I don't?'

That was a trick to find out if I had any evidence that he did not know of. It amused me.

'You will, of course. You will.' My voice hardened. 'You will pay back the arrears today. Next week, you will pay back the entire amount, I have no doubts about that. That's how psychopaths are. They have no empathy or compassion for anyone. They lie blithely, cheat anyone. Even kill. But they can never bear their masks coming loose…'

I did not wait for his reply and went straight to class. I heard nothing of that day's lectures. Two bees seemed to have got stuck in my ears and they buzzed endlessly. No Dushyanthan came to my aid. In any case, each of us better get rid of the bees that pester us – and not, like

Sakunthala, wait for Dushyanthan to appear. I asked for a sick leave, went home. The next day, Chechi and I hung about town. We called the bank; the manager told us that the arrears had been paid off. The following week, half of the principal was paid back. I called Abhilash. He did not pick up. So I went to Aruna's house and told her father that I was looking for Abhilash. He was a shrewd man; he realized that something was afoot. He questioned Abhilash. Soon the rest of the principal was paid too. I never saw him since. Never had to. For me, he was dead, long before Chechi died.

~

I told you this long story as a prelude to the story of my search for the house called Sarada Bhavanam. I took Harish's autorickshaw. I asked many, but no one really knew where it was. I even went to the post office, but the young man there did not know about it either. We found out that the old postman lived nearby. We sought him out. He recalled it with some effort: the lane to the right from the main road. There were three houses or so on the left side of the lane. Sarada Bhavanam was the second one. The owner was a legal document writer who committed suicide when his only daughter eloped with a low-caste man. It was given out on rent to some Tamils for some time. There was an old man and a young boy there.

'Was the boy called Satyaprakash?' I grew excited. He scratched his grey head.

'I can't remember, Madam. It was that Panicker's son who bought all that property. Why don't you ask them?'

Did you recognize 'Panicker's son'? Abhilash, of course! So I returned to that house once more. I cursed my would-be assassin Satyaprakash from the bottom of my heart. Why, he could have just finished me! Why did he have to push me into old mud holes? Why? Why?

FIFTY-ONE

Abhilash's house was the same, but it looked different now. The gates were rusty, the tiles in the driveway had given way to weeds. It looked like it had not been painted since the last eight or ten years, or maybe twelve. It seemed glum, silent. The yard was unswept. My mind began to feel heavier. One should, in fact, be happy to see nature unspoiled. An unswept yard is like a woman with no home and family. The state of being left alone serves both well; it is best for nature too. But what's the use of saying this? People will never agree to either of these. And, even though science confirms these, at the time when all this happened, science and life ran on divergent paths. Women like me were plants that grew in the decorative planter that was the middle class. The spunk that weeds – the mukkutti or the keezhaarnelli – show – 'I'll sprout even if you pull me a hundred times' – was positively dangerous back then.

My heart pounded as I rang the bell. There was every chance that they'd take a broom to me. The doors were open. The fading evening light still remained, and yet the insides of the house were already filled with a vague darkness. An old woman, felled by age, came to the door with difficulty. When I recognized her to be Abhilash's mother, I was shaken. She was merely four or five years older to my mother, but seemed to be at least ten times weaker than her. She had gone completely grey and walked with a stoop. Her blouse, probably stitched a long time back, hung on her body like a sack. Seeing me, she wiped her glasses, put them back on her nose again, and peered closely. I waited there, my heart weighing a ton. My voice refused to show up, but I managed to introduce myself. For a moment, she was taken aback, and then, with a sigh, said, 'Come in.' I followed her. My strength failed me. Everything became irrelevant before a sense of awkwardness.

You have perhaps noticed, or perhaps not, but the emotional misery of human beings is infectious, and it is their houses that get infected by it first. The last time I visited it, this house was bright and spotless. I should also mention everything – Abhilash was there, then.

His mother sat on the sofa opposite mine. Never before had I experienced such a block in opening a conversation with another person. She sat looking at me. The decades played tag between us. Both of us were tongue-tied.

'Did you come to see us, Satyapriya? Or had some other work around here?'

'I came somewhere close by, for something else.'

'To meet someone?'

'I came looking for a house named Sarada Bhavanam.'

'The house that used to be the second one on the left side of the lane?'

'Yes.'

'Who do you have to see there?'

'Who were its owners?'

'It was the document writer Sivan Pillai who bought that land and built a house. His daughter eloped with a low-caste fellow. He hanged himself out of shame.'

'Was Sarada the name of his daughter?'

'She was a nurse at the Taluk Hospital. Must have retired now.'

That was the first blow of the day. I froze in my seat. Amma had been right. Even people very close to us have stories that we do not know. The person Abhilash's mother had referred to was our neighbour Sarada Chechi. The grandmother of Paramarth, who firmly believed that the note ban meant the end of black money. She was near us since the past twenty years now. But to know her story, I had to meet my ex-lover's mother. Fate is so mischievous, what else is there to say?

'When Sivan Pillai died, the daughter came and took her mother away. The house was rented out for a long time.'

'Were some Tamils living here when Abhilash bought it?'

'There were many tenants. The last ones were Tamil. Vendors of pots and pans.'

'Was there someone called Satyaprakash among them?'

'Not sure if there was a Tamil tenant by that name. But Savithri Amma had a son called Prakashan.'

'Which Savithri Amma?'

She smiled once. 'Don't you know her?'

'No.'

'Ah, how would you? You weren't born when your father raped her oldest girl and the local people got mad at him.' Her voice was sharp and pointed. My head reeled. Like I was being wrested from the roots. It was my conceit that was being uprooted, though, my pride that this investigation was coming to a successful close. I was now like stale tea. The shock clouded my brain. Standing before me was another thirteen-year-old girl, like a chick with its neck broken, in a torn petticoat, faded shirt and half-skirt with its hooks broken.

'I did not know.' My tongue slurred.

'All right, listen, then. Savithri Amma was the daughter of the younger son of a noted government official here, the pravarthyar Kuttan Pillai. He had two sons, and he built each of them two similar stately homes close to each other, in the naalukettu style, with rooms opening around a large courtyard in the middle. The older grandson sold his mansion to your grandfather – that's the house in which you were born and raised, Satyapriya. The house in the compound next to yours was Savithri Amma's.'

I sat there speechless.

'Her eldest daughter was a small little thing. Your father ruined her – enough said.'

I had survived worse moments in my life. But like those weeds which pushed their way upwards despite the tiles that covered the ground, shame sprouted. I staggered as though my veins were being sliced.

'Savithri Amma's husband had high blood sugar and his leg had to be amputated. They were in hospital when this happened. Her sons were really little back then. But they witnessed the crime. People came to know. Your grandfather drove that family away. But then, I have to say this, he paid them more than they asked. They took the money, came here, and leased out a house.'

I trembled like I used to while listening to horror stories as a child; shook inwardly, wondering what was coming my way next. Abhilash's mother began to say something, but then, the sound of a mixer from the kitchen drew her attention, and she got up.

'Come in. There's someone inside who's been waiting for you, Satyapriya.'

She showed me the way. I followed her. When I stepped into the hall, an indiscernible bolt of lightning shot through me. The table upon which I had flung the photos was messy. The whole room stank of stale curd. She led me to a bedroom on the side. Someone was sitting on the cot and wheezing badly. 'Hhh ... who's there, Thankam?' he asked. It was Abhilash's father. I waited, anxious, wondering how Abhilash's mother would introduce me.

'Sivaprasad Muthalaali's daughter,' she said.

'Sivaprasad of Vasanthamaalika!' he asked, unable to believe his ears. Aiyo, his face was worth seeing then! Disbelief, awe, fervid delight! The way he sat, still, staring intently at me. 'You two can talk,' she said, going to the kitchen. I felt as stiff as a piece of wood.

'You've come?' he asked, extending a trembling hand towards me. I was reluctant, but I reached out and took it.

Have you ever experienced the romantic passion of an eighty-year-old? Have you felt flummoxed at the sight of the pangs of separation and its aching joys in eyeballs turned whitish with age? Have you been held by arms from which the skin drooped like sackcloth hung up to dry on a clothes line? Have you known the sting of the cold when your breasts press against a frail chest and brittle ribs? A pity, if you haven't, for then how would you know the immensity of the desire that refuses to die? It is like a man drowning in quicksand, and when the wet sand has reached his neck, he is thrashing desperately for a kiss. This man looked like an overly dried and smoked piece of kokum. The stubble on his face looked like mould on stale bread. I realized then that the brush of aged chin-hair felt like the shavings left over from rubbing a sheet of paper with an eraser. He smelled like termite mounds. What threw me was his greed. Like one starving for long, devouring a plate of rice in stealth. He was not strong enough to even hold me close. His trembling fingers caressed my chest and back, timidly. Had I even foreseen such a thing? I turned into a piece of wood, colder still. The termites began to gnaw and scrape at me.

'I knew that you'd come,' he muttered.

I remembered guiltily the day I had stormed into their house, angry enough to murder Abhilash. It was the day after I cut my veins. It had been my metaphor. It had not healed, the bandage was still there, I could feel my veins throb desperately. When I kissed this man who had been in his fifties at the time, when I caressed his cheek – I had felt the agony from a dagger plunged deep into my flesh. I had kicked down my pain and pushed him into a chair. Like a tiger knocks its prey senseless with a blow to its breastbone, I had run my fingers over his neck. There was a kerchief folded and tucked in between his collar and neck – I had pulled it out and flung it away. Later, I had wondered whether rapists think the same way. I had dragged him towards the office room like the tiger drags its kill into thickets. I had thrown him on to the sofa. His half-alarmed, half-perplexed face had given me a high. His shock, shudder, failure – how intoxicating! I had delighted in my cruelty. I had raised my voice deliberately. Abhilash, his mother, his sisters – all of them had come running. He was totally discomfited. He lost his self-respect that day; he was enfeebled. He used to be this bespectacled man in a spotless white shirt and mundu. Did anyone of his age expect such a thing? He must have lost face in front of his wife and children. He must have been deeply ashamed. Must have been sleepless for a long time. But I did not know what I was doing back then.

This was twenty or so years ago. The pitiful fellow waited this long. He did not know that I had forced myself on him vengefully. He could not make out the difference between romance and revenge. Maybe he was never really loved, ever. He had never experienced the pride in a woman deriving pleasure from his body and his presence. I felt sorry. The intensity of his passion convinced me of the depth of my wrongdoing. I shrank with guilt. He was weeping, like Majnu who had recovered his Laila. Hearing Abhilash's mother return, I sprang back. The man kept staring at me, his chest heaving, his desire still smouldering. She had brought tea. 'Mole, sit down, sit down,' said the man, making me sit next to him. Then I noticed: even at this age, he was trying his best to hide his passion. He did not hesitate, even, to make his seniority into a veil for it. It irritated me. But Abhilash's mother looked completely unperturbed. She came in and sat on a chair. I was still trembling. She let out a sigh and said, 'The poor man, let him die in peace.'

Not having a clue as to how to respond in such a situation, I froze further. Should I run away? Crack a joke? Try to play the smart alec? But I could do just one thing: drink that tea. Abhilash's father was still stroking my hand while I sipped the tea. It mortified me no end, but I pretended not to notice. Acting as though it wasn't my hand that he was stroking, I asked, 'Amma, you didn't finish what you were saying. How old were the children when Savithri Amma came here to stay?'

'The older girl must have been ten or twelve. She had a younger sister – eight years old. Pratapan was younger to her, and the youngest was Prakashan.'

'Prakashan has an older brother?'

'Good grief! What a question! Wasn't it he who took a dagger to your father!'

My fingers around the teacup tightened. This head had already been cracked by Prakashan's blow … and after that, it had taken so many more! Now, on top of all that, a whack with an iron brick? The theories which I had been building carefully until that moment came loose and flew all over, like pages from a book with its spine undone.

'Who told you this?'

'Dinakaran Pillai. He was the sub-inspector of police back then.' It was Abhilash's father who said this; he clearly wanted to lift my spirits.

'Why did he tell you this, Uncle?'

'Wasn't I running a bank here? And it was mostly of his deposits! He would have gone to jail if I'd put my mind to it!'

'But he did not file a case against this Pratapan!'

'How could that be, since he, too, was in the know of it? He was part of it!'

I fell quiet for a few moments, trying to get my breath back. I pulled myself together. 'Did he tell you about marrying a woman called Satyaprabha?'

'A Tamil. A mad one. The poor man had a lot of trouble with her,' he sympathized.

'Why did he marry the Tamil woman, then?'

'Someone played a trick on him. And she was very beautiful too.'

'Ah, leave it. Tell me, where is this Pratapan now?'

'Oh, that was a big case! The communists hacked him to death when he was returning from the shakha!'

Lightning flashed in my mind. That was the case in which the guy who had won the second prize in the Gita class competition was an accused.

'So Savithri Amma and her children were already in Sarada Bhavanam before I was born?'

'They were here until that girl killed herself with poison,' said Abhilash's mother. She wasn't like I thought her to be. She was sharp, like my mother. Skilled in the art of knife-throwing. Each time, she drew blood. But I hung on.

'Which girl?'

'The one your father ruined.'

'She had a sister, you said?'

'Yes, she was a good student. When she got a job in Bangalore, she took her mother with her.'

'And Satyaprakash?'

'He was hanging around, here and there.'

'That is, his family was in Bangalore?'

'Don't know if Savithri Amma is still alive. Maybe the sister and her kids are in Bangalore…'

But the conversation was interrupted when a woman came in calling to her, 'Icchechiye…' and Abhilash's mother got up and went out asking, 'Hey Malati, why are you so late?'

Once she left the room, Abhilash's father leaned on me again and began to kiss and caress me. The stench of the termite heap was unbearable. 'Come here, my dear, this old man has been waiting so long,' he muttered. I looked at his face and felt a rush of tenderness. I had always hated him. When I had approached him for a loan, he had been so blunt and cruel. He had said, 'Do you know how hard it is to make a lakh of rupees…?' and continued, 'Girl, you can live or die! Your old man who fucked up everything doesn't care. So why should I?' From that point onwards, in my mind, he was a malicious, nasty man. This is my experience: the greed for wealth lasts only until passion grips you from within. The claim that people will do anything for money is not true; we are driven by pleasure. And when money and pleasure become one and the same, there are no bounds to what can happen. Anyway, I grabbed the chance.

'Can I ask you something, Uncle?'

'What does my darling want to know?'

'Does Satyaprakash come here?'

'If he does, I'll rip his guts out.'

'What for!'

'What for? Indeed! Wasn't it he who killed my boy!'

I wobbled. This was knowledge to me. A kick in the chest. Another dagger-point. His eyes blazed, like dying embers leaping up. He was hinting at Abhilash's death. I did not want to hear or say anything about it, truly. Did I ever mention it? No. Why? Because I did not like to think of it even. But since things have reached this far, I have to bring it up.

~

It happened when I was working in Advaita. I was in love with Samir Sayyid. Abhilash had begun to shine in politics as a young community leader. He led a north-to-south padayatra from Kasaragod to Thiruvananthapuram. Every evening, there were huge public meetings in each district, where he delivered fiery speeches. The biggest one was in Thrissur. After it was over, he was mobbed by visitors, and by the time he went to bed, it was quite late. When his personal secretary went up to wake him at five in the morning, he found him dead – he had died in his sleep, apparently. The news appeared only after noon.

Samir and I were spending a weekend in a hut by a beach near Konark. We were in the mood for sex, and having come up after bathing in the sea at noon, gearing for it when Amma called and gave me the news – Abhilash is dead. The network was poor, so I just heard 'Abhilash'. I thought he had become a minister or something. 'Who's Abhilash?' Samir asked. 'An old lover of mine,' I said. That made him jealous. He pulled me into the bed; we had sex, and forgot ourselves. I was dozing with my head on his chest when Amma called again. 'Abhilash is dead,' she said. 'How?' I asked. 'A heart attack.' The call ended. Samir's arms were around me. My body must have stiffened in his embrace. 'What happened?' he asked. 'Someone died,' I whispered. I got up slowly. He got up too. 'Do you want to cry?' he asked. I did not answer, just leaned against his chest. No, I had no tears. But for days on end, I found it hard to laugh. For weeks, I felt a weight on my chest. But I knew that it could not have been true. He could not die of a heart attack. For he had no heart at all.

~

'Killed? What do you mean?' I asked Abhilash's father, trying to sound tactful.

'He was poisoned. He had collected a lot of funds that day. Prakashan would go to him every evening and take the amounts collected each day. Prakashan was the last to visit him that day, after everyone else was gone. They had dinner together. He was dead by morning.' His hollowed eyes filled with tears. 'They found poison in his stomach during the post-mortem.' His voice was drowned in tears and pain. He sat on the bed whimpering. I remembered Samir's words: a man has only his son to call his own. Abhilash's mother had come back to the room. She frowned seeing her husband's tears. 'Did you talk about him?' she asked. Abhilash's father broke down again.

Dusk had fallen. I just wanted to flee now.

'Wait, wait some more. When will you come again?' Abhilash's father pleaded. He tried to hug and kiss me again. I comforted him. Kissed his cheek, stroked his hair. Bid goodbye.

Abhilash's mother followed me to the door. I stopped at the veranda, took her hands in mine, looked her in the eye.

'Amme, please forgive me. I had to do many things I shouldn't have done…' My voice faltered. She smiled compassionately.

'When you first came to this house, Satyapriya, I'd hoped that you'd be my company at this age … That did not happen. I still feel sad about it.'

I could not help breaking into tears. I pressed my face on her shoulder. She held me close.

'The last time you came to this house, you said something – remember? That it would have been better if I had given birth to a crocodile and raised it?'

I tottered inwardly.

'That was true.'

Her voice and face hardened.

'I don't know what he did to you. He left the house vowing to come back only after he got back the sum that was lent to you. I tried to stop him. He didn't listen to me. The mess you made here two days later convinced me that he had done something really wrong. My dear, I never had any ill-will towards you.'

I was stunned. She cleared her throat and continued:

'Haven't you heard, he who lives by the sword dies by it? The one I bore instead of a crocodile was swallowed by his actions.'

'Aruna and the kids…?'

'Isn't she a big leader now? No, she doesn't come. Won't send the kids even.'

'So hostile? Why?'

'Our son had registered a marriage with someone else before he married her – he hid that from her. Neither she nor her family has forgiven that. After he died, they went to court for this house. The verdict was in their favour. We are allowed here only during our lifetime. But we aren't allowed to move a stone; neither of our daughters is allowed to enter the house either.'

'Didn't you file a case? Try to get his death investigated?'

'Against his wife and her father?'

'Are you sure that it was her father who was behind it?'

'Wasn't that the reason why there was no investigation? Just the claim that it was a heart attack, and why he was quickly cremated?'

I could not move; frissons of the shock from what I heard passed through me.

'When they found out that he'd registered a marriage, with your sister, Satyapriya, there was trouble every day. Aruna lost faith in him, so did her father.'

'When did they find out about it?'

'Before they got your sister killed, in that lorry accident.'

I held fast to those bony arms to stay steady. 'Chechi was…'

'It was Aruna's father who got it done. Through Prakashan. I heard him tell Abhilash with my own ears. I asked him, and he admitted it.'

~

I can't remember anything after that moment. All the tiles I had laid in my heart had come loose. Everything that had been covered – the soil, the weeds, all of it, had raised their heads. The stench of the termite heap stuck to the tip of my nose. The termites were gnawing into my flesh. I regained my senses only after the autorickshaw had reached quite a distance. When Harish's phone sounded, and he answered the call, saying, 'I'll be there very soon,' I began to slowly emerge into the present. 'Chechi, I didn't think you'd take this long,' he complained addressing me. All women on scooters in the road looked like Chechi to me. And I felt sorry that Aruna's father was long dead now.

It was ten kilometres from Abhilash's house to mine. Some ride it was. How could it not be? Every speeding lorry made me want to jump in front of it, the heartache was that bad. Only one person in the world could have shared it – my sister. There was just one way to join her: get crushed underneath the huge wheels of a truck, like an ant. My experience was: every life is an anthology of many deaths. Each death carries a story in it. It is that story that urges us to resurrect ourselves.

I leaned back in the seat, closed my eyes. 'Chechi,' Harish called me.

'What is it, Harish?' I asked, opening my eyes.

'A policeman's been following us for some time,' he said, without turning back. I sprang, my weakness evaporating. That was all we needed that day.

'How do you know?' I asked in a quivering voice.

'I know him, he's from our station. He was trailing us everywhere we went. In a mufti.'

Haven't I told you? Energy rushes into me when I attack or oppose someone? That was also the case when I found out that I was being observed. I've already said this: art is when you observe someone without them noticing you're doing so. So I did not turn around to look; merely paid attention to the rear-view mirror. Harish was right; the bike rider just behind us was a policeman. His helmet made it hard to see his face clearly. But I don't know if you have observed this: it is easy to spot a policeman no matter what he wears. The hubris of power will pervade his gait and gesture. His trying to alter his appearance is like a tiger cub acting like a kitten. An excellent example was Anurup Shetty. Even when he looked ever so lovable and spoke gently and humbly, his eyes would reveal him to be a tiger that was acting like a cat.

Anyway, with this it became clear that my investigation was not futile. It is true that I had started it seeking the assassin. But it was not him that I really wanted, for sure. I wanted his story; and through that, my own story. That day, I had sought the answer to just one question: Was Satyaprakash Satyaprabha's son? No, I had discovered. And also, that he was Savithri Amma's son. That discovery tilted the tower of my story, no doubt. But it had not collapsed. Satyaprabha did not disappear because Savithri Amma's existence had come to light. Satyaprabha's marriage to Dinakaran Pillai was still a reality. The entire web of connections – which included Pratapan who attacked my father, Prakashan who got my sister killed, Dinakaran Pillai, Satyaprabha who endured hell for ten years at a mental hospital, the children she gave birth to, and so on – was not rendered false. They were all linked.

There was someone who held them together. 'There's a missing link, Satye. Someone we have left out' – someone who would make Amma's surmise come true.

My fatigue and gloom vanished. I was now fully energized. We reached the small canal bridge before Sriram Press. A BMW on the opposite side blocked the way. All other vehicles had to make way for it. A black car. Someone was leaning comfortably in its back seat. Like my father, in our heyday. Suddenly, it happened – I knew who that missing link was.

FIFTY-TWO

So, then, I found Sarada Bhavanam. And the missing link too. But the immense tiredness that I felt after! I just remember falling on the bed. I was like the python that swallowed an elephant. 'Elephant' – here is a metaphor, okay? It's hard to use one and then announce, 'Kochetta, Icchechi, this is a metaphor!' I know that. But at the time all this happened, such things as metaphor and imagery and irony were comprehensible to only a few. And even if those few could comprehend them, they would not admit to it. The news would be that I swallowed an elephant. Or that the fury of Lord Ayyappa of Sabarimala had turned me into a python. Whatever, I was not willing to curl up on the ninety-ninth step of my search for the truth just because I feared slander. My aim was to locate that person who was the missing link.

The best way to know about people at the time this happened was surely to track them on social media. I needed just a little research. My experience is, those whom we seek in life and those who seek us, are all connected. It was easy for a link to break out of the chain, but surely, it had to become part of another.

I found the link – and without delay, pestered Amma to accompany me to town. Amma was willing – she had some shopping to do. I was vexed when I heard this. Here was her daughter whom she had brought into this world in pain, running desperately, holding her life in her hands – and she wanted to shop! Mother, indeed! Irritated, I concealed my discovery of Sarada Bhavanam and the policeman following me; also the aim of this trip. But when we neared the Sastha temple, Amma asked Shafeeq to stop the car. That amazed me, because Amma did not worship gods that Sreenarayana Guru did not acknowledge. There was a time when Chechi and I used to go there and pray much, and get many things done, too. In view of that familiarity, I whispered to Lord Sastha: 'I may be killed very soon.' My pride did not allow me to seek his protection, so I limited myself to asking for a quick and painless death. Amma returned soon, bearing packets of ada, containing the sacred food offering. Remembering how good it tasted made my mouth water. When the car started, she suddenly said, as if to no one, 'Need to see Kochannan.' That chilled me to the bone, because my first destination of the day was my younger uncle's home. That she had guessed it correctly, worried me a bit. She hadn't even attended the housewarming when he rebuilt the house. We got talking then:

'Why this sudden rush of love for your brother, Amma?'

'Getting old! Shouldn't I see them all again?'

'Let him not hear you!'

'I am not talking about him, I am talking about myself.'

'Really! Don't dream of it!'

'My only desire is to leave early, a day earlier, if possible.'

'Chechi, Amma is just fussing – no mother would want to leave her children,' Shafeeq chipped in.

'That's just a feeling, Shafeeq. So many mothers kill their newborns and run away!'

'They are not human.'

'Human or not, mothers will feel attached to their children for some time.'

'But mothers are after all mothers?'

'But you can't let your children hang from your neck for that reason!' Amma laughed.

It was clear that Shafeeq did not agree with her at all, but he just forgave her. There were so many things I myself had forgiven her for in this way. But I did not like her laughter, nor her words. Heard of sixth sense? A dagger was thrust into it; it had been twisted hard. Like it were testing a jackfruit for its ripeness. This was a premonition, something was about to happen. Let me tell you from experience – never ignore such a feeling. In the end, it is only our conscience that speaks the truth to us.

The way to Kochumaaman's seemed longer now. We were delayed because the new one-way road and the bypass slowed us down, but we reached Vasantharamam by around nine. I noticed the new nameplate. My mother got out of the car with a sigh. The dearly loved sister was meeting her brother after a very long time.

Kochumaaman's house was bigger than our family home, our tharavad. Though it looked like a massive mansion with four frontages, it was actually a complex of four houses. His children and their spouses were all doctors – they needed their own spaces, after all. The main façade was my uncle's house. It was luxurious, made of imported granite, was designed by a professional interior designer, and complete with a personal assistant. If my older uncle was a true-blue old-style industrialist and devoted to the service of our community, Kochumaaman was a devotee of globalization. He controlled his vast properties all over India through state-of-the-art technology. He lacked my older uncle's stature and good health – Kochumaaman was skinny, a bit stooped, in a T-shirt and pyjamas. He used a silver-tipped walking stick, like Appooppan. Appooppan hadn't needed it, really, but my uncle definitely did.

Amma's face flushed when she saw him. Her eyes turned moist, I thought. Kochumaaman's eyesight was rather weak. When he recognized her, the stick on which he rested the entire weight of his body quivered: it was a sight I will never forget. He was dark-skinned once; years of non-exposure to sunlight had turned him ashen.

'Ah, Vasantham! You still remember the way here?' he complained. After our great fall, Amma had tried to avoid her brothers at all times. Someone should do some good scientific research on the connection between wealth and human relationships. To destroy any web of human relationships, merely distribute wealth unequally. The one who receives more will never try to remedy the unequal distribution. The one who gets less will never forgive either. The injustice will drive them to create more wealth, sometimes illegally. The unequal distribution will continue to worsen; relationships will keep on deteriorating. We ought to recognize this about the law and justice: we all think that it is the law that guarantees justice. But no, it is the other way round: it is justice that undergirds the law.

Amma smiled – a smile that looked like it was being offered instead of tears – and handed him the packet of ada. Kochumaaman continued to laugh and cry and tremble for a few minutes. If they are sure not to become burdens on each other, siblings most often share great affection. Their faces darken only when they have to spend on the other; only then will they remember old scores. Kochumaaman was not as warm as Valyamaaman. He was still mortified by the memory of grabbing Vasanthaalayam cheap, at a time when we were down.

There was a large hall on the side of the room we were in, partitioned with glass walls. Young men in business attire sat working before computers. LED screens fixed on the walls of Kochumaaman's drawing room relayed scenes from his seafood and textile factories. His wife, my kochumaami, came in, expressed her happy astonishment, and offered us a welcome befitting of an aristocratic housewife. I have always felt tremendous respect for the wives of the rich and famous. How high their emotional quotient must be, and how competent they must be in managing household matters – to hide all their dissatisfactions, remain silent about their husbands' transgressions and act as though everything was flawless within. Kochumaami called her children and grandchildren. They ran in from their respective busy schedules, dropped a 'hi', and left. She served us cake and mixture and tea. A manager came looking for Kochumaaman. I followed him, pretending to look at the photos and paintings on the wall.

Kochumaaman was signing cheques. I waited. When he seemed free, I went up to him and we had this chat:

'Kochumaama, you got this big award from the Rotary Club?'

'Who told you?'

'It was on Facebook.'

'That's from two years back. I have not been on Facebook since my eye surgery, my dear.'

'That picture – isn't that Abey Kurian Panayambarambil who was putting the shawl around you in it?'

'How do you know him?'

'I know Rubin, who married his daughter.'

'Oh yes, his family is in Bangalore, right.'

'Do you know him personally, Kochumaama?'

'Of course I do! Panayambarambil is an important player in Idukki!'

'No, I was asking about Rubin's family.'

'Well, no. But Abeychan is not likely to marry his daughter to some small fry.'

'I wanted to visit them.'

'You can't just walk in like that. They have tight security.'

'Not even you, Kochumaama?'

'I can!'

'Then can you please take me there?'

'Today? Oh no, my dear! Too busy. We are sending the consignments today!'

'Please, Kochumaama, do me this favour. I scraped and begged in all the private banks around town to settle our debts, never bothered you even once! Can't you please do this in return?' I said, with affection. But my eyes filled. I was going to tell him next about how I sold my kidney. But that was not required because he gave in. He went inside, changed, and came out. Kochumaami came running, asking, 'Aiyodaa, where are you going so early in the morning?'

'Let me take this girl somewhere,' he said, stepping out.

'Amma must come too,' I insisted.

'Okay, then I won't say bye for now,' said Amma, coming out.

We went there in my uncle's S-class Benz. Shafeeq followed us in his car. 'Where are we going?' Amma asked me privately. 'To the house of a guy I know,' I told her. We reached a house with a gate that looked like a fortress. There was much checking and questioning after the gates opened, like in some horror movie. The house looked like Buckingham Palace. An expansive garden greeted us, complete with fountains and water-lily ponds. A broad driveway, a separate parking space for visitors. The garden teemed with workers busy decorating the place with pretty hangings and tender palm fronds. There was to be a dinner party in the evening – they had announced it on Facebook. I did not face Amma at all. I was enjoying the feeling that I had taught her a lesson. She didn't like me getting the better of her; it showed on her face.

We were ushered in once we had answered all the questions the young man at the entrance and the secretary posed us, and Panayambarambil himself came out to greet Kochumaaman. 'Why did you have to come, Panikkar Saar?' He made small talk. 'You could have just sent word?'

'What's that nice aroma?' asked Kochumaaman. 'Special dinner?'

'My daughter's baby shower,' Panayambarambil replied. 'A family party.'

Because he was in a hurry to leave, Kochumaaman came to the point quickly. 'This is my sister and her daughter,' he introduced us. 'They know Rubin. They would like to see him.'

Panayambarambil called Rubin. A very nice-looking, handsome youth of around twenty-five or twenty-six appeared, clad in a dark blue three-fourth-sleeved T-shirt, and pyjamas. I got up, shook hands.

Surprise was writ large on his face. I looked at Amma. She had the same sudoku-solver look, which she bore on her face every morning as she tackled the puzzle in the newspaper, pencil in hand. Clearly, she had figured out my plan.

'Rubin, do you recognize me?' I asked.

'No ma'am.'

'Your dad knows me.'

'Daddy and Mummy are here – I'll call them.'

'But your dad's dad knows me even better.'

'Aapchan is also here – I'll call him now.' (Rubin pronounced Appachan as 'Aapchan' in a cute, Anglicized way.)

Well-behaved chap, I thought; nicely brought up. I liked his sophistication. He took some time to fetch these relatives. This was a palace, like Kochumaaman's house, so it took time for anyone to get from one place to another. If there were battery-operated carts like at Mahipala, it would have been easier. I sat on the sofa, crossed my legs, and threw Amma a look of challenge. She looked like she had solved half of the sudoku.

'How do you know Rubin's family?' Panayambarambil asked. He looked a bit apprehensive. My theatrics were rather exaggerated, I think. Amma had fixed her eyes on the image of the crucified Christ on the wall. She now looked as though she had solved the sudoku fully, and the Vasanthalakshmi who lorded over Vasanthamaalika returned.

'Rubin's father Roy was a child who grew up right in front of my eyes,' she announced, shocking even me. I felt deflated. This was the reason why I didn't take her anywhere. She punctured your drama mercilessly. Before Panayambarambil could ask 'how', Rubin's parents, Roy John and Elsa Roy, appeared. Do I need to describe them at all? Their faces gleamed with the confidence of those who had won everything in life; the sort of people who could say without actually opening their mouths that they had a home gym, a personal trainer, a beautician, a hairstylist and a costumier. Roychan, who wore an expensive designer linen shirt and pants, was actually seven or eight years older to me. But he seemed to have bound himself to thirty-five; and Elsa, too, seemed to be stuck at thirty. It took him a couple of minutes to recognize us.

'Jesus! Isn't it Vasanthamma!' he exclaimed in amazement. 'And this is Satyapriya!' I said, pointing to myself.

By this time, Rubin had brought along his 'Aapchan'. Though he was the same age as my father, he looked just around fifty, reckoning by his face and clothes and state of health. He had given up the old, white polyester shirts and terylene pants. Now he wore a silk kurta, a silver-brocade-bordered mundu, and gold-rimmed spectacles. He wasn't clean-shaven any more. His moustache and beard were styled, well trimmed. Rich, clearly. Powerful. Roychan was merely astonished when he saw us. But Rubin's Aapchan nearly fell down.

'Ulahannan Maama…' I got up and went over to hold his hand. 'Do you remember me?'

The expression on his face was as though someone who had been dead had just woken him up in the morning. Kochumaaman's mouth flew open in shock. Amma poked him, whispered something into his ear, probably to warn him against mentioning the old times. He shut his mouth. I took Ulahannan Maaman's arm, brought him to the sofa, sat him down. I sat down next to him. Roy's face showed worry and terror. I had met his wife Elsa at their wedding; she, too, had probably recognized me. I sat there, looking intently at Ulahannan Maaman. It was like gazing at the past. Him, arriving on his spotless Hero cycle every morning, locking it securely in the garage, waiting to be given the key of the Contessa. Back then, he was a wiry man, a stickler for order and punctuality. Someone who thought of our home as his own. His eyes reached every corner of the house. When he was not driving, he was always ready to trim the branches of the jackfruit tree and clear the bases of the coconut palms. He always brought back exotic plants when they returned from Ooty and other places and planted them in our garden. There was something common between Abhilash and him – I noticed. Like Abhilash, he too was impossibly neat. No matter how long and tedious the drive was, he would always look neat and spruced up; his abundant hair would always be neatly combed. He would never be unkempt or fatigued. He was tenderly affectionate towards Chechi and me, attentive to even our tiniest needs and delights. He was always the humble servant before my parents. So many times had Chechi and I trusted him, more than we had our father. As I regarded him, my eyes overflowed. His hand was still in mine. I learned something then: there is no difference between the hands of men and women when they are scared. They turn cold; their palms sweat in the same way.

Panayambarambil's wife served us tea and cake. Rubin fetched his beautiful and very pregnant wife. Amma, Kochumaaman and I chitchatted. But Ulahannan Maaman did not utter a single word. He sat there rubbing his palms together. Doubts must have started to gather in Panayambarambil's mind. I remembered Aruna's father. I saw a truck running over Shafeeq, Amma, and me on our way home. Rich people, after all? Who knows what they'll decide to do and when? You are finished if they make up their minds that poorer and failed people are better off dead, isn't it? Other human beings are just flies to them. They can be swatted or crushed underfoot. They may be dismissed like minor debts.

'My father leaned on and trusted Ulahannan Maaman more than he did my mother!' I declared loudly to Panayambarambil. 'It was he who bought our Contessa car and helped us when Acchan's business failed.'

Kochumaaman and Amma looked thoroughly jolted. I found the picture that I had downloaded from FB the day before: Rubin and his wife posing in front of the car after their wedding. 'This was the car...'

I showed them the picture. All the blood in Ulahannan Maaman's face seemed to have turned into vapour. Kochumaaman stood up. 'Abey, let's leave these family friends be, let them talk. Shall we go over there somewhere?'

'Sure! Roy, you can chat in the drawing room that opens on to the garden. Let me share a drink with Panikkar Chettan!'

Panayambarambil took Kochumaaman to another room. Ulahannan Maaman now looked utterly terrified. Roy's face paled. But there was no other way; they got up. It was Rubin who opened the door to the drawing room for us and switched on the AC. He was not in the know of things even then. I did not let go of Ulahannan Maaman's hand. What if he pulled it away and ran? Roy pushed his way in. 'Please do rest,' I told Rubin and his wife, excusing them thus, but made sure that Elsa stayed. I was determined that she must witness it all. Not because of anything particular, but in such situations, I trusted men's wives more than the men themselves. The husbands would have just one agenda, not the wives. They would have another, of their own – one that might be useful to us.

It was a huge room. Even though he sat down on the sofa, Ulahannan Maaman was still silent. Had he decided to stay silent, I worried. 'Didn't you bring Sosa?' Amma asked.

'Ammachi died seven years ago,' Roy said.

'Aiyo, we didn't know.'

'It was cancer.'

'The poor woman.' Amma sighed.

'Is there any particular reason why you have come, Vasanthamma?'

'Ulahannan knows about it, Roy.'

'May I know, too, please?'

'Wouldn't it be better if Ulahannan spoke of it?'

All of a sudden, the expression on Roy's face changed. 'What is it that you want? We are about to celebrate something auspicious. If mother and daughter are out to ruin it trying to settle old scores, you'll be taught a lesson, I warn you! Don't tell me you weren't forewarned.'

The graciousness with which he had conducted himself until then, vanished. He went right back to being that imp of a boy who had come running with his cycle tyre in a tattered pair of knickers to ask for some coconut oil for his mother. Amma smiled.

'Calm down, Roy. I've read somewhere that even when people grow up, they don't usually forget those who have shown them tender affection in their childhood. Seems like this is not always true! How could you speak to me like this if it were.'

I also chipped in. 'Roycha, don't try to scare us. Oh, won't we be completely intimidated by your loud voice?'

He fell silent. I did not stop.

'I have just one thing to tell you both. If you are good to us, we will be good to you. If you are honest with us, we will also be honest with you. But if you're going to be like the old times – stabbing us in the back – then I don't need much time to bring down this life of yours. I can rip off your masks in no time, actually—' I paused, and continued: 'It's Ulahannan Maaman who has to decide if your life should fall apart or stay intact.'

I held Ulahannan Maaman's chin in my hand and lifted it. Helpless, he looked into my eyes.

'Ulahannan Maama, I met the film star Rajani a few days ago. She told me the story of how you drove her to Madras. That is, the story of what you did to her.'

His face looked bloodshot, like it had been scratched with a piece of smoking firewood. Roy blanched. Elsa looked completely clueless; my heart went out to her. But that was the fate of wives at the time this story happened. Conjugality was a package. There was no way you could demand just happiness in it. Either you took the whole package, or you did not.

'What do you want? I'll talk.' His speech returned. Like his form, his voice too had changed. The sugar with which he coated it while he used to work for us had disappeared. Maybe because he had aged. Or maybe because he'd climbed so great a height that he now spoke from that altitude. Speaking from above means that you can speak only in two ways: either in the command-mode or in the advice-mode. But there was this thing: if he spoke from the heights of wealth, I spoke from the peak of truth. So, I, too, gave up sweetness of tone and humility.

'The first thing I want to know is how much commission did you get for marrying Satyaprabha off to Dinakaran Pillai?'

Ulahannan Maaman looked thunderstruck. It took him a few minutes to regain his composure.

'Satyaprabha, who? Who told you all this?'

'Who could possibly have told me?' I refused to let go. He looked aghast.

'That girl had to be brought ashore ... somehow...' he whispered around a minute later.

'How did you come to know Dinakaran Pillai, Ulahannan Maama?'

'Through the ganja business...'

'You smoked? I can't believe it!'

'I never did.'

'Just sold it?'

'One did many things to hang on in life.'

'And how did you meet Acchan?'

'We were in jail together, in Madras.'

Amma and I were shaken, but we hid it well.

'Which year was this?'

'When he was studying in Madras.'

'Why was he in jail?'

'Arrested for the death of the girl who gave birth to Satyaprabha.'

'How long were you in jail for?'

'Two or two and a half years.'

'Wouldn't it have been better to just marry her off to her uncle? Wasn't it the custom anyway?'

'Just thought that Dinakaran Pillai would suit her better.'

'Who thought so?'

'Muthalaali, her father.'

'Why are you lying in your old age, Ulahannan?'

'Vasantha Chechi, I just thought it might be better for the girl – better than suffering all her life in an ironsmith's hovel...'

'How much did Dinakaran Pillai get for it?'

'Two thousand five hundred a month.'

'From 1972 onwards?'

'It stopped after Vasanthamaalika was sold.'

'How much did you get, Ulahannan?'

He did not answer.

'Okay, leave it. What did you do with Satyaprabha's newborns?'

'One was given away through Leelavallabhan Saar, to an LP School teacher near their house. I gave away the other one to an orphanage … someone adopted it.'

'Did this involve money too?'

'I paid two thousand to the orphanage…'

'It was you who found Savithri Amma a house, am I not right?' I asked. This time it was Amma's face that turned pale. I felt a stab of cruel satisfaction.

'That was on Dinakaran Pillai's orders.'

'How was Savithri Amma related to him?'

'They were distant relatives.'

'Are they still close?'

'After Muthalaali used her older girl, Dinakaran Pillai, too, tried to use her. She killed herself. They quarrelled after this.'

'His son Pratapan stabbed my father, didn't he?'

'I vow on Christ of the Lord, I know nothing of it.'

'Who set fire to the house, Ulahannan?'

'Vasantha Chechi, I do not know. The two boys were truly full of rage at Muthalaali for having pushed their sister to her death. And they were definitely under Dinakaran Pillai's thumb.'

'Did Muthalaali know that it was you who bought the Contessa?'

'Not sure. I did not see him after that. I really did not have the guts to face him.'

'Didn't he seek you, Ulahannan?'

'Before he could, I sold the house there and left for Coimbatore with Roy and the other kids. My uncle had a small shop there.'

'But Satyaprabha was moved into the mental hospital with your knowledge, surely?'

'There was no other way. She was raving mad.'

'What if it was your Rina in her place?'

'What am I to say if you ask that, Vasantha Chechi?'

'Acchan used to carry a dagger with him, didn't he?'

'Yes, a curved one. He would always tuck it into his belt, dear.'

'That one, yes. Did Satyaprabha's family make that for him?'

'I don't know. He already had it when I first met him.'

'Did you both get out of jail together?'

'No, he got out first. But we kept in touch through letters. When he came to Madras to make his first movie, he got me out.'

'How?'

'Found a hotshot lawyer, fought my case.'

'He was really attached to you, that means.'

'I have always shown my gratitude for it, Vasantha Chechi.'

'Yes, that is precisely why you did not care to give a second look when he was attacked and wounded, rendered helpless, immobilized, ruined.'

'I didn't have the strength to see him that way, Chechi.'

'You didn't need one-tenth of the strength you'd shown in doing all the dirty work till then?'

My eyes happened to fall on Elsa's face just then. My heart ached a bit. Her confidence seemed to have been wiped out, like make-up in hard rain. I felt a bit guilty. But we were of the same generation, bound to suffer idols crashing down.

I stretched my hand, touched Amma. Let's go, I told her. All my questions had been answered. We should be leaving. But Amma was not done. She continued:

'Ulahannan, tell me, have I ever hurt you? Insulted you?'

'Never, Vasantha Chechi.'

'Did I not make sure, like I did for my own family, that you were well-fed, that the kids never lacked schoolbooks, or anything?'

'Yes, Vasantha Chechi.'

'Even when we were completely ruined and when I struggled not knowing what to do with my two little girls, did I not always give you enough from my purse?' Her voice fell. Ulahannan Maaman looked even more devastated. He looked like the very personification of wretchedness.

'I have never said anything to the contrary, Vasantha Chechi.'

'And was it despite all that that you did this to me, Ulahannan? What pleasure did you get from betraying those who trusted you?'

I saw him squirm and shrink behind his silk kurta. Like an ice cube melting in the sun and yielding its square shape to a round one, I saw him shrink to his true shape. The others, however, were melting more rapidly than he was. Roy's head was bent. Elsa was weeping. I struggled to suppress a whimper. Ulahannan Maaman buried his face in his hands. Amma sighed.

'All right, Ulahannan, it was good to meet again.'

She rose. I wiped my eyes. Ulahannan Maaman got up too. All of a sudden, he fell at Amma's feet. She drew back. He had to struggle a bit to get up from there. 'Forgive me, Vasantha Chechi,' the man begged. Amma grabbed his folded palms.

'There's nothing wrong in the greed for wealth, right, Ulahannan? So why beg forgiveness? It is meaningless!'

'Vasantha Chechi, how much money will you take to forgive me?'

'Why would I need money, Ulahannan? My daughter does not need it either.'

'Then tell me just once that you have forgiven me.'

'I would have, if only you had told me something without my asking.'

'What, Vasantha Chechi?'

'About Muthalaali's will…'

That nearly knocked me out. What will? Which will? But yet again, Ulahannan Maaman became the ice cube exposed to the sun. The contempt that Elsa felt for him, evident on her face, hardened into sheer hate. Roychan looked even more listless. A disturbing silence pooled in the room.

Amma looked at him scornfully, laughed mockingly. 'Let good come to all!' she whispered. 'Satye, let us not be their killjoys today,' she announced.

Then, Ulahannan Maaman let slip that fact. The cruellest truth in this story of crime investigation.

'Vasantha Chechi, Venukkuttan has it.'

The earth split open, and I fell into a bottomless abyss. Sucked in by the abyss relentlessly, I threw a piteous glance at Amma. I felt myself falling and falling. Have you ever had such a fall? A pity, if you haven't! For then, you would not learn that the soul's release is not through its upward rise towards the sky and the clouds; it comes about from getting buried in mud and swamp. It's interesting. You will learn of a diverse world that exists underneath floors covered in black granite and behind walls on which hang expensive paintings. No one sees the faces of others there. One can have only the experience of falling into the abyss at the same speed, to the same rhythm. There's something else too: you can never return. Anyway, after falling to such depths, who can find the courage to climb back up?

'How did Venukkuttan find it?' I heard Amma ask, as though from a distant planet.

'Vasantha Chechi, he was the father of Satyaprabha's infants!'

I became the python who first swallowed the elephant and then got its head stuck in a trap. Its heart pounded hard, the neck twisted and turned in agony, the tail thrashed about on the floor involuntarily. Amid that chaos, when the phone rang and revealed the caller to be Joyo, I felt nothing. I took the call to tell him that I would call back later, but he quickly told me what he had to: 'Auntie, Inspector Shetty has returned. He needs to meet you urgently.'

I don't have to particularly tell you how I felt after. I was so full, so very full. It was like I had swallowed three or four elephants, not just one.

FIFTY-THREE

There is a point at which any investigation comes to an end. That is not the point when all of the truth is revealed. Rather, it is the point when the desire to find the truth dies. When the investigation took me to Venukkuttan Chettan, the thrill ended. What was there to know now? A will, revenge, a murder attempt – what a tired old story! It bored me. And my mother – she wasn't willing to speak of it even. She was very occupied. She was out most of the time – visiting her eldest brother, friends from school, going to town, shopping. She told me nothing. Not because I did not ask. 'Can't you just do what you believe to be right?' – this was her reply, always. I sought help from two people then – from Kallu and Sandeepa Sen. Both encouraged me to continue my search, and to meet Venukkuttan Chettan in person.

I, too, thought that it would be a bloody foolish mistake to fill the pot for ninety-nine days only to break it on the hundredth. How do we know – there might be a sub-narrative and a hidden character controlling the story's end? It was that suspense that drove me ahead. The yearning for such a suspense is akin to pining for romance. Both are organic. But that doesn't mean that they are free of pain. If there's a blade stuck in your heart, it will be painful, of course. Its point will

surely pierce the walls of the heart with each heartbeat. I was in pain.
I was like the butterfly breaking out of its pupa. The world that I had
known hitherto had suddenly changed. The world that I had known
as a caterpillar was not the world that I encountered inside the pupa.
And that world was definitely not the one that lay before the butterfly.
Does the world change so fast, you may ask. Will the world in which
the caterpillar lived change only because it spent a few days in a pupa,
you may ask. I can tell you that, from the experiences of my life. It
will change, sharply. Maybe you were a caterpillar and a pupa on the
very same bough. But the world you perceived while you crawled on
the bough is surely not the world you will get to explore with your
wings. Not only the world, but people too change. So do their ideas
and ideals. So do even idols. For example, the advertisements for khadi
that appeared at the time. Earlier, the ads used to feature a half-naked
fakir. But one day, when all this was happening, it changed to an image
of a stylishly dressed fakir. With this, khadi changed. The idea that
it stood for changed. So did the very idea of the fakir. That did not
bother me, really. But when some leaders began to demand that the
image of Gandhiji should be removed from our currency notes, I was
indeed terrified. These were notes that had been referred to as 'Gandhi'
for such a long time now. I had suffered so much when just two of
those were banned. What if the whole range was removed?

Even if the notes were withdrawn, there would still be money.
Plastic money. It would have no Gandhi on it; it could not be called
Gandhi either. Notes represent a certain idea. Venukkuttan Chettan
was a bit like that. He represented the idea of unconditional love.
The only person we could trust blindly. That this figure was going to
disappear, made me very afraid. I hesitated to go to his house. There
was another reason behind my hesitation; and it was the suspicion that
Ulahannan Maaman might have warned him by now. I was sure that
if he had been thus warned, he would not utter a single word. I would
not be able to break that fortress. Even otherwise, he was taciturn. If
we spoke now, the conversation would make sure that he would be out

of our lives forever. After all, had he not already died in our minds? We didn't know what to do with the body, that was all.

I set out when Amma was up in the morning. She did not ask me where I was going; I didn't tell her either. I didn't call for Harish's auto. 'Chechi, why're you making so many visits?' That would be his question, I anticipated. I was a woman – just a woman, after all. So, it seemed like I was duty-bound to explain all my acts to all men. The only way to avoid that was to avoid him completely, but without creating that impression.

The bus arrived as soon as I reached the bus stop. And when I got out at the bus stop near Venukkuttan Chettan's house, there was an autorickshaw ready and waiting. The gates of his house lay wide open. This meant that Madam Aswathy was visiting. Venukkuttan Chettan's car was not in the porch. It was not practical to deal with Aswathy without him. I hesitated, wondering if it wasn't a better idea to go back, but a policeman approached me, asking me who I was and why I was there. To meet Venukkuttan Chettan, I told him. He went in. Soon Venukkuttan Chettan came out, following the policeman. His face always bore a neutral, impassive look, and so the smile that took a moment to light up and the question 'Satyamole, you?' did not necessarily signify anything unusual. But I was still hesitant. 'Didn't Vasantha Chechi come?' he asked, holding his arm out to me. How as a child I used to swing holding that arm! I felt tears pricking my eyelids.

'Radha is away in Guruvayur. Aji's daughter has an exam,' he said, leading me into the house. It was an old house, still. It never bore signs that would have boasted of its inhabitants – two high-level civil servants, one from the IAS, the other from the IPS. They had just added another storey. The floor was laid with granite, the walls had been repainted, and some new furniture had been added, but the house, which always bore a withdrawn, furtive look, continued to look reticent, and even mysterious. I followed Venukkuttan Chettan into the drawing room and sat down on the sofa. It was evident that I just couldn't joke or chat in a relaxed manner like I used to. As though he had noticed it, Venukkuttan Chettan went in to ask for some coffee.

I looked around. I remembered his sixtieth birthday celebrations from five years ago. I had come down from Bhubaneswar just for that, to gift him a chain of gold-capped tulsi beads. I could see it above his half-sleeved vest now. He would drop me to school and fetch me from there since kindergarten. He was so thin back then! I would sit on the tiny seat in front of his bicycle. When he cycled back, I would be prattling non-stop. I would demand that he pluck for me every flower and fruit we chanced upon. He never refused any request Chechi or I made. Much later, when we needed the title deed of the land he'd bought at Kakkanad, as security for the private bank, he had handed it over to me without a single question.

We too never really asked about him. What to ask about someone you'd known since birth? It was generally thought that he was of Acchan's caste. He had resisted marriage for a long while. In the end, Amma called a marriage broker. It was Amma who went to see the prospective bride, Radha Chechi. Venukkuttan Chettan had agreed to the marriage rather reluctantly. It was at this time, when talks about his wedding were on, that I got to know that he was actually from Takkala, in Tamil Nadu. Until then, I had thought that he had initially joined Appooppan's seafood factory as a worker and had eventually been promoted for his diligence. Laalamma's daughter used to drop Chechi to school. By the time I was ready to go to school, Gracy Chechi was married. So Appooppan sent him over to Vasanthaalayam. He pampered me more than Acchan ever did. He would throw me up in the air and catch me, make me stand on his shoulder to pluck mangoes, tie up the swing, drag me around while I sat on a palm frond, take me to touch the elephant and sit me on top of the wooden horse during temple festivals ... He was, for me, the 'dependable adult' who would make any effort to fulfil a child's trivial dreams. The day I scored full marks in Class 1, I waited impatiently for him. The moment he appeared, I rushed up and showed him my slate. He picked me up in delight, and threw me high, jubilantly, and then caught me safely; I laughed in sheer delight. On our way back, he bought me cotton candy. He knew more about our marks in school than Amma herself. But he was very scared of Acchan. When Acchan was home, he tried his best to keep out of his way. Some of the questions that bothered me after the meeting with Ulahannan Maaman were: Why did Acchan allow him to continue in our house? Why didn't Venukkuttan Chettan finish us off then itself, when it was easier? When did Acchan write a will? Did it reach Venukkuttan Chettan's hands after Acchan was stabbed?

As I pondered these questions, Venukkuttan Chettan appeared with two cups of coffee and held one out to me. The other he placed on the teapoy, and sat down on the sofa opposite mine. And we talked:

'What is it, my dear? You look troubled?'

'A disturbing feeling, Venukkuttan Chettaa!'

'Is it because of that fellow trying to kill you? Don't worry, Achu is on it!'

'He'll kill me anyway.'

'Come on, don't be so scared. Don't you have all of us?'

'They killed Chechi despite all of us, didn't they?'

'Ohh! But wasn't that an accident?'

'What about the attack on Acchan?'

'There were people who nursed grudges against him.'

'This too is a continuation of that grudge.'

'Ah, you always had this habit of blowing up even tiny things, Satyamole!'

'Aren't we all shaped by experience, Venukkuttan Chettaa? Isn't it that which makes us blow up everything small?'

'Are you more frightened now? Is that why you are here so early?'

'I may get a job in Takkala, Venukkuttan Chettaa. I have to look for a house to stay.'

He fell silent for a few moments.

'I left the place some forty-five years back ... Where will you be working there?'

'At a management institute. Don't you have any relatives there?'

Again, a moment of silence.

'What relatives do I have other than you all?'

Then I took out my phone and showed him the photo.

'But what about these people?'

He jumped, then fell back. It was a terrible jolt to him, evidently. I felt that the concern that Ulahannan Maaman might have forewarned him was misplaced. He started up again and began to go indoors. I stopped him.

'How can you just leave like that? You have to answer me.'

He looked helpless. I made him sit on the sofa again.

'I have learned it all – I hope I don't need to tell you?'

He leaned on the sofa without looking at me. The chest on which the chain I gifted rested, was heaving.

'Venukkuttan Chettaa, I never thought you'd want to see me dead so much. Not in my wildest dreams. Could you not just tell me that? I would have died that moment of a broken heart.'

His eyes were fixed on me. They were welling.

'Do not say such things, Satyamole.'

'Then tell me, who funded Satyaprakash?'

'God be my witness, it was not me, Satyamole!'

'You know well that I want to believe that too.'

'That is the truth.'

'But, Venukkuttan Chettaa, why did you keep putting up an act like that? Why did you bury so much vengeance in your heart and pretend to be so affectionate?'

'It was not pretence.'

'Can someone be affectionate and vengeful at the same time?'

'Vengeful? Me?'

'Didn't you hate my father for marrying off Satyaprabha to someone else? Did you want revenge when you lost the three infants she gave birth to?'

'My dear, you have to be brave in order to be vengeful. How could I be brave? Vengeful towards someone as powerful as Muthalaali?'

'Why did you come down here from Madras if not to take revenge?'

'I came to find her and our children.'

'Wasn't it easier to stop her marriage from happening?'

'I did not know of it, my dear. I was in hiding.'

'Did you pick up Malayalam at that time?'

'I got used to speaking it then. Your father had taught me to read and write it. He would give me writing exercises and take my sister to his bedroom. I learned to read and write Malayalam in six months. And she became pregnant.'

'Your sister did not go to school?'

'She went to school until the third standard. The government at the time made a law that children would study in schools until noon and then be taught various crafts from their community. She dropped out after that.'

'What about you?'

'Then they began to give us midday meals in school. So I went to school. But they stopped giving meals in the higher classes, so I dropped out. I was also upset by Akka's death.'

'Did you meet my father as a neighbour?'

'It was through my father's younger brother, our chittappa.'

'And what about your parents?'

'The doctor had advised my mother never to get pregnant after she had Akka. But I was born, and Amma died in childbirth. Appa was devastated; he killed himself. We were raised by our grandmother – our paatti – and our chittappa.'

'Where is he now?'

'Died in an accident.'

'Was it murder?'

'He was crossing the road, drunk.'

'How did he and my father get close?'

'Give my chittappa a bottle, and he would do any dirty job. His line of work was finding corpses for the medical college. Your father and Chittappa also used to preserve dead snakes, fish and other creatures in oil and acid.'

'That is, preserve them in formalin?'

'In those days, our thatched hut had a room on the side, and it was filled with jars and acid with dead snakes, fish, alligators, and so on in them.'

'Did you also learn to preserve specimens?'

'After Chittappa died, we used to do it for your father.'

A curved dagger with an 'S'-shaped tip rose in my mind.

'It was you who preserved that foetus that we found in Acchan's box, isn't it?'

'That was my Azhagi's – that is Satyaprabha's – infant. My child.'

I squirmed. 'How could you have preserved your own baby's body?'

'She insisted. She wanted to see it every day, she said.'

'Good god! And you agreed to it, Venukkuttan Chetta?'

'I was more sentimental than her then...'

'Were you with her when she gave birth?'

'Just Paatti and I.'

'I was told that she passed away before?'

'No, it happened after – when I went to get her and the children.'

'Was it Acchan who killed her? Pushed her?'

'Pushed? She was hacked to death!'

'Who did that?'

'Ulahannan, and the thugs he brought there. Muthalaali was busy with shooting, he was at a movie set.'

'How did Ulahannan land up there?'

'He got to know that Azhagi had given birth, and he brought over four of the thugs. They kicked me and Paatti out, and locked her and the babies in a room.'

'I can't believe my ears!'

'For money, people will do this, and worse. I would have been killed too. I managed to flee.'

'You didn't approach the police?'

'Oh! What's the use of doing so for a poor and helpless man like me?'

'Where did you run to?'

'Tirunelveli, for a while. And later to Nagercoil.'

'And Satyaprabha?'

'I thought they would keep her in the guest house. Just wanted to make some money, rescue her and our babies, disappear. I did make a little money, came back, tried to find out from the owner of the petty shop near the guest house about them. He was very fond of me. I begged him. He offered Tyagu some liquor and he said that she had been taken to Kerala.'

'And when you knew?'

'I went straight to your seafood factories. Thought that it would be easy to find her once I reached.'

'How did you find the factory?'

'When I went looking for her, Babu Saar was in the guest house. I knew from Azhagi that he was Muthalaali's brother-in-law. The petty-shop owner helped me find his whereabouts.'

'And so you joined the factory as a worker, right?'

'I soon saw that it was impossible to locate Azhagi staying there. Moving to their house as a helper might be a better move, I thought. So I claimed that I was allergic to ice and asked for a job as a domestic helper. My boss agreed. But it was only when I shifted to your tharavad that I realized that it wasn't so easy to find things out in the homes of the rich!'

'When did you find out about Satyaprabha's marriage?'

'I went back to Madras feeling hopeless. Back to the petty-shop owner, whom I begged to help me get more information. He bribed Tyagu with more alcohol and then we knew … It broke my heart. I stopped looking for her.'

'Why did you stop?'

All of a sudden, Venukkuttan Chettan looked enraged. 'How could I keep looking? She was another man's wife by then! His wife.'

'If so, why did you return to our tharavad again?'

'I wanted my children.'

'Who told you that they were in Kerala?'

'Tyagu told the petty-shop owner, that they were removed before the wedding.'

'I have this doubt – how did that jar with the foetus end up with Acchan?'

'Most probably through Ulahannan ... He must have grabbed more money from your father with it.'

'Didn't Ulahannan recognize you?'

'No. He had of course seen me just once, and that too, at night. They were all totally drunk, anyway. And when I walked into Vasanthaalayam after five years, I was so changed, I couldn't recognize myself!'

'Acchan too could not make out who you were?'

'The last time Muthalaali had seen me was when I was just five. He ought to have recognized me in the five years I stayed there. But he never really stayed there, did he? All his visits were lightning visits! He must have thought I was dead.'

'So Acchan did not know the truth until his death?'

'That's what I believe.'

'Let me ask you something else – did Acchan come looking for Satyaprabha's mother after he gave up his studies? Or did you seek him out?'

'Paatti became too weak to work. I met our needs somehow ... selling peanuts, polishing shoes ... We were starving most of the time. One day I noticed a photo of Muthalaali posing with Sivaji Ganesan in the shop window of Top Stills Studio. I went in, found out where he was. There was a shooting happening at Gemini Studio. I took Azhagi and Paatti there.'

'Did you manage to meet him there, face to face, that is?'

'No, I was always terrified of him – he reminded me of Akka, lying dead … in a pool of blood…' He wheezed. 'I hated to have to beg before him. But we had no other way. We were starving! Pride, then, is not above a meal.'

As I tried to peer into the man's heart, my eyes smarted. I saw a child standing utterly stunned by the glare of blood. This was in 1957. The communist government ruled in Kerala. The Kamaraj government ruled in Tamil Nadu.

'When did Ulahannan recognize you, Venukkuttan Chettaa?'

'After Azhagi's death. She had willed everything to me.'

'And when did you see him?'

'He called me. Told me that I was to give Dinakaran Pillai half of the inheritance. He threatened to tell Vasantha Chechi everything if I didn't.'

'And what was your response?'

'That we should both go to her and tell her the whole truth.'

'Was Azhagi Satyaprabha's real name?'

'It was Sivappazhagi. I named her. Then, when Muthalaali admitted her to the convent school, she became Satyaprabha.'

'What was your real name?'

'Kumaran. I gave up that name when I left Madras State – that was what Tamil Nadu was called back then.'

'Who changed it to Venukkuttan?'

'I chose it – it was the name of the younger son of the man who gave me a job in Takkala.'

'When did you fall in love with Satyaprabha?' I asked, to change the subject.

'Muthalaali sent her to a big school. She got good clothes, three square meals a day … and became rosy and pretty – like her name … Sivappazhagi. Paatti did not want us to give her up … do not give her up to these Malayalis, she would say three times a day. I think that worked on my mind. And she loved me too.'

'But to make her pregnant at such a young age…'

'She wanted it. We also thought that Muthalaali wouldn't object if we had a child...'

'Where did the two of you meet?'

'In the guest house, when it was free. Sometimes Paatti would bring her to our hut too.'

'All right. After she and the babies were locked up, did you ever see her?'

'Twenty-seven years later.' He tried to smile but his eyes welled.

'In 1999?' I asked anxiously. He had to make a serious effort to nod in agreement. But before he could complete, he broke down and whimpered.

'She killed herself the week after we met again!' His voice broke as he sobbed uncontrollably. But he still completed what he was saying: 'She had clung to life only to see me again!'

He got up as though to collect himself and paced the room. His face was flushed; he stooped, looked terribly fatigued. He sat down again and rubbed his chest. Then got up again, went to the kitchen door, and asked for some water, gulped it down. My birthday present to him rose and fell to the rhythm of his chest.

'Enough, my dear. Can't bear any more...' he said upon returning to the sofa and looked at me pathetically. 'Don't ask me anything more. I can't.'

But I did not have the patience to let myself allow that request.

'Satya, you will never know my agony. True, I used to eat three meals at your house. You children and Vasantha Chechi were very warm and loving too. I lacked nothing there. But none of you knew how I burned within...'

'Please tell me at least how you came to know about Satyaprabha.'

'Later, my dear.' He sounded listless. His eyes were still welling up.

'Later ... But what if I am not around to listen to you?'

'When you went visiting a friend and did not return home for two days...'

That was a blow.

'Vasantha Chechi told me to go to town, to the house of a girl called Shanti, to find out.'

I went pale in the face but did not come apart. Amma had never mentioned this to me; I never knew about it.

'I went to this house but there was no one there. I racked my brains trying to think whom I could ask, and then a police jeep passed by, with Dinakaran Pillai and you.'

This time, it was my turn to flush hard. I did not try to hide it. My chest heaved violently too. I, too, was gripped by the urge to get up, pace about, ask for water, and then sit down again. I sat there feeling clammy with sweat.

'I went to the police station. There was no one there but a woman officer. She told me that they had picked you up from the college. I thought that they must have dropped you home. Then a policeman came in and I overheard him chatting about Dinakaran Pillai ... that his first wife was a Tamil girl, and she was now in a mental hospital. I suspected something at once. I came back as soon as I could to our local police station, got Dinakaran Pillai's address, and headed there. His younger sister was home. I learned from her the details. That very day, I went to Kuthiravattam, to the mental hospital, but there they told me that she had been discharged several years ago. She was in a home for the destitute. I rushed there.'

I listened to him amazed. The chains in which these lives of ours are strung – let me tell you from experience – they are impossible to break. Just because you manage to yank the chain hard and break it, doesn't quite mean the links come apart. Like the money plant that simply grows new roots wherever it falls, it just keeps growing seeking another of its links.

'And when you saw her?' I asked, suppressing my excitement. But then I realized at once that I shouldn't have. The man's eyes were overflowing. The unearthly radiance that the memory brought to his face revealed to me the truth that I had been seeking.

Have you ever crawled through a tunnel of darkness to reach the light? Have you known what it feels like to have freed your neck and head trapped inside a water pot? If not, it means you have never experienced life's great transformations. But yes, there is a price: you'll struggle for breath for a long time, become desperate. The skin on your chest will peel off, the hair on your head will be pulled out by their roots, and you'll be in a frenzy of agony.

'Venukkuttan Chettaa, did you find the babies which had been given away?'

'Wasn't that why I came back here?' He rubbed his chest and gave me a pained look.

'My son got a better father than I could be. He got a better mother. Though he did not know me, I watched him grow from a distance.'

'Who is he?'

'The son of the teacher ... from the Pulikkal Thekke house. Krishnakumar. Don't know if you know them. Has a printing press, an iron store...'

'I know them...' I said, trembling. The image of the Angry Hanuman popped up inside my head.

'And the other baby?'

'Why do you need to know?'

I started, hearing a heavy, commanding voice. Aswathy stood on the staircase. I was seeing her after many years. She had Venukkuttan Chettan's height and Radha Chechi's chiselled face. She wore a skirt and a pink, sleeveless, lace-embroidered top. Her hair was open. But I felt intimidated by the sight of her. Her eyes were not those of her parents; the pupils looked like the mouths of two revolvers pointing. For no reason, my throat dried up. After a moment's confusion, I regained my composure and rose respectfully from the sofa.

'Good morning, Madam!'

'Be seated.'

She strode in, radiating power, and sat on the sofa opposite mine. 'You go inside, Accha,' she ordered her father.

'I haven't finished speaking to him,' I said, still seated.

'Won't it do if I tell you the rest?'

She glowered at me. Her hatred towards me was evident on her face. Is this the little girl who once lay in my lap and read children's magazines, I asked myself in disbelief. You thought it was a lizard, but it turned out to be a dinosaur! I had only to blink, and she would crush me under the boots of power she wore. But I was not going to give up.

'All right, fine. I need to know who is talking, though: is this Venukkuttan Chettan's daughter Acchu, or Aswathy Venu IPS?'

'You can choose, Satyapriya Ma'am.'

'For the time being, I have nothing to talk to Aswathy Venu IPS about.'

'But Aswathy Venu IPS has some things to talk to Satyapriya Ma'am about.'

'For that, you will have to come over to my house.'

She became even more furious.

'Yes, then I will speak to you as Aswathy, the daughter of Venukkuttan and Radha.'

'Well, then tell me, where is the second infant born to your father's first wife?'

'Why should I tell you?' She sounded like she was throwing me a challenge.

'Because she happens to be my sister Satyaprabha's daughter.'

'Does Amma's half-sister have more authority than Acchan?'

'Yes, of course. Especially when a will that included me as well is in your father's possession!'

Her faced flushed menacingly. 'Will? What will?'

'Aswathy Ma'am, I really think that you will use Satyaprakash to knock off your parents, even.'

'Mind your words!' Her face burned. So did mine.

'Venukkuttan Chetta, all this time, Amma and I trusted you blindly, from the bottom of our hearts. I'll set aside the way you duped me, but the way you betrayed Amma was really too much…'

'I would have told Vasantha Chechi. But then, I would have had to reveal it all. I feared that she wouldn't be able to take it...' His voice grew hoarse.

'Accha, go inside, now!' Aswathy snapped.

'Acchu, I've told her quite a lot. Now let me finish.'

'The second baby...' He tried to say something, but she did not let him. She grabbed him, dragged him to an inner room, threw him inside, and bolted the door from the outside. She then came right back to where I was. I feared that she would strangle me. She looked like she might do it too – totally ruthless.

'I'll find out,' I said, managing to hide that I was shaking. 'If I could uncover so much, I'll also seek out the other infant.'

She laughed. 'I know, Satyapriya Ma'am,' she said. 'But what if before that I arrest you for Maoist connections?'

I liked the aggression in her, the way she looked.

'Try,' I said, 'try it.'

I, too, laughed. We fixed our eyes on each other's for some moments. That was the moment when the essence of this thing that we call 'masculinity' was revealed to me. In reality, it has nothing to do with being male. It is all about power. The word should actually be 'power-li-nity'. There is, however, only one way to deal with both masculinity and power-li-nity: deal out double the amount of violence, or practise a non-violence that they can never imagine. Non-violence does not mean submitting to violence; it means preventing it. I spied a clue that I had ignored until then: it lay on the lower shelf of the teapoy.

'My mother had brought to you a note torn neatly in two halves. What happened to it?' I asked. This confounded her a bit.

'We are investigating.'

'And what have you found?'

'Someone was just trying to scare you.'

'Maybe Prakashan?'

'He's the one with a grudge towards your family!'

'What grudge?'

'Against your father, for having destroyed his family.'

'But he's not the one who'll reap gains from my death.'

'What do you mean?'

'Only someone who owns a press would have printed it.'

I bent down and pulled the piece of paper out of the lower shelf. The notice of Balidan Diwas. 15 November, the day before an attempt on my life was made.

Her face went yellow. She snatched the notice out of my hand.

'Sorry, I am in a bit of a rush.'

I did not pause to bid goodbye to Venukkuttan Chettan. I was numb. I took the first autorickshaw I could find and went back home.

You may have noticed, I don't know but, like human beings, stories too are wrecked by their incongruities. There are no stories without these elements in this world either. We just pretend not to see such puzzles. Some, we fail to notice. The most important thing of all is the way some of the characters in the stories transform. The true shock of that day was not the conversation I had with Venukkuttan Chettan, nor my encounter with Aswathy, or the notice I chanced upon. It came from seeing Amma when I reached home – all dressed for a trip. My mother, who had been in a sari with her long hair knotted loosely at the tip when I left home, was now in a salwar-kameez, her hair cut short – transformed, within just two hours. I did not recognize the person seated in the veranda. The sight of her had me transfixed, astonished. Right then, Shafeeq's taxi arrived. When he climbed out and opened the gates of the house, I stared at Amma, unaware of what she was up to. She pushed forward two suitcases, a big one and a smaller one, from behind the chairs. I thought that the light was failing in my eyes. Was I dreaming? Or hallucinating? I had no idea.

When the suitcases were loaded, Shafeeq asked, 'Only Amma, no Chechi?'

'From now on, am I not going to travel by myself, Shafeeq?' she retorted, without flinching. Before she set out, she held me close once, and then, lifting my face, kissed me on the forehead and cheeks. My face was quite wet now.

'Stay happy. I'll be back as soon as I can. Will call once I reach the airport.'

She was brief. I, too, did not ask her anything further. Amma got into the car, shut the door, Shafeeq started the car, Amma waved. When the car disappeared from sight, however, I ran after it. I wanted to hug Amma, kiss her one more time. What if I could never do it again? The thought made me terribly scared. She will never return, my mind told me. I could not even make out where she was going. My limbs felt weak. I almost crawled back inside the house, feeling lesser than even a worm. The house seemed to be growing bigger, acquiring the shape and proportion of a dinosaur. It scared me even more; I shivered. But after some time, both body and mind tired of the fear and shivering. I searched for my old diary. On a new page, I wrote: '*Krishnakumar. The owner of Sriram Press. He was Satyaprabha's son. The second infant was a daughter. Of my age.*' Overall, I felt satisfied. The only thing left to know was: When and how would I be murdered by Satyaprakash?

I was tired, and felt like my head was trapped inside a water pot. I was desperate for someone to break the pot and let me out. But then, it was not a pot to be broken by another; it was a pupa which had to be broken out of in good time. Even though it was excruciatingly painful, I broke out of my pupa and emerged into the world outside. I tried to measure the changes. Then, unexpectedly, I noticed the newspaper headlines: 'No counterfeit notes in confiscated bundles'.

I felt sorry for the Reserve Bank. The state it was in resembled mine. How fervently had it hoped, and all was futile. The notes were like my truths. All of them came right back to me. That was cruel. At least some should not have – just for me to save face.

FIFTY-FOUR

I decided to meet Inspector Shetty at the earliest. I booked my flight, called Joyo and told him that I was coming the next morning, packed my bag. I wanted to meet Dr Ramakrishnan before I left. He agreed happily, promising me breakfast and an airport drop. The truth was that I was in no condition to take any major decision on my own.

On the way to the airport with him, we had a long exchange:

'Your situation looks scary, my dear. Are you sure you can go by yourself?'

'Valyaccha, have I not been travelling by myself all these years?'

'I am only too happy to come with you.'

'When you have no guarantee of returning, you must travel alone, I suppose.'

He looked sad; his eyes seemed to turn moist. For a moment I thought that this was Acchan. He had the same eyes as Acchan's, though their expressions were very different. I felt even more frail and helpless.

'You resemble my father.' I tried to lighten the mood.

'There must be something common in our DNA?'

'Yes, but your natures and histories are surely very different.'

He seemed to be pensive, rubbing his forehead, trying to smile.

'When you mentioned history – I can't help thinking – people's histories are so much more complicated than the history of nations.'

He seemed to be debating whether to tell me something or not.

'Yes, my father's history is a good example, is it not?'

'It is even more complex than you think.'

'I cannot understand why he preyed on girls of eleven or twelve.'

'My dear, the human mind is unpredictable.'

'Can you imagine what a daughter feels when she gets to know that her father was a paedophile, Valyaccha?'

'Satya, all child abuse need not stem from paedophilia. The reasons for both are still not deciphered fully.'

'And at the same time, marrying a woman like Amma, having two children by her...'

'Your father was full of such contradictions. Respectable and helpful outwardly, but totally ruthless...'

'Is it easy to lead such a double-faced life?'

'If your life's mission is to dominate others, then easy or not, that is the only way. About Sivaprasad, I had noted – he never laughed wholeheartedly or openly.'

'But why?'

'Something bothered him all the time. Like a dagger-tip stuck in the flesh.'

'Even Amma knows nothing about his childhood; his siblings won't reveal anything.'

'It was a hard childhood. Their property was snatched away by his mother's stepfather.'

'Have you seen my grandfather, Valyaccha?'

'No. I have heard that he died of tuberculosis.'

'It's all very confusing.'

'No need to be confused. Your father was Sivaprasad. His mother was Koyikkal Sarojini Amma. Her mother, Koyikkal Bhagawati Amma, was married to my grandmother's brother – his name was Narayanan.

We used to call him Grandfather Thuruthel, after our family name –
Thuruthel Appooppan.'

'But what about this Pulikkal Appooppan we kept hearing about?'

'That was a very rich tharavad; only Brahmins and Kshatriyas –
scions of the royal families – could have marital alliances with them.
They had a lot of land, naturally.'

'What was Thuruthel Appooppan like?'

'He was a reformer. Those days, married men would go to their
wives' tharavads for the night – that was normal. Women did not
follow their husbands and settle down in their homes. But he defied
this. He settled down with Bhagawati Amma, buying her a house and
property.'

'And she agreed?'

'He persuaded her. He could because he was educated and even
worked outside Kerala in those days. A man of progressive views, a
freedom fighter, someone who wanted to educate his daughter in
London!'

'Koyikkal Amma was to be educated? In London?' I gaped.

'Yes. Your grandmother was to be educated in Oxford or Cambridge
or someplace like that.'

'Did it all fail to take off because he went to meet Gandhiji?'
I asked.

Dr Ramakrishnan was staring at the signal at the junction where
the road turned towards the airport. He was silent for a few minutes.
Then he turned to look at me. 'I've been thinking of telling you
something for a few days now,' he said haltingly. 'Did you see a leader
demanding a few days back that Gandhi's image should be removed
from our currency notes?'

'I had read about it in the newspapers.'

'It reminded me of something. Wasn't sure if I should tell you – I
debated whether I should. But it might help you to make sense of
your father.'

'Is it about how Pulikkal Appooppan murdered Thuruthel Appooppan after he came back from meeting Gandhiji?'

'That was no ordinary murder. He was badly stabbed – his guts were strewn all around.'

'Stabbed…?'

The tip of the blade stuck inside my heart began to stir.

'It was a peculiar-looking blade. Curved at the top.'

I froze.

'The story of that dagger is even more bizarre. When Thuruthel Appooppan decided to go to Wardha, Pulikkal Appooppan, who was his friend, gave him his own dagger. Thuruthel used to tuck it in his waist always. Years later, when they fought, Pulikkal snatched it back and stabbed Thuruthel with it.'

I thought the entire universe was shaking.

'Why did they fight?'

'Over Gandhiji, most probably.' Dr Ramakrishnan smiled. 'One thought that he was the saviour of the nation, the other thought the contrary.'

'What was Pulikkal Appooppan's name?' I asked.

'Satyavratan.' Dr Ramakrishnan laughed. A sourness whizzed through my bones. 'Satyameva Jayate,' I whispered in my head. 'Satyam Shivam Sundaram.'

'I have felt that more than Thuruthel Appooppan, who went to meet Gandhiji, it was Pulikkal, who killed him, who was a greater influence on your father.'

'Why? For what reason?' I asked anxiously. But Dr Ramakrishnan still hesitated to speak. We had also reached the airport.

'I will tell you,' he finally said, 'when you are back.'

He patted my shoulder. I kissed him on the cheek and climbed out of the car with my bag. He waved, and soon the red car vanished from sight.

~

The rest of the story, still untold, troubled me. As I boarded the flight, I kept trying to complete it. What would have been the reason? Why did Acchan prefer the name of the man who had murdered his own father? I remembered Dinakaran Pillai then. The mouldy, cracked walls of his police quarters. When he took me there, I thought that he was going to protect me. But he acted as though I was a total stranger. 'What the fuck were you up to in that lab?' That angry bellow continued to make me shudder for years after I heard it. I stood before him completely shattered, begged him not to hurt me. But he slapped me hard first, and then, turning his organ into a knife, thrust it hard inside me. Was he taking revenge? On whom? Me? Or Acchan? Or Satyaprabha? Or on the world in general? The suffering of us three sisters, all intertwined, shot through my bones like a sharp sourness. The world and people's minds and lives assumed jumbled and scary forms in my mind. I dozed off, and dreamed of Satyaprakash. He bellowed at me. I pulled out the dagger from a bag and raised it to stab him. But he grabbed it and thrust it forcefully inside me. It went right through my ribcage. The curved end twisted hard … Someone shook me awake. The flight was landing. Because I woke up so suddenly, I could not pull the dagger out. It remained stuck in my ribs, most awkwardly.

FIFTY-FIVE

My search for the truth had started with a question: Have you ever faced an attempt on your life? I was someone who had indeed faced one. That moment was indescribable – a moment of utmost liberation. Whether you believe it or not, if an experience does not send you on a quest, then it can never liberate your soul. And there's this thing: If you want to search for the truth, retrace your steps. So I had no other way but to return to the city where, on the night of 16 November, an assassin who masked his appearance in a helmet and jacket, rode a bike and shot at me. I was sure that death awaited me, and so, I felt drained, empty.

As soon as I landed, I called Inspector Shetty. His tone lacked warmth. 'Come before lunch break,' he said curtly before hanging up. So I booked a cab from the airport for four hours and headed to the police station. Seeing the station building, I began to tremble again, my heartbeat quickened, and suddenly, I wanted to see my mother. Amma had called me a few times. Out of sheer pigheadedness, I had not picked up. Now, I wanted to call her back, but felt too weak to actually do it. The distance from the gate to the station building wasn't much, but it seemed never-ending to me. I was not even sure that it was I who was walking. Everything felt foggy. The station, its occupants, I, Inspector Shetty – everyone looked like characters in a story someone else was reading. In the end, I somehow managed to climb the steps to the police station.

I was, of course, seeing Inspector Shetty after a while. The last time we met was at the Mahipala Ashram. After that, he had cut contact completely and had never called – he had behaved rather strangely. Now, I was completely indifferent, though. All my disappointments and complaints about others had vanished. If it was the path and not the destination that mattered, then who cared about fellow travellers? I decided to act like nothing had happened. I collected myself the best I could. It was Mukta – the police constable who had come over to record my statement the day after the shooting incident – who greeted me. Her sincere pleasure at seeing me rendered me even more helpless. She led me to Inspector Shetty's room. I followed her, my heart pounding. Inspector Shetty was signing a file, his face buried in it. His head had been shaved and was covered with a dark stubbly growth. There was a long scar on his scalp, also stitch marks. It seemed certain that he had suffered some accident. I felt really guilty for having misjudged him. He raised his head slowly. His face bore a long scar too, one that covered his left brow, eye and cheek – a scar from a deep wound, it appeared. Seeing him, my heart forgot to beat, my palms went cold. He looked like someone else, yet with the same face. I remained rooted to the spot, limp, my eyes welling up. His face looked turbulent too. He gestured me to sit. This was the conversation we had that day:

'Satyapriya Ma'am, how are you, tell me.'

'Inspector, what is this? An accident?'

'Does this look like an accident?'

Smiling a sardonic smile, he turned his face towards me, so that I could see clearly. My blood turned icy; I felt like someone related to me had wounded him. I was afraid to guess who that might me. My throat felt parched. As if he knew it, he got Mukta to bring two glasses of water. I gulped it greedily. He observed me ruthlessly. The happy calm that used to play on his face seemed to have faded completely. His eyes blamed me for it.

'Please tell me clearly. What happened?' I begged.

'The wound on my scalp was from the butt of a gun,' he said. 'The one on my face is from my falling hard on rock.' He sounded impassive. 'No, not over yet. I was also wounded on my back and stomach – beaten with iron rods.'

'What for? Who…?'

'Did you try to find out where I was after we parted in Delhi?'

'I called you many, many times, but you never picked up. I also sent someone over here, to this police station, to ask after you.'

'And?'

'They said that you were on long leave.'

'You did not bother to find out more?'

'I felt bad that you weren't trying to get in touch.'

'I was in Odisha, Ma'am.'

'Inspector Sir, did you again go to Odisha from Delhi?'

'I didn't go on my own. I was taken there. They took me.'

'Who?'

'You are very bright, aren't you, Ma'am? Take a guess.'

I suspected that I peed a drop or two. My single kidney throbbed in pain. My whole body pulsated like an infected wound. I was not particularly insistent that I should hear only good things about all the men I'd loved. But I couldn't bear to hear that they were cads and rogues.

'Wasn't Samir in jail at that time?' I asked.

'Will he do such things with his own bare hands?'

'You mean to say that his cronies attacked you?'

'They captured us.'

'For what?'

'To release him.'

'But Aswathy told me that he had jumped prison?'

'We can say only that after all. We can't tell the world that we released him.'

'You mean to say that he made you a bargaining chip?'

'Ma'am, do I need to tell you that?'

I gulped down the contents of the second glass of water too. He rang the bell and asked Mukta to bring two more glasses of water.

'It should have become news ... reported in the press ... a police officer captured by Maoists...?' I asked after a pause.

'Yes,' he said. 'If only it had been just a police officer.'

'That means?'

'Do not underestimate your ex-lover. Is Samir Sayyid such a fool as to bargain using just a puny police officer?'

'Tell me clearly, Inspector Sir.'

'I was fortunate to share a cowshed for two or three days with someone whom tens of thousands of people throng to catch a glimpse of ... for whose touch they can wait endlessly ... all because of you!'

'Mahipal Shah Baba?' I said that with effort. Anurup Shetty placed his finger on his lips and gestured to me to be silent. We sat there, looking at each other. Mukta brought over two glasses of water and two cups of tea. I picked up a glass without inhibition, and yet again, downed it at one gulp.

'You seem to be drinking a lot of water, Ma'am?'

'Who won't, when they hear things that are hard to swallow?'

'Don't believe me, just ask your ex-lover.'

'Yes, after that you can put me in jail, right? Claiming that I have Maoist connections?'

'He's the state's own man now.'

'What does that mean?'

'That there's no legal hurdle in the way of contacting him.'

'I don't understand. Once you said that there was some connection between that dagger and Samir Sayyid.'

'One of the wounds on Golla Jayaramulu's body was from that dagger.'

'What does that mean?'

'Surely that Satyaprakash, or whoever hired him, is smart!'

'Why did Samir come to Kochi?'

'Satyaprakash lured him there and trapped him too.'

'So he wasn't arrested because of me.'

'The police wanted you to get the impression, that it was because of you that Samir Sayyid had been arrested.'

'What was the use of that?'

'To save Satyaprakash, what else?' Inspector Shetty laughed.

'I don't have Samir's latest number.'

'Oh, we will find it.'

'What do I need him for?'

'Don't you want to nab the assassin?'

'Have you outsourced your work to him, Inspector Sir?'

'My work is over.'

'What work, pray tell me?'

'The assassin has been found, caught.'

'Then where is he? I can't see him here anywhere!'

'Samir Sayyid did not let me bring him. My department did not support me either.'

'That is, he is still missing.'

'Not missing. He is in Samir's custody.'

'You mean he made Satyaprakash a prisoner as well?'

'Yes...'

'Impossible! How can he confine a powerful swami like Mahipal, Satyaprakash, and a police officer like you, at the same time?'

'It was very well planned. When Mahipal reached the cottage after the evening bhajan, they were waiting.'

'And you?'

'I ended up there pursuing Satyaprakash.'

'Is all this easy in the ashram compound?'

'They kidnapped us that very night using the Swami's helicopter.'

'And you just let them kidnap you?'

'I didn't, and these scars are evidence of that.'

'And Satyaprakash? Didn't he resist?'

'He and the Baba were injected with something.'

'You think the impoverished villagers can do such things?'

'We were not taken by villagers, for sure. They had commando training.'

'And this is going to be dumped on Samir. That's the only thing left!'

'You are still in love with him.'

'Even so, he isn't any more,' I snapped.

Inspector Shetty took out a packet from the drawer of his table, and from it, drew out a fine, expensive Kashmiri shawl – the type you can fold and pass through a finger ring. There was a number scrawled on its price tag.

'Leave a missed call on this number, and you'll know if he still loves you or not.'

'What if I don't?'

'You may not see Satyaprakash alive.'

I held my head in my hands, pressed my elbows on the table, sat still. The inspector supported his chin in his hand and looked intently at me. His face looked like a dented plate. I did not delay. I dialled the number from my mobile phone and, after a single ring, hung up. He smiled at me. His eyes were wet.

'Ma'am, you are truly wonderful. I never thought that there could be such a woman in this world!'

'You are yet to see the world, then.'

'Let me tell you the truth: I am in love with you.'

I blushed a bit.

'Me, too.'

'Why?'

'I have dreamt of a lover saying sweet nothings in police uniform!'

He laughed. I couldn't.

'You were a prisoner only for three days. Where were you after that, Inspector?'

'In the ICU. They had to sew up my head.'

I felt a bit foolish.

'Your family must have been worried?'

'I have only my parents. I am single. Like you.'

'You are good-looking! Did no girl try her luck?'

'Luck in love is directly proportional to submissiveness, not beauty.'

'Who told you this?'

'Didn't Mukta become your fan after she heard you say this?'

'Inspector, please tell me about your findings in this case?'

'The assassination attempt was carried out by Satyaprakash.'

'Didn't we find that out way earlier?'

'We found out where he is from, and his address too.'

'I found that too.'

'He had a grudge against you.'

'What grudge?'

'Your father raped his sister.'

'But then, he should settle that score with my father?'

'The vengeance he sought against you two girls was more than what he sought against your father.'

That took me by surprise. 'Why?'

'You two are too bold, haughty, not submissive to men.'

'By what sections of the Indian Penal Code are these crimes?'

'And you are of poor character…'

'Bad character?'

'You and your sister were morally weak,' he said. 'He said that he had evidence.'

'He should say "immorally strong", shouldn't he?'

'He thinks that the two of you are an insult to the world and femininity.'

'I am in agreement.'

'You asked for it!'

'Then why did he delay the murder so long?'

'Ma'am, whether you agree or not, women are the root of all the crime in this world.'

'*Sho*! What would the police have done without women?'

'Sita was the cause of the war in the Ramayana. And Draupadi caused the Mahabharata war.'

'What about the Kargil War? The Indo–China War? The Iraq War?'

'I can't argue with you.'

'Okay. Did Samir say that Satyaprakash will be delivered in chains if I called him?'

'Yes, you just need to identify him. I'll manage the rest.'

'Manage what?'

'Leave that to the police. I'll find ways to keep him locked up.'

'Don't think I am going to be complicit in it.'

'Will you really find peace only if you muddle up everything?'

'I need to be fully convinced.'

'What is there to be convinced about?'

'He killed my sister on another's order. There is an eyewitness.'

'Who?'

'The problem is not who. The problem is that he killed her only and only because someone else ordered him to do so. So he won't kill me until he receives a command.'

'That's foolish. He's been following you for so long.'

'What if he was instructed to do that by someone?'

'Who?'

'Someone who would profit from my death?'

'What profit?'

'Someone who stands to benefit from my father's will.'

'Did no one know about this will all this while?'

'No one tried to find out!'

'Your father died two months back. Was it written just before? Or earlier?'

'You called me here before I could find out.'

'You are safer here.'

'Why is that?'

'A police officer's intuition.'

He looked at his watch. I got up to leave. He too rose.

'How long will you be here?'

'Until the day after tomorrow.'

'Let's meet for coffee tomorrow.'

'Yes.'

'Where are you staying?'

'At Sandeepa Sen's house.'

'Let's meet tomorrow evening. Hope all this ends well.'

Inspector Shetty shook hands with me. I got into the car and mechanically handed over Sandeepa Sen's address to the driver. Joyo and Sandeepa were waiting for me. Seeing them convinced me that I was still alive. Joyo's hairdo resembled the tall, conical hats worn by whirling dervishes; I patted it. He kissed me on the cheek. 'The world's bravest woman,' said Sandeepa, as she too pecked my cheek. I turned to look at my old rented place. The night of 16 November came back to mind. The earth vibrating from the gunshot. 'Auntie, you can still feel the place shaking when you pass by it,' said Joyo. That revealed something to me: witnessing a murder attempt was harder than facing it. Joyo had not yet got over it. What if I had been killed that night? What if Satyaprakash's bullets had found their target? Joyo would have seen me in the throes of death; I may have died in his arms! My soul, too, would have borne the force of the bullet and it would have shot up into the sky. My life would have ended high up there, like the torch in the hands of the Statue of Liberty. Suddenly, I yearned for the experience of falling as ash on to the bluish expanse of the earth and fading as smoke into the bluish expanse of the sky.

But I hated death too. And that was because there were people like Joyo and Sandeepa around me in this world and in these times.

My heart was calmed by the joy they very evidently exuded at my presence. Those who should have loved me, or those whom I loved, never really loved me. But those who had no such obligation at all, did offer me much warmth. Love is indeed like currency notes. What you give is not what you receive. Notes worth fourteen lakh crore that were sent out by the Reserve Bank moved through the hands of a hundred and twenty crore people and went back there; some did not. Some surfaced in rivers, some were found in gutters. Some were hidden in the salt pots of sooty kitchens; at times they were stuffed inside burlaps of roadside beggars. And more were discovered under the mattresses of old geezers who didn't trust their children. It made no sense at all, if you thought of it.

We sat down to eat.

'Auntie, you have changed a lot.'

'Very true, you aren't the Satya of two months back.'

'I am so tired, Didi!'

'You didn't feel that way when that guy opened fire at you, Satya!'

'I had really thought he had mistaken me for someone else.'

'But that doesn't make the bullet any less dangerous, does it?'

'Would have been better to just die then!'

'Don't say that! We all love you.'

'Oh, for what?'

'Because, Auntie, you make life look very simple!'

'Good heavens! Only I know how complex my life is!'

'Satya, you are very genuine. You are no hypocrite.'

I wanted to laugh and cry at the same time. But it was clear that if we continued this way, mother and son would make me cry. And so, I changed the subject.

'Didi, how is your lecture series on demonetization going?'

'Stopped. The Vice Chancellor vetoed it.'

'Why?'

'Apparently, it would be anti-national...'

'Oh! What are you planning to do then?'

'I'll be writing a book on the experience of these times. The mess! ATMs shut, people queueing up before banks, falling dead, leaders and their statements...'

'And in the middle of it all, some guy shot at you, Auntie!'

Then Sandeepa asked me that question. 'Satya, do you think that this murder attempt has something to do with demonetization?'

That jarred me momentarily.

'Now, come to think of it, this guy Satyaprakash had been tracking you for years. But the actual attempts on your life began on 16 November. I think it could have been for money.'

A flash of lightning passed through my head. Demonetization was why Kripesh could not stab me. Did Satyaprakash make that attempt because of it? This was what I pondered when I lay down for a post-lunch nap. My blood pressure was climbing because I have this habit of exaggerating anything. I tossed and turned for a while but managed to fall asleep. Amma's call woke me up. And this was the conversation that took place between us:

'Satye, I am home.'

'So soon?'

'How much time does one need to travel to Chennai and back?'

'The way you set out...!! I thought that Vasanthalakshmi was on an all-India tour!'

'My ticket is for 15 February!'

'Oho, I didn't know that! Who are you travelling with?'

'I want to fly alone, like a bird!'

'At this age of yours?'

'One needs some freedom at least at this age!'

I felt a throb of pain inside. I did not like the idea of Amma going by herself, leaving me alone. It was more convenient for me that she stayed in a cage as nothing but a mother. I was used to that. To overcome my helplessness, I changed the subject.

'Okay. Who all did you meet there?'

'I went to Top Stills Studio.'

'For a photo?'

'To see the owner.'

'And did you see him?'

'He's dead. His son helped me out.'

'What did you need help with, Amma?'

'A copy of Acchan's will.'

'You knew about it then?'

'I smelled money in the conversation about Satyaprabha and Dinakaran Pillai.'

'Did you suspect Venukkuttan Chettan?'

'I had suspected Aswathy of having some ulterior motives … and of Venukkuttan being in the know of it.'

'Does the will mention land?'

'Four plots. In Adyar and Teynampet. Thirty-six grounds in all.'

'That means?'

'A little more than two and a half acres.'

'In cash?'

'Two hundred, almost.'

'Two hundred crore?'

'You don't get such big plots in Chennai now.'

'Who are the heirs?'

'Your father's three daughters.'

'The third daughter must be Satyaprabha?'

'Of course, who else?'

'What is the date of the will's execution?'

'15 May 2017.'

'If we did not know about these assets, they would have grabbed them, wouldn't they?'

'If you continue to live, they will have to inform you.'

'There are a few more months left. So why was my assassin in such a hurry?'

'The truth is that they are too late.'

'It's a hefty sum – around two hundred crore. It was a good deal for them even if they didn't kill me.'

'If you are eliminated, they get all of it. If not, they will get just one-third.'

'Not fifty-fifty, right?'

'According to the will, Satyaprabha gets one-third. That is just the plot at Adyar. The rest is Siva's and yours. You are to divide it between yourselves as you deem fit. If Siva or you passes away without heirs or a will before the date of execution, the survivor receives two of the three shares. If both of you pass away without a will or heirs, the whole of it goes to Satyaprabha or the heirs of her choice.'

'But you are my legal heir, Amma?'

'That is easily resolved. I am sure Venukkuttan has a stamp paper in my name with him.'

'Amme, are people so utterly avaricious?'

'Evidently, they are.'

'Are you feeling afraid to be alone?'

'Not me. You should be scared.'

'I'll look after myself.'

'Be careful when you challenge a person in power, my dear.'

'Don't worry, Amma. If I am taken, I will take them all with me.'

When Amma hung up, I felt that I had become a rubber ball that some child was playing with, one that bounced between the floor and the ceiling. Assets worth a hundred and forty crore. How much did I have to spend every year from now on for all of it to get over? I imagined the amount in currency notes. I imagined building a mansion from two-thousand-rupee notes. Right in front of it, a lake that glistened in the sun, made of five-hundred-rupee notes. The sky would be made of saffron-coloured two-hundred-rupee notes, and the garden, of violet-coloured one-hundred-rupee notes. I was enjoying this game, but at that very moment, the memory of going to Abhilash's house for a loan of one lakh rupees appeared, uninvited, like a killjoy. The mist, the sun, the tears, of that morning.

And Xavier Panakkal, at Vasanthaalayam. I saw Amma gathering the gold ornaments she had, in the middle of the night, in the bedroom at Vasanthaalayam. Abhilash strode into the chaippu next to the Koyikkal house, where the tattered cane chair lay. I, in a soiled, worn nightgown, feeling seared and burned from within, struggling to get him a cup of tea from a kitchen where we had run out of tea powder. At St Anthony's Thomachan's guest house, I greedily picked out the flesh from large pieces of pearl-spot fish, bigger than my hands put together. I experienced once again the feeling of guilt of eating it all by myself, without Amma and Chechi. But by then, Thomachan had stripped me naked. He, too, was naked. The mosaic floor of his bathroom was drenched with my blood. Rajasekhar of Saubhagya held me up by the neck, barking, 'Talk after you return my money, you daughter of a whore!' I lay erect, clad in a green surgical gown, on the operating table under a flying-saucer-like light. The crescent-shaped scar on the side of my belly tingled. Dinakaran Pillai scratched the ugly whitish fungal scabs on his thighs as he approached me. Acchan's bedpan was filled with reddish urine. There were blackish turds in his commode. The old silk shirt hung on his shrunken body like a pastor's robe. Koyikkal Amma boarded a ship to London with an elephant yam in her hands. A dagger, covered in blood and mud, pierced my chest. Not me, a rubber ball. My heart, my brain ... someone was playing with them, tossing and kicking them around. I struggled to keep myself rooted to the ground. I thrashed about for a moment of rest, peace of mind.

That night, I just could not sleep. I was counting the contradictions in our stories – Satyaprakash's and mine. And then, I heard a slight noise. A shadow moved on the other side of the window curtain. My breath stopped. I realized with a shiver that it was Satyaprakash. He slid a tool noiselessly through the side of the closed windowpane and undid the bolt, opened it soundlessly, moved the curtain aside. I reached out and turned on the light. This time, he was not jolted, he did not try to hide. And thus, we met face to face once again.

Have you ever faced a murder attempt a second time? A pity, if you haven't. It is a moment of tremendous release. Satyaprakash was in his assassin's garb: the helmet, those dark glasses, the jacket. Our eyes locked on each other's. His eyes were two wells that exuded disgust and hatred. Have you ever seen a bullet ejecting from the gun? A pity, if you haven't. What the hell have you, then, experienced in this life! The bullet bursts out of the barrel of the gun like the soul pulls itself out of the body – with a tail of fire pushing it on as it races ahead to plunge into the Brahmam and blend into it. A cloud of smoke runs after it for some distance, screaming, 'Take me along, take me!' It will then collapse, exhausted. But what amazed me was the way in which the cartridge that parted from the bullet broke past the series of karma, which involved first pulling the trigger, and then the ignition, and attained Moksha.

That night, Satyaprakash pushed the muzzle of the gun through the window grille, took aim, pulled the trigger. I – this self-willed, arrogant woman, who was 'immorally strong', and who had seen much in life – stood before him unflinchingly, baring my thirty-six-inch chest.

FIFTY-SIX

The bullet whizzed past, very close to my ear, and hit the wall. I was completely inert. At that moment, I felt no difference between life and death. I saw him to my heart's content. Pathetic fellow, a mere fool, one incapable of finishing a task even when granted any number of chances! For a moment, I even thought of grabbing the gun from his hand and killing myself. But Sandeepa was up and screaming. All the lights in the house came alive. But he still did not run. It was as though he was determined to see me dead. I saw him take aim again. Not one but two shots were fired. Both did not reach the room. All of a sudden, the curtain that he had been holding from the outside, fell with a crash and blocked the view. A call of 'Haa' sounded from beneath the window. The rest was like a dream. Bright lights everywhere. Sounds of whistles, boots. The voices of men. Sandeepa ran in, crying. She took me in her arms. Relieved to see me safe and well, she laughed and shed tears at the same time. Joyo ran in too. They covered me with hugs and kisses. But, like on the night of 16 November, my body and soul had parted. That night, death had appeared to me like the bluish-red-tinged bank of a river. Now, two months later, it appeared yellowish-red, like some red kumkum had been added to the tongue of flame rising from an oil lamp – a colour that aroused a kind of fear.

Sandeepa went to the window and moved the curtain. The whole front yard and street were full of policemen. The headlights of five or eight police jeeps were on. 'Look, Satya,' Sandeepa called to me. I went to her. Satyaprakash lay on the ground. His body was soaked in blood.

Have you ever seen a man shot, falling like a bird? Have you seen him thrash about in a pool of blood? A pity, if you haven't. Because that means the greatest enlightenment possible in this life has passed you by. There is this thing too: it is a matchless experience; nothing compares. You will feel as though you are seated on a mountaintop. It will be red, the colour of kumkum. When the rays of the rising sun will fall on it, the mountain will look like a huge block of clotted blood. Your eyes will be dazzled by the glinting blood. You will feel revolted. But then, this would be a moment of self-recognition. You will believe that it was you who fell, not he. And then your clothes will be soaked in his blood. His thirst will parch your throat.

Haven't I told you, I had inherited my mother's ability to find courage when in tight spots? I always had it. I took out a towel from my suitcase and a bottle of water that was on the table and went outside. Two policemen were helping him up. One of them grabbed his arms and two others, his legs. A fourth policeman was frisking him. I was about to reach them when Anurup Shetty stopped me.

'Ma'am, first, please congratulate the police! Didn't we catch him in the act!'

I did not look at him and went ahead. I had eyes only for Satyaprakash. I opened the bottle, held it out to him. He opened his mouth in desperation and I poured water into it. Only when his thirst was quenched did he really see me. He squirmed even more. I wiped his face – not just the blood but also the soil. He pulled himself back. It hurt him more. But I paid no attention to that and continued to lean down towards him to wipe the blood off his body. I yearned to take care of him, my hands tingled to heal him. What a great message would that send to the world! But I could not deliver that message of ahimsa effectively enough. Shouldn't the police agree?

Shouldn't Satyaprakash cooperate? He shuddered, fell on the ground again. The policemen brought a stretcher and took him away. I was left there alone, feeling disappointed, with many questions for him; after all, his story, too, was incomplete.

They took him away in an ambulance. I went back inside with the bloodstained towel. I touched the stain with the tip of my finger. It prickled, feeling the rough wetness. It let out a charred smell – one in which the smells of blood, soil and gunpowder mingled. For the average Indian woman of my generation, blood or gunshots were not new. Didn't we grow up listening to stories of the Emergency? Were we not teenagers who grew up watching the street plays protesting the murder of Safdar Hashmi? Didn't we memorize N.S. Madhavan's 'When the Big Tree Falls'? Didn't the Mumbai riots and Godhra shape our lives too? My experience tells me that the palaces of the powerful were built with mortar mixed with the blood of the people. Just that some people like Satyaprakash and I were fated to kill or be killed. In truth, our bodies were the instruments of exchange used by political strategists. That was the reason why our stories were intertwined, the reason why neither could be retold as the story of just one.

Have you ever escaped death by a mere whisker? Have you experienced the frissons that travel through the body afterwards? A pity, if you haven't, because how, then, will you ever understand the tremors of the container when the soul struggles to break free of it and fly away? My body trembled like the heart of a bird that had been caught again as it tried to escape. The whole of my body began to pound like somebody else's heart.

The sun was coming up. The sky, painted saffron, was shining. I took a quick shower, put on fresh clothes, and came out. The whizzing sound stayed in my ears. It was noisy outside anyway – walkie-talkies and beacon lights, sirens and whistles! The TV channel vans had arrived too. Sandeepa told me that the Superintendent of Police, Akhil Gupta, had arrived. He came up to me. His face was stonier now. 'Don't worry, the police are with you…' he said, and made some more comforting remarks. You may have noticed, people don't only have body language; they have 'voice language' too. It reveals the truth about them. I bid him goodbye and went over to the TV room. The sweat on my palms moistened the remote as I switched on the Malayalam channels. 'Malayali woman shot at: Murder attempt', 'Attacker nabbed', 'Conspiracy suspected', 'Prior enmity suspected' – rolled the headlines. Was this me? I was not sure even then if I were dead or alive. Then Anurup Shetty came looking for me. We sat in the room where he had first questioned me.

'So the heroine of the story is hiding here?'

'If I am the heroine, who is the storywriter?'

'The credit of writing this part of the story surely goes to me!'

'Inspector, was this twist in the tale entirely your idea?'

'I made full use of this story's possibilities.'

'My missed call was not in vain, was it?'

'No. You called him at twelve. By five, Satyaprakash was delivered to the police station.'

'You told me that you'll put him behind bars the moment he arrived?'

'If I did that, would we have been able to nab him red-handed like this?'

'He did not suspect anything when you allowed him to leave?'

'He was sure that there were powerful people helping him.'

'Why did he try to kill me now?'

'He's been after you since around 2011.'

'For what?'

'To keep track of you – that was his task.'

'For whom?'

Someone knocked at the door. Two policemen peeped inside. Inspector Shetty went to the door. They exchanged some words. 'Get the vehicle out, I am coming,' he assured them, and came back to me.

'The IG just summoned me.'

He surveyed the premises quickly and came closer to me.

'See? Many TV channels from your place are here.'

'I noticed.'

'What will you say to them?'

'No matter what I say, they'll report only the stories they like.'

He looked around once more and came even closer. The scar on his eye, brow and part of his cheek made him look more serious.

'Satyapriya Ma'am, can't you tell them a story that they'd love?'

'I don't get you.'

'Look, they are looking for a story that sells. Yours will sell well.'

That brought in me a rush of liking for the man. In the present system, men have better experience managing things. I did have a sneaking admiration for them for that. But I acted as though I wasn't interested.

'What for? What do I care what they report?'

Maybe it was the hurry or perhaps the tension, but he lost his patience.

'Dear woman, do you really think that everything is over just because we have nabbed Satyaprakash? I am going to meet the IG now. Only after that will we know who's going to be behind bars – the one who attempted to kill you, or me. If you want to save your life, you'd better be making good use of the media instead of playing high and mighty here.'

'Okay, tell me how?'

'Do I need to advise someone with a convoluted brain like yours?'

'Shouldn't we check if what I understand and what you advise are the same or not?'

'A drama that will drag on for days on end – that's what the media needs.'

The policemen peeped in again. Inspector Shetty had almost stepped out. I followed him.

'The drama must have a hero, a heroine and a villain,' I said.

Inspector Shetty whipped around, looking angry enough to slap me.

'There is no villain in this drama, it is a villainess – Aswathy Venu IPS!'

I stopped in my tracks, stupefied, my limbs suddenly feeling weak. Actually, there was no reason to be shocked; and yet, I was shocked. All that I had discovered was true – Anurup Shetty's words confirmed it. Even then, I swayed and shook; felt wounded, as though I was hearing it for the first time. I ached from head to toe.

'Will IPS officers touch one of their own?' I tried to smile, trying to mask my suffering.

'The evidence is very strong.'

'You managed to gather the evidence quickly?'

'I've been after this since 16 November.'

'I forgot to ask something. Upon whose instructions was Satyaprakash watching me since 2001? Aswathy was just fifteen then.'

'Not just Aswathy, that whole family wanted you dead – for the past seventeen years.'

Venukkuttan Chettan, Radha Chechi, Aji, Acchu – who were with us in wealth and poverty. Whom we loved, who loved us back. I tried to control myself, but my eyes brimmed. I did not notice Anurup Shetty leave. I was in some other world. But his words gnawed at my heart. I saw before my eyes Aswathy's face from when she was little to when she grew up, like in a photo album. It was Amma who'd borne the expenses of both of Radha Chechi's childbirths. It was she who celebrated their waist-thread-tying and naming ceremonies. Their birthdays were routinely celebrated at Vasanthaalayam, with sweetmeats and payasam. Venukkuttan Chettan's firstborn, Ajith, was a sickly, introverted child. But not Acchu. I was about fifteen when she was born. My vivid memories of her include the time when Radha Chechi brought her for the temple festival that year; she was not even a year old. She sat in her mother's arms and considered me for a few minutes. Then, as though proclaiming that I belonged to her, she leaned towards me, into my waiting arms. That was such a deep, spiritual acceptance. She taught me that it is only during our childhoods that we are able to love another without a care for who they are socially or the amount of money they possess. Have you noticed what sets apart human beings from other animals? The tendency to treat social status and wealth as the criteria of love and respect for another of their own kind. Aswathy had held out her arms to me constantly, at every stage of her growing up. I gave back generously all the love that Venukkuttan Chettan had bestowed upon me when I was a child. I played hide-and-seek with Aswathy, bought her balloons, played ball with her, read to her children's tales, fed her, wiped her snot, took her to the toilet and cleaned her up, and even gave her baths at times. She called me 'Sa'chechi' and would insist on coming to Vasanthaalayam to play with me. She would be cross if I spoke to someone other than her. When we'd return after visiting their house, she would throw a tantrum: 'Sa'chechi, don'ggo!' Just imagine. That child was the hand behind the assassin that I sought to expose! She was the real killer! The thought made me seethe in agony. My self-confidence was in tatters. The black cobra, which still danced even after being hacked and stabbed and crushed, was now so weak it could fall dead any moment! Before it died, I gathered myself. I sat down on a chair in Sandeepa's sit-out. And thus, the first press conference of my life happened. Journalists from various TV channels, with their mics and cameras, surrounded me. Their questions were interesting.

'Ms Satyapriya, there was an attempt on your life. What do you feel now?'

'I feel thankful.'

'To whom?'

'To my assassin.'

'Why?'

'That's why a story in which I am the heroine was born in the first place!'

'Can you be clearer?'

'Aren't you keen to hear my story because of him?'

'The police say that he has made attempts earlier too?'

'That's true.'

'Why has he attacked you repeatedly?'

'Only he can reveal that.'

'The SP said that he nursed a prior enmity towards you?'

'I saw him for the first time two months back when he tried to kill me.'

'But he says that you both belong to the same place?'

'What else did the SP tell you?'

'That the same criminal also murdered your sister, staging it as an accident.'

'And?'

'That your father was stabbed by him and his brother, he said.'

'And why?'

'He took revenge – your father had raped his sister.'

'Being a familiar tale from our movies, anyone would believe.'

'Do you mean to say that it is not true?'

'If the brothers of all raped women start setting out for revenge, how many people are likely to be left alive in our country?'

'The SP said that he has been tracking you for years.'

'The SP said only these things? Didn't he tell you that my father's will is to be executed on 15 May?'

'Which will?'

'My father owned some land in different parts of Chennai. When his business failed, it was mortgaged. He also made a closed will. It will be executed this year.'

'How much is it worth?'

'Not much. Some two hundred crore.'

'If you die, who inherits it?'

'Two people. An IAS officer in the Delhi cadre – Ajith Venu. And his sister Aswathy Venu IPS. She is in Kerala now.'

'Do you mean to say that two people in such high positions will connive in such a way to commit a crime like this?'

'Did I say that?'

'But what you meant...'

'Look, I told you what I had to. You may interpret it as you like.' I got up and folded my hands in salutation. 'We will meet. If I am still alive.'

There was a moment of silence.

'What is your next move?'

'I am going to publish my autobiography.'

'Autobiography?'

'Yes. My experiences after 16 November.'

They tried to ask some more questions, but I had had enough. It is important not to be garrulous to not just superior officers but also the media. Better to take a snake off the fence and cradle it in your lap.

I retreated inside acting as though I were tired. Sandeepa led me to the TV room. 'Attempt to shoot and kill Malayali woman', 'Suspicion falls on IAS-IPS siblings', 'Two hundred crore worth of assets at the heart of murder attempt: Suspicion' – such lines had begun to appear as breaking news and flash news. I straightened up, and as I watched the news, I dozed off. I woke up when someone knocked at the door. It was Mukta and Anurup Shetty.

'You are all right?'

'No.'

'Cheer up. It will all become better.'

'They could've killed me earlier.'

'If you had married and had children, they would have surely finished you off. Also, about your father's will – they were probably afraid that he might change it while still alive.'

'Why did they not try to kill Acchan?'

'He was completely bedridden, wasn't he? After they killed you, they would have got rid of your parents too.'

'But wasn't it easier for them to finish off Chechi and me together in an accident?'

'He said that he had tried that. You have a long life!'

'Inspector Sir, the date of the will's execution is in May. Just three months more, that is. Given that all this was so meticulously planned, didn't an IPS officer have the common sense to see that two heirs mentioned in the will dying from unnatural causes, one after the other, would surely rouse suspicion?'

'They have been trying since a long time. It didn't work. The plan was to finish you off two and a half years ago. They have been trying in many ways since then. And then came demonetization. They needed money.'

'What was the role of Aswathy's brother in this?'

'Who doesn't like some more wealth?'

'Is there someone called Dinakaran Pillai in this whole story?'

'He was in it. Not any more. He's dead.'

'Dead or killed?'

'It was an accident.'

'Then it was murder!'

'Have to investigate that.'

'Did Satyaprakash get any money?'

'Yes, surely. He lived on a monthly sum that Aswathy IPS paid.'

'Do not say such things, Satyamole!' I heard Venukkuttan Chettan's words again. In a single swish, Vasanthaalayam was back before my eyes. The lake and the villagers there came back to my mind. The house covered with weeds and trees just behind Vasanthaalayam surfaced. There, I saw a young girl, lying faint and listless, like a fowl drowned in boiling water. I imagined two little boys trying to help her up. Children who were forced to leave the house they were born in. Adolescents whose manliness was challenged every single day while they were growing up. I felt breathless, frightened. When Inspector Shetty bid goodbye, my eyes filled with tears. They made him emotional too. He promised to keep the house under police protection until I returned.

I failed to find courage, though. I wasn't scared of death or being murdered cruelly. The paths one trudges, the experiences one goes through before one becomes the assassin of another – that was what scared me. How did my father cause the ruin and death of young girls? How did Dinakaran Pillai become capable of crushing me? What reason could there be as to why Kallu's father and Sriram felt no compassion for me at all? How had Abhilash's father-in-law become my sister's murderer? For what all reasons did Aswathy, whom I raised, decide to plan and execute my murder? The terror that arises in one when they think about human beings filled me. I was going mad, I feared. I felt like seeing Amma; I called her. But she had landed in Bangalore by then. When I heard that she had got on the first flight after she saw the news, I broke down. I had wanted to see her so badly. I was ashamed of being so dependent on her – that was a sign of ageing. When people grow older, they cannot do without a mother. Actually, not as a person, but the idea of a mother. That idea will differ from person to person. For me, my mother stood for the very idea of freedom.

But the real blow of that day was not the attempt made on my life, nor was it Anurup Shetty's dashing feat or Satyaprakash's capture. It was the video call from Dr Ramakrishnan.

'Mole, are you all right?'

'Yes, almost, Valyaccha.'

'I was shocked when I saw the news – it was the worst shock of my retired life. Did you come to my house seeking your father's past and become so dear to me, only to make me so sad?'

I saw him wipe his eyes.

'Valyaccha, you said that it was not Grandfather Thuruthel but his murderer Pulikkal who had the greater influence on my father. Why did you say that?'

'Can't we discuss this later?'

'Please, Valyaccha.'

He hesitated a bit. Then, gathering himself, he said, 'That was because his actual father was Pulikkal Appooppan, not Thuruthel.'

That was shocking for sure.

'What do you mean!'

'When your grandmother Koyikkal Sarojini was some ten or twelve, Pulikkal began to abuse her. She used to come running to my grandmother, weeping. Thuruthel Appooppan heard this; he wanted to confront Pulikkal. That's when Pulikkal killed him.'

I struggled to steady myself.

'Later, Pulikkal himself found a husband for Sarojini Amma, but her first two children were his.' He sighed. 'I suppose Sivaprasad knew who his real father was. That was why he was always so insecure...'

I did not hear the rest of what he said. I saw Acchan before my eyes, sitting in his wheelchair. He called me 'Satyamole'. My body burned. Incidents from the time he was stabbed and became bedridden to the last time he called me that, just before his death, ran in my eyes like a movie reel. I did not understand what he had gone through, I did not know his mind. His childhood, the affection that he may or may not have got, the self-respect that he was denied – I knew none of it. I wasn't aware that the knife he tucked in his waist – that was not a weapon but his legacy. I don't know if you have noticed but, as they grow older, human beings find newer layers in their fathers' personalities. They use them to justify them or glorify them. Because a father, like a mother, is an idea. But that idea belongs to society.

My struggle was to understand my father. When we lost our home and faced hunger, he was shattered, helpless. But even then, he did not criticize himself, never admitted to his wrongs, never asked for forgiveness, never boasted about the will that was to be executed on 15 May. Instead, he fell silent. Lay where he was laid, sat where he was seated, ate what he was given, just obeyed what he was told. Asked for nothing but water, gave no advice or directions, made no complaints. Acchan, who used to lean in the back seat of the Contessa, clad in the spotless white silk shirt and the gold-brocade-bordered mundu, shrank into the Acchan in a cheap kaili-waistcloth. That kaili-waistcloth itself grew bigger than him each year. He became smaller. I paid no attention, never turned around to take a second look. He got what he deserved, I thought. In the end, he was like a locked room in the house. True, it was part of the house; true, I remembered its existence. But if something could not be found, there was no need to go search for it there. So, the room was largely ignored. That was a mistake. I should have gone there, at least occasionally, to search for what had been lost. We would have found many missing things there. If only that part of the story could be rewritten in another way. I could have offered my father, who had turned into merely flesh and bones that could hardly breathe, the compassion that any living creature deserved. I could have set aside the stubborn determination to give him back what he gave us. I could have realized that the bedridden man was different from the one who used to dress nattily and drive off in a fancy car. The old father died when he was felled by a dagger's thrust. I stored him in a glass jar, like he had preserved the viper and its young. He ended up like the foetus I found in his box. I carried it everywhere I went. The girl children he raped were in the jar too. They stayed deathless in the acid of love he never gave me.

I was like the python which had swallowed the elephant. The elephant's tusks bore through me; my belly lay open too. I realized that my life was destroyed not by Acchan alone but also by the governments and political parties of those times.

~

Amma reached by evening. She was remarkably calm and collected. She was used to her new hairstyle and clothes by now. I even felt like she was that way since her birth! We set off for home in an Innova car that very night. Anurup Shetty had sent a policeman with us for protection. Amma reclined the bucket seat and lay down. I ran my fingers over her hand. She yawned. Then she asked, 'So your investigation is over, isn't it?'

'There are a couple of things to clear up still.'

'What things?'

'Where is Satyaprabha's second child?'

Amma sighed. 'Wherever it is, let it be happy.'

I took out the shawl that Samir had sent and laid it over her. She looked at me.

'What is the second thing that's still unclear?'

'How did Satyaprakash get that name?'

'It's your father who made him write his first letters, at his vidyarambham ceremony. That was before he fell out with his family. I never saw them after they left this place. That is why I didn't recognize him even from the photo. I just thought that they must have grown roots somewhere else, prospered...' Amma sighed. She leaned back a little more and closed her eyes. 'Anything more to ask?'

I was a bit reluctant, but I still asked, 'Why did he prey especially on little girls?'

The reply took a few moments to arrive. 'The man was afraid of grown women.' Her voice was soft, compassionate. I pretended not to hear what she said. I wished I hadn't. But it was like a wasp had got into my ear. It drove me crazy. Amma prepared to retire, but before she did so, she asked, 'What do you plan to do with the hundred and forty crore?'

'File a case.'

I leaned my head on her shoulder.

'What case?'

'To establish the claim that I am the heir of the entire two hundred crore.'

'Why do you need so much money?'

'The first step towards disarming the enemy is to make him poor.'

'From where did you learn this?' Amma pushed my head away in irritation.

'From the note ban.' I had been joking, but she did not smile. I, too, did not smile, for, in reality, it was no joke. I was trying to manipulate myself. One person's security is the source of another's insecurity – that's the lesson I learned from my search for the truth. Wealth alone protected the woman who lived alone, not the curved dagger. Then,

Amma laughed mockingly. 'In that case, let your income tax payment be your message!'

My tongue froze.

Soon, Amma slept off. I sat looking at the lights that flashed by. The temperature inside the car kept falling. Outside, the night, clad in a helmet and a jacket, fired bullets of light at me. I, too, began to nod off a bit. Then my phone rang. It was Inspector Shetty.

'Bad news,' he said impassively. 'Satyaprakash is dead.'

I was struck dumb.

'The most important link in the case is now gone. You must remain very alert,' he warned.

My head grew numb. I rummaged in my bag – the dagger was safe inside. I wanted to fling it away somewhere. Yet again, I fell into an abyss of darkness. I imagined the cold body beginning to stiffen in the hospital mortuary. Someone who had no one to lament his death. Forsaken by friends.

Do you see now why this story of a search for the truth began with the question: 'Have you ever faced an attempt on your life?' This story began the day after Balidan Diwas. Do you know why I named this story *Assassin*? That day – it was a day of martyrdom. And besides, the moment I was about to nod off again, the mobile phone rang. And yet again, there it was:

'*Khushi rawho, Satyapriya, khushi rawho, motte bhuley na* ... as there is always going to be a third chance!'

– THE END –

K.R. MEERA is the author of five novels, six novellas, six collections of short fiction, two novels for children, and two collections of essays in Malayalam. She has been the recipient of numerous literary prizes, such as the Kerala Sahitya Akademi Award (for best novel and best short fiction), the Vayalar Award and the Odakkuzhal Award. A number of her works have been translated into English; they include *Jezebel*, *Hangwoman*, *The Poison of Love*, *The Unseeing Idol of Light*, *Yellow Is the Colour of Longing*, *The Gospel of Yudas*, *Qabar* and *The Angel's Beauty Spots*. *Hangwoman*, J. Devika's translation of the author's Kendra Sahitya Akademi Award-winning novel *Aarachaar*, was shortlisted for the DSC Prize for South Asian Literature in 2016.

J. DEVIKA is a feminist historian, social researcher and translator currently with the Centre for Development Studies, Thiruvananthapuram, Kerala. She translates literary writing from Malayalam to English and social science writing from English to Malayalam. Her literary translations include works by, among others, K.R. Meera, Sarah Joseph, Unni R., Ambikasutan Mangad and Lalithambika Antharjanam. Her website https:// swatantryavaadini.in/ contains a collection of translations of the writings of twentieth-century Malayali feminists.

30 Years *of*

 HarperCollins *Publishers* India

At HarperCollins, we believe in telling the best stories and finding the widest possible readership for our books in every format possible. We started publishing 30 years ago; a great deal has changed since then, but what has remained constant is the passion with which our authors write their books, the love with which readers receive them, and the sheer joy and excitement that we as publishers feel in being a part of the publishing process.

Over the years, we've had the pleasure of publishing some of the finest writing from the subcontinent and around the world, and some of the biggest bestsellers in India's publishing history. Our books and authors have won a phenomenal range of awards, and we ourselves have been named Publisher of the Year the greatest number of times. But nothing has meant more to us than the fact that millions of people have read the books we published, and somewhere, a book of ours might have made a difference.

As we step into our fourth decade, we go back to that one word – a word which has been a driving force for us all these years.

Read.

Harper
Collins

HARPER
PERENNIAL

HARPER
BUSINESS

HARPER
BLACK

हार्पर
हिन्दी

HarperCollins
Children's Books

HARPER
DESIGN

HARPER
VANTAGE

Harper
Sport